LONELY WEREWOLF GIRL

by

MARTIN MILLAR

Soft Skull Press
Brooklyn

Published in Great Britain by Meadow & Black in 2007

Library of Congress Cataloging-in-Publication Data is available.

ISBN 13: 978-0-9796636-6-6

Cover design by David Janik
Cover art by Simon Fraser
Printed in the United States of America

Soft Skull Press
An imprint of Counterpoint LLC
2117 Fourth Street
Suite D
Berkeley, CA 94710

www.softskullpress.com
www.counterpointpress.com

Distributed by Publishers Group West

10 9 8 7 6 5 4 3 2 1

Thanks to: *Les Carter, Martina Dervis, Alexandra Dymock, Simon Fraser, Robin Gibson, Lorraine Garland, Melanie Garside, Kirsty Gordon, Malcolm Imrie, Andrea Kerr, Andreas MacElligott, Jonathan Main, Gordon Millar, Peter Pavement, Penn Stevens, Geoff Travis.*

LONELY WEREWOLF GIRL

Kalix was lost. Tired, nervous, unable to focus, and lost. And now it was raining. She had padded her way down street after cold street, looking for the empty warehouse that was her temporary home but the streets all looked the same and she was beginning to despair.

The cold rain quickly soaked through her hair which trailed, thick, long and dank, round her bony hips. Kalix was skinny, thin like a reed, not an ounce of fat to show for her seventeen years of existence: a werewolf without an appetite. How her family had hated that. Her mother used to plead with her, beg her to eat. Until last year when Kalix attacked her father, lord of the werewolves. Now her mother had more to worry about than her daughter's poor appetite, or her violent temper, or her addictions, or her madness.

Kalix's hair, never cut, hung down to her hips. As the rain flattened it around her head her ears showed through. Her ears were never entirely normal even when, as now, she was in human form. There was something wolf-like about them, naturally.

Kalix stopped, and sniffed. Were the hunters close? She couldn't tell. Her senses were dulled. She hurried on. If the hunters caught up with her now, when she was weak, they might kill her. Kalix wondered what it would be like to be dead. Good, she thought. Better than living in an abandoned warehouse, begging for money to feed her addiction. But she wished she'd managed to kill her father. Then, she thought, she might have died satisfied.

Were she to die, she would die alone. Kalix MacRinnalch had always been alone. She'd never had a friend. She had two brothers, a sister, and many cousins; all werewolves, but none of them friends. She hated her brothers. She hated them almost as much as she hated her father. As for her sister, the Werewolf Enchantress, Kalix didn't hate her. She almost looked up to her. Had the Enchantress ever given her encouragement, Kalix might even have liked her. But the Enchantress had long ago distanced herself from the family and had no time for a sister born so many years after her, a sister who was famed from a young age as a source of trouble.

In fairness to the Enchantress, she had given Kalix the pendant which protected her. While wearing the pendant Kalix remained undetectable. She was free to scavenge on the streets of London, untroubled by the members of her family who wanted to drag her home to Scotland to face the vengeance that the attack on her father demanded. Free from the attentions of the hunters who wanted to kill her with silver bullets. Free from all harassment. It had been good while it lasted but Kalix, inevitably, had sold the pendant to raise money. Now her enemies were closing in.

Kalix pulled her ragged coat tightly round her thin frame. She shivered. When Kalix was five years old she could run naked in the snow and not feel the cold. Now she had lost her resistance. She longed to be back in the warehouse. It was empty, with nothing to make it comfortable, but it was some sort of shelter. When she reached it she could fill herself with laudanum and sink into dreams. Not many people remembered laudanum these days. It was almost gone from the world. For a few werewolves, sunk in degeneracy like Kalix, it was still obtainable. It was a further disgrace that Kalix brought on her family.

Footsteps sounded from round the corner. Kalix tensed though she knew it was not the hunters. Just two young men walking home at midnight. As soon as they caught sight of her they headed her way, intent on not letting her pass. Kalix attempted to step round them but they moved quickly to intercept her.

"Hey skinny girl," said one of the men, and they both laughed.

Kalix regarded them with loathing. It infuriated her the way drunken human males would always try and talk to her.

"Going home on your own?"

Kalix had no time to waste. She needed to find her warehouse before she collapsed from exhaustion. She growled. Even in human form, Kalix's growl was a terrifying sound, a lupine howl so chilling it seemed impossible it could come from her slender frame. The young men, startled by its ferocity, leapt to one side and regarded her uncomfortably as she hurried past.

"Freak," they muttered, but quietly, and went on their way.

2

After sixty years in England, mainly in the fashion industry, Thrix, the Werewolf Enchantress, had mostly discarded her Scottish accent. It was only really noticeable when her voice was raised in anger. Thrix was unconcerned at the loss. It further distanced her from her family and this was to her liking. The thought of her father the Thane, roaming the grounds of his castle in the remote wilds of Scotland, still made her purse her lips with distaste.

Whilst not displeased to be a werewolf, and a member of the MacRinnalch ruling family at that, Thrix did not like to associate with others of her kind. Others of her kind always meant problems. The malevolence of her uncles, the plotting of her mother, the machinations of her brothers, all these Thrix avoided. The MacRinnalch Werewolf Clan could tear itself to pieces so long as they all left her alone.

Thrix was unique among the Scottish werewolves. She was blonde, beautiful, the owner of a fashion house, and a powerful user of sorcery. No other werewolf could claim as much. The dazzling blonde hair alone had always been enough to set her apart from the rest of her clan. She was vain about this, which she knew.

A huge mirror covered the wall by Thrix's desk. She studied her reflection while talking on the phone.

"Cassandra, what are you doing in Portugal? You know I need you here for the shoot."

Thrix listened while the model related some tortuous story of missed planes and unreliable photographers.

"Fine, Cassandra," she interrupted. "It all sounds terrible. Now get back to London. Your ticket will be waiting for you at the airport."

Thrix put down the phone. Models. Not the most organised group of people, she found, though generally she liked them. Not as much as she liked the clothes, of course. The Werewolf Enchantress truly loved clothes in a way that had always mystified her family.

Thrix looked at the message on her desk. Her mother had called. Why? Surely Verasa was not expecting her to visit? Thrix had been at Castle MacRinnalch only six months ago and her mother knew that she would never visit more than once a year.

The Werewolf Enchantress studied herself in the mirror. She looked around thirty, perhaps a year or two younger. She was in fact almost eighty years old. Her youthful appearance was not the result of sorcery. The MacRinnalchs were very long lived, and eighty was still young for a werewolf. Thrix was enjoying her life. Her fashion house's reputation was growing steadily. If everything went to plan she would one day be one of the major players on the European fashion scene.

What did her mother want? Thrix sighed. No matter how she tried to distance herself from the clan, Verasa, the Mistress of the Werewolves, would never admit that she was gone. A troubling thought floated across her mind. Could her mother be calling about Kalix? There was a time when Verasa had never been off the phone about Kalix. Even before her savage attack on the Thane, life hadn't been easy for the youngest member of the family. Thrix affected not to care – she had left Castle MacRinnalch long before Kalix was born – and why the Thane and the Mistress of the Werewolves had chosen to have another child almost one hundred and fifty years after the birth of their first was a mystery – but she had some sympathy for Kalix. Life in the Scottish castle hadn't been easy. Not for a young girl anyway. No wonder it drove Kalix mad.

Kalix shouldn't be in trouble with the family. Not when Thrix had discreetly provided her with the pendant which hid her from the world. Even when she transformed into her werewolf shape, and her scent was most distinctive, she would remain hidden. She was safe to do whatever she wished which, as far as Thrix could see, was destroy herself at the earliest opportunity.

Her assistant buzzed through to let her know that the call she had been waiting for was here. A very fashionable photographer who Thrix was keen to enlist for an upcoming shoot. She clicked on the speaker phone and prepared to be at her persuasive best. Before she could launch into her speech, the door burst open. This was unexpected. Ann, her personal assistant, was much too efficient to let her be disturbed unannounced.

"Prepare to die, cursed Enchantress."

It was the Fire Queen. Flames were flickering around her eyes.

"You have angered the Fire Queen once too often, you perfidious werewolf! I am going to roast you over a fire then send you off to the deepest pits of hell where you will suffer a millennium of torment!"

Thrix sighed.

"I'll call you back," she said, and hung up the phone.

3

Kalix was trembling. It was a long time since she had tasted laudanum and Kalix's shameful addiction was very strong. Dizziness overwhelmed her and she halted to catch her breath. The rain intensified.

She shook her head to clear it and hurried on. Finally she recognised the street she was in. Not far now to the warehouse. As she turned the last corner she halted. Someone was close. Hunters. Seconds after registering their presence Kalix found herself confronted by two large figures dressed in black. Without the strength to flee, Kalix could only stand motionless as they advanced towards her. The light from the street lamp glinted on the ring that pierced her nose, a gold ring through her left nostril that was rather prominent, a size larger than would commonly be worn.

The hunters towered over her and their immense bulk cut off most of the light.

"If your father is Thane of the werewolves and you're just a little werewolf girl – "

" – a puny little junky werewolf girl – "

" – it doesn't pay to aggravate him, and get yourself banished."

The larger of the two men drew a gun from the depths of his coat.

"It's stupid of you to walk around here."

"I am stupid," muttered Kalix.

"Really, wolf whelp, you deserve to die."

"I know," said Kalix.

"And when you're dead, no one will miss you."

"It's true," said Kalix, quietly. And it was. It was all true. She deserved to die and no one would miss her.

The hunters gazed with dislike at the skinny, ragged, trembling figure, seventeen years in the world, without a friend to her name, not a single soul who would be sad to learn that she was gone. Kalix gazed down at her feet, at the cracked and broken boots she wore, now letting in water as the rain poured down from the black sky.

"I like it better when they fight," muttered the second hunter, drawing his gun. "Let's do it."

Kalix dragged her gaze up from her boots to the face of the larger man. She spoke, quite softly.

"I'll kill you."

The hunters laughed.

"You'll kill us? What with? Your werewolf strength?"

"You can't transform. No full moon, dummy," said the second hunter, pointing at the sky where the crescent of an old moon showed through a break on the clouds. Both hunters raised their weapons, preparing to fire silver bullets through the young werewolf's heart.

11

Kalix thought, as she often did, how pleasant it would be to die, and end it all on this bleak London street. But somehow, she just couldn't do it. As the hunters raised their guns she transformed in a split second from helpless adolescent runaway into the savage, bestial, werewolf who'd killed hunters from one end of Britain to the other, who'd torn the very gates from the prison the clan had held her in after she almost killed the Thane. Before the hunters had time to squeeze their triggers they were torn apart, shredded by the unparalleled savagery that had been both a gift and a curse to the lonely werewolf girl.

It was over in seconds. Kalix let out a frightful howl then shuddered as she reverted back into human form. She looked down bleakly at the carnage beneath her. Already the rain was washing the blood away.

"I don't need the full moon," she muttered. "I belong to the werewolf royal family."

Kalix breathed deeply to halt the shuddering, then set off along the dark street, disappearing down the first alley she came to.

4

Kalix wished that she was someone else. She had an elaborate fantasy in which her true parents had abandoned her at birth, leaving her at the mercy of the MacRinnalch Clan. Either that or she had been stolen away as a baby and sold to the Thane. Her favourite fantasy involved her being the secret love child of one of the Runaways, preferably Joan Jett.

'Joan Jett could well be my mother,' thought Kalix, sometimes. Except Joan Jett wasn't a werewolf, as far as anybody knew.

Her nomadic ways meant that Kalix had very few possessions. All she owned were her ragged clothes, an ancient walkman for playing tapes, and a bag for carrying her pills and her laudanum. Her clothes came from charity shops. Her boots were full of holes and her coat was worn and filthy.

Kalix had been taking laudanum for some years. Laudanum was an opium derivative dissolved in alcohol. She'd first bought it from Mac-Doig the Merchant, a strange character who regularly appeared at Castle MacRinnalch with fabulous goods for sale, goods from various realms, some of them not of this world. He was a man of some power who'd long outlived the normal short human span, and in that time travelled where few others had. Somewhere along the way, he'd located a supply of laudanum which he sold to anyone desperate for relief from their suffering. Kalix's mother, the Mistress of the Were-wolves, would have killed the MacDoig if she'd learned what he was selling to her youngest daughter. It was not cheap, and Kalix had learned to steal to finance her needs. Since she'd arrived in London she'd bought the liquid from the Young MacDoig, who carried on his father's business in the South. That was why she no longer had her pendant. She'd swapped it to the Young MacDoig for laudanum.

As for Kalix's walkman, she only had two tapes, both by the Run-aways: their eponymous first album, and *Live in Japan*. Kalix loved the Runaways even though both these albums had been recorded before she was born. She had a picture of the band, torn from a news-paper. Once, when a young man had tried to deface it she'd bitten his hand so hard he'd had to go to hospital to have it stitched together. That was while Kalix was in human form. Even as a human, Kalix was a ferocious opponent. As a werewolf she was abnormally strong, and when the battle-madness came over her, she was murderously sav-age.

Kalix had once gone to an internet café to hunt for information about the Runaways but she found very little. Not that much had been written about them and what there was, Kalix could barely read. Although the MacRinnalch werewolves were well educated as a rule, Kalix's peculiar background had left her almost illiterate. But it seemed to her, from the few sentences she could understand, that her favourite band had never been very successful. This baffled Kalix, and angered her, and made her hold the world in even greater contempt.

Kalix's bed was a bundle of old sacks. The abandoned warehouse was damp and the cold chilled her bones. Occasionally when night fell she would change into her werewolf shape just to gain warmth from her thick coat. As a purebred werewolf of the MacRinnalch Clan, Kalix could do this any night she chose, but it was hazardous now that she no longer had her pendant for protection. Changing into werewolf form made her easier to detect.

Kalix hadn't eaten for many days. This was good. Kalix didn't like to eat. There was no one here to tell her she had to. She might never eat again and no one could make her. Buoyed by this happy thought the young werewolf buried herself under the sacks and drifted off to sleep to dream about Gawain. Gawain was the most handsome of werewolves, and he had once been her lover. On her fourteenth birthday she'd crept into his bed at Castle MacRinnalch and after that they were never out of each other's company. They had a year of insane joy before he was banished. Kalix yearned to see him again, but she knew he was never coming back.

5

The Fire Queen, whose extreme beauty existed somewhere between a Babylonian death goddess and an Asian supermodel, advanced towards Thrix's desk, fire smouldering in her eyes.

"Prepare to suffer appalling and dreadful torments, you treacherous werewolf!"

Thrix raised one eyebrow.

"What exactly is the problem, Malveria?"

The Fire Queen reached back into the depths of her nether realm and dragged forth a pair of red high heeled shoes. She slammed them onto Thrix's desk.

"These shoes you sold me!" yelled the Fire Queen, "The heel broke! One moment I am walking up the volcano with a ceremonial knife in my hand, sacrifice at the ready and subjects bowing down before me – I was looking fabulous, of course – the next I'm hobbling up and down like a servant-girl with ill fitting boots!"

Thrix pursed her lips.

"Well, Malveria, these are clearly intended as dresswear only. You can't expect a fashion item to stand up to ritual sacrifice on the volcano. I've told you before about choosing the right footwear for the right occasion."

The Fire Queen exploded in a furious rage, cursing Thrix with dreadful oaths never before heard in the mortal world.

"You expect me to appear at the most important sacrifice of the year wearing some dull but sensible footwear? What sort of fashion adviser are you?"

"A very good adviser," replied Thrix, calmly. The Enchantress knew the Fire Queen very well – well enough to know her real name – and was not overly troubled by her wrath. As Queen of the Hiyasta, a race of fire elementals, Malveria was immensely powerful. Thrix would not lightly pit her skills against her, but her rages tended to subside quickly, particularly in the matter of fashion. Generally the prospect of an elegant new outfit was enough to calm her down. The intercom sounded. It was a slender silver box, delicately designed, in keeping with the decor of Thrix's elegant office which was calm and stylish, and only slightly spoiled by the untidy rail of clothes samples against the far wall.

"Your mother is on the phone."

Thrix made a face.

"Excuse me, Malveria. Mother... what is it? Kalix? No I haven't seen her. Why would I? Father's asking for me? Father can go to hell, and quickly... I have to go, I'm with a client."

Thrix ended the call.

"Family problems?" asked the Fire Queen.

"As ever."

The beautiful Hiyasta was sympathetic.

"I disposed of mine a long time ago. Is the young wolf in trouble again?"

"She is, but she won't be for long. They'll get rid of her soon."

"What does your mother want you to do?"

"Find her, I think," said Thrix, without enthusiasm.

"This is very interfering," observed the Fire Queen. "Does your mother not know you are busy making fabulous clothes for notable clients like myself?"

"My mother lets nothing stand in her way."

"How very irritating," said Malveria. "As a daughter of the were-wolf royal family, can you not simply order everyone to leave you alone?"

This brought a smile from Thrix.

"We've never actually proclaimed ourselves royalty. Well, perhaps once or twice, when we're feeling grand. *Ruling family* would be more accurate, and that's trouble enough. Now Malveria, about these shoes."

Malveria waved her hand dismissively. The scent of jasmine filled the room, as it always did when Malveria visited. Whether it was per-fume, or Malveria's natural aroma, Thrix wasn't sure.

"Pah, it is nothing. I regret ever threatening my most beautiful and valued fashion designer over such a trifle. The shame of the heel breakage was temporarily overwhelming but I have now made a strong recovery."

Malveria smiled. Though the fire elementals inhabited their own dimension, and had little contact with the world of humans, they were historical enemies of the MacRinnalchs. It was very unusual for a Hiyasta to be friends with a MacRinnalch werewolf. Despite this, the Fire Queen liked the Enchantress a great deal. Without Thrix's help the Queen would still be turning up at social events in her realm wearing really bad clothes. She still shuddered at the memory of some of her previous outfits.

6

Kalix woke with a pain in her stomach. She often suffered from this, when she hadn't eaten for a long time. She sipped some laudanum and fished her journal out of her bag. Kalix's journal was precious to her. It was a diary of sorts, used for recording both her thoughts and her actions. Yesterday's entry read: *My father is Thane of the Werewolves. I hate him.*

That, at least, was how it read to Kalix. To anyone else, it would have been an almost illegible scrawl of misspelled words and mis-shapen letters. The day before that was blank and the day before that read: *My brothers hate each other. I hate them both.* Further down the page it said: *I miss Gawain.*

Kalix wrote a new entry in her journal. *The Runaways are the Queens of Noise. Today I killed two hunters. Or yesterday.* It took her a long time to complete each word. She had to concentrate fully to form each troublesome letter. Though Kalix was naturally intelligent, she had never made up for her lack of schooling. Kalix was seventeen but in terms of education she was far behind girls of her age.

Outside it was still raining and water continued to drip through the roof. Kalix ignored it. Tired, her stomach still sore, she drifted back to sleep. When she next woke, sometime in the afternoon, she was still drowsy from the laudanum. Because her senses were dulled it took her a few moments to realise she was not alone. Duncan Douglas-MacPhee was standing next to her, staring at her with his cold dark eyes. Duncan worked for her eldest brother Sarapen. He was a large, strong werewolf, with a reputation for violence. He wore an old leather jacket and his long hair was held back by a black bandana. Alarmed, Kalix leapt to her feet, ready to defend herself.

Duncan regarded her silently. His eyes shifted to her squalid bed, then took in the rest of her surroundings. He looked down at the bottle of laudanum at his feet.

"You are disgusting, Kalix MacRinnalch. Fourth in line to the Thaneship and here you are with habits suited to the lowest scum of werewolf society."

"You'd know about the lowest scum," growled Kalix.

"I would that," agreed Duncan. His own reputation was very unsavoury, as was that of his brother Fergus and his sister Rhona. The Douglas-MacPhees were an unwholesome trio of werewolves in every respect. Kalix was worried. In daylight neither she nor Duncan could transform and in human form he was certainly more powerful than her.

"Leave me alone."

"I can't," said Duncan. His Scottish accent was stronger than Kalix's, and very harsh. "The Great Council wants you back."

"I'm not going back to be tried," said Kalix, edging away.

"You've already been tried. And found guilty. Now they want to sentence you."

He stared at her.

"Sarapen's not too concerned what condition you reach the castle in. In fact he's not too concerned if you get there at all."

From the depths of his leather jacket he drew a long machete.

"Just your heart will do."

"I'll kill you," snarled Kalix.

"I hardly think so. Not in daylight. Not when you can't transform."

Duncan Douglas-MacPhee advanced. Kalix sank into her defensive posture, ready to fight for her life. Suddenly the door to the warehouse opened and a young man appeared.

"Is this the sorting office?"

Duncan growled at the intruder. The young man was startled.

"My music magazines didn't arrive…" he said, by way of explanation.

Kalix moved like lightning. She grabbed a rock from the floor and

flung it at her assailant. It caught him sharply on the head and he collapsed. As he tried to rise Kalix kicked him savagely then ran for the
door, grabbing her coat and bag on the way. The young man looked
confused but at the sight of Duncan struggling to his feet with his
machete still in his hand, he swiftly followed Kalix out the door.

"In here!" yelled Daniel, pointing to his car.

Kalix didn't want to get into the car but the Douglas-MacPhee was
already emerging from the warehouse. Daniel flung open the passen-
ger door and Kalix leapt in, and they sped away from the murderous
attacker as fast as Daniel's ancient vehicle could take them.

Daniel was scared. He was a nineteen year old student and not used
to confronting men with machetes. He paid Kalix little attention till
he'd put several long streets between them and Duncan. When he
finally stopped the car and turned towards her, he was immediately
unsettled by the intensity of her expression. Kalix's eyes were larger
and darker than any he had ever seen, quite startling against her very
pale skin. There was something quite shocking about her appearance.
Her face was dirty, she was painfully thin, and her hair, unusually long,
was thick, filthy and matted, as if it had never been washed. The whole
effect was very unsettling.

"Drive further," she said.

"It's okay, we've lost him now."

"Drive further. He can still smell us."

Daniel was puzzled, and slightly insulted.

"Smell us? I don't really think – "

"Drive!" yelled Kalix.

Daniel put the car back into gear and drove on through South East
London, leaving the industrial area behind as he headed towards his
home in Kennington. Kalix sat in silence. She was recovering her
composure but felt no desire to enter into conversation with a stranger.
Daniel, however, did not feel like remaining silent. The whole experience was the most exciting thing that had ever happened to him and
now that his terror was receding he was starting to think quite well of
his conduct. He imagined himself describing it to his flatmate, Moonglow. She could hardly fail to be impressed.

"Who was that man?"

"He works for my brother," replied Kalix.

"Was he trying to cut you out of the family?" asked Daniel, trying
for a lightness of tone that would show he hadn't been scared.

"He was trying to cut out my heart," replied Kalix, flatly.

Daniel winced at the image.

"Any reason for that?" he said, after a while.

"The family condemned me."

They drove on in silence. Daniel found it hard to carry on the conversation. Nothing seemed quite appropriate and besides, he was becoming tongue tied, as he generally did while trying to make conversation with young women. Even in the midst of the excitement and danger, Daniel had not failed to notice the young girl's extraordinary beauty. She might be skinny, ragged, and dirty, with an air of madness about her, but she was undeniably beautiful. Daniel had never seen her like, outside of a magazine.

"Eh… we're almost where I live now…" said Daniel, and felt embarrassed in case she might think he was trying to invite her home with him. Unconsciously, he let his long hair swing in front of his face, which he always did to mask embarrassment.

"Do you want to come in… maybe call the police?"

But Kalix had gone. She'd swiftly opened the door, slid out of the car and was already disappearing along the street.

7

As leaders of the MacRinnalch Werewolf Clan the Thane's family were very wealthy. They owned property all over Britain. Verasa, wife of the Thane and Mistress of the Werewolves, held land in the Scottish highlands, more land in the Scottish isles, and considerable estates in Kent. Her London home, in Kensington, was large enough to be classed as a mansion. Verasa spent a lot of time there. Too much time, in the opinion of her husband the Thane, but it was a long time since they had agreed about anything.

Verasa was two hundred and fifty years old. In human terms, she would have passed for forty-eight. Like most female members of the clan her hair hung long and dark round her shoulders. Unlike her wayward daughter Kalix, Verasa was a frequent visitor to the salons of Edinburgh and Knightsbridge, and her thick mane was beautifully coiffured. Her clothes were elegant and her features striking. While taking tea at one of the smart little places in Kensington she sometimes favoured, she would always be the subject of a few discreet glances as the clientele wondered who she might be, what films she might have starred in when she was younger, and what wealth she might have married into.

Verasa was drinking a glass of wine from a crystal goblet that had been in the family for four hundred years. A servant entered.

"Your son, mistress."

"Send him in."

Markus strode into the chamber. Markus was her younger son, and her favourite. Markus, who didn't look much like a werewolf, having a somewhat rounder face than was usual, less lupine around the cheekbones. His hair was a little lighter, more chestnut than was common among the MacRinnalchs. Slightly feminine. Pretty even, which was unusual in a male werewolf. It didn't mean that he was weak. No werewolf with the blood of the MacRinnalchs flowing in his veins had ever been weak. He was certainly a more congenial companion for his mother than Sarapen, her eldest son, who had turned out to be the double of his father the Thane; strong and grim, and not given to shows of affection.

Markus's main residence was in Edinburgh but he was a frequent visitor to London. He embraced his mother and she responded with a warmth she felt towards no other member of her family. As Markus finally withdrew from the embrace, she looked at him questioningly.

"Kalix killed some hunters," said Markus.

"From the Guild?"

"No, just some freelancers. Of no account."

Verasa nodded. Bounty hunters were an occasional annoyance, but rarely able to trouble the powerful MacRinnalch Clan.

"And the Douglas-MacPhees?"

"Kalix encountered Duncan yesterday," answered Markus. "She escaped."

"Escaped? Was he trying to harm her?"

"No doubt. You don't send the Douglas-MacPhees after anyone unless you want to harm them."

Verasa frowned. Duncan, Fergus and Rhona were a notorious trio. It was infuriating that her own son Sarapen should employ such people. She poured wine for herself and Markus. As she handed him his glass she thought, as always, that she was fortunate to have at least one child who loved her.

20

"Poor Kalix," said Verasa, in her well modulated Scottish tones. "I admit we've had our difficulties but I'd hate to see her heart cut out."

Markus made a sound of mild contempt. He loathed the girl, and made no secret of it.

"She would deserve it. But we can't let Sarapen capture her. Or kill her. Great Mother Dulupina would never let us forget that he succeeded while we failed." He looked at his mother. "We should have tried harder to catch her."

The Mistress of the Werewolves sighed.

"I hoped she would just disappear. It's not pleasant for a mother to have her youngest daughter dragged back for sentencing, even if the Council insists on it."

Verasa stroked Markus's hair. He was such a good child. It would be difficult having him succeed as Thane instead of her older son Sarapen, but Verasa had successfully manoeuvred her way through the tortuous and occasionally murderous political strife of the werewolf clan for long enough to be confident of succeeding in her wishes.

"Incidentally," said Markus, raising his head. "We still haven't dealt with the matter of the cousins about whom we do not speak."

An expression of distaste flickered over the Mistress of the Werewolves' features.

"Please Markus. I can't think about both Kalix and the cousins about whom we do not speak. Not in the same day anyway. This family will surely send me to an early grave."

8

"Cut out her heart? Ew!"

Moonglow was appalled. So appalled that she wondered if Daniel might be making it all up to impress her. It wouldn't be the first time he'd done such a thing. When they first met, Daniel had told her he could play guitar and had an older brother who made films in Hollywood. Neither of these things had turned out to be true. And it was very unlike Daniel to rescue anybody from a machete-wielding maniac. Not that he'd be unwilling, just incapable. Last time they'd got drunk together in the student bar Daniel had offended two large rugby players and had it not been for Moonglow's tactful intervention they would certainly have pummelled him. Daniel was not the fighting type though he was good company, when he got over his shyness. She might have been inclined to dismiss his story altogether if it hadn't been for the book and the journal.

The girl – a wild beauty, according to Daniel, who'd been unusually forthcoming on the subject – had left them in his car, wrapped in a plastic carrier bag.

"The Flower Fairies of the Summer?"

It was a children's book, with pictures of fairies sitting on flowers. It was old and seemed to have been through a great deal of wear and tear. The book was stained with finger prints. And paw prints, as if a dog had walked over it.

"This proves she was there," said Daniel, aware of Moonglow's slight scepticism.

"Not entirely," Moonglow pointed out. "It could be yours."

"Very funny. And there's this as well," continued Daniel, plucking a very worn looking notebook from the carrier bag.

"It's some sort of diary."

He flicked it open and tried to read from a page near the start.

"It's kind of illegible. She can't spell a single word right. I think it says *My mother is mistress of the werewolves. My father is* – can't make out that word, something like *thin – of the werewolves.*"

They both laughed.

"*My brother is heir to the werewolf throne.*"

"She's pretty consistent with the werewolves," said Moonglow. Really, she was not unsympathetic. Moonglow was fascinated by anything otherworldly. Tales about werewolves were always interesting.

"Pity she can't spell it properly," said Daniel. "Her handwriting is really terrible."

He struggled to read more.

"*I am fourth in line to the thin ship of the Mac* – something - *clan.*"

Neither of them knew what that might mean. They didn't have time to read any further, there was work to do. Daniel and Moonglow had almost finished packing to move house. Daniel was going to pick up a rental van and when night fell they were moving to their new flat. They'd lived in this one for eight months, moving in after becoming friends in their first year at university. It wasn't a bad place but they

22

were behind on the rent and couldn't pay so they'd decided that a moonlight flit was the best solution. Moonglow was rather anxious about this. She didn't relish the prospect of being apprehended by an irate landlord. Moonglow had long black hair, soft pretty features, a firm belief in astrology, a kind nature, and no experience of irate landlords. She was certain that if she encountered one, she'd find it very awkward.

9

The early winter afternoon was already turning cold when Kalix picked up her prescription. The pharmacist looked at her suspiciously. Kalix was wearing sunglasses, as she frequently did, even in the weak winter daylight or the murky London night-time. The sunglasses always seemed to arouse the suspicion of pharmacists. As did her ragged coat which failed to cover her even more ragged T-shirt. And maybe her skinny frame, which suggested either substance abuse or an eating disorder. Her prescription was legitimate however. The werewolf clan, whilst not exactly part of normal society, were not entirely outside it either. In Scotland the MacRinnalchs had their own doctor, a werewolf who had studied medicine at Edinburgh University. Werewolves rarely fell sick, but there were often injuries to be taken care of and it was vital that they received treatment from someone who knew of their unique physiology. Certain human drugs could have a very bad effect on a werewolf. Besides, as the Scottish werewolves took great care to conceal the wolf part of their nature, it wouldn't do to have any member of the clan examined too closely by a normal doctor.

So Kalix had been registered with a doctor in Scotland, and through this she had been referred to a psychiatrist who had prescribed diazepam for her anxiety. Kalix disliked her psychiatrist but she liked the diazepam. She fretted uncomfortably while she waited for the prescription. When it finally appeared she grabbed the packet and hurried out of the shop. As soon as she opened her bag to put the pills inside she realised that something was missing.

"Where's my journal?"

She cursed out loud. The journal was one of her few possessions, and very precious to her. She remembered picking it up before she fled from Duncan Douglas-MacPhee at the warehouse. She was trying to work out where she could possibly have lost it when a familiar scent caught her attention. Duncan was close. She spun round, searching. She didn't have far to look. Duncan and his sister Rhona were no more than fifty yards away, and closing fast. Kalix ran for her life, sprinting up the street at a speed which would have left most people in her wake. The Douglas-MacPhees raced after her. As werewolves in human shape, they too possessed unusual strength and speed, but they weren't as fast as Kalix. She turned the corner only a few yards ahead of her pursuers but by the time they reached the next street she was rapidly disappearing from view.

"Come on!" yelled Duncan. "She can't keep up that pace."

Duncan doubted if the scrawny girl could keep running for long. She looked like she hadn't eaten in months, and even the primordial energy that burned inside every member of the MacRinnalch Clan couldn't support a starving werewolf forever.

Kalix ran for her life, and cursed the day she had sold her pendant. It had been foolish. With it she had been undetectable. Now she was easy prey for experienced predators like the Douglas-MacPhees.

Kalix was always doing foolish things. It had been foolish to attack her father. It had been foolish to crawl into Gawain's bed when she was fourteen. It had been foolish to drink the entire contents of her family's malt whisky cabinet when she was thirteen, though Kalix had protested that as a Scottish werewolf, she was merely exploring her heritage. And it had been foolish to eat the contents of her mother's medicine cabinet just to see what would happen, an escapade that led to her being the only teenage MacRinnalch werewolf ever taken to hospital for an emergency stomach pump. On each occasion the Mistress of the Werewolves left Kalix in no doubt as to the foolishness of her actions, and the disgrace never really went away.

After running the length of several streets Kalix knew that she had outdistanced the Douglas-MacPhees. They might still be following her scent, but in the city they couldn't track her as easily as they could in the wilds. There was too much pollution for her scent to linger for long. Kalix disappeared down an alleyway, over a fence, through several gardens and back out onto another quiet street where she stopped, and sniffed the air. She couldn't smell another werewolf. She had escaped. She sniffed again. There was another scent she recognised. The young man who had driven her in his car away from the warehouse.

Kalix remembered her journal. Could she have left it in his car? The young werewolf trotted along the street, following Daniel's scent. Escaping from the Douglas-MacPhees had left her weak. She hadn't eaten for a long time. She craved laudanum, but she had to recover her journal first. Every part of her unhappy life was recorded there. In some ways Kalix's journal was more real to her than her own being.

10

"There's nothing worse than moving," declared Daniel, who was struggling to pack plates and cutlery into an unsuitable cardboard box.

Moonglow nodded. She accepted the toil more stoically than Daniel but it wasn't something she enjoyed.

"Funny how everyone was too busy to help," said Daniel. He was staring rather forlornly at a frying pan, wondering whether to try to fit in the box or put in a plastic bag. Perhaps he could just throw it in the van. After all, what harm could come to a frying pan?

"Colin claimed he had to study for an exam. Is that a feeble excuse or what?"

Moonglow nodded. She was struggling with their CD collection. While these weren't difficult to fit into boxes there were a great many of them and she had unwisely determined to sort them out first, putting them all back in their correct covers. This was proving to be an impossible task. The covers for Daniel's Slayer CDs all seemed to be missing and there was no sign at all of the first disc from her Kate Bush boxed set.

"I notice Jay hasn't made an appearance," said Daniel, pointedly.

Moonglow was immediately defensive.

"He had to visit Stonehenge."

Jay was Moonglow's boyfriend. Daniel was jealous, though Moonglow wasn't meant to know this.

"As if Stonehenge wouldn't be there next week."

"It had to be now. Horoscope said so."

25

Daniel was derisive.

"Very convenient. Boyfriend avoids work by means of astrology."

He put down his box with a thud.

"Hey careful! Plates and glasses!"

Daniel was always mean and sarcastic about Jay. Moonglow understood this. Even if her friend Caroline hadn't informed her that, while under the influence of alcohol, Daniel had confessed to her his love for Moonglow, she would have known anyway. It was fairly obvious. At nineteen, Daniel hadn't learned how to shield his emotions.

The doorbell rang. They were immediately nervous. If it happened to be their landlord paying a surprise visit the boxes were going to be very hard to explain. Daniel crept to the front door and peered through the peephole. Seeing Kalix, he was hesitant. The bell rang again. Daniel opened the door a few inches.

"Eh… is that guy right behind you with a really big knife?"

"You have my journal," said Kalix, coldly.

"Right… come in."

Kalix marched inside. Daniel made an attempt at introducing their visitor to Moonglow.

"This is – "

"Where's my journal?" demanded Kalix brusquely.

Moonglow was startled by Kalix's appearance. So thin and ragged. In the gap between the ends of Kalix's threadbare black trousers and her boots, her ankles showed like two white twigs. And she was so intense. Her large dark eyes burned as she scanned the room for her possessions. Her gold nose ring was very noticeable, larger than normal. As for her hair, trailing down lankly to her waist, Moonglow had never seen its like, not even on the most unkempt beggar.

"Are you the werewolf girl?" asked Moonglow.

"What?" demanded Kalix, suspiciously.

Moonglow realised that this had not been the politest of greetings.

"I mean the girl who wrote the werewolf poem? I thought it was really cool. *My mother is a werewolf, my father is a werewolf*. I wrote a poem like that once, I kind of imagined my… eh…"

Moonglow ground to a halt under Kalix's withering glare. Kalix turned to Daniel.

"Where is it?"

Daniel picked up the carrier bag which contained Kalix's journal and her book. Moonglow was immediately concerned that she'd

26

offended the girl.

"Are you annoyed I read it? Sorry… it was a really good poem."

"Stop talking," snapped Kalix. "I've no time to waste."

Her voice seemed too strong to emanate from such a skinny frame. Moonglow was rather shocked. She was about to make a conciliatory response when the front door suddenly flew open and, terrifyingly, two strangers burst into the room.

"Get her," said Duncan Douglas-MacPhee.

11

The Fire Queen was always happiest when surrounded by clothes. She loved visiting Thrix's establishment and had now completely forgotten her anger towards the Enchantress. As she gazed with pleasure at Thrix's rough drafts for her new Spring catalogue, the mighty Fire Queen looked much more like a model than a powerful supernatural being who ruled her own realm. A smile spread over her dusky features as she examined some sketches for an evening gown which Thrix had promised to make exclusively for her.

"Could it be ready for a cocktail party at the Duchess Gargamond's next week?"

"Next week?" said Thrix. "Malveria, you know I can't work that quickly."

Malveria was one of the Fire Queen's names. Not the most secret of her names, but one that very few creatures of any sort were free to use. A person had to be on very, very good terms with the Fire Queen before they could call her Malveria.

Before meeting the Werewolf Enchantress, the Queen of the fire elementals had been very poorly dressed. Her wardrobe was full of dramatic but very gauche outfits which somehow never seemed to suit her. Malveria had found herself continually overshadowed at some elemental event or other by finely arrayed nether-world princesses who'd arrive in fabulous new outfits purchased from the catwalks of London, Paris, or Milan. The Fire Queen knew that her rivals were laughing at her behind her back. The young aristocrats from the Ice Kingdoms could be particularly cutting, and as for Princess Kabachetka,

Malveria's great rival from the neighbouring land of Hainusta, there was no saying what spiteful gossip she might have spread.

Thrix had changed all this. Now, dressed by the Enchantress, Queen Malveria was widely admired in the nether worlds as a Fire Spirit who really knew how to shop. Her wonderful collection of shoes was particularly envied.

"Do you know how long it takes to put a collection together?" said Thrix.

"No," admitted the Fire Queen, shaking her head. Her hair, long, black, gleaming, in perfect condition, was attended to by a salon in Kensington that Thrix had recommended; one more reason to be grateful to the Enchantress.

"It takes months. I start off with drawings, consult with my designers, cost fabrics, make up patterns, send the patterns for cutting, and that's just to get the process in motion."

Malveria frowned, and only just prevented herself from pouting.

"Furthermore," pointed out Thrix, brushing back her golden hair and pointing to the mass of paperwork on her desk. "I've got a hundred things to get done and they're all urgent. I've got people to interview, photographers to hire, models to send to assignments, and the plumber needs instructions."

"The plumber?" said Malveria, puzzled. She had little idea of what life in this world was really like.

"The pipes downstairs are leaking again."

"Surely you have minions to do these things for you?"

"I do. But the junior minion got it wrong last time and the senior minion – my property manager – is away at a conference so I have to take care of it myself."

Malveria shook her head.

"This is all very mysterious to me. If your minions get things wrong surely you should simply kill them and get new minions?"

"Tempting," admitted Thrix. "But it would lead to a lot of trouble with the union. Besides, my minions aren't so bad."

As if to demonstrate the difficulties of running a fashion empire, the plumber chose that moment to arrive. Thrix's personal assistant buzzed through to let her know he was here.

"I have to see him now," said Thrix, apologetically. "If you miss your plumber's appointment, you've no idea of the trouble it causes."

Thrix spent a long time talking to the plumber. The Fire Queen sat in her chair, still mystified by the entire process. After the plumber departed to gather his crew and sort out the pipes downstairs, she again voiced her puzzlement.

"I could not tolerate such a long discussion about such a tiresome subject. Surely your slaves could perform these tasks for you?"

"They're called employees," replied Thrix. "But there comes a time when the boss has to get her hands dirty. How do you think I get my collections together? By magic?"

"Yes," said the Fire Queen. "Isn't that how you do it?"

"Afraid not."

"Oh." Malveria looked thoughtful. "But all these lovely shoes. They arrive by sorcery, surely?"

Thrix shook her head.

"No. People make them."

"Really? No sorcery at all? People must be cleverer than I thought. Because these are beautiful shoes."

Thrix took Queen Malveria downstairs to her showrooms to find her some new clothes because really, she wouldn't want to let down such an important client. While there was no time to make something special she could certainly put together an outfit for the Fire Queen that would impress on the day. As Thrix readied some young models for an impromptu fashion display, the Fire Queen was thoughtful. Normally, being surrounded by clothes was enough to occupy her attention entirely, but an amusing thought had struck her.

"Thrix. I keep remembering something I read in one of your magazines. Vogue, I think, which has made me so happy since you procured for me a – what was the word – subscription? This article was about a designer who always worked hard. It contained a phrase I had never seen before. *Work Ethic,* I believe."

"And?"

"And I think this is something you suffer from."

The Fire Queen was entertained by the thought.

"Because really, my wonderful Enchantress, you could use your sorcerous powers to speed up much of this work. I'm sure you could have fixed your piping difficulties with a wave of your hand."

The Enchantress looked wary.

"But you don't use your sorcery nearly as much as you could. Is this because you must work? Do you suffer from this thing called *work ethic?*"

"Though there's nothing wrong with a little hard work," said Thrix, and tossed her golden hair a little.

The Fire Queen laughed. She could be shrewd when she chose to be. She had an amusing vision of Thrix's mother telling the young werewolf that a proper daughter of the Thane should work hard, and not rely on sorcery to sort out her problems.

12

The Mistress of the Werewolves and the Thane had been married for a very long time, and Verasa was long past the stage of wishing to be in her husband's presence every day. She travelled south regularly, although on the three nights a month when she was obliged to transform into full werewolf shape, London was not the easiest place to be. A MacRinnalch werewolf as pure-blooded as Verasa could transform at will any night, but on the night of the full moon and the two nights that surrounded it, there was no choice. The change was automatic.

Of course, Verasa never completely lost control. It would be unseemly. But even such a powerful and disciplined figure as Verasa could find it sorely tempting to rush out into the night-time streets when the wolfness came on, and give in to the desire to hunt for food.

Some werewolves did just that. The clan discouraged them from taking on werewolf wolf form next to any populated area. These days, it did not pay to go around killing humans any more than was absolutely necessary. With today's modern communications and the all pervading media, any mysterious killings would soon be investigated by the police. Worse than that, it would attract the attention of the Avenaris Guild, the hated hunters who made it their mission in life to kill werewolves. The MacRinnalch Clan, with its wealth and power, did not fear the police, or the Guild, but there was no point in attracting unnecessary attention. *One must adapt to the modern world,* as Verasa often said. She herself could hardly remember when she had last killed anyone. More than thirty years ago, certainly.

Verasa and her younger son Markus sat next to each other on a gilded couch, sipping wine from silver goblets. As mother and son, they were very close. Too close perhaps, by human standards, though not necessarily by the norms of werewolf society.

"Poor Kalix," sighed the Mistress of the Werewolves. "How did she manage to make such a mess of her life in only seventeen years?"

"I never thought it was wise to have another child when you were two hundred and thirty years old," said Markus.

"A little older, actually. But it was your father's idea, dear. He wanted another child. At the time he had just agreed to cede the estates in Argyll to my side of the family so I did not wish to start an argument. Unwise perhaps, in retrospect. Kalix has been a terrible burden."

"We have to find her before Sarapen does."

The Mistress of the Werewolves frowned at the mention of her eldest son.

"Quite why your father favours him so much I can't imagine."

"He always has," said Markus, with something approaching loathing.

"I do so regret that. You've always been a much nicer son. More wine?"

Markus accepted the goblet.

"Great Mother Dulupina has been baying for Kalix's blood ever since she attacked the Thane. Nothing will satisfy her but that someone brings her back to the castle."

Dulupina was the Thane's mother. As Mistress of the Werewolves, Verasa outranked her, but Dulupina was very important to the clan and couldn't be ignored. She was aged, venerable and influential, and had a seat on the Great Council.

"If only Kalix could have stayed hidden."

Kalix had been found guilty of assaulting the Thane. She'd fled from the castle while awaiting sentence. By the traditions of the clan it was now legal for another werewolf to kill her, and bring back her heart. Verasa suspected that Sarapen intended to do just that. At least if Verasa herself were to find Kalix, she could be taken back to the castle and incarcerated, till another solution was found.

"You should bring her back," she said to Markus.

31

When the two frightening strangers invaded her house Moonglow
shrank back against the wall, too terrified even to scream. Duncan
Douglas-MacPhee and his sister Rhona ignored her. They headed
straight towards Kalix, and there began a violent scene the like of
which neither Moonglow nor Daniel had ever seen.

Rhona wore a leather waistcoat which showed off the tattoo of a
snarling wolf on her shoulder, and she was very strong. Werewolves
always were, even in their human form. She tried to grab hold of
Kalix. Kalix lashed out with her foot, catching Rhona on the chest
with a kick which flung her clear across the table. It seemed to Moonglow that no one could really perform such a kick. It belonged in a
kung fu film, not here in her living room. Yet Kalix immediately did
it again, sending Duncan flying backwards into one of Moonglow's
carefully packed boxes of plates, which crashed to the floor with a
great noise of smashing crockery.

Rising swiftly, Rhona leapt at Kalix. Kalix spun round but not quite
quickly enough. Rhona smashed her fist into the side of her head sending the young werewolf stumbling across the floor. Duncan had now
recovered and managed to grab hold of Kalix. They thudded against
the table, knocking Kalix's bag flying. It landed beside Daniel, who,
like Moonglow, shrank back from the violence. Kalix bit her attacker's
wrist, forcing him to let go. Immediately she was free of his grasp.
She used her forehead to butt him brutally in the face. He reeled backwards with blood spurting from his nose. Rhona moved in to attack but
before she could land a blow Kalix caught her on the side of her neck
with her open palm and she went down as if struck by a bullet.

Just for a second, Kalix sagged. Her energy was fading fast. She
made an effort to pull herself together but it was too late. The Douglas-MacPhees were a savage family and Duncan was not put off by
his bloodied nose. He stepped up behind Kalix and rammed his forearm into the back of her head. She fell at his feet. Duncan kicked
her, then took his machete from under his coat. Daniel tried to wail
in terror but nothing came out. Moonglow then did something
she had never done in her life before, which was to offer violence
to a fellow living creature. As Duncan Douglas-MacPhee bent over
Kalix, she picked up a chair, rushed up behind him and hit him
over the head with it as hard as she could. The heavy blow sent

him crumpling to the floor. There was a long pause. Daniel looked at Moonglow.

"I can't believe you did that," he said.

Kalix hauled herself to her feet. She was tired and sore, trembling from the exertion of the fight. Moonglow and Daniel stared at her, waited for her to offer some words of explanation but nothing was forthcoming. Moonglow wondered who this strange girl was, with her skinny frame, her long dirty hair, and her incredible fighting skills.

"You want to eh... tell us what this is about?"

"My brother's werewolves are after me," said Kalix.

Daniel and Moonglow looked at each other again.

"Maybe you're taking this werewolf thing too far," said Moonglow, trying not to sound unfriendly.

Outside the moon had risen and the moment it did Duncan opened his eyes and began to transform.

"I mean, people call me a hippy," continued Moonglow. "Well some people call me a Goth, what with the black clothes and black nail varnish – a bit of a Goth hippy I suppose – but I know it's no good living in a fantasy world."

Behind Moonglow, Duncan, in werewolf form, was rising from the floor. Daniel tried to warn his friend but was too startled to speak.

"And it's no use blaming your problems on so-called werewolves," said Moonglow, and gave Kalix a supportive smile, to show that she wasn't being harsh. Duncan, now a large werewolf, strode past her. Moonglow screamed.

Night had now fallen. Kalix could transform, which she did instantly. As a werewolf she remained the same height. She still walked on two legs. But she was shaggy, bestial, and savage. She was covered in long hair and while her body still resembled something human, her face was fully animal and her hands were great taloned claws.

Strength flowed back into her fatigued muscles. As a werewolf, she was stronger than Duncan Douglas-MacPhee. As a werewolf, Kalix feared no one. It wasn't just Kalix's strength that made her such a fearsome opponent. It was her battle-madness. It made her ferocious and brutal, uncaring of pain, oblivious to danger. When Kalix's battle-madness took over her werewolf form, she became insane. She could not be stopped other than by death, and no one had ever come close to killing her.

She leapt at Duncan and overwhelmed him. Duncan knew he was

defeated and retreated swiftly, fending off his wild opponent as best as he could, trying to prevent her from fastening her jaws round his neck. His sister Rhona hauled herself off the floor but when she saw that her brother was beaten she made for the door. The Douglas-MacPhees fled, blood dripping from their wounds.

Kalix stopped. Daniel and Moonglow looked at her wide eyed with amazement, and terror, and wondered if she was about to kill them.

"You really are a…"

Kalix's form seemed to flicker and she slowly transformed back into her human shape. The contents of Kalix's bag had spilled out on the floor. Daniel tried to gather up her belongings.

"You dropped this," he said, picking up a dark, old-fashioned bottle.

"Give me!" yelled Kalix, and frantically snatched it from him.

Moonglow picked up a packet from the floor. She read the label. "You take diazepam?"

Kalix became angry. "Stop looking at everything!"

"Well it's just a bit weird you know," said Moonglow. "Werewolf… anti-depressants."

"Aren't you focusing on the wrong thing here?" said Daniel. "Remember the terrible violence."

"I have to go," said Kalix, but she was too worn-out to leave. Her head swam and she slumped heavily into the chair.

Daniel was nervous. "Is there going to be more violence? I'm really not keen on – "

"They won't come back," replied Kalix. "Not tonight."

Moonglow was overcome by sympathy for the young werewolf with her thin little body and ragged clothes, probably homeless, pursued by killers.

"Do you want some food? We don't have any meat… we have pop-tarts."

Kalix shook her head wearily. She put her arms round her meagre possessions and her head drooped. Against her will, she fell asleep in a house of strangers.

14

The cousins about whom the family did not speak were something of a disgrace to the MacRinnalchs. Quite possibly a disgrace to werewolves everywhere. Beauty's lip-piercing alone was enough to make her Aunt Verasa shudder. As for Delicious, her blue hair dye had scandalised the family and almost got her expelled from her expensive private school.

Beauty and Delicious were twins, the only children of Marwis, the Thane's youngest brother who had died some years ago in a plane crash. As Marwis's wife was also long dead, the twins were left parentless. They coped with this bravely, and some years later arrived in London a pair of cheerful, drunken, drug-taking degenerates who had started abusing their bodies when they were young and carried on happily ever since. After accidentally burning down the family home in Scotland they had decided it was time to seek new challenges and had moved south to start a band and see what fun they could have. Now twenty-two, the twins spent most of their time in an alcohol-induced haze in their house in Camden in North London, listening to music and practising guitar. Although full-blooded members of the MacRinnalch ruling family, it was years since either of them had voluntarily turned into a werewolf. They had long forgotten how to do it, though they still enjoyed the monthly full moon transformation which came on automatically. Then, for three nights they would get hideously intoxicated and run through the streets howling and laughing.

To the family's great displeasure, the twin sisters had a large private income, the inheritance from their father's estate. Bolstered by this, they flatly refused to move back to Scotland. Much as the Thane and Verasa might like to drag them back to the family estates, there was no way to do it short of kidnapping. The family had considered this. The disgrace of Beauty and Delicious could not be allowed to continue indefinitely.

The state of the werewolf younger generation had caused the Thane and Verasa some distress. Although, in truth, there were a great many of the MacRinnalch Clan still upholding the traditional ways. There were many who lived on the family lands as upright citizens, turning into werewolf form only occasionally, mainly to hunt deer. If the occasional human was killed on their lands, it was only to be expected. Tourists were notoriously careless.

Verasa's younger sister Lucia, who also lived in the castle, still defended the cousins on occasion.

"At least they're only drunks," she pointed out to Verasa, more than once. "They've never really harmed anyone."

By which Lucia meant that the cousins about whom they did not speak weren't criminally insane like Kalix. Verasa refused to go along with this. Beauty and Delicious were a disgrace to the family. The Mistress of the Werewolves regretted that they had been so frequently at Castle MacRinnalch in their childhood. Verasa always suspected that they had been a very bad influence on her youngest daughter.

15

Kalix slept in the chair. She appeared peaceful. Occasionally she would mutter a few inaudible words. Daniel and Moonglow looked at her from the far side of the room. Having seen her astonishing powers they were wary of getting too close.

"She looks so small. Sort of pathetic," said Moonglow.

"And yet only recently she was kung fu-ing opponents round the room."

Daniel shuddered. He'd been stunned by the viciousness of Kalix's fighting. The head-butt to her opponent's face had been particularly brutal.

"I really don't want to meet any more werewolves."

"Lucky we're moving tonight."

"Are we going to let her stay?" asked Daniel.

"Of course. We can't throw her out," said Moonglow.

Moonglow was such a kind soul. It was one of the things Daniel liked about her. That and her pretty face, her long black hair and the really attractive nose stud. It was a much more discreet piece of facial jewellery than Kalix's large nose ring. Though Daniel was keen to agree with Moonglow about most things, he couldn't help being nervous about having a savage werewolf slumbering in his favourite chair.

"It might be best to... you know... encourage her to leave."

"Certainly not." Moonglow was indignant. "Imagine you were a homeless young werewolf and other werewolves were trying to kill you. How would you like it?"

"I guess it might drive me to diazepam."

"I still think that's weird," said Moonglow. "If I ever met an otherworldly creature, I wasn't expecting it to be having treatment for depression."

"Where would she get the pills?" wondered Daniel. "Do you think they have werewolf psychiatrists?"

Daniel mused about this for a while, then wondered why he was talking about werewolves as if they were an everyday occurrence. Kalix murmured in her sleep again, slightly louder this time.

"Gawain... banished..."

With that she woke up, and looked at them suspiciously. Without speaking, she leapt from the chair and headed for the door.

"You don't have to go – " said Moonglow, and stretched out a friendly arm. Kalix growled fiercely at her. Startled, Moonglow stepped back. Kalix departed.

"Personal space issues," said Daniel. "It's probably a werewolf thing."

Moonglow gazed out the window at the rain, rather hoping that the werewolf might change her mind, and come back, but there was no sign of her. Eventually they got back to packing up their belongings.

Kalix spent the rest of the night in an alleyway, cold and wet. As the long minutes ticked past, she fell into a great pit of unhappiness. The depression with which she always struggled took hold of her. Kalix sipped some laudanum. Her supply was almost gone, and she didn't have enough money to buy more.

The laudanum dulled the pain in her body but it wasn't enough to take away her misery. She took another of her diazepam capsules. It still wasn't enough. The depression led, as it often did, to a terrible feeling of anxiety which she hated. Once the anxiety really set in Kalix always feared that she would soon be insane. When it had her in its grip, she always felt it would never go away. Finally, unable to take any more, Kalix took out the small kitchen knife she carried in her bag. She stared at her forearm for a few seconds then made a cut just above her elbow. Blood flowed down her arm. Kalix immediately felt a little better. She didn't really know why, but this always helped. Comforted, she managed to drift off to sleep.

She slept fitfully, with bad dreams. She had terrifying images of her family and distressing memories of Gawain.

"I will always love you," said Gawain, in her dream.

Kalix woke in tears because she knew it wasn't true. Gawain was far away; no one knew where. The Thane had banished him for his involvement with his daughter, an involvement that had started far too young for the Thane's liking. Not that the Thane would have allowed them to be together in any case. Gawain was not of a suitable class to be allowed a relationship with the Thane's daughter. He came from a respected werewolf family but even so he was not pure-blooded enough. Gawain had one wholly human grandparent. It made him an unsuitable partner for an aristocratic werewolf girl.

Gawain was strong, impervious to the elements, a skilled hunter and frightened of no one. Kalix had always felt safe with him. Yet hadn't he agreed to leave her too easily? Had he protested enough when the Thane sent him away? Kalix stirred uncomfortably in her drugged, stuporous state. Could he not have come back and rescued her when she needed him?

Her mother Verasa told Kalix she should forget Gawain because he would forget her soon enough. Kalix couldn't forget him. She loved him madly, and always would.

The wound on her arm bled for a long time. Kalix had noticed recently that her blood didn't seem to clot as quickly as it used to. Some symptom of her poor health she supposed. Kalix didn't care. She wished she might just bleed to death where she lay.

16

In the late evening the Mistress of the Werewolves and her youngest son walked through Verasa's art gallery. Verasa had a very fine collection of pictures, accumulated over the past two hundred years. Markus noticed an empty space on the wall.

"Where's the Vermeer?"

"I lent it to the National Gallery."

Markus was surprised.

"Just because I'm Mistress of the Werewolves doesn't mean I have no sense of duty to the wider public. It's the modern world dear, we all have to make a contribution."

Markus was distracted from the paintings by the family situation.

"If I bring Kalix back to the castle there will be trouble. She's so unstable. What if she breaks free and attacks the Thane again?"

The Mistress of the Werewolves came very close to smiling.

"That would be very unfortunate…"

Verasa had let it be known, to those members of the clan from whom the severity of the Thane's injuries could not be concealed, that Kalix had pushed her father down a flight of stairs, while under the influence of alcohol. The incident was supposed to have happened in daylight while they were both in human form. This was a terrible disgrace but the truth was worse. In reality Kalix had defeated the Thane at night when they were both in werewolf form. She'd have killed him if Sarapen and two of his servants had not come to his rescue. The full shocking circumstances could never be revealed to the clan. The Thane had to be respected, which he would not be if it were learned that his youngest daughter had defeated him in combat.

The Thane, though old, was an extremely powerful werewolf. Neither of his sons would have relished fighting him. Verasa was at a loss to explain Kalix's abnormal strength. Of course, Kalix was the only one of her children to be born at the time of the full moon, when Verasa was herself in werewolf shape. This was unusual. Werewolf mothers almost always gave birth while in human form. As a consequence of Verasa being werewolf at the time, Kalix had actually been born in her own werewolf shape, which was again extremely rare. Born as a werewolf by a werewolf, under a full moon. Perhaps this had contributed to her strength, though Verasa thought it was more probably a product of her insanity. This, Verasa swore, did not come from her side of the family.

The Thane's lack of emotion had alienated Verasa a long time ago. Sensing the same nature in her oldest boy Sarapen, Verasa had never warmed to him as she should. She had no qualms about planning to have her younger son Markus declared Thane when it was time for the succession. Succession to the Thaneship was rarely an entirely straightforward affair. The history of the MacRinnalch Clan was full of messy incidents.

It would take time for the Mistress of the Werewolves to bring her plans to fruition. There were many votes on the Great Council that would have to be won over before Markus could become Thane. Verasa needed to be in control of as many elements as possible. A demented daughter running out of control in the streets of London could not be tolerated.

"I'll look for her tonight," said Markus. "Is it absolutely necessary that I bring her back alive?"

"It would be better," replied Verasa.

17

Thrix worked late into the night, preparing new outfits for the Fire Queen. Models paraded before them and the Fire Queen squealed with delight when she saw something she liked, which was often.

Thrix's regular models were by now used to some of her more unconventional clients. They didn't mind. Thrix paid them very well, and treated them civilly. Possibly more civilly than she treated most people. The Enchantress had a sharp tongue and a somewhat impatient nature. She rarely lost her temper with her own workforce, but there were people in the industry who did not particularly like Thrix MacRinnalch. She was too intelligent, too beautiful and too ambitious to be universally popular.

Thrix's share of the family's great wealth was not nearly as large as she would have liked. The family money was mostly under Verasa's control and Verasa had never really supported her daughter's ambitions in the fashion industry. For a long time Thrix had struggled to pay the bills. In the last two years, this had changed. The business was now beginning to pay dividends and with the extra income generated by her work for Malveria, the Enchantress was no longer struggling. She owned a comfortable apartment in the centre of town and had recently made a down payment on a Mercedes.

Her wealth, beauty, and approaching success should have been more than enough to land the Enchantress at least one good relationship, but for some reason Thrix never managed to find a boyfriend she liked.

"Can't you just kidnap someone?" suggested the Fire Queen.

"Not if I want to build a lasting relationship," explained Thrix. The Fire Queen didn't really understand. There was much about the human realm she didn't understand. As one of the great elemental queens of

40

nature, Malveria had human devotees all around the world, but though the Queen appreciated their support, in reality she was almost as vague about the norms of human relationships as she was about plumbing.

"Is it because you are a werewolf and are required to go out with another werewolf but find this difficult because you have always tried to distance yourself from your clan?"

"That doesn't help," acknowledged the Enchantress. "But I'd settle for a nice human who'd take me to dinner and not bore me by talking about himself all the time."

Malveria nodded. This she could understand. Even in her realm, the male fire spirits did tend to be full of themselves. Her ladies-in-waiting were always complaining about it.

"Perhaps the more pleasant humans are intimidated by your beauty," suggested the Fire Queen. "It is something I also suffer from, naturally. My own fabulous attractiveness has often made suitors tremble and shake but of course, I simply take whoever I please to be my consort. You know, I had a visitor last week, a most handsome young man, part elemental but with a little Elf in him, or possibly Fairy. He had a glorious smile and some interesting tales of several realms. Would you like to meet him?"

Thrix shook her head. Her experience of blind dates had never been good. The conversation ended when Malveria was distracted by the most beautiful pair of silver slippers and practically shot from her chair with delight, a tiny flicker of flame appearing at the end of each of her fingers. Thrix shot her a warning glance. It wouldn't do to be upsetting the models by bursting into flames, and besides, there was always the danger of damaging the clothes.

"I want a hundred pairs," yelled Malveria.

"I can give you four," said Thrix.

"Four will be satisfactory," said the Fire Queen.

18

Kalix was now dangerously weak. She almost never ate while in human form but she was prevented from starving herself to death because during the three nights around the full moon when she would change into werewolf form whether she wanted to or not, the werewolf would eat.

As a werewolf, Kalix was still in control of her actions. She did not lose her powers of rational thought. But there were differences. In werewolf form, life never looked quite the same. Her problems with eating would vanish and the wolf-Kalix would spend each night gorging herself on whatever meat was available. Sometimes dogs from alleys, sometimes the contents of butcher's shops which she would enter by tearing the doors off. When she reverted back to her human form, the memory of eating made her feel nauseated. She would make herself vomit but it was too late to clear the food from her system. The three night binge was always enough to give her the strength to keep on living. The werewolf inside her was too strong to let her die.

Now, close to the full moon, Kalix had not eaten properly for weeks. She was surviving on laudanum, tranquillisers, and the occasional shot of alcohol, and her strength was almost gone.

Dawn filtered into the alley and Kalix woke with a start, still struggling with her dreams. Without warning a hand gripped her throat.

"Hello little sister."

It was Markus. Beautifully attired as always in a long overcoat and a dark suit, his long curly chestnut hair tied back neatly with a black ribbon. He picked Kalix up with one hand and threw her across the alley. She crashed into the opposite wall and slumped heavily to the ground. She attempted to rise but Markus was already standing over her. He looked down at the skinny girl with contempt.

"Another bad day for the lonely werewolf girl," he said, mockingly.

Kalix struggled to regain her feet. Markus put his foot on her chest, crushing her to the ground.

"Should I take you back?" mused Markus, out loud, "What do you think, lonely werewolf girl?"

"Don't call me that," snarled Kalix.

Markus laughed.

"Why not? Have you ever made a friend?"

He looked down, directly into her eyes. Kalix glared back at him with loathing but she felt shame at his mockery.

"Is there a single werewolf or human who cares whether you're alive or dead? Anyone to come to your rescue?"

Kalix still met his eyes, refusing to look away, but she had no answer for her brother.

"The family wants you dead. The hunters want you dead. You probably want yourself dead. Why are you still alive, lonely werewolf girl?"

Markus leant on her more heavily and Kalix struggled to breath.

"Even your ill-bred lover doesn't care about you."

At the mention of Gawain, Kalix erupted in fury and managed to heave herself free but as she scrambled to her feet Markus caught her with a blow and she slumped once more to the ground. Her brother looked at her with loathing.

"Do you realise the trouble you've caused us all, you foul girl? I almost wish the Douglas-MacPhees had cut out your heart. I'd cut it out myself if mother didn't want me to bring you back you alive."

Kalix, on her knees, sneered at him.

"And you always like to do what mother tells you, Markus."

Markus, angered, kicked out at her savagely, and Kalix fell to the ground unconscious.

19

Daniel and Moonglow trundled slowly along the street in their rented van. Moonglow was navigating; Daniel was driving. They halted at a traffic light, where Moonglow struggled to read her map.

"Did that really happen today?" said Daniel, abruptly.

"It did."

"It was a startling experience."

"Very startling."

"I thought we coped well," said Daniel. "I mean, how many people would have the presence of mind to offer a werewolf a pop-tart?"

Though meeting a werewolf had been an astonishing experience, they hadn't discussed it as much as they might have, because, suffering from the stress of packing and moving in secret, they'd had a prolonged argument which left them barely talking to each other. Tense at the thought of being caught by their landlord, Daniel had yet again found himself criticising Moonglow's huge collection of scented candles. At four in the morning it suddenly seemed unreasonable of her to own so many.

"Who needs so much lavender scent?" he complained.

"I do," declared Moonglow, who was in no mood to take criticism over a few candles. "The main reason for this experience being hell on earth is your music collection."

Daniel had an enormous collection of CDs plus a healthy amount of old records and tapes. He'd started collecting when he was nine and never lost the habit.

"At least they're useful," said Daniel.

"Three different copies of one Slayer album is not useful," declared Moonglow.

"They have slightly different covers," countered Daniel, defensively.

Daniel dumped the box of candles in the back of the van.

"You just have so many because Jay likes them," he said, accusingly.

"Will you get off my back about Jay?"

Moonglow's mood was worsened by her memory of Kalix. She supposed she would never see the young werewolf again and would never know what became of her. Moonglow was troubled by the thought of her running through the streets, pursued by who knew what.

By the time they finished packing they were barely talking to each other and Moonglow was wondering if maybe she should have found a place of her own to live. But she liked sharing with Daniel. He was a good flatmate. Funny, interesting, and reasonably considerate in household matters, which is to say he didn't mind that Moonglow was extremely untidy. So was he. Both of them were quite prepared to let the dirty dishes pile up to alarming levels. It didn't bother them at all. As flatmates, they were well suited. It was just unfortunate that Daniel was jealous of her boyfriend.

As far as Moonglow could gather, Daniel had never actually had a girlfriend. That was a strange thought. Moonglow, who'd grown up in Winchester, had been surrounded by boys since she was fourteen, when she'd first dyed her hair black and gone to the local Goth club. Her mother had paid for her hair dye. And she'd let Moonglow have her ears pierced on her tenth birthday, feeling that it was always good to let her daughter express herself.

"Which turning?" asked Daniel.

"Wait a minute," said Moonglow, who was still studying the map.

"I can't wait a minute, the traffic light's turned green. I knew you

44

couldn't read a street map."

"I could read it if you'd let me concentrate," retorted Moonglow.

"Look – " said Daniel.

"Be quiet!" said Moonglow, loudly. "I've almost got it."

"There's a – "

"Will you shut up!"

"In the street!" screamed Daniel. "The werewolf girl!"

Moonglow finally noticed that Daniel was pointing in front of them. There, at the mouth of an alleyway, a man was dragging the young werewolf girl along the ground.

"We have to help!" yelled Moonglow, and opened her door. Hearing this, the man looked over and as he did so Kalix, regaining consciousness, broke free of his grasp and started to run. The man ran after her but Kalix, now having a little room to manoeuvre, planted one foot firmly on the ground and raised her leg to deliver a fierce kick into her assailant's midriff. He fell to the ground.

"Over here!" screamed Moonglow.

Kalix ran towards them. Behind her Markus was already rising to pursue her. Kalix made it to the van and leapt onto Moonglow's lap. Moonglow slammed the door shut and screamed for Daniel to drive. Daniel was already putting the van in gear but by the time he'd got them underway their pursuer was alongside. He struck out at the window and Moonglow gasped as the glass broke, showering her with fragments. Daniel put his foot down and they sped away, no longer worrying about which direction they were going.

Kalix squirmed off Moonglow's lap. In the front of the van there was plenty of room for her slender frame. They drove quickly in silence through the empty morning streets.

"So," said Daniel, finally. "Another of your brother's employees trying to kill you?"

"Different brother," replied Kalix.

Daniel and Moonglow mused on this for a while.

"You have a really bad family," said Daniel, eventually.

By the time they reached their new flat Kalix had fallen asleep.

"For a person who's always being pursued by murderous relatives this girl spends a lot of time sleeping," said Daniel, as they carried her inside.

"Perhaps it's the stress," suggested Moonglow. "Remember how much we slept during the exams?"

They laid Kalix on the couch then went back to the van to start unloading their belongings.

"Do you think maybe we should wake her up?" said Daniel, after they'd made a few trips. "She could help us unload the van with her mighty werewolf strength."

Moonglow looked at Kalix, thin, ragged and filthy, asleep on their couch. Blood had congealed around her nose and mouth.

"Don't be heartless," she said. "She needs to rest."

"So do I," muttered Daniel, and went back for another box. He was convinced that he was doing all the work, though really he had done no more than Moonglow.

When Kalix woke up Moonglow helped her to wash the blood from her wounds. The werewolf, surprisingly, did not object.

"Maybe you should take a bath," suggested Moonglow. She tried not to sound insistent though she couldn't help noticing that Kalix smelled really badly. It was a long time since she'd washed properly.

Kalix felt that she should be moving on. She wasn't safe here. But she wasn't safe anywhere. She gazed longingly at the bath, white and clean, then nodded. While Moonglow ran the water Kalix slipped out of her rags and for the first time since Moonglow had met her, something resembling a smile appeared on her face. Moonglow went to hunt through her boxes for her shampoo and bath oils. Downstairs Daniel was finally bringing in the last of their possessions. He was very red in the face. As a first year English student he wasn't used to a lot of exercise. Two days a week his lectures started at nine in the morning and he always felt that this deprived him of a lot of sleep.

"She's taking a bath," said Moonglow. "I'm going to help her wash her hair."

"Do you want me to help?"

"You? Don't you think there might be a problem there? Young naked girl in the bath?"

"She's a werewolf," said Daniel. "She might look at these things differently."

Moonglow told Daniel to stay out the bathroom.

"You called her a wild beauty. That disqualifies you from seeing her naked. It's no longer innocent. Make us some tea instead."

Daniel did as Moonglow requested. Moonglow meanwhile returned to the bathroom to find Kalix lying contentedly in a bath full of hot water. When Daniel arrived upstairs with tea, Moonglow had started on the exceedingly difficult task of washing Kalix's hair.

"I think you have a world record for tangles," said Moonglow. "When did you last wash it?"

Kalix couldn't remember. She screwed up her eyes and protested as some shampoo trickled down her forehead. Moonglow had the sudden feeling that she was bathing a child.

"How old are you?"

"Seventeen," said Kalix.

"How long have you been a werewolf?"

Kalix looked insulted.

"What do you mean?"

"When were you turned into a werewolf?"

Kalix emitted a small snarl, enough to make Moonglow draw back.

"Did I say something wrong?"

"I was not *turned into a werewolf*. I was born a werewolf, fourth child of the Thane, a pure-blooded wolf of the Royal Family of Clan MacRinnalch."

"Sorry," said Moonglow. "I thought you had to be bitten."

"A werewolf can be created that way," conceded Kalix. "But it's an insult to a pure-blooded wolf to accuse them of being bitten."

Naked, Kalix's ribs were clearly visible. She was painfully thin. It made Moonglow worry that if she washed her too hard she might break. Moonglow ran water over Kalix's hair. It was so thick and tangled that working her fingers through it was next to impossible.

"I think we'll have to cut some of these tangles out," she said.

Kalix snarled again, even more alarmingly.

"Another insult?" said Moonglow, nervously.

"My hair has never been cut," said Kalix, rather haughtily. "And no human will approach it with scissors."

"Sorry."

"Everything going all right in there?" called Daniel, who was sitting

47

outside the door, drinking tea.

"Fine," called Moonglow. "Put some music on."

She rinsed the shampoo out of Kalix's hair.

"Do you want me to condition it? It might make it easier to brush afterwards."

Kalix snarled again.

"What's wrong now?" wailed Moonglow.

"You are not brushing my hair," said Kalix, aggressively.

"I didn't mean I was going to brush it," protested Moonglow. "You can do it yourself."

She started to feel aggrieved.

"And could you stop snarling at me? I'm only trying to help."

Kalix looked surprised, but she didn't apologise.

"I don't see what's so bad about having your hair brushed anyway," said Moonglow, still a little annoyed. "Is it another pure-bred werewolf thing?"

"No," said Kalix. "I just don't like it."

"My mother used to brush my hair when I was little," said Moonglow. "Didn't yours?"

"No."

When the difficult process of washing Kalix's hair was completed Moonglow gently bathed her nose ring, checking that the accumulated dirt had not caused an infection. It seemed healthy enough and when she complimented Kalix on it the werewolf seemed pleased.

Some time later Kalix appeared downstairs wearing one of Moonglow's dressing gowns, looking clean and fresh. Without her layering of dirt she was extremely pale. It made her huge dark eyes even more prominent and now that the lines of her cheekbones could be seen clearly, Moonglow agreed with Daniel's description of Kalix. She was an extraordinary beauty. Her mouth was unusually wide and her hair, now clean and untangled, was astonishingly long. As she dried and brushed it, it increased in volume so that it swirled round her body, a huge dark mane that made Moonglow rather envious even though her own long black hair was widely admired.

"Do you have anything to drink?" asked Kalix, suddenly.

"We have some beer," said Daniel, who'd packed a few cans to help him recover from the stress of moving home.

"Do you want anything to eat?" asked Moonglow.

Kalix shook her head. She only wanted beer.

48

"You should eat," said Moonglow, but Kalix didn't respond.

There was a gas fire on the wall which was giving off a lot of heat and Kalix sat next to it, drinking beer and taking in the warmth.

"Do you want to stay with us?" asked Moonglow, unexpectedly.

Kalix looked round, surprised.

"What?"

"You could live with us."

Kalix shook her head.

"I can't. It's stupid of you to ask me."

21

The doorbell rang. Kalix tensed, ready to fight or to flee.

"Relax. We phoned for a pizza."

Daniel paid for the pizza and brought it upstairs. They looked at the box for a few moments.

"It's a big moment," announced Moonglow.

"Our first pizza delivery in our new flat."

Daniel and Moonglow were very dependent on take-away pizza. They had healthy teenage appetites but no desire to cook, ever. Daniel opened the box, tore a slice of with his fingers and shoved it in his mouth.

"It's good," he said, with his mouth full.

"It's a good omen," said Moonglow. Having their first pizza for breakfast made their new place feel like home. They were pleased to have moved. This shabby flat, above a small shop, was no better than their last one really, but at least they were out of debt.

"Why can't you stay?" asked Moonglow.

Kalix said that it was too dangerous, but wouldn't elaborate.

"Why are your relatives trying to kill you?" ventured Daniel.

"That's the private business of the MacRinnalchs," said Kalix.

"But can't we give you sanctuary?"

Kalix shook her head.

"They can find me anywhere."

"How have you stayed alive this long?"

"I used to have a charm, a pendant. My sister gave it to me. It hid me. But I lost it. Now I can't hide. Especially when I'm a werewolf."

"If you don't mind me asking," said Moonglow. "How could you be a werewolf tonight? It's not the full moon."

Kalix looked at Moonglow slightly contemptuously.

"A pure-blooded MacRinnalch werewolf can be a werewolf under any moon."

"Oh. Are there some that can't?"

Apparently there were. According to Kalix, many of the Scottish werewolves did need the full moon to transform. Those not so pure-blooded as Kalix could change on the night before the full moon, the night of the full moon, and the night after.

"These are the wolf nights. But I don't need a wolf night. I can do it any night."

"Can all werewolves do kung fu?" asked Daniel.

"What?"

"The way you kicked these guys. How come you can fight like that? Does it just come naturally to werewolves?"

"No. Someone taught me."

"Who?"

But this seemed to be another bad question and Kalix looked displeased. She refused to say anymore about anything. Under questioning she became first sulky and then hostile, till Daniel and Moonglow had to leave her be. When it was time for her to dress Kalix accepted a pair of black jeans from Moonglow, and a belt to keep them up. She took a sweater that was also too big for her but she refused to replace her ragged coat. Moonglow looked at the shabby garment.

"It used to be nice," said Kalix.

"I can see that. It's a shame it's got so ragged."

Moonglow looked inside at the label.

"Thrix Fashions?"

Kalix snatched the coat from Moonglow.

"Give me."

Kalix had been mellowed by the hot bath and the temporary refuge but now her mood was worsening and she was agitated at having two strangers fingering her belongings and asking her questions. It had been a mistake to stay here for so long. She picked up her bag and put on her coat.

"Are you leaving?"

"Yes."

Kalix strode out of their flat in silence. Daniel and Moonglow watched her go.

"Not even a goodbye?" said Daniel.

"Or a thank you?"

"She's not what you'd call polite."

"Very pretty though," said Moonglow, slightly teasingly. She knew it embarrassed Daniel even to admit he found any girl attractive.

It was time for them to go to lectures. Both of them were due to attend a class on Shakespeare's *Timon of Athens*.

"Which is a good play," said Moonglow. "Or so I hear."

"Probably one of his best," agreed Daniel. "Are you going to the lecture?"

"No. I'm too tired. We've been moving all night."

"My thoughts exactly," said Daniel.

They unpacked their duvets and headed towards their new bedrooms where they threw them on their beds, and crawled underneath to sleep away the day. Daniel and Moonglow had known each other for almost a year. They'd met while both lost on their first day at university. Daniel had been immediately attracted to Moonglow but had been too shy to do anything about it. So they became friends, and then flatmates. That was good, but Daniel couldn't help regretting that Moonglow only regarded him as a friend.

22

After his failure to apprehend Kalix, Markus had to explain his lack of success to his mother. Verasa would rarely criticise Markus but she was adept in letting him know when she was disappointed.

"I would have brought her had it not been for the interference of the two young humans."

It was very strange that two teenagers had rescued Kalix. She had no friends, as far as anyone knew. After letting Markus know that she was displeased, Verasa consoled him.

"Don't look so disappointed about Kalix, dear. I'm sure you'll find her again. Will you come with me to see Thrix tomorrow?"

"You know I don't get on well with Thrix," protested Markus.

Verasa sighed. Sometimes it was a trial, the way that none of her children liked each other.

"I cannot be in London without paying a visit to my eldest daughter."

Markus couldn't understand why his mother still took the trouble.

"She does everything she can to distance herself from the clan. If she doesn't want to know us then why not just let her be?"

"Someone has to hold this family together, Markus. Your father won't do it, so it's up to me. Would you have me suffer the indignity of admitting to my sister Lucia that I couldn't see my own daughter?"

"I suppose not. But Thrix had better not try any of her enchantments while I'm there. Is she still friends with that fire elemental?"

Verasa looked pained. There was considerable ill-will among the MacRinnalch werewolves towards the Hiyasta. It was to be expected that a daughter who was so adept at sorcery might make the acquaintance of various strange creatures but there was no reason to befriend them. Verasa regretted that her daughter had proved to be so talented at sorcery. It was a rare attribute for a werewolf, and hardly a fitting one for a daughter of the Thane.

"I spoke to your father today."

"How is the Thane?"

"Weak. But recovering."

Markus believed his mother was deluding herself. Since Kalix's savage attack the Thane had never been the same. Markus did not think that he would ever recover. Age and injury were catching up with him. Each full moon he gained some revitalising power but afterwards he was weaker. He couldn't go on for all that much longer. Markus had little love for his father. The Thane had always been far closer to Sarapen, and Markus had always felt excluded. Markus was jealous, and it added to the hatred he felt for his older brother. Sarapen had always attempted to dominate him. Soon, with the help of Verasa, Markus might be Thane, chief of the MacRinnalchs, lord of MacRinnalch Castle. That would be suitable revenge on Sarapen.

Though he liked the castle in Scotland, and his rather grand town house in Charlotte Square in Edinburgh, Markus was a frequent visitor to London. His girlfriend Talixia lived here, and he was very fond of her. Recently he'd realised that he might be in love with her, which was a surprise. He was certainly close enough to her to discuss matters which his mother would rather had remained within the confines of the castle. The approaching row over the succession, for instance.

Talixia wondered if he really wanted the Thaneship. It seemed like a position which would interfere with the things he enjoyed in life. Markus liked painting, and he had some talent for it, talent which might blossom if he applied himself.

"If you become Thane," said Talixia. "Will you have time to paint? Time to go to the opera?"

Markus wasn't sure. Perhaps he could be the first artistic Thane? It was an amusing thought. Markus had a sense of humour, something which distinguished him from Sarapen, who was so grim it seemed like he might pass his entire life without laughing.

Markus was not without his cruel side. He had learned to hunt deer and stags on the family estates, and early in his life had become used to the feel of tearing flesh between his jaws. He had a capacity for violence, and it was this which had led to the bad feeling between him and Kalix. When Kalix was around eight years old she'd stolen a watch from his chambers. It was hard to explain why Kalix stole things from around the castle. She just did. Markus tracked her down in the woods and recovered his watch. That might have been the end of it had Kalix not spitefully called Markus a mummy's boy, this being the best insult the young Kalix could think of. Unfortunately it seemed to strike a very bad chord with Markus and he lashed out at her. Despite being far smaller than her brother, Kalix promptly bit him. Markus responded quite savagely. The sorry affair ended with an unrepentant Kalix being left battered and bleeding in the woods, howling for revenge.

After this Kalix had always loathed Markus and as she grew stronger she sought opportunities to pick fights with him. Eventually the Thane, frustrated by Kalix's insane assaults on Markus, had completely lost his temper and brutally chastised her, which only made Kalix hate him and Markus even more.

23

Daniel and Moonglow both studied English at King's College. Daniel minored in social studies while Moonglow took Sumerian history. The main part of the university was in the Strand, in the centre of London.

53

After taking a day off to recover from moving, Moonglow went in early the next day though Daniel, still fatigued, felt he needed another morning in bed. He did make it in around lunch time and waited in the student bar to meet her. When Moonglow arrived she was excited. She brandished her laptop computer.

"Look at this."

"It's your MacBook," said Daniel. "I've seen it before."

Moonglow's MacBook was a present from her parents. Moonglow's parents were quite wealthy, and she had more money than Daniel. She connected to the internet and directed Daniel's attention away from his pint and towards the screen.

"I mean look at this website. Thrix Fashions. A small fashion house, on the rise or so it says."

"So?"

"Don't you see?"

"That's a lot of money for a pair of shoes," said Daniel.

"It's – "

"I mean, £500? For shoes? Are they serious?"

"Yes, it is on the pricey side," admitted Moonglow. "Though they are very nice shoes. But you're missing the point. Remember the label on Kalix's coat? It said *Thrix Fashions*. Well take a look at Thrix."

Moonglow brought up a picture of the owner of the fashion house. Daniel was impressed.

"What a babe."

"Are you wilfully missing the point?" demanded Moonglow. "This woman is obviously related to Kalix."

"How do you know?"

"Just look at her."

Daniel looked. He could see what Moonglow meant. Despite the fashion designer's spectacular blonde hair she did indeed look rather like Kalix. The same large eyes, the same fine cheekbones, the same wide mouth. Not quite so wide as Kalix's perhaps, but there was certainly a resemblance.

"Isn't it great?" said Moonglow.

Daniel wasn't really sure why Moonglow was so pleased.

"So the owner of Thrix Fashions is possibly a werewolf relation. So what?"

"We can go and visit her and tell her Kalix is in trouble and she might help. Didn't Kalix say she got her protection charm from her sister? This might be that sister. She can give her a new charm. Then Kalix will be able to hide again."

Throughout this Daniel had been becoming agitated.

"Slow down, Moonglow. Is this really a good idea? Meeting these werewolves hasn't been that much fun. As far as I can see they're all violent lunatics. I don't want to go waltzing into this woman's office and announce that we know she's a werewolf and we're looking for one of her relatives. How's she going to take that? Badly, I imagine."

"We have to help Kalix."

"No, we don't."

"We can't abandon her."

Daniel pointed out to Moonglow that Kalix had showed no desire to be helped by them. Quite the opposite. She'd walked out without a word of thanks. Moonglow became agitated.

"How can you just desert her like this?"

"I'm not deserting her."

"You are."

"Moonglow. Does it mean anything to you that I don't want to be chopped up with a machete or eaten by a werewolf? Does this have any bearing on things at all?"

"Of course. I don't want you to be chopped up or eaten. I'd miss you terribly."

"Really? You'd miss me terribly?"

"Of course."

Daniel was pleased to hear Moonglow say he'd miss him. Not wanting to spoil her good opinion of him, he found himself agreeing to the plan, against his better judgement. Just then one of Moonglow's friends, a girl called Alicia, appeared at their side.

"What you looking at?" she asked, seeing the MacBook.

"Shoes," answered Daniel. "Isn't it ridiculous having shoes that cost £500?"

"No," said Alicia. "Not for shoes as beautiful as that. I'd buy them if I had the money." She looked at Daniel as if he was a man who didn't understand the important things in life. Daniel was crushed. Yet again he had failed to impress one of Moonglow's friends. It was unfair. Who ever knew the right thing to say to them? Later in the day, when Moonglow's boyfriend Jay arrived and, openly and in public, kissed her on the lips, Daniel found himself thinking that being ripped to shreds by savage werewolves might not be all that bad.

24

Thrix Fashions had its headquarters in Wardour Street, in Soho, in the heart of London. Though the door at street level was discreet, Thrix Fashions occupied all of the third and fourth floors, where Daniel and Moonglow now sat in a reception room. Daniel had been secretly hoping that he might find himself surrounded by young models but he was disappointed. Here in Thrix's suite of offices there were no models, though the people who did walk by – designers perhaps – were attractive enough to make Daniel feel shabby and out of place, in his baggy student doom-metal-fan clothes. Moonglow, in her customary gothic garb of long black skirt and black top, looked even more out of place.

Thrix's assistant Ann arrived and spoke to them brusquely.

"This way."

Daniel and Moonglow trooped after her. She ushered them into an office so coolly and expensively furnished, in which sat a woman so elegant, that Daniel immediately felt intimidated. Faced with this female he knew he would be unable to say a single sensible word and wished he was back in the student bar.

Thrix eyed them coldly.

"Well?" she said, finally.

Moonglow and Daniel stood there in silence. Now that they were actually here, it didn't seem all that easy to raise the subject of werewolves. Thrix looked impatient.

"You told my assistant you needed to speak to me about an important family matter. What is it?"

Moonglow had planned to work up to things gradually but the unfamiliar surroundings unsettled her. Instead of a calm discussion leading up to a possible question about the whereabouts of Kalix, Moonglow was horrified to find herself blurting out that the young werewolf girl needed help before her family killed her.

Thrix narrowed her eyes a fraction of an inch.

"Pardon?"

"Kalix. Your young sister. Her brother is trying to kill her and cut out her heart. You have to give her another pendant."

"I have no idea what you're talking about."

"Yes, you do," responded Moonglow. "I can tell."

'She can, unfortunately,' thought the Enchantress. 'The girl has some powers of intuition.' Thrix regarded them for a half minute longer, then leaned forward a few inches. She spoke coolly, showing no more emotion than she would while ordering a glass of wine.

"If you become involved with my family, you'll die," she said, and sat back in her chair.

"Eh…" said Daniel, and looked back at the door.

"But I will give you this opportunity to leave, and forget all about it," continued Thrix, calmly.

"Okay," said Daniel, clapping his hands together. "That's good enough for me. We gave it our best shot."

He grabbed Moonglow's arm and started to retreat swiftly. Moonglow shook him off.

"We want to help," she insisted.

"I'm quite serious about your deaths," said Thrix, this time with just the slightest shade of emotion. Moonglow felt quite certain that inside this woman there was a werewolf of some power but she would not be put off.

"I gave her a bath. She was filthy and skinny and she hadn't eaten for weeks and she had cuts and blood and ragged clothes and tranquillisers and murderous brothers trying to cut her heart out. She was a total mess and what sort of person are you that threatens to kill people who're trying to help your sister?"

Daniel looked at Moonglow in amazement. Thrix was obviously angered. She spoke into the intercom.

"Hold my calls."

25

The MacRinnalchs had two conflicting myths about their origins. One story said that the werewolf clan had been started by Gavur Rinnal at the time of the Roman occupation of Britain, two thousand years ago. According to this story, Gavur, after being badly wounded in battle with the Romans during their northernmost expedition into Scotland, at Cree, had ridden back to the hills and hidden in a cave, while the victorious Roman army combed the area. While hiding in the cave he had been visited by a Pictish medicine woman. She told him that she could save his life, though his life would never be the same again.

57

Gavur accepted her offer. His tribe had been all but wiped out at the battle of Cree and he yearned to take revenge. The Pictish healer put herbs on his wounds, and chanted a spell over him. Gavur Rinnal fell asleep. When he woke, he felt refreshed. At that moment two Roman soldiers entered the cave. Gavur flew at them and to his amazement he found himself rending their throats with his jaws. He had been transformed into a wolf. Gavur killed many of his enemies in the hills, and ever afterwards he retained the power of transforming into a wolf-like creature at will. From Gavur Rinnal and his wife, the whole MacRinnalch Clan was descended.

But another story said that the MacRinnalchs had come originally from Sumeria, from the same plains that saw the rise of the first cities ever built by men. They had emerged from the mists of prehistory among the people of Ur, formed by some strange mingling of beasts and men, when supernatural powers still walked the earth. From Ur the werewolves had spread through Mesopotamia, travelling west and north. Many had settled in Turkey and Southern France, but a few had travelled on, eventually crossing the English Channel and migrating northwards towards the isolated mountains and forests of Scotland. While werewolves had died out in many of the areas they used to inhabit, the MacRinnalch Clan had remained strong in the north.

No one knew which, if either, of these stories was true. However, it was certainly true that the MacRinnalchs could trace their historical ancestors as far back as the Great Grey Wolf himself, Avreg MacRinnalch, who fought against the Viking invaders in the latter part of the ninth century. Avreg was buried in Colburn Wood, and his broadsword was preserved in the museum at Castle MacRinnalch.

26

Thrix studied the young couple in front of her. She'd encountered humans before who seemed fascinated by her kind. Were these two like the others, looking to add some excitement to their lives by mingling with werewolves? Worse, might they be the type who actually wished to be transformed? Thrix hoped not. Such people usually had strange ideas about werewolves; romantic notions about prowling through forests and suchlike. Thrix had no interest in prowling through forests. Nor did she feel particularly in tune with nature. In London, nature rarely entered her life and that was fine with the cosmopolitan fashion designer.

Thrix had once killed a man who had threatened to expose her as a werewolf. It wasn't a memory she was proud of, if only because it reminded her of her carelessness in letting him find out her secret in the first place. Since then she had been very careful. As far as Thrix knew, the only human who knew she was a werewolf was her personal assistant Ann. Now these two were here, having been alerted to her existence by her aggravating sister Kalix. Ever since Kalix arrived in London Thrix had feared that this would happen. Really, that was why she had provided Kalix with the pendant. More to stop her from causing bother than to protect her. The Enchantress was putting all her efforts into building a fashion empire and did not want to be distracted by the werewolf madness that always surrounded her young sister.

"You gave her a bath?"

"Yes. And she was filthy and skinny and – "

Thrix waved Moonglow quiet.

"I heard you the first time."

Thrix's lipstick was bright red, accentuating the width of her mouth; it made Daniel worry about the size of her jaws should she transform into a werewolf. Already the light outside was starting to fade. He was eager to leave and tried to hurry things along.

"We can see you're busy. So could we have a new pendant and we'll be on our way?"

He smiled brightly as if he'd solved all their problems. Daniel had an attractive smile. The Enchantress didn't notice.

"You think I can give you a new pendant just like that? Do you think it was easy to find an object which could mask my sister's presence from her hunters? It wasn't easy. What happened to it anyway?"

"I think she lost it," said Moonglow.

"Sold it more likely," said Thrix, angrily. She could hardly believe she was having this conversation. It was taboo for a member of the MacRinnalch Clan to discuss werewolf affairs with any human. She rose from her desk. Despite his discomfort Daniel was impressed at her slender elegance. The sight of Thrix's long blonde hair tumbling over her shoulders made him a little more enthusiastic about the whole subject of werewolves. Take away the savage eating part and they were undeniably attractive.

"I'll think about this in private," said Thrix.

"There's no time to think," protested Moonglow. "Kalix is too weak. The next time anyone attacks her she'll die for sure."

Thrix stared Moonglow straight in the eye and told her the matter was not open for discussion.

"You have to help," said Moonglow, stubbornly. The Enchantress looked annoyed. It crossed her mind that it might be best to use a little sorcery to confuse these humans' memories.

"I don't have to do anything. I'm extremely busy and you have no idea what you're dealing with. It's time for you to leave."

Moonglow had come this far and didn't intend to give up so easily. Trying to show no fear, she faced up to the werewolf.

"You should help your sister. She's in bad trouble. And she looks up to you. She kept the coat you gave her. If you don't help her then I'll always know that werewolves are weak and dishonourable creatures."

Thrix gaped. It wasn't what she was expecting to hear. No werewolf of the MacRinnalch ruling family, no matter how self-controlled or integrated with human society, could tolerate abuse like this from a human. Thrix debated whether to blast the girl with a spell or simply use her own strength to pick her up and throw her out on the street. Before she could make up her mind the door burst open. Thrix whirled round, enraged because she had asked not to be disturbed.

It was the Fire Queen. Even Ann couldn't keep her out when she had made up her mind to enter.

"Enchantress!" she screamed. "The slippers were a disaster! You won't get away with this!"

The Fire Queen burst into a series of unintelligible oaths, then broke down in hysterical tears.

Daniel and Moonglow looked on, quite astonished.

"This really isn't the best time – " said Thrix.

"Everyone's against me," sobbed the Fire Queen. "Princess Kaba-chetka, all the other elementals, all fashion designers, everyone. It is tremendously unfair!" Tears poured from her eyes.

'How am I ever meant to get my Spring collection together in these circumstances?' wondered Thrix, and cursed Kalix for making her life difficult.

27

Sarapen MacRinnalch flew from Inverness to London with Decembrius at his side. Decembrius was the son of Lucia, Verasa's younger sister, who was a member of the Great Council. At thirty years old Decembrius was young in werewolf terms, and looked no older than twenty-one. He was pleased to be doing important work for the next Thane of the clan.

Decembrius had more than just good connections and intelligence to recommend him to Sarapen. From a young age he had demonstrated powers of prescience. Occasionally, he could see into the future. These powers were limited but he had a way of learning things that could not otherwise be known. It was enough to make him useful to Sarapen, though Sarapen had not yet admitted him into his inner circle. There were things about Decembrius that annoyed him. His appearance mainly. Decembrius had red hair, which he couldn't help, but he swept it back in a mannered way. He had an irritating tendency to wear sunglasses at inappropriate times, and an earring, discreet but noticeable. Sarapen MacRinnalch was the most traditional of werewolves. Until Decembrius grew out of his youthful vanity, he would not be fully accepted.

Decembrius admired Sarapen and tried not to let it show that Sarapen made him feel nervous. The large werewolf smouldered with such power that it was difficult to feel otherwise. Even the airline stewardesses, used to dealing with the most awkward of customers, didn't seem entirely comfortable in his presence.

"When we reach London you must locate Kalix quickly," Sarapen said. "The Douglas-MacPhees have lost track of her."

While Decembrius located Kalix it was Sarapen's intention to visit his sister Thrix. Possibly he could learn something of Kalix's whereabouts from her. Sarapen did not look forward to the encounter. He disliked his sister and he disapproved of her lifestyle.

"Do you want me to visit – " Decembrius broke off, feeling the matter to be rather delicate.

"The cousins about whom the family does not speak?" said Sarapen, finishing the sentence for him. Sarapen had not made up his mind. He felt that it would be as well if he made the visit in person but he barely trusted himself to control his actions were he actually to be brought face to face with the twins. If Sarapen could have had his way they would have been cut off entirely from the clan, never to be admitted again. Sadly, this was not possible. Tradition forbade it. As the daughters of the Thane's brother, they could not be cut off. They were members of the Great Council, the highest governing body of the MacRinnalch Clan. Technically, at least. In practice they had not been to a meeting of the council for many years.

Decembrius felt that the Thane had not long to live. That worried Sarapen. When he died the council must meet to elect a new Thane. This should be a formality. Sarapen, as eldest son, was the natural successor. However, it was a situation that demanded careful handling. Another werewolf might make a bid for power. Tupan, one of the Thane's brothers, had long been manoeuvring for influence. Sarapen did not intend to have two potential council votes adrift in an intoxicated haze in London. What if Tupan were to attempt to bribe the twins with drugs or alcohol? They must be visited. Perhaps it would be better to send Decembrius.

As for Kalix, she must be brought back to face justice. Hard as it was to believe, Kalix had also been entitled to a seat on the Great Council though she'd never taken up her position. Since the attack on the Thane, she'd been suspended from the council. She had been declared guilty, and would have been sentenced already had she not fled the castle. The council had issued an order for her to be brought back. This order, while not exactly sanctioning her death, could be construed as reason enough for a member of the family to take extreme measures against her if she refused to return. There were historical precedents.

Any member of the family who did either kill her or drag her back would gain credit with the Great Council. Dulupina wasn't the only werewolf who was furious at Kalix's continuing freedom. The three Barons who sat on the council were all steeped in tradition, and they wanted to see Kalix punished.

Sarapen frowned. Anyone who tried to deny him his rightful position as Thane had better take care. His Uncle Tupan, for instance. Sarapen would remove him if necessary. And Tupan's vile daughter Dominil. Sarapen's mouth flickered in the slightest of smiles. He would not be adverse to getting rid of her, white-haired bitch with the frozen soul that she was.

28

When the library closed Kalix didn't know what to do with herself. She'd looked at pictures of fairies and then she'd tried to find things about the Runaways in the Encyclopaedia Britannica but there didn't seem to be anything there. She wasn't sure if she was reading the index correctly and was too embarrassed to ask for help. She wondered what she should do now. She wished she could go back to the warehouse but the Douglas-MacPhees might be waiting for her. Duncan and Rhona would probably have been joined by their brother Fergus, and he was even stronger than his siblings.

Perhaps she should just go there anyway. She wasn't scared of the Douglas-MacPhees. It might be good to die in combat. But the warehouse was a long way away. She couldn't face the journey. She couldn't face anything.

The light faded quickly in the winter afternoon. As Kalix walked down the street she was hit by a sudden wave of depression as powerful as any she'd ever felt before. It poured down like a heavy black rain, covering her till she staggered under its weight. Kalix tried to keep on walking but it was difficult. The tide of depression was frightening in its intensity. Kalix realised that this was the final attack which was going to kill her. The thought flashed through her mind that it was happening now because she had dropped her guard for an instant. She had accepted help from the two young students and now that moment of weakness would destroy her. Ever since Gawain left, she'd cut herself off from her emotions but in Moonglow's house she'd felt a flicker of gratitude, the tiniest spark of contact with another creature. The moment of contact had brought home to Kalix that she was the loneliest, most hopeless creature on the planet, without friends, hopes, or purpose. As a consequence of this she was about to fall down and die.

She needed to find some private place. The waves of depression brought on a terrible anxiety which began to affect her senses. Her heart pounded, breathing became difficult and her vision was blurred. She searched right and left for an alleyway to crawl into. She couldn't find one. Kalix swayed on her feet and reached out her arm to steady herself against the wall. If anyone noticed her plight, no one stopped to help as she stumbled along.

Kalix didn't even notice when she reached the end of the pavement and stepped onto the road. She didn't see the truck that hit her. There was a screeching of tyres, a crash, and she was thrown into the air. She landed, broken and bleeding, on the other side of the road. Now people ran to her aid but Kalix couldn't make out any of the individual figures, just a frightening blur of motion as people gathered around, pressing in on her.

She couldn't die like this, with a crowd of people staring at her. She was far beyond her human endurance but the werewolf inside her gave her one last surge of strength and she rose to her feet. She took a few blind steps and then broke into a run.

Kalix turned a corner. She rubbed her hand over her eyes and there in front of her was the opening she'd been searching for. Kalix threw herself into the alleyway. Her legs gave way. She had to get further. She started to crawl. She dragged herself as far as she could up the alleyway. At the very end she found a pile of stinking, rotting boxes and she tried to pull them over her.

"Now I'll die," she thought. She could feel the blood oozing out of her body. She thought about Gawain and tears came to her eyes because he'd never know what happened to her. Kalix whispered a goodbye to him, then everything went dark.

29

The cousins about whom the family did not speak were twins, very similar in appearance though not quite identical. Beauty's hair was dyed blue while Delicious's was a very bright pink. They both played guitar and sang, quite well, and this, along with their MacRinnalch good looks, might have been enough to bring them some success, had they not been too intoxicated to ever make progress with their band. The twins' rapid descent into rock and roll degeneracy had shocked the rather staid elders of the clan.

Beauty and Delicious were playing their guitars in the front room of the house they shared in Camden. It was going well till Beauty, reaching for her bottle of wine, tripped over her guitar lead and fell into Delicious. Both girls ended up in a heap on the floor in amongst the bottles, glasses, and cigarette papers.

"Damn," said Beauty.

"Damn," said Delicious.

They lay in silence for a few moments.

"It's a good song anyway," said Beauty. "We should write another verse."

She started scrabbling around in the mess on the floor, looking for their marihuana. The sisters smoked a lot of this, and washed it down with beer, cider and wine. Their capacity for intoxicants was famous throughout North London. Although such behaviour might have had a very bad effect on any normal person, Beauty and Delicious were protected by their inner werewolf strength. The same strength which allowed Sarapen to roam the moors for days on end allowed the twins to indulge their desire for stimulants to an alarming degree. It did have some consequences. Though they remained reasonably healthy, the twins could no longer change at will into werewolf form. They had forgotten how. They still transformed on the wolf nights around the full moon but that was all. They didn't care. There was plenty of fun to be had in this part of London for a pair of attractive girls who could play guitar and drink anyone under the table.

Some way through sharing a very large joint, constructed quite expertly by Delicious, Beauty wondered what the ringing sound was.

"Feedback?"

Delicious turned down the volume control on her guitar. The feedback stopped.

"There's still something ringing."

"It's the doorbell."

Interested, Beauty started crawling towards the door to investigate.

"Maybe we ordered some food?"

She reached up with difficulty to open the door. Decembrius looked down at her in surprise. Beauty was perplexed.

"We paid the TV license," she said. "And the council tax."

"May I come in?" ventured Decembrius, not entirely at ease.

Beauty didn't answer. Delicious appeared at her side, also apparently unable to stand. Decembrius felt uncomfortable. It was some years since he'd seen the twins and they obviously didn't remember him. He introduced himself. They still looked blank.

"Decembrius? Never heard of you."

Feeling some explanation might help things along, he told them that he'd come to see them on behalf of Sarapen. Both sisters howled with laughter.

"Sarapen!" cried Delicious, as if the very name was enough to make her roar, while her sister Beauty wiped tears of mirth from her eyes.

Decembrius frowned. Looking down at the girls, with their gaudy blue and pink hair, their ripped and shiny clothes and their advanced state of intoxication, he could see why Sarapen had been unwilling to make this journey himself.

30

"Another shoe humiliation!" wailed the Fire Queen.

Thrix was at a loss. She hadn't got over her displeasure at being called a weak and dishonourable creature and strongly wished to deal with Moonglow. Unfortunately it was impossible to do anything when Malveria was alternately ranting and sobbing in her office.

"Leave now," said Thrix to Moonglow, harshly.

"No," replied Moonglow.

The Fire Queen leapt to her feet and started waving her hands around dramatically.

"I will roast you in the great volcano you cursed werewolf."

Daniel took a long step backwards. Thrix brought a protection spell to mind, just in case the Fire Queen was serious. As it was, Malveria was in too much anguish to roast anybody. She started sobbing again and leant against Daniel for support.

"There there," said Daniel. "I'm sure it will be all right."

"All right? How can it be all right? Do you know what happened to me? This creature – " Malveria pointed accusingly at Thrix. " – sold me new silver slippers and she swore – absolutely swore – that she had just designed them. And what happened when I turned up at the Igan Frost Queen's ball? Everybody was wearing them. And I mean everybody, even that slutty little Igan Princess who's always trying to steal my followers."

The Fire Queen looked accusingly at the Enchantress.

"How could this be? You swore they were new. Are you trying to make me the laughing stock?"

Thrix was finding this hard to cope with. On one side she had two humans making unwelcome enquiries about werewolf affairs and on the other she had a furious fire elemental making complaints which could not be true. Because Thrix had just designed the slippers. It was not possible that any one else could have been wearing them. Any successful designer became used to being plagiarised but not on the same day that the stock left the company.

The Fire Queen started sobbing on Daniel's shoulder again. Daniel, perplexed, wondered what he should do. He presumed that this exotic beauty was some supermodel who had been upset at a fashion show. He tried patting her hand.

"There there," he said.

Malveria looked at him, tears running down her cheeks.

"Is it not appalling?" she said. "To turn up at a ball and be the laughing stock because everyone already has your shoes?"

Daniel was touched. His kindly nature was upset at the sight of the woman's distress. Though it was contrary to his natural shyness he strained to think of something pleasant to say which might make her feel better.

"But you're so… eh… so… eh… you're so beautiful surely no one would mind what shoes you were wearing?"

The Fire Queen stopped crying, rather suddenly.

"You think I'm beautiful?"

Daniel blushed.

"Eh… yes…"

"Thank you," said the Fire Queen, and rested her head on his shoulder. "At least there is someone who is not against me."

"Please Jane," said Thrix, calling the Fire Queen by the name that was used whenever there were humans around. "These people have come to see me about a personal matter. Could you perhaps give us a few minutes?"

"Your personal matter is more important than my utter disgrace with shoes?" demanded the Queen. There was an awkward silence.

"It's about her sister," said Moonglow, attempting to be helpful. Daniel winced as he saw the look of fury which flickered across Thrix's face.

"The little wolf?" said the Fire Queen. "Is she in trouble again?"

"Terrible trouble," replied Moonglow. "She needs a new pendant."

"Really?"

"But her sister won't give us one," added Moonglow, feeling for some reason that this woman might be an ally against the unwilling Thrix.

"Of course she will not," said Malveria. "She is entirely without

67

heart. How can you expect her to do kindness to her sister when she quite on purpose sends me out with inferior shoes?"

"Really!" said Thrix. "I did not send you out with inferior shoes. They were an exclusive design. I'm baffled as to how anyone else could have a similar pair. I promise I'll sort it out for you, Jane, only I must – "

But the Fire Queen had now become interested in Thrix's visitors. They did not seem to be the sort of people with whom she was familiar. She looked at Moonglow. She studied her long black hair, black nail varnish and black clothes. The only humans the Fire Queen had ever seen dressed in this fashion had been her own devotees, who seemed to favour it.

"Is she one of mine?" she enquired of the Enchantress.

"I don't think so."

"Oh. I thought I did not recognise her."

"I'm Moonglow."

"Moonglow? A pretty name."

The Fire Queen turned her attention back to Daniel.

"And you, young man who thinks I am beautiful. What is your name?"

Daniel blushed deeply. The Fire Queen laughed, very entertained. She raised her hand to brush back his hair to look at his face and his complexion grew even redder.

"I'm eh... Daniel... eh... Jane."

"Please, call me Malveria," she said, rolling the 'r' in an exotic manner. "Fire Queen of the Hiyasta, Mistress of the Volcanoes, Protector of the Flame, Lady of the Inferno, Ruler of the Burning Element, and Persecutor of Mankind."

Daniel and Moonglow took a nervous step back, wondering if they were about to be persecuted. The Queen, however, seemed to regard them sympathetically.

"So why won't you give them a pendant?" asked Malveria.

"I didn't say I wouldn't. I was just explaining that it was very difficult. Who even knows where another Pendant of Tamol might be?"

"I'm sure I could find one," said the Fire Queen, casually. After her shoe disgrace she was rather enjoying the opportunity of discomfiting the Enchantress, who obviously wished to be rid of them all.

"No doubt you could," said Thrix, acidly. "However I'm not certain it's a good idea."

"She just doesn't seem to want to help," said Moonglow to the Fire Queen.

"I would be very wary of getting on the wrong side of me!" snarled the Enchantress.

"You are being very rude to your guests," said Malveria. "Is it perhaps to cover your guilt and shame over the recent shoe atrocity?"

"It has nothing to do with that! This girl called me a weak and dishonourable creature."

Malveria laughed heartily.

"Excellent! I could not have put it better myself."

Thrix sighed. This was all going very badly. The intercom buzzed. Ann's voice sounded very urgent.

"Sarapen is on his way!"

The Enchantress put her hand to her forehead. This was all she needed. There was no putting Sarapen off. Her older brother would stride straight out of the lift and into her office without pausing. She turned to the Fire Queen.

"Malveria. I will, I promise, sort out this business with the shoes. Someone must have stolen my design. Meanwhile, I have to talk to my brother and I'd rather he didn't find you all here."

Malveria nodded. This was reasonable. She knew all about Sarapen's forceful personality.

"Please take these two into the far corner of the room and I'll hide you," said Thrix.

Not understanding what was happening, Daniel and Moonglow found themselves being shepherded across the large office. When the reached the far corner the Enchantress waved her hand. Nothing seemed to change.

"What's going on?" asked Moonglow.

"She has hidden us with a spell," explained Malveria.

"Why?"

A very large and brutal looking man threw the door open and marched into Thrix's office.

"That is why," said the Fire Queen. "And it is quite wise. You do not want to encounter Sarapen. He is not what I would call a civilised werewolf. Not that werewolves are the most civilised of creatures as a rule – one rather despairs of them at times – but even by their low standards he is a brute. I always regret that my darling Thrix has to associate with them so."

69

31

The alleyway was long and narrow, and turned at a right angle to run along behind the shops on the streetfront. At the end it was dark, damp, cluttered with boxes which had lain untouched for years. Nobody came here. Kalix crawled under the boxes, still bleeding, and lay down in the accumulated years of city dirt. If it was not a good place to die, at least it would be quiet.

Even her werewolf strength could not protect her from the impact of a truck. Kalix's ribs were cracked and she was damaged inside. Blood seeped from her mouth and her nose. She hurt badly. She fumbled around in her bag and found her laudanum. It was hard raising her arm and Kalix drank with difficulty.

A song played in her head. *Hello Dad, Hello Mom, I'm your ch ch ch ch ch ch ch ch Cherry Bomb!* The Runaways first single. She wished she could have seen them onstage. And maybe – it occurred to her for the first time in her life – maybe it would have been good to have met someone who actually liked them. Kalix had sometimes overheard young people talking about music, discussing bands they liked, but she'd never joined in. Perhaps that would have been fun.

The laudanum started to enter her system, giving her the familiar warm glow. Now ready to die, Kalix slipped into unconsciousness.

32

Huddling in the corner of the office, Moonglow and Daniel both found it hard to believe they were really hidden from Sarapen but they were glad that they were. They had never seen a man who radiated such primeval power. He was six feet six inches tall, broad shouldered and very muscular. His face was weather-beaten and his features, though not exactly handsome, were sharp and striking, with a prominent scar running over the left side of his jaw. His thick black hair, rather long, was pushed back roughly from his brow, and he wore a black leather coat that reached down to his ankles. Despite his size he moved easily. As for his eyes, they were dark and penetrating. When he turned his gaze to the corner of the room in which they were hidden Moonglow shrank back behind the Fire Queen and Daniel hid behind them both. Malveria was amused by the situation. She was not at all frightened of Sarapen but she was always entertained by plots and stratagems.

Sarapen towered over his sister, taller by ten inches and at least twice her weight.

"Good day, sister."

Sarapen sniffed. He could tell that there was someone else concealed in the room. His sister's sorcery could not fool him completely. But it was not Kalix's scent so he paid it little heed.

"Good day, brother."

They regarded each other coolly. Thrix and Sarapen had never been friends. Sarapen had been over one hundred years old when Thrix was born. Throughout her life at the castle Thrix could never remember Sarapen paying her much attention. He had at least seldom troubled her. There was no bitter argument in their past, no wound which still festered, as there was between Thrix and Markus. Still, Sarapen made no secret of his disapproval of her lifestyle. Sarapen honestly could not understand either her desire to distance herself from the clan or her attempts to build a career in the outside world. Both things went against tradition and therefore irritated him.

"What brings you here, brother?" said Thrix.

"Kalix," replied Sarapen, curtly. "She must return to the castle."

"So?"

"So kindly tell me where she is."

"And why would I know that?"

"You are the only member of the family who's been in contact with her."

Thrix realised she had not offered her brother any token of hospitality. This was bad. Though she did not want to associate herself with the family, neither did Thrix want to be seen as a werewolf who had become degenerate. Feeling that perhaps in the circumstances it was a little absurd, she crossed over to her cabinet and produced a bottle of whisky. The MacRinnalch malt, distilled on the family estates using barley from the fields to the north of the castle and water from the pure stream that ran through Colburn Wood. She poured two glasses and passed one to Sarapen. Sarapen thanked her politely. He did not think this was absurd. Had his

71

sister failed to offer him any token of hospitality he would have been deeply offended.

"You shouldn't have given her the pendant. You had no business hiding her from the justice of the clan."

"I don't believe Kalix received much justice during her life at the castle!" said Thrix, suddenly flaring up.

She lowered her voice.

"Besides, there was no reason not to give it to her. She has not yet been sentenced.

"Only because she fled the castle. Was it of no import to you that she nearly killed the Thane?"

Sarapen too had intended not to lose his temper but as always the memory of the attack on their father roused him to a fury.

"We've fully discussed this already," said Thrix. "And to answer your original question, I've no idea where Kalix is."

Sarapen regarded her grimly. He sipped the rest of his whisky.

"Sister. We are not enemies. For the good of the family, I appeal to you to help me locate Kalix."

"So that she can be taken home and killed?"

"If the council decides it's appropriate. Why are you protecting the girl? I was under the impression you also found her annoying."

"I do," admitted the Enchantress. "But finding my sister annoying is not the same as wanting her dead. I repeat, I do not believe she was well treated at the castle."

This was something which Sarapen did not want to hear and his eyes blazed.

"You will not refer to that child's foolish fantasies. You know as well as I do that she was mad from birth. The very notion of her making such vile accusations is enough to make any decent member of the family sick. Had I got my hands on her before you hid her, Thrix, I would have ripped her apart."

"But you did get your hands on her," retorted Thrix. "You pulled her off the Thane before she could kill him. And as I heard the story she then fixed her teeth around your werewolf throat and would have kept them there if your servants hadn't dragged her off.

"No one has ever put their teeth around my werewolf throat," growled Sarapen. His eyes narrowed. He had had enough of this conversation.

"Where is she?"

"I don't know."

Sarapen seemed on the point of springing. Behind the mystical shield the Fire Queen got ready to intervene. She was uncertain if Thrix's sorcerous powers were strong enough to hold off her brother. Strong enough in daylight while he was human, she imagined, but the light was now fading outside.

"Tell me all you know of Kalix," demanded Sarapen.

It would have been easy for Thrix to defuse the situation. She could have told Sarapen that Kalix no longer had her pendant and was not well hidden. Armed with this information, Sarapen would simply have departed to sniff her out himself. But Thrix was annoyed at the arrogant way her brother had marched into her office, demanding information. She suggested that perhaps it was time for him to leave.

"You're asking me to leave?" said Sarapen, as if unable to believe his ears.

"I'm a busy woman," said Thrix, pointing to the sketches on her desk.

Sarapen swept his arm over her desk, dragging every drawing onto the floor. Thrix gasped. She could barely believe that her brother had done such a thing. To sweep her designs from her desk like they were so many scraps of worthless paper. The Enchantress was furious. She uttered a word, and a bolt of power threw Sarapen across the room. He thudded into the far wall. As he came to a halt his eyes held a look of incredulity. He could not believe that his younger sister had dared to assault him. At that moment night fell. Both Sarapen and Thrix, fully in tune with the moon, felt it in their bones. Sarapen growled and by the time his growl faded he had transformed into his werewolf shape.

Behind the magical barrier, Moonglow quailed. Sarapen in his werewolf form was the scariest thing she had ever seen. Immense, bestial, his wolf's face was huge, his jaws like a steel trap, a nightmare vision, far more frightening than either Kalix or her attackers had been. When Kalix had transformed she had retained her youthful grace but Sarapen was a monster to stalk a girl's nightmares.

In the same instant Thrix transformed. Daniel was fascinated to see that as a werewolf Thrix was still blonde. Long golden hair hung down from her head, and from her arms and shoulders.

"I'll kill you," roared Sarapen, and leapt forward. He grimaced as the Enchantress fired off another spell but such was his strength it barely impaired his progress. The Fire Queen was on the point of revealing herself when the office door opened. Ann put her head through the door.

"Your brother Markus," she announced.

33

Before falling for Talixia, Markus had had a string of lovers. With his combination of male strength and feminine looks Markus had always been attractive to women. These were usually casual affairs but with Talixia it had become serious. They'd been to the opera, the theatre, and the cinema. They'd even discussed plans for decorating a house together.

Markus had risen late, waiting till Talixia had gone to work. She had gone off to photograph children's clothes for a catalogue. It wasn't a job she was especially pleased to be doing but it brought in money. Talixia's werewolf family were not wealthy. She struggled to pay the rent each month. Markus found this interesting. He admired Talixia for her efforts, and for always refusing when he tried to give her money, no matter how discreet he attempted to make it seem.

He paced naked around her small flat. He looked through her wardrobe. He regretted that Talixia did not have a better collection of clothes. He'd have bought her anything she wanted but she wouldn't accept extravagant gifts. She did have one new item, a short blue dress she'd brought home from a shoot. Markus studied it. It wasn't a bad dress. Well cut, and the colour was quite suitable. He would have liked to have tried it on but Talixia was smaller than him so he knew it wouldn't fit. It would not do for her to discover that he had stretched her new dress. It could lead to awkwardness.

Whilst dressing in his own clothes, he frowned, and wondered again if he should talk to Talixia. Generally it was a difficult topic to raise. Markus knew this from experience. He still winced at the memory of a previous girlfriend who'd coped well with the discovery that he was a werewolf but had thrown him out after catching him wearing one of her blouses. He shrugged. Today he had other things to worry about. He'd promised his mother he would visit Thrix. Markus was not looking forward to this. He hated his sister. For reasons he could not explain to his mother, Markus would have been far happier never to see Thrix again.

The moment he entered Thrix's office and found himself in the presence of two growling werewolves he transformed into his own werewolf shape.

"So. My beloved siblings are already fighting."

Sarapen, who had been attempting to land his great claws on Thrix's neck, was not pleased at the interruption. Thrix, busy fending him off with her own considerable strength aided by some sorcery, stepped back and growled.

"Did I fail to make it clear I wasn't keen on family visits?"

Daniel and Moonglow were still hidden in the corner. They didn't realise that they were seeing something never before seen by human eyes; three werewolves of the MacRinnalch ruling family together in werewolf form. If they did not appreciate the uniqueness of the event they certainly were riveted, and scared.

"Is this barrier strong enough?" whispered Daniel, as the werewolves continued to talk angrily to each other.

"Possibly not," muttered the Fire Queen. "Are you frightened?"

"Yes," admitted Daniel.

Malveria smiled indulgently.

"I will strengthen it," she said, and made a slight motion with her hand, adding her own mystic strength to the barrier. "There. Now you are very undetectable. And I will leave you so for the meantime, because my darling Thrix is now confronted by two angry brothers and I fear for her safety."

With that Malveria passed through the barrier, instantly materialising at the Enchantress's shoulder. Sarapen growled angrily. He regarded fire elementals as low forms of life, and particularly disliked the Hiyasta.

"So it was you who skulked in the corner."

"Excuse me," replied the Fire Queen. "I do not skulk. I remained hidden out of politeness. I am a guest of Thrix, unlike you."

"Do not interfere with family business, Hiyasta," warned Sarapen.

"I have no inclination to interfere in werewolf business," retorted

75

Malveria, wrinkling her nose slightly as she uttered the word *were-wolf*. "But I dislike to see anyone picking on my good friend."

"Werewolves do not make friends with Hiyastas," said Sarapen.

"She's a better friend than you ever were," said Thrix. The Fire Queen looked delighted. It was so nice to have a really loyal friend, even a werewolf.

Despite the hostility between their races, Markus did not really dislike Malveria. On the few occasions they'd met he'd found her to be quite an attractive character. He tried to make some sort of friendly greeting. It was difficult to smile as a werewolf, but his tone was conciliatory.

"Greetings, Fire Queen," he said. "I'm sorry to meet you while engaged in this quarrel. No doubt you're aware of the trouble our young sister has caused us."

"You will not discuss our clan matters with her!" roared Sarapen.

"I'm sure she's heard most of it already," said Markus. He faced his brother and looked him in the eye. Though Sarapen was the stronger Markus would never back down to him. The brothers started growling at each other and Thrix growled at both of them. Sarapen seemed on the point of striking his brother when the intercom sounded.

"Your mother is on the phone. She says it's extremely important."

Thrix sighed. There was no occasion which her mother did not see fit to interrupt. She picked up the phone in her werewolf paw, not without difficulty.

"Yes?"

Thrix listened for a few minutes while her brothers looked on. They were frustrated at the interruption but could hardly start fighting when their mother was on the phone.

"I will," said Thrix, and put down the phone.

She spoke softly to her brothers.

"The Thane is dead."

34

An hour or so later, Daniel and Moonglow were still sitting behind the magical barrier in the corner of the office. The room was empty. On hearing of the Thane's death Sarapen had departed, almost without a word. The MacRinnalch Clan was now leaderless and it was his duty to return to the castle. Everything else could wait.

Thrix and Markus were also making plans to travel back to Scotland. There would be a meeting of the Great Council as soon as its members could be assembled. Markus had departed to gather his belongings. He and Thrix had temporarily suspended hostilities and would fly home with their Mother, the Mistress of the Werewolves. The flight from London to Scotland would only take an hour or so. Thrix didn't want to go but knew she couldn't get out of it. Not turning up for the Thane's funeral and the subsequent council meeting would be quite unthinkable, as her mother had pointed out.

"Don't worry mother," Thrix told her. "I won't miss the funeral."

As Ann made travel arrangements Thrix was gathering together computer discs and making sure that all her current files were on her laptop. With luck, she could continue her work while at the castle. She instructed the efficient Ann to rearrange her schedule.

"It's come at a bad time but I should be back in three days. See if the people from Milan can reschedule. If they can't I'll try and set up a video conference link from the castle."

"What about the children?" enquired Malveria.

"The children?"

"The children who are still concealed in your office."

"I'd forgotten about them. I'll send them away."

"And what about Kalix?"

"She can take care of herself."

The Fire Queen looked at her.

"Really, it seems that she cannot."

The Enchantress wondered out loud why Malveria had suddenly developed some concern for Kalix. The Queen shrugged.

"I have not. But I am amused by the boy who called me beautiful and then blushed. You know when we were hiding he said he was scared. Is that not funny?"

Thrix didn't quite see why it was funny. She really had no time to indulge the Fire Queen and her strange fancies.

"I'm just too rushed to do anything, Malveria."

"Perhaps I could provide the young people with another Pendant of Tamol to give to your errant sister? If you don't object?"

"Why would you do that?" asked Thrix. Fire elementals were not particularly friendly to humans as a rule. Besides, the required pendant was not an everyday object. It was a prized item. Its sorcerous uses were many and even a powerful being like Malveria would not lightly give one away.

The Fire Queen shrugged. She didn't exactly know why she would do it. But she had been entertained by the arguments between the were-wolves and she could see some amusement to follow if Kalix remained hidden. Malveria had been very bored recently. Who knew what interesting things might occur if she gave the two young humans a pendant for Kalix?

"Do it if you want," said Thrix.

Markus arrived back at the offices. Their mother would be here shortly. Thrix told Markus that she had some arrangements still to make with her designers and buyers and asked him if he'd mind waiting upstairs in her office for a little while.

In the office, Daniel and Moonglow were becoming restive.

"This has been a really bad day," complained Daniel.

"Do you think they've forgotten us?" asked Moonglow.

They were uncertain whether to stay where they were or venture out.

"I suppose we should be safe," said Moonglow. "After all, we're in the middle of a busy office building. They can't just eat us."

They looked at each other, doubtfully.

"Let's wait here a while," suggested Daniel.

The door opened. Markus entered. Daniel and Moonglow were hidden behind a barrier of very strong sorcery and even Markus's werewolf senses did not detect them. Markus was dressed for a funeral in a sober black suit. While making his quick journey home he'd taken time to brush his curly chestnut hair and was now looking his best. They watched as he paced the room. He seemed to be interested in the rail of clothes in the far corner. Now that he was on his own, Moonglow thought him quite attractive. Strong and handsome, but feminine, in a way. His hair hung in curls over his brow and shoulders, reminding her of an old picture of Marc Bolan that Daniel had on a T-shirt.

Markus was fingering the rack of clothes. Suddenly he seemed to make a decision. He crossed quickly to the door, locked it, then took off his jacket and shirt. His torso, Moonglow noted, was lean and muscular. He then took a blouse from the rack and slipped into it with practised ease.

Daniel and Moonglow looked at each other, astounded. The blouse was of flowing yellow silk, an extremely feminine article. Markus was now examining himself in the large mirror. Not preening, or parading around, or doing anything extravagant. Just examining himself. Apparently satisfied, he swiftly removed the blouse, hung it up carefully then put his own shirt and jacket back on. He unlocked the office door just as Thrix and Malveria appeared.

Daniel and Moonglow were utterly astonished.

"What a freak," hissed Daniel. Moonglow nodded her head vaguely, as if in agreement. But what Moonglow was actually thinking was that Markus in the yellow silk blouse was one of the most beautiful things she had ever seen.

35

Kalix and Gawain had been wild lovers. At fourteen Kalix had been skinny but healthy, vigorous and enthusiastic. Gawain had been a frequent visitor to the castle while his father was still alive. His father, an honoured member of the MacRinnalch Clan, had been a friend of the ruling family.

Kalix would creep through the stone corridors of Castle MacRinnalch to Gawain's room in the chambers where guests were housed. She was cunning, and extremely stealthy, capable of flattening herself into the dark shadows when anyone was near and remaining there in silence till they'd gone. She went so quietly that not even the castle mice were aware of her passing. Finally she'd arrive at Gawain's chamber, sometimes in werewolf form or sometimes as human, depending on her mood. Gawain would be waiting for her, catching her scent as she approached the door and hurriedly letting her in. Gawain, eighteen at the time, had some misgivings about what the Thane might say were he to catch them but Kalix allowed him little time to dwell on his thoughts. She'd leap onto the bed and they would make love for the rest of the night till finally Gawain was exhausted and Kalix would lie like a wolf, panting and growling in satisfaction. Just before the long Scottish night ended Kalix would make the return journey and then sleep late into the day. This never aroused suspicion though it brought criticism from her mother.

"It's no wonder her tutor refuses to teach her," Verasa complained to Kalix's brothers. "She is the laziest girl you could ever imagine."

Her brothers indulged their mother's complaints but they had no real interest in Kalix or her activities. As for the Thane, he never seemed to pay any attention to her at all.

Now Kalix lay starved, broken and bleeding under a rotting pile of cardboard boxes in a dank alleyway in South London. She had passed into unconsciousness some time ago. She dreamed that she was with Gawain, running through Colburn Wood in pursuit of a stag. They killed the stag and ate it by a campfire in a clearing, then washed the blood from their mouths in a stream. Then they lay on the bank under a full moon, watching the dark water flow by. They discussed what they might do together and Gawain said he always wanted to travel the world. Kalix was enthusiastic, and said she'd travel with him. She would go anywhere with Gawain.

36

Decembrius found his visit to the twins extremely trying. There was no meeting of minds. There was very little sensible conversation at all. The two young werewolves appeared to inhabit a world of their own to which Decembrius was not invited. Beauty and Delicious carried on a continual dialogue with each other which Decembrius had some difficulty in even understanding.

"Pass the skunk, bitch."

"It's under your guitar, ho-bag."

And so on. Used to the more formal ways of the castle, Decembrius was perplexed. The sisters would insult each other and then laugh uproariously at things which did not seem to be at all funny. When he addressed them by their real names, Butix and Delix, they laughed so hard he thought they might never stop.

"Butix and Delix? Who's that?"

"I don't like the sound of them!"

The twins seemed completely unconcerned that the head of the clan was gravely ill.

"Clan? What clan?"

"The MacRinnalchs."

"That's a funny name for a clan."

"Thane," said Beauty.

"Thane," said Delicious. "Thane Thane Thane Thane Thane."

"Thane Thane Thane Thane," added Beauty.

Beauty's hair was long, and a violent shade of blue. Delicious's hair was also long, and a very shocking pink. Decembrius found himself wondering if the colour remained when they transformed. He could hardly imagine what their behaviour might be like when they were werewolves.

Delicious burrowed into the mess on the floor, looking for something or other. She tossed some empty pizza cartons out the way and uncovered a great wad of money, a huge pile of £20 notes held together with a rubber band, several thousand pounds worth of currency. She threw it at her sister.

"Go and buy something."

Beauty threw the bundle of money back. The rubber band split and £20 notes fluttered across the room. The sisters dissolved in laughter. They were, Decembrius recalled, very rich. Their father had multiplied his wealth by astute investments in the stock market and the sisters were shrewd enough to leave their capital in the hands of their London brokers, living off the substantial income it generated. They would never be short of money.

"Would you be interested in attending the next meeting of the Great Council?" he ventured. "You are still members of course."

"Who are you?" asked Beauty, and looked puzzled.

Decembrius sighed. His mobile phone rang. It was Sarapen.

"The Thane is dead," said Sarapen. "Return home immediately. Have you made any progress with the cousins?"

"No," admitted Decembrius.

He took his leave, saluting the sisters politely on the way out. No matter how degenerate, they were still members of the MacRinnalch ruling family, after all. Decembrius left their house feeling dissatisfied. Not just because he had failed in his mission. Decembrius regarded himself as one of the more fashionable of the young MacRinnalch werewolves. Compared to the twins however, he felt as old-fashioned as the Thane. He wondered if he might have another ear

81

piercing.

"Do you think he could get us a gig in Scotland?" asked Delicious, after he'd gone.

"Our band broke up," her sister pointed out.

"So it did. What happened?"

They couldn't remember. But night had now fallen and it was time to go out and visit the local bars so they hurried to their bedrooms and started dragging out clothes from every drawer and cupboard. Beauty and Delicious had a lot of clothes. They always wanted to look good when they hit the town, and they generally succeeded.

37

"You intend to nominate Markus for Thane?"

Thrix was taken aback. She knew well that her mother was closer to her second son but it had never occurred to her that there would be any serious opposition to Sarapen.

"This will tear the family apart."

"Our family is not close, dear. You know that."

They were flying to Scotland, together with Markus. On a signal from his mother, Markus had left Verasa alone with her daughter.

"Mother, I'm shocked."

"I know this is all very sudden. I had intended to do a good deal more in the way of preparation but the Thane's death has come much quicker than I expected."

"Do you really expect the Great Council to vote for Markus? You know what Sarapen is going to do when he learns of this?"

"He will accept the decision of the Great Council like the traditionally minded werewolf he is."

"I doubt that very much. Thanks for the warning mother. I'm walking into that council chamber with a protection spell ready and I'd advise you to take a bodyguard."

Verasa pretended to be shocked.

"The son of the Mistress of the Werewolves does not attack his mother."

"The daughter of the Thane doesn't attack her father either but that didn't stop Kalix. Mother, have you really thought this through?"

"I have given it a great deal of consideration."

Thrix was too surprised by the suggestion to easily marshal her thoughts. She certainly did not like Sarapen. But she didn't like Markus either. They had suspended hostilities temporarily while they returned to the castle but she saw no prospect of a lasting friendship.

"Why are you so set against Sarapen? Just because you like Markus better?"

"I love all my children equally," replied Verasa. "But Sarapen has not adapted to the modern world. Markus will be a much better figure to take the clan forward."

Thrix shook her head. She found it hard not to smile at the notion of her mother loving all her children equally. In reality Markus came a long way above them all and always had done.

"I really don't want to be involved in this. If Sarapen and his followers start fighting Markus and his followers it will quite likely spill out from the estates. I don't want one of my fashion shows to be interrupted by a crowd of brawling werewolves. The magazine editors wouldn't like it."

"Perhaps it would give them something new and engaging to write about, dear," said Verasa, who was not entirely without a sense of humour.

The Thane's death had come too quickly for Verasa. The Great Council consisted of seventeen members and the new Thane required nine votes to be elected. The Mistress of the Werewolves was not yet in a position to guarantee Markus enough of these votes.

"I understand that the American editors of Deportment magazine are staging a European fashion show in New York in a few months time," said Verasa.

"So?"

"So think how beneficial it would be for you to show your designs there."

"The show is only for Italian designers," said Thrix, a little surprised that her mother even knew of the event.

"That was the plan," said Verasa. "However I was talking to the chairman of the board of the company which owns the magazine just the other week, while I was giving a substantial donation to a charity of which he's the patron. I really feel that the magazine might be willing to extend their foreign fashion week to include one or two select

British designers."

Thrix looked at her mother.

"Are you trying to bribe me?"

"Bribe you?" The Mistress of the Werewolves looked shocked. "My goodness, Thrix. You do surprise me sometimes with the amusing things you say. You know I'm always on the lookout for the welfare of my children."

38

Daniel and Moonglow travelled home on the bus.

"Just to clarify matters in my own mind," said Daniel. "We are attempting to help a crazy young Scottish werewolf with a long history of anti-social behaviour. The other werewolves can't help us right now because they have to elect a new leader. But a fire spirit – or elemental, whatever that is – who's queen of a different dimension but just pops over to the Earth to get her clothes made by one of these werewolves, is on her way back to her own dimension to find a new mystic pendant and then she's going to help us find the young werewolf who is presumably roaming the streets at this moment."

"That seems to be about right," said Moonglow.

"Did we perhaps go insane?" wondered Daniel.

"I don't think so."

"Because if we did, you know, we might not realise. This bus might be an ambulance taking us to the asylum and we wouldn't know anything about it because we're insane."

"But we're both here thinking the same thoughts," pointed out Moonglow. "I don't think we'd both get struck by the same kind of insanity right at the same time."

"What if you're not here?" said Daniel. "It might just be me that's crazy."

He started to look worried. Moonglow pinched him hard on the arm.

"Ow! Why did you do that?"

"To let you know it was real."

"Pinching only works when you think you're dreaming," said

84

Daniel, crossly. "It doesn't work when you think you're crazy."

When they arrived home Moonglow reapplied her nail varnish because she'd become self-conscious about the poor state of her nails while conversing with Thrix and the Fire Queen, both of whose nail varnish was absolutely perfect. Meanwhile Daniel lay on the couch listening to Slayer and pretending that none of this was really happening. The door bell rang. Moonglow opened the door to find Malveria looking pleased with herself.

"Once I was confused by door bells but now I have quite mastered the art. Shall we go?"

"Please come in," said Moonglow. "Daniel isn't quite ready yet."

Malveria, who was perhaps eight hundred years old, though time in her dimension was not exactly the same as time on earth, tripped into the little apartment with the enthusiasm of a young girl. Really, she had been bored in her dimension for a long time. Since getting rid of her family and destroying all of her serious rivals with her immense power she hadn't known what to do with herself. It was good being absolute mistress of her realm but for the last fifty years or more she'd been suffering from a troubling sense of tedium. Meeting Thrix and entering the world of Haute Couture had greatly improved her life. And now this visit to Daniel and Moonglow promised to be very entertaining. She hoped that Daniel would blush again. It amused her so. And perhaps the girl Moonglow might explain why she only wore black clothes. Could she be a sorceress?

"Mind the steps," said Moonglow, leading Malveria upstairs. "The light isn't working."

Malveria snapped her fingers and light appeared, illuminating the narrow staircase.

"Eh... thank you," said Moonglow.

In the living room Daniel was still lying on the couch. Malveria was a little offended by this, which Moonglow sensed.

"Get up," she said. "We have a visitor."

Daniel roused himself to a sitting position.

"Would you like something to eat?" asked Moonglow, who was always a polite hostess. "We have pop-tarts."

"I absolutely want a pop-tart," said the Fire Queen, enthusiastically. "What is it?"

"I'll just put one in the toaster for you," said Moonglow, and went off to the kitchen. Malveria followed at her heels, eager to see what a toaster was. Daniel trooped after them. The kitchen in their new flat was just large enough for three people, a fridge and a small cooker.

"I'm sorry about the mess," said Moonglow.

"Have you dismissed your servants?"

"Eh… no, we don't have any servants."

"No servants at all?"

Malveria looked at them suspiciously, wondering if they were lying.

"Not a servant to be found," said Daniel.

"That is so strange. Do you make your own food?"

"Well, we generally get pizza delivered."

"By slaves?"

Moonglow made tea while the pop-tart cooked in the toaster.

"Did you bring a pendant for Kalix?" she asked.

"I did," replied the Fire Queen.

The Pendant of Tamol had cost Malveria a lot. To get it she'd had to trade with a neighbouring king and his asking price had been a great deal of gold, several secret spells and the return of two hostages. Malveria had paid his price, substantial though it was. She produced a small pendant from her handbag.

"This will hide Kalix."

"It's very nice of you to bring it," said Moonglow.

The Fire Queen was pleased that Moonglow showed some appreciation. Noticing that Daniel was being very quiet, she turned to face him.

"Did you like the little werewolf girl?" she asked him.

"Eh… well…"

"He called her a wild beauty," said Moonglow. Daniel blushed. Malveria laughed. In the tiny kitchen it was easy for her to press up against Daniel. She put her dusky face only a few inches from his.

"But surely you must meet many wild beauties?"

Malveria was so beautiful that Daniel hardly knew where to look. He blushed a deeper colour and tried unsuccessfully to withdraw from the slight pressure on his chest created by the Fire Queen's breasts. Malveria laughed again. Already she was enjoying herself.

"But it is true what the Enchantress said to you, young humans. People who involve themselves with the werewolf clan will very probably be killed."

"Okay, let's not do it," said Daniel.

"Too late," said Malveria. "You went to visit Thrix."

86

"I knew it was a mistake."

"It was not a mistake," insisted Moonglow. "Kalix needs our help. Why is it every other werewolf hates her?"

"Of that I am not certain," answered Malveria. "My race, which is called *Hiyasta*, does not get along with werewolves as a rule. In particular, we are enemies of the MacRinnalchs. Really, my friendship with Thrix is quite extraordinary. And as to their motivations, who can say?"

"What about people who get involved with Fire Spirits? Do they get killed too?" asked Daniel. "I couldn't help noticing one of your titles was *Persecutor of Mankind.*"

Malveria smiled.

"We do not do so much persecuting of mankind these days. Though it is true we do not regard them kindly, in general. It dates back to the time when humans discovered how to make fire, which my ancestors resented, as fire is our preserve. But these days, our paths rarely cross, unless there is an erupting volcano, which we have to take care of."

The pop-tart popped up from the toaster. The Fire Queen, who at her last grand banquet had turned away every exquisite dish with a bored sigh, picked it up from her plate with interest. She nibbled at it.

"I like the pop-tart," she said. "Make me another one."

39

Beside the stream Gawain rolled off of Kalix and lay panting for breath. He took his human form and lay there, staring up at the clouds. Kalix nuzzled him with her wolf's nose and raised up her head to look at him. Gawain was so handsome, as wolf or human. He frowned like a poet, she'd tell him, cheerfully mocking his slightly brooding nature. And Gawain, who was on occasion given to brooding, would laugh. He had never met anyone like the young Kalix who could make him laugh so easily before.

Suddenly, and shockingly, a knife flew through the air to thud into Gawain's back. He pitched forward and Kalix could smell the blood pumping out of his heart. Worse, she could sense that the blade that had pierced Gawain was made of silver, and would kill him.

"I told you to stay away from that man-cub," growled the Thane, who'd appeared from the darkness of the river bank.

Gawain had one human grandparent. He wasn't a man cub. He was as strong and fierce as any pure bred werewolf. But the silver dagger thrown by the Thane was deadly to him. Kalix could feel Gawain dying in her arms.

Kalix shrieked, then woke up in the alley. The young werewolf was now so weak and disorientated that it took her a long time to realise that she had been dreaming. The horror of the dream wouldn't leave her. She felt herself slipping back into unconsciousness and as she did so she could again see the Thane killing her lover.

"He's not dead," she tried to say. "He's not dead. He went away."

But Kalix couldn't remember if Gawain was dead or if he had just gone away. It was too confusing. The laudanum-fuelled dream still gripped her senses. She tried to move, but didn't have the energy. As her mind slowly cleared she realised that dying was not as easy as she thought it would be. The wolf inside her was very strong. Though her injuries would certainly kill her, it was proving to be a long and difficult process. She coughed up more blood, shuddering with pain from her broken ribs, then fell back into another dark dream.

40

There were hundreds of werewolves in the MacRinnalch Clan and hundreds more who gave their allegiance to the Thane. The MacRinnalchs were not the only werewolf clan currently surviving in Britain, but they were the strongest, and the oldest. Many of the clan members lived either in the castle or on the surrounding estates, but some had settled in other parts of world. There were pockets of MacRinnalchs all over the globe, in Australia, the USA, Canada, New Zealand; anywhere the Scots had travelled. Now they were coming home. The Thane's funeral would draw MacRinnalchs from all over the world. In two days time the estates would be packed full of werewolves, come to mourn the passing of the old Thane and celebrate the accession of the new.

It was the responsibility of the Great Council to choose the new

Thane. There were seventeen members of the council: Dulupina, Verasa, Sarapen, Markus, Thrix, Kalix, Tupan, Dominil, Kurian, Marwanis, Kertal, Lucia, Butix, Delix, Baron MacAllister, Baron MacGregor and Baron MacPhee.

Dulupina was the mother of the recently deceased Thane. Tupan was the eldest of the Thane's three younger brothers. Dominil was Tupan's daughter. Kurian was the youngest brother of the Thane. Marwanis was Kurian's daughter and Kertal his son. Lucia was Verasa's younger sister. Butix and Delix – Beauty and Delicious – were daughters of the Thane's middle brother Marwis, who had died with his wife some years ago. The three noblemen – Baron MacAllister, Baron MacGregor and Baron MacPhee – were not members of the ruling family, but their clans had been represented on the Great Council for longer than anyone could remember.

Of these seventeen, fourteen now sat in the great hall, the massive vaulted chamber at the heart of Castle MacRinnalch. The three missing members were Kalix, Beauty, and Delicious. In the next chamber the Thane lay in state. His burial would take place the day after tomorrow. The service would be officiated over by the new Thane. The Thane had to be elected by a majority of the Great Council and would require nine votes. Though it had most often been the case that succession passed from the Thane to his eldest son, it was not a formality. There had been several occasions in the past thousand years when the council had refused to endorse the heir apparent and chosen another. On each of these occasions, bloody war between the factions had been the result.

A great log fire burned at one end of the long stone hall. Clan banners decorated the walls. Torches cast a flickering light over the werewolves who sat at the great circular oak table. No servants attended them; servants were banished from such an important meeting. The only werewolf in attendance apart from the council members was clan secretary Rainal, the well-respected administrator whose duties included the recording of all proceedings of the council. In front of each werewolf was a crystal decanter of whisky and another of spring water from the clan's estates. It was midnight, and the meeting had just begun. Most of the werewolves were in wolf form but some had retained their human shape. Thrix sat as a human, her long golden hair gleaming in the torch light, but across the table from her Sarapen sat huge and black in his werewolf form, eager to get on with business. He turned his head toward Great Mother Dulupina, a werewolf of such tremendous age that she rarely left the confines of her chambers.

Dulupina was no longer strong. Her hair was grey, and even in werewolf shape she looked fragile. Though she was closest to the great fire her legs were covered by a woollen blanket, woven in the dark green MacRinnalch tartan. Her voice was rather soft. Since her son died she had spoken little. The death of the Thane had been a terrible blow to the old werewolf. Dulupina held Kalix responsible. He had never recovered from her brutal assault.

Tupan and his daughter Dominil were talking to each other in low voices. The Great Mother looked at them for a while. Tupan, her second son, had always made her proud, almost as proud as the Thane. In his werewolf form he was strong, upright, a true MacRinnalch. As for his daughter Dominil, she was rather different. Dominil was a very striking figure both as human and werewolf. She was tall, and her hair was white, as it had been from birth. Not an albino; rather, it was if she had somehow inherited the genes of an arctic snow-wolf. Dominil's eyes were deepest black. With her long white hair, the effect was startling, which Dominil knew.

Quite what her granddaughter's thoughts were, Dulupina had never been certain. Dominil seemed close to no one. It had been rumoured at one time that she had some involvement with Sarapen but if that were true, nothing ever came of it. Dulupina had never seen them show any signs of familiarity. If anything, a slight enmity seemed to exist between them and they had exchanged only the briefest of greetings when entering the chamber. Sarapen was as often at the castle as he was at his own keep, but Dominil rarely encountered him during his visits. She had her own chambers which she seldom left.

Baron MacPhee, a huge, fat man and an even fatter werewolf, coughed rather pointedly in Dulupina's direction. Dulupina smiled. The Baron was a friend and supporter of very long standing and she understood him well. There were stags roasting in the banqueting hall and he wished to get the meeting over with so he could proceed to the eating. Dulupina looked towards the Mistress of the Werewolves. She in turn looked towards Rainal.

"We will begin the meeting," said the clan secretary.

The hall fell silent. Verasa, Mistress of the Werewolves, transformed from her human shape.

"It is time," said Rainal. "To elect the new Thane."

90

41

"Who makes nomination for the new Thane?"

There were a few seconds silence, then Baron MacPhee spoke up.

"I nominate Sarapen MacRinnalch."

This was good. It was fitting that the nomination should come from the loyal supporters of the clan rather than a member of the ruling family. Baron MacPhee had been a great friend and companion of the Old Thane. There were murmurs of agreement from around the table and the Barons prepared to raise their glasses to Sarapen as the new chief of the clan.

"I accept the nomination," said Sarapen, which was the only correct response.

"Are there any other nominations?" asked Rainal, merely as a matter of form. More seconds passed in silence. The huge fire crackled in the corner. Sarapen began to rise. Then, as if she had been waiting for that moment to discomfort him, Dominil spoke up.

"I nominate Markus MacRinnalch," she said.

There were more murmurs, a little louder. Sarapen sat down firmly. He glared at Dominil. Dominil, still human, still with her mane of straight white hair spilling over her shoulders, stared back at him with her black eyes. Though he was angry at the delay, Sarapen was not yet perturbed. Nor was he overly surprised at Dominil's words. There was something of a history between Sarapen and Dominil and relations between them were now very cool. Sarapen was surprised that she chose to bring her dislike of him into this meeting where it would surely do nothing but cause her embarrassment, but he could put up with it. He waited for Rainal to speak.

"Do you accept the nomination?" asked Rainal, looking to Markus.

Sarapen did not believe for a moment that he would. When Markus calmly echoed his own words of a few moments before, the huge werewolf was stunned.

"I accept the nomination."

The murmurs round the table became louder.

"You accept?" growled Sarapen.

"I do."

"Who do you expect to vote for you?" said Sarapen, angrily, his temper already beginning to give way. Markus did not reply. The Barons looked uncomfortable. They hadn't expected that there would be any need to vote.

Verasa remained silent. She had known that Tupan's daughter planned to nominate Markus. Verasa herself had suggested it to her some time ago. Such was Dominil's dislike for Sarapen that she needed little persuasion.

It was not a time for speeches. Whatever campaigning, plotting or arguing had to be done was done outside the council chamber. Here, there would simply be a vote. The clan secretary frowned. He hadn't been expecting this either, and he hoped the meeting might end without rancour.

"Those in favour of Sarapen MacRinnalch please raise their hands."

Rainal counted the votes.

"Those in favour of Markus MacRinnalch."

The secretary again counted while the werewolves sat in uneasy silence.

"And those abstaining."

The only sound to be heard over the roaring fire was the heavy breath of Sarapen as he struggled to control his emotions.

"There are seven votes for Sarapen MacRinnalch. There are five votes for Markus MacRinnalch. There are two abstentions. Three members of the council are absent. Since no member of the Great Council has received the required nine votes, I declare, in accordance with the laws of Clan MacRinnalch, that we'll vote again tomorrow."

Sarapen exploded. He smashed his fist on the table.

"You dare to oppose me!" he yelled at his younger brother. "You will regret this!"

Markus remained seated, expressionless but not cowed. Sarapen turned his eyes on his mother. He struggled to control himself. He knew that she had organised the opposition to him. She herself had voted against him. Against Sarapen, her oldest son. It was beyond belief. Unable to contain his anger and fearing that he might become violent, Sarapen threw back his chair and marched out of the room.

Those seven who had voted for Sarapen were Sarapen himself, Kurian, Kertal, Marwanis, and the three Barons. Those five who had voted for Markus were Verasa, Tupan, Dominil, Lucia and Markus. Thrix had abstained from the vote. So, inexplicably, had Great Mother Dulupina.

42

"Are there no more pop-tarts?" enquired the Fire Queen.

"Eh… shouldn't we look for Kalix now?" said Moonglow.

The Fire Queen pouted, which she liked to do, when her lips were looking their best. Malveria never left her palace without a careful application of several layers of lipstick. Today she'd used an undercoat of deep plum overlaid with a layer of Russian red, and was pleased with the dramatic effect. She looked at Daniel.

"Do you want to rush off to find the young werewolf?"

Daniel saw Moonglow directing a pointed look in his direction.

"I suppose we should look. After all, you went to all the trouble of getting a new pendant."

Malveria nodded. It was true. She had gone to a lot of trouble. And while she did not much care if Kalix lived or died, it would be wasteful not to use it.

"It is easier to track a werewolf in werewolf shape than it is to track a werewolf in human shape," explained Malveria. "But I am a skilful enough hunter to find either. So let us hunt. Young man, I believe you have a car?"

Daniel nodded. He didn't much like being addressed as young man, particularly as Malveria looked only few years older than him, but he was prepared to put up with it. Malveria was a famed beauty and her voice was soft and sweet like an exotic musical instrument. Daniel felt he could put up with a lot from her.

The Fire Queen had been in a car before but it was still sufficiently novel for her to feel some anxiety that Moonglow might take the front seat, and she hurried to claim it for herself. Daniel turned the key in the ignition. The Fire Queen struggled to open her window. Daniel tried to help and she giggled as he leaned over her. In the back seat Moonglow frowned. For a powerful ruler of an alien dimension, Malveria could be extremely helpless when it suited her.

"How entertaining this is," said Malveria, as they drove slowly through the grey London streets. "I am hunting for a werewolf! It is just like ancient times in my kingdom, though then of course any Hiyasta hunting a werewolf would have been attempting to kill this werewolf. How strange that I am seeking to save one's life."

"Did Hiyastas and Werewolves fight each other?" asked Moonglow.

"At one time."

"Why?"

"The original reasons are now a little obscure," replied Malveria. "Though the bad feelings between us became worse during a wedding hosted by the Fairy Queen."

Moonglow was agog at the thought.

"There really is a Fairy Queen?"

"Of course. There are several – "

Before Malveria could elaborate further something caught her attention and she looked sharply to the left.

"That way," she said. "I can sense her."

They drove for another ten minutes, the Fire Queen now concentrating on the hunt. Moonglow was becoming anxious.

"Should we try the hospitals?" she wondered out loud.

"If she has been taken to hospital she will surely be dead," said the Fire Queen.

"Why?"

"Different blood. You can't cure a werewolf in a human hospital. Anything they gave her would poison her."

Malveria laid her hand on Daniel's leg.

"Stop here."

"I can't. No parking."

"Stop here."

Daniel stopped.

"She is in that alleyway," said Malveria, indicating a dark and narrow opening. They hurried from the car, shivering in the cold winter air.

When they found Kalix she was almost dead. She lay stiff and cold at the very end of the filthy alley. The Fire Queen had to check her frozen body carefully before discovering the tiniest flicker of life.

"But she will die very soon."

"What will we do?"

Malveria shrugged. There was nothing to be done. In a few minutes Kalix's life would ebb away and that was the end of it.

"Perhaps we could eat more pop-tarts?" suggested Malveria.

Moonglow glared at her.

"Do you have no feelings at all?" she said angrily.

Malveria was astonished. She was not used to that tone of voice being used against her. She started to utter an angry retort but Moonglow wasn't listening. She was hastily pulling the boxes off Kalix's body and telling Daniel to help her carry the werewolf to the car.

"But she is going to die," said the Fire Queen, matter-of-factly.

"No she isn't," said Moonglow. "We're taking her home and she's going to recover."

Malveria looked towards Daniel, expecting him to agree with her. It was obviously hopeless. Daniel, however, was too busy helping Moonglow. Malveria noticed for the first time that Daniel was in love with Moonglow. And yet she had heard Moonglow speak of her involvement with another young man called Jay. Her mood brightened. This was surely entertaining.

"Very well," she said. "If you wish to take her home."

Malveria muttered a few words. In an instant all four of them were transported back to the new flat. Daniel was open-mouthed with astonishment. He had just been teleported through space. Life was becoming stranger all the time.

"How did you do that?"

"Never mind how," said Moonglow. "Help me to get Kalix warm. Get a quilt. Make a hot water bottle."

Malveria laughed.

"You hope to save her life with a hot water bottle?"

"I'll try my best."

Watching Moonglow forlornly rubbing Kalix's wrists, trying to bring life back into her, the Queen felt an odd twinge of emotion. Sympathy for the werewolf? Surely not. Sympathy for the girl? Again, that would be strange. Malveria had not forgiven Moonglow for talking sharply to her. No one in her kingdom would have dared to do so. Yet this girl apparently felt quite free to take an angry tone with her even though the Fire Queen could have blasted her out of existence with a wave of her hand.

"Perhaps this is amusing also," thought Malveria. "I am interested in this girl, and her strong spirit."

She attempted to venture a word of sympathy, and did her best to sound sincere.

"The werewolf really is going to die. I'm sorry, she is beyond your help. She has been broken inside, in many places. Bones and organs are shattered. She doesn't work any more."

Moonglow's eyes misted over. She took Kalix in her arms as if trying to lend her warmth from her own life force. Kalix was cold, colder than anybody Moonglow had ever touched. Her skin was like ice and

95

the blood that covered her nose and mouth was hard and black. Moon-glow raised her head to look at Malveria.

"Can't you help? You have power."

The Fire Queen said nothing. Daniel arrived back with a quilt and a hot water bottle. He stood and watched helplessly as Kalix lay dying and Moonglow hugged her, now in tears.

"Fetch water and a cloth," said Malveria abruptly. Daniel hurried off.

"You understand if I were to help this werewolf it would cost me dearly?" said the Fire Queen to Moonglow. "She is so far down the path of death that she cannot easily be brought back. Already her soul is communicating with the other souls in the forests of the werewolf dead. And though I have great power it would cost me much to reach out so far towards these forests. I would not be a welcome visitor there. The effort would…"

Malveria searched for words to explain what she meant. There was nothing in human language to communicate it exactly.

"It would hurt me," she said, simply. "And weaken me."

"But you'd get better?" said Moonglow, eagerly, seeing some hope.

"I would get better. But I would not forget the pain. Pain which I would suffer for a werewolf, who is not my friend or ally."

"Please help," said Moonglow.

"And what would you pay for my help, young girl who spoke angrily to me?" said Malveria. "For an action which costs me so much, you cannot expect to receive it for nothing."

For a moment Moonglow had the unpleasant thought that Malveria was going to ask for her soul. This was not what Malveria meant.

"But you will have to pay a price."

The Fire Queen did not intend to weaken herself, even temporarily, without receiving something in return. That was not the way of her dimension. What would her peers say if they learned she had been giving out favours for no reward? On behalf of a werewolf, of all things? They would ridicule her. Empress Asaratanti in the neighbouring realm would never let her hear the end of it. There had to be payment. Malveria knew that Moonglow could not provide her with anything of real value, but she might provide her with some amusement in the future.

"The young boy Daniel. He loves you."

Moonglow found herself nodding, though this seemed to be of no relevance as Kalix's life slipped quickly away.

"But you do not love him?"

"No. Of course not."

"And you never will?"

"No. We're just friends."

Malveria paused.

"I think you might, one day."

"I won't," insisted Moonglow.

"Very well. My price for saving Kalix is your love for Daniel. Which means that if one day you do find yourself in love with him you will not be able to have him for your own."

Moonglow was confused.

"But I'll never want him. I'm not going to fall in love with Daniel."

"Then you will have no price to pay," said the Fire Queen. "Do you agree to my terms?"

Moonglow didn't even have to think. She had to save Kalix's life, and she never wanted to be Daniel's lover. It was hardly a price at all. Perhaps the Fire Queen was not great at making bargains.

"I agree."

"Very well," said the Queen. "I will attempt to save Kalix's life. But remember, no matter what you feel, you can never have Daniel for your own."

Daniel now returned with a cloth and warm water. Malveria instructed him to wash Kalix's mouth, which he did, as carefully as he could. Chunks of hardened blood broke off in a sickening manner. Beneath the blood the skin was blue. The Fire Queen leant over the body and put her lips to Kalix's for a few seconds. She raised her head an inch, spoke some words, then placed her lips back on the werewolf's mouth, this time for longer. The air in the room seemed to grow quickly colder. Malveria stayed in contact with Kalix for a long time. There was silence in the room and the temperature continued to drop. Malveria withdrew her head, spoke another sentence, then placed her hands on Kalix's heart. Moonglow looked on anxiously, and shivered. Finally Malveria withdrew, and shuddered. She controlled herself with an effort and moved away from Kalix's body. The pupils of Malveria's eyes had shrunk to tiny dots and the colour had drained from her face. She rose to her feet, very unsteadily. She looked as if she had used up all her energy and could barely stay upright.

"She will live. I must go now."

The Fire Queen flickered out of the living room, fading slowly, as if too tired to even teleport at her normal speed. Daniel and Moonglow gazed down at Kalix. Daniel put his hand on Kalix's wrist.

"She's warming up," he said.

Kalix had not quite made it to the forests of the werewolf dead. Colour was returning to her face. Though the werewolf did not open her eyes, she no longer seemed to be slipping away. Moonglow carefully hung the new pendant Malveria had given them around Kalix's neck. Now she was safe. Later Moonglow melted a little sugar in some warm water and dripped some of the solution into Kalix's mouth to give her strength. She wrapped Kalix in the quilt and stayed beside her for the rest of the day and all of the night.

43

Castle MacRinnalch simmered with fury. As the werewolves came to terms with the inconclusive vote, there was dissatisfaction on all sides, and, in some places, utter rage.

"How dare my mother vote against me!" roared Sarapen. Still in his werewolf form, he paced the great stone chambers of the north tower. His advisor Mirasen stood silently by the window, listening to the tirade, with Decembrius beside him.

"She planned this," continued Sarapen. "She put that bitch Dominil up to it. Damn her! And damn that brother of mine. I ought to go down there and rip his heart out!"

Mirasen was a prudent werewolf. Ever since the meeting he'd been trying to calm Sarapen. It would be far better for the clan if the matter could be decided peaceably.

"The meeting will resume tomorrow," Mirasen pointed out. "We'll muster sufficient votes."

Sarapen was not placated. The Thaneship was his by right and he hated having to scrabble around for votes like a politician.

"You get me the votes then, Mirasen. But afterwards I will have my revenge."

Mirasen studied his list of all the votes cast. There were no surprises in those who had voted for Sarapen. Kurian, youngest brother of the Thane, had never been a strong werewolf but he had always been a traditionalist so would naturally support the Thane's eldest son. As would his offspring, Kertal and Marwanis. The Barons' support was also to be expected. They were more traditional than anyone.

Though Sarapen professed to be horrified by his mother's support for Markus, Mirasen was not really surprised. It was plain the Mistress of the Werewolves had long preferred her younger son. As for the other three who had voted for Markus – Tupan, Dominil, and Lucia – well, none of them were so strange, when you looked at it. Tupan had pretensions to the Thaneship himself. Better for Tupan's own ambitions to have a weaker Thane. Dominil might be expected to go along with her father, and anyway, her dislike of Sarapen was well known. As for Lucia, she was Verasa's younger sister, and Verasa would undoubtedly have offered her a substantial bribe.

That left the two abstentions, Thrix and Dulupina. Mirasen had no idea why the venerable Dulupina had abstained but he'd learn the reason soon enough. Thrix had been absent from the castle for a long time and it was possible she had no strong preference for either brother. Mirasen would make enquiries, and learn if her vote could be secured.

"How are matters between you and Thrix?"

"Not good," admitted Sarapen, and related the tale of his last encounter with her.

Mirasen considered this.

"A regrettable argument, but surely not irreparable. I'll talk to her."

The full moon was tomorrow. Tonight was the first of the wolf nights. Everyone in the castle would change into their werewolf form. The MacRinnalch werewolf during the three wolf nights was not quite the same as the MacRinnalch werewolf on other nights. More passionate, and less rational. Sarapen almost felt that he didn't care about another vote. Killing his opponents would suit him nearly as well.

44

Sitting in the lecture theatre, Daniel wasn't convinced he'd got the best of the deal. Moonglow was at home taking care of Kalix while he was at university taking notes on *Timon of Athens*. And not just the few scrawled lines that usually passed for Daniel's notes. Extensive notes. Moonglow had insisted.

"Don't come back without a complete record of the lecture," she'd instructed him. "And see if you can have a few insights of your own." This last part may have been a joke by Moonglow.

Daniel was finding it tough. His hand hurt from writing and it was difficult to concentrate. Given the events of the past few days this was understandable. Werewolves, elementals, teleportation and a really expensive parking ticket, the result of leaving the car in a no parking zone while rescuing Kalix. Moonglow shared the cost of the ticket but she had more money than Daniel. He could ill afford the expense.

He'd suggested to Moonglow that maybe he should stay home with her to watch over Kalix but Moonglow wouldn't hear of it. One of them had to go in and take notes and as Moonglow wasn't about to leave Kalix that meant him. Daniel, of course, could not be the one to stay home looking after a sick werewolf. As Moonglow pointed out, he wasn't responsible enough. There was no denying it, he wasn't. Daniel shook his head and tried to concentrate. He wondered if Jay would visit today. Moonglow's boyfriend was back from Stonehenge.

'Probably he'll have to call round and spend some time being handsome and interesting,' thought Daniel, with some bitterness. 'And tell Moonglow some stupid dull story about how his father was British ambassador to Brazil and he spent his early years growing up right next to the rain forest. The guy is such a phoney.'

Moonglow's friend Alicia was sitting only a few seats away. She was an attractive girl. Not as attractive to Daniel as Moonglow, but if he had to accept a substitute, she'd be his first choice. Daniel wondered about making a brave bid to talk to her when the lecture ended, but dismissed the idea. It wouldn't go well. He'd end either boring her or saying something stupid. Probably both.

Moonglow was currently trying to feed soup to Kalix. Kalix was resisting. She'd woken up, declared herself unhappy to be alive, and lain back down in front of the fire in a hopeless, bleak depression. She refused everything except water, and sipped some laudanum when Moonglow was out of the room.

"You should have some soup," said Moonglow, encouragingly. It was no use. Kalix did not want soup, or anything. She just lay miserably in front of the fire, curled up in her quilt. Moonglow was distressed.

"You're safe," Moonglow told her. "The Fire Queen brought you a new pendant."

Kalix showed no signs of pleasure or gratitude that she had a new pendant. Whatever she was thinking she kept to herself.

Moonglow had checked her astrological chart. The full moon was due soon. What would happen when Kalix turned into a werewolf? Would she want to eat? To hunt perhaps? Moonglow wondered if she should buy some steaks. Did werewolves eat steaks? Maybe they needed their meat raw and fresh. She shuddered at the thought. But Kalix might not want to stay at all. As soon as the young werewolf regained her strength she might just leave again and then surely she would die. Moonglow couldn't bear the thought. She was determined that Kalix would live.

45

Verasa and Markus had withdrawn to the west wing of the vast castle, which was Verasa's domain, staffed with her servants and advisors.

"Well?" she said.

"I'm satisfied," replied Markus.

The Mistress of the Werewolves was pleased. She had secretly feared that her younger son might have been intimidated. But Markus had stood up to Sarapen. His mother had always admired him for that.

Since the meeting ended Verasa had been busy. She knew that she had been fortunate in the voting. She'd expected Great Mother Dulupina to vote for Sarapen. As she had abstained, there was obviously room for negotiation. Verasa scanned her list. Nine votes were required and she only had five. How to find four more votes, that was the question. Quite a challenge, with the whole MacRinnalch Clan assembling on the estates for the funeral of the old Thane, and Verasa having all the duties of her position to perform.

Verasa felt that the five votes for Markus were all secure. Tupan and Dominil would not support Sarapen. As for Lucia, Verasa had promised her sister that if she voted for Markus then Lucia's son, Decembrius, could have the next vacant place on the Great Council. This place was Verasa's to give by right. It was a powerful bribe, and Lucia was well pleased at the prospect.

Another great fire burned in Verasa's room. She had reverted to her human shape though Markus remained as a werewolf. He sat on one of the old oak chairs that were a feature of the castle's decor.

"We need four more votes," declared Verasa. "I have some hopes of the Barons."

Markus was doubtful. "They'll always support the eldest son."

"I haven't been idle you know. I've been working on them. Had your father's death not come so inconveniently quickly, I may even have won them over before the vote. Two of them anyway. Baron MacPhee was such a friend of your father he'll probably support Sarapen in any circumstances. No doubt he thinks of Sarapen as very like the old Thane. But MacAllister is a modern sort of werewolf. Besides, he's sorely in debt and I've been dangling a very favourable loan in front of his eyes. I may well have his vote by tomorrow. Which would make six for us and six for Sarapen."

Verasa pursed her lips.

"It is rather a shame that you're not on better terms with your sister Thrix." The Mistress of the Werewolves eyed Markus. "What did happen between you and her?"

Markus would not say. It was one of the very few things concerning the family that Verasa didn't know. It irked her.

"Is it so terrible that you cannot tell your mother?"

Markus remained silent.

"Whatever it was, you must try to make things up with her. We need her vote."

Verasa moved away from the heat of the fire. She had a glass of wine in one hand and her list in the other. She put down her wine to light a cigarette. She smoked occasionally, at times of stress.

"What will happen if neither of us get nine votes?" asked Markus.

"I'll officiate at the funeral and carry on as acting head of the clan. The Council will reassemble in a month's time. Much may be accomplished in a month. Remember, not all the council members were in attendance. Butix, Delix and Kalix are all entitled to vote."

Markus was surprised.

"Mother, none of these three are going to come to Scotland. Kalix can't, she's under sentence of arrest."

"True. But as for Butix and Delix, who knows? I understand that Decembrius went to visit them on Sarapen's behalf. But Sarapen wouldn't know what to offer the twins."

Verasa stubbed out her cigarette.

"Whatever Butix and Delix are up to in London, there's no doubt something they need. Perhaps I can provide it. Do you know anything about their music band?"

Markus did not.

"Well you must learn. Look it up on the internet. Find out whatever you can about them while I visit Dulupina. And be ready to be charming to Thrix."

46

Of all the various werewolf hunters that existed around the world, The Avenaris Guild were by far the most proficient. They had hunted werewolves for more than a thousand years. To them it was a holy mission. The leaders of the Avenaris Guild were keenly aware of the importance of Castle MacRinnalch. For now, it remained too strong to attack, but they kept an attentive eye on everything that went on around the estates. Informants across the world had already notified them of a general movement of MacRinnalch werewolves back towards Scotland and that could only mean one thing.

"The Thane is dead," said Albert Carmichael, chairman of the Guild. "And now the werewolves are going home to bury him."

Guild members were even now undergoing the dangerous work of trying to intercept werewolves on their way to the castle. It was always a risk confronting a werewolf. Their strength and savagery were so great that no man could defeat one in combat. Not in wolf form, certainly. During the day, when the werewolf could not transform, it was a different matter. However the Guild hesitated to attack a werewolf in human form. One had to be very sure of one's target. If the victim turned out to be not wolf but human, the hunter had no excuse in court. Thinking that a person was a werewolf was no defence against a charge of murder. So it was more customary to attack the werewolf at night, though this meant dealing with the wolf's dreadful power. Firing a silver bullet through the werewolf's heart was the only sure way of killing it but this was not easy. Missing the heart by even a fraction was likely to be the last mistake a hunter ever made. The bullet would injure the werewolf but not kill it and the enraged beast would then tear its attacker to pieces.

Werewolves had great powers of recovery. There were many of them around the world who had felt the bite of a silver bullet but survived to tell the tale.

At their headquarters in London, Albert Carmichael sat with the six other members of the board of directors of the Avenaris Guild.

"The MacRinnalch Princess?" asked Carmichael, referring to Kalix by a title that was not really accurate.

"The trail has gone cold."

"Cold? How?"

The reason was unknown. Hunters from the Guild had come close to apprehending her but now they'd let her slip out of their grasp. She had somehow managed to hide herself again.

"Instruct our men to keep looking," said Carmichael. "We have a unique opportunity to kill a member of the royal family and I don't intend to let it slip."

Another member of the board reported that a werewolf had been killed after landing on a flight from Toronto. This was excellent news. On the negative side, one of their hunters had been killed in an abortive attack on a family of werewolves who'd flown in from Australia the previous day. It was to be expected. At a time like this, there would be more casualties to come, on both sides.

"Perhaps," suggested another member of the board. "In the matter of the werewolf princess, it might be time to call on the services of Mr Mikulanec?"

Mr Carmichael thought for a few moments.

"Perhaps. Mr Mikulanec has travelled a long way to be with us. "

Mikulanec was a native of Croatia. It was a region of central Europe where werewolves had once been very common. Mikulanec had grown up hunting werewolves. His father had done so, and his father before him. The Guild, though aware of his reputation, had nonetheless been hesitant about working with him. They preferred to use their own men. However, it seemed a shame to waste the Croatian's obvious talents, particularly at a time like this.

"I'll mention it to him," said Mr Carmichael.

47

Kalix didn't like being in a house of humans but she couldn't muster enough energy to leave. She could hardly move. The young werewolf had been so close to death that she had no right to be alive. The Fire Queen had intervened at the very last second, wrenching her back from the forests of the werewolf dead even as the inhabitants of the forest came to greet her. Now she lay in front of the warm gas fire, staring into space and trying to ignore Moonglow's offers of soup. Kalix seemed to have no enthusiasm for life. Moonglow was concerned.

"Isn't it great you're still alive?" she said, by way of opening a conversation. Kalix didn't reply.

"And you have a new pendant," added Moonglow, brightly. "The Fire Queen brought it. We met her at your sister's fashion house. Now you're safe here with a new pendant I'm sure you'll be back to full strength in no time."

Even the disturbing news that Moonglow had been to visit Thrix was not enough to rouse Kalix. She turned her face to the fire and tried to block out Moonglow's voice. Moonglow, undeterred, kept at her task.

"I can see you fitting in really well here. You won't have to do anything. I mean, it's not like me and Daniel are bothered about keeping the place tidy. If you want to spread a few werewolf items around the living room it's fine with us. Did you bring your journal with you? Have you been writing in it much?"

Kalix rose on one elbow.

"Be quiet!" she growled.

Moonglow thought this was progress. Better to be angry than just to lie there hopelessly and die.

"You know it's the full moon tomorrow?"

"So?"

"So you'll turn into a werewolf."

Kalix would also turn into a werewolf tonight but she could not be bothered to explain this to the irritating Moonglow.

"Is there anything special we should get you? Meat, for instance? We can always phone for a pizza but I sort of thought you might want to eat steaks. I'm a vegetarian, I don't know much about meat. Should I go to the butcher's?"

"Be quiet," said Kalix, who was starting to feel desperate.

Moonglow smiled.

"I'll get you a joint of beef. Isn't it good to have friends?"

"No," replied Kalix.

"Of course it is. Everybody needs friends. I'm sure werewolves are no different. Everyone thought I was weird at primary school but later when I started going to Goth clubs I made a lot of friends. Have you ever been to a Goth club? No? I thought you might have, being a werewolf. I'm sure you'd be popular."

Kalix looked despairingly at Moonglow.

"Why won't you be quiet?"

"Because I want you to live."

"I don't want to live," said Kalix.

"That's what you think now," countered Moonglow. "But who knows what you'll think in a few days time? Would you like some soup?"

"No," said Kalix, and turned her face back to the fire.

"I expect Daniel will be home soon," continued Moonglow. "He went to a lecture. We're doing the same course. You'll like Daniel."

"No I won't."

"You will, really. Everyone likes Daniel, he's a really good friend. I think I'll ask him to go to the butcher's shop, he probably knows more about meat than me. He eats burgers sometimes."

Kalix pulled her quilt over head and wished that she was dead. Moonglow's continual conversation was unbearable. She longed to knock herself out with laudanum but her supply was so low she daren't risk finishing it, not when she was too weak to visit the Young Mac-Doig.

"Do you dislike all Hiyastas?"

The question took Kalix by surprise. She'd never heard a human utter the word *Hiyasta* before. She half-turned her head.

"What?"

"Malveria said that Hiyastas and werewolves are never friends.

"She's right," muttered Kalix. "Stupid Hiyastas."

"What's wrong with them?"

"They're stupid," repeated Kalix, who lacked the vocabulary to construct a really telling insult.

"The Fire Queen saved your life," pointed out Moonglow.

"That just shows how stupid she is," replied Kalix, and hid under the quilt.

106

48

Daniel was fatigued when he arrived home.

"I'm in shock," he reported. "I never realised how difficult university was without you to tell me what was going on."

"Did you get the notes?"

"Extensive notes. Apparently Timon wasn't very happy in Athens. No doubt you can explain why. How's our werewolf?"

"Sleeping. I've been aggravating her."

"Pardon?"

"She's just lying there refusing to eat or make any effort to get well. I thought if I talked to her enough it might produce some reaction. You know, improve her spirit."

"Or just get her so annoyed she attacks us," suggested Daniel. "You know Moonglow, I think you're taking a far too relaxed attitude about this whole werewolf thing. First you insist they come and live with us and now you've taken up a deliberate policy of werewolf aggravating. It's dangerous."

They looked at Kalix, asleep in front of the fire.

"She does look sort of pathetic," admitted Daniel. "All right, I suppose you'd better annoy her some more if you think it'll help."

Moonglow made tea for both of them and put bread in the toaster.

"Alicia was sitting close to me in the lecture today," said Daniel. "I was going to talk to her but I lost my nerve."

Moonglow was sympathetic. She knew all about Daniel's shyness with girls. She'd given him as much encouragement as she could, so far without results.

"You should have spoken to her. Alicia is really nice and she just broke up with her boyfriend. It's the ideal time."

"Could you break the ice for me?"

"I already introduced you."

"What if she's forgotten?"

"We're at university," said Moonglow. "It's okay to speak to other students. Think of it as personal growth."

"I think of it as potential huge embarrassment," said Daniel, and looked gloomy while buttering his toast. "I never know what to say to girls."

Moonglow smiled. Poor Daniel. He really could do with a girlfriend.

"You think she likes music?" wondered Daniel.

"Wouldn't that have been a good thing to ask her?"

"Not if she said no. Which is possible. I have encountered girls who don't like music. It always leaves me struggling for conversation."

Though Daniel's taste for heavy metal was well removed from Moonglow's liking for Kate Bush, they did share an enthusiasm for progressive rock from the 1970s, which was a great help to their friendship. Late at night they could always agree to listen to some favourite album from thirty years ago: Yes or Jethro Tull. The times he'd spent lying in the living room with Moonglow listening to *Close to the Edge* were already some of Daniel's happiest memories.

"Will you be all right looking after Kalix tonight?" asked Moonglow.

"Me? Why, where are you going?"

"To Jay's house. I don't want him to come over, not with Kalix here. We should keep it quiet for a while, at least till she gets better."

As ever, Daniel was disgruntled at the thought of Moonglow visiting her boyfriend.

"How did he get on at Stonehenge? Make any important new discoveries? Maybe do some repairs?"

"No, he just camped there and looked at the stars. He sounded really inspired on the phone."

Daniel swallowed the numerous caustic things he could think of to say about Jay receiving inspiration from the stars. He thought it was probably best to hide his huge dislike of Jay from Moonglow, something which, of course, he had completely failed to do.

Moonglow went off to take a bath leaving Kalix sleeping uneasily in front of the fire. As Moonglow lit some of her favourite scented candles in the bathroom, she wondered what exactly was the source of Kalix's misery. If Kalix had been the only werewolf Moonglow had met she might have assumed that just being a werewolf was enough to make a person unhappy. Obviously it wasn't. Thrix hadn't seemed to be suffering from internal torment. Quite the opposite. If Thrix was anything to go by, it was quite possible to be a werewolf and not be miserable.

49

It was a long time since the huge, dark walls of Castle MacRinnalch had housed so much activity. The grey morning light ushered in a day of talking, plotting, threats, and bribery as the two sides each considered how best to improve their position. There was not much time; the Great Council would meet again at midnight. The night that followed would be taken up by the Thane's funeral. If the council had not reached a decision by then, the funeral would be presided over by the Mistress of the Werewolves. Once that happened it would be clear to everyone that the Great Council had failed to elect a new Thane. There would be a delay of at least a month, till the next council meeting. This would not go down well with the clan.

"The clan will just have to wait," said Verasa. "I've already breached tradition once and I'm quite prepared to do it again."

Verasa sat in her chambers with her son Markus as the daylight crept in. The thirteenth century castle had been built without much in the way of window space. Verasa, tiring of the gloom, had once planned to have the windows of her chambers enlarged, but the Thane would not agree to it, fearing that any such alteration would weaken the castle's defences. Verasa pointed out that in the modern world, it was unlikely there would ever be an armed assault on the castle, but the windows remained unaltered, just in case.

Verasa had been to see Dulupina.

"She's still concise when she wants to be, despite her age, I'll grant her that," reported Verasa. "Anyway, we can discount her vote."

Markus looked pointedly at the Mistress of the Werewolves.

"I repeat, we can discount her vote. I will not go along with her wishes. I'll find another way to get the votes we need."

Great Mother Dulupina had informed Verasa that she was outraged the clan had not brought Kalix to justice. Although the Great Council had decided that the young werewolf should be brought back to Castle MacRinnalch, nothing had been done about it.

"She killed my son," stated Dulupina. "I won't vote for anyone as Thane until Kalix has been dealt with."

"In other words," said Markus to his mother. "Whoever brings back her heart gets Dulupina's vote."

"That's about it," replied Verasa.

Again feeling that her son was looking at her a little questioningly, Verasa spoke angrily.

"I won't sanction the killing of my youngest daughter."

"I've heard you wish her dead," said Markus.

"Maybe in a moment of anger. But I will not have Great Mother Dulupina or anyone else tell me that my daughter must be killed."

Verasa could see a positive side.

"At least she's not going to vote for Sarapen. She'll abstain again which makes it impossible for Sarapen to get the nine votes he needs."

Markus was doubtful about his mother's calculations.

"What if Sarapen promises Dulupina he will kill Kalix? Might she not cast her vote for him?"

"I don't think so. Even if she did, he'd still be one vote short and the only free vote now belongs to Thrix. Yes, well may you scowl, Markus. A great shame you get on so badly with your sister. Fortunately for us she's getting on equally badly with Sarapen. Did you know he swept her designs onto the floor?"

"I was there when it happened mother, or just after."

"Then you should have picked them up. Thrix will not tolerate interference in her business, for which I respect her."

"I thought her fashion business annoyed you?"

"It only annoys me that she must distance herself from the family so. Now you must try and make things up with her."

Markus promised to do what he could, without much conviction. As tonight was the night before the full moon, Markus was expecting the council meeting to be a good deal stormier than the last one. Verasa saw that her son was troubled.

"Don't worry. Even if Dulupina and Thrix decide to vote against you, Sarapen will still not get his nine votes. Baron MacAllister won't be at the meeting. He has unexpectedly fallen ill."

"How did you manage that?"

Verasa and Baron MacAllister had come to terms on the loan that he required. The Baron was heading back to his own keep, claiming illness. If the election was not resolved and another meeting was called next month, he would then vote for Markus. The Mistress of the Werewolves was already swinging things in favour of her younger son. She asked him if he'd found out anything about the twins.

"As far as I can see they don't have a band any more. I read a message on a music forum wondering where they'd disappeared to. I also found a review of one of their last gigs. Apparently it was a shamble. Both sisters kept falling over, and one of them broke her guitar."

"Broke her guitar? How?"

"She jumped on it."

Verasa was perplexed.

"Was she annoyed with her guitar? Had it failed to function?"

"I don't think so."

"Then why would she destroy it?"

"Part of her stage act, perhaps."

"How odd," said Verasa, who couldn't imagine destroying a perfectly good instrument. "Of course they do have a great deal of money. She can buy a new one. But it sounds like they're making no real progress. Broken guitars and falling over onstage do not amount to much, I imagine. Presuming they wish to be successful, what would you say they most needed?"

Markus considered this.

"A responsible adviser, perhaps, to manage their affairs? Someone who knows the business and doesn't get intoxicated?"

The Mistress of the Werewolves nodded.

"Yes, I agree. A manager might be just what they need. Rather awkward, given that it would really not be safe for anyone who isn't a werewolf to be closely involved with them. I do worry terribly about them giving themselves away, and bringing the Avenaris Guild down on their heads. But I'll think about it, and see who might be suitable."

There was a knock on the door and a servant announced that Dominil was here. Verasa noticed how her son drew himself up to his full height as Dominil entered the room. It was natural enough. Few male werewolves could resist the impulse to show themselves off to their best advantage when the icily beautiful Dominil arrived.

50

Tupan's daughter Dominil had a powerful intellect and a cold demeanour. Her voice was not harsh but it was no longer warmed by the clan's Scottish accent. Dominil had discarded her accent at Oxford university some years ago, where she gained a double first in Classics and Philosophy. The neutral tone of her voice made her stand out at the castle, but Dominil would have stood out anywhere, with her high cheekbones, large dark eyes and long snow-white hair. She was slender like the rest of her generation of werewolves, but a little taller, and a good deal colder. Verasa still remembered the day when Dominil, then seven years old, had broken her leg in a fall in the woods and resolutely refused to cry, not even wincing while Dr Angus MacRinnalch examined the fracture though it surely must have been painful.

Dominil had followed this pattern through the rest of her life. She showed no pleasure on her admittance to Oxford and neither did she appear particularly pleased when she graduated with honour. Nothing seemed to excite her emotions. The younger female werewolves would routinely be stared at in the street because of their beauty but Dominil suffered this in extremis. As she strode along the pavement, tall, white-haired and dazzlingly beautiful, everyone would turn to stare. What Dominil thought of this, or if she even noticed, no one knew. No one really knew much of what Dominil thought. She had spent her youth at the castle, left for Oxford, returned four years later and now passed most of her time in her chambers in the east wing, with her books and her computers. She had no friends that anyone knew of. She seemed close to her father Tupan but if this closeness involved anything like warmth, it was hidden from outside eyes.

It was rumoured that she had an affair, or at least a liaison, with Sarapen. They now disliked each other but Dominil never showed any sign of discomfort when Sarapen made one of his frequent visits to the castle.

Verasa was not entirely ignorant of Dominil's tastes. Few goings on in or around the castle were hidden from her. Verasa knew, for instance, that Dominil had taken various human lovers while at Oxford and had carried on the practice since returning home. Dominil had formed temporary associations with several young men in the neighbouring towns. She kept this to herself, and it was almost a secret, save for Verasa's inquisitiveness. The Mistress of the Werewolves could not help wondering about the nature of Dominil's relationships with the young men. As far as she knew, none of them had actually died, but several of them were no longer around. Their families believed that they had left the district but Verasa wondered if their bones might be lying at the bottom of a peat marsh on the MacRinnalch estates.

Markus was a few years older than Dominil. Though not close they were on reasonably good terms. He greeted her politely, inquired after her health, then left the chamber to visit Thrix, as his mother had requested. Though Markus was not overly pleased to be ordered out of a meeting, he was nonetheless not too displeased to be excused from making small talk with Dominil. There was something about her company that he found very wearing. He sometimes got the impression she looked down on him. But there again, Dominil might look down on everyone.

Verasa offered Dominil wine which she accepted. Dominil had a liking for wine, and the clan whisky.

"I am so pleased you nominated Markus for Thane," began Verasa. "I'm sure you agree that Markus will make a – "

Dominil held up her hand.

"Please, let us not pretend I am a supporter of Markus. I regard him as quite unsuitable for Thane. But I'll continue to oppose Sarapen."

"So at least we know where we stand," said Verasa dryly. Already she could feel the oncoming full moon and she was trying not to let the excitement interfere with her judgement. She wondered if Dominil felt the same thrill when the wolf nights arrived. Possibly not. It would be no great surprise to learn that the werewolf state left her unmoved.

When Dominil transformed she remained white, with the mane of a great snow wolf. It was a spectacular sight, one that had rarely been seen in the clan. Verasa could remember the first time it happened, when Dominil was no more than three weeks old. When she had first transformed into a baby werewolf and her coat turned out to be white, the whole family had been entranced. Tupan had been delighted. There was nothing unlucky about a white-haired werewolf. On the contrary, it was so rare as to be regarded as a good omen. But if Dominil was a good omen for anything, that thing had yet to arrive.

"Do you feel any concern about remaining at Castle MacRinnalch?" Verasa asked Dominil.

"Why should I?"

"It may be uncomfortable now that you've come out in opposition to Sarapen."

"I do not fear Sarapen," replied Dominil. "Besides my father will remain close to the castle."

Verasa wondered if he would. Tupan had his own affairs to look after. The Mistress of the Werewolves realised she was not as confident about there being no violence as she had claimed when speaking

113

to Markus. It would suit her cause very badly if Sarapen were to dispose of Dominil.

"Sarapen will kill Kalix," said Dominil, abruptly.

"Kalix has proved remarkably hard to kill so far."

"He was not so concerned before. Now that Dulupina has made her thoughts clear he'll certainly kill her."

"Kalix is his own sister," pointed out Verasa.

"Sarapen won't let that stop him. He wants Dulupina's vote. Your eldest son is quite without feelings."

Verasa was tempted to point out that in comparison to Dominil, Sarapen had plenty of feelings, but she remained silent. She wondered what motivated Dominil. One of the very few things she could ever remember Dominil saying about her herself was that she was bored. That had been some years ago, during a vacation from university. Was it possible, wondered Verasa, that this most intelligent and beautiful werewolf still suffered from boredom? There was a knock at the door. One of Verasa's servants entered.

"Gawain MacRinnalch has been sighted on the outlying estates, Mistress."

"Gawain?"

This was most unexpected. Gawain? Ex-lover of Kalix? No one had seen Gawain for three years. He had been banished by the Thane from all the lands of the MacRinnalchs. By appearing anywhere near the castle he ran the risk of death at the hands of the clan.

"Has he been approached?"

"No Mistress. We await your instructions."

"Keep him under observation," ordered the Mistress of the Werewolves, calmly. "But don't approach him. On such a sombre occasion, it will not do to have any unpleasantness."

51

Thrix was not surprised to find Markus at her door.

"Come in," she said. "I doubt you can offer me anything mother hasn't already."

Thrix's laptop was open on the desk. She'd been busy writing email to her office in London. She trusted her assistant Ann to look after business for a few days but even so Thrix had to keep in touch. She hadn't spent all these years building up her business to have it interrupted by a funeral, even the Thane's.

Markus stood silently in the room, long enough for the silence to become uncomfortable.

"Probably you should say something," said Thrix, eventually.

Markus remained silent. The Enchantress noted that her brother was looking rather well. He was dressed in a black suit, finely tailored. The severity of the suit against his slightly feminine features made for an attractive contrast. She might have complimented him on it, but clothing was something of a sensitive subject between them.

"It's bright in here," said Markus, eventually.

"I used an illumination spell," replied Thrix. "I don't know how you live in this gloomy place."

"The clan wouldn't like you using sorcery in the castle," said Markus.

Thrix raised one eyebrow.

"Is that really the best you can do?"

"I was merely pointing out – "

"You were searching for some criticism which is what you always do when I'm around. Really Markus, this is not what mother had in mind when she sent you here."

"I'm not mother's servant," responded Markus, angrily. "And you don't frighten me with your childish spells. If you think I've come here to beg for your vote you're mistaken. I'm quite capable of managing my life without help from you, golden-haired sister who is so keen to abandon her family."

"I might be keen to abandon them but at least I don't assault them. I heard about you attacking Kalix in daylight when she was weak. That's a fine way of showing your regard for the family."

"I have good reason to dislike Kalix. And you helped her to hide, contrary to the wishes of your family. You've never have had any regard for us, Thrix."

Markus's voice was full of anger. Thrix shook her head.

"Markus. Will you stop this? I've told you often enough I don't care a damn about what clothes you wear."

Markus snarled and by the time the sound was out of his mouth he had changed into his werewolf shape. The moon had risen. Thrix transformed, and felt irritated as she did so. It was difficult to type on a computer as a werewolf. Had Markus not interrupted her she would have finished her email with far greater ease than she would now. Markus was glaring at her with loathing. He hated Thrix because she knew of his liking for female clothes. She'd known for a long time, ever since she'd caught him wearing something of hers back in the far off days before she left the castle.

"I really don't care," said Thrix.

"You don't? I seem to remember you had some very amusing comments to make at the time."

The Enchantress felt a little guilty about this. She had tormented her brother and while never giving away his secret, had threatened to, many years ago.

"I was a lot younger then," said Thrix. "It took me by surprise."

"But now you are quite prepared to accept that your brother has some peculiarities?" snarled Markus.

Thrix's long golden werewolf coat gleamed in the sorcerous light and her own eyes lit up with anger. Markus's hostility towards her over the years had left her with little sympathy for him.

"I told you, I don't care. I don't care about you, your clothes, the next Thane or the MacRinnalch Clan. I care about my fashion house and you're all keeping me from it. Now if you'd like to leave me alone, I might be able to get on with my work."

52

Daniel had been instructed by Moonglow to entertain Kalix. He didn't feel equal to the task.

"I've no experience of entertaining werewolves."

"Who has? Just keep talking to her. That's what I've been doing."

"Didn't she threaten to kill you if you didn't shut up?"

"Well yes," admitted Moonglow. "But she didn't really mean it."

Daniel was still in a bad mood because Moonglow was going to visit Jay. Her face was made up to be very pale, her lips were dark purple, she had on her favourite black dress and she'd even brought out a pair of black high heels she'd been saving for a special occasion.

116

"Why is this a special occasion?" inquired Daniel.

"I haven't seen Jay for four days," replied Moonglow, happily.

Daniel cursed under his breath, and resolved firmly to never think about Moonglow again. From now on, he would feel nothing for her. Moonglow departed.

"I have no feelings whatsoever for that girl," muttered Daniel to himself, and wandered into the living room where Kalix still lay in front of the gas fire.

"Moonglow has a really annoying boyfriend," he said. "He is just so irritating. No one likes him apart from Moonglow. He's always going on about how he's travelled the world and swum in the Amazon and his hair is dyed really badly and when he goes out with Moonglow he wears make-up which is just stupid. I hate him."

Having no interest at all in Moonglow's boyfriend, Kalix ignored this. It didn't prevent Daniel from warming to the subject.

"I mean, boys wearing make-up, what's that about? Jay looks ridiculous. It's not like he's good looking or anything. He looks like something you'd find in a graveyard. What Moonglow sees in him is beyond me. And as for his astrology, what a waste of time. The guy is a complete phoney. And where does he get his money from? From his parents I expect. No doubt daddy owns a company and Jay is just playing with make-up for a year or two before he goes off to be company director. They're all the same these types. And that's not the worst – "

"Be quiet!" said Kalix, in a surprisingly loud voice.

"What?"

"Stop talking. I'm not interested. Leave me alone."

Daniel was abashed.

"Sorry. Didn't mean to go on about it. Can I get you anything?"

"No."

Kalix turned away. Daniel searched for something else to say. Moonglow had instructed him to keep talking.

"Is it fun being a werewolf?" he ventured.

"It's great," muttered Kalix, bleakly. She was still wrapped in her quilt and she had a hot water bottle thoughtfully provided by Moonglow. Now her body was warm but inside she was still frozen. Daniel, who was just as kind as Moonglow, though not so good at showing it, suddenly felt worried that Kalix might die there and then. This would be bad. He'd feel terrible and Moonglow would probably blame him. He wondered if it might be a good idea to play her some music.

117

"Do you like music?" he asked.

Kalix didn't stir.

"I have a really big collection," continued Daniel. "Music for all tastes. Well mainly heavy rock, heavy metal, nu metal and doom metal, but branching out into darkwave, progressive rock and all associated territories."

Kalix had no idea what any of these words meant and wished fervently that Daniel would just leave her alone. She tried flexing her limbs, wondering if she might have enough strength to leave but she knew it was useless, her legs wouldn't carry her out of the door. Daniel, having moved onto his favourite subject, wasn't letting it go. He told Kalix about several of his favourite gigs – Metallica, Slayer, Motorhead – and talked enthusiastically about his forthcoming visit to the Wembley Arena to see Nine Inch Nails.

Kalix had a dim memory, from some time when she'd been lying in a stupor, of a conversation between Daniel and Moonglow in which Daniel had been complaining about not having a girlfriend. Listening to Daniel's endless monologue, she began to understand why. Kalix had little experience of human society. Unlike the other young werewolves, she'd never been to school. But even with her lack of experience, she felt it must lie outside the norms of human behaviour to inflict an endless tale of how difficult it had been to get a ticket for Nine Inch Nails on a suffering house guest.

"Be quiet," she said again.

Thinking that any reaction was better than none, Daniel kept on.

"I really like the first album better than the second one but the third is probably the best though it wasn't so well reviewed in some of the papers but of course the music papers – "

The moon rose. Kalix abruptly transformed into a werewolf. A fierce beast, part human, part wolf, and all of it very irritated with Daniel. She snarled, dragged herself almost to her feet and put her great fangs right in Daniel's face.

"If you say one more thing about your music collection I'll kill you."

Daniel took a swift step backwards, intimidated by the great fangs. Though still weak, Kalix's transformation into werewolf form gave her sufficient strength to leap on Daniel and they crashed onto the floor. Kalix put her jaws at his throat.

"Don't you like music?" wailed Daniel.

Kalix shouted something at him. As an angry werewolf, her voice was difficult to understand. It was harsh and her Scottish accent became stronger. But Daniel could have sworn he heard her say she only liked the Runaways. He looked up into Kalix's mad werewolf eyes. The werewolf was looking hungry. She opened her mouth.

"I have a large collection of Runaways albums," cried Daniel. "And most of their early singles."

Kalix closed her jaws. She looked at him suspiciously.

"Is this true?"

53

Moonglow lay in Jay's bed but she couldn't sleep. She was worrying about Kalix and Daniel. The most sympathetic of friends could not call Daniel competent at caring for others. He was well-meaning but Moonglow had a feeling he might not be able to cope. She began to fret and blame herself for leaving him there on his own. She should have known better. Here she was, selfishly enjoying herself with her boyfriend while back home Kalix might be dead. Daniel probably wouldn't notice. He'd be in his room, engrossed in one of the obscure music websites he was fond of visiting. Daniel loved everything about music. Show him a website that traced the genealogy of one of his favourite bands right back to when the singer and the guitarist first met at high school and he'd be occupied for hours.

"Oh my goodness," said Moonglow, sitting up suddenly in bed. She shook Jay.

"Wake up!"

Jay, a sound sleeper, took some time to rouse himself.

"When is the full moon?" said Moonglow, urgently.

"Tomorrow night," replied Jay.

"Oh dear," said Moonglow, and leapt out of bed and started scrambling into her clothes.

Jay looked on in surprise.

"What is it?"

Moonglow couldn't believe she'd forgotten that Kalix would automatically turn into a werewolf tonight. She'd forgotten all about the

MacRinnalchs transforming on the night before the full moon, although Kalix had mentioned it. It was unbelievably stupid of her. She raced to get ready and was phoning a cab while still struggling into her dress. Who knew what might happen when Kalix became a werewolf?

'She's bound to be hungry,' thought Moonglow. 'I don't believe her werewolf form suffers from eating problems. She might just devour the first human she sees.'

When the cab arrived Moonglow hurried out, leaving her boyfriend perplexed. Jay lived in a flat near Sloane street, quite an expensive part of London, but in the quiet night-time streets it did not take long for the taxi to cross the river and make for Kennington. Moonglow fretted at every red light, becoming more and more convinced that she was going to return home to a scene of carnage.

As they drew up outside her flat Moonglow quickly paid the driver and hurried up the stairs. She flew through the front door and the first thing she saw was werewolf Kalix coming out of the kitchen with blood dripping from her jaws. Moonglow wailed. Kalix opened her mouth in surprise and Moonglow saw that the werewolf had a mouth full of meat.

"You killed Daniel!" screamed Moonglow, and pounced on Kalix. "You monster!"

Kalix growled some unintelligible reply. Moonglow, in a blind fury, attempted to reign blows on her, though Kalix was far too agile to allow herself to be struck. The werewolf stepped back and put out one powerful arm to hold off the girl.

Daniel walked out of the kitchen with a slice of pizza in his hand.

"Moonglow? Why are you trying to hit Kalix?"

Moonglow was suddenly very embarrassed.

"I thought she'd eaten you."

Daniel was puzzled.

"Why would she do that?"

He turned to Kalix.

"See, like I said, Moonglow worries too much. That's why she gets me to take all these notes at class even though we don't really need them. You want to wash down that beef with some pizza?"

Kalix nodded and Daniel loaded a slice of pizza into her mouth. They trooped into the living room where all around the couch there were signs of consumption: empty pizza boxes, empty packets of pop-tarts, and the string that had held together the huge joint of beef which Moonglow had put in the freezer for Kalix.

"I thawed it out in the microwave," explained Daniel. "Hence the blood. Kalix likes her meat raw, but not frozen."

Kalix and Daniel had apparently become great friends. They sat down next to each other on the couch. Next to the empty food containers were a bundle of records and CDs.

"Kalix loves the Runaways."

"You do?" said Moonglow.

"My favourite band," replied Kalix.

"Oh," said Moonglow, who was still embarrassed at the fuss she'd made.

"So, what brings you back early?" asked Daniel.

"I just thought I'd see how you were getting on."

"She doesn't trust me," said Daniel, again turning to Kalix. "As if I'm not capable of looking after a sick werewolf. Have I been looking after you well?"

"Really well," said Kalix. "Can I hear more Runaways?"

It was strange to hear human words coming from the wolf's face. As Kalix spoke her lips would curl back over her long, sharp teeth. Daniel handed her a cloth to wipe the blood from her jaws, a sight which Moonglow found slightly gruesome. It was also strange to see Kalix apparently happy. When Moonglow had left the house she'd been lying miserably in front of the fire and now here she was, eating food and listening to records. Perhaps, Moonglow conceded to herself, Daniel was not so hopeless after all.

Now that the shock was over, Moonglow was pleased. It was good to have a cheerful werewolf in the house. Much better than a suicidally depressed werewolf. Moonglow fitted herself on the end of the couch and took what was left of the pizza from the box.

"I'm sorry I thought you'd eaten Daniel," she said.

"That's okay," replied Kalix.

They sat for a while, eating pizza, and listening to music.

"Thanks for letting me stay here," said Kalix.

Moonglow smiled. Now that Kalix was full of meat and transformed into a werewolf she seemed like a whole new person. Moonglow wondered if this happened every month. Or was Kalix just happy because Daniel was playing records by her favourite band? As far as Moonglow knew, Daniel didn't like the Runaways that much. Their brief heyday had happened around 1978, before he was born. He only had some of their records because he'd come across them in a second hand shop and bought them in the compulsive way he often did, before wondering why he never had any money to pay the bills. But they were certainly going down well with Kalix. Already Moonglow and Daniel had had the unusual experience of hearing a young werewolf singing along, not tunefully, to *Cherry Bomb*. Kalix had never seen the original vinyl single before and cradled it in her lap like a baby.

"I wish Joan Jett was my mother," said Kalix. "Play it again."

54

Mr Mikulanec was not tall but he was heavy, barrel-chested, and very strong. His dark hair was cropped short and there was something cruel about his features. He had killed many werewolves in his forty years of existence, and was confident of killing many more.

He preferred to keep his own company. The companionship of others quickly irritated him. When patrolling for werewolves with one or two other hunters, it was not so bad. Then, Mikulanec would be in command and there would be no unnecessary talking. But all social situations, where others were free to bore him with the senseless trivia that made up their daily lives, were an annoyance to Mr Mikulanec. The Guild had provided him with a small flat in Bayswater. They'd have provided him with something grander had he wished, as he was a fellow werewolf hunter of excellent reputation, but Mikulanec had expressly wished to be housed in a place which was both modest and unobtrusive. The flat remained exactly as the Guild provided it. He didn't rearrange the furniture, buy himself a new set of sheets, or hang a calendar on the wall. Such things were inconsequential to him. The only thing he cared about was hunting werewolves.

Mr Mikulanec had not been impressed since arriving in Britain. The great Castle MacRinnalch for instance, remained untouched, inviolate almost. The Guild considered it too difficult to attack. Mikulanec wondered what his father would have had to say about that. His father was not a man to allow a safe haven for any cursed werewolf. His father and his compatriots had all but driven them out of the country, ridded the land of the plague.

The Guild, he acknowledged, were well organised, and possessed some strength. But they had so far proved themselves unequal to the task of fighting the MacRinnalchs. Mr Carmichael had suggested to Mikulanec that perhaps he did not fully appreciate the strength of the MacRinnalchs, a suggestion which Mikulanec brushed aside. There was nothing about werewolves he did not know. And there were several things he knew which the Guild did not. He'd wanted to travel to Scotland while the Thane's funeral was in progress but the Guild had discouraged this. They had their own men there, they said, and didn't want to risk a stranger giving away their operations. Mikulanec had been angered and had considered leaving, though it would have been almost impossible for him to tear himself away from a country such as this. There were so many werewolves. Mikulanec could not leave before he had done something about it.

Now there was the matter of the werewolf princess. The Guild had been tracking her but had lost contact. Mr Carmichael had invited Mikulanec to demonstrate his skills by finding her.

'Very well,' thought Mr Mikulanec. 'I will locate the girl and kill her. Then perhaps the Guild will see that I am not a man to be excluded from their inner circle.'

55

Castle MacRinnalch and the surrounding estates were now full of werewolves. Rarely had so many been gathered in one place. It was a long time since they'd last come together for the funeral of a Thane, and the MacRinnalch Clan had grown since then.

Verasa strode into the council chamber. Even as a werewolf she was upright. It was rather difficult to carry oneself totally erect in werewolf form but Verasa refused to walk like a hulking beast. She was not expecting any surprises at the meeting. The Thane's brother Kurian was never going to vote for anyone but Sarapen. Nor was his son Kertal or his daughter Marwanis. They were the most traditional of werewolves and while Verasa found this frustrating in some respects, she admired them in a way. Marwanis in particular was an intelligent young woman of great beauty and distinction. With her dark brown hair, large hazel eyes and perfect complexion, conservatively yet tastefully dressed, she was every inch what a female member of the ruling family should be. Rather different to certain others of the younger generation, reflected Verasa, ruefully.

Verasa sat next to Rainal. She poured herself whisky from the crystal decanter in front of her. Fine whisky from the clan estates, and fine crystal from France. It had been imported more than three hundred years ago by Hughan MacRinnalch, an uncle of the late Thane.

A large portrait of Hughan MacRinnalch hung in the castle's banqueting hall. The clan had good reason to remember him fondly. He was the first werewolf of the modern era to take to business, and it was his dealings in the seventeenth and eighteenth centuries that had set the clan on the road to its present wealth. While the MacRinnalch estates were of great intrinsic value, Hughan had added immeasurably to the MacRinnalch fortune with his forays into foreign trade, banking, and the nascent stock markets in Edinburgh and London. By the time the industrial revolution got going in the 1760s Hughan was in a position to invest heavily, and the clan's wealth was further swelled by shipping, iron works, and the new manufacturing industries. Though much of the nation's aristocracy frowned on trade, the MacRinnalchs had never turned their noses up at the prospect of making money.

There were signs of impatience around the table. With everyone in werewolf form, and the moon almost full above, tempers could be expected to wear thin very quickly. Sarapen tramped heavily into the chamber, not upright, but slightly bent as if ready to spring on anyone who dared to oppose him. It was obvious that Sarapen had arrived in a poor temper.

"Greetings, cousin," said Dominil.

Sarapen did not return her salutation. Dominil merely spoke to annoy him; she was party responsible for his ill temper, as she well knew. Sarapen had visited her that afternoon. If he had been hoping to persuade her not to nominate Markus, it had been a hopeless mission from the first.

"Markus will never be Thane," Sarapen had told her, fiercely.

"Then we must look further afield, for neither will you."

"Why did you nominate him?" demanded Sarapen. "Did my mother put you up to it?"

"I need no encouragement to oppose you," replied Dominil. As she said this her eyes blazed. Faced with Sarapen, even Dominil could not keep her temper completely under control. Sarapen and Dominil had been lovers for a brief period, some years ago. It had ended very badly. Whatever had happened was secret between them but the antagonism between the pair had never lessened.

"We will begin the meeting," said Rainal.

"Where is Baron MacAllister?" demanded Sarapen.

"He has returned to his own keep," replied Rainal.

"Why?"

"A sudden illness."

"What!" Sarapen rose to his feet and pounded his fist on the table. "Why was I not informed of this?"

"He was afflicted only a short time ago," explained Rainal. "In fact I've only just received his apologies."

Sarapen glared at Verasa.

"And what do you know of this, Mistress of the Werewolves?"

The flickering light from the log fire was reflected on Sarapen's great fangs. On the opposite side of the table the two remaining Barons couldn't help flinching, and were glad that they did not oppose Sarapen. Baron MacAllister's own keep was some distance from the castle, and a stronghold that was difficult to attack. He might be glad of that before this affair was over.

"I'm just as surprised as you," replied Verasa, smoothly. "Though I believe the good Baron has been in poor health for some time."

Sarapen glowered at his mother. One of his votes was gone and he strongly suspected that she was behind it. Already Sarapen was feeling that he had had quite enough of meetings.

"Before we begin," said Rainal. "I feel it is incumbent upon me, as secretary to the clan, to inform the council that there is already some dissatisfaction outside these walls. If there is no new Thane to officiate at the funeral tomorrow, the dissatisfaction will increase. Of course, I make no effort to influence this meeting. I merely inform you of the feelings among clan members."

"Thank you Rainal," said Verasa. "As always, we appreciate your words."

Rainal shuffled some papers in front of him awkwardly with his werewolf paw.

"Before we take the vote, does anyone wish to speak?"

"I do," said Sarapen. He rose to his feet. "This matter must be decided tonight. And it must be decided in my favour. I invite those wolves who were of a different mind last night to reconsider their opinions."

As he said this, Sarapen slowly turned his head so that his gaze fell on every person present, and never did a more hostile or threatening gaze come from a MacRinnalch. Dominil met his eyes, and her lips pulled back so that her teeth showed.

"Thank you for that speech, Sarapen."

Sarapen snarled. Rainal shifted nervously in his seat. It would be quite intolerable for fighting to break out at a meeting of the Great Council. The clan members currently surrounding the castle were not expecting their visit to the MacRinnalch homelands to be marred by violence. Yet Sarapen was not the only werewolf here who showed signs of being on a short fuse. Kertal had let it be known he was none to pleased at what had happened last night. Kertal was young and vigorous, his sister Marwanis equally so. It would not take much to make them support Sarapen in a fight. Already Rainal could sense the werewolves sliding their seats back an inch or two to make it easier to leap up if necessary.

"Why don't you be quiet so we can vote," said Markus, leaning far over the table towards Sarapen. Sarapen rose from his chair and let out a ferocious growl. Beside him Kertal also rose and next moment there were six werewolves on their feet, all roaring at each other. Seeing that matters were quickly getting out of hand, the Mistress of the Werewolves banged her fist on the table and spoke with all the authority at her command.

"We will all sit down and proceed with the meeting. Now. Everyone. Sit down."

Great claws clenched and unclenched as the werewolves struggled to control their tempers. It was difficult to ignore a direct command from the Mistress of the Werewolves. They took their seats, uneasily. Sarapen was the last to sit down. Already he could feel that he was being outmanoeuvred by his mother and Markus.

Verasa looked towards Rainal. Rainal was nervous and took some time to get his words out.

"If there are no more… speeches… we will move to the vote. Who will nominate?"

"I nominate Sarapen MacRinnalch," said Baron MacPhee.

"I nominate Markus MacRinnalch," said Dominil.

126

"Very well. Those in favour of Sarapen MacRinnalch please raise their hands.

Six hands were raised. Sarapen, Kurian, Kertal, Marwanis, Baron MacPhee and Baron MacGregor. The same votes as last night, minus that of the absent Baron MacAllister.

"Those in favour of Markus MacRinnalch."

Now five hands were raised, those of Markus, Verasa, Dominil, Tupan and Lucia.

Thrix had been wondering all day what she would do. She'd rather have stayed out of the trouble that would follow another undecided vote. But her anger had grown under the moon. She couldn't forgive Sarapen for dashing her designs from her desk. Nothing could have been more disrespectful. Besides, there was the fashion show in New York to which her mother apparently had access. Thrix would like to be represented at that show. She raised her hand.

"Six votes also," said Rainal. "Are there any abstentions?"

Dulupina raised her hand.

Last night the vote had gone seven to five in Sarapen's favour. Now it was six votes for each candidate. No one had the required nine votes. Sarapen rose slowly to his feet. His face was a mask of utter fury but he did not speak. Instead, he turned on his heel and marched swiftly from the room.

"The next meeting will be at the time of the next full moon," said Rainal. The werewolves rose, and filed out of the room, each lost in their own thoughts, wondering what the outcome of this might be.

56

It was cold on the moorlands to the east of Castle MacRinnalch; cold, and very dark. The moon was hidden by clouds and it was threatening rain. Gawain knew that he shouldn't be here. He was forbidden to enter the MacRinnalch estates and risked his life in returning. His sentence of banishment by the Thane was not to be taken lightly. Gawain already had the feeling that he was being watched.

The approach to the clan estates had bought painful memories, particularly his journey through Colburn Wood. The wood was special to the MacRinnalchs: here they buried their heroes. Avreg MacRinnalch lay here, as did Gerrant Gawain MacRinnalch, Gawain's great-great-grandfather. Colburn Wood was an ancient place. It had never been forested or cultivated and remained exactly the same as it had been for thousands of years. The large, dark, tangled wood contained the spirit of the MacRinnalchs, from a time before the castle was built. It was a place full of primeval magic.

Less magical, but almost as important, it was from the stream which flowed through the woods that water was drawn to make the MacRinnalch whisky. Most importantly to Gawain, it was here that he and Kalix had come to make sport beneath the trees, unobserved and alone.

Oddly, as Gawain had traversed the wood, he'd thought for a moment that he caught the scent of a Hiyasta. That was impossible. No fire elemental would dare to trespass on the sacred territory of the MacRinnalchs. He sniffed again, and decided that he'd been mistaken.

When he broke cover and came within sight of the castle, memories flooded in again. Unhappy memories, ending with his humiliation and banishment. What was he doing here, on this cold, friendless night? Had he come for the funeral? To pay his last respects to the werewolf who'd banished him? Perhaps. The death of a Thane was momentous event for the clan. Gawain felt it as keenly as anyone. Perhaps he was here to gloat over the death of the werewolf who had caused him so much pain? But Gawain didn't think so. His anger at the Thane's actions had mostly faded. He thought he understood why the Thane has acted as he did.

Gawain knew why he was here. He was hoping to catch a glimpse of Kalix. Gawain burned with desire for Kalix, just as he burned with shame over the whole episode of their involvement and his expulsion. It had not been right, he knew, to become involved with the daughter of the Thane. She had been too young. Even if she had been older the clan was never going to approve of such a match.

Though the humiliation of his trial had been great, it was not the reason that Gawain burned with shame. He had a terrible sense of guilt for allowing the banishment to happen. He should have stayed with Kalix, and not allowed himself to be sent away. He should have stood up to them. He shouldn't have deserted Kalix.

Gawain had himself only been nineteen at the time. Difficult for a nineteen year old werewolf to defy the Thane and all his household. Gawain hated himself for not trying harder. Since then he had wandered the country. He never heard any news about Kalix. He didn't know if she was still at the castle. Even his sharp senses couldn't discern Kalix's scent at this distance. There were too many other werewolves on the estate and the castle itself was masked by an enchantment which muted the werewolf scent, to baffle their enemies. If she was still at the castle she would surely be in the funeral procession. Gawain had determined that he was going to see her again, no matter what it cost.

57

At three a.m. Kalix, Daniel and Moonglow were sprawled comfortably in the living room, surrounded by a great pile of empty food cartons, record covers, CD covers, and assorted junk that had not yet found a proper place in their new home. It could have been normal scene from any student flat, had it not been for one of them being a werewolf.

It was odd, reflected Moonglow, that here was Kalix, acting for the first time something like a normal human being, but not being in human form. The meat and the pizza had certainly improved her mood. So had the Runaways though Moonglow had pleaded with Daniel to change the music after a few hours, feeling that she couldn't take any more. Kalix had growled angrily but when Daniel explained that it was normal in human households not to listen to the same record for hours on end, she had grudgingly agreed to listen to something else. Moonglow intercepted Daniel on the way to the music shelves.

"Nothing loud. It's three in the morning," she said.

"All right," said Daniel, who was in a good mood. Kalix wasn't being crazy and Moonglow hadn't spent the night with Jay. That was enough to make Daniel cheerful.

Moonglow was also happy. After the trouble she'd gone to in rescuing Kalix it was gratifying to see her finally showing signs of responding. Kalix was bound to find life a lot less stressful now that she had a new pendant to keep her safe, and some friendly people to live with. Moonglow assumed that Kalix would want to live with them. It had to be better than skulking in alleyways and sleeping in warehouses.

"What is this music?" asked Kalix.

"Kate Bush," replied Moonglow.

"I hate it," said Kalix, who had never learned how to be tactful.

"You'll like it after you've heard it a few times," replied Moonglow, who was completely invulnerable to criticism when it came to Kate Bush. Moonglow had spent far too much time in her bedroom between the ages of twelve and fifteen reverently listening to Kate Bush to take any criticism of her seriously.

"Jay didn't used to like her but he does now," said Moonglow.

"Who's Jay?" asked Kalix, which was the first sign she'd ever shown of taking an interest in the life of either Daniel of Moonglow.

"My boyfriend."

"What's he like?"

"He's nice," enthused Moonglow. "He's good looking and he's smart and we go to gigs together and he's really good at astrology."

"What's astrology?" asked Kalix.

"It's the art of reading the future in the stars and planets," said Moonglow, a little surprised by Kalix's ignorance.

"What's going to happen?" asked Kalix.

"When?"

"In the future."

Moonglow struggled for an answer.

"Well, it's more like a sort of personal guidance thing."

"It's total rubbish," said Daniel, unable to contain himself. "They just make it all up."

Kalix lost interest and started licking the inside of a pizza box. Her tongue was alarmingly long, to match her teeth. But now they were used to her voice and could understand her, they didn't find the werewolf Kalix intimidating any more. They had both started to look on her furry form as cute and attractive. Moonglow had an urge to stroke her long coat, an urge she wisely didn't act on. She wondered about Kalix's shape. Sort of man-beast. Or woman-beast.

"Are all werewolves the same shape?"

"What?"

"Sort of half person half wolf. I was wondering if any werewolves can change into wolves. Like a complete wolf, I mean."

"I can do that," said Kalix. "All the pure-blooded MacRinnalchs can change into wolves if they want."

"Why don't you?"

"It's not so good for fighting," said Kalix. "And you just can't do anything with your paws. It's hard to even open a door. You can't talk. And you don't think so clearly."

"When did you last try being a wolf?"

"I don't want to talk about it," said Kalix. "It's not the business of humans.

"Sorry."

Unexpectedly, the doorbell rang.

"Have we been disturbing the neighbours?"

Kalix had risen swiftly and was sniffing the air.

"It's the stupid Hiyasta Queen," she said, and sat down again.

Moonglow went off to open the door. Downstairs she found the Fire Queen in an elegant blue outfit and a flood of tears. She was too upset to speak. Moonglow had to help her through the door and up the stairs. When they reached the living room Malveria simply collapsed on the couch and lay there sobbing.

"It must be really tough being a Fire Queen," whispered Daniel to Moonglow. "Every time we see this woman she's in hysterics."

Moonglow brought some tissues.

"Can I get you anything else?" said asked.

Malveria shook her head.

"It's no use," she cried. "Nothing will stop the pain."

"Would you like a cup of tea?"

"A cup of tea would be nice," sobbed Malveria, then buried her face in the tissues and got back to crying uncontrollably.

58

Moonglow returned from the kitchen with a pot of tea to find the Fire Queen still sobbing. Daniel, in an effort to comfort her, was now patting her head, which rested on his shoulder.

"There there," said Daniel. He noticed that Moonglow was regarding him with amusement. Embarrassed, he moved away a few inches at which Malveria sobbed even louder then laid her head in his lap.

"Tea?" said Moonglow.

Malveria managed to dry her eyes sufficiently to take the cup though she remained lying on Daniel's lap, which wasn't the easiest position in which to drink. For a while there was only the sound of Malveria sipping her tea in between sobs. It was quite a pathetic scene. Eventually Malveria looked up.

"I must look terrible," she said, and indeed her face was heavily smeared with make-up. Her eyeliner had not been able withstand the burning tears of a hysterical Fire Queen.

"Bring me servants and a mirror."

"I'm afraid we don't have any servants," Moonglow told her.

"How do you live in this hell?" cried the Queen, and prepared to start crying again. Moonglow quickly volunteered to take her to the bathroom and help her wash her face.

"Thank you," said Malveria, in a trembling voice. "Though no amount of face washing will remove the utter disgrace I have just suffered."

"Is this another clothes-related disaster?" enquired Moonglow, kindly.

"A catastrophe. Do you have mascara?"

"Plenty of mascara," said Moonglow, reassuringly, and helped Malveria to her feet. She led her from the room like a rescue worker helping a victim away from a serious disaster, steering her gently but firmly towards the bathroom. Kalix and Daniel watched them go.

"She's a strange woman," said Daniel.

Kalix shrugged.

"Can we stop playing Kate Bush now?" she said. "I want to hear the Runaways."

"You really love the Runaways."

"They're the best band ever," said Kalix.

Daniel changed the music and turned down the gas fire, which was overheating the room.

"Have you met the Fire Queen often?" asked Daniel.

"A few times. When I was younger."

"Does she really have any power?" said Daniel, who was curious.

"She brought me back from almost dead," Kalix pointed out.

"I suppose so. But every time we meet her she's crying about some ridiculous thing. The same ridiculous thing in fact. If she's so powerful why does she get so upset about clothes?"

Kalix shrugged.

132

"I don't know. But she is powerful. Once when I went to see Thrix, Malveria was there and she was celebrating some anniversary when she'd defeated the neighbouring Kingdom's army. She bought shoes and a coat."

Daniel mused on this. He supposed she must be powerful, if she was defeating neighbouring kingdoms. It all seemed strange to him.

After a very long time in the bathroom, Moonglow and Malveria reappeared. The Fire Queen had washed her face and re-applied her make-up. Her spirits were a little revived due to Moonglow's fine new mascara. With its extra powers of thickening and lengthening eye-lashes it was, Malveria said, a much finer product than the one she had been using. Even so she was far from happy, and was again muttering about Thrix's treachery.

"But maybe Empress Asaratanti's daughter just happens to have similar tastes?" Moonglow was saying.

Malveria sat down heavily. The heels of her shoes were so pencil thin it was difficult to stand on them for long.

"Impossible. Princess Kabachetka has no taste. Someone is dressing her and it must be Thrix. The Werewolf Enchantress is selling me clothes and then selling them to the cursed Princess as well. It is foul behaviour beyond all standards of decency and I am now going to destroy the Enchantress."

Daniel glanced at Kalix but if the young werewolf was upset at the prospect of her older sister being destroyed, she didn't show it.

"What's going on?" asked Daniel.

"What is going on?" said Malveria, her voice rising. "I will tell you what is going on, young Daniel. I have been subject to the most abject treachery. Kingdoms have fallen through less perfidious acts of treason than the shameful one that I have suffered. Have you washed your hair recently? I thought not. It is in poor condition. Really, you should let Moonglow guide you in these matters. She is a knowledgeable women on all aspects of hair care."

Daniel hadn't quite followed this explanation. He looked to Moonglow for guidance.

"Every time the Queen turns up at some event in a new outfit she finds that Princess Kabachetka has beaten her to it," explained Moonglow, who had heard the whole story at length, upstairs in the bathroom.

"Who's Princess Kabachetka?"

"A trollop from the Kingdom of the Hainusta, who are inferior elementals in every way," explained the Fire Queen. "She is daughter of the Empress Asaratanti, not that that counts for anything. Asaratanti has many children and one dreads to think who the fathers may be. But this so-called Princess has trumped my outfit on so many occasions recently that it cannot be co-incidence. Look at this blue dress. Have you ever seen anything so fine?"

Daniel was not a connoisseur of women's clothing but even so he had to admit that the dress, long, silky and clinging, was very fine, and rather unusual.

"Thrix swore she had designed it exclusively for me. Yet the whorish Princess Kabachetka was wearing one exactly the same when I turned up to the cocktail party thrown by the Sorceress Livia to celebrate the death of her third-born son. I did not know what to do with myself. I am sure everyone was talking about me behind my back. I simply had to flee."

The Fire Queen sighed.

"Soon I will be the laughing stock of all kingdoms." Her face set in a malevolent expression. "But Queen Malveria will not accept treachery from werewolf enchantresses. I will destroy her."

Moonglow was troubled. While Thrix had not exactly been friendly towards her, she was Kalix's sister, and she had provided the original pendant which had kept her safe.

"If you don't mind me saying so, there might be another explanation. I don't get the impression that Thrix would commit treachery against you."

"What other explanation could there be?"

"Maybe a spy."

"A spy?"

Moonglow nodded.

"It's quite common in the fashion world. I read about it in *Elle*."

Malveria looked interested.

"The edition with Ellie MacPherson on the cover?"

"I think it was Kate Moss. The article said that some fashion houses were taking on extra security because other designers were spying on them. Maybe this Princess has sent a spy into Thrix Fashions?"

The Fire Queen considered this, concentrating deeply for a while.

"This is possible. Such filthy and deplorable behaviour would be entirely in keeping with Princess Kabachetka's character. I must

134

contact Thrix immediately. I will summon a spirit to take my words to her. Although a messenger from the Hiyasta will not be welcome at this time, when there is a funeral at Castle MacRinnalch."

Malveria rolled the word MacRinnalch round her tongue in her exotic way, making it sound quite magical.

"You could just email her," suggested Moonglow.

"I do not understand this process."

"I'll show you if you like," said Moonglow.

As a fire elemental, Malveria was never comfortable with human technology, but such was the crisis she agreed to Moonglow's suggestion, and followed her upstairs to her room. She looked around Moonglow's small bedroom with interest. Dark posters, and a great deal of beads, candles, feathers, concert tickets, and other ephemera hung on the walls or covered the table. The small dark space reminded Malveria of a cave.

"You do not like the light?"

Moonglow shrugged.

"It feels comfy."

The Fire Queen could understand this. In her younger days, as a fugitive, she had often slept in caves for safety.

"I'm sorry Kalix didn't say thank you," said Moonglow, suddenly.

"Pardon?"

"She didn't say thank you for saving her life. Or for the new pendant. Which is quite rude, I know, but she's not really herself yet."

The Fire Queen waved this away.

"I did not suppose she would thank me. I know what Kalix is like. She has always been troubled. Often when I am visiting Thrix her mother phones her and there is some bother about Kalix. Thrix does not care but the mother will not realise this. Do you have a mother?"

"Yes."

"Is she an enemy?"

"Definitely not," replied Moonglow. "We get on really well."

"Really?" said Malveria. "I was at war with my mother for almost twenty years. You would not believe the stratagems and alliances it took to defeat her."

She looked slightly wistful.

"Of course, my dimension was a more exciting place in those days. At one point there were six armies competing for control. Volcanoes threw flame all over the land. My younger brother, what a warrior he

135

was. Before I overcame him he had killed almost all of my bodyguard, and they were all great fighters. Since I wiped out my enemies, things have been quiet. Apart from…" Malveria's lip trembled. "Apart from… Princess Kabachetka… she keeps stealing…"

The Fire Queen was unable to go on.

"Don't worry," said Moonglow, and tried her best to be reassuring. "We'll send an email to Thrix now."

"You are very kind," said the Fire Queen, and bravely wiped away her tears. She noticed a postcard that was stuck onto Moonglow's large mirror. It showed a fairy resting on a flower.

"She looks familiar. Do you know the fairies?"

"Are there really fairies?"

Malveria looked at her with surprise. Humans, they were so strange.

"Of course there are fairies. Why else would there be pictures of them?"

Malveria studied the picture.

"It looks like one of the MacKenzie Wallace MacLouds. We Hiyastas know them well. It was partly because of a regrettable incident at the wedding of Florazel MacLoud that the Hiyastas and the MacRinnalchs get on so badly today.

"Really?" Moonglow was fascinated. "What happened?"

"The Thane at the time, Murdo MacRinnalch – who would be Kalix's great-grandfather, I think – became shockingly drunk and insulted the great Queen Malgravane, my grandmother – may she happily walk the pathways of eternal flame."

"What did he say?"

"It was rather what he did not say. He left her out while toasting the beauty of those at the bride's table. My grandmother was a famous beauty and it was a terrible insult for Murdo MacRinnalch to ignore her. Had it not been a fairy wedding, where good behaviour is essential unless you want your cattle to start dying, Malgravane would have taken immediate revenge. But she got her revenge later."

"What did she do?"

"She waited till the wedding was over then turned all the whisky at Castle MacRinnalch into water." The Fire Queen laughed. "The poor werewolves! How they suffered. Because the werewolves are very particular about their whisky, and do not like having to drink any other type than their own. And of course, this was nine hundred years ago, a time when the situation around the castle was confused, with warfare between the human kings of Scotland and England. One could not simply visit the nearest shop to replenish supplies. Really, it was a very funny revenge by Malgravane."

Malveria frowned. "But it did lead to some deaths later, when Hiyastas and werewolves encountered each other and started to fight. We are both hot tempered peoples, and never friends."

"Apart from you and Thrix?"

"Indeed. But you can see why a messenger from me would not be welcome at the castle."

Moonglow opened up her laptop and got on with the job of composing Malveria's email.

59

A repeated knocking and ringing on the doorbell eventually brought Beauty out of her slumber. It was close to midday and the werewolf was annoyed to have been woken so early. It couldn't be anything good. No friend would disturb them before midday.

Despite the earliness of the hour, and the astonishing amount of wine she had consumed last night, Beauty was feeling exceptionally well. Last night she had transformed into a werewolf and this always gave her a lift. No matter what deprivations Beauty and Delicious carried out on their own bodies they were always restored to health by the monthly werewolf event. It was really convenient.

She wrapped her dressing gown around her and headed for the door. The ringing continued. Someone was keen to get their attention.

That someone was a delivery man, and part of the instructions on his delivery sheet were *continue ringing bell until you get an answer.* This had been specially instructed by the customer. Eventually the door was yanked open by a young woman with a lot of blue hair and a dressing gown that had seen better days.

"What is it?"

"Special delivery."

Beauty studied the delivery sheet suspiciously. Her experience of taking things in at the door was that it was always some bill or other she'd forgotten to pay. This however, was a large box. Maybe her sister

Delicious had ordered something and forgotten to tell her. She signed the sheet, and took the box from the courier, hoisting it easily with one hand though the courier had struggled to carry it.

Delicious arrived in the living room a few minutes later.

"What's for breakfast?" she asked.

"Whisky," replied her sister.

"Really? Why?"

"The Mistress of the Werewolves just sent us an extra large crate."

Delicious whooped with glee and dived towards the crate of MacRinnalch whisky. Seventy-two bottles. *The MacRinnalch,* a very select malt, was drunk mainly on the clan estates and none was ever made available to the public. It was one of the few things from home the twins truly missed.

"Why would Verasa be sending us presents?" wondered Beauty.

"Who cares?" replied Delicious, who was already drinking. "It's a good present."

"Certainly is," agreed Beauty. "An excellent present. I missed this."

The sisters got down to drinking. Had Verasa been there to witness the scene, she would have been gratified to see how much the twins appreciated her gift.

60

The Enchantress was utterly astonished to receive an email from the Fire Queen. Malveria? At a computer? It defied belief. What crisis could possibly have driven her to such measures?

From Malveria, Fire Queen of the Hiyasta, Mistress of the Volcanoes, Protector of the Flame, Lady of the Inferno, Ruler of the Burning Element, Persecutor of Mankind, Conqueror of the Ice Dwarves, Destroyer of the Iron Giants...

Thrix skipped ahead. Malveria's full list of names and titles could be quite daunting.

Dearest Thrix, most celebrated of werewolves, most revered and trusted friend. You have once more led me into the paths of damnation by sending me into the halls of mockery and derision where Princess Kabachetka rules supreme. I have again suffered the unquenchable

agonies of finding myself not the leader of fashion, but a mere fol-
lower of the Princess...

The email went on like this for a while, but the gist of it was, as
Thrix soon realised, that Malveria had again arrived at some important
social event to find Princess Kabachetka wearing the same outfit.
Thrix frowned, very deeply. This was serious. Perhaps not quite as
disastrous as the Fire Queen made out, but serious nonetheless. Thrix
provided original designs for Malveria and it was inexplicable that
they were being copied.

My young human friend suggests that you may have a spy in your
fashion house, continued Malveria. *I trust you will root out this*
deplorable, despicable, treacherous, malicious vermin at the earliest
opportunity. Have you met a nice werewolf at the castle my dear? I do
worry about you being lonely.

Thrix's reading was interrupted by the sound of someone attempting to forcibly enter her room. She swiftly put her laptop to sleep and
crossed over to the great wooden door which she had treated with a
locking spell.

"Yes, brother?" she called.

"Open this door," demanded Sarapen.

"Have you forgotten how to knock?"

"Open this door or I'll tear it from its hinges."

It was an hour or so before dawn. Thrix and Sarapen were both in
werewolf form. Thrix didn't think that Sarapen could break through
her locking spell but she couldn't be sure. She brought a few other
spells into her mind, in case she was forced to defend herself.

"Are you ashamed to face me after voting for my brother?"

"I'm not ashamed of anything I do," replied Thrix, and muttered
the word which ended the locking spell. The door flew open and Sarapen marched into the room.

"How nice to see you, brother. Anything on your mind?"

"How dare you conspire against me, Enchantress."

"I didn't conspire. I voted. I'm free to vote any way I want."

Sarapen bent down to place his face close enough to Thrix's for
their snouts to touch. Thrix stood her ground.

"Were it not for the entreaties of my advisors," growled Sarapen.
"The Great Council would already be short of several members. I warn
you sister, I will not allow my mother to cheat me of my birthright. She
may feel herself invulnerable to my wrath but you are not."

"Get your snout out of my face, Sarapen, or I'll send you out of here with such force that the castle walls will buckle."

"You think your small magicks can affect me?" roared Sarapen.

"You think your threats can change my mind?" countered Thrix.

"I do not come to change your mind, sister. I come to warn you. The Council will meet again at the next full moon. And they will elect me as Thane. You would be wise to remember that."

Sarapen took a step backwards.

"You admit that you have no interest in the family."

Thrix remained silent.

"So will it not be easier for you to simply vote for me? After I am Thane I assure you that we will not trouble you."

In other circumstance Thrix might have smiled. It was so like her brother to leave his diplomacy until after he'd made his threats.

61

"I would like you to go to London and look after Butix and Delix."

Dominil stared at the Mistress of the Werewolves.

"Look after Beauty and Delicious? Why would I do that?"

"They may need protecting. While the vote is so delicately balanced, I fear for them," explained Verasa.

It was mid-day. Castle MacRinnalch simmered with anger, anger that couldn't be properly expressed because the Thane's funeral could not be disrupted. Verasa had been busy making calculations. Sarapen would very likely try to kill Kalix in order to secure Dulupina's vote. Probably he would try to either bribe or intimidate Baron MacAllister to realign himself with him. Verasa thought she could deal with that. But the twins were a problem. Though she thought it extremely unlikely that Sarapen could offer them anything which would make them come to the next meeting of the Great Council and vote for him, it couldn't be discounted altogether. Worse, though, was the prospect that he might try to kill them.

The next position on the Great Council was Verasa's to choose, and she had already promised her sister Lucia that her son Decembrius could have the post. This had been an effective bribe, securing Lucia's vote for Markus. Unfortunately the replacement for the next place to fall vacant would be chosen by Dulupina and she would almost certainly award the position to the third child of Kurian, brother of the late Thane. Last night Sarapen had received six votes. If he succeeded in killing Kalix he would receive the vote of Dulupina, which would make seven. Once Kalix was dead her position on the council would be taken by Decembrius. He would also vote for Sarapen, making eight. If Sarapen managed to remove one of the twins, and Kurian's third child was elevated to the council, he would have his nine votes.

"Why," enquired Dominil, "did you promise to appoint Decembrius? He supports Sarapen."

"It was the only way I could ensure his mother Lucia voted for Markus."

"Reasonable, I suppose. But I still don't see why I should leave the castle to look after Beauty and Delicious. I've heard tales of their degeneracy. I do not think I would enjoy the task."

"Do you enjoy your life at the castle?"

"No," admitted Dominil. "But it is a home."

"I thought you might appreciate the chance to put several hundred miles between yourself and Sarapen."

"I don't fear Sarapen."

"I know. Part of the problem with this family is that no one feels much fear, even when they should."

Dominil was surprised when the Mistress of the Werewolves asked her if she knew anything about rock music.

"Very little."

"You know that Butix and Delix are musicians? They play guitar, and sing. They have appeared onstage. But of course, they're too disorganised to ever make anything of it. I know nothing of the business but I'm sure there must be much to organise. Other musicians to meet, places to play, publicity, matters of that sort."

"Are you suggesting I should manage their band?" said Dominil.

"Why not? You've been bored these past three years. You are the most intelligent of the family. I've no doubt that you could organise anything you put your mind to. At least you wouldn't be bored."

Dominil finished her wine and poured herself more, brushing back her hair which reached almost to her waist; long, straight and as white as snow.

"Would this by any chance be a way of persuading the twins to vote for Markus?"

"Yes," admitted Verasa. "But whether they vote or not, they will need protecting."

62

"Why doesn't it answer?" asked the Fire Queen, petulantly. She eyed Moonglow's computer with suspicion. Although Moonglow had explained that their reply would depend on when Thrix answered her email, Malveria seemed to suspect the computer of treachery.

"I should have sent a messenger."

"You said your messenger might be harmed if he interrupted the Thane's funeral."

Malveria shrugged. A messenger was of no great account.

"I'm sure she'll answer soon," said Moonglow.

It was four in the morning. Daniel and Moonglow's energy was flagging though Kalix showed no signs of tiring. The young werewolf was currently in the kitchen, snuffling out more food.

"I have to go to bed now," said Moonglow. "I have a class tomorrow."

"Do you still go to school?" asked Malveria.

Moonglow explained that she attended university.

"A school for older people?"

"Yes."

"Who could not learn enough when they were young?"

"Not exactly," said Moonglow, but felt too tired to explain it fully. She wondered if Malveria intended to stay the night. The Fire Queen showed no inclination to leave. Occasionally a pained look would cross her face, as if she was still tormented by the sour memory of her latest fashion disaster. Moonglow wondered where she could sleep. Daniel and Moonglow used the only two bedrooms. There was another very small room but it was full of boxes which they hadn't yet unpacked. Feeling that it would be rude to ask Malveria – who was a queen after all – to sleep on the couch, in the same room as Kalix, Moonglow offered her the use of her bed.

"I can sleep in Daniel's room."

The Fire Queen seemed amused by this.

"But this is taboo, no? As I understand human customs?"

"It's okay," said Moonglow. "We're friends."

Malveria was a shrewd interpreter of other people's emotions. She could see that Daniel might think this more than a friendly gesture. She was tempted to accept the offer. Sending Moonglow into Daniel's bed might very well produce some amusing results, if only frustration from Daniel. But her sense of decorum prevented her. In her realm, it was not the done thing to turn one's host out of her own bed.

"I will sleep on your couch, which I'm sure will be acceptable."

Moonglow was surprised. Having seen Malveria in tears over the slightest setback she did not have the impression that the Queen was used to coping with discomfort. In this Moonglow was mistaken. Now that she was ruler of her realm Malveria was accustomed to a luxurious lifestyle but it had not always been so. At the time of the war between the six competing factions the Fire Queen had frequently slept in caves, and been roused in the middle of the night to engage in savage combat with her enemies. She'd marched over rocks that boiled with lava and mountains that flowed with glaciers, fighting battles against seemingly impossible odds. During that time she'd had no expectation that she would ever sleep in a comfortable bed again. Malveria was a hardened warrior, though these days, it would have been difficult for anyone to tell.

"If the computer brings a message will we know?"

"Yes, I'll set it on alert."

Moonglow busied herself bringing blankets for Malveria and checking that Kalix had everything she needed to be comfortable.

"I don't need a hot water bottle tonight," said Kalix. "I'm warm when I'm a werewolf."

"You'd better take it anyway," responded Moonglow. "There's a draft coming in the back window and you're still weak after your ordeal."

Kalix scowled. She didn't like being fussed over. Nor did she like sharing a room with Malveria. But she suddenly found herself tired. She wrapped herself in her quilt, curled up in a ball in front of the fire, and went to sleep, leaving the Fire Queen lying on the couch covered in a very attractive silk covering which Moonglow had provided. Malveria herself was not particularly tired but, feeling oddly comfortable in this house, she dropped off to sleep dreaming of a great fashion triumph at next month's meeting of the Elemental Rulers Council.

63

If Castle MacRinnalch was riven with internal dissension, it could not have been discerned from the Thane's funeral. Sarapen and Markus stood side by side at the ceremony and showed no signs of animosity. They bowed their heads respectfully as the Mistress of the Werewolves read out the traditional farewell to the Thane, the same farewell that had been used to bury every Thane since Durghaid MacRinnalch in the year 1128. Torches lit up the great hall of the castle and a piper played a lament as the pallbearers moved to pick up the great oaken casket. It was difficult to play the bagpipes in werewolf form, but at the Thane's funeral, it was done. The eerie, emotive sound echoed round the great hall as the coffin was borne outside to the place where the assembled werewolves would bid the Thane a last farewell on his journey to the forests of the werewolf dead.

The Mistress of the Werewolves led the family from the castle. As the clan saw Verasa at the head of the funeral procession there was a slight tremor among the crowd. There had been rumours that the Great Council had failed to agree on a new Thane and here was proof. Had there been a new Thane, he would have led the mourners. Many significant glances were exchanged between neighbours. There would be trouble. Everyone knew that.

It was the night of the full moon. As the Thane's coffin was brought out the werewolves set up a howling the like of which had rarely been heard in the world before. The whole clan mourned for the loss of their chieftain. Of all the werewolves there, only Thrix did not howl. Shocking though it was to admit, she realised she was pleased the Thane was gone. Life at the castle had not been easy for his daughters. 'If I'd had more spirit when I was Kalix's age, I might have attacked him myself,' thought Thrix, and then felt some shame at her reflections.

Sarapen howled loud and long but as his howls subsided he glanced over to where his brother Markus stood. 'I'll kill you brother,' thought Sarapen. 'And anyone else who stands in my way.'

Dominil howled but briefly. She was already bored. She wondered if she should agree to Verasa's request that she go to London. She could see no reason to do so. There again, she could see no reason not to do so. This was a problem that had plagued her for most of her life. Not exactly indecision, more a feeling that neither alternative was worth while.

As for Verasa, the funeral brought tears to her eyes. True, it was a long time since she had been remotely intimate with her husband but they had been together for a very long time. Almost three hundred years. They shared a history that few people could comprehend. And now he was gone. Verasa put back her head and howled, with feeling.

Among the crowd, Gawain stood with his head unbowed. He was studying the mourners. Kalix was not among them. It was a bitter disappointment. Behind Gawain were six members of the Mistress's household. They'd been watching Gawain ever since he entered the estate. Verasa had instructed them to make no disturbance during the funeral but as soon as it was over he was to be arrested.

64

Moonglow was shaken awake at some unearthly hour by Malveria.

"Your computer made a noise. Is this the answer from the Enchantress?"

Moonglow was tempted to tell Malveria to go away and let her sleep but her natural politeness prevented her. She dragged herself out of bed. The screen was flashing. Thrix had replied to Malveria's email.

"I have never had an email before," said the Queen. "This is very exciting. Is there a spy?"

"Do you want me to read it?" asked Moonglow, who was not sure if the Fire Queen could read English. Malveria could read English well – she had learned in order to be able to understand fashion catalogues and style magazines – but she asked Moonglow to read it to her, and then looked over her shoulder.

Dear Malveria, this is very distressing. You might be right. Perhaps there is spy.

"Aha!" yelled Malveria, as if this were in itself proof.

Back tomorrow. Call in and we'll see what can be done.

145

"Good," said Malveria. "I will call in."

She frowned.

"Thrix does not spend many words in this email. Should it not be longer?"

"She probably had a lot of emails to write," suggested Moonglow.

Malveria stared at the screen.

"I am unused to such brevity. Look, she has signed her name only as Thrix."

"Does she have more names?"

"Of course. Thrix Ugraich Eustacia MacPhail MacRinnalch, and several more which are private."

"That's a lot of names," commented Moonglow.

"No," said Malveria. "Only a few. I have many more names than that. How many do you have?"

"Just two."

"Surely no one can mange with only two names? It must be very difficult. You see, my dearest Thrix agrees that there is a spy. I will visit the Enchantress tomorrow and we will make a plan for catching this spy and then Princess Kabachetka will see who is the person with the better fashion sense and superior shoes!"

"Right," said Moonglow, who could feel her eyes closing with fatigue. She had only slept a few hours and she really needed more.

A peculiar sound floated into the bedroom. Something Moonglow could not exactly identify. Something painful.

"What's that?"

"Kalix," replied the Fire Queen. "Since dawn broke she has been retching in your bathroom. I would suggest you send a servant to ask what is the matter but if you do not have a servant to hand, perhaps you will have to go yourself. Meanwhile I return to my kingdom to plot my revenge on the dismal Princess. Thank you for your hospitality."

The Fire Queen waved her hand and disappeared abruptly. Moonglow draped a dressing gown over her nightdress and shuffled along to the bathroom. There she found Kalix – the human Kalix – being sick into the toilet. Moonglow's first thought was that Kalix must have picked up some form of food poisoning from the meat she'd eaten.

"What's the matter?"

The moment Kalix saw Moonglow she picked herself up and barged her way past. Moonglow sighed. This was a lot to cope with so early in the morning. She followed Kalix downstairs and found her shivering on the floor. She seemed to be suffering badly.

"What's the matter?" asked Moonglow again. "Do you need a doctor?"

"No."

"Would you like some tea?"

"Stop forcing food on me," replied Kalix, then turned her head to vomit on the carpet.

When Daniel appeared shortly afterwards, Kalix was no better. Her distress was painful to watch. Neither Daniel nor Moonglow were sure if it was psychological or physical. Moonglow had tried to clean Kalix's face but had been repulsed by a ferocious growling. Kalix was now human, and it was extremely unsettling to hear such growling coming from the girl's lips. Kalix was sweating and shaking, apparently in the grip of some powerful attack. It was a very upsetting scene and Moonglow really didn't know what to do about it. She guessed, from the few muttered comments she'd heard from Kalix, that the young werewolf was distressed about the way she had gorged herself last night. Now she was throwing up but whether deliberately or not, Moonglow couldn't tell.

"Is this like your bulimic cousin?" she whispered to Daniel. Daniel shook his head. He'd never seen anything as violent as this.

Kalix reached into her bag and brought out her bottle of laudanum. There were only a few drops left. She drank it quickly. Kalix had woken up with the realisation that last night she'd eaten far more than she had for years. The humans had fed her meat and pizzas and poptarts and who knew what else and the realisation of what she'd ingested was now driving Kalix into the grip of a terrible panic attack. She didn't have enough laudanum to control it and the young werewolf felt like her mind was about to break into tiny pieces. Suddenly feeling that the walls were closing in on her Kalix knew she had to get out of the house. She grabbed her bag and her coat and made for the door.

"Please don't go – " said Moonglow, and tried to get in her way. Kalix hit her hard and the force of the blow sent Moonglow crashing against the wall.

"Hey!" protested Daniel, but Kalix was gone. He rushed to pick Moonglow up. She was rubbing her shoulder and grimacing.

"That really hurt. She's so strong."

They looked around. Their living room was an incredible mess and

147

there was liquid on the floor and all over Kalix's quilt.

"Werewolf vomit," said Daniel, with distaste.

Moonglow didn't know what she was most upset about. Kalix's illness, Kalix's violence towards her or the fact that Kalix was gone.

"She didn't have to hit me like that. She shouldn't have left, she's not well."

"Face it Moonglow, that werewolf is a complete disaster."

Moonglow wiped away a tear. It was all very distressing.

"But she was nicer last night. We were getting on well."

Daniel admitted that they had been.

"Do you think she'll come back?"

Daniel shrugged. He didn't think so. He wasn't inclined to go and look for her again. If she didn't want to be helped by them they couldn't force her. Besides, it was becoming dangerous. He'd seen the way Kalix tossed Moonglow aside and he knew that she wasn't in control of her actions. Kalix was so strong and savage it wasn't safe to be around her.

"Maybe you're right," said Moonglow. She felt very depressed by the whole affair and even the prospect of her Sumerian Cuneiform class, usually one of her favourites, didn't cheer her up.

"At least she has the pendant now. She's safe from her family. And the werewolf hunters."

65

It was just bad luck that brought Kalix up against the Avenaris Guild. Her new pendant meant that hunters could not sense her, and nor could their trained dogs. In effect, she gave off no werewolf scent, and no one could tell she was not human. The Guild did not use sorcery, as a rule, but they did have members who through a form of mystic training could recognise a werewolf, even in human form. Even they could not now detect Kalix. Unfortunately, Kalix was not safe from being recognised by one of the hunters who had previously been tailing her.

The young werewolf made it to the end of Moonglow's street without any notion of what she was doing. Gripped by the terrible anxiety attack she fled from the confines of the house but when she went outside her condition didn't improve. The anxiety was coming in waves that made it impossible to think. Kalix hurried on, as if by fleeing she could somehow escape from herself. People stared as she passed because her face was messy from vomiting and her eyes were red with tears.

With so much werewolf activity in the country just now, the Guild had stepped up its patrols. Between Kennington and Vauxhall, Kalix walked right past a group of three hunters, and one of them recognised her. He'd followed her last month, before she evaded him. The hunter waited till the sensitive-eared werewolf was some distance away before whispering to his to companions.

"That's Kalix MacRinnalch."

"The werewolf princess?"

His companions had been expecting someone more impressive than the skinny girl with very long hair who was currently walking unsteadily down the road that led to Vauxhall Bridge.

"She doesn't look a like a princess."

"Never mind what she looks like. Let's go."

They followed on, discreetly at first, but more confidently as it became clear that Kalix was paying no attention to her surroundings. The werewolf seemed unaware of what she was doing, and more than once came close to bumping into other pedestrians. The leader knew this area well. The street that ran down to Vauxhall bridge passed under several railway bridges close to the river. Around these bridges were some desolate areas that had once contained small industrial units, now mostly empty. It was an ideal place for an attack. The hunters each had a gun concealed in a shoulder holster, loaded with silver bullets. Though the Guild preferred to kill werewolves while they were in werewolf shape, a daughter of the Thane was too important to let escape. Besides, there was no possibility that they might be attacking a human by mistake. This was Kalix MacRinnalch. When she was dead, no one was going to complain to the police. They closed in, ready for the kill. When the girl stepped into the shadows of the first bridge their leader gave an order and the three men sprinted forwards.

Kalix's dreadful anxiety had negated her normally keen senses, preventing her from scenting or hearing her pursuers. It almost got her killed. At the last second, she sensed the hunters. She whirled round, saw three men running at her, and fled. Her anxiety vanished, as did her weakness. No amount of vomiting could clear all of last night's food from her system and whether she liked it or not, Kalix was strong again. The young girl, the only member of the ruling family born as a werewolf, took flight with a speed which left her pursuers gasping. Kalix disappeared beneath the arch of the bridge before anyone could fire a shot. The hunters sped after her, hurtling round the corner before coming to a halt, straining their senses for any trace of her.

"Look down that – " began their leader, then broke off as Kalix fell on him from above. Realising she was strong again, and not wanting to run from the hated Guild, Kalix had decided to bring the fight to them. She'd scaled the wall and clung on till the hunters were right beneath her. She landed squarely on the leader and pulled his head violently to the side as they went down. Kalix sprang immediately to her feet. The hunter, his neck broken, remained where he was. The other two went to pull their guns from their shoulder holsters but Kalix was far too quick for them. She kicked one backwards then smashed her fist into the other's throat. He fell down unconscious. The third hunter, his ribs cracked from the force of Kalix's kick, tried to scramble to his feet but Kalix kicked him again full in the face and he slumped to the ground.

It was over in seconds. Kalix studied the three bodies. One dead, one maybe dying and one that would probably recover. Kalix was not inclined to let him recover. The Guild had hunted her kind and killed them without mercy. She stepped over to the man with the bloody face and stamped her heel onto his chest so hard that his ribs broke. Blood gurgled from his mouth. Before making her escape the werewolf girl quickly slipped her hand inside their jackets, taking their wallets. Satisfied, Kalix trotted off.

She felt better. Her anxiety had gone, the excess adrenaline used up in the fight. Kalix passed by a cafe and noticed her reflection in the window. She looked a mess. She wiped her face, then fished around in her bag, found her sunglasses, and put them on. Then she started jogging up the road, the words of *Cherry Bomb* playing in her head. She ran over Vauxhall Bridge, running now not out of fear, but because she felt like it. As she ran, her long hair billowed out behind her like a vast sail. On the other side of the river she hopped nimbly over a tall fence, heading down towards the river bank where she would be alone. She settled down with her feet dangling over the dark water of the Thames, took out her journal, and started to write.

66

As soon as the funeral was over Gawain was arrested. He went without a struggle. He was taken to the dungeon, which was dark and damp. It was rarely used these days but the walls were extremely thick and the doors were strong. It was a place from which even the most powerful werewolf could not escape. Gawain made no attempt to escape. He intended to see the Mistress of the Werewolves, and learn news of Kalix.

Gawain sat with his back against the wall, and thought of other, happier, times in his life when he'd visited the castle. Gawain was the great-great-grandson of the renowned warrior Gerrant Gawain MacRinnalch. His family had always been welcome guests. Their status had only been slightly diminished by Gawain's grandfather marrying a human. Gawain's one quarter human blood would not have precluded him from much though it did mean he could never ascend to a position on the Great Council. Apart from that, he was free to do anything he liked, except sleep with the Thane's adolescent daughter.

High above the dungeon, in the chambers of the Mistress of the Werewolves, Verasa was taking to Markus. Thrix had already left, keen to get back to London as soon as possible. Sarapen had also departed, heading east to his own large keep. After the funeral he had not spoken again to either Verasa or Markus. He'd left formal notice with Rainal that he would return in one month's time for the next meeting of the Great Council. As for Baron MacPhee and Baron MacGregor, their farewell salutations to the Mistress of the Werewolves had been respectful but there was no hiding their disquiet at the events of the past few days.

Verasa sighed.

"If the Thane had only managed to live for a few more months I could have delivered the Thaneship to you in one easy meeting."

Markus nodded. His mother was still confident that she could gather sufficient votes, but what would Sarapen do in the meantime?

"Attempt to capture or kill Kalix, work on Baron MacAllister, possibly make representations to Thrix," said Verasa. "No doubt if left to his own devices he'd try to kill everyone who opposes him, but he has some good advisors. Mirasen is clever."

When his mother had first mooted the idea of Markus as Thane, her younger son had been uncertain, not really thinking it was possible.

Now he believed it was. The prospect of finally gaining dominance over his brother was enticing.

"Will Dominil really go to London?"

"Yes."

Apart from her sojourn at Oxford, Markus could not remember Dominil going anywhere.

"I'm amazed, mother. The idea of Dominil rousing her languid self to travel south is astonishing. And to look after the twins?"

"She was bored, my dear. I believe that boredom may be the strongest factor in her life."

"What has she been doing for the past six years?"

"Translating Latin poetry. And studying her computers, I believe."

Verasa knew more than Markus about Dominil's private life but she did not share the information.

"But now she wants to do something. The twins need help. And who knows, perhaps Dominil will find the task to her liking."

"Does she know what she's letting herself in for?" asked Markus.

"Probably not. But I expect her to cope."

"Does she know anything about the music business?"

"She says not. But I have confidence in her. Whatever Butix and Delix need, I am sure that Dominil can provide it."

Markus didn't believe that the degenerate twins would ever appear at Castle MacRinnalch to vote for him no matter how his mother bribed them, but he agreed it was wise to protect them. If they died, their places on the council would be taken by werewolves who would vote for Sarapen.

"And now, I suppose I had better give some thought to Gawain."

"Why did he come back?" growled Markus.

"Who knows? But I'm sure he'll be keen to tell me now. The dungeon is not a comfortable place. And rarely used these days, I'm pleased to say. I don't think we've had a guest there since Baron Mac-Gregor's youngest nephew got drunk and tried to climb down the north wall of the castle. And I only incarcerated him because the Baron wanted him taught a lesson."

67

Kalix had run out of laudanum. She urgently needed more. She'd have to travel over to the east end of London where the Young MacDoig had a small premises, hidden away in Limehouse. Laudanum was virtually unknown in the world these days. The opium tincture had been replaced by other drugs, heroin or cocaine. Where the MacDoigs obtained their supply was unknown. Not from this world, perhaps. The price they charged for it was certainly high enough. When the Merchant had first sold her a bottle, back in Scotland, he'd let her have it cheaply. As a favour, he said.

Having taken the wallets from the hunters, Kalix now had enough money and she wondered which would be the quickest way to travel to Limehouse. Kalix had often walked the whole length of the city but she knew how to use the underground or the bus if necessary. The underground would be quicker. She hurried up to Victoria where she bought a ticket to Limehouse after first consulting the tube map on the wall. Kalix liked the tube map. With its different coloured lines for each route it was clear and easy to follow, even to someone with her limited reading skills. She took the circle line to Tower Hill then changed on to the Docklands light railway for the last two stops.

A hundred years ago this area by the river had been home to the capital's opium dens. These were long gone, but there were, here and there, a few pockets left which had not entirely lost their connections with the old days. Kalix walked down to Narrow Street by the river bank then disappeared into a tiny alley. Far along the alley, almost invisible in the gloom, was a black door. Kalix rang the bell four times and waited. The door opened and Kalix slipped inside.

The small room she entered was crammed full of artefacts, some ancient, some unrecognisable. Some objects were of obvious value but others appeared worthless. Probably they were of use to someone, somewhere. The Merchant was a shrewd trader with a keen eye for a profit. Kalix had occasionally sold him things she'd stolen and he'd never asked too many questions about their origin. Verasa herself had bought works of art from the Merchant and there were several pieces at Castle MacRinnalch the legality of whose origins might not have stood up to close examination.

Kalix was let in by the Young MacDoig. His father, Merchant Mac-Doig, was already in the room. Merchant MacDoig was a very stout man, corpulent, and quite effusive. In keeping with the antiquity of his surroundings he wore a suit that had gone out of fashion in the nineteenth century, and a black hat. He wore side-whiskers and carried a cane. It gave him a Dickensian appearance, though genial rather than sinister. His son, if slightly smaller, was also a man of considerable girth who favoured old-fashioned clothes. Unlike his father, his thick red hair had not yet turned grey. They beamed when they saw Kalix. Kalix looked back at them without expression. She didn't trust either of them.

"Young Kalix MacRinnalch!" cried Merchant MacDoig, as if greeting an old friend. "It's fine to see you again. Have you brought me anything today?" He winked conspiratorially, either because he was making a joke or because he really thought Kalix might have something of value. Kalix shook her head.

"I have only recently been in the company of your fine mother," continued the Merchant. He had the soft lilting voice of a Highlander. He had been born in Nairn; how long ago, no one could guess. Certainly long enough for his lifespan to be not entirely natural.

"Such a sad business about the Thane!" He shook his head. "It was a bitter blow to all who knew him, may he roam peacefully in the forests of the werewolf dead."

It was odd to hear a human use this phrase, but the Merchant was familiar with the ways of werewolves and may have thought Kalix expected it. Or he may have been mocking her.

"Still," continued the Merchant. "There was much trade to be done. Nothing but the best would do for the Thane's funeral, and I, fortunately, have access to the best."

Young MacDoig hung back in silence. Though he ran the business in London he obviously deferred to his father when the Merchant chose to visit. Kalix wanted to make her transaction and depart as quickly as possible but the Merchant was a man who liked to talk.

"You will be here for laudanum, I imagine? Excellent, excellent, we have a fresh supply in this very morning, the very best. You won't find the like of this anywhere else in the world, young Kalix MacRinnalch. Have you been in contact with your sister at all? I've frequently thought the Enchantress would do well to use my services for her sorcerous supplies, though she's never shown any such inclination. But she's a fine young woman, I'll give her that, and becoming quite a force in the world, so they say."

Kalix tried to suppress her agitation. No matter how aggravating the Merchant or his son were, she could not afford to lose her temper. To be cut off from her supply would be disastrous. She fumbled in her pockets for money.

"Ah," said the Merchant, turning to his son. "The young wolf's in a hurry to be off. She was always a secretive one!"

"She is, father," agreed the Young MacDoig, only slightly less effusively. "But she's a fine customer, visits me often."

"I'm pleased to hear it boy!" he said, clapping his son on the shoulder. "Tell me, Kalix, are you settled in London? Have you a good place to stay?"

"Why?" said Kalix.

"No reason, no reason. I'm just anxious for your health."

"I'm fine," muttered the werewolf, who didn't intend giving away any personal details to the Merchant. When the Young MacDoig produced her laudanum, Kalix handed over the money and departed as fast as she could, declining Merchant MacDoig's offer of a glass of whisky to warm her against the cold.

"Hurry back," said the Merchant. "We're always pleased to see you here, young Kalix."

Kalix hastened away from the MacDoig's. She spent the rest of the day on the bank of the river. She walked all the way back to Vauxhall Bridge, just north of where she had encountered the hunters. Occasionally she sipped from her bottle but she felt healthy, and reasonably content, so did not require too much in the way of chemical sedation. Here, just south of Pimlico, the riverbank was not open to the public. It was overgrown, and hidden from the road above. She wandered around, pausing to make entries laboriously in her journal. She wrote about how she had fought with hunters, then visited the Mac-Doigs, and how she had stood on Westminster Bridge and looked at the Houses of Parliament. She also wrote some harsh words about Moon-glow, who'd tricked her into eating so much food.

There were tourist boats on the river, and a few long flat barges loaded with cargo. As far as Kalix could remember she had never been on a boat. She wondered what it would be like. The MacRinnalchs had property on various islands in Scotland and she remembered that her parents had sometimes sailed over to visit, but they'd never taken her with them. A rat ran over her foot and Kalix chased it for fun, scooping it up to look at it before letting it go.

Kalix did not meet anyone else. By her standards it was a good day. But as dusk was falling she was struck by a peculiar feeling which she could not quite identify. She felt healthy, healthier than she had done for a long time. She had gained energy from her werewolf transformation. She'd taken enough laudanum to satisfy her craving. The battle with the hunters had bolstered her spirit. She felt good, apart from... apart from what?

The young werewolf sat down and looked at the water. There was something troubling her. Not the ever present yearning for Gawain. Not the bad memories about growing up in the castle that sometimes overwhelmed her. Something else. Kalix realised she felt lonely. She shrugged. She always felt lonely. Or did she? When she tried examining the feeling she couldn't say for sure if she was always lonely or not. Usually she was sick, or running, or hiding. Now, on this rare day when she was feeling healthier, she seemed to have a little more time to notice her emotions. She thought that she might indeed be lonely.

Kalix looked down at her new pendant. For the first time it struck her that it must have been difficult to find it for her. Kalix wasn't certain who was responsible for giving it to her. Thrix? Or the Fire Queen? Or Moonglow? She thought about Moonglow and felt something close to regret that she'd hit her that morning. Kalix had been in a panic but she knew the human wouldn't understand. It meant she couldn't go back. Such was her life. Anywhere Kalix went, she was never welcomed back.

Kalix had an idea that if she saw Moonglow again she might have to apologise, and she would never do that, particularly to someone who had made her eat food when her resolve was weak. Kalix grew quite angry. Who did the girl think she was, forcing food down her throat? Kalix growled. Moonglow was as bad as everyone else. There again, she had brought her a hot water bottle to keep her warm at night. Whichever way Kalix looked at that, it seemed like a kind act.

The werewolf frowned. Daniel had talked to her about Joan Jett. She'd liked that. She'd have liked to hear more Runaways records. She tried listening to her favourite Runaways tape but the battery on her walkman was running low. She decided to remain where she was for tonight. The riverbank was quiet and no one would disturb her.

68

Moonglow spent an arduous afternoon at university studying Sumerian history and cuneiform. Later she had attend a seminar on the legal code of Hamurrabi, which, she was interested to learn, was the first code of laws ever to be written down. After the classes and seminar Moonglow now knew that the largest city in ancient Sumeria was Ur, the penalty for adultery in the time of Hamurrabi was four goats, and cuneiform, a form of writing somewhere between hieroglyphics and an alphabet, was really difficult to learn.

She concentrated during her lectures as she always did, apart from one moment when she noticed that a girl a few seats in front of her was wearing a yellow blouse. It reminded her of the yellow blouse that she'd seen Markus put on. How peculiar that had been. Moonglow still thought he'd looked attractive.

The daylight was fading by the time Moonglow caught the underground home. Her shoulder was sore where Kalix had hit her. Every time Moonglow thought about that she became annoyed. After saving her life she deserved better than to be assaulted. She tried to banish her annoyance. 'Kalix is only young. Her life is difficult,' she thought. At nineteen, Moonglow was only two years older than Kalix, but Moonglow thought of her as much younger, somehow.

Daniel was cheerful after an afternoon sleeping on the couch. He offered to make Moonglow tea, as he generally did. Moonglow placed her bag on the table and sank into a chair.

"Cuneiform is just terrible," she said.

"Of course it is," agreed Daniel. "Only a mad woman would dream of learning it. Do you want some biscuits?"

Moonglow nodded and Daniel went off to the kitchen. He returned a few moments later, looking thoughtful.

"There's a werewolf frolicking in the back yard."

"Frolicking?"

"Yes. Well maybe not frolicking exactly. But definitely moving around with enthusiasm."

Moonglow hurried to the kitchen. She peered out of the window. Their flat was above a shop, and the back yard was a small unused square of concrete, one floor below. There, in the dim evening light, a werewolf appeared to be playing with something. A tennis ball, perhaps. Moonglow tried to open the window. It was stuck where some previous tenant had painted the frame. After some effort she managed to wrench it open.

"Kalix?"

The werewolf looked up.

"Hello," said Kalix. Then, as if it was quite natural for her to be in Moonglow's back yard, she started playing with the tennis ball again.

"Have you come back to visit us?" asked Moonglow.

"No."

"Then why are you here?"

Kalix shrugged. She had of course come back to visit Daniel and Moonglow but was not about to admit it, even if it meant carrying on some absurd pretence that she had ended up in the yard by accident.

"I'm just wandering around."

Moonglow sensed that Kalix didn't want to acknowledge she had come back specifically to see them. She smiled.

"Would you like to come up anyway? We'd like to see you."

Kalix pretended to consider it for a while.

"Well okay," she said, eventually. Moonglow was expecting Kalix to climb back over the fence into the street before calling at the front door but Kalix simply scrambled up the fence then leapt for the kitchen window, grabbing onto the sill and hauling herself through. It was an impressively athletic feat. Once inside the kitchen, she attempted to look diffident, though this expression was difficult to pull off in werewolf form.

"It's good to see you again," said Moonglow, who had quite forgotten her previous annoyance.

"It is," said Daniel. "Do you want some tea?"

69

Moonglow didn't expect an apology from Kalix for hitting her which was just as well. Kalix didn't mention it. The werewolf was still pretending that it was some sort of co-incidence she'd ended up in their back yard. She stood awkwardly around the kitchen for a while but as she saw that Moonglow was not going to lecture her, or demand an apology, she began to relax.

"I saw boats," she said, unexpectedly.

"Boats?"

"On the river."

Kalix told them about her day by the river, though she didn't mention her encounter with the hunters.

"Why does the water in the river get higher and lower?" asked Kalix.

"It's tidal," Daniel told her, explaining that the level of the River Thames would rise and fall as the tide came in and out. Kalix seemed very vague on the subject of tides, which struck Moonglow as odd. The tides were affected by the moon and she would have assumed that any werewolf would know all about the moon and its effects. But Kalix, as soon became evident, was not well acquainted with life around her. The young werewolf was ignorant of many things. She didn't know who the Prime Minister was or what nuclear energy meant. She'd never learned maths beyond the most basic arithmetic, and her grasp of history was so shaky that she imagined almost everyone she'd heard of to be still alive. Shakespeare, for instance, she understood to be still writing film scripts because she'd once sneaked into a cinema to watch Romeo and Juliet.

The young werewolves of the MacRinnalch Clan were privately educated for the first years of their lives but for the past hundred years or so Verasa had established the custom of sending them to normal schools to complete their education. The Mistress of the Werewolves thought this was a better way for them to learn the ways of society. As soon as the family felt confident that one of their young werewolves was responsible enough not to give their true nature away they would be enrolled. This had never happened with Kalix.

"I never got sent to school," she confessed. "They said I'd bite the teachers. I was meant to have a tutor at the castle but I didn't like him so I never went. But it doesn't matter, I learned everything I need. Gawain taught me how to fight."

Moonglow glanced at the cover of Kalix's journal which was hanging out of her tattered bag.

kalix jurnil privt. kalix diry doont rede

There was something pathetic in the young werewolf's attempts to write, particularly as she was so keen on keeping a journal. She was so bad at it. The first time Moonglow had seen her handwriting she had assumed that it was some sort of joke. Everything was spelled so badly it reminded her of an adult cartoon mocking the spelling of a child. From the extreme shakiness of the letters she wondered if it might have been written when Kalix was in werewolf form, and was finding it difficult to hold a pen. But apparently it was her best effort. Moonglow felt overwhelmingly sad about this. She had a strong urge to offer to teach Kalix to read and write better. She held off from mentioning it, suspecting that Kalix would be insulted, but determined to help her if she could find a way of doing it tactfully.

"Can I have another pizza?" asked Kalix. "With extra meat?"

"Okay," said Daniel. "I'll call them."

Kalix was familiar with money because she rarely had any. Her face fell.

"I can't pay for it," she said.

"Don't worry about it, you're our guest," said Daniel reassuringly. It struck him for the first time that if Kalix stayed with them she was going to cost a lot to feed, if last night was anything to go by. Her appetite in werewolf form was immense. Daniel didn't mind in theory, being a generous sort of person, but he had very little spare money.

"I want to watch TV," said Kalix, while they waited for the pizza.

Moonglow and Daniel rarely watched TV. Moonglow didn't like it. Daniel did but didn't want Moonglow thinking he was the sort of person who wanted to watch TV all the time. Kalix was keen however, and as soon as they switched it on she sat down right in front of it like a child. Daniel showed her how the remote control worked. She struggled a little with her large paw and the small buttons but finally mastered it. Moonglow went upstairs to dump her books in her room and Daniel followed her up.

"She likes TV and pizza," said Daniel. "We seem to have adopted a child."

"You like TV and pizza," pointed out Moonglow.

"Well I never claimed to be mature. You think she'll be the same tomorrow?"

"The same how?"

"Vomiting and attacking us."

"I hope not," replied Moonglow, dubiously. "I can't go through all that again."

Despite her doubts, Moonglow was delighted that Kalix had returned.

"I really hope she stays this time."

Daniel arrived back downstairs just in time to prevent the werewolf Kalix from answering the door to the pizza delivery man. When the food was paid for she grabbed it eagerly and hurried back to the television.

"What's the rush?"

"This is the best programme ever," said Kalix, "I never knew they made such a good programme."

She crawled even closer to the screen.

"What is it?" asked Daniel.

"Sabrina the Teenage Witch."

Daniel sat down on the couch.

"Also one of my favourites. Move over, you're blocking my view."

70

The morning after the funeral Gawain was brought before Verasa. She stared at him coldly. This young werewolf had caused her a great deal of trouble. Indeed, it would not be stretching things too far to say that his affair with Kalix had directly contributed to Kalix's subsequent attack on the Thane. It was after Gawain's banishment that Kalix's madness had really become severe.

Verasa was surprised to find the thought floating into her mind that Gawain was in fact very handsome. Such a thought would not normally have occurred to her. She had seen too many young werewolves grow up to pay any particular note to their looks any more. Yet there was something about Gawain. Something brooding. Something poetic perhaps, though he was a strong young wolf. She could see why her youngest daughter had fallen for him. Perhaps if she had noticed Gawain's attractiveness before she'd have taken care not to let Kalix be alone with him, though as his family were so respectable, she couldn't really have prevented them from visiting the castle. It was Gawain's great-great-grandfather who had brought the Begravar knife to the clan. This was one of the MacRinnalchs' most treasured possessions and the tale of its finding was among their legendary exploits.

"I could have you killed."

It was true. Gawain remained silent.

"Under the terms of your banishment you were forbidden to return to the castle. Why did you come?"

Gawain looked the Mistress of the Werewolves straight in the eye. "I wanted to see Kalix," he said.

"How very romantic," retorted Verasa. "Unfortunately my daughter has no wish to see you."

"I'd like to hear her say that herself."

"What you would like is of no consequence," said Verasa, harshly, and rose from her chair. It was rare for the Mistress of the Werewolves to give vent to her anger but when she did she was an intimidating woman. Verasa swiftly brought her temper under control. She had less time than she would have liked to deal with Gawain. There were many werewolves to see before they left the castle, and much to be done in the matter of strengthening support for Markus.

"Are you here looking for your sentence to be commuted? Do you regret your behaviour?"

Gawain took a step forward, again meeting Verasa's eye.

"The only thing I regret is that I accepted the banishment. I should have taken Kalix away from the castle. When I find her, I'll take her away with me and no one will stop me."

"Such bravado," said Verasa dryly. "Had I time to talk to you, I might be impressed. But probably not."

She motioned to her guards.

"Put him in the small cell beneath my chambers. I'll question him later."

Gawain was led off to the cell. While not as dank and gloomy as the dungeon, it was not a comfortable place. The key turned in the lock and Gawain was once more incarcerated.

71

Thrix arrived back in her offices like a woman with a mission. She had work to do and a spy to find.

"Ann. I need to see our designers and our marketing people. Have them in my office in thirty minutes. Get Milan on the phone and then place a call to the agency in New York. We have a new show to do and not much time to prepare. Then bring me the personal files of everyone that works here."

Ann nodded and went off to organise the schedule. Thrix hoped that the spy didn't turn out to be Ann. Ann was the most efficient personal assistant she'd ever had. If she was the traitor it would be a crushing blow. At the castle it had been hard to concentrate on her business. The meetings of the Great Council had been fraught and the atmosphere afterwards had been worse. Thrix cursed the whole sorry business and hoped that it might no longer affect her. She knew this hope to be in vain. Sarapen wasn't going to roll over and let their mother manoeuvre him out of the Thaneship. There would be trouble.

The Enchantress shook her head, trying to banish all thoughts of her family. She wondered if the Fire Queen might be exaggerating her recent experiences of fashion piracy. Might Princess Kabachetka have simply been turning up to events in clothes of which Malveria was envious? It was possible. When it came to fashion Malveria was very passionate and jealous, and might mistake another's good dress sense for theft of her own style.

Thrix took a small silver bowl from her drawer, dropped some herbs into it and waved her hand, causing the herbs to ignite. She was sending a message to Malveria's realm and she hoped that the Fire Queen would not be too busy to answer. She began to mutter the words of the spell.

"I call thee, Malver – "

"You're back!" cried the Fire Queen, instantly materialising in front of the desk. "Splendid! I've been waiting for your call. How was the gloomy castle?"

"Gloomier than ever, and very stressful. Mother managed to make sure Sarapen wasn't elected."

"Then who is the new Thane?"

"Still undecided. Sarapen or Markus."

"Ah," said Malveria. "Then there will be a war. Do you want me to bring troops?"

"No, Malveria. If there's a war I'm staying well out of it."

Malveria perched herself elegantly on the edge of Thrix's desk, checking herself in the wall mirror as she did so. She was particularly pleased with the area of stocking beneath her skirt which showed between her knee and ankle. Stockings had until quite recently been unknown among the Hiyasta. The Queen had taken some back to her realm where they were examined by elemental tailors who then sub-contracted the work out to fairy weavers. The result was some fabulously sheer stockings, finer than could be found anywhere in London.

"Did you pick up any fashion ideas? But no, they are all tartan-clad barbarians at your Scottish castle, yes? Were you obliged to wear a kilt?"

The Fire Queen knew perfectly well that this was not the case but liked to pretend that Thrix had escaped from a land of barbarians before making her way south.

"Malveria, on those recent occasions when you've arrived here in tears – "

"In tears? Surely you exaggerate. A slight moistening of the eyes, perhaps."

"Yes, well, have you giving me an accurate description of events? Was there really someone there in an exact copy of the clothes I designed for you?"

"Absolutely. In a percent. How many percent is absolutely?"

"One hundred."

"Then it is one hundred percent. Copies, every item. The blue dress, the silver slippers, the little yellow shawl with the beautiful stitching which you swore had come that day from your own embroiderer."

"It had. Malveria, this is very serious. And not just for you. If my designs are being copied by someone with enough connections to get them into your dimension what chance do I have here in this world? I'm meant to be showing clothes in Milan and New York soon. If this carries on it'll ruin my business."

"What will you do?"

Thrix wasn't entirely sure.

"It would help if we knew where Princess Kabachetka gets her clothes. Presumably her designer is the person who's stealing my ideas. We might find a link between her designer and some spy in my operation."

The Fire Queen was following this closely. When it came to planning and strategy, Malveria had a lot of experience. Her frivolous manner entirely forgotten for the moment, she considered Thrix's words.

"It would be difficult for me to learn this. I have no easy way of obtaining information about the Princess. Relations between myself and her mother the Empress Asaratanti are not good."

"I thought everything was peaceful in your realms these days?"

"We will not go to war. But we do not like each other. The Empress heard that I had been casting doubts on the naturalness of her figure – she went to Los Angeles to have her breasts lifted, you know – and since then relations have been very cool. But really, I do not understand how she thought she could get away with it undetected. The Empress is two thousand years old if she's a day and now she has the breasts of a teenager. One could not help but notice. As for her whorish little daughter Kabachetka, she has never forgiven me for stealing three of the five lovers she was scheduled to meet on the last solstice."

Thrix looked at Malveria pointedly.

"What? I left her two. That was more than enough for a woman like her. I doubt very much if even these two were satisfied."

The Enchantress smiled.

"So you can't find out anything about the Princess's clothes designer?"

"I did not say that. It will be difficult, but for a woman who once defeated the three-headed crimson dragon alone and unaided, nothing is impossible. Still they sing songs of that incredible exploit. Do you like my stockings?"

"They're beautiful," said Thrix, appreciatively.

"Each pair costs three pieces of gold. The fairies, they do not work for nothing. But it is worth three pieces of gold to make each leg look fabulous. Even Agrivex complimented them, and Agrivex, as a rule, does not care for stockings."

"Agrivex? Who's that?"

"My niece. Have I never mentioned her to you?"

"I thought you'd done away with all your family?" said Thrix.

"I have. Really Agrivex is not related to me. But I've come to regard her as a niece and may even one day adopt her in some way. She would be, I suppose, around seventeen in human terms, though our years are somewhat different as you know."

The Enchantress was surprised to hear Malveria speak with warmth about any of her subjects. Normally when she talked of her realm, she just sounded bored.

"She was an orphan, the illegitimate – is that the right word? – daughter of a fire temple prostitute who died in childbirth. Around ten years ago, when Agrivex was seven, she was due to be sacrificed in the normal way. And yet, while the other children were queuing in an orderly fashion, prior to be thrown into the small volcano, which is considered quite an honour, she attracted my attention by marching around in an angry fashion, stamping her feet and saying over and over that we could not sacrifice her, as she was a *little princess*. She was very insistent, and refused absolutely to co-operate, calling me some very bad names and threatening terrible revenge. For instance, she said that if she was sacrificed she would never speak to me again. Naturally I was attracted to a child of such spirit, and spared her life. Since when she has moved into the palace where she plagues every-one, including me. I fear that she may one day attempt to steal my fine clothes, but she is at present going through a phase which involves wearing only the shabbiest of apparel. Yes, I am fond of young Agrivex's spirit, though I was obliged to punish her for wearing ripped trousers to my last banquet. One has one's limits, after all."

The Fire Queen rose lightly to her feet.

"I now depart to consider the matter of the evil Princess and her filthy spy."

Malveria smiled, waved her hand, and disappeared, leaving behind the scent of jasmine. Thrix had been meaning to ask her what hap-pened with Kalix but she'd forgotten. She had more important things to think about. She used her intercom and asked Ann about the person-nel files and Ann said she'd be right in with them.

72

Dominil put on the black leather coat which reached down to her ankles, packed a few extra clothes in one bag, her Latin poetry and her laptop in another, and flew to London. Her mission was to protect and assist the cousins about whom the family did not speak. She was not sure what to expect. At twenty-eight she was only six years older than the twins but Dominil had never had much to do with them. She mainly remembered them as a noisy pair of cubs who went around the castle wearing headphones all the time, listening to music and playing air guitar. Verasa believed that if Dominil could help the twins' musi-cal career, it might be enough to persuade them to vote for Markus. Dominil had agreed to the mission, partly because she was bored, and partly to help thwart Sarapen.

Dominil and Sarapen had fallen into a passionate relationship the year after she returned from Oxford. After being surrounded by students Dominil was surprised to find herself suddenly so attracted to the large, forceful werewolf. Their clandestine affair had been so intense that it was not uncommon for them both to wake up with their human bodies scarred from the attentions of their werewolf claws the night before. Then Sarapen had found out about an affair she was having with a young man in a neighbouring town. The young man had subsequently gone missing. Sarapen denied all involvement but Dominil was certain Sarapen had killed him. Dominil would never forgive Sarapen for that. She would have her revenge.

Dominil had not been in London for several years, not since Verasa had sponsored an exhibition of Byzantine art at the Courtauld Gallery. Dominil had liked the early religious paintings with their austere saints; liked them enough to later buy something similar from Merchant MacDoig and hang it in her chambers. It was one of the very few decorative items she possessed. Dominil was not fond of colourful trinkets. Under her black leather coat she wore black trousers and a black shirt, and no jewellery.

Dominil knew almost nothing about rock music. She'd been looking at some music websites, trying to gain an insight into the world she was about to enter. She was not impressed. Poor design, poor grammar and poor use of language, she thought. She hoped the music was better.

From Heathrow airport she took a hired car into London. She stopped off first at an apartment close to Regent's Park, one of the family properties to which Verasa had given her the keys. The apartment was large and well appointed and quite satisfactory for her needs. She phoned the sisters but there was no reply, so she set off towards Camden, ready to encounter the decadent side of the family.

73

Sarapen stared over the battlements of his keep. Down below, workmen were rebuilding the old east wall. Human workmen, but the company was owned by a werewolf of the MacAndris Clan, who were historical allies of the MacRinnalchs. Sarapen's keep dated back to the fourteenth century and the last occupant, an uncle of the late Thane, had not kept it in good repair. Sarapen was attending to the restoration, putting it back as close as possible to its original fourteenth century state. It was slow, laborious work, but Sarapen believed that the clan should preserve all of its historical buildings. He withdrew his head and turned to his companions.

"Kalix will have to die."

He was quite certain of this. Kalix's death would secure Dulupina's vote. The alternative, bringing her back to the castle, would be difficult. Once she was there who knew what might happen. Sarapen would not put it beyond his mother to somehow secure Kalix's release so that she could sit at the next council meeting and vote against him. It was best to get rid of her. In this, Sarapen's interests merged perfectly with his emotions. Kalix had attacked the Thane. She had also attacked Sarapen when he went to rescue his father. She deserved to die for that.

"That means you'll have one more vote, from Dulupina," said Mirasen. "And provided it's done before the next meeting of the Great Council, Kalix's death will bring Decembrius onto the council. Another vote for you. Eight in total."

Sarapen's black-stoned keep was forty miles west of Castle MacRinnalch. A cold, hard place, built for defence rather than comfort. It was a coincidence that Sarapen should be at this moment repairing the outside walls. He had not foreseen that he may have to go to war. A happy co-incidence however; at this time it would be as well to have one's fortifications in good repair.

The repairs were prohibitively expensive. Each stone had to be cut by masons skilled in the traditional crafts. He could have made basic structural repairs at less expense but Sarapen didn't see any point in carrying out work which did not restore his keep to its original condition. The bills were huge, however, and this was a source of some anger to Sarapen. He thought the clan should be paying for the work, but the Mistress of the Werewolves would not sanction this. She controlled the clan finances. Sarapen didn't believe that his mother had allocated him his due allowance of the family money over the years, though Verasa insisted that Sarapen had received everything to which he was entitled.

Sarapen had a huge fur-trimmed cloak around his shoulders, a traditional garment of the ruling MacRinnalchs, lined with cloth in the clan tartan, woven on the estates. It kept out the cold wind that whistled over the battlements. Sarapen's keep stood at the top of a steep hill. Around the hill were farmlands which were worked by werewolves, all Sarapen's supporters. If necessary Sarapen could gather a great many werewolves to his cause.

If he could garner nine votes at the next meeting there would not have to be a war. The prospect of war didn't trouble Sarapen, but he was willing to go along with his advisors for now, and seek a more peaceful victory, if it could be done.

"Baron MacAllister?" said Mirasen.

Sarapen growled. He was outraged at the Baron's perfidy in feigning illness.

"Were this last century I would have pursued him and killed him," snarled Sarapen. "And if he does not assure me that he'll vote for me at the next meeting I'll do it anyway."

If Baron MacAllister were to die, his son would accede to his place on the council.

"The young MacAllister would have no truck with my mother's plotting," declared Sarapen. "He would vote for me."

"Probably," agreed Mirasen. "But let me try to win back the Baron before we do anything too drastic. Remember, we have six votes already. Dulupina and Decembrius will make eight. It may be possible to persuade the Baron that it would be best for him if he voted for you."

Sarapen looked to Decembrius. Decembrius shook his head.

"I don't see Baron MacAllister changing his vote now. But I agree that Mirasen should talk to him. What about the other available votes? Might we persuade Thrix to come round?"

"My sister has a powerful dislike of me."

"She also has a powerful dislike of Markus. It may be worth approaching her again."

Sarapen growled again. None of this was to his liking.

"The next Thane should not have to grovel for votes," he declared, loudly. "The position is mine by right! Damn this family! Damn them all, particularly these women! What is the matter with them?"

"It's interesting that the death of another council member after Kalix would ensure your victory," commented Mirasen. "Because it will be Dulupina's turn to appoint a replacement, and she'll pick another of Kurian's children. Who will certainly vote for you."

"I'm aware of this," said Sarapen, coldly. "And were it not for my advisors I might have attended to it already."

74

Mr Mikulanec spoke on the phone to Mr Carmichael, chairman of the Guild.

"Three of your members dead?"

"Two are dead, one may recover."

"Killed in daylight, I understand."

"In daylight, yes."

"So if this was the work of werewolves, they were strong, even in human form," said Mikulanec.

"Werewolves are always strong in human form," replied Mr Carmichael. He had to concede that it had been unexpected. For hunters to be killed in daylight was uncommon.

"You say the hunters were patrolling at random, not in pursuit of any target. So you presume they came across a group of werewolves, in human form, and the werewolves killed them."

"Yes. With the Thane's funeral, there have been a lot of werewolves passing through London," said Mr Carmichael.

"But I understand that Kennington is not a place you would pass through on your way to an airport?"

This was true. It was a peculiar occurrence, for which Mr Carmichael had no ready explanation.

"What about the werewolf princess?" asked Mr Mikulanec. "Is that not close to the area in which she was last sighted?"

"Yes. But we're sure she's an outcast. She wouldn't have been travelling with companions."

"Perhaps not," agreed Mr Mikulanec. "But what if she was on her own?"

"She couldn't have beaten three hunters on her own, not in daylight. All reports say she's a small girl, practically malnourished."

"Perhaps you have never seen what a small werewolf, practically malnourished, can do, when the circumstances are right," suggested

Mikulanec.

Mr Carmichael was irritated. The deaths were bad enough without a foreign hunter implying that the Guild didn't know its own business.

"I don't think she was responsible. It must have been a werewolf gang we haven't encountered before. We're sending more men to patrol the area."

The Guild had had some success in the past week. Several werewolves had been killed as they journeyed to and from the MacRinnalch Estates. Too few, of course, to hurt the clan, but enough to make the Guild feel that it was doing its work successfully. Until the matter of the hunters' deaths in London. That was a major blow.

Mr Mikulanec still thought the werewolf princess might have killed them.

"I will find her and eradicate her."

He hung up the phone. Mikulanec was under no illusions as to what a small, malnourished werewolf could do. Ten years ago a lone young werewolf had eliminated many of Mikulanec's associates in Croatia. They too had been experienced werewolf hunters, but the wolf had been moon-born, a son of the oldest family of werewolves in Central Europe. Even in human form he had been a savage opponent. 'And so,' mused Mikulanec, 'So it may be with this princess, if she was born on the full moon as a wolf, and has the purest of blood, and perhaps the same sort of wolf madness I encountered in Croatia.'

Mikulanec had killed the Croatian werewolf, though not with a silver bullet. He took out his knife and looked at it fondly. The Begravar knife. The only one of its kind left in existence, as far as he knew. It was a great advantage when it came to slaying werewolves. None could stand against it, no matter how strong or savage they were.

75

"I want to see more Sabrina the Teenage Witch," said Kalix, eagerly.

Daniel was apologetic.

"No more till next week."

"No more?" Kalix was cross. "But it's the best programme. They must show more."

She looked appealingly at Daniel as if he could somehow make the show appear again. Kalix was unfamiliar with TV scheduling and found it hard to believe that a programme she liked so much could only be shown once a week. Looking at the TV, which was currently showing a gardening programme she found deeply unappealing, she felt baffled.

"Is it on another station?" she asked, and worked the remote control.

"Not till Saturday," repeated Daniel.

"But it's better than these programmes," complained Kalix. "Why won't they show it again?"

"It's TV," said Daniel. "Lots of the programmes are bad."

"Could we phone them up and ask them to show more?"

Daniel laughed. He suggested that Kalix might email the channel with her request. Kalix bounded upstairs. Moonglow was sitting at her computer, translating Sumerian Cuneiform.

"Daniel says if I email the television they might show more Sabrina," she said, enthusiastically.

"Well, I'm kind of busy – " began Moonglow, but stopped. Realising she'd never seen Kalix so enthusiastic about anything before, and thinking that it was probably a good thing, she obliged the young werewolf by finding the website of the relevant channel. Kalix watched, interested in the process.

"Do you want to write the email?" asked Moonglow.

"My paws are too big for the keyboard," said Kalix.

Moonglow composed the email. She read it out loud to Kalix, knowing that the werewolf could not really read much of what was written, even though Kalix pretended she could. When Kalix was satisfied, Moonglow sent off her heartfelt plea for more Sabrina. Kalix thanked her then bounded downstairs again to tell Daniel that there would soon be more teenage witch adventures on TV.

"Do you think they'll show more tonight?" she asked.

"It might take a bit longer for your email to reach the executives."

Kalix nodded. She supposed it might. Daniel had a TV listings magazine which Kalix wanted to read. She made an attempt but again found it difficult. She had an urge to ask Daniel to check it, just in case he was misinformed about Sabrina, but held back. The young werewolf was ashamed of her poor reading skills.

Daniel also had work to do. He was meant to be speaking tomorrow at a seminar on *Timon of Athens*. Deciding that he could probably write something later, he put it out of his mind and went off to make tea and toast. Kalix followed him into the kitchen.

"Meat?" she said.

There was meat in the fridge for Kalix though both Daniel and Moonglow were nervous about what might happen tomorrow if the werewolf gorged herself again tonight. Would it lead to more vomiting and hysteria? Whether it did or not, it seemed best to provide her with anything she wanted. Moonglow had the accurate impression that this might be the only time in the whole month that she would actually eat. Kalix had shown amazing powers of recovery. Only two nights ago she had lain broken and bleeding in the alleyway. Now she was bounding around like an athlete. It was an indication of Kalix's great inner vitality. If she looked after herself properly there was no telling how vigorous she might be.

Daniel made tea. Kalix hung around talking enthusiastically about Sabrina the Teenage Witch. Daniel felt close to laughing. She was funny when she was enthusiastic and even her werewolf face with its alarmingly large teeth did not prevent her from sounding like an eager child. Spontaneously, he reached out to pat her furry head. Kalix looked shocked, and growled. Daniel hurriedly withdrew his hand.

"Too friendly?" he said.

"It's all right," said Kalix, and relaxed again.

She took her plate of meat and went to sit close to the TV, hoping for another good programme. Daniel called upstairs to Moonglow, telling her that she had to take a break.

"Too much cuneiform isn't good for you."

Moonglow, agreeing with this, appeared downstairs, and gratefully accepted a cup of tea.

"How's your seminar going?"

"Great," replied Daniel.

"You haven't started yet, have you?"

Daniel admitted that he hadn't.

"But I'm close. And I'm really making progress with Kalix. You see how cheerful she is?"

A savage growling noise caused them to turn round hurriedly.

"I hate this programme," said Kalix, and banged her paw on the remote control. "I want cartoons."

76

Beauty and Delicious lived in a quiet residential street, a little way from the centre of Camden. Knowing that she was unlikely to find a parking space, Dominil had left her car at a car park and walked the rest of the way. Heads turned as she strode past Camden tube station. Even in this part of the city, where an unusual appearance was not uncommon, Dominil's severely beautiful face and ice-white hair drew attention.

Having memorised her street map, Dominil reached the house easily enough. It was larger and in better repair than she had been expecting. There was nothing to distinguish it from the other houses in the street, apart from the curtains being closed. She rang the bell for a long time. No one answered, though Dominil's sharp ears could hear noises within. She stretched over from the steps and rapped her fist on the front window. The door eventually opened. Beauty stood looking at her, her eyes not quite focused.

"Dominil?"

"Yes. You were expecting me, I believe."

"Was I?"

"I understand the Mistress of the Werewolves informed you – "

Beauty fell backwards, landing heavily on the floor. Dominil stepped inside. The house stank of whisky. The twins had been indulging heavily in the MacRinnalch malt sent by Verasa. Dominil closed the door, stepped over Beauty and walked into the front room where she found Delicious lying unconscious on the floor with a young man lying beside her, also unconscious. There were empty bottles of whisky everywhere, and the floor was so covered with every sort of junk that it was hard to find a place to put her feet. Dominil stared without expression at the scene. Obviously, reports of the twins' behaviour were not exaggerated. Dominil bent down to check on Delicious, and turned her on her side, in case she vomited while asleep. She returned to the hall, did the same for Beauty, then opened a window to let some air into the fetid rooms.

Dominil located the kitchen, intending to make coffee. The mess she found was beyond description. It looked as if no one had ever cleaned any plate, table, or kitchen surface. No one had ever mopped the floor no matter what was spilled on it and no one had taken out the rubbish. Even filling the kettle was a daunting task. There was so much debris in the sink that it took some time to clear enough space for the kettle to fit under the tap.

Dominil took this all in. She saw already that the twins' behaviour would have to be modified if she was to help them. As she arrived back in the living room carrying a tray of coffee, the young man stirred, and opened his eyes.

"Do you live here?" enquired the werewolf.

"No," he mumbled, and reached toward a quarter-full bottle of whisky that lay close by. Dominil intercepted his hand and hauled him to his feet.

"Then it's time to go," she said, and propelled him towards the front door. He protested, but though he was some inches taller than Dominil his strength was as nothing compared to hers. She placed him on the front step, closed the door, then picked up Beauty from the hallway and carried her into the main room. She swept some clutter from the couch and sat both the twins down.

"Wake up," said Dominil. "We have things to do."

77

"Can't you cancel for me?" said Thrix, almost plaintively.

"Absolutely not," said Ann, and sounded stern.

"New York might phone back, it's still business hours there."

"I can take a message."

"You will not take a message," insisted Thrix. "Put the call through to me at the restaurant."

Ann agreed, though unwillingly. She felt that Thrix's date wouldn't want their dinner to be spoiled by a business phone call. The Enchantress was adamant.

"I have to speak to them soon. I really shouldn't be going out to dinner."

"Stop looking for excuses," said Ann. "You're going on this date and that's final."

"Since when was it part of your job description to bully me into going out on dates?"

"Since you started moping round the office and complaining about not having a man," answered Ann.

"I never moped. The occasional comment, maybe."

Thrix was still searching for reasons not to go, but apart from saying that she wasn't really in the mood, she could find no further objections.

"Once you get to the restaurant, you'll be in the mood. It's almost a year since you had a date. Now go out and have a good time."

Ann was not certain why her employer, so successful in other fields, had such difficulties in dating. Someone as beautiful, intelligent and successful as Thrix shouldn't have so much trouble finding a suitable man. Unfortunately, after a string of failed romances Thrix now seemed to have lost all confidence.

"The last man I had dinner with turned out to be a divorce casualty. All he wanted to talk about was his ex-wife. After an hour I felt like calling her and congratulating her on getting rid of him."

Ann brushed this aside.

"Donald Carver is very eligible and he's never been married. And he's attractive and he works in films so you'll have something interesting to talk about."

"What if I don't want to talk about films? And why did he ask me out anyway? Is he on the rebound from some doomed relationship? Are you sure about this outfit?"

"As sure as I was the other ten times you asked me. And he isn't on the rebound from a relationship, he hasn't had a girlfriend for a while."

"So what's the matter with him?" asked Thrix. "Is he really dull?"

"Your taxi is waiting," said Ann, and ushered the Enchantress out of the office. "Have a good time. "

Thrix took the lift to the ground floor and stepped unwillingly into her taxi. Donald Carver was indeed a personable man, and reasonably attractive. Unfortunately Thrix's run of bad luck in romance had left her pessimistic. She was expecting something to go wrong. She wondered how old he was. Around thirty, she thought. Which was about what Thrix was in human terms, although she was actually almost eighty years old. She wondered what her date would say if he knew he was about to have dinner with an eighty year old werewolf.

The clan frowned on werewolves dating humans, fearing that their true nature might be discovered. Thrix disregarded this. No one could tell that the blonde-haired fashion designer was a werewolf, not even an experienced hunter. The Enchantress was too well masked by her

176

own sorcery ever to be discovered. Except by Malveria, of course. She had known right away. It was very difficult to hide anything from the Fire Queen by sorcery. In her own dimension she was virtually invulnerable to its effects, and even in this world, only the most powerful spells could work against her.

Malveria had walked up to Thrix at an after-show party and said in a loud voice, "I've never met a werewolf fashion designer before." Thrix had been alarmed, thinking at first this must be a hunter, till her senses told her otherwise. She leaned over to whisper in Malveria's ear. "And I've never met a Hiyasta at a fashion show before. But I'm prepared to be discreet about it if you'll stop yelling out in public that I'm a werewolf."

"Is it a secret?"

"Yes."

"Then it will be our secret," said Malveria, smiling sweetly. "Of course we Hiyastas are never in the best of friendship with werewolves, but who could not like a werewolf who designed such a beautiful collection of frocks?"

They had hit it off right away, becoming friends on the spot. Their mutual love for fashion seemed to make their historical antagonism quite irrelevant. Because, as the Fire Queen said, when you considered how important one's outfits were, what did it really matter if, nine hundred years ago, Murdo MacRinnalch had grossly insulted her grandmother Queen Malgravane? And Thrix agreed, saying that if Queen Malgravane had quite unnecessarily taken offence at a mere slip of the tongue by her great-grandfather Murdo, it really wasn't something to be troubling oneself over these days. Soon afterwards Malveria adopted the Enchantress as her fashion advisor, designer and supplier, an association which had proved beneficial to them both.

Thrix fell to thinking about her designs for Malveria being stolen. She was still preoccupied when she arrived at the restaurant and looked blankly at the man who strode up to her.

"Yes?"

"I'm your date."

"Of course," said Thrix, and smiled, though she was now feeling distracted by her problems. As she had arrived slightly late, they sat down immediately at their table. The waiter brought them their menus.

"I think I'll – " began Donald, when Thrix's phone rang.

"Sorry," said Thrix. "Important business call, it won't take long."

It wasn't her business call. It was her mother.

"Thrix," began Verasa. "Have you checked on Kalix yet? I believe that Sarapen may – "

"Mother, I can't talk about this just now."

"Why not?"

"I'm in a restaurant."

"Are you so hungry you cannot delay eating for a moment?"

"I'm not on my own."

"Ah," said the Mistress of the Werewolves. "Are you with Ann?"

"No."

"You mean you're on a date? With a human?"

"Yes."

"My dear daughter, is that wise? I know you haven't been able to attract a suitable werewolf but consider the difficulties. Humans are very short lived you know, and rarely react well to learning that they're associating with a werewolf."

"Mother, this is really not the time – "

"I'm just trying to be helpful. If you'd said you were trying to meet someone I would have introduced you to that nice Andrew MacRinnalch who was at the castle for the funeral. He's qualified as a lawyer now, you know."

Thrix groaned inside. Andrew MacRinnalch, a distant cousin, was possibly the most boring werewolf in the clan.

"With his own practice in Edinburgh," continued Verasa.

"I really have to go," said Thrix, sharply. "I'll call you later about Kalix. Bye."

Thrix put her phone away and apologised to her partner at the table.

"My mother. Always picks the wrong time to call."

Donald took this all calmly, naturally. He'd been wanting to ask Thrix out for some time and having finally worked up his nerve, after some discreet encouragement from Ann, he wasn't going to spoil things by objecting to a phone call. They studied their menus while making some small talk about the business they'd been involved in that day.

"I have some fabric coming from Korea – "

Thrix broke off as her phone rang. It had to be New York.

"Hello?"

"Thrix. It's Markus. I'm coming to London and there's a lot we should discuss. Mother wants you to – "

"I'm busy," said Thrix. "I'm at dinner."

"Business?"

"No."

"You mean you're on a date?" Markus sounded amused. "Then I should certainly not detain you, sister. After all, it's not often you go out on a date."

"No, it isn't," said Thrix, pointedly, and hung up the phone.

"My brother," she said, apologetically to Donald. "Shall we order?"

It was the night after the full moon. All of the MacRinnalchs were in werewolf form, except Thrix. She remained as human, by her own choice. She could prevent the change by sorcery. It took some effort, but it might be worth it if the date went well.

78

Thrix was not the only member of family trying to combine their personal life with the demands of the clan. Markus was on the phone to Talixia, telling her that he would be back in London shortly. Dominil was sobering up the twins and attempting to make them understand that she was here to help. Sarapen was consulting his advisors, rebuilding his walls and gathering his troops. At the castle Lucia was saying goodbye to some of the werewolves who had travelled over the oceans to be at the funeral. She assured them that the matter of the Thaneship would be sorted out as quickly as possible. Lucia was a very charming werewolf, and quite reassuring.

Tupan sat in his chambers and reflected that, all things considered, the meetings of the Great Council had gone rather well. If the weakling Markus was ever installed as Thane, the clan would surely find him an unsatisfactory leader, and look for another.

Kalix, in werewolf form, was sitting on the couch at Daniel and Moonglow's with the TV guide in her lap, trying to decipher the columns of writing, most of which were as illegible to her as Moonglow's Sumerian cuneiform. She wondered if Daniel might be misleading her about the frequency of Sabrina the Teenage Witch. Kalix was used to people misleading her. She studied the word *Sabrina,* fixing it in her mind so she could recognise it again, then awkwardly turned the pages with her werewolf paw, searching for the name.

"Aha!" she yelled, suddenly.

So strange was it to hear a werewolf shout *A ha!* that Daniel and Moonglow both burst out laughing.

"What's funny?" said Kalix, self-consciously.

"Nothing," said Moonglow. "What is it?"

Kalix pointed eagerly to a page in the TV guide which, she was quite certain, contained the word *Sabrina* twice in a row. On the next page, which she thought meant the next day, it appeared twice again.

"It's on more!"

Daniel shook his head ruefully. He explained to Kalix that while it was true the channel in the listings she was studying did show more Sabrina, they didn't have that channel.

"It's a cable channel. We only have terrestrial."

Kalix found this baffling.

"Get it now!" she said, enthusiastically.

"I'm afraid it costs money. Yes, there are ninety channels in that TV guide but we only have five of them."

Kalix looked crushed.

"But they show more Sabrina," she said. "And cartoons in the day."

"We wouldn't want ninety TV channels," said Moonglow. "TV is bad, you shouldn't waste all your time watching it."

"I don't understand," said Kalix.

"Well may you not," said Daniel. "Who wouldn't want more TV channels? But Moonglow's sort of anti-TV. So anti-TV in fact that when her mother offered to pay for a cable connection as a birthday present, she refused."

Kalix stared at Moonglow.

"Is that true?"

Moonglow admitted it was, repeating that it was not good to watch too much television. Kalix became agitated. She started pacing round the room. Then she sat down next to Moonglow and looked appealing,

"Can we get cable TV?"

Moonglow shook her head.

"Who needs ninety channels? Believe me Kalix, it's a waste of time."

Kalix found this all very strange, and when Moonglow turned down her repeated requests she began to sulk. She rose to her feet and left the room noisily.

"Now you've made her angry," said Daniel.

"Not really angry. She's just sulking. If she's joining the household, she has to learn to get along with us," pointed out Moonglow.

"I'm not certain that this werewolf will ever be really communal," said Daniel.

"Of course she will. Look how much progress she's made already."

It was true. Kalix had started to act more like a young flatmate rather than a crazed werewolf. She seemed to be enjoying their company. She'd eaten a lot and listened to music with them. She'd even found a new record she liked, *I Want Your Love* by Transvision Vamp which she'd played approximately thirty times in a row till Daniel managed to divert her attention by finding a Runaways single he hadn't played yet.

Moonglow had tried to ask Kalix details of her life as a werewolf but Kalix was very unforthcoming. In response to Moonglow's question about what state her mind was in after she transformed into a werewolf, Kalix had merely shrugged her shoulders.

"You'd think a person would have more to say about being a werewolf," said Moonglow to Daniel. "You know, communing with nature and stuff like that."

"Maybe that's only in books," replied Daniel. "Perhaps if you've always been a werewolf it's just part of the daily grind."

"I wonder if Kalix will ever change into her full wolf shape?" Moonglow wondered. "I'd love to see her as a wolf."

Daniel cautioned against asking. "If she thinks we're trying to treat her like a puppy she'll be outraged and leave."

"You're right."

The phone rang. It was Jay, Moonglow's boyfriend, calling to arrange their next date. Daniel immediately started sulking, and went to join Kalix in the kitchen.

79

The Enchantress made it as far as nibbling an entree before her phone rang again. She answered it rather self-consciously. It was Malveria.

"I have progress. The cursed Princess Crab-apple – ha ha, I am making a joke with her name, do you understand it? – the vile Princess has just received a clothes delivery from London. I learn this from the daughter of my ambassador to their court. This daughter will now attempt to see what label is on the clothes when the Princess disports her unpleasant figure at the Empress Asaratanti's party celebrating the one thousandth anniversary of her victory over the ice dwarves from the north. I am invited to this party but will not go to because it is common knowledge that the Empress Asaratanti would not have secured any victory over the ice dwarves were it not for help from my mother, Queen Malgabar, but the ungrateful Empress will not admit this."

Thrix was interested to hear that Malveria was making progress though she would have preferred not to have had the history lesson.

"When the ice dwarves flooded down over the northern glaciers, my mother – "

"I can't speak for long, I'm at dinner," said Thrix, interrupting.

"At dinner?" The Fire Queen sounded surprised. "But you so rarely go out to dinner. Is it business?"

Thrix hesitated.

"You're on a date!" said Malveria immediately. "How splendid! It is a great worry to me that you so rarely have relations with the opposite sex. Your lack of sexual activity is quite terrifying."

Thrix thought that there would be precious little chance of relations with the opposite sex if she didn't get Malveria off the phone.

"I have to go now. Please keep me informed of any developments."

Thrix ended the call and looked apologetically at Donald Carver, who was politely waiting for Thrix to finish her entree.

"Sorry, another business call."

"I can see you're busy with your work," said her companion, a little dubiously.

"Tell me more about the film you're producing," said Thrix, to get Donald's mind off her phone calls and back on to the conversation. He told her about the meeting he'd just been to with his backers, and their attempts to raise the millions of pounds they needed. Funding a film was a difficult business in Britain and even an experienced producer like himself never found it easy to raise the money.

"I've got them interested because I have an American actress – "

Thrix's phone rang. An expression of annoyance flickered across Donald's face though he stifled it as best he could. By now, Thrix was regretting coming out to dinner while expecting her business call from

New York.

"Hello?"

"This is Dominil."

The Enchantress was surprised. She couldn't remember her cousin Dominil ever calling her before.

"I am in London. I have some news I'd rather not discuss on the phone."

Thrix made an arrangement to meet Dominil the next day. Her cousin did not engage in the small talk which had so far blighted her date but even so by the time the call was finished, the main course had gone cold and Donald Carver was looking impatient.

"That was my cousin."

"You're a very close family."

"Not exactly. But you know, family business, after the funeral."

"The funeral?"

"My father. That's why I was in Scotland."

Donald looked shocked. Thrix cursed herself for mentioning it.

"You've just been to your father's funeral? I had no idea. I'm sorry, I really wouldn't have asked you out if I'd known."

"No, it's fine. I mean… once he's gone, just get on with life, you know?"

Thrix thought she hadn't phrased this particularly well. Donald looked at her rather strangely. She was rescued by the appearance of the waiter. By now Thrix had completely lost her appetite but searched for some desert she could manage, not wishing to appear unenthusiastic about the restaurant's food, or her date. At least she hadn't been unenthusiastic about the wine, she reflected, as she refilled her glass and asked the waiter to bring another bottle.

Thrix looked at the menu rather glumly. Being a werewolf, the Enchantress had a healthy appetite, but she was so used to being with models and designers, none of whom were large eaters, that it was unusual for her to be eating a dessert which would be packed full of calories.

'Not that I need to worry about that,' Thrix told herself. 'I haven't put on a pound in years.' Yet there was something about the desserts which made her uncomfortable. What if she did put on some weight? She didn't want to end up flying to New York looking like a pudding. She waved away the menu.

"I'll just have coffee," she said, in a tone of voice which attempted to imply that not having a dessert did not mean she wasn't having an excellent time with Donald. She tried to concentrate on his conversation but it was difficult, with thoughts of Malveria, fashion espionage, Dominil and her mother all floating round in her head. What did her mother mean, *she hadn't been able to attract a suitable werewolf?* Since when was her mother keeping score? Thrix realised that Donald was talking to her and tried to drag her attention back to the matters in hand. He was asking her about her possible show in New York.

"It would be a very good opportunity for me to break into the market – " began Thrix. Her phone rang. It was New York. For what seemed like the fiftieth time, Thrix looked apologetically at her date. About thirty seconds later, when she was deep in a conversation with the woman who was organising the show, she had forgotten all about him. Once Thrix was discussing business she was oblivious to the outside world. The call was a very long one, longer than all the others put together. When she finally put her phone back in her bag she noticed that Donald was looking bored.

"Sorry. Was I on the phone for long?"

"Very long," said Donald, rather sharply.

80

The Enchantress paid the cab driver and walked quickly up the steps to her apartment block. The doorman let her in and she thanked him politely. She took the lift up to her floor with a middle aged couple who had just returned from the opera. The couple stood close to each other, quiet, but affectionate. Thrix endeavoured not to look like a woman coming back from a really bad date. The Enchantress walked slowly from the elevator to her apartment. As she was about to put the key in the door she halted, sensing someone.

"Malveria?"

The Fire Queen materialised beside her, dressed in a pale lilac evening dress which set of her dark skin to breathtaking effect.

"Hello my darling Enchantress."

"What brings you here, Malveria?"

"Nothing, nothing."

"You wanted to see if I was engaging in some sexual relations?"

"Also that," admitted Malveria. "Is your man presently parking the car prior to rushing up the stairs where he will fling you on the bed or maybe the floor of the hallway if he cannot contain his passion?"

"The man is on his way home regretting he ever had such a dull date as me."

"Oh." The Fire Queen looked disappointed. "This is not the result I was hoping for. And why are you unable to open the door?"

Thrix was fumbling with her key. She realised she had drunk more wine than she intended, and had hardly eaten anything. When she finally managed to get the door open the Fire Queen put a hand on her shoulder to steady her.

"What went wrong?"

"Everything. Too many interruptions. I hardly listened to a word he said. By the fifth phone call he was looking bored and by the seventh he was asking for the cheque. I've never seen a man disappear so quickly."

The Enchantress waved her hand in the direction of the kitchen and the coffee machine sprang into life. When a woman badly needed coffee it was a blessing being a sorceress.

"Perhaps the situation could be repaired?" suggested Malveria.

Thrix shook her head.

"You can't ignore a man for the entire evening. It hurts their pride."

"I am pleased I do not have to participate in this ritual you call dating," said Malveria. "Really, it sounds so tiresome."

When the coffee was ready Malveria offered to bring it through, which was an indication of the warmth of her friendship for the Enchantress. There were very few people for whom the Fire Queen would carry a tray.

"We could work spells to make him love you," suggested Malveria.

"Forget it Malveria. I've gone off the whole idea. I've got plenty of other things to think about."

"True, you are very busy," agreed the Fire Queen. "The Sorceress Livia's 500th birthday celebration is only two months away."

Malveria had commissioned Thrix to make her clothes for the event. It was one of the highlights of the Hiyasta social calendar. Livia's 400th birthday celebration had been a legendary affair, and this one promised to be even grander. It would last for five days, and the Fire Queen would need several different outfits for each day. In addition, Thrix was designing clothes for the handmaidens and page boys who would attend Malveria throughout the event.

"Is there any chance, Enchantress, that with your upcoming engagements in Milan and New York, and the interference of your family feud that you may – " Malveria's lip trembled.

"Your clothes will be ready," said Thrix, emphatically. "Everything is on schedule."

"Will we make fittings tomorrow?"

"I'm sorry I can't. Not in the morning anyway. I have to meet Dominil. Mother has some insane idea that she can get the twins to vote for Markus. It all seems very unlikely to me. Have you ever met Dominil?"

"The white-haired one? No. But I have heard of her. Very beautiful, I understand?"

"Yes, very beautiful. But completely cold. I've no idea how mother persuaded her to do this. Meanwhile I'm supposed to look after Kalix which is just about the last think I want to do."

The Mistress of the Werewolves expected Thrix to protect Kalix. Thrix had refused to commit herself, but could see that she would probably end up doing it anyway.

"Kalix is in danger from Sarapen," said Malveria, who was now abreast of the situation regarding the Thaneship. "So it is fortunate that I provided her with a pendant, yes? Perhaps she will be safe now?"

Thrix sipped her coffee, rather wearily.

"Perhaps. I suppose I should make more effort to protect her but you know I've never liked her much. I gave her the first pendant just so she wouldn't bother me any more."

"I do not know if I like her or not," said Malveria. "But she is interesting. I feel there is the prospect of some entertainment while she remains in the humans' house."

"Is that why you went to so much trouble?" asked the Enchantress. She had been very surprised to learn that not only had Malveria obtained a new pendant for Kalix, she had summoned her back from the outskirts of the forests of the werewolf dead. The Enchantress was aware of the expenditure of power this must have required. However she was not aware of the price Malveria had extracted from Moonglow, and believed that Malveria had saved Kalix as a favour to her. The bargain with Moonglow was Malveria's secret, for her future amusement.

"Do you mind if I remain when Dominil comes to visit? I am curious about this white-haired wolf before whom all tremble."

Thrix looked at Malveria.

"Just how bored are you these days?"

"Very bored," admitted Malveria. "Sometimes I regret that I so completely vanquished my enemies. But I am forgetting – tomorrow I will meet the daughter of my ambassador to the cursed Empress Asaratanti. I may learn of the spy who torments us. How I will make the culprit suffer!"

Thrix's head was drooping. She muttered a word and released the spell that was preventing her transformation. As the werewolf form came upon her she sighed like a woman slipping off an uncomfortable pair of shoes after a long day's shopping.

"Ah, Thrix, you feel the effects of too much wine? I hope you did not put the man off with drunkenness? It is never ladylike, you know."

"He was put off long before I got drunk."

"Drink more coffee and become awake," said Malveria. "Because tonight, if my memory does not play cruel tricks, is the night of the wonderful Japanese fashion show on your excellent television of many, many channels."

The Fire Queen switched on the television and worked the remote control with the triumphant air of a woman who, although living in a realm where technology was very basic, had nonetheless mastered the art. She shrieked with excitement as a young Japanese model floated across the screen in a black kimono. The Queen was even more obsessed with clothes than usual. Nothing in her life was more important than the prospect of securing a great fashion triumph at the Sorceress Livia's upcoming birthday celebration.

81

Kalix woke up and wondered where she was. She remembered that she was in Daniel and Moonglow's flat. She thought about watching TV, and smiled. Then she thought about all the food she'd eaten the night before and immediately felt ill.

Moonglow put her head through the door of the bathroom as Kalix was vomiting profusely. Wary of being struck again, she let Kalix be. Kalix threw up for a long time then trooped past Moonglow without even looking at her. Kalix was once more a mess. Her hair was matted with sweat and the front of her T-shirt was stained with her vomit. The young werewolf went downstairs, took water from the kitchen, then wrapped herself up in her quilt on the floor, and sipped from her new bottle of laudanum. Kalix was again feeling anxious. Though the attack was not as severe as the previous day, she was sweating and trembling. She took more laudanum and a pill. She could sense Daniel and Moonglow hovering in the background and wanted them to go away. Kalix felt deeply suspicious of their motives and wondered why they had asked her to remain. Once her strength returned she resolved that she would leave and never come back.

Daniel and Moonglow withdrew to the kitchen to confer.

"Things can't go on like this," whispered Moonglow.

"She likes eating when she's a werewolf and then it drives her crazy when she's human."

"What's in that bottle she drinks from?"

They didn't know. Werewolf medicine perhaps. Kalix was very protective of her bottle and wouldn't let anyone near it.

"We really have to do something," said Moonglow. "Perhaps we should go to see Thrix again."

Daniel was not enthusiastic. Last time they'd visited Thrix, not only had the blonde-haired werewolf been hostile but they'd had to hide from other scary werewolves.

"Anyway, I felt self-conscious being surrounded by all that fashion and glamour."

"Hey, I'm suffering too," said Moonglow. "Between Kalix, Thrix and the Fire Queen I'm starting to feel fat. How come they're all so slender?"

"You're slender too," said Daniel, loyally. This was true, but after exposure to the extreme glamour of the Enchantress and the Fire Queen, and the wild and youthful beauty of Kalix, anyone was entitled to feel a little threatened.

They were interrupted by a noise outside. Kalix was limping towards the front door, her tattered bag in her hand and her ragged coat draped round her shoulders. Moonglow marched quickly to the door and stood in front of Kalix, barring her way.

"This has got to stop," she said. "And don't you dare try and hit me again after I looked after you and gave you somewhere to sleep."

Daniel looked round for something to use as a weapon in case Kalix sprang at Moonglow and started savaging her. But Kalix seemed drowsier than she had yesterday morning.

"Stay here and we can sort out your problems," said Moonglow.

"Stupid human," muttered Kalix.

"Well maybe," responded Moonglow. "But I'm a better alternative than anything else you have. Why do you want to go and live in a warehouse again when you can stay here where it's warm and comfy?"

"And watch Sabrina the Teenage Witch," added Daniel.

"We'll clear out the small room for you," continued Moonglow. "And you can stay there and it'll be nice."

"You can play your music," said Daniel, and smiled, without drawing any response.

"Really you should stay," insisted Moonglow.

Kalix swayed on her feet and abruptly collapsed on the floor. Her eyes remained open for a few seconds then closed as she drifted into unconsciousness. They carried her back to the front room, taking care not to trample on her hair which splayed out beneath her.

"It's funny," said Daniel. "A few weeks ago, I'd never have expected to be wrapping a werewolf in a quilt and giving her a hot water bottle. Now it's almost second nature."

82

North of the river in Camden, MacRinnalch werewolves were involved in another unfriendly scene. Beauty and Delicious, recovering swiftly from their whisky-soaked celebrations of the night before, regarded Dominil with the same sense of derision they felt towards the rest of the family.

"I mean, you've got nice hair," said Beauty. "Good leather coat as well. But really, why would we want you to help us?"

"It's ridiculous," added Delicious. "The Mistress of the Werewolves must be losing her mind. She thinks some hick from a castle in Scotland is going to help our band to succeed?"

"Tell her thanks but no thanks."

"But say we really enjoyed the whisky."

"Ask her to send us more."

Dominil was untroubled by being refereed to as a hick from a castle. She was not even troubled by the sisters' failure to offer her anything to drink, a breach of MacRinnalch hospitality. Having accepted the mission from Verasa, she didn't intend to be put off by the girls' poor manners.

"The MacRinnalchs have considerable resources to put behind you," she pointed out.

"So what?" scoffed Beauty. "We have considerable resources of our own."

This was true. The sisters were wealthy, far wealthier than Dominil. Her share of the family money was still controlled by her father Tupan. While he had never denied her anything she wanted, neither had he turned over any substantial portion to her control.

"Yes, I understand you are not short of funds. I also understand that you have been living here for several years and in that time have made the acquaintance of many musicians. Presumably you have also made the acquaintance of those people who are involved in the production side of the industry. I see from this room alone that you have a great deal in the way of instruments. And if your own claims may be believed, you are both excellent musicians and singers."

Dominil sipped at her coffee and, uninvited, picked up a bottle of whisky from the floor and poured the remnants into her cup.

"So why is it," she continued. "That you have failed to make any impression? You no longer even have a band. In the short walk between Camden High Street and here I saw posters everywhere advertising gigs at small venues. It would seem that it's not difficult to at least make a start. You do not yet appear to have done so."

"Well…" said Beauty, and paused. She looked at her sister.

"It takes time," said Delicious.

Dominil let her eyes roam round the room, at the mess and clutter everywhere, and the signs of continual partying. She could see very clearly why the sisters were not making any progress.

"You did play onstage several times in the past. So you have in fact gone backwards. The reasons for this are obvious. You have no application and no direction. In reality you have very little prospects of success. No normal manager would be able to tolerate you for more than a few days. Left to your own devices you will remain in this house

190

getting drunker and drunker, talking about the great music you're going to make in the future, without ever going so far as walking onto a stage again. I imagine that within a short time you'll become a laughing stock as the boys you brag to in the local taverns realise you are nothing but talk. I understand that being *nothing but talk* is a common attribute among musicians. Is this what you desire?"

Beauty and Delicious looked at each other uncomfortably. Hearing their future mapped out in Dominil's cold, authoritative tones was not pleasant.

"Why don't you just go back to Scotland, bitch?" growled Beauty.

Delicious also growled a hostile, wolfish growl, but when it ended she looked at Dominil with just a flicker of interest. Delicious had once, a few months ago, thought something very similar to what Dominil had just said. She'd suppressed the thought and almost forgotten all about it. Now she remembered her own apprehensions about never walking onto a stage again.

"So what would you do?" she asked.

"You will explain to me what is required and I will make it happen," replied Dominil.

83

Thrix woke up a little hungover and very depressed.

'Poor Donald,' she thought. 'That was probably the worst date of his life. How am I going to explain it to Ann?'

"I should never have agreed to go," she muttered, wrapping herself in a dressing gown and heading for the shower. Malveria had stayed last night in the guest bedroom. As Thrix emerged from the shower the Fire Queen appeared, a broad smile on her face, to wish her a good morning.

"Have you got over the disappointment of last night's calamitous encounter?"

"Just about."

"I will make coffee. Do you have any pop-tarts?"

The Enchantress shook her head, bemused that the Fire Queen should make such a request.

The door buzzer rang. Thrix made a face.

"Dominil. I forgot she was coming."

Thrix hurried to dress while Dominil rode up in the lift. The Fire Queen opened the door to her and greeted her politely. As Dominil walked into the room Malveria eyed her ankle length leather coat with envy. She had several herself, made in her own realm, but she felt that none was quite so finely cut as Dominil's.

"Thrix will be out shortly. Would you like tea?" asked Malveria, who had decided to play the part of an excellent host.

Dominil nodded. She took a seat and sat in silence. Dominil sat very elegantly, her back straight. As Malveria brought her tea she tried to read her aura. Hiyastas could often learn a lot about a person just by examining them. Dominil's aura, however, was not very revealing. The white-haired werewolf's emotions were buried very deeply, too deeply to reveal themselves to a cursory examination from even such a mistress of interpretation as Malveria.

Thrix emerged, looking, Malveria noticed, rather radiant. 'Ah,' thought the Fire Queen. 'She does not wish to suffer in comparison to her cousin's beauty.'

"Good morning, Dominil. This is an early visit. Are you already settled in London?"

"The Mistress of the Werewolves has made satisfactory arrangements for me," replied Dominil. "If you will excuse my brevity, I will not remain here for long. I have much to do today."

"Helping the twins?"

"Yes."

The Enchantress was as puzzled as everyone else by Dominil's acceptance of the task, and wondered how she intended to go about it.

"Are you going to make them pop stars?"

"That is not what they require," replied Dominil. "At least, not yet. First they wish to obtain credibility among their peers."

"Credibility?"

Dominil nodded.

"It appears that success is not everything. When I suggested that a large sum of money from the MacRinnalch vaults might be enough to buy them successful music careers, they were unenthusiastic. I was surprised. I had assumed it would be possible to purchase everything that was necessary. Songs, musicians, advertising, radio play and such like. And indeed after talking to them I learn that it is possible to gain success of a sort by these methods, but it is not what they wish."

Thrix, despite being put off by her cousin's rather formal manner, found herself interested in what she had to say. Dominil explained that the sisters desperately wanted the respect of the people they knew in Camden.

"They live in a community which is full of struggling musicians. Were they to buy their way to success the other struggling musicians would simply hate them. To avoid this it is apparently necessary to do things in a rather more difficult manner. They must play small gigs at which people they know must acknowledge them to be worthwhile. They must attract attention from journalists and record companies on their own merits, rather than by bribery. In short, they must do things with credibility."

"In particular," continued Dominil. "They wish to surpass the achievements of four boys who live above a shop not far from them. The twins dislike them. The four boys once mocked them for being rich girls, another reason they refuse to buy their way to success. These four boys have a band of their own and are beginning to generate interest. Beauty and Delicious are eaten up with jealousy. I believe if I can put them on a footing which is even slightly superior to that of their rivals, they may actually be grateful enough to do what the Mistress of the Werewolves wishes, and vote for Markus.

The Enchantress was impressed. Dominil seemed to know what she was talking about.

"You really seem to be making quick progress, Dominil."

Thrix asked Dominil if she could bring her anything, food or drink, but the white werewolf shook her head.

"If you do get the twins back onstage, isn't Verasa worried that they might become visible to the hunters?"

"That would be for the Mistress of the Werewolves to worry about," responded Dominil. "However, this brings me to my reason for visiting you. I have some information. While spending my last night at the castle I hacked into the computers of the Avenaris Guild."

"You can do that?" said Thrix, surprised.

"Yes."

"What is this?" asked Malveria.

"I broke through their security system to read their computer files."

There was a slight delay while Thrix explained it to Malveria, as best she could. Thrix was impressed. She knew that Dominil was the intelligent one of the family but hadn't been aware that computing at a high level was among her achievements.

"I discovered that the Guild has no knowledge of Butix and Delix. Their files on the MacRinnalchs are extensive but very incomplete. They have no knowledge of me though my father's name is listed."

"Do they mention me?" asked Malveria, eagerly.

"No."

Malveria looked disappointed,

"They're only interested in werewolves," said Thrix, reassuringly. She looked at Dominil. "Are you about to tell me they know about me?"

"They know a little. Not your name or location but there was a report that an unknown fashion designer in London could be a MacRinnalch werewolf. Other than that they had no details. I thought I had better warn you. Furthermore, they have a great deal of information about Kalix. Up until a few weeks ago they were actively tailing her and they have a very accurate description of her. They've now lost contact, but they're aware of her status as daughter of the Thane. They count it as a very high priority to kill her."

Dominil paused, and sipped her tea.

"The Mistress of the Werewolves asked me to inform you of anything I learned about Kalix. It is your job, I believe, to protect her?"

"No," said Thrix. "It isn't."

"I understood from the Mistress that it was."

"My mother suggested it," admitted the Enchantress.

"Then it would seem sensible to do it," said Dominil, pointedly.

Thrix was not pleased to hear Dominil tell her what was sensible for her to do but didn't want to get into a discussion about it. She thanked Dominil for bringing her the information.

"There is one more thing," said Dominil. "The Guild have formed an association with a man from Croatia who has a great reputation among the werewolf hunters of Central Europe. His name is Mikulanec."

"No hunter will ever trouble me," stated Thrix.

"Yet he might trouble Kalix."

"Yes all right, I'll check on her," responded Thrix, not very graciously.

The phone rang. Expecting it to be her early morning call from Ann, Thrix picked it up. It was the Mistress of the Werewolves. Thrix listened for a few minutes.

"Dominil is here. I'll tell her." She put the phone down. "Baron MacAllister is dead."

"Already? I was not expecting Sarapen to act so quickly."

The Baron on whom Verasa had worked so assiduously to gain his vote was now dead. The war for the Thaneship had claimed its first casualty.

84

Gawain sat for a day and a night in the small cell, thinking. He had come to the castle looking for Kalix. She was not here, and he had gained no information as to her whereabouts. He watched from the small barred window as far below, the castle grounds emptied of visitors. The werewolves were going home. Dissatisfied, most probably, with their visit to the ancestral home of the MacRinnalchs. The cell door opened and Marwanis strode in. Marwanis was the daughter of the Thane's youngest brother Kurian. Though she was not striking like Kalix and Thrix, with their dramatic cheekbones and overly wide mouths, she was beautiful still, and in the opinion of many of the clan, far more what a MacRinnalch woman should be. Gawain rose to his feet, out of respect for her.

"Hello Gawain."

"I wasn't expecting to see you," said Gawain, awkwardly.

"No doubt. It's a long time since you've been pleased to see me, Gawain."

"I didn't say I was not pleased to see you."

Marwanis regarded him for a few moments, as if musing on something. Gawain felt uncomfortable. He had reason to.

"Why did you come back to the castle?"

"I'm looking for Kalix."

"Still? You've left it rather late, haven't you?"

"I've never stopped looking for Kalix."

"I heard you were working on a croft on the Shetland Isles," said Marwanis, with a faint smile. "Did you expect her to be hiding there in a peat bog?"

Gawain didn't reply. Marwanis seemed to be implying that he had not looked hard enough. There was some truth in this. For a while he had lost heart, his spirit defeated by the long search.

"You should have stayed with me," continued Marwanis. "Instead of transferring your affections to the Thane's daughter. Things would have gone better for you."

Not knowing how to reply, Gawain remained silent.

"Still, that is all in the past. Do you want to know where Kalix is?"

"Can you tell me?"

"Not exactly. But I can probably point you in the right direction."

"Why would you do that?"

Marwanis shrugged.

"I still remember you reasonably fondly. They were enjoyable nights, before you decided I was not quite good enough for you."

"That's not what I felt at all," protested Gawain. He was extremely uncomfortable to be confronted by the lover he had abandoned for Kalix.

"I could see the attraction, I suppose. She is wild. No doubt I was rather dull in comparison."

"Marwanis, I'm sorry if I hurt you – "

"You could not hurt me, Gawain. There are a hundred MacRinnalchs more worthy than you. Do you want me to tell you about Kalix?"

"Yes."

"She's in London. She fled there after she attacked her father. No one knows exactly where she is but the Enchantress could probably tell you more. She gave Kalix a charm which hides her. That should be enough for you to find her, if you really want to."

Marwanis turned to go, then stopped.

"If you need more help, you might try the Young MacDoig."

"The Merchant's son? Why?"

"Because Kalix stinks of laudanum these days. Did you not know that?"

Marwanis slipped out of the cell, locking the door behind her. Gawain wondered if she'd been telling the truth. Historically some werewolves had shown a liking for laudanum but it was a rare affliction, and very degenerate. Gawain didn't like to think of Kalix being involved in it. He wasted no time wondering why Marwanis had chosen to give him information. Kalix was in London. Gawain had searched there before, two years ago, without success. But on that occasion, Thrix had sworn she had no knowledge of Kalix at all.

'That's as much as I'm going to learn here,' he thought. 'So it's time to leave.'

He examined his cell. The window was much too small for him to squeeze through and the walls were of thick stone. The cell door was made of layers of hard wood, reinforced by iron bands. It was some hours till darkness so he sat on the cot in the corner of the cell, and waited.

Night came and the moon rose. It was two nights after the full moon. Only pure-blooded MacRinnalch werewolves could now change at will. With one human grandparent, Gawain should not have been able to do this. Gawain however, was a werewolf of unusual determination, with exceptional powers of concentration. He meditated briefly, then let the werewolf form come over his body. He walked towards the door and stooped to place his great jaws over the handle. Then he bit so fiercely that the handle and the wood around it was torn from the door. Gawain took one step back then kicked with all his strength. The door flew open sending shards of wood and metal flying out into the corridor. Gawain leapt out of the cell.

The two guards outside were startled. They had not been expecting that Gawain would be a werewolf this night. Gawain brushed them aside before running down the corridor to where the torch light flickered on a large window. Without breaking stride Gawain leapt at the window, crashing through the thick glass to fall all the way from the highest level of the castle into the moat below. He hit the water with tremendous force but surfaced quickly and struck out for the far side. He was hauling himself onto the far bank while the guards were still raising the alarm. By the time they'd rushed down the staircases, flooding out of the great gate of Castle MacRinnalch with torches in their hands, Gawain had long since disappeared into the darkness.

In the west wing a very flustered attendant rushed into the chambers of the Mistress of the Werewolves.

"Mistress, the prisoner has escaped."

"Escaped?" said Verasa. "How?"

"He became werewolf and tore the door from his cell then leapt for the moat."

"Really?"

Verasa took this calmly enough but Markus, who was with her in

197

the chamber, was furious. He berated the attendant and instructed him to gather all available werewolves and hunt for Gawain. The attendant nodded and left the chamber as quickly as he could, glad to escape from Markus's wrath.

The Mistress of the Werewolves was not exhibiting much wrath.

"Markus, it's quite all right. I rather expected him to escape. That's why I put him in that cell, rather than the dungeon. He is a vigorous young wolf, despite his human blood."

"Why did you want him to escape?"

"Well," said Verasa. "He was no use to me here. What was I going to do with him? Have him executed?"

"That is what he deserves," answered Markus.

"Perhaps. But Markus, do we really want to be executing MacRinnalchs in this day and age? We are trying to modernise the clan, after all."

"What if he finds Kalix?"

"Then he'll lead us to her. Thrix claims not to know where Kalix lives. I'm not sure if she's being honest. It's disturbing that we still don't know where Kalix is. And if Gawain does find her, then he'll try to protect her from Sarapen, which would be no bad thing."

Markus did not totally approve of this. He had never liked Gawain.

"I was not aware that he could transform into a werewolf at will, on any night."

"Weren't you? Gawain comes from a very strong lineage. His great-great-grandfather brought back the Begravar knife from Mesopotamia when he went overseas with the Black Douglas. And he was one of the MacRinnalchs who helped win the day for Robert the Bruce at Bannockburn. As of course was your own great-great-grandfather."

The Mistress of the Werewolves might not have been so calm had she been aware of the phone call Marwanis made to Sarapen a short time later.

"I gave Gawain the information about Kalix, as you wished. He then managed to escape."

"Already?" Sarapen sounded pleased. This was better than he had expected. Even if Decembrius failed to locate Kalix, Gawain might well lead them to her. He congratulated Marwanis on her work. Marwanis took his praise calmly, though she glowed inside. These days, she found herself increasingly attracted to her cousin Sarapen.

Verasa's calm was soon to be shattered. A messenger arrived with news from the MacAllister keep.

"The Baron is dead."

"What!" yelled Markus, and leapt to his feet.

Verasa's face was grim.

"Tell us what happened," she said, though she already knew in her bones who was responsible for the death.

85

Pete was extremely surprised to find himself being roused from his bed at nine o'clock in the morning. Usually he slept until noon. He was even more surprised to find that the person responsible for ringing the doorbell in such a remorseless manner was one of the most beautiful women he had ever seen, with hair so long and white that he wondered if it could possibly be real.

"Are you Pete, who plays guitar?"

"Eh… yes…"

"Good. Beauty and Delicious are re-forming their band. They again require your services. Turn up for rehearsal at three o'clock tomorrow afternoon at the Huge Sound studio in Leyton Street. Bring your guitar, do not be late and do not be intoxicated. Is there anything else you need to know?"

"Beauty and Delicious? I thought they'd given up."

"They have reactivated their career."

Dominil looked deeply into Pete's eyes. He flinched under the intensity of her stare.

"Can I count on you to be there?"

Pete nodded. He'd planned to spend tomorrow handing out fliers to earn a little money, but whoever this woman was, she didn't seem like someone he wanted to argue with.

Dominil turned on her heel and departed, her long black coat swaying gently round her ankles. Having repeated this scene at various flats around Camden, she walked calmly through the cold drizzle back to the twins' house. The sisters were as surprised as Pete to find themselves roused so early but Dominil brushed aside their protests.

"I've made contact with all the musicians you wanted to play with again. They will be there tomorrow at three."

The sisters were surprised.

"Even Adam?"

Adam had been their last drummer. He'd sworn never to speak to them again after they'd blamed him, quite unfairly, for ruining their last gig. While his timing on the night may not have been perfect, their own intake of red wine and vicodin had contributed far more to the general shambles.

"He was reluctant. I persuaded him."

Dominil looked round the living room.

"Whatever you want to salvage from this mess, I advise you to take to your rooms and store safely. The cleaners will be here shortly."

"Cleaners?"

"You cannot focus on anything while living in this sorry wasteland. I have engaged some cleaners to rectify matters. They will be here in thirty minutes so I advise you to get busy."

Beauty and Delicious protested vigorously. Dominil was unmoved.

"You now have twenty-nine minutes. I estimate that the cleansing of this house will take most of the day but we can use the time well. You can take me to the venues in which you wish to play."

"But it's raining outside."

"You are werewolves of the MacRinnalch Clan. Nieces of the late Thane. You can stand a little rain. It's necessary for you to show me these places in order that I may procure gigs for you."

"Gigs? Aren't you going a bit fast here?"

"No," said Dominil. "You assure me that you are fine musicians. Tomorrow you will be rehearsing with other musicians with whom you are already familiar. I have been reading about the bands you told me you admire, and it seems to be a common thread that they did not rehearse for an overly long time before placing their music before the public. To do so, I understand, can lead to a certain staleness, which is to be avoided. John Lydon was particularly insistent on this point. Now you really must make ready for the cleaners."

86

Many werewolves and men now hunted for the lonely werewolf girl. Sarapen wanted her dead and sent the cunning and far-sighted Decembrius to London to find her. Markus, feeling that it would be good to know where Kalix was, dispatched his trusted lieutenant Gregor to search for her, though he did not tell his mother that he'd done this. Meanwhile the Avenaris Guild redoubled their efforts. Mr Carmichael made it his highest priority. He was determined that his organisation should not be beaten to the task by Mr Mikulanec. Mikulanec himself prowled the streets, the Begravar knife in his pocket. So far Kalix had eluded him, but the knife would tell him when she was close. Mikulanec had a strong suspicion that the werewolf girl was now hidden from the world in some way with which he was not familiar. Nonetheless, he remained confident. The knife would not let him down.

Against these enemies Kalix had only Thrix to protect her, and Thrix was an unwilling guardian. Today Kalix's anxiety was less but she was still very suspicious of Daniel and Moonglow. After passing out at the doorway she'd found herself back in front of the fire, wrapped in her quilt. Now Kalix was wondering what these humans wanted from her. It was very strange the way they kept wrapping her in a quilt and giving her a hot water bottle. Various ideas of what might be behind it flitted through her mind. They might be being paid by her mother to watch her till she was brought back to the castle. They might be in the employ of one of her hated brothers. What if they were being paid by the Guild to lull her into a false sense of security before handing her over to be killed?

Kalix examined and rejected all these ideas but couldn't help feeling it was a bad idea to remain here. But she was warm and comfortable and though she cursed herself for her weakness she just couldn't bring herself to leave again right away. She'd taken too much laudanum for one thing, gorging herself on the new bottle, and her senses were very dull. She felt a shadow fall across her and looked up to find Daniel standing over her with a mug in his hand.

"Do you want tea?"

Kalix shook her head.

"How are you feeling?"

Kalix refused to answer. She had already given these humans too much information. Daniel put the tea down and sat beside her. He asked her if she'd like to hear some music. She shook her head.

"Is there anything we can do to make you feel better? Do you want another pillow?"

Kalix regarded him suspiciously. She wondered if he might be trying to have sex with her. She'd experienced offers of hospitality from men on these terms before. She made ready to fight him off.

Daniel was unaware of Kalix's suspicions. Last night she had been far more friendly, and he didn't realise that Kalix's moods could oscillate so wildly in a short space of time. So he spoke to her as if nothing was wrong, apart from her again being ill.

"Me and Moonglow will clear out the small room tonight and then you can move in there. I've got a little CD player you can have. We don't have a spare TV unfortunately but maybe we could find one. Are you sure you don't want this tea?"

Kalix raised herself on one elbow and looked him directly in the eye.

"Why do you keep trying to help me?" she demanded.

Daniel was surprised. It seemed like a difficult question to answer.

"I don't know," he said, and shrugged. "Just because we like you, I suppose."

"Is someone paying you?"

This made Daniel laugh.

"Of course not. Who would pay us?"

Kalix looked unhappy. Daniel fell silent. Given the amount they'd done to help her, he might have been justified in thinking that this was a very ungrateful werewolf. Daniel didn't really think this. There was something so pathetic about the skinny girl that he couldn't help wanting to assist her.

"Are you going to stay with us now?" he asked.

"No," said Kalix.

"Oh. That's a pity. I was hoping you might help me persuade Moonglow to get cable TV."

"What?"

"Moonglow is a fine woman in almost every way, but she does have this irrational dislike of television. It's criminal the way she refused that gift from her mother. If you stay around we might be able to work on her, you know, gang up till she gives in." Daniel smiled. "So really, I need you here."

Kalix was quite surprised at the thought of helping someone. It was

202

a long time since she'd done that.

"I'm not staying," said Kalix.

"All right," said Daniel. "We'll miss you."

"No you won't."

"You're right, we won't. After all, who wants a nasty clumsy were-wolf cluttering up the place, particularly one who likes really bad music like the Runaways?"

Kalix's eyes widened.

"The Runaways are not – "

She stopped. She realised that Daniel was joking. It was such a strange feeling to have someone joking with her. She couldn't remember when that had last happened. Despite herself, she smiled, then tried to erase it quickly so Daniel didn't see.

"I'm leaving right away," she said, but made no attempt to get up.

87

Verasa, Markus, Rainal and several trusted advisors sat in the outer room of Verasa's chambers. It was the room she used for her private conferences and in homage to this there was a painting on the wall by Velasquez of two ambassadors. This was one of the finest pictures by Velasquez in private hands, and did not appear in any of the standard lists of the painter's works.

"I did not expect Sarapen to do this. Not so suddenly anyway," admitted Verasa.

"It seems that Sarapen didn't even attempt to negotiate with Baron MacAllister before removing him," said Rainal.

According to the MacAllister Clan, their Baron had tragically lost his life after accidentally falling from the highest part of the east wall of his keep. The Baron had been on his own at the time, in human form, and had been killed instantly. The Baron's eldest son had now sorrowfully acceded to the leadership of his clan.

No one in Castle MacRinnalch believed this story for a minute. The old Baron had obviously been murdered, probably by agents of Sarapen.

"The Baron's son will now join the Great Council," said Rainal.

"But surely he won't vote for Sarapen? A werewolf who just killed his father?"

Verasa made a genteel noise of derision.

"Rainal, you're being naive. The Baron's son was in on the assassination."

"How can you know that?"

"Because the MacAllister keep is a strong place with high walls. Sarapen's werewolves couldn't have entered without help from the inside. It's obvious that young MacAllister decided his best interests lie in siding with Sarapen."

Each werewolf had a decanter of whisky before them. Verasa sipped hers slowly as her advisors considered her words. There was an air of shock around the castle as the werewolves realised that war had now begun.

"Sarapen is trying to bring matters to an end quickly," said Markus. "He gains the vote of the new Baron by this action and is hoping it will intimidate others."

"He doesn't need much more intimidation," pointed out Rainal. "If the new Baron votes for him, Sarapen will have seven votes. If Sarapen kills Kalix then Dulupina will give him her vote. And Kalix's death will open the way for Decembrius which will give him the required tally of nine."

Consternation showed on the faces of Verasa's advisors. All Sarapen had to do was remove Kalix and the Thaneship was his. They did not relish the thought, not after they had thrown in their lot with Markus. Everyone looked to Verasa for guidance.

"I've provided Kalix with protection. And I've taken other measures. Don't forget, Kalix is not the only werewolf whose vote is still unsecured."

"Are you referring to Butix and Delix?" asked Rainal. "I must say it seems very unlikely to me that we'll ever see them at the castle again."

"It seems likely to me that we shall," countered Verasa.

"I had six votes at the last meeting," said Markus. "If you could somehow succeed in bringing the twins that would give me eight. Which means…"

Markus paused.

"Which mean what?" said Verasa.

"Which means that if we ourselves were to deal with Kalix,

Dulupina would add her vote to these eight, giving me the Thaneship."

Verasa took Markus's suggestion calmly though in truth she was not at all pleased.

"It will not be necessary for us to assassinate my youngest daughter."

"I didn't say we should," protested Markus. "Dulupina may be satisfied if she were merely returned and incarcerated."

"I doubt that very much," said Verasa. "Dulupina is set in her ways. Leave the gaining of votes to me, Markus. Don't forget, there are others in the castle on whom we may bring pressure to bear."

"Kurian and his brood? Nothing will persuade them to change their minds."

"Who knows what may happen to change their minds?" said the Mistress of the Werewolves.

Later that night Verasa received a second piece of bad news. Beneath the south tower of the castle was a vault in which the clan kept various private relics. One of these was the banner the MacRinnalchs had carried into battle at Bannockburn. The clan believed that this was the only remaining standard which had been present in 1314, when Robert the Bruce, King of Scotland, defeated Edward I of England. Another precious relic was the axe belonging to MacDoig MacRinnalch, who had fought a pitched battle with Danish Vikings in 1172, and driven them from the family lands. The Vikings had come to rule much of the surrounding country but had never ruled over the werewolves.

Also in the vault was the Begravar knife, brought back by the werewolf knight Gerrant Gawain MacRinnalch, after he had travelled overseas with the Black Douglas. When Douglas died in Jerusalem, Gerrant MacRinnalch travelled on to the far off lands of the biblical Mesopotamia, where the ancient cities of Sumeria had emerged on the plains more than four thousand years ago. There, Gerrant had come across the Begravar knife, taking it from a Persian Knight who had a reputation as a killer of shape changers. No one knew what the shape changers of ancient Sumeria had been like, but the MacRinnalchs believed they had been in some ways similar to themselves, and may even have been their ancestors. Certainly the Begravar knife was as effective against werewolves as it had been against any ancient shape changer. It was virtually impossible to kill a werewolf with a normal blade, but a cut from the Begravar knife was fatal. Whoever made the knife had given it properties that had kept it sharp and deadly through-out all its long history.

It was no longer in the vault. Verasa was astonished. No one could enter the vault but her. She had the only set of keys. For a while she simply could not believe that it had disappeared, and looked round the small stone chamber as if it might somehow have been mislaid. It was not there. Someone had taken it. She checked the lock. It was undam-aged. If anyone had entered it could only have been with a duplicate key. Verasa wore the key on a chain which she kept round her neck and no one could have taken it without her noticing. The Mistress of the Werewolves was baffled. Her suspicions fell on Sarapen, and she was troubled at the thought of him now having the Begravar knife.

88

Thrix picked up the latest copy of Elle from the reception desk and flicked it open in the lift up to her floor. When she arrived at work she had been feeling rather depressed. By the time the elevator doors were sliding open she was in a rage.

"Ann!" she yelled. "My office!"

Ann hurried after her. Thrix threw the magazine down on the desk and let out a growl that could not have come from a human throat. She pointed to a page in the magazine, a photo of a young model wearing a pretty and elegant white summer dress.

"I designed that!" yelled Thrix. "And I haven't shown it yet! It was meant to be new for the show in Milan. Someone's stolen my work!"

Thrix paced around her desk, extremely agitated, and then she did something which startled Ann. It would have startled anyone, even a member of the MacRinnalch Clan. She transformed into a werewolf, though it was daylight outside. Thrix threw back her head and howled in fury. Ann rushed to lock the door. No one else knew that Thrix was a werewolf and it seemed unwise to advertise it to the world. The Enchantress growled a few more times then transformed back into human form.

"I didn't know you could do that in daylight," said Ann.

"Sorry if I startled you."

Ann shrugged. Having learned about a year ago that she was working for a werewolf, a werewolf with magical powers at that, she was beyond being much surprised at anything. Which was just as well, for at that moment Malveria materialised in the room.

"Did I hear you call?" she asked, sweetly, before noticing there was something strange about Thrix's aura.

"You have been a werewolf? In daylight? My goodness Thrix, this is very exceptional anger. Has another of your models been taken to the substance abuse clinic?"

"No."

"Ah," Malveria nodded sagely. "Still upset over the romantic dinner which went so sadly wrong."

"The dinner went wrong?" said Ann.

"Terribly wrong," replied the Fire Queen. "Poor Thrix was quite desolate when her man abandoned her at the earliest opportunity."

"He abandoned you?" said Ann.

"He did not abandon me! I asked for a cab home."

"Really, it is too bad," said Malveria. "But perhaps this Donald was not the right man. You know the Enchantress is very hard to please. I have searched my realm for a suitable – "

"Could we get back to the topic in hand here!" demanded Thrix, loudly. "I did not howl as a werewolf because my date went disast… eh… not that well. I'm annoyed because my designs have been stolen!"

"Ah," said the Fire Queen. "Now I understand. Of course, when it is Malveria who is suffering such cruel indignities there is no great crisis but now it happens to you, you begin to see the full horror of the sufferings."

"When I find out who's responsible I'll make them suffer!" cried Thrix.

Ann, who had kept a calmer head in the midst of the crisis, picked up the magazine.

"But isn't this a step forward?"

"What? How?"

"Well, before we only knew of the espionage because the Fire Queen was turning up at events and finding that her clothes were already there. But now we have a picture of one of our outfits in a magazine. So now we should know who's behind the whole thing."

"Of course," cried Thrix, grabbing the magazine. "I was too upset by the picture to even read the caption. Who's the designer?"

She scanned the page, then frowned deeply.

"It would be."

The dress had been designed, or so the magazine claimed, by Alan Zatek. Zatek, whose house occupied a place in the fashion world not dissimilar to Thrix Fashions, was one of her main rivals.

"Alan Zatek will be showing his new collection in Milan next season," read the Enchantress. "Will he now? Not if I blast him off the face of the earth, he won't."

"He very much deserves to be blasted," agreed the Fire Queen. "Not least because when I wore a pair of trousers designed by him my hips looked bulky, for which I will never forgive him. But consider. Should we not make more investigations before we take action against him?"

Thrix could see no reason not to hurry over to Alan Zatek's fashion house and launch an attack but Malveria, more used to the art of war, urged caution.

"It does not do to fly at your enemy before you have a clear idea of his strength. This Alan Zatek is most obviously not a standard human designer. If he were, he would not be sending clothes to the vile Princess Kabachetka. He must be a man with connections to the other realms. Perhaps he does not realise your power, and doesn't know the risks he takes. But it is also possible that he does. He may be aware of all your sorcery, and all your werewolfness, and still believe he has enough strength to defeat you. There are other sorcerers in this world, some of them not to be taken lightly."

After this speech by Malveria, Thrix nodded her head.

"You're right Malveria. Leaping in blindly would be foolish. I should find out more about Zatek."

"And we still don't know who the spy is in our own office," said Ann. "Except it's not me."

"It better not be," said Thrix. "I rely on you too much to lose you. Malveria, have you learned anything in your realm?"

"I have indeed. Due to her monstrous appetites Princess Kabachetka has put on several pounds in the past month and is obliged to have her clothes secretly adjusted."

"Malveria!"

"That is not all. The adjuster of the clothes is an elemental tailor of some skill who has on occasion visited my palace. Of course, this has been to tighten clothes after I lost weight following my exercise programme last winter when I astonished my thousands of devotees by turning up for the solstice sacrifice looking even more fabulously slender than before. The daughter of my ambassador to the Empress Asaratanti has learned from this tailor that the Princess has recently been transporting clothes between the dimensions by way of a large man who wears a strange and unappealing hat. This man is known as the Merchant and has a talisman which allows him to contact our realms."

Thrix was listening intently.

"The Merchant? MacDoig!"

"You know him?"

"I do. He's a dealer in the sort of goods you can't get anywhere else. This is interesting news Malveria. Though it still doesn't tell us who the spy is."

Thrix and Ann had gone through every employees personnel file without coming across anything suspicious. Really, they had not much idea what they might be looking for. Ann had suggested bringing in an investigator but Thrix was reluctant to have any human detective closely examining her business.

"Are there no werewolf detectives?" enquired Malveria.

"No. Well yes, actually. There is a MacRinnalch who dabbles in investigation I believe, but that would be too close to my family. I don't want my mother finding out any more of my private business.

"I have a suggestion," said the Fire Queen. "Permit me to take a stealthy look at Zatek's offices. Perhaps there I will find a clue to the culprit."

The Enchantress thought that was a good idea. There was little chance of so strong a being as the Fire Queen coming to any harm, no matter what secret power Alan Zatek may have.

Ann went off to bring them both coffee. Thrix looked questioningly at Malveria.

"When did you buy a pair of trousers made by Zatek?"

"Years ago. Do not be insulted. It was before I met you, and they were of a very inferior cut. I gave them away to one of my ladies-in-waiting who was equipped with more robust hips than I. Incidentally, could you provide me with several pots of slime green nail varnish?"

Thrix was alarmed. Slime green was a particularly virulent shade. Having succeeded in getting Malveria into elegant attire and make-up, she feared that the Fire Queen may be slipping back into her old ways.

"Do not worry," said Malveria, sensing Thrix's thoughts. "It is not for me, it's for Agrivex. My young almost-adopted niece has spent five days sulking in her room and I have finally learned that this is because she hates all her nail varnish. And while I am determined not to give in to all of young Vex's whims and fancies, I must admit I am again impressed by her spirit. Five days is a long time to sulk in one's room, and perhaps deserves new nail varnish."

The Fire Queen looked at her own nails and frowned.

"I'll make you an appointment," said the Enchantress. "And I'll ask Ann to bring us some slime green for Agrivex."

"Would seventeen be a normal age for intense sulking?" asked the Fire Queen.

"Possibly. Depends on the seventeen year old. I take it Agrivex is not full of serious thoughts?"

Malveria shook her head.

"No serious thought has ever approached her. She is a..." Malveria struggled to find the right word.

"An airhead?" suggested Thrix.

"Exactly!" The Fire Queen was pleased. "That is the perfect expression. Her head is full of air. But this is not so bad. While she will plague me to death for nail varnish and clothes, she will never desire to usurp the throne. Relatives are so bad at that, Enchantress. Sometimes I wonder why we ever have relatives in the first place."

"I sometimes wonder that too," agreed the Enchantress.

89

Neither Gregor nor Decembrius, agents of Markus and Sarapen, had so far found any trace of Kalix. Decembrius however, had powers of finding which went beyond the normal acute senses of a werewolf. While crossing the city he became aware of Dominil's presence. He located her, trailed her discreetly to the twins' house, then reported this to Sarapen.

Thrix finally made the effort to visit her young sister. Short of time, and with other matters to occupy her, Thrix made the journey unwillingly. Kalix was in the flat on her own when the Enchantress arrived.

Both were unsmiling as they faced each other on the stairs. Thrix noticed that Kalix was looking a good deal better than the last time she'd seen her. She was clean. Her hair was washed, something which Thrix could hardly remember having seen since Kalix was a child. She'd forgotten how long and thick it was. She almost complimented Kalix on it, but held back.

"What do you want?" asked Kalix.

"You have your new pendant?"

"Yes," muttered Kalix, looking at the floor.

"You have the Fire Queen to thank more than me. I'm here because our mother wanted me to check on your safety."

Kalix's lip curled.

"Don't look at me like that," said Thrix, sharply. "Without me you wouldn't have made it this far. Really Kalix, you're so ungrateful. Is it any wonder that you've ended up without a friend in the world?"

Kalix didn't reply. She turned on her heel and disappeared up the stairs. Thrix followed her, uninvited. Kalix had retreated into the small room which Daniel and Moonglow had cleared for her. She had a single bed, a CD player, and a lamp. Her bag lay beside the bed. Piled on a chair were some clothes they'd given her from their own wardrobes. Most of these did not fit but next weekend they intended to visit the local charity shops and see what they could find.

Thrix glanced around the small, bare room, undecorated save for three pictures of the Runaways which Moonglow had printed for Kalix. The Enchantress repressed a shudder at the sight of the clothes, student cast-offs which she would rather have died than been forced to wear.

"Well I suppose it's comfortable enough."

"I didn't invite you in," said Kalix. "What do you want?"

"Nothing. But mother wants me to protect you."

"I don't need your protection."

Thrix advanced a pace or two.

"Kalix, believe me, I'd rather not be here. So just listen, and spare me your comments. Have you heard any news of the Great Council?"

Kalix shook her head.

"You know the Thane died?"

Kalix did know. She stared at the wall.

"Have you nothing to say? He was our father, after all."

"I wish he'd died sooner," said Kalix.

It was a shock to hear these words, though Thrix herself couldn't pretend to be full of grief over their father's death. She'd spent the last fifty years trying to avoid him, and hadn't shed a tear at the funeral.

"The Great Council couldn't agree on a new Thane."

"I thought it would be Sarapen."

"So did everyone else except our mother. But he hasn't been elected yet. There was a split between Sarapen and Markus. Mother is backing Markus and you can imagine how Sarapen has taken that. Now he wants to kill you to get your vote."

Kalix appeared unconcerned.

"He always wanted to kill me."

"Well now he really intends to do it. I doubt you'd be interested in all the details of the vote but believe me, Sarapen regards it as vital to his interests that you die, and quickly. So I'm here to warn you. Don't take the pendant off under any circumstances. And stay here, it's the safest place for you."

"I'm going to leave when I feel better," said Kalix, defiantly.

"Kalix you're a fool. I've no time for your petulance. God knows why these humans want to look after you but it seems they do and you ought to realise when you're well off. If you go wandering off again I'm not going to waste my time running after you."

Thrix stopped. This wasn't going the way she had intended. She hadn't meant to come here and insult Kalix. It was difficult. The girl's sulky, hostile demeanour had always annoyed her. She tried to inject some sisterly concern into her voice.

"Kalix. You really should stay. You're better off here than anywhere else. The pendant will conceal you and I'll add my sorcery to it." Thrix handed Kalix a card. "Here are my phone numbers. Let me know if you need anything."

Thrix sniffed the air.

"Are you still taking laudanum?"

Kalix looked fixedly at the wall.

"It'll kill you."

They were interrupted by the arrival of Daniel and Moonglow who made their way noisily up the stairs and collapsed with exaggerated exhaustion on the couch.

"Poetry of the Renaissance will kill me, I'm sure of it," said Daniel. "Hey, Kalix, are you in?"

Thrix stepped out of Kalix's room. In her immaculate clothes she looked startlingly out of place in their scruffy flat. Daniel and Moon-glow were quite perturbed, given the hostility she'd displayed towards them the last time they met.

"I came to check on my sister," said Thrix, awkwardly. "Thank you for giving her somewhere to live."

The two students looked at her nervously. The Enchantress did not know what to say to make the situation less tense. She was unversed in the ways of students. She could deal with crazy models but when it came to other sorts of teenagers, she was on unsteady ground.

"Do you need anything?"

"Like what?" said Daniel.

"Like a better haircut," retorted Thrix, annoyed at his tone. "Or money for looking after Kalix."

They shook their heads. They could have done with some extra money but they weren't about to accept it from a person whom neither of them liked.

"Fine," said Thrix. "Kalix has my phone number. I'll be in touch."

The Enchantress hurried off. She didn't feel that her visit had been a great success, but at least she'd done what her mother asked. For a while she was free to concentrate on her own life.

90

Gawain boarded a train for London. Paying for his ticket took up quite a large proportion of his money. Gawain's family had never been wealthy and what money there was he judged better to leave for the use of his young sister, a student at St Andrews University. She was his only surviving relative and it was more than a year since he'd seen her. She had her own life to get on with, and prob-ably not much time for an older brother who wandered the land in disgrace.

As he took the money from his wallet he found a scrap of paper. It contained a poem he'd written about Kalix while he was sitting alone on a hillside. He tore the paper into small pieces and dropped them in a bin. It was time to stop writing poems and start making some progress in finding Kalix. It had been weak of him to abandon

213

the quest. When he reached London he intended to visit Thrix, and he would not be put off with her lies again.

Gawain had not seen Kalix for three years. Might she have changed? Somehow, he doubted it. Her hair would be longer and she would still be skinny. Too skinny, as he'd told her. She'd laughed, and told him if he didn't like skinny werewolves he'd better find another werewolf. When he'd first met her she was quiet, and troubled. Later she'd started to laugh a lot. He wondered if she still did. He wondered if she'd met anyone else. This thought was too distressing to dwell on for long.

Deep in his soul Gawain didn't really believe that Kalix would have found anyone else. Surely there was no one else for her but him, just as there was no one else for him but Kalix.

Gawain was the only werewolf on the train but he was not unobserved. When Sarapen learned that he had escaped he'd sent agents to watch the railway stations. Gawain had been spotted quickly and then followed, though not by a werewolf. Gawain would scent any werewolf who tailed him. Sarapen sent a man called Madrigal who had worked for him before, and could be relied on. His mission was to follow Gawain and see if he led them to Kalix.

Gawain was also observed by two werewolf hunters from the Guild, on their way back to London after completing their duties in Scotland. They were immediately suspicious of him. He had the look of a MacRinnalch and there was something in his movements that suggested werewolf to the experienced hunters. They kept a discreet eye on him as the train travelled south. Nothing about their appearance or behaviour gave them away as members of the Guild, but inside each of their briefcases was a gun loaded with silver bullets.

91

Kalix was in an extremely bad mood after Thrix's visit. As Daniel reported to Moonglow, she was sulking in her room and refused to come out.

"She says we must never let Thrix in again because she's an evil witch and if we keep inviting her enemies here then she's going to

214

leave right away. Also, she hates us for not having enough TV channels and she suspects we're deliberately preventing her from watching Sabrina the Teenage Witch, probably because we're too stupid to realise what a great programme it is. Also she loathes the way my hair flops in front of my eyes and she says if you wear any more make-up it's going to make her ill, and maybe you could try wearing something that wasn't black once in a while. Also her bed isn't comfy, the CD player I gave her doesn't work properly and apart from this, she doesn't much like the colour of the walls. Also, she – "

"Please stop," said Moonglow, holding up her hand. "So she's all right, really?"

"Pretty much," said Daniel. "I guess she just finds it hard to cope with her family."

He glanced in the small mirror above the fireplace.

"Is it really nauseous the way my hair flops in front of my eyes?"

"Totally," said Moonglow. "I've often wanted to mention it."

She was relieved that Kalix, despite her long list of complaints, had not decided to pack her bag and leave. Really, the young werewolf was settling down quite well, in a bad-tempered, full-of-complaints sort of way. Moonglow suggested to Daniel that possibly Kalix's continual whining was the best she could do in the way of relating to them.

"I don't think she has much experience of being happy in company. When she gets used to it, things will become easier."

Daniel hoped Moonglow was right. At least Kalix hadn't been violent, and nor had she seemed to suffer another attack of anxiety recently.

"She's seemed calmer since she filled up her bottle," he said. "I wonder what's in it?"

According to Kalix her bottle was full of a herbal drink which werewolves were partial to.

"All MacRinnalchs drink it," said Kalix, but made sure that neither Daniel nor Moonglow ever came near the bottle.

"Are you coming to the party tomorrow?" asked Moonglow.

Daniel shook his head.

"I was going to but now I'm feeling bad about my hair."

"Don't be silly. You have nice hair. When you wash it. Which you will, if Alicia is going to be there.

"I don't care if Alicia is there," replied Daniel. "Is Alicia going to be there?"

"Yes."

"I'm not going to speak to her. She thinks I'm an idiot."

"No she doesn't. She likes you."

"How do you know?" asked Daniel. "Did she say that?"

"Well, no."

"So she said she doesn't like me?"

"No."

"Then how do you expect me to get to know this girl?" said Daniel. "She obviously has no interest in me at all."

Moonglow shook her head. She had decided to make an effort to help Daniel find a girlfriend. It was becoming a little tedious the way he kept sulking when Moonglow went to visit Jay. Sharing a house with a sulking flatmate and a sulking werewolf was hard on a girl. Moonglow could see that Daniel would be attractive to girls if he could only muster a little confidence. And maybe cut down on the music lectures. And not talk about cricket.

Daniel was gloomy at the prospect of going to Moonglow's friend's party. If Alicia was there he could foresee great embarrassment, particularly if Moonglow pressured him into talking to her, as she was threatening to do. Daniel's mood became worse when Jay phoned. He went off to sulk in the kitchen, but finding that Kalix had beaten him to it and was already there, sulking furiously, he retreated to his room, selected the noisiest CD he could find, and put it on.

92

Sitting on her splendid throne, in her fabulous throne room, in her enormous palace, the Fire Queen was dissatisfied. It was barely lunch time and she had nothing to do.

'It is a matter of regret,' she mused. 'That I am so splendidly competent. Not only did I defeat my enemies so completely that there seems no prospect of war ever breaking out again, I then proceeded to organise my kingdom so efficiently that matters of state now run so smoothly as to never cause me any problems.'

Finding that she did not care to be continually tending to each minor volcano, of which there were many, or take care of distributing gold, blood and sacrifices to her loyal subjects, the Fire Queen had taken care to appoint the best elementals to do these tedious tasks for her. They did this so well that very little ever arose which needed the Queen's attention. Malveria drummed her fingers on her throne. She called for Xakthan, her First Minister. He arrived seconds later, in a flash of blue lightening.

"Has anything happened to disturb my realm?" she enquired.

"No, Mighty Queen," he replied.

"Is there any matter before the courts of justice which requires my judgement?"

"I do not believe so, Mighty Queen."

"Oh." Malveria was disappointed. "Any sign of rebel activity on the borders?"

"The rebels are all dead, Mighty Queen. So superb was your leadership that none remain."

"Just checking," sighed Malveria.

Her First Minister was a very loyal ally. He had been one of her original supporters. Malveria had fine memories of these days. When the old King died and every member of the family scrambled for power, she had been commonly supposed to be the fire elemental with least chance of success. Her mother and several of her brothers had vast armies at their disposal, while Malveria had almost no support. She spent many long years hiding in the terrible wastelands at the edge of the kingdom, evading her pursuers. Yet the Fire Queen, by dint of her skill, intelligence, bravery and indomitable spirit, had led her tiny force from victory to victory, gaining strength each time.

Eventually, having amassed a great army of her own, she defeated the combined forces of her remaining enemies at the Battle of Askalion, an affair of such unparalleled ferocity that it breached the walls of several neighbouring dimensions. After four days of fighting, Malveria, sword in hand, had finally waded through a river of blood to despatch the most terrible of her enemies, her uncle, known as the Dragon of Despair. Malveria had severed his head and thrown it into the great volcano. It was the final triumph. Great celebrations followed, and Malveria had ruled the kingdom ever since.

She sighed. Happy days. She had rewarded her supporters well and her First Minister proved to be worthy of her trust. Malveria had never really cared for the blue flames which occasionally blazed from his left ear – it gave his head such a lopsided look – but he'd proved to be

217

as good an administrator as he had a fighter.

"Is my water here?" she enquired.

"It has been delivered to the Royal Baths," replied Xakthan.

Malveria had the water she bathed in brought to her from outside her kingdom. From outside her dimension, even. When she bathed she added crystals to the water to keep her looking young, crystals treated with sorcery which reacted with the water. It had to be water of the greatest purity from an untainted source, preferably one which had been blessed by a Fairy Queen. These days Malveria's bathing water came from an excellent source: the untainted, magical spring which flowed through Colburn Wood, on the lands of the MacRinnalchs.

"Remind my gatherers that they must take great care. One can imagine the fuss the werewolves will make if they discover I am using their water."

Xakthan nodded, and Malveria dismissed him. She still felt bored. Really, it was too bad. No rebels, no justice to be dispensed and nothing of any real significance in her social calendar till the sorceress Livia's 500th birthday celebration.

Daniel and Moonglow floated into her mind. They were unlike anyone she had encountered before. Really quite cheerful in their way, despite having to make do with no servants and very little in the way of comfort. Not at all like her own human worshippers. Malveria valued her human devotees because they were a source of power for her, but she didn't like them that much. Far too obsequious. You could never trust them for an honest opinion on a dress or a pair of shoes. They occasionally made her feel like returning to the old days of persecuting mankind. But as for Daniel and Moonglow, she rather liked them. They were honest, and hospitable.

The Fire Queen was quite certain that Moonglow would one day fall for Daniel. It would be very entertaining. Moonglow had agreed that she could never have him. Of all the permutations of romantic entanglements there were to be observed in the world, Malveria liked it best when someone was in love with another and knew they couldn't have them. It was the stuff of tragedy and it led to the most interesting things. Rage, madness, death; she had often been very entertained. Malveria smiled. All it needed was for Moonglow to realise she liked Daniel which she surely would if she were to see Daniel with another woman. Then, Malveria knew, jealousy might rear its head. It was one thing for Moonglow to think nothing of Daniel while he was alone. Would she feel quite so sanguine about things if Daniel were involved with another woman?

Malveria could see a problem. Daniel's extreme shyness made the prospect of him ever meeting a girl rather remote.

'While he remains single Moonglow will never fall for him,' she mused. 'What can I do to move things along?'

Really, in terms of the Queen's bargain with Moonglow, it was cheating for Malveria to do anything to move things along. Certainly a breach of the spirit of the agreement. But no one would ever know. She sent for Agrivex, her not-quite-adopted niece.

Vex, a young girl with skin the colour of dark honey, spiky blonde hair, and an inappropriately large pair of boots, appeared minutes later.

"If this is about the broken windows in your private gardens, I had nothing to do with it," said Vex. "Nor the overturned plants and stuff."

"Forget the broken windows and destroyed plants. I have already deducted the money from your allowance."

"Hey! That's not – "

"Silence!" said Malveria, raising her hand. "I have a mission for you."

"A mission?"

Agrivex looked surprised. The Queen had never sent her on a mission before.

"Will it be fun?"

"Whether or not it is fun is of no importance. I want you to – "

"But will it be?" said Vex, eagerly.

Malveria frowned. "Yes, it may be fun. But please attend to my words. You must dress entirely in black and – "

"What, am I going to be sacrificed?" demanded Vex. "This is way too harsh, I mean it was only a few plants and a window. You can't kill a girl for a minor – "

"Will you stop interrupting!" roared Malveria. "One more inappropriate word and I will cut off your clothes allowance for a year! And possibly your head as well. Now pay attention. There is no sacrificing in prospect. The black clothes are by way of a fashion statement. One which seems to be common among the people I am now about to send you among. Even those preposterously clumpy boots of yours will not be inappropriate. You are to attend a party in the human realm, and there you must make the acquaintance of a young man called Daniel."

Gawain arrived at Euston station. As he disembarked from the train he was followed by the two hunters, and by Madrigal, Sarapen's agent. It was five o'clock and already dark. In London the temperature was a few degrees warmer than it had been in Scotland but the early winter evening felt cold after the warmth of the train.

Gawain remembered that Thrix's offices were in the centre of the city. He set off on foot, keen to stretch his legs after the five hour train journey. He walked south, past the buildings of University College, heading for Holborn then turning right towards Oxford Street. The pavements were full as the capital's shops and offices closed for the day and workers headed for the tube stations and congregated at bus stops. Unused to being among such a crowd, Gawain left the main road to make his way to Soho by what he hoped would be a less busy route. The hunters from the Guild followed discretely, looking for a quiet place to confront the werewolf. When they saw him turn off the main road they hurried to the next side street, hoping to overtake him and block his path.

The hunters moved fast. They sprinted round the corner with their guns drawn, ready to attack the werewolf who should now be appearing in front of them. Gawain wasn't there. He was behind them, concealed in a doorway. Though it was dark he had not troubled to change into his werewolf form. Gawain sprang, and smote each hunter on the back of the neck. They crumpled unconscious to the ground. He picked their guns up from the pavement, slipped them in his pocket and hurried off. Really, it had been absurd. Did the hunters think they could take him by surprise so easily? He shook his head. In this city they must not be used to dealing with warriors. Gawain threw the guns in an industrial skip a few blocks away and carried on towards Soho.

When the hunters regained their senses and realised that the werewolf had outmanoeuvred them they wondered why they were still alive. Gawain didn't like to kill unnecessarily. Unlike many of his clan, including Kalix, Gawain would not lightly take a life, even that of a werewolf hunter. Besides, he was in a hurry, and they were not worth wasting time over. Madrigal, a rather better tracker, was more used to the ways of werewolves. He saw what happened, and continued to trail Gawain, unobserved.

At two minutes past three o'clock, at the Huge Sound rehearsal studios, under the arches just south of London Bridge, Dominil stood outside the door, a look of displeasure on her face.

"Where are they?" she growled.

"It's only two minutes past three," Beauty pointed out. "You can't expect people to arrive right on time.

"Why not? We were here at three and I expect others to be punctual."

Beauty and Delicious had only arrived on time due to Dominil dragging them out of bed at some unearthly hour and forcing them to get ready. It was the latest in a number of shocks the sisters had received since agreeing to let the white-haired werewolf help them. The house cleaning had been extremely traumatic. It had taken a long time and resulted in a house that was disconcertingly tidy. There was a funny lemon smell everywhere that didn't seem right. The twins had protested mightily about the whole process but when the cleaners unearthed their favourite demo CD, which had been lost for months, they were obliged to admit that perhaps it wasn't such a bad idea after all.

On the day of the cleaning Beauty and Delicious took Dominil to all the small venues in Camden where they might play. There were many of these. One of them had a poster outside advertising a gig for their rivals, the four boys who lived above a shop. Beauty and Delicious growled with jealousy.

"Do not fret," said Dominil. "You will have the opportunity to outshine them."

The twins sniggered. *Do not fret.* Sometimes they couldn't help laughing at Dominil's choice of words.

Unfortunately, it had not proved easy to procure a gig for the sisters. This was partly because many of the venues booked their bands through agencies, and partly because of the twins' bad reputation.

"The last time they played here," said the manager of one venue. "They set fire to the stage and started a fight with the audience. It was the only time we've ever had to call the police, the fire brigade and an ambulance all in one evening.

"Is this not acceptable behaviour in the world of music?" asked Dominil. "Good publicity perhaps?"

"There are limits. The police nearly closed me down and I had a lot of explaining to do when my license was up for renewal. What's more, someone stole some crates of whisky from my storeroom and I've got a strong suspicion who might have done it."

Beauty and Delicious had by this time departed the scene, to hang around outside looking guilty.

"Can't you give them another chance?" asked Dominil. "After all, they are an excellent band."

"No they aren't. The gig was terrible."

Dominil nodded her head, and walked thoughtfully out of the venue to the street outside.

"You did not inform me that your behaviour had been so abominable you would never be welcomed back."

"It wasn't so bad," protested Beauty. "The guy just doesn't understand our music."

"Did you steal several crates of whisky?"

"We were helping to salvage things from the fire. No point letting it get burned, was there?"

It was a scene that was repeated all over Camden. Even in an area where musicians were not expected to behave all that well, the sisters' incredible debauchery had made them unwelcome everywhere. Several venues would not even let them through the door. Dominil eventually sent them home and retired to a cafe to consider the situation. She was still considering it the next day when she dragged the sisters from their beds and drove them south of the river. The busy streets of London were very different from the quiet roads around Castle MacRinnalch. Dominil had not fully adapted yet and drove carefully, too carefully for the sisters' liking. They sat in the back, and criticised her driving. Dominil ignored them.

At six minutes past three Pete turned up in a car with his friend Adam who was the sisters' last drummer, Simon, their bass player, and Hamil, who played some keyboards and took his computer onstage to trigger their samples. Dominil scowled at them.

"You are six minutes late. I'll overlook your tardiness on this occasion but don't let it happen again."

The boys started to smile, thinking that Dominil was joking. When they noticed her hard black eyes boring into them, and realised she wasn't, they hurried inside. The sisters were already in their rehearsal room, making noise.

"Who is that frozen woman from hell?" Pete asked.

"Our cousin Dominil. She's completely insane. We've really been suffering."

Pete, Adam, Simon and Hamil could believe it. Who made a fuss about being six minutes late?

"You wouldn't believe how evil she is," said Beauty.

"So why are you working with her?" asked Pete. "Is she some sort of music biz person? Does she have good contacts?"

"No," said Delicious. "But she gets things done."

It was true. Here they all were, ready to rehearse, only days after Dominil had arrived. It was quite an achievement.

"You know we're not going to be able to play anywhere?" said Simon. He himself was still unwelcome in several establishments due to his association with the twins.

Beauty shrugged her shoulders.

"Dominil will sort something out."

95

Though Markus was worried about leaving his mother at the castle, Verasa still would not countenance the thought that she might be in danger.

"Sarapen will not return to Castle MacRinnalch. Anyway, I'm very well protected by my retinue, Markus. You should go to London."

"Why? You've already sent some werewolves down there to keep an eye on things."

"None of them know the city as well as you, dear. And there's Thrix, Dominil, Kalix and the twins to look out for, and who knows what Sarapen might attempt next? And don't you want to make sure Talixia is safe?"

"Surely you don't think she's in danger?" said Markus, alarmed.

"Not really. But she is associated with you. Perhaps it would be as well to be with her for a few days. Unless she cares to visit us at the castle?"

Markus explained that Talixia couldn't leave London just now as she was engaged on a photo shoot.

223

"It's going to be awkward for her to be the bride of the Thane if this carries on, Markus."

Markus frowned. He was very keen on Talixia but he hadn't been thinking of asking her to marry him yet. Verasa didn't press the point. About forty years ago the Mistress of the Werewolves had realised that the world she had grown up in had gone forever. A profound change had taken place in the country's manners. Affluence had arrived along with technology. Werewolves, like people, no longer expected to live in the same way their parents had. She could no longer expect her children to settle down quickly with the first suitable werewolf their parents approved of. The young werewolves today, like humans, were free in a way they had never been before. Verasa, who remembered back to the days before motor transport, before telephones, before electricity even, regretted much of what was lost in the old world. Never again would a werewolf set out on horseback from the port at Leith to bring news from abroad to Castle MacRinnalch. And never again, thought Verasa, would a writer like Samuel Johnson arise in the world. Or if he did, few people would notice. Verasa had met the great Doctor Johnson when she was eighteen, when Johnson, with his friend Boswell, had travelled through Scotland. They had been guests of the old Thane at Castle MacRinnalch. The Mistress of the Werewolves still remembered with pleasure the power and wit of the Doctor's conversation at the dinner table.

Verasa adapted to the modern world as she always did. If Markus needed to run through twenty or so girlfriends before settling down with a bride, so be it.

Though he was worried about leaving his mother, Markus was looking forward to seeing Talixia. 'Perhaps mother is right. Maybe I should marry her.' It was a novel thought. He called to let her know he'd be in London later today. Talixia was pleased. She told him that her work had been going well.

"But I'm worried."

"Worried? Why?"

"I think someone might have been in my flat."

Markus was instantly alarmed.

"Why? Was there a burglary?"

"I can't see any sign of a break-in," Talixia told him. "But my clothes have been disturbed. I had a red dress in the wardrobe and it was moved. Other things as well."

Markus frowned. And then he shrugged. He supposed that it would be as good a time as any to have Talixia tell him she never wanted to see him again.

"I moved them," admitted Markus.

"What?"

"I moved them. I thought I put them all back in the right places but obviously I didn't."

Talixia was puzzled.

"Why were you moving my clothes?"

"I was trying them on," said Markus.

"What?"

There was a long pause.

"Is that something you generally do?" said Talixia, eventually.

"Yes."

"You should have mentioned it to me before," she said.

"Do you still want me to come down?"

"Of course I still want you to come down," said Talixia.

96

The two American werewolves walking through Trafalgar Square were enjoying the last few days of their vacation. The werewolves, husband and wife, had spent the last week travelling round Scotland where they'd seen numerous places of interest to any member of the MacRinnalch Clan. Among these was the harbour at Greenock where Roy MacRinnalch, one of their grandfathers, had set off for America on a sailing ship in 1868. They'd been particularly pleased to visit Castle MacRinnalch, home to so much of their heritage. The election of a new Thane had not gone as smoothly as expected but still, it was fine to see the traditional estates of the clan; the mountains to the north, the great stretches of moorlands to the south, and Colburn Wood, rich with MacRinnalch history.

After completing their tour of Scottish sites they'd flown south to complete their vacation in London. Here they'd visited the Tower where William James MacRinnalch had been imprisoned after the suppression of the Scottish rebellion of 1745. William MacRinnalch had fortunately not been held in prison for long, and his werewolf identity had not been discovered. The MacRinnalchs had not been enthusiastic supporters of Bonnie Prince Charlie, deeming his rebellion to have little chance of success. William's involvement had been very minor, but he'd written a poem about his time in the tower of London which was still well known in the clan.

From Trafalgar Square they walked along the Strand to Waterloo Bridge then turned south. Between Waterloo Brigade and the South Bank Centre there were a series of underground passages, slightly confusing for visitors. They stopped to study the signs.

"I think we have to go through this tunnel and – "

The werewolf stopped, and looked troubled.

"What's the matter?" said his wife.

"Just felt funny for a moment, it's – "

He stopped again, and this time his wife did not speak, because she too was feeling strange. As if the world around her was muffled somehow. She shook her head, trying to clear it. It was the last thing she ever did. Mr Mikulanec stepped out up behind them and slashed down with his Begravar knife, cutting the back of her shoulder. Though it was a deep wound it should not have been fatal for a werewolf, but she fell down dead on the spot. Her husband tried to defend himself but his actions were unnaturally slow. Something was making it difficult to move. The last thing he saw was Mr Mikulanec's knife heading for his chest then he too fell down dead.

Mr Mikulanec turned on his heel and disappeared up the next flight of stairs. Two werewolves located, and two werewolves killed. He was satisfied. He'd come across them by chance while prowling the streets looking for Kalix. Though there was nothing in their appearance to give them away as werewolves, the knife had told him. In the presence of a werewolf it would hum and vibrate. Then the power in the knife would confuse their senses, and the unnatural blade would kill them.

Mr Mikulanec reported his success to the Guild, and continued to hunt for Kalix.

97

Kalix declined Moonglow's invitation to the party. She didn't feel she could cope with mingling with so many people. Kalix was feeling unwell again. After the full moon she'd stopped eating and had suffered from some attacks of anxiety. Not as serious as those which had driven her in terror out onto the streets, but unpleasant enough. She suppressed them with diazepam and laudanum, and fell into a semi-stupor in which she dreamed about Gawain. Around midnight, as the laudanum wore off, she felt slightly more active. Daniel had showed her how to programme the small CD player. Kalix could quickly pick up anything she was taught, and now knew how to set the machine to play her favourites tracks over and over again. Moonglow and Daniel had burned a CD of her favourite songs. She put it on, then lay on her small bed and stared at the ceiling.

She tried to work out how she was feeling. Better, she thought. After eight days in this house she was already used to being warm and clean, which she liked. It still felt strange to be living with humans but her suspicions of them were lessening, though they hadn't disappeared. Kalix still found it difficult to believe that anyone would help her without some ulterior motive.

She thought about Gawain and became unhappy. She knew she would never see him again. So no matter what happened, there would be no point to her life. She took out her journal and wrote this down. *There is no point to my life.* When she put her journal back in her bag she noticed her knife and wondered if she should cut herself. She usually did this when she thought there was no point to her life. She considered it for a while, as the Runaways and Transvision Vamp played endlessly on. Finally deciding that it would be a good idea, she took out the knife and made a long cut on her arm and watched it bleed.

Kalix heard the front door open. It was Moonglow, who came up the stairs very noisily.

"Kalix? Are you there?"

Kalix thrust her arm quickly under her quilt as Moonglow entered her room.

"Guess what happened at the party?"

Moonglow was clearly suffering, or enjoying, the effects of alcohol. Kalix was surprised. Moonglow sat down on the edge of the bed.

"A really beautiful girl picked Daniel up!"

"What do you mean?"

"I mean this beautiful girl that nobody knew just walked up to Daniel and asked him to dance! She was so pretty. She had a sort of foreign accent. And she had on this green make-up which was quite strange but she was really beautiful. She wouldn't let Daniel go, she practically dragged him onto the dance floor and then into the kitchen to get drinks and everybody was like, well, amazed, because you know, it was Daniel, and here was this girl throwing herself at him."

Kalix was surprised to find Moonglow on the side of her bed, gossiping. It wasn't something she was used to.

"So I just left them to it," enthused Moonglow. "I got a taxi back myself, I didn't even ask Daniel if he wanted to leave because obviously he wouldn't want some other girl butting in when he was onto a good thing. What's that stain?"

Moonglow stared in alarm at Kalix's quilt which was turning red.

"Nothing," said Kalix, quickly.

"What is it?" demanded Moonglow. She reached to pull down the quilt. Kalix moved swiftly to prevent her. She growled. Moonglow looked Kalix straight in the eye.

"Let me see," she demanded.

Kalix scowled, but let go of Moonglow's hand. Moonglow drew back the quilt. Blood was seeping out of the long cut in Kalix's arm.

"Did you do that?" asked Moonglow.

"Yes," said Kalix, defiantly. "So what?"

Moonglow sighed.

"You really shouldn't," she said. And then, trying not to make too much of it, she suggested to Kalix that they go to the bathroom and treat the wound.

98

Malveria drifted ethereally on the fringes of the world. She floated over the rooftops of London, not quite fully merged with the human dimension. When she found Alan Zatek's offices in Constitution Street, not too far from Thrix's own headquarters, she sank through the roof, materialising silently in an upstairs storeroom. She had masked herself very carefully by sorcery, and could not be observed. The security cameras in the corridors would not see her as she passed. Malveria was searching for Zatek's private office. Once there she would examine his files. And possibly his computer, although this might be a problem. Malveria would not be able to search on a computer. However, if there were discs she could steal them and let the Enchantress examine them. She paused. There were voices coming from a room nearby.

"You were born to wear this dress."

Someone was discussing clothes. Malveria boosted the power of her masking spells and slipped inside.

'I am the Mistress of Stealth,' she thought, with satisfaction. As soon as she entered the room Malveria came to an abrupt halt. Princess Kabachetka was there, talking to a small man with a shaved head who wore a black T-shirt and an earring in each ear. Forgetting that she was meant to be the mistress of stealth, the Fire Queen immediately cast off her spells of concealment.

"Aha!" she cried. "So here you are, you disgraceful fashion thief. I have caught you red handed in the act of piracy!"

"Malveria!" exclaimed the Princess, very surprised. "What are you doing here?"

Kabachetka looked like she had just stepped off the cover of Vogue. She was beautifully dressed, beautifully made up, and pencil thin, all of which increased Malveria's irritation. The Fire Queen eyed her with loathing.

"Have you had liposuction?"

"Certainly not! The Princess Kabachetka does not need to resort to such procedures. I repeat, what are you going here?"

"I am confronting you about the disgraceful thefts of my fashion you have been carrying out."

Queen Malveria pointed at Alan Zatek and there were flames flickering around her fingers.

"You cannot deny that you have been stealing designs from Thrix and giving them to this... this..." Malveria struggled to find words that were bad enough to describe Princess Kabachetka.

The Princess turned to Zatek and spoke apologetically.

"You must excuse the Queen. She has been upset since I began eclipsing her on the social calendar."

"Eclipsing me? The day you eclipse me will be the day the moon

229

runs backwards!"

Princess Kabachetka was a fire elemental, like Malveria, though from a different race, the Hainusta. Her hair was golden blonde, which made her the only blonde in her kingdom. Malveria knew that she went every week to have her roots dyed, to which she could make no objection, but the Princess then blatantly misled her followers into believing it was natural.

"Admit it, you have been stealing clothes that were intended for me!"

"Kabachetka does not require clothes that were made for you," sniffed the Princess. "One hardly imagines that they would fit at all well, given the Queen's generous proportions."

"You dare call my proportions generous? Compared to you I am the slender willow beside the over-stuffed dragon. And I would not be at all surprised to find traces of rhinoplasty around your nose were I to examine it with a spell."

"You will leave my nose alone!"

Princess Kabachetka, who was not short of power herself, stepped forward to confront Malveria and an ugly scene seemed inevitable till Alan Zatek held his hands up and screeched in a loud voice.

"Please! Stop this! How can I be expected to work in these conditions?"

Queen Malveria and Princess Kabachetka drew back, abashed. It was, after all, very bad form to cause a scene in front of a fashion designer. They were notoriously delicate. Even a designer like Alan Zatek, an enemy, should not be upset unnecessarily. If word got round, Malveria might find herself missing from the guest list at several important fashion shows.

"Perhaps there has been some misunderstanding?" said the designer.

"There is no misunderstanding," replied Malveria. "This so-called Princess has been stealing my fashions and I strongly suspect that you have been copying them from Thrix."

"From Thrix? Thrix Fashions?" Zatek laughed. "Please. Why would I need to do that?"

"Because this slut will stoop to any depths to get the better of me."

"I've never stolen a design from you," stated Kabachetka, emphatically. "They would be quite unsuitable for my slender frame."

"You dare to once more imply that I am overweight, you daughter

230

of a troll? You wish you were as slender as Malveria!"

"Please. Do not try to pretend you are not at this moment using several powerful spells to hide the rest of your bulk in another dimension."

Malveria realised that her mission was a failure. She had meant to carry out her reconnaissance in secret and instead had ended up trading insults with her enemy.

"Well, Kabachetka. We shall see who is the best dressed at the Sorceress Livia's 500th birthday celebration!"

"We shall indeed," retorted Kabachetka. "And it will be me."

"It will be me," said Malveria, and dematerialised before the Princess could reply.

The Fire Queen flew back to her own dimension in an exceedingly bad temper. To have actually met the Princess while she tried on clothes was unbearable. And she had called her fat! Malveria would have her revenge. As soon as she entered her throne room her First Minister Xakthan hurried in.

"Mighty Queen, I've been awaiting your return. Today there has been a most interesting development in the courts of justice. A case of such complexity has arisen that it will take all of your great wisdom to resolve the matter. It seems that – "

"What is this?" yelled the Fire Queen. "You expect me to trouble myself with petty matters of justice? Do I not have people to do these things for me?"

"Well yes, Mighty Queen, but I thought you would be eager to – "

"Enough!" roared Malveria. "Do not waste my time with these trivial affairs. Sort it out yourself! That's what I pay you for. And have you ever considered doing something about the flames which emerge from one ear? Do you have any idea how strange it is? The lack of symmetry is quite appalling."

The First Minister looked abashed.

"I am sorry, mighty Queen, I did not realise…"

"Go," snapped Malveria, waving her hand. "And when you have gone, send me Agrivex."

Shortly afterwards Vex appeared in the throne room.

"Hi," said Vex.

"Hi?" said the Fire Queen. "Is that how you greet me? The ruler of this realm and your benefactor?"

"Sorry Aunt Malvie."

"Do not refer to me as *Aunt Malvie,* miserable niece! It is high time you learned some respect for your Queen."

Vex, seeing that Malveria was angry, began the appropriate bowing and curtseying.

"Will you please stop that?" said Malveria, crossly. "You look ridiculous. What happened at the human's party?"

Vex looked apologetic.

"It didn't go that well."

"Not that well? What do you mean, not that well?"

"I met Daniel and did as you instructed, you know, threw myself at him basically, but well, it just didn't work."

The Fire Queen frowned ominously.

"Explain yourself, dismal niece. Why did it not work?"

"I tried my best," said Vex, defiantly. "I did everything you instructed. I was fitting in really well at the party – have you noticed the humans have sparkly nail varnish? – how come we don't have that?"

"It is rather attractive, isn't it?" agreed Malveria. "Sadly, my fashion advisor maintains – stop diverting me with your nonsense, girl. Continue with your sorry tale of failure."

"Well everything seemed to be going fine. I asked Daniel to dance – which he was very bad at – and then, following your instructions closely, I steered him towards the kitchen, poured drinks and prepared to listen to his conversation. But this wasn't so easy. He's not great at conversation. Have you ever had an awkward silence? It was a new experience for me. I mean, what is there to be silent about? Anyway, finally he began to speak about music and this was better. I nodded occasionally, and smiled. And what more can a girl do? Once you've got a boy on his favourite topic and you're nodding and smiling you should be home and dry. That's what it says in Cosmo Junior anyway, and if you can't trust Cosmo Junior I don't know what to think."

Vex paused, and looked troubled.

"I thought it was in the bag. Any moment now he asks me home and it's mission successful and Aunt Malvie buys me new boots. You remember you promised me new boots, right? Anyway, he still seemed hesitant so I said I'd never met any boy I liked so much as Daniel and then I told him how good looking he was. Then I looked into his eyes and asked him if he knew anywhere I could spend the night."

"And what happened?" demanded Malveria.

232

"He ran away."

"What do you mean, *ran away?*"

Agrivex looked puzzled. If her aunt didn't know what *ran away* meant, it was difficult to know where to start.

"Well, you know, like walking, but much faster, in the opposite direction – "

"Silence, imbecile!" roared Malveria. "I do not need an explanation!"

The Fire Queen frowned, very deeply.

"You'd didn't go to the party with vivid orange skin, did you?"

Agrivex shook her head.

"Absolutely not. I was my normal alluring honey colour. He's just a hopeless case."

Malveria was bewildered. She couldn't understand it. Of course Vex was not an accomplished seductress, but for a young man like Daniel, an accomplished seductress would have been quite unsuitable. Someone young and bright was what was required. Agrivex should have been ideal.

Vex smiled brightly at the Fire Queen. She had a lovely smile. Her spiky blonde hair gave her a boyish look.

"So can I have my new boots now? I saw this fabulous pair at the party. Sort of clumpy but with these really nice silver buckles – "

"The boots were a reward for success. You have failed."

"But I did everything I could," protested Vex.

"Foolish girl," said the Fire Queen ominously. "Do not trouble me at this time."

"It's no trouble," said Vex, brightly. "I just need the boots."

"Begone!" roared the Fire Queen.

Vex looked hurt.

"But I want the boots."

"Get out before I call the guards, dismal niece," said Malveria.

"I hate you!" cried Vex, then stormed out of the throne room, complaining loudly that her life would have been better if she'd been thrown into the volcano when she was eight.

Malveria sighed. Today had been very unsatisfactory.

99

While the band rehearsed Dominil sat outside in the small reception room at the front of the studio. It was not a comfortable room, having only one ripped sofa and a coffee machine that had stopped working years ago. Dominil didn't mind. She took a notebook from her pocket and jotted down a few phrases in Latin. For some time Dominil had been working on a new translation of the poetry of the Tibullus, a Roman poet from the first century BC. He was quite a minor poet, but Dominil liked his light style, and was amused by his tales of mistresses and prostitutes.

She looked in on the band occasionally and was pleased to find that they were busy. Dominil had wondered if the twins might indeed be nothing but talk but now, guitars in hand, microphones in front of them and a rhythm section behind them, they were working hard. Dominil didn't find the sisters' harsh music appealing but she hadn't expected to. It didn't matter. It only mattered that she could place it before the public in some way. She wondered what to do about finding gigs. No venue in the Camden area would let them play. There were other small venues around London but the twins weren't keen.

"It's no use getting us a gig south of the river," Beauty had said. "Who wants to go south of the river?"

"There are a few places for bands to play in the west of the city."

"West London? Who goes there? You might as well get us a gig on the moon."

Dominil mulled over the problem. As most of the local venues only accepted bands through booking agencies, she wondered if she might find an agent who was willing to represent them. That was a possibility, but it might take a long time. Dominil needed to find them a gig soon. For now, it seemed best to keep looking by herself. As the Mistress of the Werewolves had suspected, she was taking to her task with something approaching enthusiasm. Dominil had spent far too many years doing nothing. Now, with something to accomplish, she was almost enjoying herself. She turned her mind to the matter of a name for the twins' band. They'd last played gigs under the name of Urban Death Syndrome but wanted something new.

"We want something aggressive," said Delicious. "We want to let people know they're in for a hard time."

The sisters' four-hour rehearsal session was almost at an end. As

Dominil sat with her notebook the owner of the studio arrived to confer with his staff. He looked at Dominil curiously as he passed by but did not speak. At seven o'clock Dominil put her head inside the thick, padded door of the rehearsal room to tell the band it was time to leave.

"Did it go well?" she asked.

"Really well!" enthused Beauty and Delicious. For the very first time Dominil felt some small amount of regard for the twins. They had worked hard and their faces were flushed with excitement. Here in the studio, with their bright pink and blue hair, and their guitars in their hands, they looked comfortable. Happy, and quite pretty, Dominil thought, in her objective way.

Beauty hunted around in the large black bag she used to carry her book of lyrics.

"Rehearsal tiring. Need sustenance."

"Also need sustenance," said Delicious, and helped with the search. They brought out chocolate, ripping the wrapping paper off and cramming it in their mouths like children.

"Yum yum," said Beauty.

"Sugary snacks," said Delicious.

Dominil paused. She watched the twins shoving chocolate into their mouths. Even by werewolf standards, it was an inelegant sight.

"That's what you should call your band," she said.

"What?"

"Yum Yum Sugary Snacks."

Delicious nearly choked.

"Are you serious?"

"We were looking for something aggressive, remember?" said Beauty, scornfully.

"There are too many doom-ridden and aggressive names already," replied Dominil. "My suggestion would be ironic, and attractive."

"Do you have any idea what you're talking about?" demanded Delicious. Dominil had to admit she was treading in an area in which she had no experience. Nonetheless, she felt that it was a good suggestion. It suited the twin sisters, somehow. The sisters remained unconvinced.

"Please Dominil, thanks for getting us to the studio but don't come up with any more names."

Peter was carefully putting his guitar in its large black case.

"I think it's a good name," he said.

235

"That's cos you're lame-brained," said Beauty.

They carried their instruments out to the car. If the four young men noticed that Beauty, Delicious and Dominil were all unusually strong when it came to carrying things, they didn't comment. They were pleased at the day's events. None of them had ever expected to be rehearsing with the notorious twins again but now it had happened, it felt good. Already they could see that the sisters were right about Dominil. She wasn't a lot of fun to be with but she did get things done.

After they departed, the owner of the studio made a phone call. When the call was answered he spoke a password and was put through to the private switchboard of the Avenaris Guild.

"I'd like to speak to Mr Carmichael. I have some information. About creatures who can change their shape, you understand?"

100

Gawain arrived at Thrix's building at the same time as a motorbike courier delivering documents. As the door was opened for the courier Gawain strode in and made for the stairs. The receptionist called after him angrily and the security guard rushed to intercept him. Gawain brushed the guard aside and ran up the stairs.

Thrix was waiting for him. She had been alerted by the security guard that an intruder was heading her way. She hoped it wasn't Sarapen. If it was, her staff were going to see her displaying a lot of power she'd rather they didn't know she had. It was a surprise when the invader turned out to be not Sarapen but Gawain. He halted when he saw her.

"You couldn't phone for an appointment?"

"My business is very urgent," said Gawain.

"Or course," retorted Thrix. "Everyone's business is urgent, apart from mine. This way."

The Enchantress turned and led Gawain towards her office. She was extremely displeased to have her premises invaded by an uninvited werewolf.

"Congratulations on breaking out of the cell. They should've kept you in the dungeon."

She crossed over to her cabinet and took out a bottle of the MacRinnalch malt. This, she felt, was ridiculous. She had no reason to welcome Gawain and had no desire whatsoever to offer him any hospitality. But he was a MacRinnalch, and the tradition of offering a guest from the clan a drink was too deeply embedded in her to break. Gawain accepted the whisky.

"I want to know where Kalix is," he said.

Thrix placed the bottle on her desk and sat down.

"I may be missing something here Gawain, but weren't you banished? I don't give out information to banished werewolves."

Gawain was not intimidated by the Enchantress and didn't intend to bandy words with her.

"Where is Kalix?" he asked, again.

"I've no idea," said Thrix.

Gawain looked at her for a few seconds, as if considering his next words carefully.

"Thrix. I once appealed to you for help. You told me then you didn't know where your sister was. I doubt that was true. This time I know Kalix is in London. I was told by a reliable family source."

"Marwanis, no doubt," said Thrix, surprising Gawain. "No one else at the castle would tell you anything. You should have stayed with Marwanis. She'd have been a much better partner than my underage sister."

Gawain scowled but did not respond to the jibe.

"If Kalix is in London you know where she is. So kindly tell me."

Gawain's voice had risen a fraction. Thrix knew that he would not easily be put off. She was momentarily uncertain of what to do. While she hadn't exactly approved of his association with Kalix, neither had she been as outraged by it as the rest of the family. Indeed, as it had seemed to make Kalix happy, Thrix had occasionally thought it may have been better to let it continue. It crossed her mind to simply tell Gawain where Kalix was. It would get him out of her office. But would that really be for the best? Verasa wouldn't like it and it would mean endless recriminations. Besides, Gawain might simply lead Sarapen to Kalix.

"She was in London but she's gone," said Thrix, coolly. "I gave her a new pendant to hide her and she left the city. I think she intended to go to France."

"France? Why?"

"Who knows? With you out of the picture, there hasn't been much here for her."

"I will not be put off by lies. I'll find Kalix."

"Good luck," said Thrix.

"If you're lying to me I'll be back."

"Are you attempting to threaten me?"

"I am threatening you," said Gawain, menacingly. "Nothing will keep me from Kalix."

"Yes fine, you're a romantic hero," said Thrix. "So go find your heroine. Shut the door on your way out."

Gawain rose to his feet and strode swiftly from the room. Behind him the Enchantress was thoughtful. Thoughtful and displeased. Another insolent werewolf who felt free to threaten her in her own domain.

"If didn't have a business to run I'd blast them all to hell," she muttered. She reached for the phone, intending to inform the Mistress of the Werewolves of her encounter but before she could pick it up Ann buzzed through from outside.

"Who was the handsome stranger?" she asked.

"Just another werewolf I didn't want to see."

"Was he looking for a date?"

"Sorry Ann," said Thrix. "He's already got an obsession."

"Your brother is on line one."

"Which brother?"

"Markus."

Thrix shook her head as she took the call. There seemed to be no end to her family's interference in her life.

"Markus? What do you want? I'm busy."

"Talixia is dead."

"What?"

"She's dead. She's been murdered."

"Who by?"

"I don't know."

"I'll be right there," said the Enchantress.

101

Thrix found Markus sitting in the hallway, numb with shock. Talixia lay dead on the floor. She had suffered a cut across her ribs and some blood had congealed around her body. It was a serious wound but Thrix saw immediately it shouldn't have been fatal for a werewolf. She knelt down over the body.

"Tell me what happened."

Markus spoke with some difficulty. He'd arrived at the flat around an hour ago and the first thing he encountered was his lover's dead body lying in the hallway. He was profoundly shocked and could say little more. When Thrix asked him if the body had been cold when he arrived he nodded and tears formed in his eyes.

"This wound," said Thrix. "It shouldn't have killed her."

She checked the body for any other injuries but found none. She sniffed the air, then concentrated on the area around the body for a few moments, trying to discern if sorcery might have been involved. She couldn't say for sure but she thought she could sense something not entirely of this world.

"She's been killed by the Begravar knife," said Markus.

Thrix shook her head. That was impossible. The Begravar knife was locked away in the vaults of Castle MacRinnalch.

"It's not," said Markus. "It's missing."

"Missing? Since when?"

"Mother noticed it was gone a few days ago. She thinks Sarapen took it."

Thrix frowned, very deeply.

"Sarapen couldn't have done this."

"Why could he not?"

Thrix struggled to find an answer. Was it possible? Could Sarapen have gone so far as to murder his brother's girlfriend? A werewolf who had no say in the struggle for the Thaneship? If he had it was a far more shocking occurrence than anything Thrix was expecting.

"I don't believe he's responsible," she said, but there was uncertainty in her voice.

"You think not?" Markus suddenly became animated. "Who else could it have been? Only the Begravar knife could have killed her. Sarapen has the knife! My brother has murdered her to get at me! I'll kill him!"

Markus rose to his feet and let out a dreadful howl. His face was contorted with rage and hatred.

"Markus. We don't know for sure what happened. We must speak to mother and – "

Markus wasn't listening. He ran to the front door and rushed from the building. Thrix sighed. There was no point pursuing him. It would not be possible to reason with Markus just now. Thrix wasn't certain that he should be reasoned with. If he was now seeking bloody revenge, what member of the MacRinnalch Clan could say he didn't have the right to do so?

It was as well that she was here. Someone had to clear up the mess. The murder couldn't be reported to the police. They must not become involved in the internal feuding of the MacRinnalchs. The body would have to be taken discreetly to Scotland for the clan and Talixia's family to deal with, as was fitting. The Enchantress, with her powers, could see that this was done without outside interference.

She took out her phone and called the Mistress of the Werewolves. While waiting for Verasa to answer, Thrix sniffed out Talixia's supply of the clan whisky and poured herself a large glass. The battle for the Thaneship was already spiralling out of control and there was no saying what the final consequences would be.

102

Moonglow had already transformed the small bathroom in their new flat into a pleasant space. The shelves were full of natural beauty products, there was a warm rug on the floor and a cheerful poster of dolphins on the wall. Kalix perched on the edge of the bath while Moonglow washed the werewolf's self-inflicted wound.

"Why do you do this?" she asked.

"It makes me feel better," said Kalix.

"Why?"

"I don't know. It just does."

Moonglow didn't press the point. When the wound was clean and dry she led Kalix back into the living room and offered to make her some tea, which Kalix accepted.

"But no milk or sugar."

While waiting for the kettle to boil Moonglow wondered what, if anything, she should do about Kalix's self-cutting. It obviously wasn't something she could be dissuaded from by a few kind words. Moonglow wondered if Kalix's mental state might improve if she started to feel more secure in her surroundings.

"Here's your tea. Do you want anything to eat?"

Kalix shook her head.

"You should eat. You haven't eaten all day."

"Don't lecture me about it," growled Kalix.

"Okay," said Moonglow.

Kalix wanted to watch TV so they sat quietly in front of the screen for a while.

"I wonder if Daniel went home with that girl?" said Moonglow, during the adverts. "She just homed in on Daniel. I've never seen such an instant attraction."

It was an odd thought, Daniel with a woman. Moonglow couldn't quite picture it.

"Why are there no good programmes on at night?" complained Kalix. "We need more channels. Can we get more TV channels?"

"Definitely not," said Moonglow.

"I'll stop cutting myself if we get more channels," said Kalix.

"Is that really true?" demanded Moonglow.

"No," admitted Kalix. Moonglow laughed. At four a.m. they heard the front door open. Daniel had returned. As he entered the room he found Moonglow and Kalix both eyeing him with unusual interest, and immediately felt uncomfortable.

"What are you doing back here?" asked Moonglow. "I thought you'd gone off with Miss Dark Mysterious Stranger."

Daniel attempted to look casual.

"Well, I thought about it. But, you know…"

"What?"

"I decided not to."

"Why not?"

"What is this, an interrogation?" said Daniel, sounding exasperated. "Do I have to tell you every detail of my personal life? Is a man not entitled to the slightest bit of privacy round here?"

Daniel went to the kitchen and hunted in the fridge, returning with a large plastic bottle of cheap lager purchased from the small supermarket on the corner, and they all sat watching TV and drinking from the bottle.

"There's nothing good on," said Kalix, looking for support from Daniel. "Moonglow, if Daniel tells you all about his failure with the girl can we get cable TV?"

"I did not have a failure!" said Daniel.

"And no we can't get cable TV," said Moonglow. "But I'd like to hear about the failure."

"There was no failure. I simply decided to come home alone. Is there some law says I have to go home with any really attractive girl who asks me?"

"You lost your nerve, didn't you?" said Moonglow.

"Completely. I mean, it was all too strange."

Daniel looked very unhappy.

"Never mind," said Moonglow soothingly. "It looked impressive anyway. Probably Alicia's thinking about you in a whole new light, what with exotic girls pursuing you all over the party."

"You think so?"

"Definitely."

Perhaps this was true. It couldn't be denied that an exotic girl had pursued him all over the party. Daniel looked slightly less unhappy.

It was very late the next day before any of them rose from their beds. Kalix arrived in the living room in the early afternoon to find Moonglow drinking her first cup of tea of the day. Moonglow was civilised in the matter of tea drinking, and had the tea pot, a small milk jug and a cup all placed neatly on a tray.

"Tea?" she said to Kalix.

"I've never drunk so much tea before," said Kalix.

They sat in silence for a little while. Kalix played with her nose ring. The gleaming piece of gold was the only jewellery she owned. The young werewolf looked better than she had for a long time. Her hair, still unusually long, was now thick and well conditioned due to liberal use of Moonglow's hair products. Moonglow noticed how good Kalix looked, and hoped it would last. She had something to tell to Kalix that was going to be a little awkward. She didn't want to offend her but it had to be said.

"Kalix, I've invited my boyfriend Jay round tonight. He's been wondering why I haven't asked him over recently and it's starting to look a bit odd. But there's just one thing…"

242

"Yes?" said Kalix.

"Well, the reason I've been going to his place rather than inviting him here is because you're here. Not that I don't want to introduce you to my boyfriend of course but…"

Moonglow paused. This felt very awkward.

"You're worried I'll do something weird?" suggested Kalix.

"Yes. If you turn into a werewolf when Jay is here it'll really be hard to explain. It's best that no one else knows you're a werewolf. Not that I don't trust Jay of course, but…"

"All right, I won't turn into a werewolf," said Kalix.

"And please don't eat raw meat straight from the fridge."

"Is that strange?"

"Unusual," answered Moonglow. "And probably quite distressing for Jay. He's a vegetarian."

"Okay, I won't."

"Also it'll seem weird if you cut yourself, throw up on the floor or assault us in the midst of an anxiety attack."

"Hey!" said Kalix. "It's not like I do these things all the time. Maybe once or twice."

Kalix started to sulk.

"And please don't sulk," said Moonglow. "Not that it would be so unusual, having a person sulking in the house. Daniel does it all the time. But I want Jay to feel comfortable when he visits. You know, I really like him."

Kalix looked thoughtful for a second. She could understand the concept of really liking someone. She smiled.

"I promise not to do anything strange. I don't want to make your boyfriend uncomfortable."

"Good," said Moonglow. "Thanks for being understanding."

Moonglow went off to her bedroom to put on her make-up and start the long process of getting her hair in good order. Shortly afterwards Daniel appeared in the living room, obviously not in the best of moods.

"Isn't it annoying the way Moonglow keeps inviting this guy over here?" he said. "You can't turn round but Jay's cluttering up the place."

"He's never been here before," Kalix pointed out.

"Hasn't he? Well he was at our last house all the time. You couldn't move without trampling over him. It's completely inconsiderate of Moonglow to invite him over."

"Why?"

"Why? Plenty of ways. There's you to think about. Is it right for a sick werewolf to have to put up with this sort of thing? I'd have thought Moonglow would have been more considerate than to fill up the house with annoying visitors."

Kalix laughed.

"Moonglow asked me about it first."

Daniel was unconvinced. A cunning look came into his eye.

"Do you think you could scare him off?"

"What? How?"

"You know, maybe turn into a werewolf when he's here, and growl at him? No? Perhaps that would be a bit much. How about just having an anxiety attack and running round attacking everyone? Maybe cut yourself a bit, make it look realistic? Or you could just vomit everywhere, that'll spoil his visit."

"Certainly not," said Kalix. "I wouldn't do that."

Daniel was disappointed. Having saved this werewolf's life, he might have expected her to be a little more co-operative.

"Well what about bringing in some raw meat and wolfing it down? Jay would hate that."

Kalix shook her head and departed from the room, leaving Daniel to plot Jay's downfall on his own. Moonglow was on her way to the shops, and asked Kalix if she wanted anything.

"Beer or whisky or cider," said Kalix.

"You know you're technically not old enough to drink alcohol?"

"I've had a very hard life as a werewolf," said Kalix.

Moonglow laughed. She'd realised recently that when Kalix was not suffering from anxiety attacks or running from her pursuers, she could actually be quite funny.

"Can I use your computer and the internet?" asked Kalix.

Moonglow agreed, though she was a little nervous about letting Kalix use her new MacBook unattended.

"I'll be careful," said Kalix.

Moonglow turned on her computer.

"Daniel really doesn't like Jay does he?"

"No," admitted Moonglow. "He doesn't."

"Why not?"

"I don't know," said Moonglow, though really she knew very well.

"Did you ever sleep with Daniel?" asked Kalix.

"No. We just met and became friends."

Kalix nodded.

"My mother hated Gawain," she said, unexpectedly. "So did my father. They banished him from the castle."

Kalix looked sad.

"I thought he'd come back for me. But he didn't."

Moonglow was unsure of what to say.

"Being banished by the werewolf clan must be serious. Would it be dangerous for him to come back?"

"Yes. But I thought he would anyway. Do you think he thinks about me?"

"Of course. He probably thinks about you every day."

"I don't think he remembers me," said Kalix.

Kalix seemed to have no more to say on the subject. To prevent her from sinking deeper into gloom Moonglow found some fan sites for Transvision Vamp and the Runaways. Kalix was diverted by this, particularly when Moonglow showed her how to download music from the page. Moonglow left her to it, and went off to the shop.

As Moonglow left the house it was already getting dark. The only shop nearby that was open at this time on a Sunday was a very small supermarket, not cheap but fairly well stocked. Moonglow bought vegetables and spices she needed for cooking. At the checkout till the attendant greeted her with a smile. Moonglow had quickly got to know the staff. She always did, even in an anonymous city like London. She returned home, dumped the food in the kitchen and went upstairs to change. There she found Kalix, now in werewolf form, apparently trying to eat her computer.

"Hey!" yelled Moonglow, and leapt to retrieve her MacBook before it disappeared between Kalix's great jaws.

"What's going on?"

Kalix looked back at her angrily.

"Explain this," demanded Moonglow.

Kalix slowly changed back into her human shape and then stood looking at the floor.

"Well? Why were you trying to eat my computer?"

"It wouldn't work," muttered Kalix.

"So you thought you'd bite it?"

"Yes."

"Kalix, this is precious to me. You promised to be careful. If I'd got home thirty seconds later you'd have crushed it."

Moonglow quickly inspected her computer. It seemed to have survived the experience.

"What was so annoying?"

"I couldn't read it properly," admitted Kalix. "There was something wrong with the writing."

"There was nothing wrong with the writing, Kalix," said Moonglow. "The truth is you just can't read very well."

"I can so."

"No you can't."

"There's no need to keep lecturing me about everything," snarled Kalix, and departed swiftly from the room.

Moonglow sighed. She'd known it would be a sensitive subject. But perhaps, she thought, now she'd raised it she could do something about it. She picked up her laptop and walked down to Kalix's room.

"Go away," said Kalix.

"Look, instead of trying to destroy my computer why don't you use it to learn to read better?"

"I can read fine," said Kalix, stubbornly.

Moonglow was already busy logging on to a website she'd found recently which she thought might help. Unless of course it just insulted the young werewolf more.

"You shouldn't be embarrassed about not reading well," said Moonglow. "It doesn't mean you're not clever. I already know you're intelligent. It's just because you didn't get to school much. Look at this."

Moonglow had logged on to a remedial *learning to read* website. It was very cheerful and involved a lot of colourful pictures of animals and flowers. It was like a simple infants reading book, but brightly animated. When you got things right the animals danced around the screen, and congratulated the user on their performance. When you got things wrong, the colourful animals encouraged you to try again.

"Start using this site and you'll be reading and writing in no time and won't that be better than just getting angry about it?"

"I don't need any help," said Kalix.

"Well you should take a look anyway," said Moonglow. "I have to go and start cooking for Jay now. If I leave my computer here will you promise not to damage it?"

"All right."

Fervently hoping that this would not be the last time she saw her MacBook in good working order, Moonglow went off to the kitchen.

103

Maddened with rage, Markus ran through the streets of London. Anyone unfortunate enough to get in his way was flung roughly aside as the crazed werewolf sprinted north towards Hyde Park. Sarapen's town house overlooked the park, and Markus had only one thought in his mind: to kill Sarapen. Sarapen had stolen the Begravar knife and killed Talixia. Now Markus would kill him. Markus had no thought of the Thaneship, no thoughts of the effect his action might have on the clan. He did not even think of what Verasa would say. His older brother had to die. That was all that mattered.

Markus arrived at Hyde Park just as the moon rose. He transformed into his werewolf shape and leapt the tall fence with a bound that would have been beyond the power of any man. A few people outside the park rubbed their eyes, shook their heads and hurried off, not wanting to believe that they'd seen a wolf-beast hurdle the fence.

The park had closed at dusk and no one else saw Markus as he raced over the grass. Now he could see the block in which Sarapen lived. Markus raised his snout and howled, the howl of a MacRinnalch werewolf going to war. He sprang over the fence which separated the grass from the houses beyond then raced through the bushes towards Sarapen's door. Already he could scent the werewolves inside. Alarms went off in the house as the intruder approached. Seconds later the back door was torn from its hinges and Markus stormed in, roaring for Sarapen to come and face him.

Two werewolves hurried to confront Markus. They tried to grapple with him but Markus was too strong. He sunk his teeth into the neck of one opponent, killing him instantly, then smashed the other werewolf him into the wall, knocking him unconscious.

"Where is Sarapen!" screamed Markus, and ran forward through the hallway.

"Markus!"

Markus turned to find himself confronted by Decembrius and Mirasen.

"What is the meaning of this!" demanded Mirasen.

"I'm going to kill Sarapen!" yelled Markus.

Mirasen tried to reply but Markus was too maddened to listen. He threw himself at Sarapen's advisor. Decembrius leapt on Markus's back and the three werewolves fell in a struggling, growling heap onto the floor. The struggle was fierce but brief. When it was over Markus jumped to his feet. Mirasen lay dead and Decembrius was barely alive. A huge pool of werewolf blood spread out over the tiled hallway.

Markus ran through the house, screaming for Sarapen to come and face him. Unable to find his brother he began to wreck everything he came across, throwing furniture across the room and hauling down shelves and bookcases, smashing everything with his claws and his mighty jaws. Everywhere he went he caused destruction, but he couldn't find Sarapen. Finally realising that his brother was not here, he ran back to the hallway. Decembrius was struggling to rise. Markus grabbed him by the throat and dragged him to his feet.

"Tell Sarapen I'll kill him next!" snarled Markus, then threw Decembrius from him. Decembrius crashed into a marble statue and slumped to the floor. Markus stormed out of the house, disappearing over the fence into the darkness, still enraged, and still howling.

104

Thrix arrived home very late. She'd cleaned up the mess at Talixia's house, sending the body home to Scotland for burial. The process had involved various pieces of sorcery and several long phone calls to her mother. Thrix was unable to get on with any of her own work and was in consequence extremely disgruntled when she arrived home. She hoped she could work through the night and make up for some of the lost time.

It had not taken long for the murderous feud to reach London. Thrix still found it hard to believe that Sarapen had really killed Talixia but what other explanation was there? The Mistress of the Werewolves seemed quite certain that Sarapen had stolen the Begravar knife from the castle, and no other weapon could have caused Talixia's death.

Verasa asked Thrix to find Markus. Verasa did not want her younger son to confront Sarapen. She feared for his life. Thrix had agreed to look but she hadn't done so. She'd already been to visit Kalix, and spent a long time at Talixia's apartment. She couldn't afford to waste more of her time chasing Markus around the city. As Thrix put her key in her front door she sensed her flat was not empty. Malveria was inside, sitting languidly on the couch, surrounded by magazines, with the TV on and a bottle of wine suspended in mid-air within easy reach.

"Make yourself at home," said Thrix, dryly.

"Thrix!" said the Fire Queen, welcoming her joyfully. "I have been eager to see you. But you are so late coming home. Have you been working all day or is it perhaps another date with the eligible young men of town?"

"No date. No work."

Thrix slumped on the couch and brought the Fire Queen up to date with the latest events. Malveria nodded sympathetically. She knew that Thrix was hating this.

"As you should. You have the far more important business of clothes designing to be getting on with. Some wine?"

Malveria nodded to the bottle and it travelled steadily through the air to pour itself into a glass which Malveria floated over to Thrix. Thrix accepted it gratefully.

"Or something a little stronger?" suggested Malveria, and raised a bottle of the MacRinnalch whisky a few inches off the nearest shelf.

Thrix shook her head.

"Not yet, I have to stay up all night and work."

"You are making me fine outfits for the Sorceress Livia's birthday celebration?" said Malveria, eagerly.

The Enchantress nodded, rather wearily.

"Splendid," said Malveria. "But I am forgetting. I have encountered the great whore Princess Kabachetka while spying at the office of Zatek the treacherous."

"You did? What did you learn?"

"Her hair is definitely dyed. I have suspected this for some time though she resolutely denies it. But it was quite uneven around the roots, no doubt because the Princess is too mean to pay the best hairdressers. But that is typical of the Princess, a cheap elemental to the core."

Malveria frowned.

"I would so much like to kill that Princess. Do you know she had the effrontery to insinuate that I was generously proportioned? She accused me of hiding my excess weight! Which is absurd. Of course it can be done – I believe her mother the Empress Asaratanti has long concealed several hundred pounds of ugly fat in another dimension – but such tactics are not necessary for the extremely slim Queen Malveria. Last year my devotees added the title *Slenderest of Queens* to my many existing names, quite unbidden by myself."

"But of course I cannot kill the Princess," sighed Malveria. "If I did then it would be said that I had done so out of jealousy at her superior fashion sense. You wouldn't believe, my dearest Thrix, how cruel they can be in my dimension. Those harpies who flock around the Sorceress Livia simply live for gossip."

The Enchantress, well used to Malveria's ways, waited patiently for the Fire Queen to get to the point.

"But I must admit to some slight failure in my spying. When I saw the harlot Kabachetka I was unable to conceal my rage and we had a great argument which may have become violent had I not been unwilling to resort to violence in front of a fashion designer. If my front row seats for the Vogue fashion awards were to be withdrawn I would simply not be able to carry on living."

"So you didn't learn anything?"

Malveria swept her arm expansively through the air.

"Please, Enchantress. You disparage me. I did not say that I didn't learn anything. In Zatek's building I sensed a very particular form of sorcery, sorcery I would not have expected to find there. It's called the *Seeing of Asiex* and by its use a sorcerer can see very far, even through a strong magical barrier."

"You mean there isn't a traitor in my organisation? Zatek is just using a spell to spy on me?"

"I believe so."

Thrix gulped her wine down and poured herself some more.

"I've never come across this *Seeing of Asiex*."

"It is very obscure. Indeed, I would not have thought that Kabachetka could provide this spell for Zatek. Some forms of sorcery are very difficult to transport to this dimension."

"Perhaps," suggested Thrix. "Merchant MacDoig is involved? He'd know how to do it."

Thrix pursed her lips. So Zatek could use sorcery, and Princess Kabachetka was prepared to hire the Merchant to import obscure spells for him.

"Can you help me block it off?"

"Of course, Enchantress. I know to how to negate its effects."

"Excellent. Malveria, that's the best news I've had all day. No more spying from Zatek and no more Kabachetka stealing my designs."

"Indeed it is excellent, dearest Enchantress. But I remain troubled. A person who can use this spell may have other resources to hand. We must be ready for his next move."

Malveria looked longingly at a yellow cocktail dress in the pages of Tatler.

"I would like a dress like that. But as you know, yellow has always refused to suit me. I count it as a great misfortune in my life."

"Yes," agreed Thrix. "It is a burden."

"I so wanted these yellow shoes last year," said Malveria, and started to look quite unhappy. When she turned the page and found a picture of the same model now wearing a tiny yet exquisite yellow hat, a tear formed in her eye.

"Oh look how beautiful she is in her yellow hat. She is so lucky."

"I know that model Malveria. She's a heroin addict and the only place she ever goes is to see her psychiatrist."

"But she really suits her yellow hat," stated Malveria. "She is the most fortunate of women."

It was time for the Japanese fashion show on cable TV. They settled down to watch. Although Thrix had been determined to spend the night working, the Fire Queen would not leave before the show was over and besides, an hour of relaxation would do her good. She nodded towards the bottle of whisky, bringing it floating towards them.

"The young man Daniel," said Malveria.

"What about him?"

"Do you think he could be… What is the word that describes those two designers you recommended to redecorate my reception room?"

"Homosexual?"

"That is correct. Could this apply to Daniel?"

"I don't know. Why?"

"For no reason. I just wonder at his aversion to women. I sent him my niece who is not unattractive. Yet he fled the scene. I admit myself to be baffled."

Thrix was puzzled.

"Why did you send her to Daniel?"

"I felt that he deserved some reward," explained Malveria, untruthfully. "You will remember that he called me beautiful. And do not forget, he is the guardian of young Kalix, in a way."

Thrix sighed.

"I've been trying to forget about Kalix. My mother keeps asking me to check on her."

Malveria wondered why the Mistress of the Werewolves could not send someone else. Thrix admitted that she hadn't told her mother exactly where Kalix was.

"My mother would tell Markus. And I don't trust Markus."

"Perhaps we could visit Kalix together?" suggested Malveria, who had an urge to see Daniel again, that she might judge for herself why he'd fled from Agrivex.

105

Kalix played on Moonglow's computer for a long time. She enjoyed the *learning to read* website. Each page was a like a game and Kalix, by choosing the right words, led hopping frogs across a pond, and goats safely over a mountain. The young werewolf had never played any sort of computer game before and even though this was all rather simple, she was entranced. Without her really noticing, Kalix's reading skills began to improve. The next page involved helping a kitten crawl back into its basket. *Cat – mat – sat – bat – hat,* typed Kalix, triumphantly leading the kitten to safety by spelling all the words correctly.

Kalix was vaguely aware that Moonglow's boyfriend was now in the house. She wondered if she should go down and say hello. Daniel knocked on the door. Kalix immediately felt self-conscious. While she had been quite happy using the website alone, Daniel's appearance made her realise that she was playing a child's game, and learning very simple words. Daniel was bound to think she was stupid if he found her typing out *cat, bat,* and *mat.*

"What are you doing?"

"Nothing," mumbled Kalix.

Daniel walked across the room. Kalix's poor computer skills meant she was unable to close the website before he saw it.

"What's this?"

"Nothing," mumbled Kalix again, now feeling very embarrassed.

"You have to get the kitten back into the basket?" said Daniel, picking up the idea the moment he looked at it. "Let me try."

Daniel sat beside her and typed in the right words, soon succeeding in taking the kitten safely home.

"What's next?"

They clicked on the link for the next page. This page, containing some words of four letters, looked very challenging to Kalix.

"Okay, lets get that buffalo safely across the prairie," said Daniel.

"It looks hard," said Kalix, doubtfully.

"Hard? To a smart werewolf like you? Definitely not. You better make a start, the buffalo's looking anxious."

Kalix smiled a very small smile, and made a start.

Downstairs Moonglow was feeling happy. Life had been stressful but now she was settling into her new house and her boyfriend was visiting for the first time. She'd cooked a meal and Jay had eaten it appreciatively, as he always did. They were sitting on the couch listening to Kate Bush and Jay was telling her about the astrological chart he'd drawn up for a friend of his which had several interesting insights. Moonglow listened attentively, and twined her fingers in Jay's long black hair.

Upstairs, Kalix, with a little help from Daniel, had now led the buffalo safely across the prairie. In addition she'd helped a baby kangaroo back to its mother's pouch and a lion cub back to its den. In the process she had learned to spell several new words and was feeling pleased with herself. Daniel was a good companion for this sort of thing. He enjoyed all computer games, from the simplest to the most complex, and for some reason it didn't make her feel stupid that he was sitting beside her when she was struggling to spell *lion*.

After the lion cub adventure, Kalix felt fatigued.

"I can't do any more.

Daniel nodded in agreement.

"You shouldn't do too much at once, it's a bad idea. I follow much the same philosophy at university."

"Is Jay here?" asked Kalix.

"He's currently eating every scrap of food in the house and droning on about the time he went to the Dracula Festival in Whitby," said Daniel, morosely. "You'd think Moonglow would have better taste."

"Should I say hello?"

"Probably. Moonglow told him you were my young cousin come to London for a visit."

Daniel went off to his room to listen to music and lie on the bed being unhappy about Jay and Moonglow. Kalix shut down the computer. So Daniel said she should say hello to Jay. In that case it must be the right thing to do. Maybe if she didn't say hello, it would be rude. Kalix suddenly remembered all the things Moonglow had instructed her not to do. Now she felt nervous. What if she did something weird and upset Jay? Moonglow would be annoyed. Just thinking about going downstairs began to make her anxious. She was bound to do something weird.

'No matter what I do,' thought Kalix, 'It'll be wrong. Everyone will hate me.'

She decided she'd better just stay in her room where she was safe. But Daniel had said she really should go and say hello. Kalix growled. Living with humans was too stressful. To quell the rising tide of panic Kalix took her bottle of laudanum from her bag. She took a large swig and waited for it to calm her nerves. A memory of life at Castle MacRinnalch floated into her mind. Once, when she was twelve or so, guests had been gathered round the banqueting table. Kalix had by this time developed her aversion to food and wouldn't eat. Verasa later berated Kalix about embarrassing her in front of her guests. She'd been banished to her room in disgrace. Thinking of this now, Kalix had the confused notion that if she went downstairs, Moonglow would offer her food and then berate her if she refused to eat in front of Jay. The thought made her anxious so she drank some more laudanum.

In the living room Moonglow and Jay were studying an astrological chart. The door opened and Kalix walked in.

"Hello," said Moonglow brightly. "Jay, this is Kalix."

Kalix advanced with a smile on her face. Unfortunately, as she was now under the influence of a huge dose of laudanum, she was unable to stop. She stumbled over Jay's outstretched legs, bounced off the couch and plummeted to the floor.

"It's okay I'm fine," said Kalix, quite gamely, attempting to rise. Her legs gave way and she fell again, this time onto the table where she tore the astrological chart in half and took the remnants with her onto the floor, along with two glasses, a bottle of wine, and several dishes. Jay seemed rather shocked. At that moment the doorbell rang. Moonglow shouted for Daniel to answer it but he was listening to music in his room and didn't hear.

"I'll be back in a minute," said Moonglow, and hurried off.

At the door she found the Fire Queen and the Enchantress with their

254

arms round each other's shoulders.

"Oh… hello…" said Moonglow.

"We've come to…" began the Enchantress, then stopped. She turned her head towards Malveria.

"Why have we come here?"

"To enquire after the health of Kalix."

"Of course. We've come to enquire after the health of Kalix."

"It's not really a very good – " began Moonglow, but the Enchantress and the Fire Queen were already brushing past her and climbing the stairs. Moonglow caught the powerful aroma of whisky. As she watched their unsteady progress up the stairs she realised, rather desperately, that they were both under the influence of alcohol. Moonglow gritted her teeth and set off in pursuit. The evening had taken an unexpectedly bad turn.

The Fire Queen snapped her fingers as she walked up the stairs, causing the light to come on.

"I have a visitor," said Moonglow, urgently. "Please don't use any magic, it's – "

She broke off as they entered the living room. Thrix and Malveria were bemused at the sight of Kalix, who was sprawled on the floor in the midst of a great mess of plates, cutlery, and glasses.

"Is this the best you could look after her?" said Thrix.

"Has there been a fight?" asked the Fire Queen.

"No, Kalix is just…" Moonglow stopped. She wasn't sure what Kalix was. Drunk? Collapsing from lack of food?

The Fire Queen sniffed the air.

"Ah," she said, knowingly. "Laudanum."

"Laudanum?" said Jay, who up till now had been too busy brushing food scraps from his clothes to pay attention their visitors. "There isn't any laudanum any more."

"No laudanum?" said the Fire Queen, immediately displeased at being contradicted. "What a strange thing to say."

"It hasn't been made for a century or more," said Jay, knowledgeably. "Not since morphine and heroin arrived."

"You are quite mistaken," said Malveria.

Daniel, having now heard the commotion, arrived in the room to see what was happening.

"Daniel!" cried Malveria. "How well you are looking! Very like a young man who would attract girls. You are a young man who wishes

255

to attract girls, yes?"

Kalix tried to stand, gave up the attempt, and slumped heavily on the couch. The Fire Queen wondered if there might be a pop-tart in the toaster, waiting to be eaten. Thrix apologised for troubling them but wondered if it might be possible for her to have a cup of coffee as she was feeling rather tired. When Malveria noticed the TV guide on the floor she asked if they subscribed to the Japanese fashion show and was surprised to learn that they did not.

"No cable? My dears, how do you manage?"

106

When Sarapen heard of Markus's savage attack he immediately flew to London. Sarapen was incensed by the destruction of his property and the killing of his counsellor Mirasen. He was furious that Markus had so easily invaded his house in London. Of the four werewolves who had been there, two were now dead, and Decembrius was badly injured. It was unfortunate that Andris MacAndris had not been at the house. Andris, the head of Sarapen's household, was a fierce warrior, almost as strong as the mighty Wallace MacGregor, son of the Baron. If Andris had been there he might have ridded Sarapen of Markus for good, and Verasa could not have held Sarapen responsible. It would have been ideal.

Sarapen was baffled as to Markus's motives. It was a far more adventurous exploit than he would have expected from his young brother. Despite his fury, Sarapen realised that he could turn the situation to his advantage. Markus had killed Sarapen's advisor. Sarapen was now free to kill Markus. The clan could not protest because the revenge would be justified.

Now that Sarapen was free to seek out Markus, he knew he'd have less time to hunt for Kalix. Decembrius, his chief hope of finding her, lay wounded, so Sarapen called ahead to instruct Andris MacAndris to summon the Douglas-MacPhees.

At Castle MacRinnalch Verasa was agitated. She had just learned from her informants in Sarapen's camp of events in London. She cursed Markus for flying off in a rage. Talixia's death had been a severe shock but really, it was no time to lose control of one's emotions. She didn't think Markus could defeat Sarapen in combat and was relieved that Sarapen had not been at his house when Markus attacked. She urged Thrix to find Markus and take him to safety. Not entirely trusting Thrix to do this, she sent more of her werewolves to London.

"This is all very bad," said Verasa Rainal, in her chambers. "Particularly the assault on Decembrius."

Rainal nodded. Verasa's sister Lucia was not going to be pleased. Lucia had voted for Markus and would be furious to learn that he'd subsequently attacked her son.

"It's fortunate Decembrius wasn't killed but even so it might cost Markus her vote."

"Sarapen is to blame for this outbreak of violence," Rainal pointed out. "He was behind the murder of Baron MacAllister and he seems to be responsible for Talixia's murder."

Verasa pursed her lips. She wasn't certain that Sarapen had been responsible for Talixia's death.

"Although now that Markus has acted so rashly, it hardly matters."

Verasa clenched her fists. All Markus had to do was stay out of the way till Verasa had collected enough votes. Now he'd put himself in danger and quite probably alienated Lucia. It was all very aggravating.

"Most irritating," agreed Rainal. "Particularly as Dominil has been making such good progress. Do we have news of Kalix?"

"She's safe, according to Thrix. Though I don't believe Thrix is putting as much effort as she should into protecting her. I don't believe she doesn't know exactly where she is, either."

107

Sarapen's werewolves had done what they could to clear up the mess but Sarapen could still smell the blood. He asked for news of Decembrius and was told that the young werewolf was being cared for in another apartment nearby. He was not in danger. His injuries had been serious but his inborn werewolf vitality would allow him to recover.

Sarapen was eager to search for Markus and take vengeance but there was another task to attend to first.

"Bring in the Douglas-MacPhees."

The door opened and three sullen werewolves were shepherded into the room. Duncan, Rhona, and the huge, lumbering Fergus. Duncan was the eldest, around forty, the others a few years his junior. They were thieves and quite probably murderers. Baron MacPhee had banished them from his keep and all surrounding lands. After being run out of Scotland they'd established themselves in London and were busy with various criminal enterprises of their own. They gazed sullenly at Sarapen. They had no respect for any other werewolf, member of the ruling family or not. Duncan, Rhona and Fergus had little regard for clan tradition, and no regard at all for humans.

Sarapen stared at them with open dislike. They were almost as objectionable as the cousins about whom the family did not speak. The Douglas-MacPhees were all dark, heavy browed, and dressed in black. Not well dressed like Markus, or formally dressed like Sarapen, but shabbily and aggressively dressed, with leather jackets and bandanas, and tattoos.

"I sent you to capture Kalix MacRinnalch. You failed."

Duncan shrugged.

"We went back for her next day. But the humans had moved."

"I want you to find her again."

"We're busy."

"You will do this for me."

"We've got other things to do."

Sarapen strode forward and took Duncan by the throat, lifting him from the floor so he couldn't move. Duncan stared straight back into his eyes, refusing to show fear. Sarapen wrinkled his nose. The Douglas-MacPhee wore a leather jacket that reeked of age, blood and death.

"You have no other things to do," said Sarapen, raising his voice. "You're a vicious little gang and if I didn't want your help I'd snap your necks now. Baron MacPhee would thank me. But I do want your help. Find Kalix MacRinnalch."

"What if we don't want to?" said Rhona, defiantly.

"Then I'll run you out of London. And if you annoy me any more I'll kill you."

Sarapen released Duncan.

"Andris MacAndris will arrange for you to be paid. Now get out of

258

my sight."

After they'd gone Andris looked questioningly at Sarapen.

"They're a vicious trio, Sarapen. Not trustworthy."

"I know. But they fear me and they'll do as I tell them."

Andris nodded. It made sense. But he shuddered inside at the thought of Sarapen setting such a gang on the trail of his sister Kalix. They weren't the sort of werewolves to show mercy.

Sarapen selected four strong MacAndris werewolves from his entourage.

"Now," he told them. "It's time to attend to Markus."

108

Dominil made ready to drive the sisters to the rehearsal studio. It was no easier to get them out of bed than it had been before. They seemed to have a great disinclination to rise before three o'clock in the afternoon, something which Dominil found very frustrating. Werewolves did have a tendency to nocturnal living but there was no need to take it to ridiculous extremes. Not when there was work to be done. She dragged the pair from their beds, ignoring their protests.

"Get ready. We have to leave soon."

"Can't leave now," muttered Delix. "Hair's a mess."

"Then wear a hat."

Delix seemed scandalised by the idea.

"There's no way I'm leaving the house till my hair's exactly right and you can scowl all you want you white-haired bitch it doesn't make any difference."

Beauty and Delicious headed for the bathroom to attend to their hair. The sisters' excessive vanity was infuriating. Neither of them could so much as step out into the street without preening themselves for hours in front of the mirror. Even a trip to the shops to buy a pint of milk had to be preceded by a long session with their make-up bags.

While waiting for the sisters to get ready Dominil worked at her computer. She'd downloaded some new hacking software and was modifying it. A few days ago Dominil had attempted to break into the Guild's computers but she'd been unsuccessful. Since her last cyber spying mission the Guild had increased their protection. Dominil was now upgrading her own software to penetrate the Guild's new security encryption.

Twenty minutes later she knocked heavily on the bathroom door.

"It's time to go. Finish your hair. We're only going to the rehearsal studio. Have you considered the matter of a name for your band yet? If I'm to book you gigs you need a name."

Dominil noticed a familiar aroma.

"Are you drinking whisky in there?"

"Yes. And we're almost finished our hair. We haven't thought of a name yet. What was that stupid one you suggested?"

"Yum Yum Sugary Snacks. I still like it. It employs irony, and also alliteration. Alliteration has been a powerful poetic tool for a long time. The Anglo-Saxon poets – "

"Will you shut up?" yelled Beauty.

"We'll call the band anything just so long as you don't go on about these damned Anglo-Saxon poets again," added Delicious.

When the twins were finally ready Dominil bundled them into her car and set off. They were late, though it probably wouldn't matter. The others would also be late. No matter how scared everyone was of Dominil – and they were all scared of her – it seemed that no power on earth could get musicians to turn up anywhere on time.

Dominil drove down to London Bridge with a lot on her mind. She would have had a great deal more on her mind if she'd known that the owner of the studio, having recognised them as werewolves due to his previous association with the Guild, had already alerted Mr Carmichael. The hunters were waiting for Yum Yum Sugary Snacks.

109

Gawain's next destination was the lair of the Young MacDoig. If Kalix was using laudanum it could only have come from the MacDoigs. There was no other known source. The night was cold and the rain was coming down heavily by the time Gawain arrived at the narrow alleyway in Limehouse.

"Who is it?"

"Gawain MacRinnalch. Here to see the Young MacDoig."

"The Young MacDoig is not here," came the reply.

Gawain called back loudly. "Open this door or I'll remove it from its hinges."

There was a pause. Gawain prepared to transform into his werewolf shape but before he could tear the door down it swung open and he found himself confronted not by the Young MacDoig but his father, the Merchant himself. The Merchant beamed at him.

"Gawain MacRinnalch! An unexpected pleasure. Come in man, and have a glass!"

Gawain entered the shop. He paid no heed to the clutter of artefacts, and shook his head at the offer of a drink.

"What brings you round these parts?" asked the Merchant. He smiled jovially, as if nothing could have pleased him more than a visit from Gawain. Despite being indoors he still wore his black hat and even though Gawain was fixated on his task he could not help but notice that MacDoig, with his side-whiskers and cane, was a notably strange figure. Micawber come to life perhaps, or Mr Pickwick.

"I'm looking for Kalix."

"Kalix MacRinnalch? I'm afraid you've come to the wrong place, young Gawain. I've not seen Kalix for many a long year. I'm sorry I can't help you."

The Merchant looked at Gawain, a benevolent expression on his red, cheerful face. MacDoig knew well that the Mistress of the Werewolves had banished Gawain, and he didn't intend to do anything which might upset the clan. He might have been prevailed upon to sell information but he surmised, quite correctly, that Gawain had no money to spare.

"I think you must have some knowledge of her," declared Gawain. "I was told that Kalix has been taking laudanum. No one sells laudanum these days but you and your son."

"Laudanum? It's a fine product, I grant you that. It suits the temperament of the poetic man, and indeed the poetic werewolf. I'm not one to partake of it myself, of course, but I believe it has fuelled the imagination of many an artist. Are you sure you won't take a glass of whisky with me?"

"Never mind the whisky," growled Gawain. "Where's Kalix?"

The Merchant chuckled, and placed his thumbs in the pockets of his pattered waistcoat.

"Not been here, Gawain, not been here at all."

"You're lying," said Gawain. "Her scent is in this room."

The Merchant chuckled again.

"There's no scent of any werewolf in this room, not even yours."

MacDoig the Merchant was telling the truth. Though he was not a sorcerer, MacDoig had a great deal of esoteric knowledge. He had traded for many spells from various realms. There was one in place here which prevented anyone from sensing who might have visited recently. Gawain was bluffing. He couldn't sense Kalix. Gawain gave a long low snarl and transformed into a werewolf.

"I won't ask you politely again," he said. "Tell me about Kalix."

"Gawain, you are fine young werewolf. One of the finest, I've always said. I knew your father well. What a warrior, and his father before him. I was always sorry you found yourself in trouble with the clan. My advice – "

He broke off as Gawain hurled himself towards him. Before he reached the Merchant, Gawain was flung backwards with great force. He crashed against the wall and found himself looking rather foolishly at the MacDoig, who continued to grin affably.

"Ah, Gawain, you always did have a streak of impatience in you. You know, young sir, that the MacDoigs are valued trading partners in many places, and when a man goes to some of these places, he picks up a thing of two. I wear a charm that will protect me from any were-wolf. Not that I expect any werewolf to attack me. After all I'm a great friend of the MacRinnalchs."

MacDoig picked up a bottle and a glass from a table nearby.

"Are you sure you won't have a drink?"

Gawain growled, and shook his head.

"Then I suppose it's time for you to leave," said the Merchant, and opened the door.

Later the Merchant chuckled to himself. Gawain. An impetuous wolf. Heading for a bad end, he was sure. To whom would it most profit him to transmit news of Gawain? The Mistress of the Were-wolves? Or her son Sarapen? Both perhaps? Like any good business-man, MacDoig was always keen to keep in with his customers, and if in doing so he could turn a profit, that was all to the good.

110

Kalix woke up the next day a little vague about what had happened the night before. Feeling thirsty, she dressed quickly and went downstairs. When Kalix crossed through the living room she was surprised to see Moonglow and Jay huddled together on the floor, under a quilt. They were still asleep but somehow they didn't look comfortable. The young werewolf crept past silently, took water from the kitchen and went back upstairs. As she reached her room, Daniel's bedroom door opened and he peered out.

"Are they awake yet?" he whispered.

Kalix shook her head. Daniel tiptoed along the corridor with exaggerated stealth and slipped into Kalix's small room.

"Good," he said. "I'm leaving the house before Moonglow gets up."

"Why?" said Kalix, puzzled.

"After last night's debacle I figure she might need a few hours to cool off."

"What's a debacle?"

"A general disaster in which everything goes wrong. You don't remember?"

Kalix shook her head.

"What went wrong?"

"Well, there was you collapsing all over her boyfriend for one thing."

Daniel looked pointedly at Kalix's bag.

"So the mysterious werewolf herbal concoction turns out to be laudanum. Powerful stuff, by all accounts. Yes, well may you hang your head in shame, Kalix, the way you plummeted to the ground, upsetting Moonglow's carefully laid dinner arrangements."

Noticing that this had made Kalix much more agitated than he intended, Daniel hurried to reassure her.

"Don't worry about it. Your collapse was no more than a side show compared to my performance."

"What did you do?"

It was Daniel's turn to look ashamed.

"Started an argument with Jay and, quite possibly, tried to pick a fight with him."

"You tried to pick a fight?" said Kalix, quite astonished at the thought. She couldn't imagine Daniel fighting with anyone.

"I was severely provoked. He criticised Motorhead. You can't do that in this house. Not when I've been drinking cider, anyway. I guess I didn't really try to fight him. Just abused him verbally for a while…"

Kalix looked sympathetically at Daniel.

"Is this all because you're in love with Moonglow?"

"How did you know that?" cried Daniel, agitated.

"It's the most obvious thing in the world."

"Is it? I suppose it is. Well, maybe that was why. But it's not just me that doesn't like Jay. Malveria really took against him. They had an argument about astrology and then when he had the nerve to spout some rubbish about Stonehenge she put him pretty soundly in his place. You can't argue with Malveria about Stonehenge, her grandmother knew the people who built it."

Daniel paused, and looked troubled.

"It all seemed funny at the time but I don't think Moonglow was very pleased. No girl likes to see her boyfriend harassed from every direction."

"Why are they sleeping downstairs?"

"Because Malveria accepted Moonglow's offer of a bed for the night. Not that Moonglow actually made the offer. Malveria just said she was tired and she much appreciated Moonglow's hospitality. Then she disappeared up to Moonglow's room. Jay was surprised."

Daniel stood up.

"I'm actually planning to arrive at university two hours before my first lecture, so you'll appreciate how much I don't want to meet Moonglow right now."

Daniel crept away and soon afterward Kalix heard him going as quietly as he could down the stairs and out of the house. She smiled. It sounded as if last night had been fun. She was sorry she couldn't remember it very well.

'But now they know about the laudanum,' she thought, and became worried. 'And Moonglow will be angry at me for collapsing on her boyfriend.' She wondered if she should follow Daniel's example and vacate the flat for a while. Deciding it would be a good idea, she put on her ragged coat, slung her bag over her shoulder and slipped out silently. She had nowhere to go, but, remembering how she had enjoyed looking at the boats, she decided to head for the river.

As Kalix walked swiftly northwards she attracted plenty of attention, though not the sort that she'd attracted recently. Then people had

264

wondered who the sick, trembling girl might be. Now they looked at her with admiration. She was still very pale, but she was healthier, and clean. With her large dark eyes, her perfect cheekbones and her incredibly long dark glossy hair, she looked like a teenage model walking down the catwalk to exhibit some new collection of ragged urban clothing. Kalix was exceptionally beautiful, the most beautiful of the ruling family of the MacRinnalchs, who were, as everyone acknowledged, a notably beautiful family.

111

Wary in case hunters from the Avenaris Guild were patrolling the same area, Kalix took a different route towards the river. She turned north east, became slightly lost, and ended up heading towards London Bridge. It was now well into the afternoon and the rain began to come down heavily. Kalix pulled her coat around her and put on her sunglasses. She still enjoyed wearing shades at inappropriate times.

A hundred yards from the river, she stopped, and sniffed the air. She could smell werewolves. Who was it? Someone whose scent she hadn't encountered for a long time. She sniffed again. More than one werewolf. There were too many other scents around for her to distinguish them properly. She walked on, intrigued. As she neared London Bridge and the scents became clearer she realised with surprise that it was her cousin Dominil. What could she be doing here?

Kalix halted, and wondered if she should turn back. Dominil had never tried to pursue her before but why else would she be here? Kalix's mother must have sent her. Kalix scowled and was about to go back when she suddenly recognised the other werewolf scents. Butix and Delix. Kalix remembered them with more fondness that any other members of her family. They had always been creating havoc in the castle and it was they who'd given Kalix her first taste of whisky. Kalix was sure that Beauty and Delicious wouldn't be in pursuit of her. 'Perhaps,' she thought, 'They've fled from the clan and that horrible white wolf Dominil has come to attack them.' Dominil had always treated Kalix with contempt and Kalix could believe anything bad about her. She trotted forward, prepared to rescue Beauty and

Delicious from the evil Dominil.

Kalix found herself in a small back street full of shabby looking premises. A builders yard, a boarded up cafe, a few empty shops in a bad state of repair. She concealed herself behind a white van and looked on curiously as several young men came out of a building nearby carrying instruments. They loaded them into a car. Kalix managed to catch a few of their words.

"That white-haired maniac never gives us a break."

"She's insane. She belongs in an asylum."

"Hey, don't knock it," said the third young man. "She got us back in the studio didn't she?"

The rest of their words were lost as they drove off. So they were musicians. And Dominil was helping them. Kalix stood on her own on the pavement in the rain, wondering if she should go inside. It would be good to see Beauty and Delicious, perhaps. Kalix suddenly remembered that even though the twins had given her whisky at the castle, they hadn't really been her friends. They had been too involved in their own affairs to pay her much attention. Sometimes when they'd been up to some mischief and Kalix had wanted to go along, they'd sent her away, telling her she was too young.

It was becoming dark and Kalix didn't like this gloomy street with the boarded up buildings. Deciding she didn't want to meet three werewolves who'd probably not want to talk to her, she turned to leave. Then several things happened in quick succession. First Kalix caught the scent of Sarapen. Before she could move Sarapen dropped from the sky having apparently travelled over the rooftops. As he landed beside her he seemed surprised.

"Kalix? It was not your scent I followed. Indeed, you seem to have no scent."

Sarapen took a step towards her, as darkness fell.

"But it's as good a place to meet you as anywhere, sister."

Kalix prepared to defend herself but they were interrupted by a great commotion as several vans raced into the street. A crowd of men with dogs emerged from the vehicles and swarmed into the rehearsal studios.

"Dominil," muttered Sarapen. He immediately changed into his immense werewolf form and sprinted towards the rehearsal studio. Kalix transformed and ran after him. Seeing members of her clan in peril she forgot about the danger she was in from Sarapen, and hurried

266

to assist them.

The two werewolves crashed through the front door of the studio to find the place in uproar. The corridor leading to the rehearsal rooms was full of men with snarling dogs who were heading for a room at the far end. The mighty Sarapen in his terrifying werewolf form fell on them with fury, sending one crushed body spinning away before picking up another and tossing it like a child's doll onto the heads of the men in front. The hunters, surprised by the unexpected assault from behind, yelled as they turned to face their attackers. Kalix fixed her jaws to the neck of a hunter and her teeth tore great wounds on his throat. She tossed the body away and leapt for the next. Her battle-madness descended on her and she bit, clawed, kicked and beat her way down the corridor in a savage fury, arriving at the door of the rehearsal room over a pile of broken and bloody bodies.

Sarapen was already there. He rushed into the rehearsal room where Dominil was disappearing under the weight of her attackers. There were men with guns, trying to get a clear shot at the savagely resisting werewolf, and dogs hanging on to her legs, snarling and barking. Beauty and Delicious, who for some reason had not transformed into their werewolf shape, were trying to beat off their attackers with their guitars. This was futile. The sisters were thrown back and hunters leapt to grab hold of them. Kalix jumped across the rehearsal studio, tearing the gun from one hunter's hand then smashing her taloned foot brutally into the face of another. A dog tried to sink its teeth into her leg and Kalix stamped downwards, breaking its neck.

Sarapen leapt into the heaving mass of bodies around Dominil, dragging them from her and tossing them against the walls. Two shots rang out and he flinched slightly before his jaws were around the neck of the man who had fired them, almost decapitating him with the strength of his bite. Seizing he opportunity, Dominil leapt to her feet. Her white werewolf coat was stained with blood but she threw herself back into the fray, tearing and rending the men from the Guild. They began to fall back, finding themselves confronted by a great deal more werewolf strength than they'd been expecting. They had not anticipated the savage, bestial fury of Kalix, Sarapen and Dominil. When Kalix finished off the hunters who had been attacking the twins, and turned to fall upon the men confronting Sarapen and Dominil, they broke and ran.

The rehearsal room was now a grim scene of destruction. Broken and bleeding bodies lay everywhere. Men and dogs moaned in pain among the smashed remains of the studio equipment. Ruined amplifiers and speakers littered the floor. Dominil wasted no time in examining the aftermath of the battle.

"Outside," she said. "My car."

Beauty and Delicious seemed shocked by the events. They were not warlike. Dominil grabbed them and dragged them from the building.

"You drive," she said, thrusting Delicious into the front seat. Delicious put the key in the ignition and pulled away from the kerb like a racing driver, and Dominil didn't protest. There was no telling if reinforcements from the Guild might be on the way.

In the back of the car Kalix found herself in the unusual position of being separated only by Dominil from her older brother. She remained in her werewolf form, ready to fight him off. Dominil turned her white head towards her.

"A timely intervention," she said, calmly. She turned to Sarapen.

"And a timely intervention from you, cousin."

If Dominil was surprised to see Kalix and Sarapen together she didn't show it, concentrating instead on giving some brisk instructions to Delicious as to the quickest route away from the studio. When they were some way north of the river, she told Delicious to turn down a side street and stop the car.

"This is as far as you go, Sarapen."

There was a trickle of blood on Sarapen's arm where he'd been grazed by a silver bullet. It wasn't a serious wound but even so, it was painful. An injury caused by silver was always painful for a werewolf. He ignored it. Sarapen changed back into his human shape, and looked over at Kalix.

"Well fought, sister. Like a MacRinnalch."

It was a strange fortune of war, thought Sarapen. Only days ago he had sent out the Douglas-MacPhees to find Kalix. Now Sarapen had encountered her, but honour prevented him from taking her prisoner. He could not resume hostilities so soon after she'd fought by his side. But it was interesting that something was masking her scent, and he would pass on the information to the MacPhees. He turned back to Dominil and they stared into each other's eyes for a long moment. Then Sarapen opened the door and exited into the street. Unexpectedly, Dominil followed him.

"Cousin," she said, quietly, so those in the car couldn't hear. "What brought you to the scene?"

Sarapen didn't answer. The rain poured down but it didn't wash away the tension than flowed between Dominil and Sarapen.

"Were you tracking me?" demanded Dominil.

"No. I was hunting Markus. But I warn you, the situation has now become worse. If you continue to support Markus you may come to harm."

Dominil's face was hard and emotionless.

"You need not fear for me. Why has the situation become worse?"

"Markus killed my counsellor Mirasen. I'll make him pay for it."

Sarapen stared into the dark, dark eyes of his former lover. His look was so intense than Dominil made ready to defend herself. Sarapen stepped forward. Dominil held her ground. There faces were only inches apart. They remained like that for several seconds. Abruptly, he turned on his heel to vanish into the rain. Dominil climbed back into the car.

"Drive," she said. "Quickly. I don't trust him not to follow us."

112

Thrix had spent the day trying to make up for lost time. As she had important shows in Milan and New York coming up, Ann suggested that she delegate some of Malveria's outfits to other designers. Thrix rejected the idea.

"You can't delegate Malveria. She'd have a fit. Besides, Malveria's money has been keeping me afloat for the past year. Without her I'd never have made it this far. I owe her."

For Livia's 500th birthday party, the Fire Queen's outfits had to be perfect. The sorceress's party would be the highlight of the social calendar. Her four hundredth birthday celebration had gone down in legend and this one was set to surpass it. Everyone of importance would be there, even the ladies from the court of the iron elementals, and they hardly ever went out to social events. Last night at Thrix's apartment a tear had formed in Malveria's eye at the thought of Princess Kabachetka once more outdoing her in the fashion stakes.

"If she is judged to be better dressed than me I shall simply die," said Malveria, dabbing her eyes with a small handkerchief. "There are many jealous elementals who are now envious of my excellent style. It is not easy, darling Thrix, to be the fashion leader in the realm of the Hiyasta. Jealousy lurks around every corner. Apthalia the Grim would like nothing better than a chance to gossip about my poor garments, if poor they were."

"Doesn't Apthalia the Grim spend her time waiting on quiet roads, trying to ambush lonely travellers?" asked Thrix.

"Not so much now," replied Malveria. "These days she's more interested in fashion. And since she had her warts removed and her nose done, and started buying her clothes from Dior, rather than simply robbing the corpses of her victims, she is not so bad looking, I admit. But she is a terrible gossip. When the Duchess Gargamond, Lady of Blazing Destruction, wore the same aquamarine frock with matching shoes and handbag to two separate sacrifices, Apthalia the Grim had spread it all round the realms before the day was out. Poor Duchess Gargamond was forced to retreat to her castle in shame and has never been the same since."

"I see," said Thrix. "That would explain why she hasn't been responding to summonses recently. I understand her devotees are devastated."

"Indeed they are," agreed Malveria. "But really, who can blame the Duchess? One cannot be answering requests to deal out blazing destruction when one's frocks are the subject of public ridicule."

Thrix showed her most recent sketches to Ann.

"What do you think of this line for Malveria? I mean a formal coat like this in dark blue for her arrival in the horse drawn carriage, then a dress something like this for the start of the evening?"

"It's a beautiful dress but Malveria will probably want something a little more daring."

Thrix nodded. It was a continual problem, trying to merge Thrix's good taste with the Fire Queen's liking for the dramatic and the revealing.

"I think I can persuade her, particularly as I've been working on these for the night-time carnival."

The Sorceress Livia's birthday party was spread over five days – which was appropriate, as the birth of the sorceress had taken five days – and Malveria would need a lot of outfits. Ann nodded with approval as she saw Thrix's design for carnival night, a short golden skirt and halter top which might have been worn by a dancer in a video on MTV.

"She'll like that."

"She will. Malveria's been doing sit ups for the past three months and is keen to show off her flat abdominal muscles. Ever since she read about Heidi Klum's exercise regime she's been hard at it."

Malveria would need around twenty complete outfits. It was a major task for Thrix, and she was already falling behind schedule. At the end of her working day she only had time for a hastily eaten sandwich before hurrying out with Ann to a fashion show she could not afford to miss. When she had settled down in her seat – not as important a seat as she would have liked – she noticed with displeasure that Donald Carver was in the audience.

"My last miserable date," she whispered to Ann, with some suspicion. "Are you trying to set me up again?"

Ann shook her head.

"I couldn't if I wanted. You messed it up too badly."

At the drinks party after the show Thrix studiously tried to avoid coming into contact with Donald Carver and consequently bumped into him every time she turned round. She felt embarrassed, and the fact that he seemed to have become very close to the new accessories editor at Cosmopolitan didn't make it any better. Thrix took refuge with Ann behind a phalanx of Japanese buyers who were grouped together near the bar.

"Every time I take a step I'm practically falling over him."

"Don't worry," said Ann. "You didn't like him that much anyway."

"What's that got to do with it? He never called me back. Which he should have. A woman is entitled to at least one phone call even after the worst dinner date. So now I'm standing here on my own while the man who never phoned me back is waltzing round with a new date. I might as well just carry a sign saying *don't date Thrix MacRinnalch she's a complete waste of time.*"

Thrix took a glass of wine from the tray of a passing waiter, downed it quickly enough to replace the glass on the tray of the next waiter and take another, then walked to the bar to see what they had in the way of whisky.

"You never find a decent whisky at these things," she complained to her assistant.

"There's not that many Scottish werewolves wanting service, I suppose," said Ann.

By the time she took a taxi home, Thrix was in a very bad mood. The strain of over-work, the annoyance of dealing with her family and the embarrassment of meeting Donald all combined to put her in a foul temper which was exacerbated by her intake of alcohol. She regretted going to the show, particularly as they hadn't even provided her with a good seat. Thrix felt the familiar resentment of the outsider who couldn't quite force her way in. She drummed her fingers on her lap. She would triumph in Milan and New York and then perhaps she might get the respect she deserved.

Thrix noticed where they were and abruptly instructed the driver to stop the cab. She paid for her ride, climbed out of the taxi then looked around her with a malevolent expression. It was cold, and teeming with rain, but Thrix paid no attention to the weather. This small street, just north of Oxford Street, was home to Zatek's head-quarters. It was now two in the morning and no one was around apart from a tramp who slept in a doorway nearby, wrapped in a filthy blanket with a layer of cardboard beneath him. Thrix scanned the dark buildings around her. She soon found what she was looking for. One of the buildings positively radiated magic. Thrix marched towards it, her high heels clicking on the pavement, her eyes narrowed to slits. So Zatek thought he could spy on the Enchantress. A bad mistake.

Thrix stood in front of his building. It was protected by a spell. A very minor spell, thought Thrix, examining it with her own sorcery. Not nearly enough to protect Zatek from the wrath of Thrix MacRinnalch: werewolf, enchantress, and currently in a really bad mood. Zatek was about to learn the power of a true sorceress. The Enchantress brushed her wet hair from her face, then chanted a spell to burst through Zatek's protection. The magic Thrix used was powerful. It would cause such devastation in Zatek's headquarters that he would never dare meddle with the Enchantress again. A bolt of energy flashed from her fingertips towards the building. Thrix laughed. This felt good. She should have done it before.

Unexpectedly, the bolt of energy bounced off the wall, and struck Thrix. She was thrown all the way across the street and landed unconscious on the opposite pavement. Sparks of blue light flickered around her body. The Enchantress lay motionless in the rain, her golden hair splayed out around her. Further up the road the tramp slumbered on undisturbed. In the next street, a few late night travellers, seeing the

272

flashes of light, thought that a thunderstorm had begun. They pulled their coats around them and hurried home as quickly as they could.

113

As Daniel had predicted, Moonglow was not in the best of moods. When she woke up on the floor of the living room beside Jay she was stiff, cold, and very dissatisfied with last night's events. The evening had started off well, but from the moment Kalix stumbled in and crashed into Jay, it had gone terribly wrong. It had been bad enough having an intoxicated girl falling all over the place, but why had Daniel insisted on starting a foolish argument about Motorhead? Daniel's music obsessions were usually quite funny but there was no excuse for using them to harass her boyfriend. And why had Malveria and Thrix chosen that moment to arrive? The Fire Queen hadn't really seemed to take to Jay. That was no reason to mock his theories on Stonehenge thought Moonglow, angrily. Worst of all had been Malveria's unexpected decision to stay the night in Moonglow's bed. In response to Jay's questioning look Moonglow could only explain, rather lamely, that her friend Jane was slightly eccentric, and needed to have her whims indulged.

"Couldn't you indulge them another time?" suggested Jay.

"Sorry," said Moonglow. "But I'm sure we can be comfy on the floor."

They hadn't been. Moonglow had tried to make the best of it, even suggesting that it was quite romantic, but Jay hadn't seen it that way. When Moonglow tried to get close to him he'd claimed to be tired, and turned over.

Moonglow's resentment did not last for long. Really, she was too good-natured for that. By the time she was getting off the bus outside college, she was almost back to her normal self. She gave her seminar, leading a small group of students through a translation of a Sumerian text. The text in itself was not that interesting, being mainly a list of the crops produced by farms belonging to the King of Ur, but it had been a challenging task. She was gratified when her tutor congratulated her on her excellent work.

273

Almost next door to King's College was Brettenham House, a large Georgian building which had been renovated a few years ago. It was hidden away behind a small doorway in the Strand, but once through the door a visitor arrived in a grand courtyard full of fountains. Today was damp and chilly, and not really the time for admiring architecture, but after her seminar Moonglow took a walk there anyway, wanting some fresh air before her afternoon classes. There were few people in the courtyard. Moonglow shivered in the cold. She decided against sitting down. She'd just walk round before heading back.

A tramp sat on one of the chairs in the courtyard. Not old, but lost and hopeless looking. Dirty and unshaven, he looked forlornly at the paving stones in front of him. A pathetic young man with the weight of the world on his shoulders, from the looks of him. Moonglow felt sorry for him. She fished in her quaint little purse for some money. The young man did not look up. Moonglow noticed that he was wearing what had once been a smart suit, though it was now very ragged. His hair was rather long, matted, and seemed to be stained with blood.

"Do you want – " began Moonglow, trying to attract his attention so he would take the coins.

The tramp looked up. Moonglow took a step back. She almost ran away but there was something too hopeless about him for her to run.

"Markus?" she said.

Markus looked right through her. He didn't recognise her. Moonglow stood there staring, not knowing what to do. She should leave. This was the werewolf who had brutally attacked Kalix. He couldn't be trusted. But he looked so pathetic.

"Markus? What happened?"

Markus didn't answer. Moonglow stood in front of him, unsure whether to leave him there or help him. She didn't know why she should be helping him. It was foolish to get involved with Kalix's enemies. The rain intensified. Moonglow was too moved by sympathy to just walk away.

"Do you need help?" she asked.

Markus didn't respond. Moonglow could see that he was in shock.

"Markus," she said, quite loudly. "What's the matter?"

Markus lifted his face a fraction of an inch.

"Talixia," he said. A look of anguish spread over his features. Moonglow didn't know what *Talixia* meant. As far as she could see, Markus's injuries weren't serious. If she could just get him home, he

274

could rest and recover. She'd already seen the healing powers that the werewolves had.

"Where do you live?"

Markus didn't respond. Moonglow had now had enough of standing in the rain so she took Markus's hand and helped him gently to his feet. He didn't protest. She led him back to King's College, downstairs to one of the men's washrooms. Moonglow would probably have to take Markus home in a taxi and she knew that a London taxi driver would object to picking up a fare with blood on his face.

"Wash your face," she instructed, "And then you can go home."

Markus stood dumbly in front of the basin. Moonglow sighed, and took a handkerchief from her bag. Here she was, washing another werewolf. It was very strange, when you thought about it. She gently dabbed the dirt and blood from his face. All the while he stood unprotesting like a man in a trance. Soon he was looking better. Not great, with his suit ripped, but not so bad that a taxi driver would refuse to pick him up.

"Now," said Moonglow. "I'm going to check your wallet. Don't do anything crazy."

She felt around inside Markus's jacket and found his wallet.

"Is this where you live?"

Markus nodded.

"Then let's go."

As they crawled through the heavy London traffic, Moonglow again wondered why she was doing this. She couldn't have explained why exactly. The taxi dropped them off in Bayswater and Moonglow led Markus towards the door of his apartment block. She was about to start hunting in his pockets for keys when she found herself abruptly confronted by two men, both dark haired, both with the look of the MacRinnalchs about them. They regarded Moonglow with suspicion.

"Who are you?"

"I found him sitting on a bench," replied Moonglow, not wanting to give out her name.

"We'll take him from here."

Moonglow moved protectively in front of Markus.

"Why? Who are you?"

"Gregor MacRinnalch," said one of the men. "I work for Markus."

Markus seemed to come back into the contact with the real world. He spoke to Moonglow in a quiet voice.

"It's all right," he said. "I know Gregor. He'll look after me now. Thanks for helping me."

With that, Markus left, led of by Gregor. Moonglow watched as they took him inside. She couldn't afford a taxi back to college so she headed for the nearest tube station. She had missed her first English lecture of the afternoon but if she hurried she might make the next.

114

Thrix woke up in her office. Gawain was standing over her. She leapt to her feet.

"What happened?"

"I found you unconscious in the street. I brought you here."

The Enchantress remembered her spell bouncing back off Zatek's building. Not only had her spell been deflected it had come back onto Thrix with terrific force and were it not for the strength of her own magical protection it might well have killed her. Obviously she had seriously underestimated Zatek's power. It was something to worry about later, after she'd dealt with Gawain.

Thrix's outfit was ruined and her hair was streaked with muddy water. It was humiliating to have Gawain see her in this condition. Fortunately she was uninjured, apart from a few bruises.

"Were you following me?" she demanded.

Gawain shook his head.

"I was travelling through the city when I scented a werewolf in trouble. It turned out to be you."

"An odd co-incidence," said Thrix, suspiciously.

"Perhaps," admitted Gawain.

The Enchantress realised that she was being ungrateful. It had been quite gallant of him to pick her up off the street and carry her to safety. She thanked him, a little stiffly, then brought out her MacRinnalch whisky from her cabinet. She poured herself a very large drink and offered a glass to Gawain which he accepted. Gawain did not ask what had happened to the Enchantress, regarding it as not his business. He did look pointedly at her.

"I was intending to visit you again."

"About Kalix, I suppose?"

After the aggravation which Thrix had suffered this night, she was not pleased to find herself once more subject to interrogation. It occurred to her to blast Gawain with a spell. That would teach him to annoy her with questions. But then she felt tired of it all. 'To hell with it,' she thought. 'I don't care if he knows where Kalix is or not. Mother can sort it out, she's the one that cares about all this.' She finished her whisky and poured herself another. Her supply of the MacRinnalch malt was running low, a result of the stress she'd been feeling recently. She'd either have to stop feeling so stressed or, more likely, ask her mother to send another crate.

"Gawain. There is nothing in the world that you could do to force information out of me. Apart from maybe bore me to death, which is possible. If I wanted to I'd send you out my office as a small pile of ashes. But to tell you the truth, I can't be bothered. And, I suppose, I owe you for the rescue. If you want to see Kalix, fine, go and see her. No doubt disaster will ensue but that's not my problem."

The Enchantress told Gawain the address in Kennington.

"She's living with two students. Don't harm them, they've been looking after her well."

Gawain nodded. As he was leaving the office he paused, and looked over to the sketches on her desk.

"You're a fine artist, Thrix MacRinnalch," he said, then disappeared.

'A rather incongruous time for a compliment,' thought Thrix. Perhaps it was Gawain's way of thanking her for her help. He did have something of the gentleman about him, though he was still young and rough round the edges.

Thrix felt too tired to go home. She removed her wet outer garments, took a coat from the clothes rack and lay down on the couch, using the coat as a blanket and a cushion as a pillow. It wasn't the first time she'd spent the night in her office. At least it would allow her to make an early start in the morning. Before she fell asleep she wondered what her old teacher Minerva MacRinnalch would have had to say about the night's events. Thrix had originally learned her sorcery from Minerva, studying with her for almost six years. Since then Thrix had learned a good deal more, but the foundation of everything she knew came from Minerva. Including, Thrix now recalled, the advice never to take petty revenge by means of sorcery. Followed by the advice that if you were unable to resist taking petty revenge, then make sure you did it right. Thrix shuddered to think what old Minerva would have to say about her student ending up unconscious in a puddle. Fortunately Minerva had retired to a very remote mountain top and rarely ventured into the world these days.

The Enchantress transformed into her werewolf shape. It would renew her strength. By morning she would be fine. She drifted off to sleep, comforted by thoughts of her old teacher, whom she had liked a good deal more than any member of her family.

115

Delicious drove back to Camden. By the time they reached their house the twins were in good spirits. The danger was over, they were safe, and no werewolf would dwell for too long on an attack by the Avenaris Guild.

Dominil was thoughtful, and remained silent all the way home. Kalix was intrigued to meet them all, though nervous. It was strange, meeting werewolves from her family who weren't trying to drag her back to Scotland. It was still a surprise to find Dominil associating with the twins. They were outcasts from the family. Not hated perhaps, and not hunted like Kalix, but outcasts all the same.

From their conversation she gathered that they were in a band. They played guitar and sang and they were soon going to be stars. They were cheerful and confident. Kalix felt some admiration, and some jealousy. The twins were free, and doing what they wanted. The family wasn't chasing them and they had their own house to live in. They never had to hide in alleyways. They talked about going out and drinking with friends. Kalix could tell just by looking at their brightly coloured hair that their lives were good. Suddenly she felt much younger than them, and quite inferior. When Kalix asked what their band was called, her voice came out surprisingly weak, and the sisters didn't hear her over the traffic. Kalix felt stupid to have spoken and not received an answer. She was too shy to repeat the question.

By the time they reached Camden Kalix was regretting that she'd come. She dreaded them asking her what she did with her life. The fact that she'd fought savagely to save them only an hour ago was quite forgotten by Kalix, because the sisters weren't talking about fighting. They were talking about lyrics, amplifiers and shiny new clothes to wear onstage. It sounded a lot more interesting than Kalix's life. When they arrived at their house, Beauty and Delicious tumbled out of the car and headed inside. Kalix remained where she was.

"Do you want to come in?" asked Dominil.

"I don't know," mumbled Kalix.

"What do you mean you don't know?"

"All right," said Kalix, and followed her from the car.

Dominil had not mentioned the fight. Nor had she commented on the odd fact that the sisters hadn't transformed into werewolves when they were under attack. Kalix was curious about this. She couldn't imagine why the sisters had chosen to face the hunters in human form. They would have been much stronger as werewolves.

The house was now tidy. The cleaners had done an efficient job and Beauty and Delicious were surprisingly hesitant about messing the place up again. Dominil would nag at them if they did. This was the down side to their involvement with her. In revenge, they were writing songs about her. *Evil White-Haired Slut* was already completed, and *Stupid Werewolf Bitch* was coming along well.

"What's your band called?" asked Kalix, again.

"Yum Yum Sugary Snacks."

"That's a good name," said Kalix. "It suits you."

The twins didn't seem interested in her opinion. Kalix sat quietly and looked round at the array of guitars neatly stored on racks, and the huge collection of CDs on the walls, and music magazines and papers on shelves.

Dominil was already getting down to business.

"I'll find another rehearsal studio. Do you have any preferences?"

Beauty and Delicious began a long conversation about all the rehearsal studios they'd been in; which ones they liked and which ones they were banned from. After that they all moved on to a discussion about venues. By the time they started discussing the new software Dominil was installing on their sampler, Kalix was feeling thoroughly left out of things. Dominil acted like she wasn't there. Even though Kalix was a werewolf like them, and a member of the family, the musicians and their manager seemed to have no time for her. Kalix felt like a young and very boring werewolf with nothing interesting to say. She wanted to leave but she couldn't seem to find an opportunity even to say goodbye. Finally, when Beauty and Delicious went to the kitchen to make coffee and Dominil followed them in, Kalix just slipped quietly out of the house and headed for home.

She felt depressed. It hadn't been that much fun meeting the twins, and she didn't like Dominil at all.

116

Verasa studied her new Perugino with little pleasure. She'd bought it last month, intending to have a copy made before loaning the original to the National Gallery of Scotland. Normally this would have brought Verasa a good deal of satisfaction. Two years ago the Scottish Arts Council had held a dinner for her, honouring her contribution to the Scottish arts. It remained a very pleasurable memory. Unfortunately the news from England was too bad to allow her to indulge herself in any form of artistic pleasure at the moment.

Her sister Lucia was furious at Markus's attack on her son Decembrius. Verasa pointed out that Markus had been maddened by the death of Talixia but it had not mollified Lucia. She doted on her son. And, as she forcefully reminded the Mistress of the Werewolves, Decembrius had not been responsible for Talixia's death.

Verasa herself had been extremely concerned when Markus had gone missing after the attack. She'd spent a few very anxious days till news arrived that he'd been brought home by a young woman who no one knew. Again she felt a flicker of annoyance at her younger son. He owed it to her to keep her informed. She understood that Markus was upset about Talixia but that was no reason to lose control.

Dominil had reported the events at the rehearsal studio. That was a strange story. An attack by a large group of hunters followed by a rescue by Sarapen and Kalix. Dominil believed they had met by chance outside the studio. Sarapen, having encountered Kalix, would now pursue her, of that Verasa was sure. She consulted with Rainal and they sat deep into the night, sipping whisky and eating from a dish of venison from a stag that had been killed that day.

"What will Sarapen do now?" wondered Rainal. "Now that Markus has killed Mirasen?"

"He'll try to kill Markus of course. Sarapen will regard it as justifiable revenge, and he might be right, by clan tradition."

"Not if he started the violence by killing Talixia."

"True. But we can't prove he did."

Verasa had sent more werewolves from her estates down to London to stay by Markus's side.

"Only two weeks till the next meeting of the Great Council," said Rainal. "It will certainly be an interesting affair."

"Too interesting, possibly. I'm thinking of postponing it."

Rainal protested. "The meeting cannot be postponed."

"I am the acting head of the clan. In exceptional circumstances the head of the clan may delay the meeting. There are precedents."

"Only in time of war."

"This is now war."

Rainal didn't like it but Verasa was adamant.

"I need more time. Dominil needs more time. And I don't want to risk Lucia changing her vote. Far better to let her forget her anger at the attack on Decembrius."

117

Kalix trudged home in the rain. She had no money so she faced a long walk from Camden to Kennington, all the way through town and over the river. She wondered if she should try to take the underground without buying a ticket but decided against it. She didn't feel like fleeing from a ticket inspector.

Kalix had felt some elation after the fight but it had now faded, leaving her depressed. The meeting with Beauty, Delicious and Dominil had left her feeling inadequate. She wasn't looking forward to arriving home. The young werewolf had now convinced herself that Moonglow hated her for crashing into Jay. Probably she would be thrown out the house. If it wasn't for her journal and her walkman she wouldn't even go back. She cursed Moonglow for being so unreasonable, and cursed herself for ever getting involved with humans. But she didn't seem to get on much better with werewolves. Dominil had hardly spoken a word to her and the twins obviously regarded her as an idiot.

Kalix tried to cheer herself up with the thought that she might never eat again. It worked for a while but by the time she reached the river her depression was turning into anxiety and she wished she had her laudanum with her. Kalix plodded on through the rain. When she finally arrived in Kennington she took out the shiny new key Daniel had cut for her and opened the door as quietly as she could. Moonglow wasn't in. Daniel was slumped on the couch in front of the TV.

"Kalix. I'm glad you've come home."

This took Kalix by surprise.

"Are you?"

"Of course. I've had a terrible day."

"Is Moonglow throwing me out?" said Kalix.

"What?" Daniel laughed. "Of course not. She wasn't that mad. Moonglow can't stay in a bad mood for long. She's gone over to Jay's to have a better evening, that'll cheer her up."

"Oh."

"You better dry your hair," said Daniel.

Kalix went up to her room and hastily drank some laudanum. Because Daniel had suggested it, she dried her hair with a towel before going back downstairs.

"Are you sure Moonglow doesn't want me to leave?" she asked.

Daniel almost laughed again but when he saw Kalix was very concerned about this he reassured her.

"It was really nothing. Moonglow likes you."

"Does she?"

"Of course. How could you think she didn't?"

"No one likes me."

"We like you a lot."

Kalix had difficulty accepting this.

"Why?"

Daniel shrugged.

"Why would anyone not like a bouncy young werewolf like you?"

The word *bouncy* was so unexpected and so inappropriate that Kalix laughed. She wanted to tell Daniel that she liked him but it felt like an awkward thing to say.

"Did you have a good time at college today?" was the best she could manage.

Daniel looked glum, and sank further into the couch.

"No. It was a bad day."

"Were the lectures hard?"

"The lectures? I didn't really notice, to be honest. What made today an especially bad day was that I went and talked to Alicia after Moonglow practically forced me into it, and when I was talking to her she looked bored and said she had to go and do something else."

"What did she have to do?"

"She didn't specify."

Daniel sighed.

"I am the number one loser when it comes to talking to girls, it has to be said."

"Lots of girls must like you," said Kalix, who didn't like to see Daniel depressed.

"Well no. Not lots of girls. Very few girls. Actually no girls like me. Not Moonglow and not Alicia and not any of the hundreds who wander around King's College every day."

"What about the girl at the party?"

Remembering this sorry experience, Daniel became more depressed than ever.

"I'm going to eat everything in the fridge then drink the last of my wine."

Daniel headed for the kitchen, looking sad. Kalix sat for a while, puzzled. She didn't like it that Daniel was sad. He was always so nice to her. She couldn't understand why no girls liked him. Kalix wished that she could cheer him up but she wasn't sure how to go about it. Usually she was the one who was depressed. She had no experience of bringing cheer to anyone.

Kalix rose from her chair, a little unsteadily. The day had taken a lot out of her. The fight had been very violent and though turning into a werewolf had given her energy, this had now faded. She'd not eaten for several days. The laudanum she'd drunk when she came in was coursing through her system, making her drowsy and euphoric by turns. She followed Daniel into the kitchen.

"I like you," she said, then took him in a tight embrace and kissed him.

Daniel was startled. So startled that he failed to move. He really didn't think he should be kissing the young werewolf but he was too surprised to break away. Besides, Kalix's embrace was very strong.

Also, it was so long since anyone had kissed Daniel that he wasn't finding it that unpleasant.

"Eh... hello..." came a voice from only a few feet away.

Daniel leapt backwards, banging himself quite painfully against the sink. To his horror he found Moonglow regarding them with a shocked expression.

"Hi!" said Daniel. He was grinning wildly in an attempt to appear unruffled, meanwhile wishing that he might be instantly teleported to another dimension.

"What's going on?" said Moonglow.

"I think I'll go to my room now," said Kalix, and trotted off.

Moonglow watched her go then turned to Daniel.

"You kissed her?"

"Absolutely not."

"What do you mean absolutely not? I saw you!"

"She just grabbed me and kissed me, it took me by surprise."

Moonglow frowned.

"I didn't see you fighting her off."

"I didn't mean it!" said Daniel. "It just happened!"

Moonglow emptied the contents of her shopping bag into the fridge. She didn't know what to think about Daniel kissing Kalix. It was certainly an unexpected development. It surprised her so much that she forgot all about the suspicious looking young man she'd seen loitering outside their house. When she'd reached the front door and turned back to check, he'd disappeared.

"I mean, she's been sick," said Moonglow. "And she's only seventeen."

"Isn't that older in werewolf years?" said Daniel. "You know, like cats?"

Daniel was mortified by the whole event. He was aware that he hadn't exactly struggled to avoid it, though he tried to pretend he had.

"Just walked up and grabbed me. I was ending it right then when you came in, just about to push her away..."

"Stop babbling," said Moonglow, and almost smiled. "Hey, you're both adults, more or less."

In the small back yard outside the kitchen, Gawain was watching. He had seen everything through the kitchen window. He'd seen Kalix kissing another man. The werewolf stood in silence for a long time. He'd yearned to see Kalix for three years.

'Well now I've seen her,' he thought, bitterly. He leapt over the fence and hurried away, with no destination in mind, but a desire to put as much distance as possible between himself and the unbearably painful sight of Kalix in someone else's arms.

At her office in the centre of London, Thrix was sleeping on her couch. She woke suddenly. No matter how deep her sleep, the Enchantress could not be taken unawares. She awoke knowing that someone was nearby. She looked round the room, her werewolf eyes adjusting instantly to the dark. There was no one in her office but a slight scrabbling noise outside made he look round in alarm. She was four floors up and no one could possibly be outside her window.

Clinging on to the small window ledge, apparently trying to attract her attention, was a werewolf.

"Gawain? What are you doing here?"

"I need to talk."

"You need to talk?" The Enchantress was mystified and considered closing the window again. But when she looked into Gawain's werewolf eyes she could see that they had recently been wet with tears. She stepped back to let him in. Gawain stood awkwardly in the room. Thrix regarded him without sympathy.

"This had better be good, Gawain."

The Enchantress was angered to have been wakened in this way, angered by Gawain's effrontery in appearing outside her window. Her limbs were still sore from the unfortunate experience at Zatek's and this annoyed her more.

"What's so important that you're climbing the outside of my building? Did you damage anything out there?"

Gawain looked utterly hopeless.

"Kalix," he said, eventually.

"Is she dead?"

Gawain shook his head. He seemed unwilling to say more. Thrix's patience was wearing very thin. She had no great liking for Gawain.

"Tell me the problem or get out."

"I saw her kissing someone," said Gawain.

Thrix was tempted to laugh. 'So much for the grand passion,' she thought. 'Perhaps Gawain will now realise that Kalix is not a suitable werewolf to fall in love with.'

"Gawain, you never did have a true understanding of Kalix."

Gawain sat down very heavily. Such was his obvious misery that even the Enchantress, who had little sympathy to spare, could not quite bring herself to throw him out. She transformed back into her human shape, crossed to her cabinet and brought out her whisky.

"The MacRinnalchs generally find this helpful for all problems," she said, dryly, and poured two glasses.

118

Sarapen thought for a long time about his encounter with Dominil. It had raised some disturbing emotions. Even though Sarapen had focused his will on the Thaneship, to the exclusion of all else, images of the white-haired werewolf kept interrupting his thoughts. He'd been surprised at the strength of feeling he still had for Dominil. When he saw the hunters heading into the studio, Sarapen had abandoned all thoughts of Kalix and the Thaneship and rushed to save her.

He hated Dominil. Unfortunately, his passion for her had never abated. He remembered their closeness in the car as they left the studio, and how near their faces had come as they faced each other in the street. Had he not turned to go at that moment, Sarapen might have tried to put his arms round her.

"And how the bitch would've laughed at that," he muttered, furious with himself. To feel such emotions for the werewolf who had nominated his cursed brother for the Thaneship. It was beyond belief. Sarapen kept his thoughts to himself. His chief councillor Mirasen was dead. Even if Mirasen had still been here, he probably wouldn't have spoken to him. Sarapen wasn't in the habit of discussing his emotions.

Decembrius was on his way back to Scotland to be nursed by his mother, which was unfortunate. Sarapen could have made use of his superior talent for finding things. Sarapen's werewolves couldn't find Markus, though Sarapen couldn't understand why Markus would be hiding. Having worked up the courage to attack Sarapen's house, why would he now go missing? It made no sense. Sarapen cursed his werewolf guard and instructed them to keep hunting till they found him. As for Kalix, Sarapen still intended to kill her. She deserved to die, and her death would bring him the Thaneship.

Dominil floated back into his mind. What was she doing with those

286

degenerate twins? They were not worthy of her company. Dominil had been magnificent in the battle. Her savagery had been a credit to the fighting MacRinnalchs. Sarapen shook his head and tried not to think about her.

Dominil was not thinking about Sarapen. She was busy booking a new rehearsal studio and still trying to find a venue for the sisters to play. The encounter with the Avenaris Guild had been an inconvenience but it had not altered her schedule. She'd once again infiltrated their computers and she was satisfied that the Guild had no real information about either the twins or herself. It was just chance that someone at the rehearsal studio had recognised them as werewolves.

If Dominil did think of Sarapen at all, it was only to acknowledge briefly that he was a fine warrior; a good werewolf to have on your side in a battle. That could also be said of Kalix. After observing the savagery with which the werewolf Kalix fought, Dominil had been surprised to see how skinny she was when she changed back to human. She didn't look capable of inflicting violence on anyone. She had done so however, most effectively.

Dominil didn't know why Kalix had left the twins' house without saying goodbye. Perhaps she'd been bored. Or perhaps it was just her way; Kalix was known to be irrational. It was no concern of Dominil's. As she'd told Verasa, she didn't intend to play nursemaid to another young werewolf. It was bad enough looking after Butix and Delix. They'd got hopelessly drunk after coming back from the fight at the studio. Not that their fighting had been very effective, unable to transform as they were. Still, even in their human form they were stronger than most men, and to their credit they hadn't shirked the battle.

Though Dominil didn't like the sisters' music, she thought she understood their motivation. Beauty and Delicious shared the vocals, because each of them had too large an ego to allow her sister to be sole frontwoman. Though they enjoyed posing with their guitars, for the last few songs of their set they abandoned their instruments, preferring just to sing, or shout, at the audience. Dominil didn't think this was unreasonable. It was probably necessary to have a large ego to front a band. In her practical way, Dominil had been assisting the group with their sampling software, to fill in the sound when the sisters put down their guitars.

Dominil left the house in the early morning, determined to find a place for the twins to play. First, however, she had to pay a visit to

East London, to the premises of the Young MacDoig. Her supply of laudanum had nearly run out and she needed more. Laudanum was Dominil's secret vice. No one knew of it, not even Verasa.

119

Ann arrived at work early. She took the lift to the fourth floor and used her key to open up the offices. She collected the day's post, sorted it into various bundles, then took Thrix's mail to her office so that it would be there for her when she arrived.

Ann opened Thrix's door, switched on the light, and came to an abrupt halt. Her employer was lying on the couch. A young man, whom Ann recognised but couldn't name, was lying beside her. They appeared to be naked, and the coat they were using as a blanket wasn't covering much. Thrix immediately woke up. She opened her eyes to find her personal assistant smiling broadly at her.

"Coffee?" said Ann.

"Oh God," said Thrix, and looked appalled.

The young man opened his eyes.

"I'll just leave you two alone for a while," said Ann. "You have a meeting in thirty minutes, do you want me to reschedule?"

"No!" said Thrix, loudly. "Bring coffee."

"We could reschedule," said Ann brightly.

"Just get the hell out of my office and bring me coffee," snarled Thrix, who had already had quite enough of her assistant's amused gaze.

"Good morning," said Gawain, awkwardly, after Ann left. The Enchantress regarded him with great displeasure.

"I have a meeting. Get dressed."

Thrix leapt from the couch and hurried to put her clothes on. She looked in the large mirror and was horrified at the mess she was in. Normally she turned up to work immaculately attired. Now she looked like... she looked like a woman who had started the evening by being thrown across the road by a spell and finished it by having sex on the couch. It was a poor way to prepare for meeting an important client.

Gawain was hanging around looking awkward.

"You should go," said Thrix.

"All right," said Gawain.

"And don't mention this to anyone," said Thrix.

"I won't."

Gawain departed. Thrix took her make-up bag to the small bath-room adjoining her office and hurried to do her face. As she put on a covering of foundation – a little thicker than normal – she smelled the aroma of Jasmine, and suddenly Malveria was standing beside her.

"Bravo!" cried the Fire Queen, with some enthusiasm. "You have had sex!"

The Enchantress was pained.

"Do I have no privacy at all? Were you watching?"

"Of course not. As soon you were removing your lingerie, I politely left, almost immediately. I had come to discuss various matters, but finding you in the strong and passionate embraces of Gawain the hand-some young werewolf I naturally did not wish to disturb you. He's certainly a most attractive young wolf and I can quite understand why your sister Kalix is in love with him. Do you think it might be a prob-lem that your sister Kalix is in love with him?"

The Enchantress interrupted her eye-liner application to cast a hos-tile glance at Malveria.

"What do you think? Of course it might be a problem. A big prob-lem, if she ever got to hear about it, which she won't."

"I of course would never breathe a word," said Malveria. "Though it's a shame to keep this a secret because as all the world knows, you have been very short of sex recently. Will he come and visit you again?"

"Absolutely not," stated Thrix.

"Why not? Was it not satisfactory?"

"What sort of question is that?"

"The sort of question which means it is time for you tell me every detail of the sexual encounter," replied Malveria, meanwhile borrow-ing Thrix's mascara to make a few minor repairs.

"No details."

"Not even one? This is very poor spirited, Enchantress. Did you have sex on your desk?"

"No."

"On the floor?"

Thrix halted her make-up application.

"Malveria, I'm not going to tell you any details. I'm trying to forget the details. It was a disastrous mistake to sleep with Gawain and I'm now about to suppress the memory."

Malveria couldn't understand Thrix's attitude. She'd just slept with a handsome and healthy young werewolf. She should be happy.

"If you are not pleased, why did you do it?"

"I don't know. He just came here to talk and things got out of hand." Malveria sniffed the air.

"Much alcohol was involved I suppose? Yes, it's a powerful aphrodisiac, in my realm too. But I am not satisfied. You are not a woman who will lose control of yourself, so why have sex with him? Do you seek to control him?"

"No."

"Do you wish to break your sister's heart and trample on her dreams?"

"No!"

"Then why?"

Thrix was frustrated at the Fire Queen's refusal to drop the subject.

"I slept with him because I drank too much whisky, he's very good looking, he has an excellent body, and I haven't had sex for a long time. Will that do?" she said, marching out of the rest room.

She found herself confronted by Ann, a tray of coffee in her hands.

"It seems reasonable enough," said Ann. "I've slept with men for far less than that."

Thrix scowled at Ann and grabbed a mug of coffee.

"Are you all right?" asked Ann.

"She is fine!" said Malveria, appearing from the bathroom. "May I have some coffee? Thank you. Is this not very entertaining, Ann, esteemed personal assistant to my friend Thrix? That the Enchantress should sleep with the werewolf who is so entangled with her sister Kalix, is so full of ramifications that one can hardly imagine what it may lead to."

"It won't lead to anything," retorted Thrix. "Because no one is going to know. You're not to tell anyone.

"But Thrix my dear," protested. Malveria. "You are being unreasonable. I'm a Hiyasta. We are not famed for our discretion."

"Not a word, Malveria, or I swear I'll never design another frock for you."

The Fire Queen pouted, looking, as she did so, exactly like a model in a magazine.

"Really Enchantress, you are so cold. What happened to the famous werewolf passion? This is something to be talked about yet you are swearing me to secrecy and not only this, you refuse to tell me any details. And did I not entertain you with the tale of my sexual encounter with three frost spirits only last month?"

The Fire Queen smiled at the memory.

"It will be a while before they can cool down enough to make frost again!"

Malveria laughed heartily at her own joke.

"Three at once?" said Ann.

"Yes. You have never done this?"

"Enough!" roared Thrix. "No more talk about sex. I've a meeting to attend. Ann, get me my papers. And don't gossip about this round the office."

"I wouldn't dream of it," said Ann.

120

Moonglow was troubled by Kalix kissing Daniel. Or Daniel kissing Kalix, depending on how you looked at it. Her natural inclination was to blame Daniel, as he was older, but perhaps that wasn't fair. Kalix had demonstrated her forceful personality before.

After the kiss the atmosphere in the house was slightly strained. Daniel was embarrassed and Kalix stayed in her room, assuming that Moonglow was annoyed with her. 'Probably she's drinking laudanum,' thought Moonglow, which was another problem. Moonglow wondered if she should talk to Kalix about it, but it was so difficult raising anything with the young werewolf. The merest hint of criticism made her retreat into an angry silence. Perhaps she should just let Kalix get on with her life. Take as much laudanum as she wanted, cut herself, and never eat. Moonglow wasn't comfortable with that. Kalix would surely come to harm if she carried on like this.

Jay had noticed that Moonglow was pre-occupied. It was harming their relationship, just to add to her problems. It was a relief to arrive in college. The cuneiform script was baffling enough to drive everything else from her mind. Daniel wasn't in college till the afternoon so Moonglow ate lunch on her own in the canteen, sitting at a table with a book propped in front of her. She was engrossed with her reading and didn't notice when someone sat down at her table.

"You study even when you're eating?"

Moonglow looked up abruptly, recognising the Scottish accent. It was Markus.

"What are you doing here?"

"I came to thank you," said Markus, in his soft voice.

Markus was now clean, well dressed, his wounds healed. His chestnut hair hung over his brow, soft and thick. There were slight shadows under his eyes but otherwise he looked almost as good as he had before, apart from the sadness of his expression. They looked in silence at each other for a little while.

"My girlfriend was killed," said Markus, suddenly.

Moonglow didn't know how to reply.

"You know of our family problems?" said Markus.

Moonglow nodded.

"She got caught in the middle. I think we would have been married one day."

Markus tried to say more, but the words died on his lips. A tear formed in the corner of one eye. Moonglow was overwhelmed with compassion. She stretched out her hand and put it over Markus's hand to comfort him. Markus looked hopeless, and hung his head.

"Are you in danger?" asked Moonglow.

"My friends moved me to a safe house. But I can't bear to go back there. All I do is sit and think of Talixia."

People at nearby tables were watching but Moonglow didn't notice them. She didn't notice anything except Markus.

"Should I take you there?" she asked.

Markus didn't reply. He just sat there looking miserable. Moonglow rose, took Markus by the hand, and led him from the canteen. Alicia, entering at that moment, had only the briefest of glimpses of Moonglow as she left, but even so she couldn't help noticing that her friend was leaving the cafeteria hand in hand with one of the most beautiful men she'd ever seen.

"Lucky Moonglow," she said to her companions. "Do you think Jay knows about this?"

Outside the college Moonglow waved down a taxi and told the

292

driver to take them south, away from the centre of the city, to Markus's safe house.

121

Kalix wrote in her journal. She was making a list of all the reasons she was unhappy. She still felt upset about her visit to the twins. It seemed to Kalix that they had deliberately excluded her from their conversation. This sort of small incident was just the sort of thing to have a ruinous effect on Kalix's fragile confidence.

Gawain is never coming back, she wrote, in her laborious handwriting, still struggling over every word. *And Sarapen will kill me.* It was another painful reminder of how badly Kalix had messed everything up. Her lover was gone, her brothers wanted to kill her and her cousins wouldn't talk to her. She wrote again. *Moonglow hates me because I kissed Daniel.* Any moment Kalix was expecting Moonglow to tell her to leave. When that happened, Kalix would go. It wasn't comfortable to stay here anyway. Even Daniel was acting strangely since they'd kissed.

Kalix took her knife and made a small cut on the inside of her thigh, and watched it bleed. It made her feel a little better. She drank some laudanum and crawled into her bed, covering her head with her quilt. The laudanum lulled her to sleep but she slept uneasily, with bad dreams of her childhood. Her father was chasing her through the castle and she couldn't get away. No matter how fast she ran he was always getting closer. She fled round a corner and the way was blocked, though there should have been a door. Kalix moaned in her sleep. This was a recurrent dream, where she was being pursued through the corridors of Castle MacRinnalch and suddenly the familiar passageways would change and she'd find herself trapped. She woke, dripping with sweat, and looked round the room fearfully, thinking that the Thane was there.

Kalix shuddered, and dragged herself into a sitting position, trying now not to sleep, but the laudanum had her in its grip and she couldn't keep her eyes open. The minute she nodded off she plunged into a terrifying dream in which she was with Gawain in the forest but the moon overhead was breaking into pieces and raining down on their heads, crushing Gawain.

Kalix woke again with a start and this time threw herself from her bed. She stumbled into the wooden chair that was her only piece of furniture and the painful blow on her shin brought her back to reality. She shivered. Her whole body was damp from sweat and there was blood congealing on her thigh. She had the frightening impression that the room was smaller than it used to be. Kalix backed into a corner, trembling with fear. She could feel the anxiety overwhelming her. She struggled to breathe as the walls began to move towards her. Kalix burst into tears and backed into a corner then slid down the wall, ending up curled up on the floor, her hands over her head, shivering, and crying, and quite certain that this was the time when she was finally going to go insane.

122

When Thrix returned from her meeting, Malveria was sitting in her office reading Harpers and Queen. The Enchantress put down her briefcase and sighed.

"Is there absolutely nothing for you to do in your own realm? You know, queen stuff?"

"Very little. The crushing of all enemies was a terrible mistake. I was thinking of re-decorating the throne room. Perhaps Louis XV?"

"An excellent idea," said Thrix. "Let me introduce you to some interior designers. You could visit them now."

Malveria looked pained.

"Dearest Enchantress, are you trying to make me go away?"

"I'm not telling you any more about my night with Gawain."

"Really, Enchantress. Do you think that is why I've returned? I have not such a great interest in the affair. Was it entertaining?"

"Malveria, I'm really very busy. Yes it was quite entertaining, what I remember of it. But if you want me to come up with a range of outfits for Livia's birthday party, you must let me get to work."

"Aha. So you admit it was entertaining. One day you must tell me all. Although I have very little interest, I assure you. But it is not why

I have returned. More important matters have come to my attention. Why did you not tell me you were defeated by a spell outside the headquarters of the vile Zatek?"

The Enchantress looked surprised, then deflated. She sat down heavily at her desk.

"Because I was embarrassed, that's why. I got flung across the road like a novice. I wasn't in a fit state to be working magic. I was hoping you wouldn't hear about it."

The Fire Queen looked concerned. This was a serious matter.

"A man of Zatek's limited capabilities should not have been able to harm you, dearest Thrix, no matter what state you were in. My agents report that more powerful sorcery has been transported from the Empress Asaratanti's realm into this one by Merchant MacDoig. Undoubtedly Princess Kabachetka has given this sorcery to Zatek, so we're now faced with a far more dangerous opponent than we anticipated. He may be able to employ spells even more potent than the *Seeing of Asiex*."

"Why would Princess Kabachetka do that for Zatek?"

"The disgusting Princess will stop at nothing to outshine me in terms of fabulous clothing. Already she's been spreading a rumour that I wore – "

The Fire Queen stopped, an expression of fury on her face.

"I cannot repeat what she said. The very idea that I would wear shoulder pads almost fifteen years after they were last fashionable is too hurtful for words. Were any of my subjects to repeat such a rumour I would have them executed."

The Fire Queen began to stride round the room, muttering threats, curses and insults.

"I wouldn't have thought the Empress would be very pleased to learn her daughter has been peddling her secrets to Zatek," said Thrix.

"She would not. But Kabachetka is a desperate woman. Faced with the unmatchable Queen Malveria, she has thrown caution to the sea."

"So we have a problem," said Thrix.

"Indeed we do," agreed Malveria. "If Zatek is armed with the *Gilded Asaratanti Protection Spell* for instance, it will be very difficult to attack him. And if he's using the Empress's own *Spell of Wondrous Spying,* it will be almost impossible to prevent him from seeing everything that goes on in this building. I can negate the effects of these sorceries in my own realm, Enchantress, but in this world it is different. I am not as strong. Even our combined power may not be enough to block all espionage."

Malveria smoothed a tiny crease on her new jacket. She glanced at herself in the mirror and smiled. Another fine outfit.

"So I suppose we must go to war," continued the Fire Queen.

"What?"

"We should attack Zatek. He must not know in advance what clothes I am to wear to Livia's celebration. I will bring forty warriors, and start preparing the *Deadly Wall Breaching Spell*."

"That's a tempting idea, Malveria. I'd like to see Zatek's fashion house disappear off the face of the earth. But an operation like that would take a lot of planning and I don't have much time to spare."

"But what else can we do?"

"The Pendant of Tamol can hide anything."

The Fire Queen considered this for a few moments.

"It is true. The Pendant would hide all things from Zatek. It is the most powerful means of concealment known to work in your world. No sorcery can penetrate its field, not even the Empress's *Spell of Wondrous Spying*. But consider, Enchantress. If it is removed from Kalix, she will be found and killed."

Malveria shrugged her elegant shoulders.

"Still, our need is greater. I will get it back."

"I wasn't actually thinking of taking it back," said Thrix. "My mother would never let me hear the end of it. I have a better idea."

123

Kalix was whimpering on the floor when the door burst open and a strange girl walked in.

"I thought I sensed a werewolf in here," she said.

Kalix looked up. The girl was around seventeen, slender, boyish and pretty, with brown skin, her hair cut short and spiky, bleached almost white. Bleached rather badly, so that the dark roots showed quite clearly. She was rather oddly dressed, with a shiny silver corset that looked expensive, and a pair of ragged army trousers that looked like they had been through a series of bad accidents.

"Hi! I'm Vex," said the girl, smiling broadly, apparently not noticing that Kalix was curled up in a ball, sweating and trembling.

Kalix scrambled to her feet. All of a sudden she felt embarrassed to be in such a poor state in front of a stranger.

"You're so skinny!" cried Agrivex. "It's fabulous! I'd just die to be that skinny!"

Kalix stared at her in surprise. She could sense that she was a Hiyasta, just as the girl could identify her as a werewolf. What was another Hiyasta doing here?

Daniel entered the room.

"Sorry Kalix," he said. "She just ran up the stairs ahead of me."

"You have such fantastic hair," enthused Vex. "It's so long. Is it sorcery? Or is it just a werewolf thing?"

She turned to Daniel.

"Doesn't she have fabulous hair? Have you ever seen anything like it? Isn't it wonderful?"

Daniel nodded dubiously. He could see that Kalix was not in the greatest of states and was worried about their unannounced intrusion. Agrivex meanwhile looked round her with interest.

"This is a small room. Is this where you live? Did your mother cut off your allowance? Aunt Malvie gives me practically nothing you know, it's a scandal, really."

Vex stopped, and looked concerned, remembering that she wasn't meant to mention Malveria. Agrivex's mission to seduce Daniel was supposed to be a secret.

"Who are you?" asked Kalix.

"Just an exchange student who's come home with Daniel. We're going to sleep together."

Daniel blushed as she said this. Vex carried on brightly.

"It's so cool to meet a werewolf especially one who's so skinny. Not that I'm fat, do you think I'm fat? How do you get your hair so long and thick? It's just fabulous. You're so pretty!"

Without her even noticing it, Kalix's terrible anxiety attack was fading. Under the relentless onslaught of Vex's compliments, her anxiety just seemed to melt away.

"Can we be friends?" said Vex. "I don't like anyone in my realm much, they're all so annoying. Do you like this nail varnish?"

"One moment," said Daniel. "What do you mean your realm? You said you were from India."

Vex looked momentarily confused. Malveria had once more sent her to ensnare Daniel, and she was not meant to let it be known that she was anything other than a normal girl.

"Forget I mentioned it," she said, and grinned.

"How come you can recognise a werewolf?"

Vex frowned.

"What is this, an interrogation? Am I not young, beautiful and about to sleep with you? Is this the time to be asking hundreds of questions?"

"We met at a gig at college," said Daniel, by way of explanation to Kalix. "Moonglow didn't show up."

"Malveria never mentioned you lived with a werewolf," said Vex. She paused. "Forget I said that."

"Malveria? Are you a Hiyasta?" demanded Daniel.

"Absolutely not! What a ridiculous idea. Ha ha ha. I'm just your average – "

" – complete imbecile," came a familiar voice. They looked round to find Malveria and Thrix standing in the doorway. The Fire Queen was frowning.

"Agrivex, you are an idiot."

Daniel stepped back abruptly.

"So you are a Hiyasta."

"Hey," protested Vex. "There's no need to make it sound like I've got the plague."

"I sent my not-yet-adopted niece to check on your safety," explained Malveria, improvising swiftly. "It has been a matter of some concern to me how the companions of Kalix were faring. It can be dangerous to become involved with the MacRinnalchs, as you know."

Vex was struggling to keep up. Eventually catching Malveria's drift, she smiled again and told Daniel she'd been worried about him so she decided to escort him home safely. It was something of a blow to Daniel's ego to discover that the girl who'd attached herself to him so enthusiastically had in fact been sent by Malveria to look after him. For a few happy hours Daniel had felt attractive, which he very rarely did. When Vex had put her arms around him, he could tell that the other students were impressed. Now, it didn't seem the same.

"And look what I found here!" continued Vex, who had no idea she'd crushed Daniel's ego. "A really pretty werewolf! We're going to be best friends, I can tell. Her mother cut off her allowance so she has to live in this small room. Could you give me more money and I'll share it with her?"

Endeavouring to follow Moonglow's example of hospitality, Daniel asked his guests if he could bring them anything. He departed to the kitchen to make tea, and look for wine. Whilst there he tried not to think too much about being alone in the house with two fire elementals and two werewolves; each, it seemed, more exotic than the other.

Daniel soon found himself with more to think about. The werewolf fashion designer wanted to store clothes in their attic. Without going into much detail, Thrix explained that she required the power of Kalix's pendant to hide her designs from an enemy designer. Daniel was not enthusiastic. He didn't like the prospect of the abrasive Thrix spending time in their house. Nor did he relish getting involved in a war between fashion designers. It wasn't something a person would willingly step into.

"It's not going to be very convenient, is it?" he protested. "You'll be here all the time making clothes. I've got important studying to do."

Thrix looked pointedly at Daniel.

"Well, Moonglow has important studying to do."

"We won't be here all the time," said Thrix. "My visits will be brief. I only want to store some finished items here."

Daniel wished that Moonglow was here. She'd know what to do. Unfortunately Moonglow was missing, which was troubling. She should have been at the gig but she hadn't shown up. It was very unlike Moonglow to break an arrangement, and she wasn't answering her mobile. Daniel supposed she was with Jay, and too busy to answer.

Kalix was no more keen than Daniel to have her sister around. When Thrix informed them that the only alternative was for Kalix to return the pendant, Kalix was only prevented from flinging it back at her by the intervention of Daniel.

"You need the pendant," he said. "Without it we'll have your older brother here and he's really scary and he'll probably kill you."

"I'll kill him first."

Daniel looked pained.

"Well maybe. But I'll probably get in the way and he'll kill me."

This seemed to carry some weight with Kalix. She didn't want Daniel killed. She assented, grudgingly.

"But don't give me a hard time about anything," she warned her sister. "I'm not taking any lectures."

"I've got better things to do than lecture you," retorted Thrix.

Before visiting, Thrix had taken great care to remove all traces of Gawain from her. A werewolf like Kalix might pick up Gawain's scent from her body and that would never do. Thrix had bathed carefully, and strengthened her magical protection. Thrix once more cursed herself for her stupidity in sleeping with Gawain. No partner could have been less appropriate.

"Splendid," said Malveria. "We are now back in the business of outwitting the evil Zatek and the harlot Kabachetka. Is there more wine?"

She looked at Daniel expectantly.

"I think we have some cider."

Malveria was unimpressed.

"I did not become ruler of my realm to drink apple juice. One must draw the line somewhere."

"I like cider," said Vex.

"That is no surprise, abominable niece. Have these clothes you are wearing ever been washed?"

Malveria looked at her empty glass.

"I'll bring you some wine from the shop," volunteered Daniel.

The Fire Queen looked immensely pleased.

"You are such a pleasant young man," she said, and sounded like she meant it. Daniel blushed, and left the room.

The attic was small and full of junk. Thrix put her head through the trapdoor in the ceiling, wrinkled her nose in disgust, then waved her hand. The junk disappeared, the room became light, and seemed somehow bigger. She climbed inside. Malveria, who generally affected a manner which suggested she would be incapable of walking more than ten yards without tripping over her high heels, followed her up the ladder with a good deal more ease than might have been expected.

"It's safe," said Thrix.

Malveria smiled in agreement.

"It is. The pendant is already blocking all outside intrusion. Zatek won't be able to see anything that's stored here, no matter what spells he uses. We can boost the protection to cover for the times Kalix leaves the house."

"You know, if you hadn't given the only available pendant of Tamol to Kalix we wouldn't have to do this," said Thrix.

"True. But Kalix would soon be dead, and is that what you wish?"

Thrix didn't reply. She suddenly remembered something that Gawain had said.

"Malveria, do you know of any reason why Hiyastas might be in Colburn Wood?"

"Colburn Wood? The sacred collection of werewolf graves and ancient trees? Why do you ask?"

"Gawain told me he thought he sensed Hiyastas there."

"This is most unlikely," replied Malveria. "Hiyastas would not be welcome there. And why would they visit such a place?"

"I wondered if you might know."

Malveria shook her head.

"No Hiyastas have been there."

Kalix retreated to her room, followed by Agrivex. Kalix was feeling overwhelmed by the number of visitors in the house and wanted to be alone but Vex was very bad at noticing the needs of others.

"So," said Vex. "Are you sleeping with Daniel?"

"No."

"Oh. I thought you might be. Do you want to?"

"No."

"Do you mind if I do?"

"Is that what you're here for?"

"No. Or yes. I forget. Don't you have a TV?"

Kalix shook her head. The only TV was in the living room. Vex seemed disappointed.

"We should have our own TV to watch."

"What do you mean we?" demanded Kalix.

"For when I visit of course."

Vex grinned eagerly at Kalix. Kalix felt at a loss. She still hadn't got used to the idea of having human friends and now this young fire elemental just seemed to assume she was going to be coming round to watch TV. She was about to tell Vex that she didn't want her to visit when Vex asked if they had cable, a question which distracted Kalix, due to her ongoing dissatisfaction concerning Sabrina.

"No cable. They won't get it."

"Why not?"

"Moonglow – the girl – doesn't approve of it. Even though her mother offered to pay for it."

"That's very strange," said Vex.

Kalix nodded, and explained to Vex that Moonglow was quite a strange person.

"She doesn't like TV. Not even Sabrina the Teenage Witch and it's such a good programme. She let me write an email to the TV station but I don't think she really sent it because they didn't change the schedules afterwards. And she dresses all in black and she'd got this weird boyfriend and she doesn't eat meat and her bedroom is really dark. I think she might be mad, really."

"She sounds strange," agreed Vex, and sat down comfortably on Kalix's bed. "But old people are like that. Malveria is very strange. She disapproves of practically everything I do. Last month she wouldn't give me any money at all just because I broke some antique vase. Which is insane. She's the ruler of a whole kingdom, it's not like she couldn't afford a new one. Why don't you persuade Moonglow to get cable?"

"How?"

"I don't know. But there's bound to be a way. I'm always having to persuade Aunt Malvie to get me stuff. Tell me more about Moonglow, I'll think of something."

124

Dominil was used to dealing with the Merchant in Scotland and knew that his son ran the business in London. Had this not been so, it would have been difficult for her to make the journey to England. Dominil had the strength of character to keep her addiction secret but it would have been very difficult for her to manage without laudanum for long.

The MacDoigs knew from experience that Dominil was not one for banter. She entered their shop, paid for her merchandise, and left quickly. They didn't attempt to detain her. There was much about Dominil to make a man nervous. And yet, as Dominil left his premises, there was an expression of satisfaction in the Merchant's eyes. He knew Dominil despised him. But while she was taking laudanum she was dependent on him. Even though MacDoig knew better than to push Dominil too far, he had not shirked from raising the price. There was a fine profit to be made here, and Merchant MacDoig never backed away from making a profit.

"She's an odd one," was his only comment to his son, as the white-haired werewolf strode silently away.

"The most intelligent of the clan, so they say," responded his son.

"So they say. But not so intelligent that she won't need us for the rest of her life."

A perceptive person might have observed a change in Dominil's demeanour when she came back from the Merchant's shop. The twins were not perceptive, and didn't notice the slight slowness of her actions. Sarapen would have noticed had he been close enough, but he was watching from a distance. It hadn't taken him long to track her down. The huge werewolf gazed after her as she entered the twins' house and he remained there a long time, staring at the curtained windows, wondering what she was doing inside.

Sarapen should have been busy hunting for Markus. Or hunting for Kalix. But here he was, perched on an uncomfortable vantage point, looking at the house which contained Dominil. He told himself it was all part of his campaign to win the Thaneship. The votes of Dominil, Butix and Delix were all important. Sarapen knew he was lying to himself. He hadn't tracked Dominil because of her influence on the voting. He'd tracked her down because ever since he'd seen the savage way she'd dealt with her attackers, he'd burned with desire for her.

Dominil was not the only non-human to visit to the Merchant that day. As night fell Princes Kabachetka made an appearance, wrapped in golden fur.

"You understand that this is a confidential transaction?" she said.

"Aye, Princess. Don't worry, there's no one more tight-lipped than old MacDoig."

MacDoig was importing more magical items from the Princess's realm. Some of these items were very delicate. It needed a specialist to bring them across the dimensions safely. The Empress Asaratanti would not have approved of her nation's sorcerous secrets being brought to this realm, but Princess Kabachetka was prepared to go to any lengths to defeat Queen Malveria.

From the Merchant's shop the items were taken to Alan Zatek.

"Now you have Asaratanti's *Spell of Wondrous Spying,*" she told him. "Thrix MacRinnalch can hide nothing from you. Do whatever is necessary to ensure that I surpass Malveria at the Sorceress Livia's 500th birthday celebration."

125

Verasa was surprised to receive an early morning phone call from the twins. She knew it must be bad news.

"She's gone."

"Who?"

"Dominil."

"What do you mean she's gone?"

"Sarapen kidnapped her."

Beauty and Delicious had been wakened by the noise of struggling in the hallway. They'd arrived to find Dominil being dragged from the house by Sarapen and bundled into a car.

"Who else was involved?" demanded Verasa.

"Just Sarapen."

Verasa was perplexed. In human form, Sarapen was certainly stronger than Dominil; even so, Verasa would not have expected that she could simply be picked up and carried off.

"She didn't seem to be properly awake," explained Beauty. "I don't know why."

"We don't know what to do," added Delicious.

"Remain where you are," instructed Verasa. "I'll contact Thrix."

The household in Kennington was thrown into uproar by the news. Had the neighbours been able to see the scene as Thrix hurried into the living room, rousing the Fire Queen, while Vex and Kalix wandered out to see what the fuss was about, and Daniel tried to wipe the sleep from his eyes, they might have wondered what they were doing living next to such a household.

"The brutal Sarapen has kidnapped the white-haired wolf?" said Malveria, a hint of admiration in her voice. "Such a decisive action! What will you do?"

"Get her back," muttered Thrix.

"Not without re-doing your make-up, I trust," said Malveria.

"Where's Moonglow?" said Daniel.

"How would I know? Is she missing?"

"Maybe," said Daniel. He'd tried calling her mobile, with no success, and was now phoning Jay. When Jay informed him that he hadn't seen Moonglow for two days, Daniel became frantic with worry.

"I'm sure Moonglow is not involved..." began Thrix, but halted. It was possible she was. Moonglow might somehow have been caught up in events. To Daniel's frustration, Thrix was touching up her make-up in the mirror.

"Don't do that, find Moonglow," he demanded.

"I'm thinking," retorted Thrix.

"Why would Dominil let herself be kidnapped?" wondered Malveria, aloud. "Even confronted by Sarapen I would have expected her to repel him for long enough for help to arrive."

No one could answer this.

"And why has he kidnapped her anyway?" continued the Fire Queen. "A swift killing at the doorstep I could understand. But kidnap? For what?"

"Malveria, I'm going home. I'll use a spell to find her."

"That werewolf can work spells?" said Vex to Kalix. "That's really unusual. Can you do it?"

Kalix shook her head.

"It's quite thrilling really," said Vex. "A kidnapping. Did you ever kidnap anyone, Aunt Malvie?"

"Yes," responded Malveria. "And have I not instructed you not to call me Aunt Malvie? But my kidnappings were usually for sound strategic reasons. Maybe once or twice just as humorous escapades. And once for passion, when that handsome air elemental – "

She paused, and looked towards Thrix.

"Does the werewolf Sarapen have a passion for Dominil?"

"Sarapen has no passion for anything except the Thaneship," said Thrix.

Malveria looked thoughtful, but kept her own counsel. Daniel was not satisfied. Surely no one was taking Moonglow's disappearance seriously enough.

"She's probably not involved," repeated Thrix. "If she is, I'll find her and let you know."

"What will I do?" asked Vex, as the Queen made to leave.

"You? You will return home and continue your studies. I believe you have several lessons in history today."

Vex looked aghast, then outraged.

"You can't send me to lessons. Not when everything is so interesting here."

Malveria eyed her pointedly.

"The werewolves do not want another Hiyasta poking her nose into their affairs. Particularly one so dramatically incompetent as you. Now

305

go to your lessons. If I hear from your tutor that you have not spent the day studying assiduously I will be most displeased, dismal niece."

With that, Malveria waved her hand and both she and Thrix disappeared from view.

"I'm not going to school," said Vex. "It's a ridiculous idea. What's for breakfast?"

"I have to find Moonglow!" blurted Daniel.

So far Kalix had remained unaffected by the uproar, not caring one way or the other for Dominil, but at Daniel's distress she felt a twinge of sympathy.

"I'll help you look," she said.

"Excellent," said Vex. "I'll come too."

"The MacRinnalchs don't need more Hiyastas interfering in their affairs," retorted Kalix, rather grandly.

Vex chortled merrily. "You werewolves are so funny," she said. "So, where will we look first?"

Kalix was baffled and defeated by Vex's good humour. She couldn't think of a suitable response.

"Can you teleport us like Malveria?" asked Daniel.

"Teleportation is the speciality of the Hiyastas," replied Vex.

"But can you do it?"

"Well not very well actually."

"Then we'll have to drive," muttered Daniel. "I'm going to college to find out if anyone's seen Moonglow."

Daniel dressed very quickly then hurried to his car, pursued by Kalix and Vex. Kalix and Vex struggled over who was to sit in the front, an argument over which neither would back down, and they ended up sharing the seat as Daniel headed north of the river as fast as he could.

126

Dominil was now Sarapen's prisoner, locked in a cell in the basement of his London mansion. Her rage against Sarapen was immense and her rage against herself was worse. Sarapen had fallen upon her as she opened her front door, struck her unconscious and carried her off. As simple as that. She hadn't even detected his approach. Dominil's senses had let her down because last night she'd overindulged in laudanum. After arriving home with a fresh bottle she'd been unable to resist taking more than her normal dose, even though she knew that now was not a good time to do so. Dominil sat on the bench in the cell and cursed herself for her weakness.

She'd already tried breaking out. Her great strength had made no impression on the door but come tonight, when the moon rose and she could transform, she would rip the door from its frame, then find Sarapen, and tear him to pieces. Dominil wiped a bead of sweat from her forehead. Already she was missing her laudanum. It was many years since she'd been forcibly separated from her supply. She didn't know exactly what the effect of an enforced abstinence would be, but feared it would be severe.

Several floors above, Sarapen sat alone, brooding, and wondering at his actions. He was surprised at the ease with which it had been accomplished. Dominil had grown careless since leaving the castle. Either that or she'd been indulging too freely in the MacRinnalch malt, something to which Sarapen knew she was occasionally prone.

Since bringing Dominil to his mansion, he hadn't spoken to her. When the moon rose the white-haired werewolf would try to tear her way to freedom. Let her. The cell was of stronger construction than even her werewolf jaws could break. 'She can languish in that cell for a long time,' thought Sarapen. 'She can stay there till she decides it's not such a good idea to nominate Markus as Thane.' He felt some satisfaction at the image of Dominil languishing. His satisfaction faded as unwelcome memories of his passion for Dominil flooded into his mind. Again he wondered whether he'd kidnapped Dominil as a strategic move in the war for the Thaneship, or simply because he couldn't bear to be separated from her. He rose to his feet, determined to rush downstairs and tell Dominil he loved her. He sat down, angry with himself, then rose to his feet once more, determined to go and tell her he despised her and she could stay in the cell forever. He sat down, rose again, and then wondered what he, Sarapen MacRinnalch, was doing bobbing up and down like a child at a funfair. It was a relief when Andris MacAndris interrupted him with news that Verasa was on the phone.

"I won't talk to her," said Sarapen. "Tell her you don't know where I am, or when I'll be back."

127

Moonglow didn't know what to think when she woke up naked in bed with Markus. It surely hadn't been a good idea to sleep with him but she couldn't convince herself that she regretted it. She was strongly attracted to Markus and had been since she first laid eyes on him. When she'd taken him home for the second time she'd refused point blank to relinquish him into the care of his fellow werewolves. She didn't trust them to look after him properly. Obviously he was traumatised and needed someone to care for him.

Markus had indicated to his werewolf companions that it was all right for her to enter the house. Moonglow had stayed with Markus for the rest of the evening. She sat on the couch beside him, comforting him, and finally soothed him sufficiently for him to drift off to sleep. She sat like that for a long time and when Markus woke up, deep into the night, she kissed him, without even thinking about it. It was she who suggested that she stayed the night.

Now, with the morning light barely penetrating the heavy curtains in the bedroom of Markus's London hideout, they lay in each other's arms with no one to disturb them. There were werewolves in the apartment next door, but here there were just Moonglow and Markus, and Moonglow felt satisfied. She thought of Jay, and didn't feel guilty. She was too passionately attracted to Markus to feel any guilt. He turned over in bed, moving a little uneasily in his sleep. Moonglow stroked his arm, and he became quieter, then Moonglow fell asleep again, still content.

128

No one at College had seen Moonglow. Daniel feared the worst, and despaired.

"She's been eaten by a werewolf."

Kalix and Vex remained silent.

"Well?" demanded Daniel, angrily.

"Were we meant to contradict you?" asked Vex.

"Yes."

"Okay," said Vex, brightly. "I'm sure she's still alive. Sarapen would probably kill any friend of Kalix's without a second thought. But that doesn't mean Moonglow's dead. She may just have had a bad accident and be in hospital. What's that machine that makes noises?"

Vex was gazing at the pinball machine in the student's union. Daniel, normally not adverse to a few hours on the pinball machine, ignored both it and the young Hiyasta. He spoke urgently to Kalix.

"Can you pick up Moonglow's scent?"

"It's difficult in the city, with all the traffic and people."

Kalix sniffed the air.

"Markus has been here," she announced. "Maybe yesterday or the day before."

"Markus? Are you sure?"

Now even more worried, Daniel hurried back to his car which he'd left in a garage in Holborn. Agrivex bounded after him but Kalix followed on less enthusiastically. She'd suddenly started to wonder what she was doing here. She still didn't care that much for Moonglow, who was always ordering her about, and telling her to eat. It struck her how much more Daniel liked Moonglow than herself and she felt some resentment. No one ever liked Kalix best, so it seemed. There was always someone they liked better.

By the time Kalix reached the car she had started to sulk. The young werewolf looked bored while Daniel negotiated the ramp back onto the street.

"Where are we going?" asked Vex.

"To see Thrix," replied Daniel.

"Why?"

"To find out where Markus lives."

"That's a stupid plan," said Kalix. "Thrix won't be there."

"Then we'll ask her secretary where she is."

"She won't know," said Kalix.

"Well do you have any better ideas?" demanded Daniel, rather harshly.

Kalix's lip curled. People always ended up speaking harshly to her. She didn't like being here. She didn't like being ordered around by Daniel and she didn't like being in the same car as the ridiculously bubbly Vex. It seemed to her that Daniel already liked Vex better than her. Kalix wished that she could go home and take laudanum.

They drove off, with Kalix now in a bad mood. Outside the cold rain was starting to fall. The heater in the old car took a long time to warm up and Kalix shivered as they crawled through the busy afternoon traffic towards Soho. Daniel swore in frustration as they became tangled up in a great jam of buses and taxis as they inched their way through Piccadilly. Kalix looked at the small statue of Eros in the centre of Piccadilly. When the weather was better crowds of people would sit around the statue: tourists, or just young people with nothing better to do. Kalix had sat there herself, when she had nothing better to do. It didn't hold any good memories for her.

Daniel's language became worse. He shouted abuse as a bus trundled so slowly through the traffic lights that they changed back to red before they could make it through.

"Stop shouting," muttered Kalix. "It's annoying."

"What do you mean?" demanded Daniel. "I'm trying to get to Thrix's to find Moonglow."

"Shouting isn't going to get us there any quicker," said Kalix.

"Stop complaining," said Daniel, now frustrated at everything, because he was frightened for Moonglow.

"You stop complaining," echoed Kalix, like a child.

Daniel turned in his seat and looked at Kalix angrily.

"This wouldn't have happened if it wasn't for your crazy family."

Kalix snarled, and felt a wolf-like anger descending on her.

"So it's my fault," she said. "Fine."

Kalix got out of the car. She hopped nimbly through the lines of traffic, pleased to be away from them. Daniel was so annoying. She decided to walk home, pick up her bag and journal, and leave the house. It had been a mistake to ever become involved with humans. She put on her sunglasses, pulled her coat tight against the rain, and set off towards Kennington.

129

Even as a werewolf, Dominil could make no impression on the cell door. The metal was strong and the cell had been cunningly engineered so that there was nowhere for a werewolf's claws or jaws to grip. Dominil couldn't get out. When Sarapen arrived in the basement she was still pounding on the door.

"You won't escape," said Sarapen, calmly. "This cell is specially constructed to hold werewolves and it's a good deal more sophisticated than anything at the castle."

Dominil glared through the small window at her captor.

"How dare you kidnap me. I'll kill you for this!"

Sarapen looked at her in silence for a moment. He still hadn't been able to make up his mind exactly what to say to Dominil. He tried to reason with her.

"I will be Thane, Dominil. The Mistress of the Werewolves can't prevent me. Withdraw your nomination of Markus and I'll let you go."

Dominil refused to even answer this.

"Why side with Markus anyway? He's weak. You know he's weak. Everybody knows, except the Mistress of the Werewolves. Do you really think he'd make a better Thane than me?"

"Any half bred dog-wolf would make a better Thane than you."

As always, Sarapen could not argue without becoming angry.

"I will be Thane. And you can rot in this cell if you like!"

"I'd rather rot here than vote for you."

"Why is that?" yelled Sarapen. "You have no reason to hate me. Is this all because of what happened to your human lover?"

Dominil's eyes burned at the memory.

"You killed him."

"I did not."

"You're a liar."

Sarapen put his snout close to the small window.

"No one can call me a liar and live."

"Open the door then, liar, and let's see who lives."

But as Dominil said this, her voice faltered and for a second she seemed to sag. She recovered quickly but not before Sarapen noticed. He was puzzled. Perhaps Dominil was not as strong as she used to be. Perhaps living with the twins had corrupted her. He felt contempt for her, and then sympathy. Sarapen shook his head furiously. Every time he felt something about Dominil the opposite feeling seemed to arrive at the same time. It was a relief when his phone rang, informing him of a visitor upstairs. Sarapen looked balefully at Dominil then hurried off. Much longer in her company and he'd have been telling her he loved her.

Dominil sagged onto the small bed in the cell. She was now feeling very unwell. She'd expended a great deal of energy in trying to break out. Worse, she needed laudanum. Lack of the opiate was starting to make her feverish. She sat on the bed and tried to compose herself. If she couldn't have laudanum then she would just have to do without it. Dominil would not allow Sarapen to see that she was suffering.

Madrigal had arrived upstairs. A thin, non-descript sort of man of average height, thirty years old, with light brown hair. Not a man to stand out anywhere. He told Sarapen of Gawain's encounter with the hunters, how he'd tossed them aside as if they were nothing, before going on to visit Thrix.

"After that he travelled east to Limehouse."

Sarapen nodded. "The premises of the Young MacDoig. No need to wonder why Gawain searched for news of Kalix there. And then?"

"He returned to Thrix's establishment in Soho. But after that…" Madrigal paused. "I lost him."

Sarapen frowned. "How?"

"I can't explain. It was as if I became disorientated. As Gawain left Thrix's I suddenly couldn't track him. I don't know why it happened."

Madrigal looked abashed. He was good at his job, and not used to failure. He shifted uncomfortably. Madrigal had worked for Sarapen often enough to know that he was not a werewolf with an even temper. Sarapen frowned deeply, pondering this. Though displeased, he knew his agent well enough to appreciate that he didn't lose concentration for no reason. He was exceptionally reliable, and he had good reason for serving Sarapen well. Madrigal wanted to be a werewolf. He'd grown up in the region of Castle MacRinnalch and had played with the young MacRinnalchs and MacAndrises when he was a child. Though the young werewolves took care not to divulge their secret to humans, it so happened that Madrigal had learned of it. Now he wanted to be a werewolf, which was not impossible, if a werewolf like Sarapen agreed to make it happen.

"Could you have been entranced by sorcery?"

"Sorcery? I didn't feel anything."

"The Enchantress may have been responsible for your disorientation. She could have placed some spell on Gawain as he left the building, rendering him impossible to follow."

Sarapen didn't like the way he was being forced to encounter sorcery. Not just from Thrix. There was the Queen of the Hiyasta to contend with as well.

"Keep looking for Gawain," he instructed. "When you find him, keep following. He'll lead us to Kalix. Have you reported your findings to the Douglas-MacPhees?"

"I have."

From his tone, Sarapen knew that Madrigal did not care for the Douglas-MacPhees. That was not surprising. Few humans would.

130

Sarapen sat all night alone on the upstairs balcony, sipping whisky from a glass. Sometimes at night he'd change into werewolf form and roam in the park. It was a poor substitute for his own lands in Scotland. Here the air wasn't clean and even on the clearest night, there were few stars in the sky. His thoughts turned again to Dominil. What was she thinking, helping the detestable twins? It was bad enough supporting Markus without becoming involved with Butix and Delix. Was she conniving with them, encouraging them to vote for Markus? Sarapen didn't believe there was any chance of the twins ever returning to the castle to vote, but perhaps the Mistress of the Werewolves thought otherwise. Perhaps that was exactly what Verasa and Dominil were plotting. Sarapen was suddenly filled with loathing for the twins. He should make it clear to them just how unwise it would be to get in his way.

The great werewolf scowled, suddenly remembering the jealousy he'd felt at Dominil taking other lovers. He couldn't go on like this, indecisive and uncertain.

"She's going to join with me or I'm going to kill her," he muttered.

Sarapen drained his glass then headed towards the basement. Dominil was slumped on the bed in her cell but as Sarapen entered she rose to her feet and glared defiantly at him.

"Release me," she demanded.

Sarapen glared back at her.

"Were this door not between us I'd kill you now, dog," spat Dominil.

'Who else would dare to call me a dog to my face?' thought Sarapen. Dominil had not threatened to complain to the Mistress of the Werewolves about her abduction, as might have been expected. She simply stated her intention of killing him. She was a fine werewolf.

"Join me," he said, abruptly.

"What?"

"Join me. I'll be Thane and you'll be Mistress of the Werewolves." Dominil was astonished.

"Sarapen," she said, speaking slowly. "You are a dog who deserves to be put down. As a man and a werewolf you're a brute and as a lover you were a failure. I'd rather dally with a farm-hand on the MacRinnalch estates than spend a minute in your company."

Sarapen roared with fury and threw open the cell door. Before Dominil could move he struck her full in the face and she tumbled to the ground. As soon as she hit the floor she transformed into her werewolf shape but even as she leapt for Sarapen's throat she could feel the sapping of her strength brought on by the lack of laudanum. Her jaws were still a long way from Sarapen's neck when he transformed and stuck her again, harder this time. Dominil hurled herself once more at her captor but Sarapen, furious and no longer in control of his actions, fastened his jaws around her neck and wrestled her to the ground. He inflicted savage wounds on her with his teeth and claws, biting and striking her again and again till the white werewolf's coat was a mass of bloodied fur.

Sarapen might have killed her had he not been interrupted by Andris arriving in the basement. Thinking that Sarapen would regret killing Dominil when he regained his senses, Andris called out in alarm, but made ready to flee in case Sarapen's rage was such that he turned on him as well. Sarapen looked round. For a moment he seemed undecided. He looked down at Dominil's broken body, unconscious at his feet, then rushed from he cell.

"Lock the door," he ordered, then left the basement.

Sarapen's fury had subsided just enough to prevent him from killing Dominil but it flared up again when he found the three Douglas-MacPhees waiting for him upstairs.

"Well?" demanded Sarapen. "Have you found Kalix?"

"No," responded Duncan Douglas-MacPhee, shaking his head so the black feather earring that hung from his right ear touched his chin.

"So what are you doing here?"

"We need money."

314

"I gave you money," said Sarapen.

"It's expensive in London," said Rhona. "You expect us to live like dogs?"

Sarapen roared and snatched Duncan and Rhona from their chairs, lifting them into the air, one in each hand.

"I expect you to do as I tell you!"

He flung them from him and they skidded over the wooden floor to clatter into the far wall.

"You bunch of petty thieves. Show me results or you'll regret it."

"It's not our fault," protested Duncan, picking himself off the floor. "She's hidden. She doesn't even have a scent."

"You haven't been looking hard enough!" roared Sarapen. "Kalix skulks in alleys and so do you. Find her for me!"

The Douglas-MacPhees backed away. Sarapen held up his hand, halting them.

"Listen well. Before you resume your hunt for Kalix, I have another task for you. Do it, and you'll be paid. I want you to visit someone."

Outside, the air was cold, and the winter rain was threatening to turn into sleet. In Camden, Butix and Delix shivered, and turned up the heating. They had quickly relapsed into their old ways. Beauty lay on the couch with a bottle of the MacRinnalch whisky in one hand and a large joint in the other.

"So much for the great musical revival," she muttered.

"It's all over," agreed Delicious.

Pete called up to ask about their next rehearsal.

"No rehearsal ever," Delicious told him. "We'll never play again."

She put the phone down with a heavy sigh. After the initial excitement, Yum Yum Sugary Snacks were now heading the way of all the twins' other bands, rapidly into oblivion. The cousins about whom the family did not speak had come to rely completely on Dominil. Now she was gone they had no idea what to do, apart from curse all the MacRinnalchs for their ridiculous family feuds.

They watched TV till they passed into unconsciousness in a haze of marihuana and whisky. Both would have slumbered late into the day had they not been wakened before dawn by an extremely loud banging. Wondering if it might be Dominil, Beauty struggled to her feet and made her way unsteadily to the door.

It wasn't Dominil. It was the Douglas-MacPhees. They marched into the front room, pushing Beauty before them. Delicious tried to

315

rise but Rhona MacPhee kicked her back onto the couch. Beauty attempted to help her sister but was clubbed to the floor by Duncan.

"A message from Sarapen," he said.

The Douglas-MacPhees changed into werewolf shape and began to wreck the house. The sisters were powerless to prevent them. They couldn't transform. Their protests were met with violence and in a space of only a few seconds Beauty and Delicious lay battered on the floor and the MacPhees were smashing furniture and hurling guitars around the room. The destruction was swift and thorough.

Fergus put his foot through the twins' DVD player and kicked the remnants at Beauty's head.

"Don't vote against Sarapen," he said. "Don't do anything that might annoy him. If you do we'll kill you."

"Dominil won't be coming back to protect you," added Rhona. "The white bitch is dead and so will you be if you misbehave."

The Douglas-MacPhees marched out of the house, slipping into their filthy black transit van and driving off.

Beauty and Delicious helped each other to the couch. Neither of them had wanted to cry while the Douglas-MacPhees were there but now they gave in to the urge. Finally Beauty rose. She locked all the doors and windows and phoned Castle MacRinnalch.

"The Mistress of the Werewolves. Quickly. We're in trouble."

131

Andris MacAndris looked dubiously at Dominil. She was lying motionless on the concrete floor. Was she dead? He entered the cell and leant over her carefully.

Dominil was still in her werewolf shape. She wasn't unconscious. She'd passed out briefly under Sarapen's terrible assault but had regained consciousness in time to hear him leave. She lay still, aware that Andris was entering the cell. Dominil ached. Her body, already weakened by the laudanum withdrawal, had been severely damaged by the cruel talons and fangs of Sarapen. She felt as if her life was draining away. Dominil banished this thought. As she sensed Andris bending over her, she sprang. She clamped her jaws round his throat, lifted him from the ground and threw him against the wall. She followed up with a crushing blow to the head that rendered him senseless.

She slung her coat over her werewolf shoulders and limped from the cell. She could hardly walk. Sarapen's jaws had torn a great gash in her leg, ripping her thigh muscles. Despite her poor physical state, Dominil was now thinking clearly. At the foot of the stairs she sniffed the air. There were many werewolves upstairs, but not Sarapen. Dominil made her way painfully up the stairs and crept through the door. The corridor was empty. She swiftly advanced, entering the first empty room she came to. Dominil had to escape without encountering anyone because she knew she didn't have the strength to fight again. Blood continued to seep from her wounds, and her white coat was stained red in many places.

She found herself in a small room overlooking the park. The window was locked. Dominil swayed. Her injured leg would barely support her.

'This,' she thought in her calm way, 'is difficult.'

It would have been better to leave quietly but Dominil had no time to work on the window fastenings. She picked up a heavy chair, smashed the window, leapt through the ragged gap, and fled into the park. The moon above gave her strength and she struggled on for as long as she could before her damaged leg gave way. She sank into a clump of bushes. Her strength was almost gone. Dominil summoned her last reserves. She hadn't put enough distance between herself and Sarapen's mansion. She gritted her teeth and began to crawl. At this moment, though she had troubles enough, a terrible craving for laudanum washed over her, followed by a feverish heat that brought sweat oozing from her pores. She felt that if she didn't have laudanum soon she would burn up and die. Dominil wiped the sweat from her eyes and kept on crawling.

132

Daniel couldn't find Moonglow. Thrix was not at her office, and no one else who knew Moonglow had seen her.

"No sign of her?" asked Vex.

"No. And I think I've managed to panic her parents."

"What now?"

Daniel didn't know. Once he'd looked in the obvious places he had no inspiration about what to do next. Vex was now feeling bored.

"Maybe we should just go home and wait for Aunt Malvie and Thrix to come back," she suggested. "They know spells and stuff. They'll find her."

"They're busy looking for Dominil. They don't care about Moonglow."

"I suppose you're right," said Vex. "Could we go back and play on the pinball machine? It looked really entertaining."

Daniel was aghast.

"We have to keep looking," he said, sternly.

Vex shrugged, and ran her fingers through her spiky blonde hair, pushing some strands back into vertical position.

"Okay."

She looked at her feet.

"I'm not completely satisfied with these boots."

Elsewhere in London the hunt for Dominil continued. The Enchantress and the Fire Queen were interrupted several times by anxious calls from the Mistress of the Werewolves. Thrix told her that she was on her way to Sarapen's mansion.

"I've just learned that Sarapen has taken Dominil there."

"Learned? By sorcery?" said Verasa, disapprovingly.

"Yes, by sorcery."

"Was there no other way?"

"You do want me to find her quickly, don't you?"

Verasa was worried about her daughter.

"Please be careful. Sarapen has obviously descended into madness."

Thrix doubted that Sarapen had lost his reason. He was just acting like Sarapen. Violent and impetuous. No matter what the state of Sarapen's mind, there was good reason for Verasa to worry.

"Remember, he has the Begravar knife. It's a lethal weapon."

"We don't know for sure he took it."

Verasa was frustrated by her daughter's words.

"Talixia's death was proof enough. If Sarapen didn't wield the knife then one of his henchmen did."

"Don't worry, Malveria's here. We've enough power to protect ourselves."

For the first time Verasa didn't find herself disapproving of her daughter's association with the Hiyasta Queen. Thrix asked her mother if she had heard from Markus. Verasa told her he was resting at a concealed location, and would remain there till she told him to leave. Thrix wondered if this was true. She half-suspected that Markus had lost his nerve in the face of Sarapen's fury, and fled the city.

The Mistress of the Werewolves had other news, also serious.

"The new young Baron MacAllister has been prowling around the edges of Colburn Wood. Perhaps he's eager to show his allegiance to Sarapen. He's there with a whole company of MacAllisters."

"Are they heading for the castle?"

"No. They're still in the wood. Don't worry, they're not a threat. They wouldn't dare advance on the castle. Please find Dominil as quickly as you can. Let me know if she's alive."

Verasa feared that Sarapen would kill Dominil. So did Thrix, but Malveria was doubtful.

"I believe he has a mighty passion for her. He won't kill her. Not on purpose. But possibly the mighty passion may spill over into violent death. I have known it to happen."

"Was that meant to be re-assuring?" asked Thrix.

"Is it not re-assuring?" said Malveria brightly. "Perhaps it is not. Shall we proceed? Before the violent death should occur?"

Malveria made ready to teleport them, but paused.

"Are we making progress towards a series of fabulous outfits for the Sorceress Livia's party?"

"Kind of."

The Fire Queen looked alarmed.

"*Kind of* does not sound like good progress."

"Malveria, you know the interruptions I've had. I'd be designing for you now if we didn't have to look for Dominil."

Malveria sighed, then waved her hand, transporting them to the edge of Hyde Park where Sarapen's imposing mansion was set back in its own grounds. Thrix sniffed the air.

"No sorcerous protection. Sarapen's inside. Other werewolves too."

"Including the white-haired one?"

"I can smell her blood."

"Then perhaps we should enter quickly?"

Malveria took them into the mansion. They materialised just inside the front door and were immediately confronted by two members of

319

the MacAndris Clan. Thrix pointed a finger at them and they were thrown violently across the hallway.

"This way," said Thrix.

They hurried down the stair that led to the basement. Thrix's heart was beating quickly. She was surprised to find that she was excited. Though she'd rather have avoided becoming involved in the struggle for the Thaneship, something in her MacRinnalch blood couldn't help responding to the adventure. Here she was, invading the domain of Sarapen, most feared of the clan. In days gone by such an escapade would have been suitable material for an epic song.

They found the cell, and in it Andris MacAndris, still unconscious. There was a lot of blood on the floor.

"That's not his blood," said Thrix. "It's Dominil's."

"Has Sarapen killed her?"

"No," came a voice from behind them, "I have not."

Thrix was startled. As she whirled round to face her older brother she felt confused and guilty, as if she was a child caught out in some mischievous prank. She quickly buried the emotion.

"What are you doing in my house?" demanded Sarapen.

"Checking your decor. We don't like it. Where's Dominil?"

"You dare to invade my lair? With a Hiyasta? Are you seeking death, sister?"

Malveria tapped her foot impatiently.

"Please tell us where Dominil is so we may return to designing beautiful clothes."

Sarapen looked beyond them to where Andris lay unconscious on the cell floor. He scowled.

"Did you do that?"

Thrix shook her head.

"No. Isn't he one of your victims, brother?"

"He is not. Though he may soon be."

"Dominil has escaped, hasn't she?" asked Thrix, who could sense that Sarapen was himself confused by events. Sarapen did not deign to reply. Instead he roared, and charged towards them. Malveria waved her hand and both she and Thrix dematerialised, appearing seconds later in Thrix's offices in Soho.

"I did not see any profit in fighting him," she said to Thrix. "Unless you wished to fight him? I could take us back?"

The Enchantress shook her head. "No. Dominil wasn't there. She escaped, apparently. From the smell of blood in the basement I'd say she was in bad shape."

Malveria nodded. "He has attacked her. Most probably he made a statement of passion and she rejected him. Passion and violence will often be found together."

"It's probably as well I'm not dating anyone right now," said Thrix.

133

Kalix was feeling disturbed. She was very bad at interpreting other people's emotions and the slightest criticism could wound her deeply. The few sharp words spoken to her by Daniel had convinced her that Daniel hated her. Probably he had only valued her as an oddity. Now that Daniel had a new freakish companion – the young elemental Vex – he didn't need a werewolf around any more.

She picked up her bag and her journal from the empty house in Kennington and left, intending never to return. Winter was setting in, the night was damp and Kalix shivered. She felt like changing into her werewolf shape, partly to warm her and partly so she could disassociate herself from all humans. She looked for a park where she could transform without being observed.

She walked a long way north, sometimes passing small groups of people waiting for night buses. Once or twice cars drew up beside her, mini cabs, the drivers said, looking for fares. Kalix scowled at them and sent them away without speaking. She made an interesting figure, striding quickly and silently along, her long coat hanging from her thin frame, her extraordinarily long hair wet with the rain, a few strands falling over her sunglasses. Her large nose ring reflected light from the street lamps. Outside the Houses of Parliament policemen watched her pass, imagining her to be a student returning from a late-night club. Or maybe a young prostitute, looking for drug money, desperate as the night became older and customers fewer.

She carried on north, scenting an expanse of open land in front of her. Hyde Park, where there were trees, long stretches of grass and dark clumps of bushes. Kalix knew that Sarapen had a house nearby but she was feeling reckless. She vaulted the perimeter fence and took

321

on her werewolf shape. A welcome strength flowed through her veins, energy from the moon that warmed and comforted her. Feeling herself free from all human interference, she even considered howling, something she very rarely did. Suddenly she halted, her nose twitching. She could smell blood. Dominil's blood. Curious, she snuffled around for a second or two, picking up the direction of the scent, then set off. She didn't have far to go. Dominil was slumped under a tree only fifty yards or so inside the park. As Kalix drew near Dominil pulled herself along a few inches more.

"Dominil," said Kalix.

Dominil looked up.

"Kalix?" she whispered. There was blood coming out of her nose and blood all over her white fur. She dragged one leg behind her as if it was broken.

"What happened?"

"Sarapen," muttered Dominil. "Have to get out of here."

Dominil clearly was not going to make it out of the park. Kalix sniffed the air. There were other werewolves about. Upwind of them, fortunately, which meant that they might not yet have caught Dominil's scent. Soon they would. Kalix didn't know what to do. At first it didn't register with her that she should do anything. Not till Dominil muttered *help me* did it strike Kalix that perhaps she should.

Unfortunately Kalix still didn't know what to do. If Sarapen had arrived that moment, Kalix would have stood up to him without a second thought. But faced with the injured Dominil, far from home, she felt bewildered. It was baffling to have responsibility for another creature and Kalix felt some anxiety creeping up on her. Should she pull Dominil out of the park? Was that a good idea? Dominil had so many wounds Kalix wasn't sure. Suddenly Dominil half rose and clutched at Kalix's leg.

"You have laudanum," she said, taking Kalix by surprise.

"So?" said Kalix, defensively, thinking that Dominil was about to lecture her.

"I need it," said Dominil.

Kalix was startled.

"You take laudanum?"

Dominil nodded, then sagged back to the ground. Kalix rebelled against handing her precious laudanum over to anyone. But it was something helpful to do, and Kalix was by this time feeling very anxious about not knowing what to do. So she took out her bottle and gave it to Dominil. Dominil drank from the bottle. She shuddered, then sipped a little more. She muttered a *thank you* and handed the bottle back. There was a moment's silence.

"What should I do?" asked Kalix.

"Get me away from Sarapen," replied Dominil. She sagged again. The laudanum was taking away the pain of her wounds but in her weakened state it quickly made her drowsy. Kalix looked up sharply. The scent of werewolves was coming closer. Kalix picked up Dominil and made towards the fence. In her werewolf form, Dominil was a burden, too heavy for her to make fast progress. Now Kalix could hear sounds of pursuit. By the time they reached the fence she knew they weren't going to make it over, not without a fight. She laid Dominil on the grass and spun round. Three werewolves were running towards her. They halted just yards away.

"Step away from Dominil," said the largest of the werewolves, who was large indeed, towering over Kalix. His coat was dark and shaggy and his teeth were very long and sharp.

"No," said Kalix.

"We work for Sarapen MacRinnalch," growled the werewolf, in a manner which suggested that this should end all argument.

"So what?" said Kalix. "Sarapen's a dog."

The werewolves looked as surprised and offended as it was possible to look in werewolf shape.

"You dare call Sarapen MacRinnalch a dog? Who are you?"

"I am Kalix MacRinnalch," declared Kalix, imperiously.

The large werewolf grinned.

"Kalix? Sarapen will be grateful when we drag you in front of him."

The three werewolves fanned out and advanced. Each of them was larger than Kalix, trusted guards from Sarapen's household. Any one of them on his own would have felt no qualms about attacking the rather small werewolf who now confronted them.

"I'll kill you all," said Kalix, not raising her voice. The werewolves laughed. It was the last thing the attacker on the right ever did because as he leapt for Kalix she put her taloned claw to his neck and tore his throat open. The other two werewolves pounced on her and then learned, too late, that Kalix's battle-madness was not just the stuff of idle tales. Kalix, born as a werewolf on the night of the full moon, simply tore them apart, moving so quickly and with such strength that the fight lasted only seconds.

When it was over Kalix stared at the three bodies in front of her. She watched as their dead werewolf forms reverted to human. She bent down towards Dominil.

"I'll take you away," said Kalix, now thinking more clearly. "Change into human."

Dominil did so. Kalix picked her up and hauled her over the fence, dropping heavily to the pavement outside. She still wasn't sure what to do for the best. The only person Kalix could think of that might help was the Fire Queen. Or maybe Thrix. But they were out hunting for Dominil. Could Moonglow help? Kalix again felt confused. She had to do something. Soon more werewolves would come. Kalix decided to take Dominil to Daniel's house. Surely there would be someone there to help.

"I need money for a taxi," she muttered.

Dominil was by now almost unconscious. Kalix felt in the pockets of her coat and found a wallet, then set about the difficult business of looking for a cab to take them to South London in the early hours of the morning.

134

Daniel was extremely agitated when he arrived home. Vex was still accompanying him. She had been no help at all and Daniel was now aggravated by her presence. The young elemental started rummaging through Daniel's music collection while he made phone call after phone call, still trying to find Moonglow. Finally he decided to call the police.

At that moment Moonglow walked into the room. She'd opened the front door very quietly and crept up the stairs, as if coming home without disturbing anyone might remove the necessity of explaining where she'd been. Daniel bounded across the room and hugged her.

"I was so worried! Where have you been?"

Moonglow had had almost two days to think of an explanation but she hadn't come up with anything very convincing.

"I had some things to do."

Daniel looked at her eagerly, waiting to hear.

"I really need a cup of tea," said Moonglow.

Daniel wrinkled his brow, very slightly. He shrugged.

"I'll make you tea."

No doubt Moonglow would tell him soon enough. Vex's presence might be putting her off, if it was some personal affair.

"I must get changed," said Moonglow, and hurried up to her room. Behind her Daniel looked puzzled.

"Things to do? What sort of things?"

"Probably something to do with the werewolf she's been with," said Vex. "Look, this Led Zeppelin CD says it came out in 1969. Was there music then?"

"What werewolf?" asked Daniel.

"I just don't see the point in old music," continued Vex. "I mean, who was born in 1969?"

"What werewolf?" screamed Daniel.

Vex looked confused.

"What werewolf what?"

"You said Moonglow had been with a werewolf."

"Of course she has," said Vex. "Can't you sense the aura – no wait don't tell me – my tutor once taught me something – humans can't really sense auras, right? Can't tell if a person has been with a werewolf, for instance. Is that right?"

Vex beamed, pleased to have remembered something from her lessons.

"That's right. So tell me all about it."

"Hey, I'm not psychic. But Moonglow has definitely been with a werewolf recently. I can see traces of its aura."

"You mean Kalix? Or Thrix?"

"No. Some werewolf I've never met."

Daniel was very perturbed. Moonglow, missing for two days, returns home, acts mysteriously, and now Vex was claiming she'd been with a werewolf.

"When you say *been with,*" he said, awkwardly. "Do you mean *been with* as in having a cup of tea in a cafe, or *been with* in a biblical sense?"

Vex had no idea what Daniel meant.

"You know - intimate," he explained.

"Oh."

Moonglow appeared in the room, having changed her clothes. Vex looked at her, then at Daniel.

"The biblical sense," she said, cheerfully.

Daniel glared at Moonglow, open-mouthed.

"What's up?" said Moonglow.

"What's up? Have you been sleeping with a werewolf?"

"Of course not!" replied Moonglow. "What makes you say that?"

"Vex can sense it."

Moonglow rounded on Vex. "Can't you mind your own business?"

"Sorry. Was it a secret?"

Daniel had never felt so irate.

"I've been chasing all over town looking for you! I thought you were dead! And it turns out you've been sleeping with a werewolf! What werewolf? How did it happen?"

Moonglow backed away. This had quickly turned worse than she'd anticipated. She cursed the young elemental.

"Don't blame me," protested Vex. "I didn't ask you to go around trailing your *I've had sex with a werewolf* aura all over the place."

"Whatever you are being blamed for you are no doubt guilty," declared Malveria, materialising in the room. "Have you remained here all day? Against my express instructions that you were to attend your classes?"

Vex searched frantically for an excuse.

"We had to rescue Moonglow," she said, cunningly. "She was being ravished by a werewolf."

"I was not ravished!" protested Moonglow.

"What is going on?" asked Malveria, and looked puzzled, till she glanced at Moonglow. Malveria could interpret auras far more accurately than Agrivex, and she laughed.

"Well well! This is unexpected. An intimate encounter with Markus? How very bold!"

Daniel was appalled.

"You had an intimate encounter with Markus? Markus? The psycho werewolf? Are you crazy?"

"He's not a psycho," retorted Moonglow heatedly, upset at hearing her private actions bandied around the room. Moonglow had realised she might have some explaining to do but she hadn't been expecting to encounter Hiyastas who could apparently read her every action.

"What are you doing here, if you don't mind me asking?"

"Returning from an unsuccessful hunt for Dominil," replied the Fire Queen. "I teleported ahead while Thrix parked the car. I always find the process of parking very tedious. Thrix is not skilled in this area."

"Did you find Dominil?"

"No. We fear for her life."

"Yes it's a worry," said Daniel. "Now getting back to Markus, what's it all about?"

Moonglow fell silent. The doorbell rang.

"I'll get it," said Vex and rushed downstairs.

Malveria was hardly less curious than Daniel about Moonglow's dalliance with Markus. She looked pointedly at the girl. So did Daniel.

"I refuse to discuss it," said Moonglow.

Vex bounded back into the room, followed by Thrix. The instant Thrix entered she halted, looked at Moonglow, and sniffed the air.

"You slept with Markus? How did that happen?"

"Will you all stop smelling me?" protested Moonglow, who was now feeling quite frantic. "I have washed, you know."

"I did not smell you," said Malveria, rather offended. "The Hiyasta Queen does not smell people. Rather, I studied your aura."

"Well I smelled you," said Thrix. "It would take more than a shower to hide the mating scent of Markus from me."

Unlike Malveria, Thrix was not at all jovial.

"This is not good. How did it happen?"

"It's none of your business."

The Enchantress's deep blue eyes bored into Moonglow.

"None of my business? You sleep with my brother while my family is in the middle of a murderous feud? I'd say it is my business."

"Just leave me alone!" yelled Moonglow, and stormed out the room.

Malveria turned her coldest stare on Vex.

"You are in substantial amounts of trouble for missing your lessons, foul niece."

Vex was outraged.

"Weren't you listening? We had to save Moonglow from being ravished."

"Pah!" replied Malveria. "Begone!"

She snapped her fingers and sent Vex back to her own dimension.

"I despair of the girl. I have been too soft with her. Really I should throw her into the volcano."

"No, don't do that," protested Daniel.

327

Malveria smiled, and crossed over to Daniel, placing her face close to his which immediately made him uncomfortable.

"You are being kind," said Malveria, and stroked Daniel's cheek. "You are always very kind."

Daniel blushed a brilliant shade of red. He was spared further embarrassment by Thrix's angry interruption.

"Malveria, please stop tormenting him. We're still meant to be looking for Dominil."

Moonglow strode back into the room.

"Kalix has gone," she announced. "She's taken her stuff and left."

"Again?"

"The MacRinnalchs," sighed Malveria. "They are such trouble."

Really, she didn't sound too displeased. Troublesome werewolves were very entertaining, in their way.

135

There was more trouble among the MacRinnalchs than Malveria realised. The MacAllisters had encroached on their lands and refused to withdraw. The Mistress of the Werewolves sent a message to the new Baron MacAllister instructing him to remove himself from MacRinnalch territory. The Baron had sent back a message which, in the politest of terms, pointed out that the MacAllisters were engaged in hunting on their own territory and had every right to be there.

Verasa was furious. It was true, as clan secretary Rainal pointed out, that there was a strip of land between Baron MacAllister's lands and the MacRinnalch estates the ownership of which had long been disputed. The dispute belonged to a bygone age, but as the land in question contained the eastern fringes of Colburn Wood it was still a matter which could raise strong emotions.

"We own all of Colburn Wood," declared the Mistress of the Werewolves.

Rainal felt obliged to disagree.

"The matter has never been satisfactorily settled. Thane Pictus MacRinnalch granted the land beyond the wood to the MacAllisters more than twelve hundred years ago but the original deeds have been lost. The new Baron MacAllister is not the first to claim that the original grant included the eastern side of Colburn Wood. In recent times the matter has never been seen as important, but now…"

Rainal let the sentence hang unfinished. Now, obviously, the MacAllisters wanted to show some defiance towards the Mistress of the Werewolves.

"Which they would not be doing without encouragement from Sarapen. Damn that wolf. Does my son intend to plunge us into civil war?"

Verasa poured herself a glass of wine and lit a cigarette.

"I will not be threatened. If the Baron refuses to withdraw I'll make him. Instruct Eskandor to assemble my MacRinnalch Guard."

Rainal was hesitant. He could see events running quickly out of control.

"Would further negotiation not be preferable? If we send a force to encounter the MacAllisters, things may get out of hand. Werewolves are not good at restraint while facing an enemy."

"We are not," agreed Verasa. "But I refuse to be intimidated by some upstart Baron who's hardly finished burying the father he helped to assassinate. Call Eskandor."

136

Andris MacAndris wondered if he might be executed. It had been foolish to approach Dominil in the cell, laying himself open to her attack,

"MacAndris. You have let me down. Have you anything to say?"

The MacAndris wolf held his head up high, not wishing to leave this life in a shameful manner.

"No, Lord Sarapen. I have no excuse."

Sarapen was furious with Andris for allowing Dominil to escape. However he was pleased that he didn't offer an excuse, or plead for his life.

"I'm disappointed in your conduct," said Sarapen.

He dealt the MacAndris a tremendous blow. The werewolf fell to the floor.

"Get up," said Sarapen.

Andris hauled himself to his feet.

"Will you ever let me down again?"

"No, Lord Sarapen."

"Very well," said Sarapen. "Now go, and find out how the hunt for Dominil progresses."

MacAndris bowed, then hurried out of Sarapen's presence. From force of habit Sarapen stood in front of the fireplace, as he would do at his own keep. Here in London however, there was no blazing fire. Bylaws prevented it and the mansion was centrally heated. It was comfortable enough but not suitable for a werewolf. Not in Sarapen's opinion anyway.

Dominil had escaped. Worse, his mansion had again been invaded, this time by Thrix and the cursed Hiyasta Queen. Sarapen bridled to think that these creatures could simply appear in his own house by use of their unclean sorcery. Had they not teleported out again, Sarapen would have torn them apart.

"But that," he muttered, "is just the point. They did teleport out again. While Thrix and the Fire Queen are ranged against me I'm at the mercy of their sorcerous powers. I need some protection."

Sarapen was averse to sorcery. However, he was also pragmatic. It was no use ignoring the problem. He instructed his secretary to contact Decembrius, who was now making a good recovery at his mother Lucia's lodge on the castle Grounds. When the call was connected Sarapen inquired briefly as to his advisor's health and was satisfied to learn that Decembrius would be rejoining him soon.

"I need some way of preventing the Enchantress and her ally from entering my house, or spying on me. For all I know they could be watching my every move. Do you have any suggestions?"

"Are you considering using sorcery yourself?" asked Decembrius.

"If necessary."

Decembrius thought for a while.

"Thrix has been troubled by a rival designer with sorcerous powers," he said. "I saw the power of her rival knock her senseless and throw her across the street."

Sarapen was interested. Anyone who could send the Enchantress flying across the street should be worth talking to.

Andris returned to report that the three werewolves who had left Sarapen's house to pursue Dominil had not come back.

"Very well," said Sarapen. "Assemble my bodyguard. We'll hunt for her ourselves."

137

Kalix was worried that Dominil was going to die. She couldn't find a taxi to take them to Kennington. There were few cabs around and those that were refused to go south of the river. Kalix picked up Dominil and started to walk. She had to put more distance between them and Sarapen's mansion. She struggled on through the rain, walking down a dark street she didn't recognise, pausing frequently to rest. She knew she couldn't make it far with Dominil. The white werewolf was taller than her; even her human form was too heavy for Kalix to carry for long.

Kalix felt panic welling up, threatening to overwhelm her. She made an effort to control it, breathing deeply and sipping from her laudanum. The situation was new to her. She'd taken on responsibility for someone else and now she had to save Dominil and she didn't know how to do it. The panic became stronger, urging Kalix to leave Dominil where she was and flee. She tried to fight off the fear but only succeeded in plunging into anxious depression. Depression because she was too stupid to know what to do. Her brothers would have known what to do. So would Thrix. But Kalix couldn't think clearly. She hung her head and stared at the pavement, now running with water from the heavy rain.

Dominil moaned. Kalix clenched her fists and started to feel angry. Why had she got involved in this? It was none of her business. She should just run away and leave Dominil here. She'd done enough already, saving her from the werewolves in the park. It wasn't as if Dominil had ever been friendly towards her. On their last encounter she'd all but ignored her, even though Kalix had helped her fight off the hunters. Kalix became quite irate thinking about this. Dominil was not a nice werewolf.

She remembered how Dominil had asked her for laudanum. That was so unexpected. Kalix felt more kindly towards her. She realised she didn't want to leave her dying in the street, in the rain, cold and bleeding. She had to forget her anxiety, stop being stupid, and think of something to do. She had to get Dominil back to Daniel's house.

Unfortunately this reminded Kalix of how annoyed she'd been with Daniel. So annoyed that she'd picked up her bag and left. Now Daniel and Moonglow would hate her. Kalix sighed. Why was it everyone always ended up disliking her?

"It's because I'm no use for anything," she muttered, quite seriously. "I'll just take Dominil there and leave before they can say anything."

How could she get there? She noticed a phone box on the corner. Kalix remembered that Moonglow had written her telephone number in the back of her journal, saying she might need it sometime. Kalix fetched her journal from her bag, found the number and went to the phone. She dialled very hesitantly. By now her feelings of alienation were so strong that she expected whoever answered to simply hang up on her.

Daniel answered the phone very quickly.

"Hello?"

There was a long pause.

"Hello?"

"It's Kalix."

"Kalix! Where are you?"

"I'm with Dominil. She's hurt. I don't know what to do."

As she spoke Kalix felt a tear forming in her eye. She blinked, annoyed that this should happen.

"I'll get Thrix," said Daniel.

The Enchantress took the phone.

"What happened?"

"I rescued Dominil. Sarapen attacked her. I think she's dying."

"Where are you?"

"Near Hyde Park."

"Where exactly?"

Kalix didn't know. The Enchantress recognised the rising panic in her young sister's voice and spoke to her quite calmly.

"Look at the sign in the phone box. There should be a notice giving the address. If you tell me that we'll come and pick you up right away."

Kalix looked for the sign but this was not so easy. There were many cards in the phone box, adverts left by prostitutes, and Kalix, with her poor reading skills, wasn't sure what she should be looking for.

332

"There are lots of cards," she said. "I don't know where the address is. And – "

Kalix broke off, sniffing the air.

" – there are werewolves coming."

The Enchantress remained calm.

"The notice telling you the address of the phone box will be right next to the phone. It's white with black letters, with a red border."

"I see it."

"What is it?"

There was a long silence.

"What's the address?" urged Thrix.

"I can't read it," admitted Kalix, miserably. Dominil was going to die because Kalix couldn't read the address.

"Can you spell it out?"

Kalix made an effort, though the small sign wasn't all that legible in the poor light.

"L-Y-A-L-L-S-T-R-E-"

"Lyall Street. South of the park. I know it. Don't move, I'm coming with Malveria right now."

Thrix rang off. On the pavement beside the phone box Dominil moaned again. The blood on her limbs and body had now congealed in dark red clumps but it still flowed from her nose, a very bad sign. Dominil was damaged inside, like Kalix had been.

"The Fire Queen saved me when I was hurt," said Kalix, in an effort to be re-assuring. "And she's coming here now."

The scent of werewolves was stronger. They were getting nearer. Dominil's eyes were now shut. Kalix had the notion that she should talk to Dominil, to keep her alive, to prevent her from journeying to the forests of the werewolf dead.

"Wake up," she urged, but Dominil didn't respond. Kalix was sure she was going to die before Thrix arrived. The young werewolf struggled to think of something else to say, but her mind was blank. In the silence, she could sense Dominil's life slipping away.

"I saved Puffy the Puffin," said Kalix, suddenly.

Dominil's eyes opened a fraction.

"What?"

"I saved Puffy the Puffin. On Moonglow's computer. It's a game. I saved Puffy the Puffin."

Dominil stared at Kalix through her half-closed eyes. Then, for the

333

first time that Kalix could remember, she smiled.

"Well done," whispered Dominil.

Kalix smiled back, hesitantly.

"It was good," said Kalix. "I like Puffy. I saved him."

"Then I'm sure you can save me too," whispered Dominil.

The scent of werewolves was now very strong. Kalix scanned the street anxiously.

"Thrix will be here soon. And Malveria. They'll heal you. Do you want more laudanum?"

Dominil nodded. Kalix let her have a sip.

"Take care of my bottle," said Kalix. "There are werewolves coming along the street and I have to fight them now."

Sarapen was striding towards them; huge, dark and menacing. Andris MacAndris was at his side. In his werewolf form he was almost as large as Sarapen. Behind them marched five others, all in werewolf shape, though it was not a night of the full moon. Too heavy odds, even for Kalix. Kalix walked a few paces up the road to meet them. Now that the enemy was here, she felt quite calm. Her battle-madness often began with a feeling of tranquillity. She transformed into her werewolf form.

"Keep back," she said.

Sarapen looked huge, a vast dark shape under the streetlights.

"Was it you who killed my wolves in the park?" he asked, his voice low and full of menace.

Kalix growled at him.

"Kill her and take Dominil," said Sarapen.

The werewolves charged. Kalix opened her jaws wide and raised her claws as her madness took over. Suddenly her attackers flew backwards, landing heavily. The Fire Queen stood on one side of Kalix and the Enchantress on the other. Kalix was confused. In her werewolf battle state she wasn't ready for unexpected assistance, and didn't immediately realise that she'd been rescued. She continued to growl.

The Enchantress gave a small smile.

"We should go."

Kalix growled again, indicating that she'd rather stay and fight.

"Yes, you're a fierce little werewolf, no doubt about that," said Thrix, rather kindly. "But we'd be better just leaving. Dominil needs attention."

With that, Malveria waved her hand and wafted them all back to

Daniel and Moonglow's house in a haze of jasmine. They materialised in the front room where Daniel and Moonglow were waiting anxiously.

"I am quite exhausted," exclaimed Malveria. "My teleporting powers are not endless, I must confess. Taking others around is not so easy. Daniel dear, please bring me one of your pop-tarts and perhaps a glass of wine?"

"Later," said Thrix. "Dominil isn't far from the forests of the werewolf dead."

Malveria made a face.

"Really, I do not wish to visit that place again. Its guardians are most inhospitable towards the Hiyasta. But very well, let us see what has to be done. Please bring me some refreshments anyway. Soon I will be so worn-out I will be as wrinkled as the disgusting Empress Asaratanti. And who will care then that I am so fabulously dressed?"

Malveria bent over the prone figure of Dominil, and pursed her lips.

"Bad," she muttered, shaking her head.

"How bad?" asked Thrix. A few spots of rain had dampened her golden hair. Not many though. It had been a very swift rescue.

"In human terms, several fatal wounds and dead some time ago. In werewolf terms, not quite so bad. She is not yet so near to the forests though if blood keeps pouring out at this alarming rate she soon will be. Look, it has stained my blouse and it is my favourite."

"It's not your favourite at all," said Thrix.

"Very well it is not my absolute favourite but it remains high on my list of favourites."

"I'll make you a new one."

"Thank you," said Malveria.

After being plucked from battle and teleported through space as a werewolf, Kalix felt confused. Disorientated, she looked around her suspiciously, still half-expecting to be called on to fight. When she finally realised that she'd saved Dominil she felt pleased. Then she felt hungry. She was still in her werewolf shape and the wolf needed feeding. Kalix headed for the kitchen.

As Daniel and Moonglow looked on, Malveria once more knelt over the figure of a damaged werewolf, placing her hands and then her lips on the face of her patient. It seemed to Moonglow that Dominil couldn't be as badly hurt as Kalix had been, because the air in the room did not grow so cold and Malveria didn't seem to have to expend so much effort as she had before. Even so, it was some time before the Fire Queen withdrew her lips from Dominil's, and when she did she again looked drained.

"She will be well," said Malveria. "Now I must go."

"Please don't," said Moonglow, stepping forward quickly.

"I need time to recover. It is an effort, this medicinal assistance for werewolves. In replacing their fire, I diminish my own."

"Recover here," suggested Moonglow, who felt that they owed the Fire Queen. "You can have my bed."

Malveria was touched. Again, looking at Moonglow's long black hair, long black skirt and heavy make-up, she felt that this must be one of her devotees, but apparently she was not. It made the offer of hospitality all the more gratifying.

"Very well," said Malveria. "I will stay."

With that, she lay on the couch, and closed her eyes.

"Where's Kalix?" asked Daniel. "Has she left again?"

"I think she's in the kitchen," said Moonglow.

Daniel, Thrix and Moonglow all trooped through to the kitchen where they found the young werewolf with her nose in the bin, eating the remains of a pizza. Moonglow and Daniel burst out laughing. Kalix looked up, and changed back into her human form.

"What's funny?" she demanded.

"There's more food in the fridge," said Moonglow, but Kalix looked offended because they'd laughed at her, and said she wasn't hungry.

"You're a hero," said Moonglow.

"What?"

"You are," said Daniel, enthusiastically. "You rescued Dominil. It was heroic."

Kalix looked uncomfortable.

"It was very well done, sister," added Thrix.

Daniel put his arms round Kalix. Kalix still looked uncomfortable but there was nowhere to retreat in the crowded kitchen. She came close to smiling.

"Thanks," she mumbled.

"Tea," said Moonglow. "We need tea for Malveria. That woman is a great healer, don't you think?"

"She is," agreed the Enchantress. "Though it's fortunate that Dominil was not so near to death."

"Why?"

336

"Because if Dominil had been closer to the forests of the werewolf dead Malveria would have had to expend much more effort in bringing her back. A fire elemental won't do that without demanding some sort of payment in return. Even from a friend the price could be severe. I might have had to enter into some bargain I'd have regretted."

Moonglow was filling the kettle. She paused.

"Do you think you would have regretted it?"

"Certainly," said Thrix. "You must never strike a bargain with the Queen of the Hiyasta."

"But you make clothes for her. Isn't that some sort of bargain?"

Thrix shook her head.

"That's a clearly defined commercial transaction, which is fine. But a bargain concerning any matter where the outcome is unclear must be avoided. Malveria will always get the better of you, and you'll regret it."

"She brought me back," said Kalix. "I didn't make any bargain."

"She did that as a favour to me," said Thrix.

Moonglow knew this wasn't true, and worried a little about her bargain with the Fire Queen.

138

Sarapen was keen to see the man whose sorcery had repelled the Enchantress. He went to visit Zatek. Zatek was not willing to give details of his power to a stranger, but did go so far as to refer Sarapen to Merchant MacDoig.

"Your sorcery comes from MacDoig?"

"In a way. He might be able to help you."

Zatek showed no nervousness during their meeting, though the designer could tell he was a werewolf. Zatek obviously had confidence in his protection spells. Too much confidence, perhaps. In his full rage Sarapen was difficult to repel, even by sorcery. As Sarapen walked back to his car he was thoughtful. Early this morning Madrigal had brought news. He had been tailing Gawain around London. So far this hadn't led him to Kalix, which was surprising. Gawain should surely have found her by now. But if he had, he wasn't visiting her. However he was visiting Thrix.

Madrigal thought that Gawain was sleeping with Thrix. Sarapen found this almost impossible to accept. He had little regard for his sister but he could hardly believe that any member of the MacRinnalch ruling family would stoop so low as to form a relationship with a banished werewolf. Could it possibly be true? Even Sarapen, the very last person to show an interest in scandal, realised how potentially explosive the situation was. Gawain, the great love of Kalix, now in bed with the brat's older sister? What would Kalix make of that, he wondered?

Sarapen scowled as he drove slowly through London towards the Merchant's. His sisters were almost as degenerate as the twins. At least the twins wouldn't be poking their noses into the dispute over the Thaneship. The Douglas-MacPhees had scared them off.

The hunt for Markus continued. Though Markus's disappearance was annoying it was not necessarily of desperate importance, as Decembrius had pointed out. After all, it hardly reflected well on Markus MacRinnalch to be in hiding, afraid to face his brother. It would not impress his followers. Sarapen found himself concentrating more coolly now that there was action in Scotland. Following his instructions the new Baron MacAllister had planted himself in Colburn Wood and was defying the Mistress of the Werewolves' orders to withdraw. Let his mother deal with that if she could.

Sarapen wondered where Dominil was. Her escape had cost him the lives of several of his guards but he admired her for her courage. Kalix too, in a way. There was no denying her fighting spirit. But he would certainly kill her now. No one could be allowed to live after slaughtering his followers. If Sarapen did not exact vengeance his status would suffer.

He arrived in Limehouse and made his way along the curiously old-fashioned alleyway that led to MacDoig's. Rats scuttled away from Sarapen, sensing that he was a creature to be avoided. If the rats showed nervousness at Sarapen's approach, the MacDoig did not. Sarapen was displeased to find himself once more confronting a human who was aware of his reputation yet, like Zatek, showed no signs of unease. Obviously the Merchant also believed himself to be well protected.

"Come in, Sarapen MacRinnalch. Will you have a drink with me?"

Sarapen shook his head. The Merchant seemed disappointed.

338

"Are you sure? You won't mind if I have one myself? It's a shame my son has just stepped out on business, he'd have been pleased to meet you. What can I do for you?"

"The protection you gave to Zatek. I want it."

MacDoig stopped grinning.

"Sorcerous protection? That's not a thing I ever expected to hear from you, if you don't mind me saying so, Sarapen MacRinnalch."

Sarapen frowned. Already he was feeling that this was an affront to his dignity and wished that Decembrius had been in London so that he could have made the visit instead.

"I need something to protect me from prying eyes."

"Who's prying eyes, might I ask?" said the Merchant, and sipped from a large tumbler of whisky. The MacDoig was as fond of whisky as the MacRinnalchs, and though he had no access to the werewolves' own excellent malt, he had a cellar full of other fine old bottles.

"I am not here to discuss my business with you, Merchant."

"Of course, of course. But if you need some protection, I'll need some idea of what you're up against."

Sarapen considered this. It probably wouldn't do any harm to tell MacDoig. It was likely he knew most of the background to the family feud already, unfortunately.

"The Enchantress. And the Hiyasta Queen."

"Ah." MacDoig nodded, and tapped his silver headed cane lightly on the ancient floorboards of his shop. "The Enchantress. I did hear some rumours that things were not altogether well between you. Aye, she's a powerful woman, Thrix MacRinnalch. And the Hiyasta Queen, she's another. It takes a lot of sorcery to protect a man from those two."

A sly expression settled on MacDoig's face.

"A lot of expensive sorcery."

Sarapen took a purse from inside his great black coat. The purse contained gold, to which the Merchant was very partial. Even though his business now encompassed the modern world of the stock market and the internet, MacDoig was old enough to remember when all transactions were done in coin of the realm. Gold had never lost its attraction for him.

"Let's talk about sorcery," said Sarapen.

139

Realising that she had rather neglected affairs of state recently, the Fire Queen summoned First Minister Xakthan to her throne room. He arrived wearing his finest blue robe and carrying the silver mace that denoted his rank. Thanks to the application of some sorcerous surgery, flames no longer rose from one ear. He looked a good deal more symmetrical. Malveria was pleased with the result, and so would Xakthan be, when it all healed properly, and the pain subsided.

Xakthan was surprised to be asked for a detailed description of the state of the nation. Queen Malveria was being rather inconsistent these days, he noted, though he did not disapprove. Xakthan was far too loyal to disapprove of anything Malveria did. She had saved his life on numerous occasions during the wars, and rewarded him very handsomely afterwards. Malveria listened intently while he described the affairs of each of her ministries. When he finished, Malveria nodded, though Xakthan noted that the Queen did not look particularly happy.

"Does this not please you?"

"It pleases me well, Xakthan. But you know, I am occasionally bored by the lack of stirring events. We grew up fighting, and sometimes it does not sit so well, these long years of peace."

"It is a consequence of your excellent rule, Mighty Queen."

"It is. And of your excellent ministry. I apologise for shouting at you recently."

Xakthan was overwhelmed to hear Malveria apologise to him, and hardly knew how to respond.

"I have been spending time in the human realm," said Malveria. "Too much time perhaps, but I find it diverting. They are often amusing creatures."

Xakthan, with his fire elemental's traditional dislike of humans, couldn't quite understand this. The only humans he ever encountered were Malveria's devotees, and they never seemed amusing. Always very serious, and far too fond of chanting.

"I don't mean my devotees," explained Malveria. "I have encountered some other young humans who I find very funny, and even charming. And the MacRinnalch werewolves, who are not funny or charming, but are full of intrigue, stratagems, and violence."

Xakthan was troubled.

"I admire intrigue, stratagems and violence, Mighty Queen. But

I've never regarded werewolves as honourable creatures, particularly the MacRinnalchs. They would stab you in the back, every last one."

"Well, our last battle with the MacRinnalchs was some hundreds of years ago," Malveria pointed out. "The world in which they live has changed substantially in that time. Really, Xakthan, you would hardly recognise it these days. The humans have such machines, machines of doing and machines of thinking. And such weapons, and such entertainments, and such clothes. I do not understand how a race which lives for such a short time makes such changes, but they do. As if each human, living for only a few years, must invent something to make their world different."

"And do the werewolves invent things?"

"No," said Malveria. "They do not. That is part of their problem. Some of the MacRinnalchs want to join in with the modern world, and some of them don't. There is strife between the modern and the old."

"Are you involved in this strife?" enquired Xakthan.

"To some degree. But only because of my liking for the Werewolf Enchantress. Do not wrinkle your brow, First Minister. You know that the Enchantress has provided me with wonderful clothes which have brought me great happiness, and increased my status."

Malveria described the struggle for the Thaneship of the MacRinnalchs. Her First Minister listened intently.

"If you had no involvement, Queen, who would win?"

"Sarapen," replied Malveria. "His enemies have underestimated his power, particularly his mother. Sarapen is not a werewolf who can be put off by the vote of a council."

Malveria paused.

"Which is interesting. Sarapen is, after all, the werewolf who sets most store by tradition, and clan law. MacRinnalch law dictates that the decision of their Great Council is final."

"But he will not accept it," said Xakthan. "Neither would we, in his position."

"Indeed we would not," agreed Malveria, and smiled, remembering all the pronouncements and judgements that had been handed down against her when she was an outlaw princess.

"It all comes down to power in the end, I suppose. As it is with the Hiyasta, so it is with the MacRinnalchs."

"I don't like the sound of this younger son Markus," said Xakthan. "He seems an unsuitable leader. You say he dresses in fancy clothes?"

341

"I dress in fancy clothes, First Minister."

"It is appropriate now you're Queen. When we slept in caves by day and fought by night, we wore whatever rags we had left after battle."

Xakthan's eyes showed some fondness for his memories.

"You are right," agreed Malveria. "But his mother believes Markus is better suited to leading the clan in the modern age, and she might have a point."

Xakthan wondered if Malveria cared about the MacRinnalchs. She admitted that she didn't care a great deal, as long as Thrix was safe.

"Though I have some interest in another. Thrix's sister Kalix, the youngest of the ruling family. I saved her life."

"Why?"

"As a favour to Thrix."

Malveria halted.

"No, that is not quite true. It was more as a favour to a young girl, Moonglow by name. And I did extract an entertaining price from her."

Malveria explained her price to Xakthan, who nodded his understanding. A tormented human was always entertaining, he had to agree.

"But will this Moonglow ever really love Daniel? He sounds quite unappealing."

"He is appealing in his own way, I think. Moonglow may yet fall in love with him, and then of course she will be tormented, as I have forbidden her ever to have him."

"Of course," continued Malveria, frowning deeply. "My scheme has not been helped by the appalling Agrivex."

The First Minister was surprised. He knew Vex well. Only last week she had stormed into a meeting of the ministers of state, demanding they pass a law to substantially increase her clothes allowance, and another law to have her history tutor thrown into the great volcano. Neither had been approved. Agrivex had then stormed out with threats and curses, spoiling the effect by tripping over a small table, banging her elbow quite painfully and bursting into tears.

"You asked Agrivex to help in your scheme?"

"Yes. And I know what you're thinking. Any plan which involves the foolish young Agrivex is doomed to failure. But in the human world, she does not seem so unsuitable a candidate for turning Daniel's head. I will tell her to keep trying. Once Daniel is involved with another, Moonglow will become jealous, I am sure of it."

The Queen gazed into the distance for a while.

"When I saw Vex and Kalix together I felt old. Do I look old to you?"

Xakthan had fielded this question many times in the past.

"Mighty Queen, you look like the fresh-faced daughter of a wealthy nobleman, a young girl who has never suffered a care in the world."

Malveria was pleased.

"Really?"

"I promise."

"Good. But be sure to tell the gatherers of my rejuvenating water to take extra care. With the MacRinnalch Clan in such uproar, they must use great caution when entering Colburn Wood."

140

Dominil spent only one night at Moonglow's. On hearing news of the attack on the twins' house she insisted on returning there as soon as possible. Verasa had called both Thrix and Dominil, informing them of events.

"These vile creatures," raged the Mistress of the Werewolves. "The Douglas-MacPhees should have been put down long ago. Their father was an evil werewolf and they are no better."

Apparently the twins were unharmed, but were shaken and intimidated. Dominil knew she had to get back there immediately. Her injuries were severe and Thrix was convinced that she should rest for longer but Dominil wouldn't hear of it.

"I will recover swiftly."

Thrix herself was too busy to look after the twins so she dropped the subject. Moonglow was more concerned. She really didn't think that Dominil was in a fit state to return home.

"Let her go," said Daniel to his friend, privately. "She's a werewolf. They recover fast. Anyway Dominil makes me nervous."

Moonglow knew what he meant. There was something unsettling about Dominil. She didn't smile. Her dark eyes bored into a person and never seemed to soften. If she was in pain from her injuries she wasn't admitting it. She spent the night on the couch in her werewolf form, renewing her strength, then limped into Daniel's car to be driven back to Camden. Before she left, she spoke to Kalix, quite formally.

"Thank you for your assistance, cousin. I appreciate it."

With that she departed.

"Thank you for your assistance?" said Moonglow. "Is that all she could say?"

"She was never chatty," explained Kalix.

After being congratulated by everyone for rescuing Dominil, Kalix had seemed pleased, but embarrassed, unsure how to react. She'd never been the hero before. It was good but it made her feel self-conscious so she retreated to her room to write in her journal.

Dominil had been spending part of her time in the apartment provided by Verasa. She decided it would be better if she now moved in with the twins to protect them, even though this didn't sit that well with her. Dominil found it trying to be with them for too long. Nothing she could do could make them act like civilised werewolves.

The house in Camden was still a shambles after the attack. Beauty and Delicious had made half-hearted attempts to clear up the mess, but had become depressed and given up. When Dominil returned, the sisters' gloom lifted and they greeted her enthusiastically.

"We thought Sarapen was going to kill you."

"I am fine," said Dominil. "Were you hurt by the Douglas-MacPhees?"

"No, but they wrecked a lot of stuff."

"So I can see."

"Can you organise a cleaner again?"

Dominil said she would. She was relieved to see the twins apparently unharmed. Not in as poor a state as she had expected, given what had happened. Beauty picked up her guitar and posed dramatically on top of an armchair.

"We're back. Yum Yum Sugary Snacks rise like a – " she halted. "What is it things rise like?"

"A phoenix from the ashes, usually," said Dominil.

"Excellent. Like a phoenix from the ashes. We wrote a new song. Want to hear it?"

Dominil sighed. Musicians were always writing new songs and they always seemed to think you wanted to hear them.

141

Markus was still traumatised by Talixia's death, too shaken to make sense of what had happened in the past few weeks. He sat all day in a chair by the window, wrapped in a silver dressing gown, gazing out into the gardens where those few small birds that remained in London in winter fluttered around the trees. This apartment wasn't far from Crystal Palace, rather a green part of the city. Grey squirrels would sometimes make their way from the park to the garden. Markus watched them as they scurried up trees, always busy with something. At night foxes would emerge from their hiding places and Markus would hear them in the garden below, listening to their shrill calls while he lay in his bed, unable to sleep.

"How is he?" asked Verasa, on the phone to Gregor MacRinnalch, who was charged with looking after him.

"A little better," said Gregor.

"Don't lie to me," said Verasa, brusquely.

Gregor frowned. The Mistress of the Werewolves was very hard to fool, even when she was hundreds of miles away. He admitted that Markus was no better. He was still in shock and not capable of much apart from staring out into the garden.

Verasa was frustrated. She understood that Markus had suffered a severe trauma but even so, this was not the behaviour required from a claimant to the Thaneship. Were the werewolves around the castle to learn that Markus MacRinnalch was at present hiding in a safe house, watching squirrels, they would not be impressed. The Great Council wouldn't elect a Thane whom the entire clan despised as weak.

Gregor was a loyal MacRinnalch, but his first loyalty was to Markus rather than Verasa, so there were some things he hadn't told her. He hadn't told her that Markus had instructed him to look for Kalix. And he hadn't told the Mistress of the Werewolves that Markus had recently slept with a human girl. This, he reasoned, was really none of Verasa's business, though Verasa herself wouldn't have seen it that way.

The day after Moonglow had been with Markus, he'd seemed better. Livelier, at least for a while, before he sank again into the blank numbness that enfolded him these days. Perhaps, thought Gregor, sex was what Markus needed to bring him out of his gloom. Or maybe it wasn't even sex. Markus was more sensitive than most MacRinnalchs.

Perhaps the human girl was good at listening, or talking, or something like that.

"Did anyone call?" asked Markus, when Gregor went to tell him there was food ready.

"Your mother."

Markus didn't respond. It wasn't the call he was waiting for. Dusk was coming. Werewolves were creatures of the night but somehow Markus no longer felt so comfortable when the darkness came. He wished that the daylight hours were not so short in winter. He wished he could see Moonglow again.

142

Young Baron MacAllister was camped on the eastern edge of Colburn Wood with fifty of his followers. Eskandor MacRinnalch, captain of the castle guard, advanced on the Wood with a force of eighty werewolves to eject them. The Mistress of the Werewolves had instructed Eskandor to advance cautiously but resolutely, and to enter into no negotiations with the Baron. He was to be removed from the Wood. If the Baron wanted to discuss the boundaries of his lands he could come in peace to Castle MacRinnalch and confer with the Great Council. He would not be permitted to force the issue by show of strength.

It was noteworthy that the new Baron had only fifty werewolves with him, and that this force included MacAndrises as well as MacAllisters. Baron MacAllister had many more werewolves under his command but many of these could only assume their wolf shape on the nights around the full moon. Presumably the Baron had brought with him only those who could make the change on any night. In this, the MacRinnalchs had an advantage. There were many more MacRinnalchs who could transform every night. All of Eskandor's force could.

The MacRinnalchs left the castle in the early afternoon. Buvalis MacGregor, head of Verasa's household, watched them go.

"A fine sight," she said to Verasa. Buvalis was too young to have seen a battalion of werewolves march to war. Verasa nodded. She'd seen far larger forces leave the castle on the way to battle. She had also seen forces arrive back, badly depleted from the fighting. Not for a long time though. These days the clans no longer went to war. It was many years since a clan dispute had led to serious fighting. Verasa never thought it would happen again. Yet here she was, sending out the army. It was Sarapen's fault. He was dragging the clan back to the old days of violence, as she knew he would.

Verasa trusted Buvalis MacGregor. She'd been head of Verasa's household for seven years. Buvalis, however, was troubled. She had recently formed an attachment with Kertal MacRinnalch, son of Kurian, brother of the late Thane. With her intimate knowledge of Verasa's movements, Buvalis had so far managed to keep this relationship secret. Buvalis was loyal to the Mistress of the Werewolves, but Kertal opposed her. Kertal supported Sarapen, not Markus. It was troubling for young Buvalis, and she fretted as she watched Verasa's werewolves march off to fight against the MacAllisters, whose cause her lover favoured.

Eskandor's force travelled through the MacRinnalch lands and marched into Colburn Wood as night was falling. As one, they took on their werewolf shapes. The woods were silent as they passed. All wildlife had fled or taken sanctuary. Only a few birds and squirrels, safe in the tree tops, watched their progress. The stream that flowed through the wood, the burn itself, was no more than fifteen feet wide but the banks were steep in places. The werewolves followed the main path and reached the bridge that led to the eastern side of the wood. Eskandor halted before crossing the bridge and waited for the return of his scouts. They brought news that the MacAllisters had not withdrawn. Eskandor spoke to his werewolves.

"We will now eject the MacAllisters. Prepare to advance."

143

Thrix stretched from her bed to pick up her mobile phone, which was bleeping. Someone had sent her a message.

Dearest Thrix I have learned how to send a text message is it not good??? Will be with you soon. Malveria.

Thrix hurried to send a reply, warning the Fire Queen that now was not a good time to visit. She got no further than the second word before

347

Malveria appeared in her bedroom.

"Damn it Malveria, can't you warn me when you're coming?"

"I sent a message. Did you not admire the way I have triumphantly mastered this complicated technology? I learned from Agrivex, who, I believed, learned from Moonglow. It is very dark in here."

Malveria waved her hand and the room lit up.

"Hello Gawain," said Malveria, smiling broadly. "How nice to see you again."

Gawain, next to Thrix in bed, looked pained.

"Don't you believe in privacy?" demanded Thrix.

Malveria looked puzzled.

"This is not a word I am familiar with. Please explain?"

"I should be going," muttered Gawain.

"I urge you not to not leave on my account," said Malveria graciously. "The Enchantress almost certainly has sufficient energy for more lovemaking. She has had so little opportunity recently."

"Will you get out of my bedroom!" demanded Thrix, frustrated at Malveria's appalling lack of tact, and embarrassed to be caught in bed with Gawain.

"I really should go," said Gawain, pointedly, looking at Malveria.

"And?" said Malveria.

"He wants you to leave the room while he dresses," said Thrix, crossly.

"Ah… I forgot that werewolves these days have adopted the nakedness taboos of humans. Very well, I shall retire to the kitchen and make coffee on your machine, if it will co-operate. Since Agrivex has been plaguing the human lands, I have learned more about the machines of humans. I really feel I may be able to utilise the coffee device."

Malveria strode out the bedroom.

"Does she always interrupt like this?" wondered Gawain.

"Probably," replied Thrix. "I haven't actually had a lover since I've known her…"

She broke off. That hadn't been quite what she'd meant to say. Thrix felt annoyed and embarrassed as Gawain rose and dressed swiftly. He slipped out of the bedroom with only the briefest of goodbyes and disappeared from Thrix's apartment without saying anything to Malveria. When the Fire Queen arrived back in the bedroom, triumphantly carrying a tray of coffee, she found the Enchantress, now wrapped in a white silk robe, glaring at her furiously.

348

"Coffee?"

"Malveria!"

"Yes?"

"How dare you burst in here like that!"

Malveria looked hurt.

"But I sent you a message. Did you not receive it?"

"I got it about three seconds before you appeared."

Malveria waved this away.

"Well, time in this dimension does run rather differently, I understand."

Thrix angrily took her coffee.

"How would you like it if I burst in on you when you were in bed with someone?"

Malveria shrugged.

"I would not mind at all. Is it very taboo among the MacRinnalchs?"

"Yes. And worse, it's extremely rude. And even more worse, what am I doing sleeping with Gawain again?"

"Ah," Malveria nodded. "This is still an embarrassing secret?"

"Yes. Don't mention it to anyone."

Malveria promised not to, though that didn't prevent her from closely questioning Thrix on every aspect of the encounter.

"How did it come about? Did he call you?"

"No."

"Did you meet by accident in some romantic spot for instance the Beautiful Frosted Fairy Glade or the jewellery counter at Tiffany?"

"No."

"Then how?"

"He rang the bell," said Thrix. "And I let him in, which was a mistake."

Thrix shook her head and sat down heavily on the side of the bed.

"I don't know what I'm doing. Why am I sleeping with him?"

"Does it matter why?" enquired Malveria. "He is rather attractive. A little sallow perhaps, but it gives him a poetic look. Does he write poetry?"

"No. Well, maybe a little. But I haven't read any of it."

"Probably that is just as well," said Malveria. "It may be all about Kalix. Unless he has now transferred his affections entirely to you."

"I doubt it. He's still mad about Kalix."

"Ah," The Fire Queen nodded sagely. "In that case I understand your attraction. There is surely nothing more desirable than a man – or werewolf – or elemental – who is more attracted to another than to you. Why this is remains a mystery but I have experienced it, most certainly. The Elvish bard Gwonthin had at one time an attachment to my lady-in-waiting Rendolin. I tried everything in my power to seduce him but he was only interested in Rendolin. It quite drove me into a frenzy of desire, I assure you."

"And how did that romance end?"

"Badly," admitted the Fire Queen. "But if an Elvish bard wishes to avoid being thrown into the volcano, he should not persist in visiting my palace and refusing to respond to my advances. It was simply asking for trouble."

Thrix sipped her coffee. She hadn't had much sleep and she was tired.

"You still haven't told me what you're doing here."

"I am here by arrangement. Have you forgotten?"

Thrix looked blank.

"What arrangement?"

"We are to visit your office, pick up finished designs and take them to Moonglow's house where they will be hidden by Kalix's pendant."

The Fire Queen's voice took on a more serious tone.

"You did not remember this?"

Malveria wasn't pleased. It was good for the Enchantress to be having a little romance, but not at the expense of Malveria's clothes.

"There is not much time till the Sorceress Livia's celebration."

"I know. Sorry, I'm getting behind with things."

Malveria couldn't conceal her displeasure. She didn't want to criticise her friend, but really, one had to have one's priorities. While Thrix dressed, Malveria asked her more questions about Gawain, which Thrix tried to deflect. Trying to change the subject she asked the Fire Queen what had become of Vex after her recent misdemeanours.

"Did you punish her?"

"Alas no," replied Malveria. "She tricked me. Before I could inflict the substantial chastisement she deserved for refusing to attend her lessons, she approached me with a copy of Italian Vogue and I became so interested in the magazine I forgot about her wide-ranging crimes."

Malveria shook her head sadly.

"You simply would not believe the outfit she wore this morning.

350

As well as the great black boots she had the gold corset I wore last year to the Igan Frost Queen's Ball – as delicate and expensive a garment as any in my last year's wardrobe – and a pair of – a pair of – " the Fire Queen groped for the word. "I really do not know what they were. Like some sort of undergarment, but to the ankles."

"Long Johns?" suggested Thrix.

Malveria shuddered at the very sound.

"That is right. And the hideous slime green nail varnish. I was obliged to send her away before I became nauseous. I despair of her."

The Enchantress laughed.

"She's young. Wait till she's stealing this year's outfits, then you'll really regret it."

144

The atmosphere in the house was bad. Kalix didn't know why. Daniel was angry at Moonglow for sleeping with Markus and Moonglow was angry with Daniel for interfering in her business. Neither of them explained to Kalix what their argument was about, and she remained unaware of Moonglow's encounter with Markus. Moonglow found it impossible to tell Kalix, and Daniel just couldn't bear to mention it.

Unfortunately, whenever there was tension in the air, Kalix always assumed that she was the cause. She retreated to her room to mope, and write in her journal how miserable everything was. She was interrupted by a loud crashing noise in the back yard, and a yell of pain. Thinking that Sarapen might be mounting an attack, she rushed to the kitchen to peer out the window. Down below, Vex was tangled up in the rubbish bins.

"What are you doing?"

"Practising my teleporting."

Vex rubbed her elbow ruefully, and brushed off some debris.

"Go away you stupid Hiyasta," shouted Kalix.

"Okay I'll be right up," replied Vex, and clambered over the fence in the direction of the front door. Kalix wouldn't have let her in but Moonglow appeared back from the shops at that moment and Vex came up the stairs with her. Vex was looking miserable and clutching her arm. Unlike Malveria, Agrivex was not the sort of elemental who spouted flames in times of emotion, but her unhappiness over her injury did give her a slightly pink hue.

"I bumped my elbow."

"I'm sorry," replied Moonglow.

"It's really sore," said Vex.

Moonglow noticed that Vex was still holding her arm out.

"Eh... do you want me to rub it better?"

Vex nodded enthusiastically. Moonglow rubbed it better. By the time Kalix arrived Vex had recovered and she greeted the werewolf cheerfully.

"So what's happening?"

"Go away you stupid Hiyasta no one wants you here," said Kalix, forcefully.

"Right. So what'll we do? Watch TV? Listen to music? Maybe go shopping?"

Kalix was perplexed. Vex was apparently impervious to insult. Hoping that she might just go away, Kalix turned on her heel and hurried back to her room. She slammed the door then turned to find Vex standing on her bed, looking pleased with herself.

"Look, I just teleported from the kitchen to your bedroom, totally successfully. So, what's on TV?"

Kalix gave up the struggle. She couldn't get rid of Vex and would just have to put up with her for a while.

"There's nothing on TV. TV is awful. I need more channels."

Kalix was annoyed because she hadn't seen Sabrina the Teenage Witch for several days. It was only on once a week, with a repeat on Saturday, and this just wasn't enough. The cable channels ran it twice every day. As for SpongeBob SquarePants, Kalix's favourite cartoon, that was hardly ever on terrestrial television. There were so many programmes and their TV could receive so few of them. Vex was sure that Moonglow was behaving unreasonably.

"The girl just doesn't understand how you need more TV. I mean, it's fine for her, gallivanting around at college and learning stuff but that's not how other people want to behave. Other people want to watch television and she has a moral duty to help them."

Vex shook her head.

"Adults have no morals. Aunt Malvie promised me new boots and would she come through with them? She would not. It's a scandal. So what's the plan for persuading Moonglow to go with cable?"

Kalix didn't have a plan.

"She just won't do it. Last time Daniel mentioned it she got really annoyed."

"Well it's your lucky day," announced Vex. "I have an idea."

"You do?"

Kalix, despite herself, felt impressed. She'd failed to think of anything at all. Vex put her head close to Kalix's and began to whisper, careful not to let anyone overhear. From Kalix's descriptions of Moonglow's unreasonableness, Vex wouldn't have been surprised to learn that Moonglow had planted a listening device in the room.

"That's maybe not a bad plan," muttered Kalix.

145

Gawain hadn't recovered from the shock of seeing Kalix kissing Daniel. Sleeping with Thrix hadn't made him feel better. He didn't know why he did it. Thrix was very beautiful but she was not a sympathetic companion, and Gawain felt she was no more pleased about the affair than he was. Gawain had romantic ideals of love, and his affair with Thrix didn't seem to fit in with any notions of romance he was familiar with.

He spent most of his time hanging around the fringes of Kennington, secretly guarding Kalix. To atone for abandoning her at the castle, Gawain had decided to protect her in London, even though she was now no longer his. As dusk came Gawain would prowl the streets and alleyways of South London, looking for anyone who might be trying to harm her. He'd already noticed Gregor MacRinnalch sniffing round the area. Gawain had not confronted him, but followed him at a distance. The three Douglas-MacPhees had also made an appearance. Gawain loathed them. So far they had not come near Kalix's house. If they did, Gawain was determined to kill them.

Hostile werewolves were not the only creatures spotted by Gawain. He was certain he'd seen some hunters, sometimes driving, sometimes on foot. There was one in particular, a stocky, powerful man who several times had walked down streets close to where Kalix lived, and paused, as if he almost sensed something, before moving on. Gawain had the uncomfortable feeling that this man knew a lot about werewolves, and was a danger to Kalix.

Gawain told Thrix about these encounters. She seemed interested. Though she took information from him she was very reticent about handing any over in return. She wouldn't tell him what was happening in the clan feud, or who exactly was hunting for Kalix. And she wouldn't tell him much about Kalix's new lover. Thrix said that it was better for Gawain to try and forget Kalix. Kalix had moved on. Thrix was vague on details, but Gawain understood from her that Kalix and her new boyfriend were in love.

So Gawain spent his cold days and nights on patrol, never going too close to Kalix's house for fear of leading anyone to her. Occasionally he'd withdraw for warmth to the cafe at the Imperial War Museum, in the large park in Kennington, but he never stayed long. He'd be too troubled by the thought that at any moment Kalix might be in danger, so he'd hurry back into the streets and continue with his lonely work.

Further north in the city, Dominil was also continuing with her work, though she ached so much she could hardly rise from her bed. Strong as her regenerative powers were, they couldn't heal her as fast as she'd have liked. Muscles that had been ripped open by Sarapen's teeth needed time to heal, even for a MacRinnalch. Three days had passed since the kidnapping. Three days lost. Dominil refused to rest any longer. She dragged herself to her feet and headed for the shower. She briefly regarded her wounds in the long mirror. There was a bloody scar on her thigh and her body was covered with scratches and bruises. She also had a black eye, which she found faintly amusing. She hadn't had a black eye since she was a very young werewolf.

The shower took away some of the pain. Dominil took the opportunity to wash her hair. Her long white hair was one of the few things she was vain about, vainer than anyone would have guessed. She dressed as quickly as she could and breakfasted alone in the kitchen. It was late morning and the twins were still asleep.

Dominil planned to have her revenge on Sarapen but she'd filed away her fury for later. At this moment she had other things to do. Dominil finished her breakfast with a small sip of laudanum. She took a pair of Beauty's sunglasses to hide her black eye and limped out into the grey morning drizzle, already concentrating on the task in hand.

146

Baron MacAllister had intended to withdraw his werewolves from Colburn Wood without fighting. He had been instructed by Sarapen to demonstrate his defiance to the Mistress of the Werewolves but not to engage in combat. As soon as Eskandor's werewolves crossed the bridge, the Baron was meant to pull back, remain on the borders of his own lands, and await further instructions.

Unfortunately, as Rainal had pointed out to Verasa, werewolves were not good at restraint when faced by an enemy. The Baron tarried longer than was wise. The moon was up, his force was all in werewolf shape and he delayed his retreat till the MacRinnalchs were in sight. He planned to march his company away in good order, showing that they were not afraid. This was a mistake. The new Baron was young and had never been in battle before. He didn't know how a large group of werewolves, faced by an opposing group of werewolves, would react. As soon as the MacRinnalchs caught sight of the MacAllisters, they set up a terrible howling, and began to rush forward.

Eskandor MacRinnalch was also partly to blame. He had intended to order the Baron out of the woods, and give him time to leave. He should have sent a messenger ahead, instead of leading his whole force so close to the enemy. Before Eskandor or Baron MacAllister could do anything to prevent it, battle was joined. The whole host of werewolves met in the middle of a clearing and began to fight, some on two feet, laying about them with their claws, and some as full wolves, rushing forward to rend with their jaws. There was no stopping the werewolves now. It was a fight to the death, a battle on a scale not seen among the Scottish werewolves for more than a century. The fifty MacAllisters were outnumbered by the eighty MacRinnalchs but no one hung back from the fray.

Each side flung itself on the other in a flurry of terrible violence. Werewolf hides, almost impossible for human weapons to penetrate, split open freely under the werewolves' own jaws and claws. All over the clearing they rolled on the ground, trampled and bit each other, clawed at each other's flesh, inflicting dreadful wounds and sending werewolf after werewolf off to the forests of the werewolf dead.

The fighting spread from the clearing to the ground beneath the trees, ground that was thick with bushes, dead wood, and thorns. The werewolves crashed through the undergrowth, snarling and biting all the while. Some of them found themselves flung back into the stream and there they fought furiously, seeking to drag their opponents under water and drown them before scrambling ashore and heading back into battle.

There was terrible slaughter. When the battle was over, many werewolves lay dead, including the new Baron MacAllister. Eskandor was badly injured. The surviving MacAllisters retreated and there were few MacRinnalchs in a fit state to pursue them. The wood, normally alive with the night-time activities of its animal inhabitants, lay eerily silent, as the squirrels, foxes and badges hid in their lairs, waiting for the violence to pass.

147

Moonglow sat on her bed, reading *Bleak House,* a lengthy work by Dickens. She'd dragged her quilt over her legs for warmth and was propped up comfortably on her pillows, making good progress. Unusually, Daniel was at this moment doing much the same, in his room. It had been intimated to him by his tutor that while the English Department did not expect their first year students to perform academic miracles, they did expect them at least to read some of the course books. Daniel had arrived home with the look of a condemned man on his face, and a copy of *Bleak House* in his bag.

He realised he might have made a strategic mistake in being so annoyed with Moonglow over Markus. It meant he couldn't really ask her for help. He considered approaching Moonglow with a full apology, and begging her to hand over her notes. But Daniel set his mind firmly against this. He was furious with Moonglow and was even prepared to go to the lengths of reading Dickens to demonstrate his displeasure.

Moonglow was interrupted by a peculiar snuffling noise outside her bedroom door. She put down her book and turned her head. She was momentarily alarmed to see a snout appearing through the door. A large wolf padded into her room.

"Eh..." Moonglow didn't know whether to panic or not. But there was something friendly about the wolf. It was medium brown, shaggy even by wolf standards, and it seemed to be wagging its tail. The wolf bounded onto the bed and started licking Moonglow's face.

"Kalix!" cried Moonglow, and began to laugh. "You're a wolf!"

Kalix, in her full wolf form, licked Moonglow's face again, and pawed at the bedclothes. Moonglow patted her on the head. The wolf seemed to enjoy this. In fact, wolf-Kalix seemed far more enthusiastically friendly than werewolf-Kalix ever had. After licking Moonglow's face some more, she bounded round the room, in a manner which could almost be described at frolicking. Moonglow laughed as Kalix rolled over. She thought she'd never seen anything as beautiful as Kalix in her full wolf form. Abruptly Kalix departed, leaving Moonglow delighted at the whole event. She loved Kalix as a wolf.

Wolf-Kalix hurried back to her own room where Vex was waiting.

"Did it go well?" asked the young elemental.

Kalix nodded enthusiastically.

"Okay," said Vex. She knew they had to act quickly. In the form of a full wolf, Kalix would soon forget what she was meant to be doing. Vex picked up the TV guide, rolled it up and stuffed it between Kalix's jaws.

"Go get her," she said.

Kalix bounded back along the corridor and into Moonglow's room then leapt on the bed, wagging her tail furiously.

"You're back," cried Moonglow. "What's this?"

She took the magazine from Kalix's jaws.

"The TV guide?"

The wolf looked at Moonglow as appealing as she could, which was very appealingly indeed. Her wolf face was really so beautiful. She licked Moonglow's nose. Realising that this was a plot by Kalix to persuade her to install cable TV, Moonglow burst out laughing. It was a funny idea. She stroked Kalix's coat.

"You think you can persuade me to get more TV by being such a beautiful wolf?"

Kalix nodded her head enthusiastically.

"Well maybe," said Moonglow. "I'll think about it."

Kalix rolled around on the bed some more then rushed back to her own room. There she continued to bound around.

"Hey, stop it," said Vex, as Kalix started growling and sniffing around under the bed. "Change back."

Kalix, by now forgetting all her human thoughts, looked suspiciously at Vex, and growled. Vex rolled up another TV guide and whacked Kalix on the nose.

"Change back you idiot."

Kalix yelped and transformed into her werewolf shape, then, after a moment or two, back into human.

"So how did it go?" asked Vex.

"Quite well, I think. Moonglow laughed."

"That's a good sign. Did you remember to frolic?"

"I frolicked loads. And licked her face."

They looked at the TV guides.

"So it's cable TV any time now," said Vex, with satisfaction. "A master plan, though I say it myself."

Kalix agreed. It had been a good plan. Vex, with all her experience of manipulating her Aunt Malveria, had picked out a weak spot in Moonglow's armour.

"You were pretty cute," said Vex. "There's just no way a gothy girl who likes romantic poetry can say no to a friendly wolf."

Vex suddenly looked worried.

"Uh-oh. Aunt Malvie. Pretend I'm not here."

The doorbell rang and they heard Moonglow tramping downstairs to answer it. Moonglow had been expecting Thrix and Malveria to visit earlier in the day, bringing with them a consignment of clothes.

"We were delayed," explained Thrix, and made ready to nudge Malveria in the ribs if she showed any sign of explaining the reason for the delay. Thrix had again erased all traces of Gawain from her by means of sorcery.

Malveria and Thrix had several long cases with them. Malveria cradled her case like a precious infant.

"Clothes for the party?" enquired Moonglow. "Can I see?"

"No," replied Malveria and Thrix, simultaneously. "They're for storage in the attic and are not to be touched under any circumstances."

Malveria's nose twitched. She snapped her fingers and Vex materialised in the room with a quilt over her head.

"Please stop trying to hide under the bedclothes," said the Fire Queen, exasperated. "It is not a convincing disguise. What are you doing here?"

Vex struggled out from under the quilt and smiled brightly.

"Hi auntie."

"Well?"

Vex thought briefly.

"I was checking the house was safe for storing your clothes."

"Did I not instruct you to attend to your historical studies with your tutor today?"

"Something came up."

"And what would that be, dismal niece?" said Malveria, glowering at her.

"I was watching a DVD with Kalix. We saw nine episodes of the Simpsons."

"That is not historical, vile girl."

"Well I think they were mostly from last season."

"Pah." Malveria snapped her fingers again and Vex flew back to her own dimension, protesting bitterly.

Thrix and Malveria climbed up to the attic. This small, dusty space had now been transformed into a cool, clean, storage area. They were relying on Kalix's pendant to prevent it being breached by hostile sorcery. The Enchantress and Malveria had set up a complicated spell to maintain the pendant's protection even if Kalix left the house. The loft was now so secure that nothing within it could possibly be observed from outside. It was safer than Thrix's offices, safer even than Malveria's palace. The new clothes would be brought here and stored until Malveria needed them. The Fire Queen was in an excellent mood as they returned downstairs.

"When I arrive in the new formal coat the Princess Kabachetka will simply fade away in comparison. Dearest Thrix, you have excelled yourself again."

Livia's celebration was on the fourteenth of next month, just five weeks away. Enough time, provided Thrix suffered no more interruptions.

"Kalix is doing well," said Moonglow, who'd noticed that neither of her visitors had asked about her.

The Enchantress nodded.

"Good. It's important she stays here. It wouldn't do for Sarapen to find her just now."

"She hasn't been vomiting so much," said Moonglow. This was true. After rescuing Dominil, Kalix had eaten pizza while still in werewolf form, and afterwards had not thrown up. Moonglow was hoping for further improvements if she would just stay around, and perhaps start to feel more secure. But in truth, neither Thrix nor Malveria seemed very interested in hearing about Kalix. They were too involved in plans concerning clothes.

"I will dazzle the assembled multitudes at the Sorceress Livia's 500th birthday celebration. Already my spirits are revived. I have quite forgotten my previous fashion disasters."

148

"Werewolves are not keen gamblers, as a rule," said Merchant Mac-Doig. "Not in my experience anyway. I don't think it's in the blood."

"Aye, father," replied the Young MacDoig. "I'd agree with that."

The Merchant slid a picture from the wall to reveal a safe.

"But that's not to say you won't find the occasional werewolf who's fond of a wager. Kertal MacRinnalch, for instance. He's a gambling werewolf, sure enough."

Kertal, nephew of the late Thane, son of Kurian, and brother of Marwanis. A member of the Great Council, a strong supporter of Sarapen, and a respectable werewolf. Apart from his gambling habit.

The Merchant opened the safe.

"And a bad gambling habit will inevitably lead a man – or a werewolf – into debt. Your mother was strongly against it, son."

Father and son paused respectfully at the mention of the Merchant's late wife.

The Merchant took something from the safe, a small object wrapped in a tartan cloth. He unwrapped the cloth to reveal a knife, very old, but still bright and sharp, and etched with curious symbols.

"The great Begravar knife," said MacDoig, with satisfaction.

The Merchant had bought the knife from Kertal, who'd removed it from the castle vaults after cunningly making a copy of the key that hung round Verasa's neck by taking an impression with a soft clay pad while he embraced her in greeting. It had been slyly done.

It had cost the Merchant a large sum of money to buy the knife. Even so, he'd paid well below the market value. The knife was a relic of ancient Mesopotamia and would have been sought after by any museum.

"An expensive item," muttered MacDoig. "But when a werewolf

360

like Kertal urgently needs money to clear his debts and doesn't want his father to learn of it, the price isn't so great, all things considered."

"It's a beautiful artefact," said the Young MacDoig.

"It is," agreed the Merchant. "Glows when a werewolf's close, and confuses the wolf, so they say."

"And kills easily," added his son.

"It does. Not that we would want any werewolf to be killed, them being such fine customers of ours."

"Who will you sell it to?"

The Merchant scratched his chin.

"Well that's a tricky one, son. There's many a werewolf might be pleased to have this weapon. They're all going to end up fighting each other, sooner or later. But we have to take care. There's some of them as might want it, yet we couldn't afford to let them know we had it."

"You mean Sarapen?"

MacDoig nodded. Sarapen would not take kindly to anyone trying to sell him a stolen MacRinnalch relic. That was not to say the transaction couldn't be made. The Merchant might claim, for instance, that the person who stole the knife had contacted him, and wondered if the Merchant might be willing to act as intermediary in the return of the knife, for a price. That had worked for the MacDoig before.

"I'll think on it a while, lad, and see who might be prepared to pay most. A lot of the MacRinnalchs have money of their own."

"The Avenaris Guild is also rich," suggested the Young MacDoig.

"The Guild? True, they have money. It's a possibility."

The Merchant's son pursed his lips.

"Perhaps we should sell it soon, father. Before the MacRinnalch feud ends. It will lose some value if they make peace."

The MacDoig chuckled.

"I don't think that's very likely, lad. I heard today that there's been fighting in Colburn Wood. The new Baron MacAllister is already dead and the captain of the castle guard is gravely wounded. There will be no peace among the MacRinnalchs for a long time to come."

149

The Mistress of the Werewolves cancelled the next meeting of the Great Council. Rainal was doubtful about the legality of this but Verasa overruled him.

"Rainal, do you really expect me to hold a meeting of the Great Council when one member of the council has kidnapped and nearly killed another member? When that same member has induced Baron MacAllister to launch an attack on the MacRinnalchs in Colburn Wood?"

Rainal did admit that the situation was awkward. How Sarapen, Dominil and Markus could ever again sit together in the council chamber could hardly be imagined. As for the MacAllisters, their new Baron was now dead after only three weeks in office. His place would be taken by his younger brother; another supporter of Sarapen, and no less rash, by all accounts.

Eskandor, the captain of the castle guard, lay wounded in the state rooms which had been converted into a hospital ward for the victims of the battle. Verasa had not been expecting such injury and loss of life, and blamed Eskandor for his lack of caution. There was no way that the council could meet at the next full moon, only five days away.

"But what then?" asked Rainal. "You can't keep postponing meetings."

"By the time of the following full moon I'll have enough votes to declare Markus Thane."

"The longer we wait," pointed out Rainal. "The more time Sarapen has to dispose of his enemies."

"I know. But I can't bring Markus to the castle just now."

Rainal nodded. It was a delicate subject. He knew that Verasa regretted her second son's lack of strength.

Tupan was wholly in agreement with Verasa's decision to cancel the next council meeting. He even suggested to the Mistress of the Werewolves that she expel Sarapen from the clan. After all, Sarapen had committed violence against other council members. Verasa was tempted, though she held off from taking this drastic step, still feeling that she could procure a vote in favour of Markus. Once that was done, everyone would fall into line. Postponing the meeting gave her another five weeks in which to work. By then Markus's health would have improved and the twins might have been persuaded. That left her need-

ing only one more vote, and she hadn't been idle. She was still working on Dulupina and Kurian.

Verasa transmitted her decision to postpone the next meeting. It
brought polite but concerned responses from Barons MacPhee and
MacGregor. The new Baron MacAllister, busy burying his older
brother, did not reply. Sarapen sent a cold response through Decembrius. It was illegal, he said, to postpone the next meeting, and Sarapen would come to the castle if he chose.

An odd report had come back from Colburn Wood. Two of those
who fought there were quite certain that as they struggled with the
MacAllisters near the river, they had caught the scent of Hiyastas. This
was hard to believe. It was the very last place you would expect to
find them. Verasa made a mental note to ask Thrix about it. Perhaps
she could enlighten her.

150

Dominil limped back to the twins' house in the early evening. She had
been walking the streets for several hours and her injured leg was very
painful. The sisters were lying on the couch watching old videos on
VH1. As Dominil entered the room they were hurling abuse at Van
Halen.

"I have found you a gig," said Dominil.

The twins were so excited that they sat up.

"Where?"

"The King's Head."

The King's Head was a good venue, very suitable. An old pub now
converted into a rock venue, the room upstairs where bands played
was busy most nights of the week. It was one of the places Dominil
had tried to book before, with no success.

"How did you do it?"

"I threatened the manager," replied Dominil.

"Really?"

The twins were impressed, and pleased. The manager of the King's
Head deserved to be threatened. He had once banned them from his
establishment for very little reason.

It wasn't true that Dominil had threatened him, though she would have if necessary. She had actually bribed the promoter who looked after Wednesday nights at the venue, using Verasa's money. It had been easy enough and was something she'd have done before had the sisters not been so anxious to avoid any accusations of buying their way to success. However, after making enquiries, Dominil had learned that bribing a promoter was not particularly unusual. It did not place the twins outside the norms of behaviour for any small band making a start. But she let the twins believe she'd threatened the manager, knowing they'd like that better.

"When is it?"

"About five weeks from now. Wednesday the fourteenth."

The twins grumbled about playing on a Wednesday. It wasn't the best night for attracting people to see an unknown band. Dominil pointed out that it had been hard enough to find anything. Besides, the fourteenth was two nights before the full moon, which meant it was the last night they could play. On the wolf nights of Thursday, Friday and Saturday, they'd be in werewolf shape.

"Couldn't we have played after the full moon?" wondered Delicious.

"No," replied Dominil, but didn't offer an explanation. The Mistress of the Werewolves had cancelled the next council meeting. But at the meeting after that, in five weeks' time, Verasa believed she'd be able to secure Markus's election, if the twins voted. There was no chance of them doing that unless they were so grateful to Dominil for helping them that they'd be willing to travel to the castle. This meant that the twins had to play some time in the next five weeks. Dominil had this clear in her mind, though she was not yet pressuring them to vote. She'd leave that until she'd made more progress.

"Tomorrow I will make a start on publicity and whatever else needs to be done. You will rehearse at the new studio."

With that Dominil left them, heading upstairs to her room to rest. The twins were already on the phone, bragging to their friends about their gig. Afterwards they went out to celebrate and had one of the most satisfying and raucous nights they'd had for months.

Dominil had not forgotten about Kalix rescuing her. She'd been surprised to find herself lectured on the topic by Beauty and Delicious. When the twins learned that Kalix had saved Dominil, quite heroically, they'd been disappointed to learn that Dominil had not been more effusive in her thanks.

"Shouldn't you buy her a present or something?"

"A present? Why?"

"To say thanks, idiot. She fought some fierce werewolves to save you."

"I would do the same for her," protested Dominil.

The sisters weren't impressed.

"You really take this cold emotionless thing way too far, Dominil. Send her a present."

151

"There's a fire elemental here to see you," announced Decembrius.

"A Hiyasta?"

"No, a Hainusta. Princess Kabachetka. Shall I send her away?"

"No. Send her in."

The Princess walked very coolly into the room. She was dressed in a coat that would feature on the cover of next month's Vanity Fair; a small fashion coup, which Sarapen could not appreciate.

Before visiting Sarapen the Princess had learned what she could of him. From what the Merchant told her, he was not a werewolf who was keen on small talk, so she came straight to the point.

"You approached the Merchant for sorcerous assistance?"

"I did."

"The sorcery you require to protect you from the eyes of the Werewolf Enchantress and Queen Malveria could not be worked by you or anyone you know. The spells are too complicated and need an experienced hand to set them in place."

Sarapen looked at her in silence, waiting.

"I will assist you with this," continued the Princess.

"Why would you do that?"

"Because I'm their enemy."

Sarapen nodded.

"Please take a seat," he said, brusquely but politely.

Sarapen hadn't noticed Kabachetka's exquisite coat or her exquisite shoes. Her dazzling blonde hair and red lips made no impression on him at all. However he was very interested in anything that might give him an advantage over the Enchantress.

152

Kalix was excited. The cable company was coming to connect their TV. She rose early and paced the living room. She felt some anxiety but not the sort of anxiety that drove her mad, more a kind of anxiety that made her want to talk all the time.

"Do you think they'll come? What if they can't find our house? What if Moonglow's changed her mind? What if it doesn't work? Do you think they're still showing Sabrina? Is SpongeBob still on? Where are they, shouldn't they be here now?"

Kalix hurried to the window to scan the street.

"Relax," said Daniel, who was taking the day off college to supervise the installation. "You can rely on a cable company. They never let you down."

Moonglow had refused to stay home for the installation. Though she'd acceded to Kalix's request and told her mother she would accept the gift, she wasn't about to change her life for a TV company.

"I'm going in to college."

"Thanks for the TV!" said Kalix.

"You tricked me," replied Moonglow.

Moonglow wasn't really that upset. Kalix seemed so much better these days that she was prepared to compromise a little to keep her happy. It was now three weeks since the last full moon. During that time Kalix had several times assumed her werewolf shape, and eaten. Afterwards she'd vomited, but less, and on two occasions, not at all. Her food intake still seemed frighteningly small but she wasn't fainting and fading away as she had been before the last full moon. It all seemed like a great improvement. Since being universally praised for rescuing Dominil, Kalix had become more settled. Now that Moonglow had agreed to the TV request, Kalix had even been smiling.

Kalix had a new book in her room, a rock yearbook from 1979. It had several large pictures of the Runaways, and an interview with the band. Dominil had bought it on eBay, and posted it to Kalix as a thank you for her efforts on her behalf. Kalix was fascinated, and slept with it beside her. It was the first new Runaways item she'd had for years. Encouraged by having a new book, she continued to play reading games on Moonglow's computer and was making progress.

Moonglow headed off to college. She wasn't about to wait in for cable engineers. There again, she wasn't actually going to college either. She was on her way to meet Markus, something she'd decided not to mention to Daniel. Or to Jay, with whom she was, of course, still in a relationship.

Kalix looked out the window for the tenth time. Now she was worried.

"Shouldn't they be here by now? Maybe they can't find our house, you know it's quite hard to find if you haven't been here before. Why is this house so hard to find? It's stupid. Why aren't they here yet?"

Kalix suddenly felt unwell and had to sit down.

"What's wrong?" asked Daniel, concerned.

"I don't know. I'm sick."

"Your not sick, you're hyperventilating. You're getting overexcited. Calm down."

Kalix felt distressed at this unfamiliar feeling. It was so rare for her to feel excited about anything good that it began to make her uncomfortable. The excitement reminded her of the anxiety she felt over bad things, and she started to feel confused.

"Tell the cable men not to come," she said, and looked worried. "I don't want to see them."

Daniel realised what was happening. He sat down beside her and took her hand.

"Don't worry. This is good. Cable TV arrives at the end of it."

Kalix was a little comforted but still didn't feel right. It was difficult, when her feelings became mixed up. Good feelings seemed to bring on bad feelings.

"You should be feeling great," said Daniel, reassuringly. "It was a brilliant plan to change into a wolf and lick Moonglow's face."

He looked thoughtful for a moment.

"What happens to your clothes? How come they disappear when you become a werewolf and reappear when you change back?"

Kalix shrugged.

"I don't know."

"You don't know? Don't you wonder about it?"

"Not really. Thrix says it's something to do with the mystical origin and nature of the MacRinnalchs. I don't think even she really understands it. We just take it for granted."

The doorbell rang.

"The cable guys are here!" shouted Daniel, and rushed downstairs to answer the door, with Kalix close behind him.

153

Moonglow stood in the foyer of the Tate Modern, waiting for Markus.

'I'm dating a werewolf,' she thought. 'Can I tell Alicia that? No, definitely not. Is this a bad idea? I'm meant to be going out with Jay. It's all going to end in disaster. I should end it.'

Moonglow's doubts disappeared as Markus walked into the foyer. He wore a long black coat of perfect cut. Under the coat he wore a delicate peach coloured blouse, a woman's garment, though shaped to fit him. He'd let his hair hang loose around his shoulders and some stray curls hung over his forehead. His skin was pale and clear, his eyes were large and dark and his face was quite beautiful. As he strode into the foyer everyone stared. Not only was Markus beautiful, he was extremely charismatic. Several women, walking by with their partners, simply abandoned their men and edged forward, wanting to get closer.

'I'm going out with Lord Byron,' thought Moonglow, with pleasure.

He kissed her lightly on the cheek. Moonglow glowed with happiness.

"So," said Markus, and smiled, very faintly. "Convince me about this place."

"Don't you like it?"

The Tate Modern was housed in a converted power station on the south bank of the Thames. The conversion of the old building into a modern gallery had been widely acclaimed. The first room was magnificent in itself, a vast space where the old turbines had been.

"I like the building," said Markus. "I'm not sure about the contents."

The gallery only housed art from the late nineteenth century to the present. Much of it was still strange to the public, and controversial.

"Mother has tried to show an interest but nothing is going to convince her that an installation made out of twisted metal is the equivalent of her favourite Titian."

Moonglow noted how Markus, Thrix and Kalix always said *mother.* It sounded curiously formal.

"So do you only like art your mother likes?"

Moonglow was surprised to find herself teasing Markus. Despite being awe-struck by his beauty there was something about him that made her feel comfortable enough to do that. Markus smiled.

"I hope not. Take me to the installations."

As they headed upstairs to the first series of galleries, Moonglow wasn't thinking much about art. She took Markus's arm, pressed herself closely to him, and felt madly in love.

154

Two nights before the full moon, Gawain was patrolling the streets of Kennington. It was almost November and the winter had turned very cold. He had now rented a small room, over towards Camberwell; close enough to make patrolling convenient, far enough away for him not to encounter Kalix accidentally. Gawain generally retained his human shape while patrolling the streets but sometimes, late at night, he'd take on his werewolf form and swiftly climb to the rooftops. He sat now, high up on top of a tenement block on one of the old estates. To his right was the Oval cricket ground. On his left were the small streets that led to Kalix's house.

He spied two small figures down below. They were too far away to make out their faces but Gawain recognised Kalix immediately, with her old coat and her long hair trailing past her waist. She was accompanied by a girl he didn't know, with spiky blonde hair and large boots. Kalix and her companion went into the only shop on the street below which was still open, an off-licence. Gawain stayed on the rooftops, not wanting to come close enough for Kalix to scent him. His heart was pounding. He had an overpowering urge to confront her, to tell her he loved her. Before he could give this much thought Gawain became aware that there was someone else abroad on this cold night. Further along the street, a figure was lurking in the shadows.

Kalix and the blonde-haired girl emerged from the shop, each with a carrier bag. From above Gawain could hear the clinking of bottles as they hurried home. He glanced along the street to see if the anyone emerged from the shadows. Someone did. It was the man who'd once looked into his eyes and known him for a werewolf. Gawain slipped over the edge of the roof and swung himself onto the balcony of the highest flat, heading for street level as fast as he could. By the time he reached the road below, Kalix had disappeared from sight and the stocky man was some distance away. Gawain hurried after him. He took care not to let himself be seen but he didn't appreciate the experience of the man he was dealing with. As Gawain turned a corner the hunter emerged suddenly from a doorway. Gawain halted, frowning. There was something about this he didn't like.

Mr Mikulanec walked towards him. He took a knife from inside his jacket. This was curious. No knife wielded by a human was going to seriously damage a strong werewolf like Gawain. The man muttered a few words and the blade glowed faintly. Gawain's eyes were drawn towards it. There were symbols etched on the knife. Fascinating symbols. He watched as they drew nearer. Suddenly the knife was heading for his chest. Shocked into action, Gawain vaulted backwards. Realising he was being attacked by some sort of sorcery, he tried not to focus on the knife but even being near to it seemed to bring on confusion. Mikulanec advanced with surprising speed for such a stocky man. Gawain leapt away again, scrambling on top of a bus shelter and placing himself out of reach. Never before had Gawain had to flee from a hunter.

"You think you're safe on top of the bus shelter, werewolf?"

Mikulanec grinned, and pointed the knife.

"This will bring you down."

Gawain felt his strength draining away. He knew now what the man carried. A Begravar knife. Gawain's great-great-grandfather had brought such a knife back to Scotland. He hadn't known that another one existed. It seemed like it might be the last thing he ever learned in this world.

On the verge of passing out, Gawain roused himself with a tremendous mental effort. He howled furiously and leapt directly at Mikulanec, using all his willpower to break through the knife's mystic shield. Mikulanec slashed with the blade and it caught Gawain's arm. It caused no more than a scratch but Gawain felt as if he'd been hit by a volley of silver bullets. His arm burned then went dead. He lashed out desperately, catching Mikulanec with his claw. The blow sent Mikulanec backwards into the bus shelter but even so, he didn't fall. He raised the knife in front of him. Gawain knew he couldn't break through the weapon's sorcery again. If he stayed here he would certainly die. He turned on his heel and fled, taking the hunter away from the direction in which Kalix had gone.

155

"Isn't Thrix just fabulously beautiful?" said Vex to Daniel. "Her hair is so golden. And it's natural. You know how much bleach I have to use?"

Vex's natural colouring was dark but her hair was glittering, metallic, yellow gold, the result of a determined campaign of bleaching that had been going on for some years. It stood up around her head, each spiky strand around eight inches long, not so much set in place as welded into position by a combination of Malveria's expensive hair products and handfuls of gel from Moonglow's bathroom.

"She looks all right," conceded Daniel, grudgingly. Thrix and Malveria were in the attic, storing dresses, and while Daniel liked the Fire Queen, he hadn't yet warmed to the Enchantress.

Daniel, Vex and Kalix were sitting on the couch, immersed in the new cable TV. They had some wine, bought after much scrambling around in pockets and under the couch, looking for loose change. The shopkeeper had not been hugely impressed by several pounds worth of pennies.

"Isn't Thrix fabulously beautiful?" repeated Vex, turning to Kalix.

Kalix grunted. Daniel looked at her.

"What's wrong? It's the big TV inauguration night. You should be cheerful."

Kalix wasn't cheerful, and not just because she didn't know what inauguration meant. Outside, for a second, she'd thought she sensed Gawain. Then it was gone and she knew she'd imagined it. It was

371

enough to depress her.

"She's thinking about Gawain," said Vex, who never realised that there were some topics best left alone. "Haven't you noticed how every time she thinks about Gawain she goes weird?"

Daniel didn't reply, knowing that Kalix wouldn't want to discuss it.

"Of course," added Vex. "Kalix goes weird for plenty other reasons as well."

"Be quiet you stupid Hiyasta," said Kalix.

"It's okay, you can't help being weird," continued Vex, brightly. "You should see some of the people where I come from. Three eyes, extra limbs, flames belching everywhere, you name it. Compared to them you're normal. Well, maybe you're more depressed. So what's on next?"

Vex grabbed the TV guide from Daniel, part of an ongoing struggle.

"Who's paying for this cable?" demanded Daniel, fighting to regain the guide.

"Moonglow's mother," said Vex, securing victory and opening it up. "So, more Voyager? Or cartoons or the late night sex show?"

Vex turned to Kalix.

"Any preferences?"

Kalix shook her head. Vex was dissatisfied.

"When I got you this cable TV with my superb cunning plan I wasn't expecting you to sit here being gloomy about it. Lighten up. So your boyfriend got banished and you'll never see him again. At least you can watch Sabrina every day."

Kalix abruptly burst into tears and ran out of the room. The young Hiyasta was mystified.

"What? I didn't say anything."

"What has my appalling niece been doing now?" demanded Malveria, appearing in the room with Thrix.

"Upsetting Kalix."

"It's not true," said Vex, defensively. "She's just being weird about Gawain again. She thought she sensed him outside."

"Did she?" said Thrix, sharply. "That's impossible."

"That's what I tried to tell her but you know Kalix, always lost in some fantasy. Hey, could we get a space ship like Star Trek Enterprise?"

Malveria was interested in the new cable service.

"Is there more fashion?"

"Who needs fashion?" said Daniel, dismissively.

"Ah," said Malveria, sliding onto the couch beside him. "I'm sensing Daniel is not truly in a good mood, despite the excellent new TV. What is the matter?"

Malveria pressed herself against Daniel, making him uncomfortable.

"Is it sadness over Moonglow?"

"Malveria will you please stop tormenting him," said Thrix. "Your interest in all this is very unhealthy."

Thrix suddenly looked concerned.

"Where's Moonglow? She hasn't gone to see Markus has she? Doesn't she realise how dangerous it is?"

"She can't keep away," said Daniel, bitterly.

Moonglow hadn't told Daniel that she was going to meet Markus but Daniel knew she had.

"What does she see in him?" he cried, exploding suddenly. "I just don't understand it."

"You don't?" said Vex. "It's obvious."

"Why is it obvious?"

"Well he looks all romantic, and he's pretty and sensitive and vulnerable. All very attractive, naturally. But he's also a werewolf, so he's really tough as well. He could protect Moonglow from anything. I mean, pretty and sensitive and tough as well? He's the ideal boyfriend. You can't compete with that."

"Thank you," said Daniel, and felt crushed.

"You shouldn't be depressed," said Vex. "It's not your fault Moonglow is insanely happy now she's with Markus."

"Is Moonglow with Markus?"

Kalix had arrived in the room and heard the end of the conversation. She was astonished.

"Didn't you know that?" said Vex.

"Moonglow's with Markus?"

Kalix was distressed. The last time she'd seen Markus he was throwing her around an alleyway. She quickly left the room again.

"A word in private, niece," said Malveria, and dragged Vex into the kitchen.

"Am I in trouble? It's not my fault if Kalix keeps breaking down in tears. I got her cable TV, what more does she want?"

"That is not my immediate concern," replied Malveria. "Why are you attempting to destroy Daniel's confidence? I wish Daniel to be attractive, not some crushed and broken spirit whom no one could love."

"Well I'm confused," said Vex. "I don't know what you want me to do with him."

"Make him into a happy confident person Moonglow might be attracted to."

Vex shrugged.

"I'll do my best."

156

Gregor was hunting for Kalix. As soon as he emerged from the tube station at Kennington he sensed that werewolves had been here recently. This unfashionable part of town was quickly becoming a popular haunt for his kind. After prowling the streets for less than thirty minutes, he scented another werewolf nearby. Knowing that Sarapen's wolves were hunting in the same area, he advanced carefully. Far more carefully than Gawain, who appeared round a corner and almost crashed into him. They drew back, each recognising the other.

"Gawain MacRinnalch."

"Gregor MacRinnalch," responded Gawain suspiciously, knowing Gregor to be Markus's lieutenant.

Gawain was holding his arm and appeared to be in distress.

"Hunters?" asked Gregor.

Gawain nodded. Gregor was puzzled. Gawain had the slightest of scratches on his arm yet he seemed to be in great pain.

"What's wrong?"

"Begravar knife," said Gawain, surprising Gregor. But he'd heard that Sarapen had stolen the knife from the castle. He looked round anxiously in case Sarapen was approaching. Gawain leaned against the wall. His arm was numb to the shoulder. Gregor was about to lead him to safety when a car pulled up alongside them.

"It's a popular place for werewolves these days," said a familiar voice. "Soon we'll be a tourist attraction."

It was Thrix, making her way home from Kalix's house.

The three werewolves, all in human form, only occupants of the dark street, regarded each other.

"Gregor MacRinnalch," said Thrix. "Doing Markus's work, no doubt."

She turned her head towards Gawain, and was immediately concerned because she could sense that his wound came from a Begravar knife. She told Gawain to get in the car.

"I need to speak a spell over that wound. If I don't it will kill you."

Gawain didn't protest. Already the numbness was spreading into his chest. Thrix asked Gregor if he wanted to be taken from the area. Gregor shook his head. There was much here that he could learn, and report to Markus or Verasa. He watched as Thrix and Gawain drove away. Gregor guessed that Thrix might have come from wherever Kalix lived so he started walking in that direction. He hadn't gone far when a slight breeze brought a scent to his nostrils that sent him diving into a garden for cover. Sarapen. Thrix was right, Kennington was becoming a popular destination for werewolves. Gregor wondered what the slumbering inhabitants of the terraces and tenements might say if they knew that Scottish werewolves were carrying on their feud in the night-time streets outside.

Gregor took out his phone and quickly composed a text message. *Kennington. Met Gawain and Thrix. Sarapen near.* He sent the message to Markus. Though Markus probably wouldn't read it till the next day it was as well to let him know what had happened in case he didn't return. He retreated, creeping through a garden, and climbing the wall. On the other side of the wall Sarapen was waiting. The instant Gregor caught sight of him he transformed into his werewolf shape. Sarapen remained as human, six inches taller and far broader than Gregor.

"Gregor MacRinnalch. What brings you here, I wonder?"

Gregor remained silent and tried not to show he was nervous.

"Looking for Kalix, no doubt."

Suddenly Sarapen transformed and as he did so he reached out a great claw, grasping Gregor by the throat. The smaller werewolf couldn't break free. Sarapen drew him close, and stared into his eyes.

"You don't know where she is, do you? You haven't found her."

Gregor shook his head. Sarapen drew him closer so that their snouts almost touched.

"But you know where Markus is, don't you?"

Gregor remained silent. Though he was facing death he wasn't about to betray Markus. Sarapen opened his jaws as if about to bite, then closed them just as quickly. Abruptly he let Gregor go.

"You know your master is skulking, hiding from me? Does that make you proud to serve him?"

"Markus MacRinnalch does not hide from anyone," declared Gregor, loyally.

Sarapen almost smiled.

"Well give him a message. Tell him I remain in my mansion. I'm not hiding. If he wishes to confront me he knows what to do."

"I'll take your message," replied Gregor.

"I admire a loyal wolf," said Sarapen. "When I'm Thane and Markus is dead, you can work for me."

With that Sarapen turned and walked away. Frustrated by the failures of the Douglas-MacPhees, he had come to conduct the search, and had no more time to waste on his brother's underlings. Gregor went swiftly in the opposite direction, hurrying through the side streets. A few flakes of snow drifted down from the dark grey sky. Suddenly he felt confused. He seemed to have lost his bearings. Was this the street he'd been in before? Puzzled, Gregor turned the corner. A man stood facing him. Gregor wondered why he hadn't sensed him. He was still wondering when the man plunged a knife into his chest. Gregor collapsed to the ground.

Mikulanec looked down at Gregor. He counted it is as reasonably successful night. The first werewolf had been unusually resourceful, making an escape even though Mikulanec had touched him with the Begravar knife. He'd probably die from the wound anyway. And this werewolf wasn't about to escape. Mikulanec watched as Gregor transformed back into his human form, as werewolves did at the moment of death. He left Gregor dead on the pavement, blood still seeping from the fatal wound.

157

Moonglow and Markus had a perfect date. Though Markus's views on the art in the Tate Modern were harsh, uncompromising, and hostile, it hadn't prevented them from having a blissful day.

Whenever they approached an exhibit, be it a collection of tangled metal, a looping piece of video, or an unmade bed, Moonglow would look at it, refer to her catalogue, muse briefly, and then say either "interesting," or "I like this." Markus would invariably reply "I hate it, it's not art." The ninth or tenth time Markus told her he hated something and it wasn't art, Moonglow burst out laughing.

"You hate everything!"

Finding himself laughed at by a young human girl, Markus was about to reply harshly when he realised that he wasn't really offended at all. He could see that it was funny, in a way.

"I don't hate everything. I just hate everything in this building."

"Even the unmade bed?"

"Especially the unmade bed."

"I liked it," said Moonglow.

Markus had the good grace to smile.

"I'm sorry, I've been involved in mother's collection of Titians and El Grecos for too long. I don't really understand any of this."

Moonglow took his hand. Thinking she might have inflicted enough galleries on her companion she led him towards the restaurant.

"So werewolves in general aren't enthusiastic about contemporary art?"

"Not as a rule. But I don't know if the humans who live around the MacRinnalch estates would be very impressed either. I mean, nothing here looks like anything."

"Well let's leave it till we've had some tea," said Moonglow. "After that I'll bring you up to date with the last century of art."

Markus smiled.

"You know you should never lecture your date about art?"

Moonglow felt her heart pounding with excitement. He'd said they were on a date. Not just a visit to an art gallery.

'I'm dating a werewolf prince,' she thought, happily. 'That's even better than Lord Byron.'

They drank tea in the cafe, and ate cake. Markus paid for it and carried the tray, gallantly. As they sat at the table Moonglow knew that the eyes of every women in the cafe were fixed on her companion. With his striking looks, his glorious hair, his long black coat and feminine blouse, he was so attractive. Moonglow had an odd giddy feeling that she had never experienced with Jay, or anyone else.

Markus seemed happy. Something about Moonglow made him forget his recent traumas, almost. Though not as striking as the MacRinnalch women, she was pretty, she was intelligent, and she was – what was she? Markus couldn't exactly put his finger on it. The phrase *fun to be with* came to mind. It was a good description though somehow he'd have been embarrassed to utter something so trite. Trite or not, it was true. Moonglow was fun to be with. He asked her if she'd like to come home with him and Moonglow said she would. She said this quite calmly, though really she felt like climbing over the table, flinging her arms round Markus and dragging him onto the floor to commence love-making immediately, and never mind the onlookers.

158

By four a.m. Vex had fallen asleep on the couch. Daniel and Kalix sat on either side of her, watching a repeat of Buffy. Neither spoke for a long time. Finally Daniel picked up a bottle, drained the dregs, and sighed.

"Well it's hard to believe, but cable TV doesn't bring happiness in all circumstances."

Daniel had developed a deep, maudlin gloom about Moonglow. He stared at the carpet, contemplating the unfairness of life.

"The girl I love is a werewolf groupie."

Kalix was just as unhappy as Daniel. The news that Moonglow was seeing Markus had come as a terrible shock. She hated Markus. Markus hated her. He wanted to take Kalix back to Castle MacRinnalch to face punishment. And now Moonglow was dating him. Kalix could hardly believe it.

"Moonglow will make me go back to the castle," she said.

Daniel shook his head.

"No, that won't happen."

"It will. Markus wants me to go there. If Moonglow is his girlfriend she'll want the same."

Daniel shook his head again. He knew Moonglow would want nothing of the sort but he was too wrapped up in his own gloom to spend much time comforting Kalix. Kalix felt herself becoming anxious. She hurried to her room for laudanum. The opiate calmed Kalix a little but it didn't help her confused state of mind. She imagined Markus and Moonglow bursting in and trying to take her away to Scotland. She thought of fighting them. She'd kill Markus, and Moonglow as well if she tried to help him. Moonglow was bad. Look how much she'd upset Daniel. Kalix liked Daniel and didn't like to see him upset. She put her hands to her head. She was full of wine and laudanum and she couldn't think straight. Her anxiety was threatening to burst through the protective shield of intoxicants. She hunted round for something to do to take her mind of her problems.

Kalix suddenly remembered how she'd felt good after helping Dominil. Maybe if she helped someone right now she might feel better. So she decided to help Daniel. She'd heard him trudge past her door on his way to his bedroom and Kalix knew that he was depressed and lonely now that Moonglow was more out of reach than ever. It struck Kalix quite forcefully that sleeping with Daniel would be a very good thing to do. He'd stop feeling lonely. Kalix herself might not be so lonely. She might forget about everything long enough for her anxiety to pass.

Kalix had a knife in her hand, ready to cut her own arm. Now, pleased with her plan, she laid it down unused. Already this was making her feel better. She hurried into the corridor and along to Daniel's door. She halted, realising that she wasn't certain how best to bring this about. Should she just creep into Daniel's bed? Should she ask first? That felt awkward. Kalix didn't know what to do. She became discouraged and returned to her room.

A new anxiety descended on Kalix, one she hadn't encountered for a while. The fear of being unattractive. How could she expect Daniel to want to sleep with her? Kalix looked in the mirror and shuddered. She was sure she'd put on weight. Kalix realised she'd been eating far too much and resolved to put a stop to it right away.

She still wanted to sleep with Daniel. It would take away her loneliness. Kalix took a substantial drink of laudanum and set off again, determined to carry it through. This time she didn't hesitate. She marched into Daniel's room.

"Daniel – " she began, before grinding to a halt. Daniel's room was lit by a single candle, plenty of light for a sharp-eyed werewolf to make out everything. Daniel and Vex were in bed together. They halted, turning their heads to look at the intruder.

"Eh – " said Daniel.

"Hi Kalix," said Vex, cheerfully. "Are you here to watch?"

Kalix fled. She rushed downstairs, sank into the couch, and switched on the TV. At least her anxiety was gone.

'I've reached a new low point of misery, humiliation and uselessness,' thought Kalix. 'Through which even anxiety can't penetrate.'

159

"What is this?" demanded Dominil, picking a disc off the floor.

"A CD," replied Beauty.

"I know it's a CD," said Dominil, coldly. "It's the CD of your last rehearsal which I burned for you. You're meant to be listening to it to seek ways of improving your performance, not using it as a beer mat."

"Lighten up," protested Delicious. "We know the songs."

"You don't know them. You have an acquaintance with them. The last rehearsal was far from satisfactory and if you're going onstage in four and a half weeks time you'll have to do better."

Delicious shared a pained look with her sister. It hadn't taken Dominil long to get back to being her mean, domineering self.

"Can't you give us a moment's rest? We're trying to relax here."

"You have relaxed for five hours today. That's enough."

"You're actually counting?" said Beauty, incredulously.

"Yes. And it's time you got to work."

Beauty yawned.

"I've always thought work was overrated."

"We're skinny and we have fabulous hair," added Delicious. "I figure that's enough."

"Camden is full of girls who're skinny and have fabulous hair. And they're all closer to success than you are. So clear this mess off the floor, listen to the CD then get to work."

The twins scowled at her angrily but gave up the argument. Satisfied that she'd made an impression on them, Dominil retreated upstairs to her room, where she had other matters to think about. She'd been wondering about the morality of using some of Verasa's money for her own purposes. The Mistress of the Werewolves had given Dominil access to a large sum. As the twins wouldn't allow Dominil to buy them success, there was a lot of money left unused. If Dominil were to use the money herself she knew she could disguise the expense in ways the Mistress of the Werewolves would not discover.

She glanced at her notes on Tibullus. She wasn't going to find a solution to her dilemma there. Tibullus was generally busy pursuing a hopeless love. Finally deciding that she was uncomfortable with the notion of misappropriating MacRinnalch funds, Dominil phoned the Mistress of the Werewolves at the castle. Verasa welcomed her call. She held Dominil in high regard these days.

"I want to use some of the money you provided."

"Of course Dominil."

"I need a small sum for a new leather coat. Sarapen damaged my old one. And I need a larger sum for purposes of my own which I can't tell you about."

Verasa paused, very slightly.

"Dominil, you know if you say that to me I can't help wondering what you need it for."

"I know. But I can't tell you. Do you object to me using the money?"

"Of course not. Why would I? You've made such splendid progress with the twins."

"Very well."

The Mistress of the Werewolves enquired as to the likelihood of Butix and Delix appearing at the castle to vote for Markus. Dominil told her it was possible.

"If their gig goes well I think I'll be able to persuade them."

"Excellent. Does their band have a name, Dominil? Some of the young werewolves in the castle were asking about it."

"Yum Yum Sugary Snacks," answered Dominil.

Verasa was surprised.

"That seems like a very odd name. I suppose one could not expect the twins to think of anything very good. Perhaps you can find something better for them."

"I'll give it some thought," said Dominil.

Not long after this, Dominil phoned the Young MacDoig.

"I'll take the item," she said, and hung up the phone.

Dominil headed out to the nearest branch of the Royal Bank of

Scotland. There she made a large withdrawal. She was going to the MacDoigs, but not to buy laudanum. She was taking up their offer of purchasing the Begravar knife. Dominil knew that this had been removed from the vaults of Castle MacRinnalch. Her duty should have been to return it to the clan. Perhaps she would, later. But first she intended to plunge it into Sarapen's heart, and kill him.

160

Moonglow fell hopelessly in love with Markus before they left the gallery. Unless, she thought, she was hopelessly in love with him before that. As they walked round the building Markus seemed to come alive again. He attributed this to Moonglow. She knew this because he'd told her so.

"I was so far gone in misery I didn't think I was ever going to come out of it."

He'd kissed her in the foyer, in front of a crowd of people. Moonglow felt like she was floating as they left the building.

He'd also apologised to her for attacking Kalix.

"The Thaneship. It was driving me insane, even before Talixia was killed. I was acting in ways I never should have done."

"Are you going to be Thane now?" Moonglow asked.

Markus shook his head. He no longer cared about it.

"I'll withdraw. My brother can have it."

Moonglow had missed college, something she'd never done before without feeling guilty. Today, she felt no guilt at all. She'd willingly miss many more days at college to be with Markus. Now she lay in Markus's bed, in Markus's arms, enjoying the feeling of being hopelessly in love. She'd have to tell Jay she was leaving him. She didn't mind that; something that would have seemed impossibly difficult only a few days ago now seemed easy. She'd fallen in love and that was all there was to it.

161

The Fire Queen returned from dinner at the Duchess Gargamond's castle in a worried frame of mind. The Duchess, an old friend, was still hiding from the world after her disgrace in wearing the same aquamarine frock to two separate sacrifices. Poor Gargamond – until recently as powerful a fire elemental as ever crossed the dimensions, nurturing volcanoes and dealing out blazing destruction with tremendous enthusiasm – was now a shadow of her former self. She admitted tearfully to Malveria that she couldn't even bear to face her devotees.

"I'm so afraid that Apthalia may have told hateful stories about me."

Apthalia the Grim was a terrible gossip. Life had been easier when she just concentrated on killing travellers on lonely roads. Since she'd taken up with the fashion world, no one was safe. Reputations could crumble in a moment. It was a miracle, reflected Malveria, that her own status had not plunged even further, given the number of times the vile Princess Kabachetka had trumped her recently in matters of style.

"Don't worry, my dear," said the Fire Queen, re-assuringly. "I am sure it will all be forgotten soon."

Duchess Gargamond was not comforted. She could see no end to her disgrace.

"Apthalia the Grim is utterly evil," complained the Duchess.

"Well of course," said Malveria. "But one would expect that from a woman who kills lonely travellers."

"I do not mean that sort of evil. I mean in the far worse sense of being a malicious gossip. I'd like to raise a volcano on her doorstep and throw her in."

But of course, Duchess Gargamond could do no such thing. Had Apthalia the Grim offended her in some other way – stolen her cattle perhaps, or poisoned her wells – the Duchess could have taken violent revenge. However, in matters of fashion, etiquette forbade it. Anyone offering violence to a fellow elemental for mocking her outfits would be outcast forever, the subject of eternal ridicule. Violence was not permitted, and the realm's great ladies had to get by on wit and style.

"I suppose I'll just have to put up with it till some other poor unfortunate suffers an even greater disgrace," sighed the Duchess. "Then, mine may be forgotten about."

It was this thought which now preoccupied the Fire Queen. The

Sorceress Livia's celebration was only four weeks away. All the ladies of the court were preparing their wardrobes. Coats and dresses were being sewn, and shoes made to order. Some from the lands of men, some from the lands of the fairies and some from those elemental tailors who were up to date in matters of fashion. Yet Malveria's outfits were not ready. As far as Malveria could see, the Enchantress was falling seriously behind with her work, and might not finish in time. If Malveria was obliged to turn up at Livia's with a wardrobe which was in anyway deficient, it would be the end. Her shame would eclipse that of the Duchess Gargamond.

It was too bad. Malveria decided to raise the matter with Thrix. The Enchantress was slightly touchy these days but Malveria couldn't just do nothing. She must be dressed for Livia's in a style so superb as to cow and overwhelm all opposition, particularly Princess Kabachetka.

Agrivex appeared in the throne room.

"Hi auntie. Do you want the bowing and curtseying?"

Malveria frowned.

"The bowing and curtseying is not something my subjects should ask about, foolish niece. It must be done spontaneously. Otherwise the whole effect is ruined."

"All right," said Vex, and began the appropriate greeting. Malveria waved her hand.

"Stop that, idiot girl. I never saw anyone so bad at bowing and curtseying. You make the whole process a mockery."

Malveria eyed Vex with distaste. The spiky blonde hair was particularly offensive. Vex grinned at the Fire Queen in what she imagined was a winning way.

"I expect you've noticed how I've been attending my lessons, not breaking things, no outrages committed round the palace, that sort of thing."

"Nothing has occupied my attention more," replied the Fire Queen, dryly. "And to what do we owe this unexpected good behaviour?"

"I need four new pairs of boots, a new coat, some T-shirts, a leather jacket and probably some new earrings as well."

Vex held up her hand.

"Now before you protest, I should point out that not only have I attended to all my palace duties, I've also slept with Daniel."

"Pardon?"

"Daniel. You know, human, floppy hair, friends with Kalix – "

384

"Yes I know who you mean," said Malveria, sharply. The Fire Queen hadn't been expecting this, and wasn't sure how to react.

"So can we come to a sensible new boot agreement?" said Vex, happily.

"You bothersome girl. Did I tell you to do this?"

"Absolutely. *Stop making Daniel feel like a worm, crushed and broken.* Your very words. Or something like that. So I slept with him. His confidence has consequently gone through the roof. Or probably, I didn't actually wait around the next morning but hey, he's got to be feeling happier about life."

The Fire Queen was temporarily confused. In truth, she didn't really know if this accorded to her plans or not. The ultimate aim was to make Moonglow jealous but now Malveria was not so sure that a liaison between Daniel and Vex would do that. Malveria felt a great wave of dissatisfaction. It was hard to credit that she, the mighty Fire Queen, could ever be uncertain about a plan for breaking a human's heart. It was a sign of how distracted she'd become by the matter of the Sorceress Livia's celebration, with its attendant clothes anxiety.

"So, about the boots?"

"I'm not certain that you deserve any boots, my unsatisfactory niece."

"Unsatisfactory? After giving Daniel the time of his life?"

Malveria leaned forward and glared at Agrivex.

"I doubt very much that you provided him with the time of his life."

"I did too!"

Malveria continued to glare.

"Well, okay, maybe not the time of his life," admitted Vex. "Because, you know, I was wanting to get back to cable, and maybe Daniel was a little upset when I started reading the TV guide before he'd finished. But I maintain I carried out your instructions and definitely deserve new boots."

Malveria frowned. She wasn't at all sure that Vex hadn't made everything worse. Still, she had carried out her instructions, albeit rather late.

"Very well. You may have the boots. But only after you describe to me everything that happened."

"Okay," smiled Vex, pleased to be getting new boots. "Well first of all we were interrupted by Kalix – "

"Kalix? Did she want to watch?"

"That's what I thought," said Vex. "But she ran out the room looking miserable so I guess she didn't."

The Fire Queen was interested.

"Tell me everything."

162

The Fire Queen might have been even more worried had she been able to eavesdrop on the conversation between Princess Kabachetka and the designer Zatek. The Princess was making one of her frequent visits to Zatek's fashion house, where the entire production line had been turned over to ensuring that Kabachetka was fabulously dressed at Livia's celebration. Zatek was pleased with his designs but worried by developments at Thrix Fashions.

"I'm finding it impossible to get an accurate view of their preparations."

"How can that be?" said the Princess. "The Hainusta spells I've provided you with are powerful enough to penetrate anything the Enchantress might use to hide her work."

"She's placed a lot more defensive charms around the building. Even when I get through them, I'm not sure I'm seeing Thrix's latest designs."

"They have to be there. The Enchantress must already have made many clothes for the contemptible Hiyasta Queen."

Zatek agreed, but repeated that he hadn't been able to find them.

"I'm sure the designs I saw there weren't really Thrix's latest. For instance, in the storage room where Malveria's new outfits are usually kept, there was a violet dress."

Kabachetka looked up sharply, immediately suspicious.

"Impossible. Violet was last season's colour."

"Indeed."

"The Queen is trying to trick me," exploded Princess Kabachetka. "To make me arrive at Livia's in violet. As if I would make such an error!"

Kabachetka became thoughtful.

"So where," she wondered, "are her newest clothes?"

Zatek didn't know.

"There's something blocking me from finding them."

Kabachetka paused while she examined herself in the mirror. Zatek had made an evening dress for her of pale yellow silk and it was a splendid item. The Princess clicked her fingers and several more mirrors magically appeared, giving her a view from every angle.

"This matter needs thought," she said, after approving the dress. "However, if my plans are successful we will not have a problem. I have met with Sarapen MacRinnalch. He is at war with the Enchantress. And, by extension, with Malveria. So I will provide him with sorcery which will enable him to crush the Enchantress. Then we shall see who is the best dressed at Livia's birthday celebration."

163

Thrix was feeling the strain. She sat in her office deep into the night, trying to come up with original ideas for Malveria's clothes. The moon was full but Thrix remained as human, suppressing her werewolf shape in order to work more easily. It was hard making sketches and working a keyboard with werewolf paws. As far as Thrix knew, she was only the second MacRinnalch ever to be able to suppress the change. Old Minerva, her sorcery teacher, had taught her a long time ago.

Thrix was reasonably satisfied with her designs for the first three days of the event but had made minimal progress on days four and five. As for Malveria's servants, Thrix still wasn't happy with her efforts, and cursed all handmaidens and page boys for being so difficult to dress.

There were now only four weeks till Livia's celebration. Malveria had to be ready by the fourteenth of next month. It was a tight schedule and there were other matters that demanded Thrix's attention. Milan and New York were crowding in on her time, and there was the day-to-day business of running her fashion house. Ann was working hard to protect Thrix from outside distractions but even so, there were some things that couldn't be delegated.

Thrix wished she could have delegated the task of protecting Kalix.

That seemed to be hers whether she wanted it or not. She had warmed to Kalix a little after her rescue of Dominil but even so, Thrix couldn't bring herself to love her young sister. Kalix was so sullen, so hostile, and so troubled. The Enchantress believed that people should work hard, put their lives in order, and make something of themselves. That was the way to deal with your problems. Sulking and depression never got you anywhere.

Then there was Zatek. Thrix could feel the prying eyes of his sorcery attempting to scan her office, her storerooms, even her computer. The Enchantress and the Fire Queen had placed the strongest spells of defence they could around Thrix's offices but the sorcery Princess Kabachetka had provided for Zatek was so difficult to deflect. At least the clothes were safe once stored near Kalix.

'And who knows what Kalix would do if she found out I've been sleeping with Gawain,' thought Thrix. She put her hand to her brow and swept back her golden hair with a frustrated gesture. Yet again she had found herself in bed with Gawain. Thrix couldn't understand it. No matter how strongly she told herself not to do it, it just seemed to happen.

'I don't even like him that much,' Thrix told herself, angrily. 'And he's not that attractive.'

She knew this wasn't really true. Gawain was attractive.

"But that shouldn't be enough reason to keep sleeping with him," muttered Thrix. She dreaded her mother finding out. If Verasa ever discovered that her eldest daughter was now sleeping with the banished Gawain, her reaction did not bear thinking about.

The Mistress of the Werewolves had called today to inform Thrix that she'd expelled Sarapen from the clan. Thrix wasn't sure what she thought about this. She supposed there were good reasons. Verasa held Sarapen responsible for the deaths of Baron MacAllister, Talixia, and now Gregor, Markus's bodyguard. Then there was kidnap of Dominil, and the assault on the twins, all of them members of the Great Council. And Verasa blamed him for inciting the new Baron MacAllister to invade MacRinnalch lands, leading to many deaths. The Enchantress didn't know if Verasa's actions were legal, in terms of clan law. She didn't much care. Whether they were legal or not, it would only lead to more violence.

Verasa mentioned another matter which was rather puzzling. Apparently Hiyastas had been sighted in Colburn Wood. It was hard to believe that the fire elementals should have been there, but there had been more than one report of their presence.

"Do you have any idea why that might be?" her mother had asked.

Thrix had replied in the negative, but her mother, knowing of Thrix's friendship with Queen Malveria, pressed the point.

"I really don't know," protested Thrix.

"Colburn wood is sacred to the clan, dear. We can't let it be overrun with Hiyastas."

"Perhaps it's just a false rumour?"

Verasa didn't think so. Eskandor, captain of the castle guard, was a reliable witness, even though he still lay wounded in the castle. Which led to another piece of news. The Mistress of the Werewolves had decided to promote Markus to captain of the castle guard, placing him in control of the MacRinnalch forces.

"Isn't Markus currently incommunicado, suffering from severe trauma?"

Apparently he wasn't. According to the Mistress of the Werewolves he'd made a very swift recovery.

"I spoke to him today and he's in excellent spirits."

Thrix wasn't completely convinced about Markus's spirit but she was keen to get back to her work so didn't pursue it. Her mother wasn't about to let her of the phone so easily, and went back to the unexplained presence of Hiyastas in Colburn Wood.

"They're not friends of the MacRinnalchs and they're not welcome there. Fire elementals are very untrustworthy creatures. What if they set fire to the Wood?"

"The Hiyastas can control their fire, mother," said Thrix.

"Doesn't your friend the Queen regularly burst into flames over minor fashion disappointments?" asked Verasa.

"She sometimes flickers a little," admitted Thrix, and wished her mother would drop the subject. "But I'm sure none of her subjects would visit Colburn Wood."

"Well Eskandor swore he caught a glimpse of one of them filling a flagon of water from the spring." Verasa's voice rose in annoyance. "The spring water is used for the MacRinnalch whisky. It's not to be stolen or polluted by Hiyastas."

"I doubt the Hiyastas are distilling their own whisky. They generally prefer wine."

"Don't be flippant dear. The pure water of Colburn wood is a valuable resource. Your grandmother used to speak highly of its rejuvenating properties."

As soon as Verasa said this the Enchantress's heart sank. Of course. The rejuvenating properties. It would take a lot of sorcerous power to transform the water into a suitable potion but Thrix had a good idea of who might be interested in doing just that.

Thrix applied herself to her work. Suddenly she sensed someone penetrating her defensive spells. She half rose, ready to defend herself, before catching the aroma of jasmine. She relaxed.

"You are working so hard, darling Enchantress," said Malveria. "You are working hard, yes?"

"I am."

"Excellent." Malveria smiled. "Are we up to day five?"

"I'm still on day three."

Malveria frowned.

"Oh. Have we solved the vexatious problem of the handmaidens' attire? Which must be glorious but not as glorious as my own?"

"No."

"The page boys?"

"I'm still working on it."

Malveria's frown deepened.

"I understand that the contemptible handmaidens of Kabachetka are already boasting of their new finery. My own handmaidens are starting to fret."

Rather wearily the Enchantress tried to reassure the Fire Queen that everything would be ready on time. She pointed out that recently she'd had a lot of other things to attend to. This didn't go down well with Malveria.

"Can't you concentrate on me?"

Thrix became slightly irked. To listen to Malveria, a person might think that Thrix Fashions was deliberately neglecting her, which was surely the very opposite of the case. Thrix had rescued Malveria from fashion hell, but the Fire Queen seemed to have forgotten this.

"I presume you have spent no time sleeping with Gawain?"

"What do you mean by that?" responded Thrix, sharply.

"I mean you may make more progress with the fabulous costumes if you were to spend less time in the arms of Gawain. Really Thrix, one understands the need, but you must not let it interfere with the important things in life."

Thrix was becoming more and more annoyed. Here she was, up alone in the middle of the night, working on Malveria's clothes, and Malveria herself was criticising her. Not only that, she had the nerve to meddle in her love life.

"If you didn't drop in here every five minutes I might get some work done," said Thrix, quite harshly.

"If I didn't drop in here every five minutes you would no doubt be spending all your time in the embraces of Gawain."

"Malveria, I don't even like Gawain! And what does it have to do with you anyway?"

"Nothing at all," declared Malveria, rising an inch or two from the ground. "And I hope you have a splendid time with the young werewolf while I am facing disgrace at Livia's."

Thrix stood up. Not liking the way Malveria was higher than her, she levitated eight inches from the ground, and they faced each angrily in mid-air.

"You'd be facing disgrace every day if I hadn't started dressing you properly."

"And you would be out of business long ago had I not poured money into your coffers," replied Malveria, which was true enough to wound the Enchantress.

"Thrix Fashions can manage very well without your money, Malveria."

A flicker of flame now played around the Fire Queen's eyes.

"Really? Perhaps we should see if that is true, wretched werewolf. London is full of designers who would kill to have Malveria as their client."

"Then I suggest you find one," stormed Thrix. "And while you're at it, stay out of Colburn Wood."

Malveria, taken by surprise, descended a few inches.

"What?"

"You heard me. Mother told me Hiyastas have been there."

"I have no idea what you're talking about."

"Please, Malveria, if Hiyastas have been visiting Colburn Wood I'm quite sure you know the reason why. You've been stealing water from Colburn Spring and using it for rejuvenation."

Malveria was outraged, and rose higher from the floor. She completely denied the allegation, raging against the Enchantress for daring to suggest such a thing.

"Malveria requires no rejuvenation! You may count yourself fortunate that I do not blast you from this earth!"

The Enchantress levitated further, bringing herself level with Malveria.

"And you can count yourself lucky I don't sling you out my office! Have you any idea the trouble it will cause for me if you're found stealing from Colburn Wood? Do you know how important it is to the MacRinnalchs?"

"Pah!" spat Malveria. "What may be important to the barbaric Scottish werewolves is of no importance to the Queen of the Hiyasta. Good Day, Enchantress, and may you never cross my path again!"

"That's fine with me," yelled Thrix. "I should have known better than to try making elegant clothes for an elemental who's only happy when she looks like an extra from an old disco movie!"

"And I should have known better than to trust a nefarious werewolf who is no doubt treacherously in league with the repulsive Kabachetka!"

Malveria vanished, her dematerialising being so violent that she left behind a circle of fire on the carpet. Thrix snapped her fingers, putting out the flames, and floated back to ground level.

"That's the way to treat your most important client," she sighed.

The Enchantress released her spell, sinking with relief into her werewolf shape, gaining strength from the moon. Then she sat on the couch and read Vogue, in a very bad mood.

164

On the night of the full moon Sarapen called a meeting of potential supporters. Representatives from each of the three Barons flew to London, and there were delegates from the MacAndrises and other smaller clans with whom Sarapen had influence. Twenty grim-faced werewolves now sat in the largest room in his mansion. Sarapen had greeted each arrival with due courtesy. They had been provided with food and drink as hospitality required. This done, Sarapen began the meeting without further formality.

"The Mistress of the Werewolves has expelled me from the clan. I don't accept this. She does not have the authority."

No one contradicted Sarapen, though the point was far from clear. In an emergency, the Thane did have the power to expel a werewolf. Whether this power also extended to someone who was in temporary charge of the clan, as Verasa was, had never been tested.

"The Mistress of the Werewolves intends to force through the election of Markus. I say she's unfit to lead the clan, and should be removed before she foists Markus on us."

Around the table there were some expressions of concern, but many were in full agreement with Sarapen.

"We should end this farce immediately," declared Morag MacAllister, who'd seen two Baron MacAllisters die in quick succession. The new Baron Douglas, young and hot-tempered, had sent his equally fiery sister Morag to the meeting with instructions to urge Sarapen to march on the castle and take the Thaneship by force. "Expel the Mistress of the Werewolves and declare yourself Thane!"

Lachlan MacGregor, emissary from Baron MacGregor, was not keen on Morag MacAllister's suggestion.

"Baron MacGregor also inclines towards Sarapen MacRinnalch as Thane but the removal of the Mistress of the Werewolves would be illegal."

Lachlan found little support. The Mistress of the Werewolves' behaviour had caused resentment among the clans. Support for Markus had never been strong and it was fading quickly. Murdo MacPhee made it quite clear that the MacPhees preferred Sarapen over Markus.

"Baron MacPhee will back Sarapen on one condition."

"And that condition is?" asked Decembrius.

"The Baron wants justice for the old Thane. Baron MacPhee was his companion for two hundred years and he's never been reconciled to the Thane's killer walking free."

"I agree with the Baron," said Sarapen. "Kalix MacRinnalch should have been brought to justice long ago. It's only lack of will on the part of the Mistress of the Werewolves that's prevented it. As proof of my commitment to her capture – "

Sarapen paused, and drew out a leather purse. He emptied five gold coins onto the table.

"I offer these as reward for her capture. Or for her heart."

The werewolves looked with wonder at the coins. Five gold nobles, minted in the reign of King David II of Scotland, in the year 1357.

393

Ancient gold, from the legendary vaults of the MacRinnalchs. These coins were hardly known to exist in the world these days. Gold like this was coveted by any werewolf.

"Then Baron MacPhee will support you," said Murdo MacPhee.

Red Ruraich MacAndris was adamant that the MacAndrises would never follow Markus, no matter what the Great Council decided. Sarapen was pleased. He'd known from the start that Verasa had overestimated the strength of her own position. Sarapen clearly commanded the loyalty of almost all who were gathered here. It was surely enough support to defeat the Mistress of the Werewolves, if it came to a confrontation. The MacRinnalchs were strong but would the MacRinnalchs in the castle really fight for Markus? It had not gone down well with them that Markus was in hiding.

"Very good. I'm grateful for your support. At the next full moon, we'll advance on Castle MacRinnalch, demanding that the Mistress of the Werewolves rescinds my expulsion. If necessary we'll storm the castle. Then I'll call a meeting of the Great Council at which I will be declared Thane."

Morag MacAllister chafed at the delay. The next full moon was four weeks away. She wanted to know why they couldn't march earlier.

"You forget," said Decembrius, "A great many of the MacRinnalchs in the castle can take on their werewolf shape any night. The majority of werewolves under the Barons cannot."

"I can be wolf any night I choose," declared Morag, fiercely.

"Indeed. But most of your clansmen can't."

Sarapen nodded his agreement. There were other reasons to wait. Thanks to Madrigal, Sarapen now knew that Butix and Delix would be playing on the fourteenth of next month, directly before the next full moon. Dominil would be with them. It was possible that Kalix and Thrix would also be there. Five members of the Great Council, all opponents of Sarapen, all together at a venue in Camden. Sarapen planned to attack the gig. With the promise of help from Princess Kabachetka, Sarapen was confident he could defeat the sorcery of the Enchantress. Kalix would be killed and the other members of the council taken prisoner. That night Sarapen would deal his enemies a fatal blow and the next day he'd fly to Scotland to lead his troops against the castle.

Before the next moon Sarapen would send out the Barons. Though they'd hold off from attacking the castle, the threat would draw back

394

to Scotland many of the werewolves Verasa had dispatched to protect her allies in London. Then Sarapen would sweep up every MacRinnalch who opposed him. Butix, Delix, Thrix and Dominil could vote for him or they could die like Kalix. Either way, Sarapen was going to be the Thane at the next full moon.

165

With the moon being full, Kalix had gorged on pizza and raw beef. Though Moonglow was out with Markus she had not forgotten to provide well for her, which Kalix completely failed to appreciate. She hated it that Moonglow was having an affair with Markus. To spite Moonglow, she decided not to learn to read anymore.

To make matters worse, Kalix felt as if she'd betrayed Gawain. Even though her plan to sleep with Daniel had crashed in flames before she'd got started, she'd still betrayed him. It was treacherous behaviour on her part. Though it was almost impossible for a werewolf to be miserable on the night of the full moon, the uniquely troubled Kalix managed it. When the clouds parted outside the kitchen window, revealing the white moon looking down over London, Kalix scowled.

"Stupid moon," she muttered, and hunted in the fridge for more meat, and another carton of ice cream.

The atmosphere in the house between Daniel, Moonglow and Kalix was now quite awkward. On her way back from the kitchen Kalix met Daniel in the living room but headed for her own room without greeting him. Daniel wondered if he should go after her but at that moment Malveria materialised with an unusually violent flash. Something was obviously wrong. Flames were flickering around the Fire Queen's eyes, nostrils and fingers. Tears rolled from her eyes, hissing and sizzling in the heat.

"I am here to burn the Enchantress's foul designs!" she announced, and made for the stairs.

"Wait!" yelled Daniel, not liking the idea of his flat burning around his head. "Wouldn't you like to tell me about it?"

"There is nothing to tell, young human! The perfidious werewolf has deliberately delayed the making of my clothes leading to inevitable disgrace at the Sorceress Livia's birthday celebration."

"I'm sorry about that," said Daniel. "But I'm sure you'll look beautiful whatever you wear."

The Fire Queen set her mouth in a firm line.

"It is no use bombarding me with compliments, Daniel. The clothes must burn!"

The Fire Queen began to ascend the stairs with a determined gait.

"But you can't burn them. I saw you wearing the new orange dress. You looked eh... fabulous."

Daniel writhed in embarrassment as he said this but it brought Malveria to a halt. She turned her head slowly, steam still hissing from the tears that mixed with the flames in her eyes.

"I did?"

"Absolutely," said Daniel, nodding his head furiously. "Fabulous. Believe me, I've never used that word about a dress before."

The flames around Malveria's eyes and nose grew smaller. She took a step back towards Daniel.

"It is a good dress."

"It's wonderful," agreed Daniel, meanwhile searching frantically for a further compliment. He remembered something he'd heard Moonglow say about a friend she admired.

"And of course, not everyone could wear it."

Malveria nodded.

"You're right. It is a bold orange. Few elementals could carry it off. And yet the moment I laid eyes on it I knew I would look as brilliant as the midday sun."

"That's the very words I was looking for."

The flames went out. Malveria descended the stairs. Then, quite abruptly, she dissolved in tears.

"There there," said Daniel, leading her back into the living room and helping her to the couch. "Do you want to tell me about it?"

It took Daniel a while to learn exactly what had happened between Malveria and Thrix. When her tears dried Malveria descended into a deep depression. Daniel brought her wine and scanned the TV guide for any fashion-related programme which might cheer her up. Unfortunately, when he found a programme on makeovers, it only made Malveria sadder.

"I have no one to make me over," said Malveria, gripped by her maudlin emotions. "You are so lucky to live with friends who would never betray you."

Daniel nodded.

"But we're not getting on so well," he admitted. The Fire Queen seemed interested in this, so Daniel told her of his unhappiness over Moonglow and Markus.

"Moonglow is much more crazy about Markus than she was about Jay."

Daniel started the conversation as a way of diverting Malveria's attention from her own misery but it didn't take him long to forget Malveria's problems and concentrate on to his own. The Fire Queen proved to be a good listener. She was interested in everything he had to say about himself and Moonglow.

"Don't despair, young Daniel. I have much experience in the ways of lovers. Do not abandon hope. One day Moonglow will want you."

Daniel took heart. After all, Malveria was well versed in these matters. He felt sufficiently grateful to refill Malveria's wine glass, though he wouldn't have felt so grateful had he known of the Fire Queen's bargain with Moonglow. Daniel tensed as he heard the front door open, but Malveria reassured him.

"It's Moonglow on her own. She is not with Markus."

"Maybe they've broken up?" said Daniel, hopefully.

Moonglow burst into the room looking radiant.

"I love Markus!" she cried.

Daniel and Malveria regarded her sourly.

'Another MacRinnalch annoyance,' thought Malveria, and wished ill on the whole family.

"Where's Kalix?" asked Moonglow.

"Sulking in her room."

"Oh dear." Moonglow noticed that neither Daniel nor Malveria were looking very happy either.

"What's wrong?"

"Malveria argued with Thrix," explained Daniel, not wanting to refer to his own problems. Moonglow was concerned. In her happy state she didn't like to see anyone miserable. She listened as Malveria related her sorry tale. When she finished, Moonglow nodded.

"Very upsetting," she agreed. "But surely you don't really think Thrix is betraying you?"

"Of course," exclaimed Malveria. "It is the treacherous behaviour

I have come to expect from the Enchantress."

"No, really," said Moonglow, looking Malveria in the eye. "You don't really think Thrix is betraying you, do you?"

Malveria stared back at Moonglow, not liking to be contradicted. Then she shrugged.

"Possibly she is not."

"Of course she isn't," said Moonglow, in her kindly way. "Thrix would never do that to you. I expect she's just tired because she's been working too hard and when you started to argue, it all got out of hand and you both said things you didn't mean."

Malveria stared at her exquisite shoes for a moment, then at Moonglow. The girl did have a way of putting things that made sense.

"You think this is possible?"

"Definitely. Thrix is a good friend. And she's making you such beautiful clothes."

Malveria let out a long low moan and rested her head on Daniel's shoulder.

"Moonglow is right. But now it is an even worse disaster. I have accused my friend of terrible things and she'll never speak to me again."

"Why not just apologise?" suggested Moonglow.

The Fire Queen bridled at the idea.

"Apologise? Never. The Enchantress said very hurtful things to me. If I marginally overreacted it was quite understandable."

"Just apologise, it'll make things better."

"Never," insisted the Fire Queen. "I did not defeat the dragon of death and despair by apologising."

Moonglow pointed out that this was rather different. Malveria dug her pencil-thin heels in.

"Before I can apologise the Enchantress will have to beg my forgiveness."

"Well really!" said Moonglow, exasperated. She took out her phone and dialled Thrix's personal number.

"Thrix? This is Moonglow. Malveria's here and she's really upset…"

"This is outrageous!" cried the Fire Queen. "I insist you put down that phone."

"…and she wants to make up the argument."

Malveria crossed her arms in front of her chest.

"I will not speak to her," she declared.

The Enchantress suddenly appeared in the room, materialising with a much gentler flash of light than had Malveria. Moonglow was surprised to see Thrix as human, with the full moon overhead. Thrix stared at Malveria. Malveria stared at Thrix, then leapt to her feet and embraced the Enchantress.

"Dear Thrix I'm so sorry."

"I'm sorry too," said Thrix.

They embraced emotionally. Daniel turned to Moonglow.

"You're good at this sort of thing."

"Yes, it's one of my talents."

Moonglow broke off a slice of the pizza which Daniel had just microwaved for her. Kalix slunk out of her own room and made her way through to the kitchen without speaking. She didn't even acknowledge her sister.

"There goes our teenage malcontent," said Daniel. "Also in a bad mood."

Thrix and Malveria had by now stopped embracing and were talking animatedly about designs for day four, whatever that meant. Kalix traipsed heavily back into the room. Moonglow scrabbled in her bag.

"I brought you something," she said and handed over a box. Kalix took it in her werewolf paw with a show of boredom. She wasn't intending to be impressed by any gift from Moonglow. However, on finding it to be a DVD containing the whole first series of Sabrina the Teenage Witch, her face lit up. Kalix's emotions while in werewolf form were less subtle than her emotions as human. Her defences were dented by the excellent present.

"Thanks," she muttered, still attempting to show as little gratitude as possible. But she sat down on the floor beside them and eagerly opened the DVD to look at the pictures inside.

Moonglow had worked a miraculous transformation. It seemed like only minutes ago that the house was full of miserable elementals and gloomy werewolves. Now the living room was full of contented creatures. Moonglow was still puzzled at Thrix being in human shape while the moon was full.

"I can suppress it," explained Thrix.

Moonglow considered this.

"Why? Isn't it fun? Don't you get urges to run through a forest?"

"Why on earth would I want to run through a forest?" asked Thrix.

"To get close to nature?" ventured Moonglow.

The Fire Queen burst out laughing at the thought of Thrix getting close to nature.

"Thrix does not like to participate in anything which does not require high heels."

Moonglow's phone rang. She hurried out of the living room to take it in private. Malveria commented on Moonglow's capacity for bringing good cheer. Thrix looked thoughtful.

"I wonder if she's bringing good cheer to Markus?"

"One would imagine so," said Malveria. "Given that she seems so happy herself."

There was a terrible cry from the hallway. Moonglow burst into the room and collapsed sobbing onto the couch. Malveria turned to Thrix.

"These humans can be so inconsistent."

Moonglow put her head on Daniel's shoulder.

"Markus says it's all over," she wailed. "He never wants to see me again."

Moonglow cried bitterly, and it was all she could do for a long time to come.

166

The third time Markus had woken up with Moonglow beside him he realised he felt different. He felt peaceful. He was calmer than he had been for weeks. The terrible emptiness caused by the loss of Talixia didn't hurt so badly. He still grieved for her but it no longer felt like something he couldn't cope with. He had done enough grieving.

Little of the dull morning light penetrated the heavy curtains of Markus's bedroom; it was enough for a werewolf to make out his still sleeping partner. Moonglow was pretty when she was sleeping. Tranquil, with a hint of a smile on her lips. Markus looked at her appreciatively. She had brought him back from the brink. Her love for him had rescued Markus from his despair. He leaned over and kissed her lightly on the cheek. He appreciated what she'd done. It was a shame that he would now have to leave her.

He dressed silently and went downstairs to the phone, then called his mother's private chambers at Castle MacRinnalch.

"This is an early call, dear. I hope there is nothing the matter?"

"I'm better. The trauma has gone."

Verasa was surprised.

"Are you certain?"

"I'm quite certain. Tell me what's been happening."

Markus was aware that his behaviour could not have impressed his fellow werewolves. The prospective Thane did not hide away and mourn for his losses. The prospective Thane rallied his supporters and defeated his opponents. When Verasa gave a rather vague and meandering version of recent developments, Markus interrupted her.

"Mother, it's fine. You don't have to spare my feelings. Do I still have sufficient support to be Thane?"

Verasa assured him that he did. She was cautious, still surprised at the sudden change in her favourite son's demeanour.

"Did anything happen to you?"

"No," replied Markus. "I simply recovered. I am a MacRinnalch, after all. We should discuss what we're going to do next. I've been thinking it might be best if you made me captain of the castle guard."

"My thoughts exactly," said Verasa, and sounded pleased.

They spoke for a long time, till Markus was fully abreast of recent events. He was contemptuous when he heard that his older brother had called a clandestine meeting of his supporters.

"The Barons will not dare to go against us. And if they do we'll put them in their place."

Markus was healed, in body and spirit. Moonglow's attentions and the power of the moon had brought back his strength. He thought of the girl, lying upstairs in his bed. He knew that she loved him. It had happened before. Human girls of that sort always loved him. They couldn't help themselves. When Moonglow woke he'd be polite to her, and send her off kindly. But now he was well, he didn't need her any more, and the relationship was over.

167

At the headquarters of the Avenaris Guild Mr Carmichael was assessing reports. The Guild knew by now that there was a dispute going on among the MacRinnalchs; something to do with the succession to the Thaneship. This was highly significant. At such a time there might be many opportunities for killing werewolves, particularly as they had information that many of the principal characters were here in London, far from the safety of their ancestral homes.

Gregor MacRinnalch had been killed by Mr Mikulanec, and Gregor was known to the Guild as a senior member of the MacRinnalch Clan. Affairs in London must be important for him to have made an appearance. Mr Carmichael had a shrewd idea that the MacRinnalch feud might be coming to a head on their own doorstep, and sent out as many agents as he had available. Some south of the river, to continue the hunt for Kalix. Some further afield, looking for the werewolf musicians they'd fought at the rehearsal studio. The Guild was now co-operating fully with Mr Mikulanec. He'd proved his worth by killing Gregor. When the Guild made the breakthrough that was surely coming, they'd call on the services of Mr Mikulanec, and together they'd deal the MacRinnalchs a blow they'd never forget.

The werewolf hunters had increased their computer security. Their information officer reported to Mr Carmichael that whoever had hacked into their system would not be able to do so again. Sitting at her computer, upstairs in the twins' house, Dominil was only slightly inconvenienced.

"You wasted your money on the upgrade," she murmured, as she once more bypassed their security, and scanned their files. The werewolf was not pleased at what she learned. The Avenaris Guild seemed to know more about the feud for the Thaneship than they should. They still lacked details – no word of events at a meeting of the Great Council had ever reached outside ears – but they knew enough to realise that this was a good time to attack the clan.

Dominil noted with displeasure that she now appeared in their records. *A white-haired werewolf, of unknown origin. Apparently protecting the younger musicians. Assisted at the studio by two other werewolves, one of them Kalix MacRinnalch.*

Again there was mention of the man from Croatia. Now he had a name, Mr Mikulanec. He had killed Gregor MacRinnalch on the same night that Gawain was injured. Dominil knew of Gawain's injury. Thrix had told her that a human hunter now carried the Begravar knife, or something very similar. Thrix didn't know how the human came to

402

possess such a weapon. She thought it most likely that it was the MacRinnalch knife, stolen somehow from the castle by the Avenaris Guild. The Mistress of the Werewolves didn't believe the Guild were involved. She believed it had been stolen by Sarapen, and then used by one of his human hirelings.

Only Dominil knew for certain that there were two Begravar knives, because she had one of them. Kertal had stolen this knife from the MacRinnalch vaults, but if the Mistress of the Werewolves blamed Sarapen for the theft, and the deaths of Talixia and Gregor, then Dominil wasn't about to enlighten her. It suited Dominil for Sarapen to take the blame. She had been amused to learn that Verasa had expelled him from the clan. How that must have hurt Sarapen, with his liking for clan tradition.

Reaching under the bed, Dominil drew out the box. The knife wasn't large but the blade was sharp. The hilt was decorated with a plate made of bone, with cuneiform engravings. Dominil could not yet read them but she intended to learn how. As far as she knew, the knife needed activating before its dread power became fully effective. Were it active at this moment, she wouldn't even be able to hold it without its spell of bafflement affecting her senses. Presumably the writing gave some sort of instructions, some word of power, to bring the weapon to life. Dominil took a sip from her bottle of laudanum then began to hunt on the internet for translations of Sumerian cuneiform.

168

Moonglow sobbed on Daniel's shoulder. Thrix fidgeted, wanting to leave, but the Fire Queen was fascinated. She was pleased to see the way Daniel comforted Moonglow. Kalix, not that interested in Moonglow's misery, was about to head for the kitchen when Vex appeared in the room, arriving from upstairs.

"What are you doing here?" demanded Malveria.

"Practising teleporting," replied Vex. "Quite successfully really."

Vex smiled brightly, and wondered why no one was smiling back at her. She finally noticed that Moonglow was crying.

"What's the matter with her?"

"Markus has discarded Moonglow like an unwanted sacrifice," explained Malveria. "Jettisoned her like last years shoes. Thrown her out like – "

Moonglow's crying grew louder. Thrix nudged Malveria.

"Did I speak out of place?"

"Whoa!" said Vex, enthusiastically. "Bad break up? Lucky you got cable. It's just what you need to get you through. So, who's got the TV guide?"

"Be quiet, idiotic niece," said Malveria. "You will upset the girl. What good is television when you have been cast aside, abandoned, and brutally rejected by the one you love?"

Moonglow sobbed and rushed from the room.

"I really think you need TV," insisted Vex. "It's the best thing for a broken heart. I've read about people eating ice cream and chocolate but what's the point of that? I mean, then you're not only miserable you're fat as well."

"Surprisingly, my niece speaks sensibly for once," agreed the Fire Queen. "There is no point in laying on pounds of unwanted blubber as a means of dealing with rejection."

The Enchantress nodded in agreement. Vex, Malveria and Thrix were united in their antagonism towards food as a palliative for a broken heart. Daniel, feeling they were all missing the point, rose with an exasperated grunt.

"I'll go see she's all right."

"He is gallant," said Malveria, as Daniel left the room. She turned her eyes back towards Vex, and became suspicious.

"Appalling niece. When you came downstairs there was something about your aura I did not like."

Vex looked at Kalix, a pained expression on her face.

"You see what I have to put up with? Even my aura gets criticised."

"It looked to me like the aura of a girl with a guilty conscience," continued Malveria. "Of course, you often have a guilty conscience due to your numerous crimes. But I would judge this particular guilt-tinged aura to be the result of trying on my new clothes which are at this moment hidden in the attic."

Malveria glared at Agrivex.

"I completely deny it," said Vex.

"You dismal girl. If you go near these clothes again you will find yourself swimming briefly in the great volcano before disappearing

404

under a torrent of lava, and a great benefit to the Hiyasta nation that would be, now I think about it."

"We should be going," said Thrix.

"Ah, Enchantress. Moonglow's tears have discomfited you. You are not comfortable in the presence of such raw emotions, no?"

Thrix didn't reply. Malveria was correct. Thrix didn't feel comfortable when confronted by great public displays of emotion. The result of a rather cold upbringing, a therapist had once told her. But Thrix didn't really approve of therapy either, and had only gone for reasons of fashion, when a therapist seemed like a necessary accessory.

With a final stern exhortation to Agrivex not to go near any of the clothes in the attic, the Fire Queen dematerialised. The Enchantress looked at Kalix, who was sitting with Vex on the couch, watching TV.

"Are you all right?" she asked.

Kalix mumbled a reply without looking up. As a werewolf with a mouth full of pizza, her words were very hard to understand. It aggravated Thrix that Kalix couldn't tear her attention away from the TV screen for a few seconds to talk to her older sister. The Enchantress left abruptly, and was soon back in her office, hard at work.

The Fire Queen was not so direct in her journey home. After dematerialising downstairs, she rematerialised in Moonglow's room. Moonglow was now on her own, and lay crying on her bed.

"You yearn for Markus?" said Malveria.

Moonglow looked up.

"I love him," she sobbed.

"And he has ended it? Why?"

"He didn't say," wailed Moonglow. "He just ended it."

The Fire Queen nodded sagely. She was not surprised. Malveria knew Markus to be ambitious. A young human girlfriend was not what he needed to become Thane. The kind and compassionate Moonglow had exactly the right sort of character to comfort Markus, and bring him back to life. And probably, thought Malveria, she was a moderately good companion in bed, which would be a help. But once healed, Markus would no longer need her.

The Fire Queen chose her words carefully. Moonglow was distraught, and could not be comforted. But she could surely be influenced.

"You may soon come to realise that this is a good thing. Now that you have been released from Markus, you will be free to meet the person who is truly right for you."

"I want Markus."

"Indeed. But that will pass. I can sense it passing, more swiftly than you realise."

Moonglow didn't respond, She didn't think her anguish over Markus was ever going to pass.

"Meanwhile, as a way of taking your attention from you own troubles, perhaps you could attend to the troubles surrounding Daniel?"

"What troubles?"

"I believe he may be in for some awkwardness with Vex and Kalix."

Moonglow had no idea what the Fire Queen was talking about.

"Daniel slept with Vex," explained Malveria. "Did you not know that? I believe that Kalix was rather jealous and upset. It may be awkward for Daniel if these two young beauties are competing for his attention."

Moonglow looked surprised. She had no idea that Vex and Kalix were competing for Daniel's attention.

"And I understand a young woman at your college – what was her name? Agrivex did mention it to me – Alicia? – I understand that she has now been calling Daniel."

"Alicia's been phoning Daniel?"

"So Agrivex informs me. Poor Daniel may find it hard to cope with so many girls in urgent pursuit of him. As a good friend, you will be ideally situated to help him choose for the best."

The Fire Queen departed, leaving Moonglow puzzled at the thought of Vex, Kalix and Alicia all competing for Daniel. Malveria was well pleased with herself. Perhaps, she mused, Moonglow would not regard him as quite so unworthy now.

169

After the full moon there was great activity around the lands of the MacRinnalchs. The Barons' representatives arrived back from London carrying Sarapen's instructions, and now every fortified keep was alive with preparations. When Sarapen gave the order each Baron had to be ready to advance on Castle MacRinnalch.

Young Baron Douglas MacAllister, to the east of the castle, was to march through Colburn Wood. Douglas and his sister Morag were eager for war.

The MacPhees would come down from the hills to the north. Baron MacPhee was too old and obese to conduct a campaign, so they would be would led by his eldest son, Euan MacRinnalch MacPhee.

As for Baron MacGregor, his lands also hummed with activity, but so far he had neither refused nor consented to support Sarapen's insurrection. His son Wallace favoured joining with the other Barons, but Wallace was war-like by nature, better at fighting than thinking. Lachlan MacGregor still advised caution.

News of the Barons' preparations reached the castle quickly. It was time for all werewolves to choose sides, or else retire to their homes, and hope the storm might pass quickly. The Fairy Queen of Colburn Woods drew her people to her, and waited on events. Far away to the north, old Minerva MacRinnalch, now retired, turned her gaze southwards. She could see the troops gathering and the troubled times to come. She could see Lucia MacRinnalch fretting in the castle, hardly knowing which side to support, that of her sister or that of her son Decembrius. She saw her old pupil Thrix MacRinnalch struggling to maintain her grip on events in London, and watched as Marwanis left the castle to take up residence at Sarapen's keep.

The Mistress of the Werewolves did not really believe that the Barons would attack the castle, but made careful preparations nonetheless. She informed those members of the Great Council still remaining – Lucia, Kurian, Kertal, Dulupina, and Tupan – that she had recalled Markus.

"I've appointed Markus captain of the castle guard and he will direct all our troop operations."

Tupan smiled to himself. He doubted very much if young Markus would direct the troops. Verasa herself was far more experienced in the art of war.

"Is it true that Sarapen has put a price on Kalix's head?" Tupan enquired.

"Yes. Five gold nobles."

Tupan was impressed.

"A fine price. As much as has ever been offered for a werewolf, I'd say."

"So I believe," replied Verasa, stiffly.

"I wonder who'll try to collect?" said Tupan.

"No one will collect a reward for Kalix," declared Verasa. Tupan wasn't so sure. He knew many werewolves who'd do a lot to earn five gold nobles.

The Mistress of the Werewolves stared over the battlements. Beneath the great dark castle the MacRinnalch lands were green and peaceful, though the skies were overcast. The land to the north sloped gently downwards for almost a mile before giving way to the great glen that came down from the Rinnalch hills, where Baron MacPhee sat in his fortified keep, as his ancestors had done for more than a thousand years. Verasa had known the old Baron all her life. He'd been present at her christening, and her wedding. She had sent him lavish gifts when his son Euan was born. Now Euan was about to lead the MacPhees against her.

170

There were three and a half weeks till the Sorceress Livia's birthday celebration and Princess Kabachetka already had a beautiful new wardrobe. Five days' worth of exclusive shoes, coats, dresses, blouses, skirts, trousers, and accessories. It should have been enough to make her happy. It wasn't. The Princess knew there was something missing from Zatek's designs. Something that could hardly be named, but something of ultimate importance. Zatek could not provide for Princess Kabachetka the final touch of genius which Thrix could give to Queen Malveria.

For months now, Kabachetka had trumped every fashion statement made by Malveria, wearing clothes ostensibly made by Zatek, but really designed by Thrix, and swiftly stolen. Now Zatek designed on his own and the results weren't good enough. Kabachetka knew that if Malveria turned up at the party in a full array of Thrix Fashion, she would outshine her. All the great ladies would nod as the Princess passed, and congratulate her on the splendour of her attire, before raising their fans to whisper that really, she was no match for Queen Malveria.

If Princes Kabachetka's garments were seriously deficient in comparison to her rival's, then Beau DeMortalis, Duke of the Black Castle, might even raise an eyebrow. Beau DeMortalis was a fabulous dandy whose disapproval in matters of fashion was feared all over the realms. A raised eyebrow from Beau DeMortalis had been the kiss of death for many an aspiring fashion leader. The Princess grew cold at the thought. She simply couldn't bear it if Beau DeMortalis were to raise an eyebrow.

Princess Kabachetka bent all her will to discovering the hiding place of Malveria's clothes. She scanned the area around Thrix's office, widening her search, hunting for any secret places where werewolves had been. She would find out what Malveria was going to wear and Zatek would copy the ideas.

'And if I discover her clothes too late,' thought the Princess. 'If there is no time for Zatek to adapt them for me, then I will destroy Malveria's new garments, every one of them.'

171

Kalix was surprised to receive a phone call from Dominil.

"I need help handing out fliers," said Dominil.

Kalix didn't understand. Dominil explained that the twins had a gig and now Dominil needed to give out leaflets advertising it. To Dominil's mind this was a tedious task, and probably unnecessary. Using Verasa's money she could have paid for adverts in every music paper and website. That however was tantamount to buying success and the twins wouldn't allow it.

"If there's expensive ads everywhere everyone will mock us for being rich girls. We need fliers."

Not that there was any likelihood of Beauty and Delicious handing out fliers themselves.

"We're busy writing songs and stuff. We can't hand out fliers. Anyway it's cold outside."

Dominil had designed the leaflets herself. She was pleased with the result but wasn't looking forward to giving them out. Dominil knew she was certain to attract a lot of unwanted attention if she stood around outside Camden tube station. Thinking that a companion would make the work easier, she selected Kalix, and offered to pay her.

Kalix would probably have done it without being paid. The atmosphere in the house was still strained, and she'd been curious about Dominil since the eventful night in the park. Kalix put on an oversized jersey that Daniel had given her, wrapped herself in her coat, and slipped out into the cold afternoon. She took the tube from Kennington to Camden where Dominil was waiting.

"I've never done this before," said Kalix.

"Neither have I," said Dominil, taking a wad of fliers from her bag and handing them to Kalix. "Just give one to everyone who passes."

Although Camden was always full of people giving out fliers, and most people studiously avoided taking them, Dominil and Kalix had no trouble in disposing of theirs. Their combined strangeness and beauty acted as a magnet to almost everyone who passed. Their hair alone was enough to attract attention. Dominil's hung long and ice-white over her black leather coat and Kalix's, thick and lustrous, streamed down to her waist. Kalix was so skinny it seemed there was more hair than anything else. Her health had improved and though she was still very pale, her large, elfin eyes were now shining rather than dull.

The two werewolves soon found themselves on the receiving end of the sort of unwanted attention Dominil had anticipated. After chasing off the twentieth man who lingered beside them, wanting to discuss the gig, the weather, or anything else, Dominil pursed her lips.

"This is just as tedious as I imagined it would be."

Kalix shrugged.

"We've given out a lot of fliers."

They had. As a first attempt it had been a success. Dominil suggested that they retire to a bar and Kalix followed her across the street. Dominil asked Kalix if she wanted anything to eat. Kalix shook her head so the white-haired werewolf bought two bottles of beer. Kalix suddenly felt nervous. Outside she had been fine but now she wondered if Dominil was going to start lecturing her about family business. Kalix generally assumed that any family member was going to lecture her about something.

"Thanks for the book," she said.

"Thank you for saving my life," replied Dominil.

They sat rather stiffly together. Neither of them were great conversationalists. Dominil politely inquired how Kalix was getting along with her new friends.

"Everything is awful," replied Kalix, to Dominil's surprise.

"I understood you were co-existing well with Daniel and Moonglow."

"Moonglow's depressed and Daniel's unhappy and we've been arguing."

Kalix told Dominil about her recent experiences in the house.

"These do not seem like serious problems," said Dominil, dismissively. "Merely the sort of things that are to be expected when sharing a flat. I also suffer from the idiocies of Beauty and Delicious."

Kalix supposed that her experiences weren't so bad, when she considered it.

"But I hate people lecturing me," she added.

"What do they lecture you about?"

"Not eating. And I cut myself."

Kalix looked defiantly at Dominil.

"Don't lecture me about it," she said.

"I don't care if you starve and bleed yourself to death," replied Dominil, and quite obviously meant it. Kalix was surprised. Dominil handed her a small bag. Inside was some money, and a bottle of laudanum.

"Payment for your help."

Two young men in leather jackets approached rather hesitantly and asked if they could sit down at their table. Dominil showed her teeth and growled at them. They hurried off.

"Can I come to the gig?" asked Kalix.

"Of course. We'll put you on the guest list."

Kalix liked that. She'd never been on a guest list before. It felt important.

"When is it?"

"It's on the flier," said Dominil.

Kalix looked at the flier. Dominil saw immediately that she struggled to understand it.

"You can't read?"

Kalix flushed.

"I can read some."

"But not well. That must be inconvenient."

"I was getting better," said Kalix. "I was using Moonglow's computer. With Puffy the Puffin."

411

"So I recall," said Dominil. "You rescued him. What happened next?"

"I don't use Moonglow's computer any more."

"Did she prevent you?"

"No…"

"You didn't want to accept the favour?"

Kalix nodded.

"How very foolish," declared Dominil, with an alarming lack of sympathy. "If you don't look after your own interests you may be sure that no one else will."

"But I don't want to," said Kalix, rather pathetically.

"Then don't," said Dominil, bringing the subject to a swift end.

It was time to give out the rest of their fliers. They walked along to a venue where people were arriving for tonight's gig.

"It's a good design," said Kalix, who was impressed that Dominil had made the leaflets herself. "People at the castle used to say you were the cleverest MacRinnalch."

"They were right," replied Dominil. "I am."

Kalix smiled. She decided she liked Dominil.

"Do you really think I should keep learning to read?"

"I do not greatly care," said Dominil. "But it would probably make your life easier."

Kalix thought that was encouraging. She'd make another attempt.

172

Thrix woke up with Gawain beside her and immediately felt annoyed.

"What the hell are you doing here? Don't you know I'm busy? How am I meant to work with you here all the time?"

"You asked me to stay," protested Gawain.

"So what? You didn't have to accept. Don't you have any self-control?"

Thrix swung herself from the bed, donned her dressing gown and snapped her fingers, turning on the coffee maker in the kitchen.

"This has got to stop!" she said, forcefully.

In her bed, Gawain was looking perplexed.

"You asked me to stay!" he said.

"Will you stop repeating that?" said Thrix. "It's not my fault if you're always turning up here with wounds and making me feel sorry for you. Do you think I've got nothing better to do with my time than wrap you in bandages?"

Gawain had endured another hostile werewolf encounter in Kennington. He'd met two MacAndris werewolves, hunting for Kalix. Gawain had chased them off, receiving a few cuts in the process. And then, to use the Enchantress's words, he'd trotted over to her house like a sick puppy looking for attention. Gawain was stung by Thrix's criticism. He rose from the bed. The Enchantress was irritated to observe what an attractive body he had. Flat stomach muscles, and shoulders that were strong without being too broad. The male model in her last advert should have had such a good physique.

Gawain hardly knew what he was doing here. He didn't know why they kept sleeping together. It didn't seem to make either of them happy. He dressed swiftly and headed for the door.

"So that's your idea of how to behave?" cried the Enchantress. "You're just walking out of here without saying goodbye?"

"I didn't think you wanted me to say goodbye," replied Gawain.

"I don't. The sooner you're out of here the better. And next time you get injured protecting that walking personality-disorder Kalix, go somewhere else for treatment."

"I will," snarled Gawain, angered by Thrix's withering tone. Though he didn't like her very much at this moment, Gawain did still realise he owed her for her healing powers. He attempted to say as much but she cut him off.

"Are you going to stand there talking all day? Weren't you about to leave?"

"Damn you I don't know what you want!" cried Gawain. "I'm leaving." He wrenched the bedroom door open. The Enchantress snapped her fingers and the door slammed shut.

"So you're just going to walk out of here without a word of thanks?" demanded Thrix.

Gawain growled. This she-wolf was beyond his comprehension.

"Open the door!" he demanded, and dealt it a hefty blow.

"You dare to use violence in my house?" roared the Enchantress. She again snapped her fingers, making the door fly open.

"Get out and don't come back!"

413

"I won't!"

Gawain marched along the hallway and opened the front door. Before he could step outside, it flew shut again and the Enchantress was somehow in front of him, looking angry.

"Oh yes you'd just love to leave with your nose in the air, wouldn't you? Do you know how much I despise you? God knows why I ever got involved with you."

Gawain put his face close to Thrix's.

"And God knows why I ever got involved with you, you manipulating, bad-tempered, blonde-haired – "

Gawain came to an abrupt halt. For one thing he'd noticed how attractive Thrix's hair really was and for another the Enchantress had grabbed him and was now kissing him, very forcibly. She propelled him along the corridor and back into the bedroom.

"Never bother me again," demanded Thrix, as they fell onto the bed.

173

The Douglas-MacPhees prowled the south London streets in their black van. Rhona drove, and the brothers scanned the pavements. The inside of their van was dark, with various stolen items strewn on the floor. They had a new digital radio, taken from a house they'd burgled last week. It was tuned to doom-metal.com. The harsh noise suited their mood. Duncan nodded idly in time to the music, shaking his hair, which was long, lank and black. He had a snarling wolf tattooed over his shoulder as did each of his siblings.

So it was that they finally ran into Kalix. They had no warning of the meeting. No werewolf scent reached them. But there she was, walking along the pavement outside Kennington Park. The Douglas-MacPhees leapt from their van and ran to intercept her. Kalix had once again been careless. She should have scented the MacPhees well before she saw them but she was too wrapped up in thoughts of her day with Dominil to pay attention to her surroundings.

"Kalix MacRinnalch," snarled Duncan Douglas-MacPhee.

Kalix looked at him. Oddly, she didn't seem overly concerned at her plight.

"Get out of my way," she said.

"You're coming with us," said Duncan. "And your boyfriend isn't around to help you."

Kalix glanced up sharply and Duncan knew his words had got to her.

"Yes, we saw Gawain, out looking for you, no doubt."

"Maybe he wasn't looking for her," said Rhona, and they all laughed.

"What do you mean?" said Kalix, puzzled.

"Gawain MacRinnalch reeks of she-wolf but he doesn't reek of you. Your boyfriend's found another bitch to play with."

"Take her to the van," said Duncan.

Kalix sank into her fighting crouch, her knees slightly bent, her fists at shoulder level, each lightly clenched. At this the Douglas-MacPhees howled with laughter. She looked like a skinny waif who'd just watched a kung fu film, and come home from the cinema to practice. Her raised fists were as intimidating as the paws of a little kitten.

Fergus tried to grab hold of her. Kalix abruptly lashed out with a brutal kick, catching him in the groin. He howled and fell over. Then she sprang at Duncan and smashed the heel of her hand into his face. Duncan's nose erupted with blood and he stumbled backwards. As she landed Kalix was caught by a blow from Rhona but she rode it as Gawain had once taught her to, deflecting its force. Kalix chopped at Rhona's throat and drove her foot into her belly with such force that she doubled over and sank to her knees.

Fergus was on his feet in an instant with a knife in his hand. Kalix knew she couldn't fight like this for long in her human form. Her strength would give out. She took off, sprinting for all she was worth towards Kennington Park. She was over the fence in a second and disappearing into the evening gloom before the Douglas-MacPhees could come near her. The MacPhees set off in pursuit, scrambling awkwardly over the fence.

By the time Kalix reached the bushes she was short of breath. As always, her habit of not taking care of herself was costing her. Dusk was falling. Kalix kept on running. If she could evade them till the moon rose she'd transform and then she wouldn't need to run. She'd rend them to pieces. Thorns ripped her flesh as she fled through the bushes. She burst into a clearing and there was Gawain.

415

"Kalix!"

Gawain tried to take her in his arms, but Kalix remembered the mocking words of the Douglas-MacPhees. She hadn't seen her beautiful Gawain for years. She should have thrown herself into his arms as she'd dreamed of doing but instead she found herself yelling at him.

"Do you have someone else?"

Gawain hesitated. Kalix, who knew him so well, could see that it was true. He did. Kalix's world imploded. Gawain gazed at her, distressed, unable to find any words that were appropriate. Suddenly a figure emerged from the bushes. It was Decembrius, come to Kennington to guide the Douglas-MacPhees. Decembrius stepped forward, and laughed.

"How fortunate to be present at the great reunion," he said.

Decembrius's powers of seeing were often of little use. He hadn't yet learned to control them. Here, however, with such raw emotion all around, he could easily sense what had been happening.

"Yes, Kalix. Your beloved Gawain does indeed have another lover." He peered closely at Kalix. "And so, I think, do you."

Decembrius was exaggerating. Kalix didn't have a lover. But he thought it was worth exaggerating, to demoralise his enemies.

Gawain and Kalix looked at each other and didn't know what to say. This was not the reunion they'd dreamed about; it was the reunion from a nightmare. The Douglas-MacPhees burst into the clearing and it all became worse. There was an ugly fight as they rolled around on the cold damp grass, punching and kicking. Kalix found herself underneath Rhona, pinned to the ground by her far heavier opponent. Rhona drew a knife and tried to stab Kalix in the neck. Kalix grabbed Rhona's wrist but the blade came closer and closer. Kalix knew it was coated with silver, and Rhona had the strength to drive it into her. In desperation Kalix bit her wrist. Rhona yelled and the knife fell to the ground. Kalix then butted Rhona savagely on the bridge of her nose. Rhona groaned and rolled to one side. Kalix dragged herself to her feet and stamped on her, though she no longer had the strength to do it as hard as she'd have liked. She raised her foot to drive it back into Rhona's chest when a voice called out behind her.

"That's enough."

Decembrius had stayed clear of the fighting. When it seemed that Kalix and Gawain were gaining the upper hand, he drew an automatic pistol from his coat and pointed it at them. Kalix was sure the gun contained silver bullets. Decembrius wouldn't be pointing it at them otherwise. Firing a silver bullet at another werewolf, even a deadly enemy, was one of the most taboo things a werewolf could do. Apparently Decembrius was prepared to break that taboo.

Gawain was struggling with Fergus and had wrestled him to the ground. Decembrius pointed his gun first at Kalix, but seemed to change his mind, and turned it towards Gawain. Kalix leapt at Decembrius, getting a hand to the gun before it went off. There was a scream behind her and she looked round in anguish, expecting to see Gawain lying dead. The bullet hadn't hit Gawain. Thanks to Kalix's intervention it had gone through Fergus's shoulder. Fergus screamed in agony as the silver, so deadly to werewolves, burned the flesh and bones. Kalix grabbed the gun from Decembrius and tossed it away. She tried to strike him but she had no strength left. He brushed her off and she tumbled to the ground.

Gawain rushed to Kalix's side and picked her up. The Douglas-MacPhees were howling in confusion around the stricken Fergus. Decembrius was scrabbling in the bushes, trying to retrieve his gun. Gawain hoisted Kalix over his shoulder and set off at a run. He'd escaped from the clearing and reached the edge of the park when Kalix began to struggle.

"Put me down," she demanded.

He did as she asked. Kalix's body sagged, as if she was about to faint. Then the moon rose. Kalix transformed into werewolf shape. Her vitality returned and she spun round and ran away. Gawain pursued her at a distance. He saw her change back into human as she left the park to hurry away into the side streets. He followed her till she was almost home, making sure that she wasn't pursued, then retreated into an alleyway where he sat down on a wooden crate, put his head in his hands and sighed.

174

Markus returned to Castle MacRinnalch one week after the full moon. The Mistress of the Werewolves was overjoyed to see him return. By coming back to the castle while the Barons were preparing to attack,

Markus had shown himself to be a worthy MacRinnalch. Whatever stories had been spread about Markus hiding in London were false. He donned an old-fashioned cloak trimmed with fur, the appropriate garment for the captain of the castle guard, and as he walked the ramparts he looked the part. The castle's defenders were heartened. Markus was back, and it could never be said that he'd shirked his duty.

The Barons had not yet taken the field. The MacPhees and the MacAllisters were ready but there was still no word from Baron MacGregor. The MacAndrises, in the west, were impatient to make a start. Their leader, Red Ruraich MacAndris, had sent back a cold response to Verasa's demand that he declare loyalty to her. *The MacAndrises are loyal to Sarapen,* he replied. The Mistress of the Werewolves was irritated. It was bad enough for a Baron to be disloyal, but at least there was some historical precedent. It was not too outrageous for a Baron to be occasionally rebellious. The MacAndrises were a different matter. As a minor clan under the protection of the Thane, they had no right to declare loyalty to anyone else but the head of the clan.

Verasa joined Markus and Rainal on the eastern battlement. She was pleased to see how well Markus looked. Strong, and very handsome in his warrior's cloak. He would make a fine Thane.

175

Kalix lay in her room, huddled under her quilt. She was weak after the fight in the park but was refusing to turn into a werewolf because then she would eat. Kalix had made up her mind never to eat again. Gawain having a new lover was final proof that she was a worthless creature who didn't deserve to live. Her left arm was a mass of new cuts. She sipped laudanum, and slipped in and out of bad dreams.

Moonglow lay on her bed, still devastated by Markus's rejection. She'd been crying for two days and hadn't been able to attend college. She played Kate Bush constantly but though this had helped her to survive emotional emergencies in the past, it now brought her little comfort. Her misery over Markus transcended even Kate Bush. She just couldn't believe that she could be so quickly brushed aside by someone she was so much in love with.

Daniel lay in his room, between those of Kalix and Moonglow, and stared gloomily at the ceiling. Moonglow's profound unhappiness had now plunged him into deeper misery. For a while he'd tried looking at it positively. 'If Moonglow is so unhappy over Markus, maybe she'll turn to me.' He hadn't been able to maintain the idea for long.

Daniel had done what he could to comfort both Moonglow and Kalix. His efforts had been completely unsuccessful. They both seemed to be beyond comforting.

'I'm living in the unhappiest household in London,' thought Daniel. 'Possibly the world.' Daniel was also under his quilt, though for warmth rather than emotional support. All the bedrooms in the house were cold, thanks to the inefficient heating. Only the living room with its fire had any real warmth, but no one was visiting the living room. There was too much danger of meeting a flat-mate, and having to confront their misery.

Oppressed by the silence, Daniel crawled from his bed to his computer and connected to doom-metal.com. Surely the only music suitable for a time like this. He studied the radio station's play list. There was a list of genres: traditional doom, atmospheric doom, gothic doom, metal doom, progressive doom, death doom, suicidal doom, funeral doom, and various others. A wide choice. Daniel could appreciate the subtleties involved. In fact Daniel could have named a different band in every category, if anyone had asked him, which no one ever had. He turned it on and was satisfied to hear a series of loud groaning chords and an agonised voice telling him there was no hope for the future. Absolutely right. These doom metal bands, they really knew what was going on.

Next door Kalix could hear Daniel's music. She didn't like the interruption so she put on her headphones to listen to the Runaways. Night fell on the unhappiest home in South London, with neither the Runaways, Kate Bush nor the assembled hordes of doom metal bringing any real comfort to the occupants.

176

At two a.m. Thrix was still in her office. Thanks to another encounter with Gawain, a missing consignment of Chinese silk, and a further emergency plumbing problem, she had now fallen further behind with her work. The Enchantress had reluctantly resorted to sorcery to repair the heating pipes. It wasn't something old Minerva MacRinnalch would have approved of, but the Enchantress had her staff to worry about. The newly repaired heating had not yet fully warmed the office so Thrix took a long blue overcoat from the clothes wrack and draped it over her shoulders. As she returned to her desk the spells of protection that enshrouded the office started giving off their mystical alarms.

"Hello Malveria."

The Fire Queen appeared, looking very excited.

"Tremendous information from my intelligence services regarding the malodorous Princess Kabachetka!"

The Enchantress sat up alertly.

"Is she going to attack my office?"

"No, she has booked into a clinic in Los Angeles for a tummy tuck! I knew it! Aha!"

The Fire Queen marched triumphantly round the room.

"Did I not say it? Did I not claim that while the fabulous Malveria was dieting, exercising and putting her body through hell to achieve the perfect figure, the vile Hainusta Princess was all the while accumulating extra poundage? I knew she could not maintain her figure by natural means. The fake-blonde-slut-Princess is to have pounds of surplus ugly fat carved from her body like a sacrificial bullock. Aha!"

Malveria halted her triumphant marching, and smiled broadly at the Enchantress.

"Did I not say so?"

"Yes, Malveria you did. Congratulations, you've really defeated her on this one."

Malveria perched jauntily on Thrix's desk. It was some time since Thrix had seen her looking so happy.

"Did you learn anything else?" enquired the Enchantress.

"She had an affair with a gladiator. Very disreputable."

"I mean did you learn anything about her plans?"

Malveria looked puzzled.

"Her plans?"

"You know. For attacking me. Stealing my designs, ruining your grand entrance at Livia's."

Malveria pursed her lips.

420

"Hmm… Now that you mention it, no. My intelligence services do not seem to have provided me with any such information."

"Did you ask them?" enquired Thrix.

"Certainly. Perhaps not with such urgency as my enquiries into her tummy tuck. But really, I think it is fabulous news."

Malveria caught sight of her face in the large wall mirror and frowned.

"Am I looking old?"

"No."

"I'm sure I am. I'm convinced I am falling prey to disfiguring wrinkles. Who knows how harmful to the skin may be the radiation and poisons emitted by my volcano?"

"Can't you just avoid the volcano?"

"Of course not. It is my favourite volcano. I must visit every day."

Thrix knew what was on Malveria's mind.

"Malveria, please hold off on the water for a little while longer. We've got a full scale war brewing up in Scotland and if your Hiyastas keep tramping around in Colburn Wood it will only make things worse."

"But I need my rejuvenating water," protested the Fire Queen. Her eyelids trembled, threatening tears.

"Aren't there a million sources of water throughout the realms?"

"None as good as Colburn Wood. You know yourself how excellent it is. And if I'm not using it, what if the Fairy Queen decides to sell the water to someone else?"

Thrix was confused.

"The Fairy Queen? Of Colburn Wood? You mean she knows about this?"

"Well of course, dearest Enchantress. One does not go around taking water from woods without coming to some arrangement with the local fairies. Who knows what spiteful magicks they may work if they are upset? I do not intend my firstborn child to be an imbecile. I already have Agrivex to worry about."

Thrix felt irritated. It seemed to her rather disloyal of the fairies in Colburn Wood to be selling the MacRinnalch water to the first fire elemental who came along and asked.

"Well the fairies are generally good at business," pointed out the Fire Queen. "When not too busy fluttering around trees. No doubt Dithean NicRinnalch, their Queen, saw it as a sound commercial

proposition. And I'm sure she has the best interest of the MacRinnalchs at heart. Though she may have them more at heart if the werewolves were to pay her more respect."

"We pay Queen Dithean NicRinnalch plenty of respect!"

"Does this respect include a well-laden thimbleful of gold every
now and then?"

"Possibly not. But it will from now on. Really Malveria, my mother
will have a fit if she learns about this. Please hold off for a little while."

"Very well," sighed the Fire Queen. "Though when I am old and
haggard, as I will be soon, it will not matter what clothes you design
for me. I will be mocked and reviled on all sides."

"The Hiyastas will love you no matter how you look," said Thrix.
"Or respect you. Or fear you, whatever it is you prefer."

Malveria waved this away, though she was secretly pleased. She
peered at Thrix's computer screen. Since encountering Moonglow,
Malveria was not quite so computer illiterate as she had been, something which Thrix regretted.

"You are working on day four? Does this mean you have completed
day five and are now going back over the clothes for day four, lovingly
adding that final touch?"

"No it doesn't," admitted Thrix. "It means I'm still stuck on day
four."

"And what of day five?"

"I haven't started it yet."

The Fire Queen's eyes widened in great alarm.

"You have not yet started on day five? The great ball in which every
lady of my realm and the next will be dressed in the most exquisite ball
gowns ever made? With much added finery to boot? But Enchantress,
this is a disaster. Am I meant to attend the most glamourous, glittering, fabulous ball in history in an off-the-peg dress purchased in some
wretched street bazaar? Apthalia the Grim has been in fitting rooms for
a month and as for the Duchess Gargamond – "

Thrix held up her hand.

"Malveria. Everything is in hand. You'll have the finest ball gown
ever seen."

Malveria was not placated. Only yesterday Beau DeMortalis, Duke
of the Black Castle, had arrived at Queen Malveria's court and already
her courtiers were saying the Duke was on top of his form. He had
witticisms and bon mots to spare, and any poorly dressed elemental to

whom he took a dislike could expect to find herself on the end of a withering set-down.

"If I am subjected to a withering set-down from Beau DeMortalis it will be quite the end. One utterly dreads it. It will reach the ears of Princess Kabachetka and she will repeat it endlessly."

"Can't you tell the Duke of the Black Castle you'll throw him in the volcano if he speaks out of place?" suggested the Enchantress. "He is your subject, after all."

"Impossible, dearest Thrix. Were I to do such a thing it would be said that the mighty Queen Malveria fears the tongue of Beau DeMortalis because she is poorly dressed. I would be sneered at in every corner of the realm. Besides, I rather like the Duke."

"Wasn't he your enemy during the war?"

"Yes, but I forgave him because he is always so impeccably dressed. And he is very good company. Really Thrix, you cannot send me to dance with the Duke while dressed in an inferior ball gown. I will be forced to abdicate, and flee the kingdom."

Thanks to the efforts of Thrix and the other fashion designers who now attended Malveria and her rivals, most of their clothes were of an elegant and human style, but the gowns for the final evening, the great ball, were like nothing seen in the human world these days. Malveria had brought Thrix several paintings of such garments and they were extravagant items of lace, tulle, silk and satin, with great hooped skirts and flouncing bodices, belonging to a ballroom somewhere between Regency England, Gone With the Wind, and the realms of the fairies. Thrix had not flinched from the challenge of creating something special for Malveria. Unfortunately, she was now running out of time.

Thrix rose to her feet. It was time to display some confidence. More confidence than she really felt, which was something that Thrix often had to do.

"Malveria. The gown will be ready on time and it will be fabulous. Trust me, I'm your designer."

Malveria was reassured. After all, Thrix had never let her down.

"You have not been…?" murmured Malveria. "Not that it is any of my business…"

"No Malveria. I've not been seeing Gawain. I ended it."

This was not true, but the Enchantress had cleansed his aura so thoroughly from her body that not even Malveria could now detect it. Thrix had some of the clothes for the carnival night lying completed in the room next door. Knowing that it would cheer Malveria, and take her mind off the ball gown, Thrix suggested taking them over to Moonglow's house before Zatek managed to spy on them here.

"You can try them on in the attic. And the shoes for the lunch time promenade on day three arrived from Italy."

"The pink high heel sandal? I am trembling with excitement already," said Malveria. "Let us hurry to the house of the young humans."

As there were only a few clothes to carry, Malveria could teleport them. She set off enthusiastically but as they materialised in the attic the Fire Queen flinched.

"What's the matter?" asked Thrix.

"This house. It has become a place of such tremendous misery. What has been happening to the young humans?"

"Perhaps the young werewolf's eaten them," suggested Thrix.

"Where are the new shoes?"

"Right here," said the Enchantress, opening a box, while Malveria looked on eagerly.

"They're gone!" exclaimed Thrix.

Immediately their darkest suspicions were aroused. No wonder there was such an aura of doom in the house. Princess Kabachetka had discovered their hiding place and stolen the clothes, probably murdering Daniel and Moonglow in the process.

"Their blood-soaked bodies are no doubt strewn around downstairs at this moment!" cried Malveria. "If we hurry we may save the shoes!"

The Fire Queen rushed downstairs and burst into the living room, ready to fight off the Princess. The Princess wasn't there. Neither were Daniel or Moonglow, or Kalix. Sitting in front of the TV with a can of beer in one hand and a bag of crisps in the other was Vex. She was engrossed in *3rd Rock from the Sun*. She wore a ragged brown flying suit that was so tattered it looked as if its original owner might have died in a plane crash. On her feet were the new high heeled sandals, a delicate shade of pink with a dainty ankle strap.

"Aarrgghh!" roared the Fire Queen. "You have stolen my new shoes! Did I not warn you of the dire consequences? Thrix, bring me a knife! I am going to sacrifice this girl right now!"

Vex looked round.

"Hi Aunt Malvie," she said brightly. "Eh… is something wrong?"

"You villainous thief of shoes, I will kill you where you sit, you detestable, vile, obnoxious, odious – " Malveria broke off. "What is that disgusting brown thing you're wearing?" she demanded.

"A flying suit."

"Why are you wearing such an appalling garment?"

Vex shrugged.

"I like it."

Daniel arrived in the room, alarmed by the outcry.

"What's happening?"

"I am about to sacrifice Agrivex for stealing my shoes. Bring me a knife immediately."

"This is way too harsh," protested Vex. "I didn't do anything."

"What do you mean you didn't do anything, you imbecilic girl? You are wearing the shoes!"

Vex looked down at her feet.

"I like my boots better," she said.

Malveria roared in frustration, again threatening her niece with instant death.

"It's Kalix's fault," said Vex. "She made me do it."

"Don't lie to me, dismal niece. The werewolf did no such thing."

Moonglow hurried into the room, wondering what was going on.

"My never-to-be-adopted niece is about to die!" cried Malveria. As she did so something fell from Vex's pocket. The Fire Queen snatched it up and then reeled in shock.

"An earring? You stole my new earrings?"

"See, this is the mistake you always make, Aunt Malvie. The first suspicious sign and you just jump to the wrong conclusion. I never stole your earrings. I just borrowed them."

"Why?"

"To see how they looked with the shoes. After all, you're always saying you can't really judge an accessory by itself."

Thrix laughed. She couldn't help herself. She had rarely seen a fashion combination as inappropriate as Vex's tattered flying suit and the pink high heels.

"Anyway, it's not my fault," continued Vex. "Everyone here is lying around being miserable. I was bored. So I just thought I'd check a few of your new things. You know, see if they were suitable. Also, Kalix made me do it."

"Will no one bring me a knife?" cried Malveria. "Daniel, fetch me your finest sacrificial implements immediately."

425

Moonglow, rather fearing that Malveria was serious, hurried to divert her anger.

"Could I see them on?"

"What?"

"The shoes. They're so delicate. They're lovely."

"I do not wear shoes that have been besmirched by my idiot niece!" said Malveria, still very cross.

"Well they just look ridiculous on her," said Moonglow, wisely. "I really want to see them at their best advantage. Please try them on."

"I want to see too," added Daniel, who had no real interest in women's shoes, but dreaded having to clear up the mess after Malveria sacrificed Agrivex on their living room carpet.

Malveria sniffed, pointing her nose in the air and refusing to co-operate. The Enchantress took the shoes from Vex and laid them beside Malveria. Then, to Moonglow and Daniel's surprise, she muttered a spell which caused a mirror to appear in front of the Fire Queen, and altered the lighting in the room to show her off to her best advantage.

"I refuse to try them on," said Malveria. "They have been befouled."

"You should," said Moonglow. "They'll really suit you."

Malveria was unable to resist any longer. She stepped into the pink shoes. She spoke a word which caused the straps to fasten round her ankles, then looked in the mirror. A great sigh of pleasure came from her lips. Of all the delicate, exquisite high heeled sandals in this world and the next, these were the best. Malveria forgot her annoyance. Tears of happiness formed in her eyes. She hugged the Enchantress.

"I love these shoes," she said.

Daniel and Moonglow were relieved.

"Now that's all sorted out how about some wine?" suggested Vex.

177

Dominil was puzzled. When she'd arrived in London, Beauty and Delicious had been a useless pair of intoxicated losers who never got anything done. By strength of character she'd dragged them back on course. Throughout this period, the twins had never been exactly moderate in their behaviour but they had at least made an effort. They'd drunk less, attended rehearsals, and worked on their songs. Everything seemed to be going well. Neither the violent incident at the rehearsal studio nor the intimidating visit by the Douglas-MacPhees had dimmed their enthusiasm for their music. So Dominil couldn't understand why, now that she had finally got them the gig they so desperately wanted, everything had gone wrong again.

Their behaviour was now worse than ever. They were rarely in a fit state to pick up their guitars. Dominil just couldn't account for it. No matter how she railed against them, they refused to make an effort.

"We're musicians," was all Beauty would say. "We don't have to practice. It'll be fine on the night."

Dominil dismissed this. At this rate it wouldn't be fine on the night. It would be a disaster. Dominil had her pride and she abhorred the thought of anything to which she had contributed being a disaster. Frustrated, the white-haired werewolf strode out into the falling snow and hurried through Camden. Pete the guitarist was surprised to find her at his door, though not as concerned as he once might have been. No one actually liked Dominil but the band had come to trust her. He invited her in. His front room, Dominil noted, was extremely untidy.

"Was it not the case that a week ago things were looking promising for the band?"

"Eh… yes," replied Pete.

"Then why are Beauty and Delicious now acting in so destructive a manner? They refuse to do anything except drink and make fools of themselves. I cannot see any possible explanation for this."

Pete had an idea of what the problem might be but hesitated to make a suggestion. He felt intimidated by Dominil.

"Well maybe…" he began, then paused.

"Speak up," demanded Dominil. "If you are about to criticise me you may do so freely. After living with the twins I am used to it."

"I wasn't going to criticise you. You've been great. Really. I think it's just that they get nervous. You know, they're quite shy really."

Dominil stared at him in disbelief.

"Nervous? Shy? Beauty and Delicious? Everything they do is designed to call attention to themselves."

Pete shrank back a little.

"Well yes. But you know… they're probably just overcompensating. They wouldn't be the only people to do that. They were always like this before gigs. They're scared in case they get onstage and no one likes them."

"You mean they have stage fright?"

"Yes."

Dominil considered this. Was it possible the guitarist was right? If so, it was something that Dominil had completely failed to take into consideration. It hadn't occurred to her for a moment that the sisters might suffer from nervousness.

"They have no reason to be anxious. The band is sounding good and there is every reason to be optimistic."

Pete shrugged.

"I don't think that makes any difference really. You know how some people just worry anyway."

"No."

"You don't?"

"It is not something with which I can easily empathise."

"I can believe that," said Pete.

Something in his tone caught Dominil's attention.

"You think I am lacking in empathy?"

"If you go around saying things like *it is not something with which I can easily empathise* then it's probably a sign that you can't. And you always talk, you know, sort of formal."

Dominil felt irritated.

"I did not come here to discuss my diction. What is to be done to bring the twins back to normality?"

Pete didn't know. He'd seen this before, and as far as he remembered the twins kept on behaving badly till it was time to step onstage.

"And then they were all right?"

"Not really. The gigs were always a shambles."

Dominil thanked Pete for his help. She had noticed before that for a young guitarist, Pete was fairly attractive. She could even have classed him as desirable, if she wanted. Not while she had work to do, however. She walked slowly back to the twins' house, wondering what to do about their emotional fragility. There were less than three weeks left to the gig and Dominil was quite determined that it was going to be a success.

The Avenaris Guild was quite determined that it was going to fail. The Guild had managed to track down Dominil. One of their operatives who'd survived the fight at the rehearsal studio had happened to

428

see her in Camden, handing out fliers, and taken one. It was on Mr Carmichael's desk at this moment, and the small slip of paper had generated a great deal of activity. Plans were now being made for an attack on the gig.

It was reported that the white-haired werewolf had been accompanied by a girl who matched the description of Kalix. The presence of the werewolf princess made it a very important operation for the Guild. Despite this, nothing about it was entered on their computers. The Guild's information officers believed that their system was now safe but Mr Carmichael's intuition told him otherwise. Someone had hacked into their files recently. It might happen again. He gave instructions that all arrangements were to be made by word of mouth. A messenger was sent to Mr Mikulanec, informing him that his services would be required on the night. Yum Yum Sugary Snacks and all werewolves associated with them were going to be eliminated.

178

Kalix still lay on her bed with the quilt covering her head, refusing to engage in conversation with either Daniel or Moonglow. Even the relentlessly cheerful Vex failed to get through. They all wanted to talk about her problems but Kalix had had enough of talking.

Moonglow knocked on her door.

"Go away," mumbled Kalix.

"Visitor," shouted Moonglow.

"Go away," repeated Kalix.

The door swung open and Dominil marched into the room.

"I need your help," she said.

"Go away," said Kalix.

"No," said Dominil, calmly. Without asking Kalix, she opened the window.

"I do not like foul air," she said, which Kalix found quite insulting.

"Is the air foul?"

"Yes. It stinks of laudanum and an unhappy werewolf."

"I've been very unhappy," admitted Kalix, and sighed. "I was in the park and – "

429

"Yes, very well," said Dominil, interrupting her. "Perhaps you can tell me about it some other time. At this moment I need your help."

"What for?"

"The twins are suffering from a serious case of pre-gig anxiety."

Dominil looked penetratingly at Kalix.

"I have no experience of anxiety. You are prone to it. I thought you might be able to suggest something."

Kalix felt rather pleased at this. It was as if someone had come to her for help on her specialist subject.

"Why are they nervous?"

"Fear of failure, I believe. I've told them there is no point feeling anxious. Feeling anxious about an event won't change the event. However, they do not agree. In fact they will not admit to being nervous at all, but I know they are. Perhaps if they'd just acknowledge it, it might help them to overcome it. Are you ready to leave?"

"Leave?"

"Of course. I need you in Camden."

Kalix was perplexed. She had been determined to lie in bed being miserable until she died. Now Dominil wanted her to go to Camden. She was quite surprised to find herself on her feet, putting on her coat.

"I really don't know how to help the twins," she said.

"Perhaps you will think of something. After all, you outwitted Sarapen when you rescued me, did you not?"

Kalix smiled. That was a good memory. They drove slowly north through the dense London traffic. The streets were damp and there were traces of snow on the pavements.

"Do you like the snow?" asked Kalix, suddenly.

"Yes. I do. When I was very young in Scotland I used to lie in it."

"Were you hiding?" asked Kalix. "Because you're so white you could hide in it?"

"Yes."

Kalix thought about the young werewolf Dominil playing in the snow. She couldn't quite envisage Dominil ever playing. Kalix found it easier to talk to Dominil than most people. She didn't know why.

"I hated the castle."

"I know."

"Everyone gave me a bad time when I was there." Kalix looked at Dominil. "Did that happen to you?"

Dominil shrugged.

"I was often on my own. But I preferred it that way."

Kalix felt a sudden urge to tell Dominil about her problems. This was odd. When Daniel and Moonglow had encouraged her to talk, she hadn't wanted to. As they slowly negotiated the busy junction outside the Houses of Parliament she told Dominil that she'd met Gawain.

"He's got another girlfriend."

"Did he say so?"

"No. But I knew. He didn't deny it."

Dominil was still a slow and careful driver. They crawled forward.

"Is it not some years since you've been together?"

"Yes."

"Then it doesn't seem strange that he's formed another relationship. It may just be to ward off loneliness."

"Do you think so?"

"What did Gawain himself have to say?" asked Dominil.

Kalix admitted she didn't know. She'd run off before he had a chance to speak.

"That seems like a poor way to resolve a problem."

"I suppose so. Do you think he might still be in love with me?"

Dominil turned to look at Kalix.

"I have no idea. But unless you talk to him, you'll certainly never find out."

Kalix fell silent, thinking about this. She supposed it was true. She took a sip from her bottle of laudanum.

"Please keep a clear head," said Dominil.

"Okay," said Kalix, and put the bottle away.

179

Verasa's confidence that the Barons would not attack the castle was misplaced. Sarapen was already planning the assault, though he knew it would be difficult. The walls were high and strongly guarded. Humans could never scale them; werewolves might, but not in the face of determined opposition.

"There are two well-tested means of taking a castle," he pointed out to Decembrius. "Through siege, or through treachery. As a siege would be difficult and time-consuming, I prefer the latter."

Marwanis had left the castle but her father and brother remained. Kurian was old, and not well, but his son Kertal was a supporter of Sarapen's. The Mistress of the Werewolves would probably be having him watched, but even so, it might be possible for Kertal to provide the necessary help from inside.

It was fortunate for Decembrius that his stock was high with Sarapen at the moment, due to the information he'd gathered about Dominil, and the twins' gig. Had it not been, Sarapen might well have reprimanded him more severely for the affair in Kennington Park. He was very unimpressed by Decembrius firing a silver bullet into Fergus. For a werewolf to fire a silver bullet was taboo. In different circumstance Sarapen might have punished Decembrius. As it was, in time of war, there were some traditions which could perhaps be overlooked.

Sarapen didn't waste much sympathy on the injured werewolf, even though Fergus Douglas-MacPhee had endured great pain. The silver bullet, penetrating his shoulder, had burned like acid. The MacRinnalchs in London did have a werewolf doctor on whose services they could call but he was busy operating on a human patient when Fergus was shot, so it took some time for him to attend. Fergus had not taken the pain well. Sarapen had left him with his brother and sister, contemptuous of the injured werewolf's unseemly howling. He'd be better soon enough.

Sarapen was far more interested in Decembrius's latest piece of information. Markus had returned to Scotland and was now captain of the castle guard. On hearing this, Sarapen laughed. His delicate brother, head of a force of fighting MacRinnalchs.

"It becomes ever more ridiculous," he said. "When the guard learns what sort of werewolf they've got for a leader they'll probably throw him over the walls."

At least his younger brother was no longer in hiding. He'd gone to the castle to save it but he'd find that he was trapped there, and Sarapen would make sure he never left it alive.

180

Dominil drew up outside the twins' house. Kalix had been feeling more and more agitated as they approached, and now she quailed.

"I can't help them," she blurted out. "They'll just laugh at me."

"Don't worry. I'm sure your presence will have a beneficial effect."

Kalix was very dubious. She knew if the twins thought she was there to help cure their stage fright they'd mock her and refuse to listen to anything she said.

"The twins won't know you're there to help them," said Dominil. "Just observe them for a while, and perhaps later you can suggest to me some means of making them calmer."

"You promise not to say anything to them about me trying to help them?"

"Certainly," said Dominil.

Kalix trudged up the path with her coat pulled tightly around her and her shoulders hunched, feeling very awkward. Already she regretted the lack of willpower that had allowed Dominil to coerce into coming here. They entered the house, which smelled of whisky.

"I've brought a visitor," announced Dominil. Kalix shrank backwards but Dominil propelled her into the room.

"I have informed Kalix that you are both suffering from serious anxiety," said Dominil. "She is an expert in the subject and will tell you what to do about it."

Kalix reeled in shock, and turned her eyes in horror on the treacherous Dominil. The twins were staring at her in surprise, wondering what this was about.

"I don't – " spluttered Kalix, and ground to a halt.

"I have some arrangements to make for the gig," said Dominil. "So I'll leave you for a while. Now remember, listen to Kalix. She'll tell you how to get over your stage fright."

With that, Dominil strode out of the room and out of the house. Kalix watched her go with gritted teeth. She turned back towards the twins. They were staring at her with hostile expressions.

"Why does that white-haired bitch keep saying we're anxious?" demanded Delicious.

"And what do you think you're going to do about it?" demanded Beauty.

"Eh…" said Kalix, who wished she might be swallowed up by an earthquake.

"So you just felt like paying a visit and lecturing us?"

"As if Dominil isn't lecturing us enough?"

Kalix sighed. She felt weak, and had to sit down.

"I'm sorry," she said. "Dominil tricked me. I didn't know she was going to say that."

The twins weren't listening. They seemed convinced that Kalix had insisted on coming to their house and lecturing them.

"Where do these werewolves get off?" raged Delicious. "Barging into other people's homes and lecturing them about stuff?"

"What do you think this is?" shouted Beauty. "A support group for unhappy werewolves?"

Kalix flinched under the verbal assault. It was quite prolonged and seemed far more hostile than necessary. Obviously her presence had touched some nerve.

"How does Dominil think you're going to help anyway?" said Beauty. "You're the one with problems."

She took a drink straight from her whisky bottle.

"I'm not worried about the gig."

"Neither am I," declared Delicious. "We don't need any stressed-out junior MacRinnalchs coming here and lecturing us."

Kalix felt that this was going too far. She hadn't wanted to come in the first place.

"I didn't come here to lecture you," she said, more forcibly. "I just came because Dominil insisted. I don't even care if you're anxious."

"Well, we're not."

"Yes you are," said Kalix. "But I don't care."

"No we're not and it's none of your business anyway."

"You're the most stressed werewolves in London," sad Kalix, now angry. "You can't fool me, I can sense it."

"Well, so what if we are!" screamed Delicious. "Stop going on about it! No one asked you to stick your nose in!"

"That's fine!" yelled Kalix. "I don't care if you get so drunk you fall off the stage and everyone laughs at you again."

"We never fell off the stage," objected Beauty.

"Yes you did," said Kalix. "Dominil read me the review. It said the audience all laughed at you."

She stood up.

"Anyway I don't care. I'm leaving and I'm not even coming to your stupid gig. If you're as frightened as a pair of sissy little puppies that's your problem."

"What did you call us?"

"Sissy little puppies."

Beauty and Delicious were stunned by the insult. They raged at Kalix, trying to insult her back, but nothing they could say stung like Kalix's juvenile taunt.

The door opened and Dominil came in. None of them had heard her enter the house. There was an odd expression on her face. Almost as if she was about to laugh. She controlled it.

"Sissy little puppies," she said, appreciatively. "Such a perfect phrase."

"I want to go," said Kalix.

"But why? You're doing such a fine job."

"We're just arguing."

"That's good," said Dominil. "Beauty and Delicious would never argue with me. They simply refused to speak."

Kalix was confused.

"Did you just bring me here to start an argument?"

"I wanted Beauty and Delicious to acknowledge the problem. Which they now seem to have done."

"You tricked me," said Kalix. "That's not very nice."

"I am not very nice," replied Dominil. "As everyone knows."

She turned to Beauty and Delicious.

"So. Now you admit there is a problem. Good. That is progress. You have nineteen days to get over your stage fright. I suggest you talk sensibly to Kalix. If you stop trying insult her and have a rational discussion instead, you'll find it helpful."

This time when Dominil left them alone, they did manage to have a more rational discussion. Kalix had some suggestions for coping with anxiety, strategies she'd learned over the years, either from her therapist or by herself. The sisters were never going to radically change their lifestyle, but were impressed by her simple suggestion that each time they found themselves anxious, they took a series of deep breaths from their abdomen.

"And some time every day, imagine yourself walking confidently on to the stage and playing really well."

Delicious and Beauty looked at each other.

"We could probably do that. You think it will help?"

435

"It might. Sometimes it works for me. And maybe you might feel better now anyway, now you've talked about it."

Delicious nodded.

"How come we don't have therapists?" she asked her sister.

"We just never thought of it before," replied Beauty. "We should get some. Rock stars need therapists, it's part of the deal. "

Dominil arrived back in the room. Kalix scowled. She had not forgiven Dominil for tricking her. The white-haired werewolf, impervious to Kalix's glare, calmly asked the twins if they'd been making progress. Beauty and Delicious said that they had.

"Very well," said Dominil. "I will trust you both to carry out your relaxation exercises as recommended by Kalix."

In Dominil's mind, the problem was already solved, which was a mistake. Kalix knew that they wouldn't completely get rid of their nerves before the gig. They'd still need encouragement, probably from a bottle of the MacRinnalch whisky. But Dominil was at least correct in believing they'd made progress. The gig was coming closer, and she was busy with fliers, posters, mailing lists, equipment checks, rehearsals and various other things. The werewolf knew that her methodical preparation was somewhat out of the ordinary. The other unknown bands playing that night would very likely turn up having done a minimum of preparation. Dominil however, could not arrive for any event unprepared. It didn't matter if it was a small gig of little importance. Yum Yum Sugary Snacks would be ready.

Dominil had a feeling that Sarapen might come to the gig. If that happened she too would be ready. She looked forward to plunging the Begravar knife deep into her former lover's heart.

181

"Agrivex will drive me into an early grave. Her sulking is pervading the palace."

"Aren't you used to it by now?" wondered Thrix.

The Fire Queen frowned darkly.

"It has taken on an alarming new dimension. Previously the abominable niece has sulked only about clothes, make-up and lessons. Now

436

she has also decided to sulk about boys. It is wearing me quite to a shadow. I swear I can go nowhere in my palace without bumping into some part of Agrivex's miserable aura which she has left behind. The Hiyasta aura does tend to fragment, when misery strikes."

Thrix and Malveria were transporting the latest batch of clothes to Moonglow's house. There were many of them, too many for Malveria to whisk through space, so they were using Thrix's car. The car was well protected by spells but even so she drove quickly, keen to escape from Zatek's prying eyes.

"I made a profound mistake when I halted the sacrifice of Agrivex at a young age. I set in motion a tragic chain of circumstances which now threatens to engulf us all. Empires may crumble."

"Malveria, you're exaggerating."

"Perhaps a smidgen. Is smidgen correct? It sounds like a peculiar word."

"It'll do."

"Empires may not crumble but the inhabitants of the palace are suffering. My pastry chef has been complaining that Agrivex's gloom is pervading the kitchen and affecting the balance of his finest creations. I don't want my pastry chef to be unhappy. It took me a long time to find a fire elemental with such a light touch at the mixing bowl."

Thrix waited impatiently at traffic lights and sped away as soon as they changed. Malveria nodded appreciatively. She enjoyed Thrix's impatient driving.

"Which boy is she sulking about?"

"Daniel."

"Daniel? I didn't know she liked him."

"I am convinced she does not," said Malveria. "However, she wanted to stay with him after she had the effrontery to try on my new shoes. Most probably she only wished to avoid returning to the palace and facing me. I understand there was a scene of some embarrassment involving Moonglow, Kalix and Daniel all feeling awkward. Daniel told her she should probably not stay. Now Agrivex has managed to persuade herself that she has been rejected by the boy she loves most in all the world."

"Well," said Thrix. "You know, young love, it's always difficult."

"Agreed. But there are limits, and I will not allow my idiotic niece to upset my pastry chef over some boy she never cared for at all only two days ago. The almost-adopted niece of the Hiyasta Queen does

437

not sob like a little girl when perplexed in matters of love. This is beneath the dignity of the Hiyasta Royalty. I ejected her from the palace with instructions either to either make Daniel love her, or else forget about him."

"And how did that go?" asked Thrix, successfully cutting in front of a taxi that was going far too slowly for her liking.

Malveria pursed her lips.

"Very badly. Vex has now retreated to her room and refuses to communicate for any reason."

"What happened?"

"Daniel tried to explain the rules of – " Malveria paused. "What is the human game that requires white clothes and a great deal of time?"

"Cricket?"

"That is it. Cricket. Apparently the rules of this game are most puzzling and complex. Daniel tried to explain these rules to Vex. As a consequence of this I understand she almost lost consciousness, and had to be helped to a chair, in a very poor state of mind. It was some time before she could summon enough energy to return to her own dimension. She has subsequently refused to leave her room, and has only her favourite cuddly toy for comfort."

"Her favourite cuddly toy?"

"A fluffy dragon."

"It sounds comforting," said Thrix.

"Yes," agreed Malveria. "She has always found it to be a tremendous comfort. Perhaps because it is so very fluffy. A present from the First Minister on her eighth birthday, and a great favourite ever since."

Thrix was puzzled. "Did Vex want to know about cricket? I wouldn't have taken her for the sporting type."

"Indeed she is not. The Hiyasta are not great players of sport, as a rule, and Agrivex less so than anyone. Vex will trip over her own feet at the slightest excuse. But she was following her standard procedure for attracting boys. She has read these procedures in Cosmo Junior and sticks to them religiously. One of them is to find out the boy's interests and ask him about them. It was just Vex's grave misfortune that Daniel turned out to be interested in cricket. Apparently the game has a great many complicated rules and many peculiar names."

"Does it?" said Thrix, who knew nothing at all about cricket.

"So Agrivex claims. But she is prone to hysteria, and may have misunderstood some of Daniel's words. It's hard to believe that any game could involve a *silly mid-wicket,* though Vex swears that Daniel said exactly that."

Malveria sighed.

"Now things are worse than ever. Agrivex still pines for Daniel but is convinced he is mocking her with false stories about cricket. I think the whole affair may have shaken her belief in Cosmo Junior, and that is a serious matter. It's never let her down before. She's currently hunting through back issues to see if there is some loophole in the matter of asking boys about their interests."

182

Fifteen days before the full moon, the Barons marched. The MacPhees and the MacAllisters came from the south and the east while Red Ruraich MacAndris occupied the land to the west. They did not yet come near to the castle, but guarded all roads and trails then settled down to wait.

Sarapen was losing patience with Baron MacGregor. It would lend legitimacy to the rebellion if it was supported by all the Barons but MacGregor had not yet indicated if he would join them. Sarapen's natural inclination was to send a thinly veiled threat. Decembrius disagreed, and urged Sarapen to make further efforts to win the Baron's support through diplomacy.

"Time grows short," growled Sarapen.

"There are fourteen days till we attack the twins' gig. Fifteen days till the first night of the full moon and our assault on the castle. The MacGregors would need only a few days to make ready."

Sarapen was again irritated by Decembrius's appearance. His swept-back red hair, pale skin and angular features were somehow annoying. Decembrius's appearance had degenerated recently, in Sarapen's eyes. He had a new earring, which Sarapen didn't like at all, and a pair of overly-fancy motorbike boots.

"What would persuade the Baron?" asked Sarapen.

"Marwanis."

"Marwanis? Has she influence with Baron MacGregor?"

"No. But she has influence with his son Wallace."

439

Sarapen frowned. It was the first he'd heard of it. Wallace MacGregor, eldest son of the Baron, was a huge werewolf and a noted champion, but he was not, by all accounts, the smartest wolf in the clan.

"Why does Marwanis have influence with Wallace?"

"Because he's crazy about her."

Decembrius immediately regretted his choice of words. *Crazy about her* sounded very out of place in the context of planning a war. It was accurate however. Everyone knew that the Baron's eldest son was enamoured of Marwanis MacRinnalch. Everyone except Sarapen, who was above noticing this sort of thing.

"If Wallace can be persuaded to join our side his father will probably follow."

"And what about the Baron's chief advisor Lachlan?" demanded Sarapen. "We could not persuade him when he was in London."

"Send Marwanis," said Decembrius.

"Why?"

"Because Lachlan MacGregor is… also very attracted to her."

Sarapen frowned.

"Is this true?"

"Certainly. Wallace and Lachlan's rivalry over Marwanis is a source of great interest among the MacGregors, and further afield as well."

Sarapen shook his head. He was glad he never bothered himself with clan gossip. Decembrius persisted with the idea.

"Marwanis is a shrewd wolf. I'm sure she could persuade them."

Sarapen was hesitant. Like many of Decembrius's suggestions it went against the grain. Sarapen MacRinnalch did not relish the notion of using the charms of his female cousin to influence the MacGregors.

"It's worth trying before we send threats," added Decembrius. "We can always send threats the next day."

Sarapen allowed himself a rare smile.

"Yes, Decembrius. I acknowledge I may be too keen on sending threats, before trying other means. Very well, I will contact Marwanis."

Decembrius asked Sarapen if he would rather that he made the request but the offer was declined. Sarapen felt that if he was to stoop to using Marwanis to further his ends, the least he could do was ask her himself, in an honourable manner.

"Which of her suitors does she prefer? Wallace or Lachlan?"

Decembrius couldn't say. He didn't think that she favoured either of them. He had an idea that Marwanis rather favoured Sarapen himself, but he wasn't about to mention it.

183

Malveria found herself unable to concentrate on selecting her outfit to receive Beau DeMortalis.

"This is intolerable," she complained to her chief lady-in-waiting. "How can one choose an outfit when Agrivex's gloom pollutes the atmosphere?"

In their own realm, the auras of the Hiyasta were very strong, and the energetic despair of a teenager could cast a very long shadow.

"Must she choose this moment to interfere with my dressing?" cried Malveria. "When I am due to lunch with Beau DeMortalis, of all people? Does she not appreciate that the slightest ill-selected stitch of clothing can be fatal when meeting the Duke of the Black Castle? Really, one still winces at the cruel things he said last week about Countess Vesuvian. And I do not believe the Countess was really so badly dressed, although it's true that pink is not her ideal colour."

"He can be cruel," agreed her lady-in-waiting, though from the tone of her voice, Malveria guessed that she found the Duke rather exciting. Ladies-in-waiting always did. It could be hard to calm them down after he visited. The Fire Queen gave an angry exclamation as her mirror darkened around the edges, falling victim to Agrivex's miserable aura.

"This cannot be tolerated," she declared, throwing down her newest jacket and marching from her chambers in search of her almost-adopted niece. She found Agrivex slumped on a couch in the corridor that led to the kitchens. She was staring vacantly into space, sucking on the ear of her fluffy dragon. The aura around her was dark and miserable. The sight moved the Fire Queen to anger.

"Dismal niece, are you aware that your foolish gloom is casting dark shadows all over my palace?"

Vex didn't respond.

"Have you nothing to say? Why are you sucking that fluffy dragon?"

"For comfort. My life is just awful."

"Awful? You're life is far from awful."

"It is too. I've no clothes and Daniel hates me."

"You have many clothes. Daniel does not hate you. And if he did, what does that signify? You do not really care for this Daniel."

"Yes I do," said Vex, and stuck out her lower lip defiantly.

"I refuse to let you be depressed about a young man from the mortal realm!" said Malveria. "It is unbecoming."

Vex stared at her feet.

"It's all your fault," she mumbled.

The Fire Queen was taken by surprise.

"My fault? In what way?"

"You're the one who insisted I meet him. It was you that practically forced me to sleep with him. And now he hates me."

Malveria was temporarily lost for words, partly because there was some truth in her niece's accusation. She had directed Agrivex to form a relationship with Daniel. She had not foreseen these consequences.

"Agrivex. I know perfectly well that this is not a serious love affair. It will be forgotten in a day or two. Please try not to be so miserable."

"You wouldn't understand," said Vex. "You're too old to understand."

Malveria reeled. She'd never been called too old for anything before. No one else would have dared to say such a thing.

"You miserable and ungrateful creature! How dare you say that to me! Your problem is that your life is far too comfortable! When I was your age I was fighting a war and facing danger every day."

Vex looked bored. Malveria narrowed her eyes.

"If you dare to yawn because I mentioned the war I will pick you up by your toes and dip you in the great volcano."

Vex yawned, and put the dragon's ear back into her mouth. Malveria became more agitated. Really, her niece was just impossible.

"Must you behave in such an aggravating manner, idiot niece?"

Vex looked up.

"It's so harsh the way you're always calling me idiot niece. How about charming, pretty or intelligent niece?"

"You are not charming, pretty or intelligent."

"Fine," said Vex, folding her arms and crossing her legs. "Destroy my confidence. I'll be sending you the therapy bills."

"The Hiyasta do not go to therapists, vile girl."

"Then it's no wonder they've always got fire pouring out their ears. Who can be normal when their aunt just criticises them all the time? I can practically feel the fire pouring out my ears right this minute. I demand you send me to a therapist to repair the damage."

"You do not have fire pouring out your ears, foolish one. You do not need a therapist. You need to occupy your thoughts with something other than make-up and television and this Daniel who you do not really care for. And will you please stop sucking on that fluffy dragon? It's starting to make me ill."

Vex removed the dragon's ear from her mouth, but kept tight hold of the toy.

"Cosmo Junior says the number one cause of girls needing therapy is harsh criticism from their parents."

"Must you believe everything you read in Cosmo Junior? And I am not your parent. No child who sprang from my loins could ever be such an imbecile."

"I'm not an imbecile!" declared Agrivex.

"You are the biggest imbecile in all the realms of the Hiyasta," countered Malveria.

The Fire Queen was surprised at what happened next. Instead of answering back, Vex burst into tears and ran from the corridor. Malveria was bewildered. Why had Agrivex done that? The Queen reviewed their conversation. Has she said anything upsetting? No more than usual, surely. Malveria frowned. She could only put it down to her young niece's general idiocy, and dismissed it from her mind. Malveria had more important things to worry about. Lunch with Beau DeMortalis, for instance. That must go well.

The Fire Queen applied herself to dressing, and her lunch with the Duke was not unsatisfactory. He made her laugh, as always, and complimented her clothes, sincerely enough for the Queen not to have to worry about him saying anything hurtful behind her back. She always enjoyed the Duke's company and had never regretted not executing him after the war.

There was one awkward moment. Beau DeMortalis had heard that the Fire Queen had saved a young werewolf's life. The Duke of the Black Castle raised one eyebrow very slightly. Malveria retained masterful control over both her manner and her aura. No one could have discerned that she was at all discomfited, though she was. Were the Duke to suspect that Malveria had saved the life of a MacRinnalch werewolf out of kindness or affection, he would be sure to be very cutting about the incident.

"I did indeed rescue such a creature," said Malveria, smoothly. "A small affair altogether, but a necessary part of a plan to break a human heart. Though we don't do so much persecuting of Mankind these days, I like to keep in practice."

The Duke nodded. Breaking a human's heart was quite reasonable behaviour.

"I look forward to hearing of the completion of the episode."

"And I look forward to relating it," said the Queen, meanwhile making a stern mental note to make progress with the matter of tormenting Moonglow. It was a pleasant lunch. But when the Duke was gone, leaving the hearts of her ladies-in-waiting fluttering, the Fire Queen was annoyed to find that she hadn't managed to entirely dismiss the matter of Agrivex from her mind.

'Why is this troubling me?' wondered Malveria. 'I do not care if the ridiculous girl spends her worthless life in tears.'

Somehow, she wasn't satisfied. Malveria decided she would rather like to see the Enchantress. She left the palace, materialising immediately outside Thrix's apartment, and knocking on the door. It was after midnight and Thrix was surprised to find the Fire Queen on her doorstep. Malveria smiled brightly, and stepped briskly into the flat. Thrix greeted her with caution, assuming that Malveria was checking up on her. However the Fire Queen showed no sign of harassing the Enchantress about her work. Instead, she settled herself on the couch, accepted a glass of wine, and expressed an interest in watching some fashion programmes. The Enchantress, knowing Malveria so well, soon realised that there was something on her mind.

"What's wrong, Malveria?"

"Nothing," replied the Fire Queen. "I'm just making a friendly visit. It is some time since we watched the Japanese fashion programme."

Malveria noticed that Thrix didn't look convinced.

"My goodness, dearest Thrix, why are you staring me like that? This is a most frightening inquisition. Surely you can allow a close friend to relax on your couch without this merciless interrogation?"

Thrix raised her eyebrows a fraction.

"Very well," said Malveria. "Since you give me no peace, I will admit that there is a small matter about which I wished to talk to you."

Having finally got to the point, Malveria quickly described the day's

444

events. Hearing her tale, Thrix was surprised at the denouement.

"Vex ran away in tears?"

"Absolutely," replied Malveria. "It was most strange. Normally I would expect my niece to argue back relentlessly. Of course, Agrivex will sometimes cry over foolish things and is not above using hysterics to have her own way in matters of new boots and so forth, but this seemed different."

"She's suffering an unhappy love affair," Thrix pointed out. "I suppose that's a new experience for her."

Malveria was not satisfied.

"True, perhaps. But I'm not convinced. I am an expert at interpreting the auras of unhappy lovers. I believe my niece's ridiculous notion of despair concerning Daniel is a symptom of some deeper unhappiness. However I do not know what that might be."

The Fire Queen levitated the bottle of wine, refilling their glasses.

"I find myself upset. Why, I can't say. Agrivex is such an airhead – to use your most suitable term – that it can only do her good to be reminded of her foolishness. But for some reason I cannot fathom, I wish I hadn't made her cry."

Malveria stared into her glass. Thrix was surprised to see the Fire Queen actually looking depressed. An unusual emotion for her, unless clothes were involved.

"Well," said Thrix. I think the problem might be you like Vex more than you admit. A question of family feelings, I suppose. Which makes me unfit to offer any advice, because all feelings in my family are destructive, harmful and probably fatal, and I've been trying to avoid them for years."

"Well of course," agreed Malveria. "It is the wise thing to do."

They sat in silence for a few moments, watching as a pretty Japanese model strode forcefully down the catwalk wrapped in a tight red dress that neither of them really cared for.

"Perhaps this is indeed the problem," said Malveria, thoughtfully. "It is most remiss of me. I can hardly believe I've allowed myself to like my ridiculous niece to the extent that I am now upset over making her cry. Did I mention that she alleged I was too old to understand her problems? An unparalleled insult for which I would have been justified in executing her."

The Fire Queen looked at Thrix.

"Do you think I treat her harshly?"

Thrix found it hard to reply. She didn't really know how young relatives were normally treated in the realm of the Hiyasta.

"Perhaps a little."

"But I transformed her existence. One day I may even formally adopt her. All she was born to was the life of either a temple prostitute or a sacrificial victim, and now she lives in my luxurious palace."

"I suppose luxury isn't everything," replied Thrix. "I've never heard you address her as anything other than idiot niece, or dismal niece, or something similar."

"But she is an idiot. No one can dispute this."

Thrix laughed.

"I think Vex has her good points. And so do you, or you wouldn't have looked after her for so long."

"This may be possible."

They finished the bottle of wine and started on Thrix's whisky.

"Maybe the strangeness of Vex's aura had something to do with being criticised by someone she holds in high regard?" suggested Thrix.

Malveria was startled at the thought.

"If Agrivex holds me in high regard she has certainly disguised it well up till now. Please Thrix, you are making me feel guilty, and that is a most unwelcome emotion for the Queen of the Hiyasta."

Malveria pondered Thrix's words while watching the fashion programme.

"What should I do about this?"

"You could take her shopping. She'd like that."

"She would indeed. I constrain her spending, to make her realise that in life one does not always obtain everything that one desires. Were I to actually take her shopping, she would be happy." Malveria looked troubled. "But if I do that, will there ever be an end to it? Take Agrivex shopping once and she will be forever plaguing me to do it again. My life will become unbearable."

Thrix laughed.

"That's possible. But it would make her happy. Really, should you be asking me for advice anyway? I come from the most dysfunctional werewolf family in history."

184

Verasa was disturbed to hear that Marwanis had gone to Baron Mac-Gregor's keep. Markus didn't understand why she was worried.

"Marwanis holds no sway over Baron MacGregor."

"But she holds great sway over his son Wallace."

"Wallace is a fool," snorted Markus.

"Indeed he is," agreed the Mistress of the Werewolves. "But his father is fond of him and will listen to his opinion."

Markus wore his cloak, trimmed with fur. Every day he walked the battlements, scanning the horizon for the enemy. The MacRinnalchs in the castle thought much better of Markus these days. Verasa hoped they would continue to do so if it came to a fight. She didn't doubt her favourite son's bravery, but she was unsure of his qualities of leadership under pressure.

"Even if Marwanis persuades Wallace to support the rebellion, Lachlan is still against it," pointed out Rainal.

"He is," agreed Verasa. "Unfortunately Lachlan is also under Marwanis's influence."

"It seems odd that a clan should go to war merely because its leaders are besotted by one female werewolf," said Rainal.

It wasn't so odd, really. Rainal knew that it wasn't. The Scottish werewolves were a passionate breed. You didn't have to look too far into their history to find bloody disputes which had been started by lover's quarrels, or lover's ambitions.

"I've been working on Lachlan," said Verasa. "Given time I'd have brought him round to supporting our point of view."

Verasa's voice trailed off. She looked through the great windows of her chambers out onto the lands beyond.

"But now?" said clan secretary Rainal.

"Now I rather expect that Lachlan and Wallace will lead the MacGregors into the fray," admitted Verasa.

"Let them come," declared Markus. "They'll regret it."

"So will we," said Verasa. "Not as much as them, I trust."

Verasa knew that the Barons would not begin their attack until the wolf nights. Only then would their superior numbers be effective, when all of their followers could transform into werewolves. Verasa also knew that the twins were due to play in London the night before the next wolf night. Did Sarapen intend to attack the gig before returning to Scotland? It was a worrying possibility. Verasa had sent were-wolves to London to help guard all the vulnerable members of the Great Council, but since the castle came under threat she'd been obliged to recall many of them.

By her reckoning, there was still enough protection for those in England. Sarapen might even find himself defeated in London, and unable to lead his werewolves against the castle. Markus hoped that wasn't the case. He looked forward to the encounter. Markus believed that he could best his brother. Verasa was not so sure. Werewolves from her personal guard were under instructions to ensure that if battle came, Markus was never left unguarded.

185

Dominil drove Kalix home after the young werewolf's encounter with the twins. The sky over London was grey. Cold rain had been falling for most of the day, mixed with some light snow. Dominil hoped for a dry night for the gig. She was concerned that the event might be poorly attended. Several bands were playing but none of them were well known, and the gig was on a Wednesday, not the best night for attracting an audience.

"I need to give out more fliers," she said.

"I'll help," said Kalix.

"Good. I appreciate your assistance."

Kalix was pleased. She felt important. As they inched through the congested streets in the centre of town, heading towards Lambeth Bridge, she noticed that Dominil was examining her.

"You are thinner," said Dominil.

"I don't think so," replied Kalix.

"You are. I can tell."

"I really don't think I'm any thinner," protested Kalix, who had in fact been feeling fat, due to eating half a pizza yesterday.

"I have a photographic memory," said Dominil. "You are thinner."

"All right," said Kalix, and felt uncomfortable.

"I want you to eat," said Dominil.

Kalix squirmed at the unexpected assault. She didn't reply.

"If you are to help me it's necessary for you to be healthy," continued Dominil. "So you'll have to eat."

"Okay I'll eat," said Kalix, keen to bring the subject to a close.

Dominil turned towards her.

"I agree that you may be better off dead," she said.

"What?" said Kalix, startled.

"You may be better off dead. Which I presume is your ultimate aim in starving and cutting yourself. As you are so determinedly unhappy all the time, you may be right. There is little point hanging around just to be miserable."

Kalix was offended and bewildered. One minute Dominil was telling her to eat, the next she was saying that she would be better off dead.

"Make your mind up," she snarled. "Do you want me to be dead or healthy?"

"I want you to be healthy till the gig is over," said Dominil, calmly. "Can you manage that?"

"I expect so," muttered Kalix, scowling.

"Good. After that you can do whatever you please."

They drove over Lambeth Bridge into the narrower South London streets that led to Kennington. The road was busy, as it generally was, and the car crawled along.

"There's another reason why you should be healthy for the gig," said Dominil. "I suspect that Sarapen may attend."

This got Kalix's full attention.

"It would be an ideal opportunity for him to attack. There will be four members of the Great Council there, five if Thrix comes."

"Does Sarapen even know they're playing?" asked Kalix.

"Decembrius is with him, and Decembrius usually learns things his master wants to know."

Dominil advised Kalix not to mention her suspicions to anyone. There was no point in worrying Moonglow or Daniel unnecessarily, or the twins. They drove in silence for a while. Kalix watched the rain streaming down the windshield, and was amused when they splashed some pedestrians.

"Do you really think I might be better off dead?" she said, finally.

"I don't care," replied Dominil. "As long as it's not till after the gig."

Kalix scanned Dominil's face for some trace of humour, or irony.

There didn't seem to be any.

When they reached their destination Dominil strode into the flat. There she managed to further appal Kalix by informing Moonglow that she had made an agreement with the young werewolf.

"Kalix agrees to eat regularly to preserve her health until the gig."

Kalix thought that this was stretching things. Moonglow was surprised at the news, but pleased.

"I'll feed her well," she said, and smiled at Kalix. Kalix scowled. She was heartily sick of all this talk about food.

"Have you heard anything about Markus?" asked Moonglow, unexpectedly.

"He is back at the castle," replied Dominil.

"Oh," said Moonglow, and looked sad. Dominil regarded her without emotion.

"Make sure Kalix eats," she said, and strode briskly from the house, ready for the next part of her campaign.

Moonglow's misery over Markus had not diminished. As Dominil left she began to cry. She turned to Kalix for support but Kalix was gone. Kalix couldn't understand why Moonglow had fallen in love with her hated brother Markus, and felt very little sympathy for her. In her room Kalix sipped laudanum, and took out her journal. She painstakingly wrote an account of the day's events at the twins' house. After recording her efforts to help them, Kalix wrote *I like Dominil*. The she wrote *Dominil doesn't care if I die.*

She studied that for a while, but didn't know what to think about it. She drew another thick line and made another entry in her poor, ill-formed handwriting. *Moonglow is sad about Markus. Daniel is sad about Moonglow. Kalix is sad about Gawain.*

Kalix put the journal away and crawled under her quilt, then stared at the ceiling till the laudanum made her drowsy enough to go to sleep.

186

Malveria was uneasy. Today was the day she planned to be nice to Agrivex. She knew it was going to be difficult. No matter what Malveria did, her niece would inevitably say something stupid, or do something foolish, and aggravate her beyond endurance. 'Why,' Malveria wondered, 'am I even making the attempt? It is doomed to failure.' She suddenly felt annoyed at the Enchantress. It was all very well for Thrix to lecture her about being nice to her family. The werewolf was in a perpetual state of warfare with her own.

Malveria swept through her palace, halting outside Vex's room. She forced a smile onto her face, and knocked lightly on the door. There was no reply. She opened the door and walked in, finding herself in the midst of an astonishing mess. Malveria blanched. It was some time since she had dared venture into Agrivex's bedroom and she'd managed to blot out the memory of quite how bad it was. There was no inch of floor space not cluttered with clothes, toys or magazines. The dressing table sagged with make-up. The walls were covered by an incredible collection of pictures stuck on top of each other so that small pieces of Vex's favourites stared out crazily from behind each other. The only free space was the ceiling, and Malveria was startled to see that it had recently been painted silver by a very inexpert hand.

Vex was slumbering peacefully in bed, partially covered by a huge pink quilt, her fluffy dragon beside her on the pillow. Malveria coughed loudly. Vex opened her eyes.

"Go away," she said. "I'm not waking up yet."

Malveria was prepared for this. No matter how annoying Agrivex was today, Malveria intended to remain calm. It was an almost impossible task for a fire elemental but the Queen had decided to look on it as a test of character. Surely she could force herself not to yell at her niece for one day?

Malveria sat on the bed.

"Wake up. Today is a special day."

"No it's not," replied Vex. "It's another boring day in this boring palace and I'm going back to sleep."

"I really want you to wake up," urged the Fire Queen.

Agrivex scowled, then pulled her quilt over her head. Malveria was surprised. She yanked the quilt down.

"You dare ignore me you – " She halted herself. What was it the Enchantress had advised her to do? *Take a deep breath before sacrificing your niece.* She took a deep breath.

"Young niece. Today I'm going to take you shopping."

Agrivex opened her eyes. She was interested, but suspicious.

"What do you mean shopping?"

451

"Buying things."

"What things? Boring things? Like things for lessons?"

"No. Pleasant things. For you to wear."

Vex sat up. Malveria was displeased to see she was wearing Hello Kitty pyjamas. The cute little pussy cat motif was quite unsuitable for any inhabitant of the Hiyasta palace. She let it pass without comment.

"Things for me to wear? Why? Am I being sacrificed?"

Malveria frowned.

"Why do you always say that?"

"Because you're always threatening to sacrifice me."

"Well today I am not. Today I'm taking you shopping."

"For new boots?"

"Possibly…" replied Malveria.

"What do you mean *possibly?*"

"I thought it might be time for you to purchase some more presentable garments than those which you currently wear," explained Malveria. "Some garments suitable for a young lady who has the status of almost-adopted niece to the Queen."

Vex scowled.

"I see. You drag me out of bed in the middle of the night to tell me I have to wear some hideous dress with a matching handbag?"

"That is not what I mean at all," replied Malveria. "I am intending to treat you. I thought that you would enjoy being taken to some of the more elegant costumiers in the human realm. Surely you would like to see yourself elegantly attired for once?"

Vex turned to her fluffy dragon.

"She wants to stuff me into some hideous dress with a matching handbag."

Malveria took another deep breath. Already this was going wrong.

"Are you incapable of responding positively to this kind overture?"

"What kind overture? I refuse to be shovelled into a lot of boring dresses from haute-couture-for-the-aged. If we're going shopping I want to go to Camden Market."

"To buy foolish boots and ragged T-shirts?" demanded Malveria.

"Yes," replied Vex, and looked her aunt in the eye. "I want foolish boots and ragged T-shirts."

"I will not waste my money on such things."

"Fine," said Vex. "I'm going back to sleep."

Agrivex wrenched the quilt from Malveria's hand and dragged it over her head. The Fire Queen had a strong urge to call her executioner and have her niece dragged immediately to the volcano. No one else in her realm would have dared to pull a quilt over their head while the Queen was talking.

"Go ahead, get the executioner," said Vex from beneath the quilt, as if reading her thoughts. "My life sucks so badly I'd be pleased to be thrown into the volcano. If you wait till I'm ready to get up I'll walk there myself."

The Fire Queen stood up and strode round the room several times. Given the mess on the floor, this wasn't easy. After a few more deep breaths, she again sat on the bed, but found herself distracted by the silver ceiling. Malveria's palace was beautifully decorated throughout but this ceiling looked as it had been painted by a blind elemental in a great hurry.

"What happened to your ceiling?" she demanded.

"I spray-painted it," replied Vex, from beneath the quilt.

"What does *spray-painted* mean? No, do not tell me, it will no doubt distress me further."

There was a silence which quickly became oppressive. Malveria pursed her lips.

"Very well, dismal niece. We will go to this Camden market you talk of. And we will buy whatever you wish."

Vex exploded from under the quilt, an eager look on her face.

"Really?"

"Yes, really."

"And you'll buy me whatever I want?"

"I will."

"Fantastic!" cried Vex, and bounded from the bed.

"So if you will meet me after dressing – "

Vex stuffed her feet into her boots and pulled a ragged denim jacket over her Hello Kitty pyjamas.

"I'm ready!" she yelled. "Let's go!"

187

With Castle MacRinnalch now under siege, the twins' gig only ten days away, and the Sorceress Livia's celebration fast approaching, there were now many plots and stratagems among the MacRinnalchs, their associates and their enemies. The Mistress of the Werewolves hadn't given up on securing enough votes for Markus, and was hopeful of persuading Kurian to change sides. Sarapen offered Kurian's son Kertal a rich reward if he would help his werewolves enter the castle, and he promised to transform Madrigal into a werewolf once he'd carried out his part in attacking the gig. Meanwhile Marwanis was at the MacGregor's keep, working on Wallace and Lachlan. Wallace was already won over, and Lachlan found it very hard to resist.

Thrix MacRinnalch was in the midst of a crisis. Her shoe designs were delayed in Italy due to a problem obtaining the special dyes for the leather. Every day saw an agonised correspondence between London and Italy, and the Enchantress dreaded to think what Malveria would say if her shoes were not ready in time.

The ball gown was another problem. Normally the great ladies of Malveria's realm would not wear clothes which had been either sorcerously made or repaired. As Malveria said, fine tailoring was everything. One could not walk around in clothes which had been botched together by a spell. To do so would be very common. However, the ball gown was different. By ancient tradition, these fabulous dresses could have a touch of magic about them. Thrix was constructing a new spell to enhance the gown but it was a difficult piece of magic, and she struggled to bring the spell, and the garment, to fruition.

The Fire Queen herself was plotting furiously. Malveria told Thrix, quite untruthfully, that Sarapen had offered her perpetual access to the water of Colburn Wood if she would agree to end her assistance to the Enchantress. The Enchantress was obliged to report this to her mother, and Verasa in turn was forced to consider making a counter offer to Malveria, allowing her access to the water in return for her continued support. Malveria was pleased. It hadn't been too difficult a problem to sort out, to a Queen of her astuteness.

In the affair of Moonglow and Daniel, Malveria felt that the tide was turning in her favour. Moonglow was unhappy and vulnerable, and Daniel was becoming more attractive. To help this along, Malveria asked the Sorceress Livia, who had power over dreams, to send a dream to Alicia, showing her great happiness if she went out with Daniel. That wasn't breaking the rules of the bargain, or if it was, it was only a minor infringement.

Malveria promised Agrivex a speedy death if her niece ever dragged her round the whole of Camden market on a busy Saturday afternoon again. The entire affair had been very trying for Malveria. Each disreputable item of clothing that Vex purchased was like a dagger through the Queen's heart, and she despaired as Vex enthusiastically loaded her shopping bags with endless T-shirts, boots, jeans, military clothing, psychedelic items and whatever else caught her eager eye. But though Malveria complained at length, in reality, her day had not been so bad. At one point Vex had taken her hand to lead her along, something she had never done before.

It had been raining in Camden, adding to the Fire Queen's discomfort. It was raining at Castle MacRinnalch too, and it was raining outside the Merchant's shop when MacDoig opened a small portal to bring herbs, crystals and the blood of other-worldly animals into this dimension: tools which the Princess Kabachetka would need for her sorcery. It wasn't easy to bring these things to earth and the Princess paid MacDoig well for his expert help. Princess Kabachetka was satisfied. If the Werewolf Enchantress thought she could protect her allies from Sarapen's wrath on the night of the gig, she was in for an unpleasant surprise.

There were other matters about which the Princess was less satisfied. For one thing, she had become unexpectedly attracted to Sarapen, yet sensed that the great werewolf would never consider any sort of dalliance. This mildly frustrated the Princess, and she wondered what she might do about it. Worse, and more pressing, neither she nor Zatek had succeeded in locating the Fire Queen's clothes. The Princess fretted, and tried to think of a plan.

Malveria was exhausted when she arrived back at her palace. It was raining there too, which was unusual, but despite the weather the palace had a more cheerful air. Agrivex had completely forgotten her unhappiness over Daniel and was busy dressing herself in a fantastic array of outlandish garments. All over the palace, ministers of state, handmaidens, and the staff of the royal kitchens sighed in relief as Vex's misery dissipated, allowing them to get back to work without fear of envelopment in the grim aura of teenage Hiyasta gloom.

188

Dominil was waiting for Kalix in the small concourse at the top of the elevator at Camden tube station. She leant against the wall, reading a book, ignoring the many stares from passers by. Sensing Kalix's arrival, she looked up. Kalix glanced at the book.

"Sulpicia," said Dominil. "A contemporary of Tibullus. I have a bag of leaflets. Let's get to work."

There were already people handing out fliers outside the tube and they had to walk some yards up the road to find a vacant position. It was cold and wet and the leafleters outside the tube station were having little success. Again however, Dominil and Kalix attracted a lot of attention. They handed out leaflets for an hour. By this time Kalix was soaked. Dominil's long leather coat kept her dry, though her white hair hung limply over her collar. Finally Dominil announced that they'd done enough for now.

"I am uncertain if this is beneficial or not," she admitted to Kalix. "So many people hand out leaflets here. Does anyone ever read them?"

She led Kalix across the road to the same pub they had visited before. At seventeen, Kalix was technically one year too young to drink alcohol in a public house, and she didn't look any older than her real age. Younger perhaps, with her skinny frame and her pure unblemished skin. But if the barman thought anything about it, he wasn't about to do anything which might drive away two such spectacularly beautiful women from his establishment.

They sat in silence. Kalix toyed with her bottle of beer, scratching off the label. She shifted in her seat to avoid looking at the woman at the next table, who was very overweight, which upset her a little.

"I ate lunch," she said, suddenly.

"Good," said Dominil.

They relapsed back into silence. Kalix drummed her fingers on the table. She wanted to ask Dominil a question, but felt embarrassed to speak.

"If you have something to say, please say it," said Dominil, with her customary lack of sympathy.

"Could you speak to Gawain for me?" blurted Kalix, and winced, waiting for a crushing retort from the white-haired werewolf.

"Speak to him? About what?"

Kalix looked awkward, and didn't say anything.

"You want me to find out about his new lover? Perhaps discover if he still cares for you?"

Dominil stared at Kalix for a few moments. Kalix felt stupid, and wished she hadn't mentioned it.

"Very well," said Dominil. "I'll talk to him. Are you expecting him to come to the gig?"

Kalix didn't know. She didn't really know where she expected Dominil to meet Gawain.

"I think he'll be there," said Dominil. "He's been watching you closely enough. I'll speak to him."

Kalix was grateful. Dominil turned her head sharply. She'd sensed another werewolf entering the bar. It was Decembrius. He caught sight of them and walked to their table. His red hair was wet, though slicked back as it was, the style remained unaffected. He wore sunglasses like Kalix's and a long black leather coat not unlike Dominil's.

"May I sit down?" he said, politely.

Kalix bared her teeth. The last time she'd seen Decembrius he'd been pointing a gun at her.

"But I avoided shooting you," said Decembrius, as if reading her thoughts.

He took off his shades. Dominil observed that Decembrius's pupils were slightly enlarged. That, and something about his manner, made her think for a moment that he was attracted to her. Dominil was interested in the notion. Decembrius was not unattractive. Even a hint of a relationship with him would outrage Sarapen. As she continued to study him, Dominil quickly perceived that she was not the object of his desire. Decembrius was doing his best to conceal it, but he was attracted to Kalix. Dominil felt mildly irritated, but dismissed it quickly.

Kalix sat in silent discomfort. Dominil asked Decembrius what he was doing here.

"Looking for entertainment," replied Decembrius. He took one of their leaflets from his pocket. "I found this on the pavement."

"Then you'd better run home and report it to your master," said Dominil.

"Sarapen already knows about the gig," said Decembrius.

"I do not imagine the music would be to his taste."

"No, I don't see him spending a lot of time listening to Yum Yum Sugary Snacks," agreed Decembrius. "Are they any good?"

"They are excellent," replied Dominil. "But your presence here is unwelcome. Leave."

Decembrius showed no inclination to leave. He put his hand in his pocket.

"If you're intending to produce a gun, I'll break your neck before you can use it," said Dominil, calmly.

Decembrius drew out a packet of cigarettes with an expression of exaggerated innocence, and lit one.

"Maybe you should cancel the gig," he said.

"Why?"

"You won't be safe."

"Are you concerned for our safety?"

Decembrius shrugged.

"There's no real need to fight. Sarapen will be Thane soon enough, whatever happens in London."

"If Sarapen comes to the gig I'll kill him!" exploded Kalix, so loudly that the people at the next table looked over with interest.

"Or he might kill you," said Decembrius, and gazed at her. Kalix glared back at him angrily. She hadn't forgotten his mocking words when he'd interrupted her encounter with Gawain. If he made another sneering remark like that she'd attack him. Though Decembrius didn't seem to be here to mock her. She didn't know why he was here. He stubbed out his cigarette in the ashtray and rose smoothly to his feet.

"I don't think you should go to the gig," he said, to Kalix. "It's not safe."

With that he departed, leaving Kalix puzzled.

"Why did he come here?" she wondered.

"The poor way you treat yourself has dulled your werewolf senses," answered Dominil.

"What do you mean?"

"I mean Decembrius doesn't want you killed, apparently. Couldn't you sense his attraction to you?"

Kalix was bewildered. It was always puzzling to Kalix that anyone would find her attractive.

"I don't think you're right," she ventured.

Dominil almost smiled.

"I am right. Congratulations. You've made a conquest."

Not liking that her hair had gone stringy from the rain, Dominil went off to brush it before they handed out more leaflets, leaving Kalix

458

perplexed, and not at all pleased that Decembrius found her attractive.

<u>189</u>

Moonglow dragged herself into college. For the first time in her life she was behind with her work. Only two weeks ago she couldn't have imagined this happening. Now, with her intense misery over Markus, she found it almost impossible to study. The freezing rain and sleet that assailed her on her way to college was nearly enough to send her home again, and she had to summon all her reserves of energy just to reach the building.

Moonglow's life seemed to be getting worse. The pain over Markus was not diminishing and now Jay hated her as well. He had finally called round to her flat, demanding to know why Moonglow hadn't been phoning him. Moonglow told Jay the truth. She was in no state to lie convincingly. Anyway, Moonglow didn't really want to lie. She tried to say she was sorry but Jay was too irate to listen. He shouted at her, calling her names which Moonglow was surprised to hear from her once gentle boyfriend. Then he marched furiously out of her life.

In Sumerian history the Professor noticed her lack of concentration. Thinking it might be a good idea to encourage her, he asked Moonglow a simple question about the city of Nineveh. Moonglow didn't answer. Instead she picked up her bag and ran out of the room in tears. The Professor was embarrassed as his other students looked accusingly at him, as if it was his fault for picking on Moonglow.

The canteen was quiet. Moonglow sat on a chair by the window that looked out onto the Thames and tried to compose herself. Other people coped with unhappy love affairs. She should be able to as well. Moonglow tried to make it easier by hating Markus but it was useless. She couldn't hate him. She kept thinking how glorious he'd been as they walked round the art gallery, and afterwards when he took her home.

"Yes, it is very sad," came a voice Moonglow didn't recognise. She looked up. Facing her was a very striking woman, a little older than her, perhaps twenty-one or so. She had dazzling blonde hair and her eyes were deep green, quite startling in their way.

"What?" mumbled Moonglow.

"It is very sad to be discarded," said the glamourous woman. Her accent was peculiar, not one that Moonglow had ever heard before.

"What do you mean?"

"To be left by a lover. It is the most tragic thing in this world, or any world."

Moonglow stared at her.

"Who are you?"

"You may call me Kabachetka," replied the woman, rather grandly. "Would you like him back?"

"Who?"

Princess Kabachetka chuckled, though her laugh was so low and muted it sounded almost like the purring of a cat.

"You know who I mean. Markus MacRinnalch."

"How do you know about him?" demanded Moonglow.

"I know a great deal about the MacRinnalchs. A most vigorous clan of werewolves. And I would agree that Markus is one of the most beautiful. Would you like him back?"

Moonglow should have stood up and left. She'd had enough experience of the MacRinnalchs by now to realise that it wasn't a good idea to discuss their affairs with a stranger. Somehow she didn't feel like leaving.

"Could you bring him back?"

The Princess leaned forward, and smiled seductively at Moonglow.

"Yes. I could. But first, please tell me about Malveria's clothes."

190

The Fire Queen presented the Enchantress with a small cedar box, inlaid with gold.

"I thought you might like this. A good receptacle for those sorcerous herbs which need to breathe."

It was a beautiful item. The Enchantress was rather surprised. Gift-giving was not something that Malveria often did.

"From the realm of the Hiyasta?"

"No, Camden Market," said Malveria. "Though the place is full of

460

unpleasant stalls selling quite shocking garments, I discovered that there were several more agreeable shops in the side streets. Do you like it?"

"It's lovely. Thank you."

"I was shamed into the purchase by my idiot niece," admitted Malveria. "She seemed to think it necessary to buy presents."

Malveria's frankness made Thrix smile.

"I was rather taken aback by her eagerness to purchase gifts. A most un-Hiyasta like quality, though only to be expected from the sort of dismal girl who is now experimenting with thirty shades of nail varnish, and wondering if it might be a good idea to grow more fingers. She bought presents for the daughter of the First Minister, for Kalix, and for me. As I was paying for all this, it was perhaps not the most unexpected gift one has ever received, but I appreciated the thought."

"What did she buy you?" asked Thrix.

"A most unsuitable necklace comprising several small axes on a chain. However, I count myself fortunate to have escaped without receiving a sturdy pair of motorcycle boots."

"It sounds like you had a good day," said Thrix, smiling.

"A good day?" Malveria shuddered. "You quite misunderstand me. Walking around that endless market with Agrivex was most exhausting, I assure you. And do not forget the additional stress caused by the knowledge that every time she halted, it was to buy some even more appalling garment or vile trinket."

Malveria winced at the memory, and gratefully accepted both coffee and whisky from Thrix, who took the bottle from her office cupboard and poured large shots for them both. Thrix had taken her share of large shots in the past few days.

"Agrivex further embarrassed me by her chosen apparel," continued Malveria. "I know it is hard to believe, but she went out for the day dressed in pyjamas and boots, barely covered by an elderly jacket."

Malveria winced again, and sipped her whisky.

"The pyjamas have cats on them. I am informed that these cats belong to an organisation called Hello Kitty. Where she obtained them I do not know, but it ranks among the most perturbing things my niece has ever done."

"Does Hello Kitty offend you? Isn't it rather cute?"

"Cuteness is not encouraged among the Hiyasta," explained Malveria. "In fact, the concept is virtually unknown. One dreads to think what the Empress Asaratanti would say were she to learn that my niece is prancing around in Hello Kitty pyjamas. For a war-like nation, it is most unsuitable."

The Fire Queen shook her head sadly.

"Truly, Agrivex must be the least war-like Hiyasta ever born. No doubt it was profoundly misguided ever to consider adopting her as niece, and will eventually lead me into disgrace with my subjects. When they learn of her ridiculous pyjamas, they will express their outrage by storming the palace."

Thrix laughed.

"But you had a good day with her?"

"I don't admit it was a good day. But the foolish niece was certainly cheered. After I bought her a hideous T-shirt featuring some frightful music band, she actually held my hand as we progressed to the next market stall."

The Fire Queen sat upright in her chair with the air of a woman throwing off her lesser cares to concentrate on more important matters.

"Two days ago you said you hoped to be nearing completion…?"

"I'm still nearing it," said Thrix.

"I can tell you have been busy," said Malveria, pointedly. "So busy you have neglected to properly attend to the spells you use to conceal Gawain's aura. You have not managed to end the relationship?"

The Enchantress sighed, then shook her head, and looked close to despair. Malveria struggled to be understanding.

"Dearest Enchantress, I can, with some strain, sympathise with you. You have the terrible passion which cannot be denied. And though it may lead you into any number of dreadful fates, there is perhaps nothing to be done about it."

She looked Thrix in the eye.

"I'm serious about the dreadful fates. I do not just say this because your rampant passion is delaying my clothes. If you continue this dalliance with Gawain, it will end badly, of that you may be sure."

Thrix was uncomfortable, but didn't contradict Malveria. From the first time she'd slept with Gawain she'd envisaged it coming to a bad ending. Why she was still doing it, she couldn't explain. Not wishing to dwell on the subject, the Enchantress told Malveria that her ball gown was almost ready. The Queen leapt from her chair in excitement.

"Let me see me the garment!"

Thrix buzzed for Ann, asking her to bring the dress. Malveria examined the gown. She pursed her lips. It was obvious she wasn't satisfied.

"It is a beautifully cut dress. But is it not rather plain?"

The ball gown, though lavish in the way of hoops, layers and lacing, was mainly white. Malveria had expected something more extravagant.

"Wait till you try it on," said Thrix.

From the disappointed look on Malveria's face as she was laced into the dress it was clear she thought that the Enchantress had let her down. This was not the ball gown to dazzle her rivals. She turned to the huge mirror on the wall.

"Well, Enchantress, it is pleasant enough, but – "

Thrix spoke the spell to activate the dress. It fluttered gently, as if caught in a light breeze. It was a pleasing effect, but even better were the large, shimmering fairy wings which appeared at the back of the gown. The Fire Queen gasped as they folded themselves gently around her, shimmering with every colour of the rainbow. They were translucent, delicate, and utterly beautiful. Malveria's appearance was suddenly transformed from cynical supermodel into radiant fairy queen.

"It's… it's…" she gasped, but was unable to get her words out. Abruptly she fell over. The Fire Queen had fainted from pleasure.

Ann looked down at her.

"Is that good?"

"I hope so," replied Thrix.

She bent down and gently rubbed Malveria's temples to bring her round. As Malveria revived there was a quietly ecstatic expression on her face. She hobbled to the mirror.

"It's so beautiful," she gasped, and fell over again.

Thrix frowned.

"She'd better get used to it before the ball. Unless fainting with pleasure is acceptable at a Hiyasta social event. Which it might be, I suppose."

191

Moonglow was in an odd mood when she arrived home from university. Daniel was sympathetic, as ever. He brought her tea as she sat at her mirror, cleaning off her make-up.

"What a state," she muttered. Her kohl, mascara and eye shadow had all suffered from her tears. Even the highest quality products had not proved completely impervious to hours of crying. Daniel placed a cup of tea on one side of her and told her there was wine downstairs, if she needed additional comfort.

"And I brought you this nice chocolate frog in case you felt – "

Moonglow grabbed the frog and crammed it in her mouth.

"I'll get some more," said Daniel.

Unlike Malveria and Thrix, Moonglow was amenable to chocolate as a means of solace. As she was unable to eat anything like a proper meal, the effects of some extra chocolate weren't likely to be too drastic. Moonglow sipped her tea.

"Has Thrix been here today?" she asked.

Daniel wasn't sure. He'd been out part of the day. Thrix now had a key, which neither of them really approved of. The Enchantress had pointed out that they'd agreed to let her use their attic and if they didn't give her a key she could just open the front door by sorcery. Kalix had complained about Thrix and Malveria traipsing through the house at all hours. Thrix had angrily informed her young sister that if she didn't like it, she could hand back the pendant she wore and Thrix could then store everything at her own building.

It had been strange at first, living in a house which contained an attic full of magically protected clothes. They'd got used to it now. After encountering the MacRinnalchs, Daniel and Moonglow were no longer much surprised by anything. Moonglow asked Daniel what he planned to watch on TV tonight.

"We can watch it together. Maybe it wasn't such a bad idea to get cable."

"It was a great idea," enthused Daniel. "But I can't watch it with you."

"Why not?"

Daniel looked slightly embarrassed.

"I've got a date with Alicia."

Moonglow was surprised. She noticed that Daniel had washed his hair. It still flopped in front of his eyes but it was in much better condition.

"You finally worked up the nerve to talk to her?"

"No," admitted Daniel. "There was no working up of nerves. My nerves weren't up to the task. She phoned me."

Moonglow was even more surprised though she attempted not to insult Daniel by showing it.

"She told me she had a dream about me," continued Daniel. "So she thought she'd give me a call."

"Well I guess that's good," said Moonglow. "A girl dreaming about you and everything."

"I know. It's amazing."

"Wonderful."

Daniel noticed that Moonglow wasn't sounding very happy. She seemed as if she might be about to burst into tears again any moment.

"I'll stay in and watch TV with you if you want," he volunteered, loyally. "I could see Alicia another time."

"Don't be silly," said Moonglow. "You can't just stand her up."

Later, while Daniel got ready for his date, Moonglow was disconsolate. She'd been looking forward to watching TV with Daniel. She knew his presence would cheer her. Apparently Malveria's words had been true. Daniel was becoming more attractive. Moonglow had a disturbing image of Daniel's life improving in every direction while hers became worse. Soon he'd be out every night enjoying herself while she sat at home watching TV with only a bottle of wine for company.

Moonglow heard a noise downstairs. It was Vex, who'd teleported in without invitation. The young Hiyasta was holding her arm, rather miserably.

"I bumped my elbow," she said, and looked hopefully at Moonglow. "It really hurts."

Moonglow hurried to her assistance, sitting on the couch where she rubbed her elbow till Vex proclaimed it to be better.

"I hate bumping my elbow," said Vex.

"It can be very painful," agreed Moonglow.

Vex was holding a parcel.

"I brought a present for Kalix," she said. "I went shopping."

"I can see," replied Moonglow.

Vex was wearing a pair of black army trousers which had so many straps it was difficult to see where the trousers ended and the straps began. They were obviously new, as were the large boots she wore which were also black but, incongruously, had flowers round the edge of the soles and fairies on the laces. She had a bright yellow Hello Kitty T-shirt onto which were pinned several Hello Kitty badges, and an embroidered waistcoat which may have originated in India, or some point further east. Each of her nails was a different colour. Her hair, brilliant gold, stood up in spikes with the support of various new hair preparations which appeared to have been put on in their raw state, and not properly rinsed out, cementing the strands into place firmly enough to resist the most hostile environment. If Malveria ever made good on her threat to throw Agrivex into the great volcano, it was possible her hair might survive the experience.

Vex flexed her elbow and grinned.

"It's better now. Why are you so cheerful?"

"What?"

"I can read it in your aura."

Moonglow was amazed. She'd never been less cheerful in her life. Vex was extremely bad at reading auras.

"Getting over Markus, I expect?" continued Vex. "It's the right thing to do. Just move on. Are Aunt Malvie's clothes finished? I want to take a look."

"You will do no such thing, wretched girl whom I tragically considered adopting in a moment of weakness," thundered Malveria, materialising in the front room with Thrix at her side. Moonglow was surprised to see how worn Thrix looked. Malveria, in contrast, positively radiated happiness.

"The Enchantress has magnificently completed my ball gown for the Sorceress Livia's birthday celebration. It is a garment to break the hearts of all ladies not fortunate enough to be wearing it."

The Fire Queen laughed with unbridled pleasure.

"Once more Malveria rules supreme!"

"So are all your clothes ready now?" asked Moonglow.

"No," admitted Malveria. "But the Enchantress assures me that the shoes, matching accessories, outfits for the poolside breakfast, and assorted handmaidens' dresses will all be ready in time."

She frowned.

"Though there is barely more than a week to go…"

"Everything is under control," said Thrix, confidently.

"Can I see?" asked Vex, eagerly.

Malveria glared balefully at her.

"Agrivex, I have frequently threatened you with a visit to the great volcano. Please be assured that I mean it when I say to you this time, if you dare to touch any of these clothes, I will kill you. If I find that one single ill-painted finger of your poorly washed hand has befouled my glorious new raiments, you will die."

As she said this the Fire Queen looked so utterly ferocious that Moonglow shrank back into the couch.

Vex looked glumly at her arm.

"I bumped my elbow," she said, and looked hopefully at her aunt.

"Please Agrivex," sighed Malveria. "You must fight this continual need to have your elbow rubbed. A minor elbow bump is really not such a serious injury."

Malveria turned to the Enchantress.

"Let us hide these immediately. There's no telling how closely the repulsive Kabachetka and her lickspittle Zatek may be spying."

Thrix and Malveria hurried upstairs. Vex, apparently unaffected by her aunt's threats, began bouncing around on the couch.

"When's Kalix coming back? I want to give her her present."

192

Encouraged by Marwanis, Wallace and Lachlan had their way. Baron MacGregor joined the rebellion. Wallace was exultant. He was one of the very few werewolves whose strength rivalled that of Sarapen. He loved to fight and had feared that such a fine opportunity might not present itself in his lifetime. The MacGregors made their way down from the Rinnalch Hills in the north. They camped on the northern fringes of Colburn Wood, taking cover from the persistent rain, which was now turning to snow.

They were greeted by Morag MacAllister, sister of Douglas, the new Baron. She crossed quickly over the countryside to congratulate the MacGregors on their arrival, and trade banter with Wallace as to who would be first over the castle walls. A meeting was arranged for the following night between representatives of the three Barons, to co-ordinate their forces ahead of Sarapen's arrival. It was still five days till the full moon, when Sarapen would lead them to war.

Inside the castle the loyal MacRinnalchs were tense, though not because of the approaching confrontation. The MacRinnalch werewolves did not fear combat. But there were many extra werewolves in the castle, drawn in from the surrounding estates, and it was unnatural for them to be cooped up like this. At night, they transformed into their werewolf shapes and paced the walls, waiting for the enemy.

Kertal MacRinnalch had free rein to go where he pleased but the Mistress of the Werewolves had him closely watched. She didn't trust Kurian's son. However, when she was informed that Kertal had briefly encountered Buvalis MacGregor, the head of her household, on the western battlement, she thought nothing of it. Verasa would not have be so sanguine had she known that the few words Buvalis and Kertal exchanged concerned a rope long enough to reach the ground, and where it might be let down unobserved.

When Sarapen learned that the MacGregors had finally entered the fray he felt elated. One part of his plan of attack was nearing completion. He asked Decembrius if he had news from Princess Kabachetka.

"She has assembled everything she needs."

Sarapen nodded. Again, it was satisfactory. First he would smash all resistance in the south, then he would take the castle. In five days time he'd be Thane, and Markus and Kalix would be dead.

Decembrius reminded Sarapen that they owed money to Merchant MacDoig. Sarapen nodded. It was distasteful, certainly, paying that man for his help in transporting the means for Kabachetka's sorcery, but the Merchant had done the work as agreed.

"MacDoig is making a fine profit from the MacRinnalchs," noted Sarapen.

"We could decline to pay," suggested Decembrius.

Sarapen regarded Decembrius with annoyance.

"The MacRinnalchs do not default on their debts," he said, sharply. "Pay the man."

Merchant MacDoig would have been surprised to learn that several of the unfamiliar items he'd transported for Princess Kabachetka were for a new spell designed to penetrate the most skilfully wrought magical defences, and destroy any fabric that lay beyond them. Sarapen would also have been surprised. It was not something he had requested of her. Neither Sarapen nor the Merchant would have understood why the Princess had expended such effort in developing new sorcery just to destroy clothes.

193

The Enchantress and the Fire Queen were still at Moonglow's flat when Dominil brought Kalix home. Dominil wanted to speak privately to Thrix and they withdrew into the kitchen to talk in low voices. Meanwhile Vex greeted Kalix enthusiastically.

"You're back! How was the leafleting?"

"It was okay," shrugged Kalix. "I got wet."

"And cold?"

Kalix shrugged again.

"Of course you got cold," said Vex. "Probably so cold you wished you had a fine new pair of army trousers instead of these raggedy jeans you always wear."

Vex produced a bag with a triumphant flourish.

"I bought you a present!"

Kalix was surprised.

"What is it?"

"It's a surprise," cried Vex. "It's new army trousers like mine."

Kalix stared uncertainly at the bag.

"Don't you want to find out what the surprise is?" said Vex.

"Is it army trousers?" said Kalix.

"You guessed!" cried Vex, pleased. "Open the bag."

Kalix took out the trousers.

"I got the skinniest size available," explained Vex. "And I got a belt as well in case they weren't skinny enough, you being so skinny and everything. Do you like them?"

Kalix didn't know if she liked them or not. It flashed through her mind that she would never even have considered buying Vex a present. She suddenly felt quite ashamed, and didn't want to accept the gift.

"I don't need new trousers," she said.

Vex laughed.

"You're so funny. Let's go to your room and try them on."

In the tiny kitchen Dominil was conferring with Thrix.

"Mother is very impressed with what you've done for the twins," said the Enchantress. "Are you actually going to take them to Scotland to vote for Markus?"

"It is possible," replied Dominil. "If they survive the gig."

"Survive it?"

Dominil described her encounter with Decembrius in Camden. It was worrying news. Though it was no real surprise that Sarapen planed to attack the gig, the Enchantress had been so busy with her own affairs that she hadn't anticipated it.

"Why did Decembrius warn you?" wondered Thrix. "Is it some sort of trap?"

Dominil didn't think so.

"I believe he is attracted to Kalix."

"Attracted to Kalix? He can't be."

"Why not?"

"Because she's crazy."

"Perhaps Decembrius is attracted by her craziness," suggested Dominil. "More likely, he is simply attracted to her youth and beauty."

"Maybe," grunted Thrix. She was tired, and felt too old and haggard to enjoy hearing about her sister's youth and beauty.

"I don't mind meeting Sarapen again," said Dominil. "But he won't be alone. The Mistress of the Werewolves had some wolves in London to protect the twins but the trouble in Scotland has forced her to withdraw most of them."

"Do you want me to come to the gig?" asked Thrix, frowning.

"You do not appear keen," said Dominil.

"Well it could be a problem," declared Thrix. "I've no idea what to wear."

Dominil looked rather coldly at Thrix.

"I presume you could solve that dilemma with a minimum amount of effort."

Thrix stared back at Dominil.

"Do you have absolutely no sense of humour?"

"Very little, so I am informed."

"You must be having a great time with the twins."

"It is occasionally exasperating. Can you attend?"

The Enchantress nodded. Really, she didn't have any choice.

"Mother would never forgive me if I let beautiful young Kalix get shredded by Sarapen and the Douglas-MacPhees."

Thrix opened the fridge and wrinkled her nose with distaste on finding that the only alcohol on offer was a large plastic bottle of cider. Unable to find a glass, she poured some into a coffee mug. She offered the bottle to Dominil and was a little surprised when the white-haired werewolf accepted. Thrix noticed how well cared-for Dominil's hair was. It took an effort to maintain such long straight hair in such perfectly shiny condition. Thrix, who was vain about everything, was relieved to learn that Dominil was at least vain about something.

Here, in the close proximity of the tiny kitchen, the Enchantress could almost feel the cold emanating from Dominil. Had anyone from outside observed the pair, they would have been astonished to learn that the golden, elegant and beautiful Thrix was a werewolf. But as for Dominil, it might not have been such a surprise.

"Have you considered cancelling the gig?"

Dominil told Thrix she had considered it, but decided against. If this gig was postponed, the opportunity would be lost, perhaps forever. Who knew what might happen in the next month to prevent the twins from playing again? In reality, Dominil was not being completely honest. It might have been possible to delay the event. The Mistress of the Werewolves might have been amenable, and changed her plans accordingly. But Dominil didn't want to cancel the gig. She was eager to confront Sarapen.

Dominil asked the Enchantress if the Fire Queen would accompany her. Thrix shook her head. Malveria would be attending the first night of the Sorceress Livia's birthday celebration.

"Don't worry," said Thrix. "I've enough power to repel Sarapen."

"I know," replied Dominil. "Though I only require you to repel his werewolves. I intend to take care of Sarapen myself."

Kalix was pleased with her new combat trousers. She thought the straps were funny and she liked the big pockets at the sides.

"I knew you'd like them," said Vex. "You can wear them to the gig. If Gawain comes he'll like them too."

Kalix immediately looked gloomy. Vex was puzzled.

"What's the matter? You can wear something else if you like. No need to get stressed about it."

The Fire Queen was happy when she climbed down from the attic. The ball gown was fabulous and most of her outfits were now completed. If the Enchantress kept working day and night then everything should be ready on time. Malveria raised her head, sensing the atmosphere around her, testing it for intrusive sorcery. She nodded, satisfied at what she found. Kalix's pendant was doing a splendid job of hiding the clothes.

"There is nothing stronger than a pendant of Tamol for hiding," she muttered to herself. "It was an excellent idea of mine to give it to

Kalix. It has all worked out well. Ah Moonglow, how are you today?"

"All right," replied Moonglow, attempting to smile. "A bit behind at college."

Malveria could discern that Moonglow was distracted, but did not enquire why. Moonglow's aura was full of misery. It covered her like a shroud. Mixed in with the misery were feelings of resentment. And was that a hint of treachery? Very suitable, thought Malveria. No doubt Moonglow was intending to treacherously steal Daniel from his new admirers. Dominil and Thrix walked back through from the kitchen and Vex appeared from Kalix's bedroom and suddenly the main room was again full of werewolves and elementals.

"Would everyone like some tea?" asked Moonglow, politely. "Where's Kalix?"

"She's being gloomy again," replied Vex.

"What did you do to her?"

"Nothing," protested Vex. "She's just crazy. You know what were-wolves are like."

The young Hiyasta noticed that there were two werewolves in the room, currently staring at her.

"Hey, no need to look at me like that. Some of them are crazy. Moonglow, back me up. Wasn't Markus crazy when you were going out with him?"

Moonglow abruptly broke down in tears and fled from the room.

"What?" demanded Vex, looking round her with pained innocence. "It's not my fault if everyone just bursts into tears the moment I open my mouth. What's the matter with them all? Is there anything good on TV?"

"Come with me, niece," said Malveria. "I wish to talk to you."

Vex was immediately suspicious.

"Is this about your pink shoes? Because I really think it's time to get over that."

"It is not," said Malveria. "Now come with me to the palace."

As they materialised in the flower garden of small yellow flames, the Queen told Vex that she had a task for her.

"Attend to my words closely. Have you forgotten your misery over Daniel?"

"Yes."

"Good. Because I want you to entice and fascinate a young man."

"Who?"

"Daniel."

Vex looked confused.

"Yesterday you wanted me to forget him."

"Well today I want you to fascinate him. Daniel is becoming more attractive and it's time to increase the pressure. It must seem as if Daniel is the most desirable boy in the world. I want you to make Moonglow jealous."

"I don't understand."

"You do not have to understand. You simply have to do as I say."

Vex shrugged.

"Okay. Do I get a reward?"

"A reward? For carrying out the wishes of your benefactor?"

"Well do I?"

"No," said Malveria. "You do not. Because I am not at all pleased with you."

The Fire Queen produced a scroll with a flourish.

"Do you know what this is?" she demanded.

"A shoe catalogue?" suggested Agrivex, hopefully.

"It is not a shoe catalogue. It's a report from your tutors. And a most shocking piece of reading it is in every respect. You are woefully deficient in all subjects. Never has the professor of history written in such agonised terms over one of his students. As for your mathematics tutor, the paper is still damp with his tears."

Agrivex looked defiant.

"They're all against me. It's not fair."

"The only unfair thing is that your miserable self is inflicted on these most learned Hiyastas. Really Agrivex, this cannot go on. Your tutor of auras reports that you show no skill or application whatsoever. Do you appreciate how important it is for a Hiyasta to read auras? I am shocked that my almost-adopted niece is so deficient in this talent."

The Fire Queen put on her sternest expression.

"Agrivex. You wish to attend the werewolf music event in four days time. If you do not show an immediate improvement in your interpreting of auras, you shall not go."

Agrivex's mouth dropped open.

"It's not fair!"

"Life is seldom fair," replied Malveria. The Fire Queen raised her hand to silence the protesting Agrivex. "I have given you two tasks.

473

Fascinate Daniel and improve your reading of auras. Now begone, and do not disappoint me, miserable niece."

194

Merchant MacDoig settled back in his armchair in front of the fire, a satisfied smile on his face, a tumbler of whisky in his hand. A fine crystal decanter rested on the small mahogany table at his side, one of the numerous pieces of antique furniture that adorned the upstairs rooms of the Merchant's London premises. The Young MacDoig sat on the other side of the fire in another armchair which, while not quite a match for the Merchant's, was also old, and very comfortable.

"It'll be time for me to get back to Scotland soon," said the Merchant. "It's been a bitter feud, but it's coming to an end now. And it's been a profitable affair for us, son."

The Young MacDoig nodded. He inhaled on his cigar, which he preferred to the pipe smoked by his father. His father drew out a great silver hob watch and stared at the dial.

"Two days till the MacRinnalchs go to war. And not much more than a day after that, I'll wager, till the war ends."

"There are a powerful lot of werewolves on each side," his son pointed out. "I'd say it might last a while."

Merchant MacDoig shook his head.

"Sarapen MacRinnalch will sweep them all before him, son, mark my words."

The Merchant knew something about most of the affairs of the MacRinnalchs, and he'd made a profit from many of them. He'd sold the Begravar knife to Dominil and he'd helped import Kabachetka's sorcery for Sarapen. He'd sold laudanum to Kalix and Dominil, provisions to the Barons, and found a discreet source of silver bullets for Decembrius. Equally profitably, he'd sold information to various interested parties.

"The Barons have all met on the field, you know. MacGregor, MacAllister, and MacPhee's son Euan. And Red Ruraich MacAndris, who fancies himself as a Baron one day too, I'd say. Sarapen will find a way to lead them into the castle. Just like he's found a way to defeat that sister of his."

The Merchant looked thoughtful.

"It's not like the old days, of course. I remember when it took an army months to march from one end of the land to another. Now Sarapen can fight in London one day and fly to Scotland the next. It's not the same at all. It's not what a man would call a proper campaign."

He poured himself whisky from the crystal decanter.

"But the result is the same. The strongest son gets to be Thane."

He glanced at his own son.

"Be sure to reduce our order for laudanum. We'll not be selling so much of it after this. Dominil MacRinnalch is unlikely to be alive in a few days time, and Kalix certainly won't be."

The Merchant looked thoughtful.

"It's a fine reward he's put on her head. Five gold nobles. She won't last long. "

The Young MacDoig leaned forward to prod the fire with a poker, and flames leapt up the narrow chimney. It was no longer legal to light a coal fire in London, but the Merchant was too attached to the warmth of his fire to abandon the practice.

"What did Mr Carmichael want?" he asked.

"Just some information," replied his father. "As to the timing of the werewolves' music event, and suchlike. He's never been a generous payer, Mr Carmichael. It takes some negotiating to get a fair price off the man. And I'm not sure he'll be with us much longer either, to tell you the truth. I wouldn't say it was prudent for the Avenaris Guild to involve themselves with the MacRinnalchs at this moment. But he seemed confident, so perhaps he knows some things I don't. In an affair like this, there's always a lot of plots and treachery going on behind the scenes."

The Merchant drew out an unusually large gold coin from his purse and studied it fondly. Hiyasta gold, very old and very pure. It was part of his payment from Princes Kabachetka.

"The Princess is counting on profiting by some treachery she's worked up for herself. Some information she has from a youngster, I believe. She can be persuasive woman."

War was always good for trade. It was as true now as it had been when the Merchant's great-grandfather established the family business with the profits gained from selling weapons to the Scottish Covenanters before they marched south in 1640. The Merchant puffed

475

on his pipe.

"I'll miss dealing with the Mistress of the Werewolves. But no doubt Sarapen will continue to put business our way, when he's Thane."

195

The day before the gig the twins' house was in uproar. Beauty and Delicious rushed from one room to the next carrying bundles of clothes and make-up, trying on endless outfits and dismissing each quicker than the last. The sisters were not well focused. The final rehearsal had been chaotic. The other members of the band had managed to play quite competently but the sisters were over excited and had put in some of their worst performances ever. Dominil was frustrated, though not as angry as she once would have been. She knew they'd been making an effort. Unfortunately the twins were becoming overwhelmed. Even though it was only a small gig, the prospect of performing in front of an audience again had caused Beauty and Delicious to work themselves up into a state where they could hardly remember how to play the most basic chords. Dominil reminded them of their relaxation exercises, tried to prevent them from consuming too many intoxicants, and hoped for the best.

She hadn't informed them that Sarapen might attack the gig. The twins were scared of Sarapen. If they even suspected he might turn up they'd never be able to play.

"Do you like this top?" yelled Beauty, hurrying into the room wearing a small strip of red latex.

Dominil raised her eyebrows. The tiny piece of latex didn't seem large enough to qualify as a garment.

"It depends. What effect are you trying to achieve?"

"Rock'n'Roll slut."

"Then you've succeeded. Wear it."

Beauty looked in the mirror. She wasn't satisfied.

"Maybe the black one was better," she muttered, and hurried back to her bedroom to change.

There was nothing more for Dominil to do in the way of publicity or promotion. To escape from the twins' manic behaviour she retreated upstairs to her room. She took the Begravar knife from its hiding place and spoke the Sumerian words that were engraved on the handle. Dominil frowned. She wasn't certain that the knife was properly activated. It could be that her translation was wrong. She sipped sparingly from her laudanum, and logged onto the university website she'd been consulting, to check her it again.

A long way off, in the west of the city, Mr Carmichael sat with the other members of the board of the Avenaris Guild, finalising their plans for attacking the gig. They had already checked the venue, examining the upstairs room where the bands played. The Guild planned to wait till Yum Yum Sugary Snacks had finished their set and people were leaving, then attack. If the hunters moved quickly it should be possible to trap the werewolves upstairs and destroy them all in a hail of silver bullets.

196

Markus spent his days either on the walls, or planning the defence of Castle MacRinnalch with Verasa, Rainal, and Eskandor. He spent his nights with Beatrice MacRinnalch, the assistant curator of the castle relics. Verasa didn't object to Markus associating with her. She was an intelligent and respectable young werewolf, and her son needed some form of relaxation.

The Mistress of the Werewolves was pleased with her son's conduct since arriving back at the castle, but she was worried by his most recent suggestion. Markus proposed that, rather than wait for Sarapen to arrive in Scotland, the defenders should make a pre-emptive sally against the Barons. It was a bold plan, and not without its merits. The Barons wouldn't be expecting an attack. Furthermore, if it were done before the full moon, many of their followers would not be able to transform into their werewolf shape.

"Why wait?" asked Markus. "We're certain that Sarapen will fight in London tomorrow. The next day he'll be here. Let's deal them a blow before he arrives."

Rainal was against it.

"I'm not sure we'd take them by surprise. Baron MacGregor leads their forces and he's an experienced werewolf. He'd pull his troops back the moment we appeared. We might make some gains but nothing substantial. If we suffered losses we'd be weaker when Sarapen arrives."

The Barons now completely encircled the castle. The smoke from their campfires could be seen from the battlements. Markus was not so convinced of the Baron's qualities as a leader.

"MacGregor is the senior Baron on the field but are the others really following him?"

Again, it was a reasonable point. There were four factions outside the castle walls, and none of them could claim to be their natural leader. Baron Douglas MacAllister was far too young. Baron MacPhee was well respected but he was not on the field, and had sent his son Euan, who was not a noted warrior. No Baron's troops would follow the lower ranked Red Ruraich MacAndris. Which left Baron MacGregor. He was the senior Baron present, and nominal leader in Sarapen's absence, but he had arrived late, and was not thought to be such a willing participant.

The Mistress of the Werewolves came out against the plan. She still believed that they could defend the castle against assault and was unwilling to risk sending Markus into battle. That night Markus complained to Beatrice about his mother's lack of faith in him. He chafed against her restraints.

"I'm captain of the castle guard," he told her. "I should be leading the defence. It's time my mother let me have my way."

Beatrice sympathised, although she was secretly relieved that Markus was not about to lead a dangerous mission outside the castle walls. Like many before her, Beatrice was overwhelmed by Markus's beauty, and already loved him dearly.

197

The day before the gig was uncomfortable for Kalix. She dreamed of Gawain and woke up feeling warm and content but as the dream faded, her misery returned. She kept picturing him with someone else, and tormenting herself with thoughts of who it might be. She had a wild notion of hunting Gawain and his lover down and killing them both.

"No," muttered Kalix. "I won't do that. I'll kill myself."

It was momentarily comforting to think how sorry Gawain would be when she killed herself. But probably he wouldn't be sorry for long. He'd have his new love to comfort him.

Dominil didn't need any more help and Kalix couldn't find anything else to take her mind off her unhappiness. She watched her Sabrina the Teenage Witch DVD but she'd already seen it so many times it failed to distract her. She felt angry at the TV stations for not showing more new episodes. Since getting cable Kalix had learned that just because a channel showed her favourite programmes regularly it didn't always mean they were new. When the afternoon episode of Sabrina turned out to be repeat which she'd already seen several times, Kalix felt tempted to bite the television.

The atmosphere in the house was again strained. Moonglow was still unhappy. Worse, she was in a bad mood with Daniel, and they had an argument about the dirty dishes in the kitchen. This was unusual. They'd never argued about the dishes before. Now Moonglow seemed to be implying that Daniel had carelessly neglected his share of cleaning due to seeing too much of Alicia.

"Who did all the dishes when you were spending time with Markus?" retorted Daniel, which made the argument worse. Kalix didn't like to be around when Daniel and Moonglow were arguing. It made her anxious. She grabbed her laudanum, went to the kitchen, took a carton of cheap wine from a cupboard, and hurried out of the house.

Outside it was snowing. Kalix headed towards Kennington Park, looking for somewhere private. She made for an isolated clump of bushes and felt a little more secure as she crawled inside. She began to breath a little more easily. Finally noticing the cold, she transformed into her werewolf shape, then used her claws to rip off the top of the wine carton. It didn't take long for the wine to affect her. Mixed with the laudanum it quickly began to dull her senses.

Kalix put one paw to her neck. There seemed to something missing. What was it? She remembered she'd taken her pendant off to have a bath, and hadn't put it on again. She was outside without her protection, and she was in werewolf shape. Very dangerous. Kalix shrugged. She didn't care. If anyone was looking for her, let them find her.

198

The day before the gig was also the day before the start of the Sorceress Livia's 500th birthday celebration. Malveria's moods swung wildly between calm, despair, and elation. She felt calm while planning her five-day campaign of aggressive fashion warfare. Directing her dressers, handmaidens, and make-up artists was not unlike planning a military campaign, and she was good at this. As each stage of her plan was finalised, Malveria felt a great surge of happiness. She simply couldn't wait to walk into Livia's celebration wearing Thrix's wonderful clothes.

There were also moments of despair. Her final batch of shoes had not yet arrived from Italy. The Enchantress was even now on the phone, threatening the postal services with dire retribution if they didn't come up with the goods. No matter how impossible the odds against her had been as she fought to gain control of the kingdom, Malveria had never given way to despair. Now, faced with the prospect of wearing her astonishing new blue chiffon evening dress with anything other than the perfect high heeled leather sandals Thrix had designed for her, the Queen felt she could just sit down and cry. Finally she could stand it no longer. She teleported to the premises of Thrix Fashions, erupting into the Enchantress's office in a blur of flames, jasmine and burning tears.

"I must have my new shoes!" she screamed, and collapsed sobbing on the couch.

"They're here," said Thrix. "I dragged them out of the sorting office with sorcery – "

Malveria wasn't listening. Having spotted the shoes in question resting beside Thrix's desk she'd rushed towards them and was feverishly tearing open the box. Thrix took Malveria firmly by the shoulder and led her back to the couch.

"I must try on the shoes immediately," gasped the Queen.

"Malveria," said Thrix sternly, looking her in the eyes. "You're not in a fit state to try on shoes. You'll set them on fire. Calm down."

"Please!" wailed the Fire Queen, and made another move towards the shoes. Thrix flung herself in the way.

"As your fashion designer I order you to sit on the couch till you cool down," cried Thrix, even more sternly. "It's for your own good."

Malveria reluctantly did as she was told. The flames that flickered around her gradually began to fade. Thrix snapped her fingers, causing a glass of water and a glass of wine to float to her side. She helped Malveria sip from both. Malveria took some deep breaths.

"Thank you dearest Enchantress. The thought of my new shoes not arriving in time quite undermined my famous self-control. Are they really all here?"

"Yes, all of them."

Thrix had been up the whole night putting the finishing touches to the Fire Queen's new collection of handbags. In themselves the bags were a collection worthy of a page in a fashion magazine. The Fire Queen, who loved a good handbag, would derive a great deal of pleasure from them, but not until she'd spent some hours revelling in her new footwear. The Enchantress sat on the couch, briefly watched as Malveria tried on her shoes, then drifted off to sleep, exhausted by her endeavours.

199

Gawain was patrolling, as he did every night. Though he had no hope of ever being re-united with Kalix, he was still protecting her. During the past week Gawain had noticed several unfamiliar werewolves in the South London Streets. He didn't know about the price Sarapen had put on Kalix's head but he sensed that she was in more danger than ever. He patrolled for as long as he could, a lonely figure in the snow, prowling through gardens, occasionally taking to the rooftops, always ready to intercept anyone who might be a threat to Kalix.

As Gawain hurried past Kennington Park, he halted, and looked up sharply. He was so used to straining his senses for the slightest sign of danger that it was a shock to be suddenly aware of Kalix's presence. She was nearby, in werewolf form, and not making any attempt to hide. The moment he sensed her Gawain knew she was in trouble.

It was not yet the full moon. Gawain's werewolf shape would not come on naturally. Despite the urgency of the situation, he was forced to concentrate for a few moments to bring on the change. As soon as he transformed he charged through the park towards the bushes in the distance. Snow was falling, hindering visibility. Gawain didn't see his quarry till he was almost upon them. Four werewolves, all still in human shape, also heading towards the bushes. Gawain knew that Kalix was there. He snarled. The four men turned to face him.

"Back off," said one of the men. "You're not getting a share."

"A share?"

"Of the reward."

The man looked at his companions.

"Thinks he can just come here late and pick up five gold nobles. Maybe he thinks he's special because he can change without the moon?"

As he spoke the man transformed into a werewolf. One of his companions did the same. Gawain realised that these werewolves were not from Sarapen's entourage. They weren't seeking Kalix as part of the feud over the Thaneship. They weren't trying to drag Kalix home to face the Great Council. They were just vagabond werewolves, come here to kill her and pick up a reward. It filled him with fury. He leapt on the largest werewolf, dragging him down to the snow-covered ground. There was snarling and howling as Gawain engaged with his four opponents. The battle was brief. Gawain was a warrior, from a line of warriors. His opponents couldn't cope with his fighting skills. Five gold nobles was a fine reward but not worth losing their lives over. Within minutes the two who were unable to make the werewolf change had fled. Their werewolf companions followed shortly after, limping away from the scene, blood seeping from their wounds.

As soon as they were out of sight Gawain rushed into the bushes. He was frantic about Kalix. He knew she would never ignore a fight. It was so unlike her he feared she might already be dead.

He found her unconscious, an empty carton of wine by her side, an open bottle of laudanum still clutched in her paw. Gawain halted, mopped some blood and sweat from his brow, and smiled, rather grimly. This, he reflected, was very like Kalix. He put the cap back on the bottle of laudanum, and placed it carefully in his pocket. Then he picked her up in his arms, and took her out of the bushes. As they emerged into the park, Kalix woke up.

"What's happening?" she murmured.

"Werewolves hunting you," said Gawain. "We have to leave."

"Okay," said Kalix. Her eyelids drooped.

"I love you," said Gawain.

Kalix opened her eyes.

"I love you," she said, then threw up over him.

Gawain gallantly ignored it. He tenderly wiped her mouth, and carried her out of the park.

200

It was past midnight. The twins were downstairs, trying on clothes, and making a lot of noise. Dominil was both bored and irritated by their behaviour. Her translation of Tibullus was spread out before her but she was bored with that as well. Dominil hadn't been bored since arriving in London. Now her work was almost done, it was creeping up on her again.

Tomorrow would not be boring, of course. Yum Yum Sugary Snacks would be onstage, and Sarapen would be in Camden. It occurred to Dominil that she could die. Dominil didn't feel alarmed at the prospect, but it made her dissatisfied. If she was about to die, she didn't want to spend her last night on earth listening to Beauty and Delicious screaming about which pair of shades to wear onstage. She looked around for something to do. The van to take the musicians to the venue was booked. The sampling software had been upgraded. All instruments and equipment had been checked. She'd made out the set list and the guest list. There was nothing left to do and no more instructions to give.

Dominil put on her long black leather coat. She checked her hair in the mirror, brushing it down around her shoulders, then strode silently out of the house. Outside it was snowing, and the streets were quiet save for a few determined beggars around the tube station. Dominil walked past them without a glance. She crossed over Camden High Street and carried on up the road.

Pete, guitarist in Yum Yum Sugary Snacks, was surprised to find Dominil at his door in the early hours of the morning.

"What's the matter?"

"Nothing," said Dominil.

There was snow on her shoulders and some flakes rested on her brow, unmelted. With her mass of pure white hair she looked like a mythical snow queen who'd strode out of legend to bury London under a new ice age. Pete felt discomfited at the sight, and more uncomfortable at the way her black eyes stared deep into him.

"Are you alone?" asked Dominil.

"Yes. But I was about to go to sleep... you know... gig tomorrow."

Dominil walked in, uninvited. She put her hand behind Pete's head and dragged his face to within an inch of her own.

"I grow bored in the twins' house," she said.

Dominil drew Pete forward further till their lips almost met. Her touch was cold, still frozen from the snow.

"So I would like to spend this night here with you," continued Dominil. "Tomorrow you will not mention it to anyone. Do you understand?"

Pete said that he did.

"Very well," said Dominil. "Let us proceed. I trust your bedroom is not in the same deplorable state as the rest of your flat."

201

Unusually among the MacRinnalchs, Markus was not a great whisky drinker. He sat alone in his chambers, sipping water from the castle's well, and brooding over Verasa's rejection of his plan to attack the Barons. He'd started to feel that his mother did not have as much faith in him as she should. Every time he made a proposal she would overrule it. Markus began to wonder what was said about him behind his back. Might there be whispers that he was completely under his mother's thumb? He bridled at the thought.

Markus was wearing a peach coloured blouse, the same one in which he had once dazzled Moonglow. Here in the castle he took care to limit his penchant for female attire. Even a garment like the blouse, which didn't stray too far over the boundaries of normality, he would only wear in the privacy of his chambers.

He tapped his foot on the dark stone floor. Captivity in the castle was as irksome to him as the rest of the MacRinnalchs. He removed the blouse, replacing it with a black shirt, and draped his fur-trimmed cloak over his shoulders before heading out to the courtyard. From there he climbed to the walls, greeting the werewolves on guard duty.

Despite the respectful greetings he received in return, Markus couldn't help feeling suspicious. Did these werewolves really respect him? Might they all wish that Eskandor was still captain of the guard?

The courtyard below was busy, as the castle's occupants sought relief from the confinement of their living quarters. Markus glanced downwards. In a dark recess on one of the stairs he noticed two werewolves in the shadows. They whispered together, and kissed briefly. Markus grinned. He had no doubt there were a great many secret relationships of this sort going on, in the prelude to war.

Markus almost laughed when the female werewolf stepped out of the shadows and hurried down the stairs. It was Buvalis MacGregor, employed by his mother as head of her household. He could imagine why young Buvalis might want to keep any relationship away from the eyes of the Mistress of the Werewolves. Verasa always liked to know more than she should about the private lives of her employees. Markus was not so amused when the other werewolf stepped into the light. It was Kertal MacRinnalch, a supporter of Sarapen and a prime suspect for acts of treachery. Markus's suspicious were aroused.

He followed Kertal at a discreet distance as he made his way to the western chambers where Buvalis had her living quarters. By the time Markus reached Buvalis's rooms the door was closed. Suddenly he felt ridiculous. What would people say if they knew he was going round the castle spying on illicit lovers? He was about to move on when he heard an unusual sound coming from the room. A sort of tearing noise, like metal being wrenched from stone. Markus's suspicions were re-ignited. He hesitated for a second longer. 'If it turns out that Kertal and Buvalis are merely enjoying an energetic lovemaking session, this is going to be very embarrassing,' he thought, then took hold of the door handle, and pushed. The door was locked. Markus applied his shoulder and it burst open. Buvalis and Kertal looked round, startled. Markus was startled as well, because the tearing noise he'd heard had been the sound of the metal grate that covered Buvalis's window being removed. Markus stared at the open window, and then down at Buvalis's feet, where a very long coil of rope lay in readiness.

"So. Kertal. Buvalis. I see you are about to throw open the castle to the Barons."

202

Deep into the night Thrix and Malveria arrived at Moonglow's with the final batch of clothes. Thrix sensed immediately that while the pendant was here, Kalix was not.

"She's gone out without it. Now of all times."

"Do you want to hunt for her?" asked the Fire Queen.

"No," said Thrix. "I don't care if she dies or not."

"You are not serious?"

Thrix was. She was too fatigued to care about anything except depositing the last of Malveria's clothes and going home to sleep. If Kalix got herself killed through her own foolishness that was her affair.

They sat in the attic, awaiting the arrival of Malveria's chief dresser. For the next five days Malveria would be shuttling back and forth between her palace, this attic, and Livia's celebration. Thrix had given specific instructions as to the wearing of her clothes and accessories, and some advice about the appropriate make-up for each event.

"I wish you could attend to all this yourself," said Malveria. "I trust you so much more than my dresser."

"Don't worry, I'll be around most of the time," said Thrix. "But I can't be here for your opening night, I have to watch the twins play."

The Enchantress was rather worried about the gig. She really didn't know what to wear, and dreaded turning up in the wrong outfit. Thrix studied her hair in one of the many sorcerous mirrors that hung in the attic. It was a mess. She was about to hunt for a brush, but abandoned the effort. A quick brush was not going to repair the damage. She changed into her wolf form, a shape that was more comfortable for lying on the floor, and drifted off to sleep. Malveria busied herself trying on clothes, and was so absorbed that she barely sensed the door opening downstairs.

Gawain was carrying Kalix up the stairs. He took her to her room and laid her on the bed. Kalix opened her eyes.

"Don't leave me," she said.

Gawain nodded. He wouldn't leave her.

Upstairs, the Enchantress woke to find the Fire Queen in consultation with her chief dresser, a middle aged Hiyasta who emitted an orange glow.

"Ah, Enchantress, you are awake. We are discussing the order in which my clothes must be put on for my grand entrance. The entrance is so important. The imperial carriage has been newly plated with gold, and fresh blood sprinkled on the wheels."

When it was finally time to leave, Thrix bid farewell to Malveria. As soon as she descended from the attic she sensed Gawain. She walked to Kalix's room and stood outside the door. She knew that Gawain was inside with Kalix. Thrix stared at the bedroom door for a while.

"To hell with you both," she muttered, finally. She arrived home in a foul temper, and despite her previous exhaustion, required a large shot of the MacRinnalch whisky before she could sleep.

203

Baron MacGregor's son Wallace received a message from Markus MacRinnalch informing him that his scheme for entering the castle by treachery had been discovered. There would be no surreptitious ascent by rope ladder into Buvalis's chambers. But if Wallace had the stomach for an honourable battle, Markus challenged him to single combat in front of the castle gates, the following night. Wallace snarled, insulted by the suggestion that he might not have the stomach for it. He would be there. He only wished it could be now, instead of twenty-four hours hence.

Lachlan MacGregor was astonished when he heard the news. He couldn't believe the Mistress of the Werewolves had allowed her favourite son to challenge Wallace. Wallace had never been defeated in combat. He was a huge werewolf, the strongest in his clan. It was unfathomable that Markus would engage in solo combat with him.

"Why would he do it?" said Lachlan. "I can't see us even getting over the walls now that Kertal and Buvalis have been discovered. They can sit tight and wait till we go away. Why would Verasa let Markus do this?"

"Perhaps she doesn't know about it," suggested Marwanis.

Lachlan dismissed this, feeling certain that nothing happened in Castle MacRinnalch unless approved by the Mistress of the Were-wolves. But he was wrong, and Marwanis was right. Markus MacRin-nalch had not consulted his mother before issuing the challenge. He hadn't consulted anyone. He'd simply told Kertal and Buvalis that he'd have them killed unless they transmitted his challenge to Wallace. Markus planned to show his mother, and the clan, that he was a werewolf fit to be Thane.

204

Beauty woke at two o'clock in the afternoon and went to rouse Delicious.

"I'm not getting up," said Delicious.

"Why not?"

"I can't remember any of the new songs and I've forgotten how to play the old ones. Tell Dominil I'm sick."

"Dominil isn't here. We asked her to give us some peace to get ready today."

It had seemed like a good idea at the time. Though the twins had almost reached a truce with Dominil they'd decided they didn't want her hanging round as they made their final preparations. If Dominil started lecturing them when they were putting on their make-up, it could really set them back. Dominil had been a little reluctant to leave them to their own devices but in view of their recent progress had agreed to let them spend most of the day on their own.

Beauty made a further effort to rouse Delicious. They had to leave for the gig around seven p.m. which only gave them five hours to get ready, not a lot of time really, given that they still hadn't decided on their outfits, and their hair would need a lot of attention.

"It's no use," said Delicious. "We can't play and we can't sing and all our songs are really bad. I'm never going onstage again, starting from tonight."

Beauty was depressed by her sister's pessimism. She became disheartened, and went back to bed. When their drummer rang up to check that everything was all right for tonight, they didn't answer the phone.

The cousins about whom the family did not used to speak were not the only MacRinnalchs reluctant to rise that day. Kalix lay in Gawain's arms and never wanted to get up again. She pressed herself close to the still sleeping Gawain, and drifted in and out of consciousness, drowsy and happy. She didn't care that Gawain had temporarily taken another lover. He was back now and that was all that mattered.

Thrix MacRinnalch slept very late, and would have slept longer had she not been woken by a phone call from Ann.

"What's the matter? If the heating's gone again, close the building, I'll deal with it tomorrow."

"You forgot one of Malveria's handbags."

Ann had found the handbag in Thrix's office. Apparently it had been left behind in the excitement over the final batch of shoes.

"Which one?"

"Black leather, silver clasp, Hiyasta imperial motif."

Thrix groaned. That was one of the bags Malveria needed for the first day of the celebration.

"Maybe she could just substitute another one?" suggested Ann.

"No," sighed the Enchantress. "If she doesn't have the right handbag for each outfit the world will come to an end. Maybe literally. Send it over on a bike, I'll get a message to her."

Thrix dragged herself out of bed. She felt better for her long sleep, though not yet fully refreshed. A shower and perhaps a brisk transformation into werewolf shape should bring her back to life. Thrix was feeling angry. She tried to avoid acknowledging why she felt angry, but gave up after a while and faced herself squarely in the mirror.

"You don't even like Gawain," she said to her reflection. "So who gives a damn if he's currently snuggling up to your little sister, who you don't much like either?"

Thrix had difficulty in selecting her outfit for the day. She'd never been to a small rock gig before, and had to look long and hard in her walk-in wardrobes before she found anything appropriate.

Dominil MacRinnalch had slept later than she intended. It was some time since she'd had a lover and the release provided by sex, plus the laudanum she'd take the night before, sent her into a deep slumber. She awoke feeling calm and almost satisfied. Pete woke at the sound of her dressing.

"Eh... do you want breakfast?" he ventured.

"No," said Dominil. She leaned over him. "I'd rather you did not mention this to anyone."

For a brief moment the still bleary-eyed Pete had the strange illusion that a great white wolf was standing over him. He blinked, and it

489

was only Dominil, but he felt quite shaken.

"Of course," he said, and he meant it. Dominil wasn't like other women, and he wouldn't have dared go against her wishes.

"I'll see you tonight," he called, as Dominil walked out the bedroom. She didn't reply.

Markus MacRinnalch rose later than most other inhabitants of the castle. The look-outs the walls had changed and the werewolf defenders were at their posts long before the captain of the castle guard made his appearance. Markus was feeling satisfied. His only worry was that his mother might find out about his challenge to Wallace MacGregor and try to prevent it. If she did attempt to stop the fight, he'd be disgraced.

In his London mansion, Sarapen MacRinnalch was up very early, and felt vigorous and alive from the moment he opened his eyes. He was looking forward to this evening's events.

205

Gawain lay in bed with Kalix, and didn't want to leave. He only wanted to tell her he loved her, which he did, many times, and listen to Kalix say she loved him, which she also did, many times. But late in the afternoon he reminded her that she'd promised to go to the cousin's house to help Dominil.

"I don't want to go," said Kalix.

"I don't want you to go," said Gawain. "But you should."

Gawain felt that it would somehow be unlucky for them to celebrate their re-union with a broken promise. Kalix was still reluctant. Gawain encouraged her. Already he'd formed the impression that the responsibility of helping Dominil had been good for Kalix. She'd talked enthusiastically of how she was going to help carry the band's equipment.

"Dominil's designed T-shirts," said Kalix, and sounded enthusiastic again, before her voice fell. She held on tightly to Gawain.

"I don't want to leave you."

"We'll only be apart for a few hours," pointed out Gawain. "I'll come to the gig."

"And then we be together?" said Kalix.

"Yes," said Gawain. "We'll always be together."

Kalix felt intensely happy as she dressed, and for once her happiness didn't lurch into anxiety. She put on her new trousers which hung round her narrow hips, held in place by the new belt, then brushed her hair. Gawain had never seen her hair in such fine condition, so long and thick that she could wrap it around her like a cloak.

Gawain slipped quietly out of the house and made his way back to his small room in Camberwell. It was snowing and a cold wind blew through the streets but Gawain barely noticed. In the space of one night, he'd shed three years of misery. He was serious when he told Kalix they'd never be apart again. Though he'd been concerned to find that Kalix was indeed taking laudanum, he hadn't mentioned it. Perhaps, now that they were back together, she would no longer feel the need to use it.

Moonglow was surprised to arrive home and find a happy looking Kalix eating a bowl of cereal, without appearing to grimace or threaten to vomit.

"Gawain rescued me!" Kalix said, and told her all about it. It was a dramatic tale.

"I dreamed we met," said Kalix. "And then he rescued me."

Kalix danced around the room. It was so unusual to see Kalix so cheerful that Moonglow managed to forget he own misery for a while. She laughed as Kalix danced. The young werewolf looked at the clock, and realised she was going to be late.

"See you later!" she cried, and hurried from the house. Tonight she'd remembered to put on her pendant. Now that Gawain had come back, Kalix wasn't so uncaring about her own safety.

Moonglow planned to catch up on her studies before going to the gig this evening. She was hoping that seeing the infamous MacRinnalch twins onstage would distract her from her worries though it struck her, rather depressingly, that she didn't have anyone to go with. Daniel, her once reliable companion, would probably be going with Alicia, her once reliable friend. Moonglow didn't much feel like being the extra person at their side.

Later in the day she heard voices in the living room. Daniel and a girl. Alicia no doubt. Moonglow hesitated. She didn't enjoy seeing them together. She shrugged, and went downstairs. Daniel was in the living room, but not with Alicia. Vex was sitting on his lap, staring into his eyes.

"Eh hello…" said Moonglow.

Daniel looked around, awkwardly.

"She's practising reading auras," explained Daniel, and looked embarrassed. Vex turned her head towards Moonglow.

"Hi Moonglow! I'm really making progress with reading auras. I was just telling Daniel about his secret thoughts and feelings."

"With you sitting on his lap I can probably tell what he's feeling," said Moonglow.

"Aunt Malvie can't stop me going to the gig now. Are you coming? Me and Daniel are going together."

"You are?"

They were. Daniel was apparently putting Alicia on hold for the evening to go out with Vex.

'Probably Alicia's at home dreaming about him right now,' thought Moonglow, and felt irritated. She went to the kitchen to make tea, and was sufficiently annoyed not to offer a cup to Daniel or Vex.

206

Dominil had a late breakfast in a café then picked up the van she'd hired for tonight. She called in at a print shop in Camden High Street to collect the small batch of Yum Yum Sugary Snacks T-shirts she'd had made on a whim, doing the design in a moment of boredom. Tonight she planned to either give them away, or sell them if anyone expressed enough interest to hand over money. T-shirts were good publicity.

Dominil had drawn a stylised version of the twins, mostly colourful hair, put the band's name underneath, and their set list beneath that, made up of some of the twins' more notable song titles, such as *Yum Yum Cute Boys* and *Stupid Werewolf Bitch*. Dominil knew that *Stupid Werewolf Bitch* had been written about her, as had *Evil White-Haired Slut*. It didn't annoy her. Nor did it amuse her. She didn't care.

It was snowing again. Bad for tonight, unfortunately. The cold might keep people in their homes. Beauty and Delicious had better be prepared for a low turnout.

'They'd better be prepared for anything,' thought Dominil. She entered the house expecting to find a chaotic scene as the twins made themselves ready. Instead she found the house completely silent. Dominil hurried through to Beauty's room.

"What are you doing?"

"Staying in bed."

Dominil frowned.

"Are you ready for the gig?"

"We're not playing."

At that moment the doorbell rang. Dominil was scowling as she answered the door to Kalix.

"What's wrong?"

"Beauty and Delicious have lost their nerve. They refuse to leave their beds."

"Oh," said Kalix.

Dominil paced the room.

"Gawain stayed with me last night," said Kalix.

Dominil cast a frozen stare at her.

"Am I meant to care about that? I have to get the twins onstage."

Dominil headed for the door.

"Are you going to shout at them?" asked Kalix.

"Damn right I'm going to shout at them," replied Dominil.

"I don't think that's a good idea," said Kalix. The glare which Dominil now turned on her was so fierce that Kalix took a step back.

"Do you have a better suggestion?"

"Well… you could…" Kalix found it hard to get her words out.

"Get to the point," growled Dominil.

Kalix wished she hadn't started the conversation, but struggled on.

"Maybe you should encourage them. You know… sort of try being nice. If you shout at them they'll just get more nervous and refuse to play."

"Do I strike you as the sort or werewolf who can be encouraging? Or nice?" said Dominil, in a tone of voice which suggested an icy gale blowing down from the frozen north.

"Well, sometimes," said Kalix.

Dominil seemed about to give vent to another furious retort, but paused, and looked surprised.

"I think you can be quite encouraging," said Kalix.

Dominil laughed. Kalix had never heard her laugh before. It was a

493

harsh sound.

"Nice. Encouraging," she muttered, as if she'd never heard the words before. "Possibly it is worth trying. Come with me."

Beauty was still hiding under the covers. Seeing that Dominil was unsure of how to begin, Kalix made a start.

"You should get up and get ready for the gig. Because you've made all this progress. All the hard work rehearsing. It would be a shame to throw it away."

There was no reply from Beauty.

"Kalix is right," said Dominil. "I have been impressed with your efforts. It would be foolish to let it be for nothing."

Beauty stuck her head out from under the covers. There was a bottle of whisky beside her on the pillow.

"You just want us to go to the castle and vote," she said to Dominil, and looked at her accusingly.

Dominil considered this for a few moments.

"That is not entirely true," she said eventually. "It was my main motivation, I admit. But since I've been here I've been impressed by your talent. You and your sister can be successful."

Beauty didn't look entirely convinced.

"You deserve to be successful," continued Dominil, with a final effort.

Beauty still hesitated.

"I have run out of encouragement," said Dominil. "If you don't get up of your own accord, I really will pick you up and throw you in the van."

The next half hour was utter chaos as Beauty and Delicious made themselves ready. They had to cram five hours worth of hairstyling, make-up and dressing into under thirty minutes. Dominil and Kalix were forced to withdraw to the kitchen to avoid being trampled in the melee. Kalix rather hoped that after her reasonably kind words to the twins, Dominil might have something positive to say about her momentous news concerning Gawain, but Dominil didn't mention it. She glanced at her watch.

"Almost time to go. Help me load the van."

"Gawain came and rescued me," said Kalix.

"You told me that already," replied Dominil.

207

The Fire Queen appeared in Thrix's apartment in a triumphant mood.

"The Queen of the Hiyasta will tonight crush and obliterate all who spoke harshly of her fashion achievements. Princess Kabachetka will acknowledge that Malveria is supreme."

She took the Enchantress in her arms and kissed her.

"Thank you for the wonderful clothes."

The Enchantress had been expecting Malveria to send a minion for the missing handbag but the Fire Queen explained that she had journeyed here herself in order to thank Thrix once again.

"Soon it will be time to mount the imperial carriage and dazzle the assembled hordes. But my preparations are now complete, and as in time of war, there is now nothing to do but wail till the appointed moment, and then attack. "

Malveria looked thoughtful.

"And I have been struck by another thought. Tonight you will confront Sarapen, yes?"

"It seems likely," said Thrix.

"For which reason I forgive you the rather utilitarian T-shirt you are wearing. It would not do to be fighting in over elaborate clothing."

"I'm hoping there's no fighting involved," said Thrix. "I'm planning to blanket the area with protection spells and keep him out."

"Yes, this is wise. And it leads me to my other thought. Sarapen is a mighty werewolf. He will have other werewolves with him. I do not wish to insult your skills in any way, but are you certain you can keep them all out? If you have the slightest doubt, I will attempt to add some power of my own to yours."

"I'm sure I can manage," replied the Enchantress.

"The white-haired werewolf has her doubts. When I last encountered her she asked if I could lend extra protection."

Thrix was moderately displeased to learn this.

"I told Dominil I could manage."

Malveria looked squarely at Thrix. As happened on those occasions when the Fire Queen turned her attention fully to the art of war, she was serious and to the point.

"You are not completely certain if you can manage. You don't know what forces Sarapen may being with him. If you block every door you may find he has a company of wolves on the roof. Take note of my words, dearest Enchantress."

Thrix didn't like any suggestion that she might be lacking in power. Had it been anyone else warning her, she'd have thrown them out.

"I'll be fine. Dominil is strong, and there will be four or five other MacRinnalchs in the audience. That should be enough to take care of any werewolf who breaches my spells. Not that any werewolf will breach my spells."

"Very well, stubborn Enchantress. But will you be insulted if I make a brief visit during the evening?"

"To check I'm all right?"

"Yes. I worry about you. And, I confess, about my idiotic niece, who will also be there, plaguing the audience."

"I won't be insulted," said Thrix. "Though I doubt you'll have time to visit, you'll be on your way to Livia's."

"Indeed I will. The population is even now gathering to see me ride off in my most splendid carriage. But I will visit if I can spare a moment."

Malveria thanked Thrix effusively for her new clothes once more.

"It is a victory for your skill, genius, artistry and unparalleled work ethic."

She de-materialised, leaving Thrix slightly annoyed at the thought of Dominil doubting her powers.

208

Clan secretary Rainal had rarely seen Verasa so livid.

"Markus challenged Wallace to single combat? Without consulting me?"

Verasa slammed her fist on a table. The table was a hefty old piece of wood, but no match for a werewolf's temper, and it split apart.

"Is my son losing his mind? Does he want to die?"

"He wants to prove himself," said Rainal.

Verasa growled, and kicked out at a small chair. It too disintegrated. The sound of it smashing jerked Verasa back to her senses. She looked at the pieces of wood.

"That chair," she said calmly, "has been in the family for five hundred years, and is quite irreplaceable. You see, Rainal, what a fury this has driven me to? I'm sure I never before broke two pieces of furniture in such a short space of time."

Rainal had found out most of the story concerning Markus's challenge. Soon it would be known by everyone.

"I can't believe Buvalis planned to betray the castle," said the Mistress of the Werewolves. "Damn that Kertal for corrupting her."

She shook her head.

"What a mess this all is."

Verasa was terrified at the thought of Markus falling before the awesome strength of Wallace MacGregor. Her immediate inclination had been to forbid the duel even if it meant putting Markus under guard. Now, as her reason returned, she realised that it was not so easy. If she were to ban the fight, Markus would be disgraced. He'd be regarded as a werewolf who hid behind his mother's skirts. No MacRinnalch would support him as Thane. She cursed her son for getting them into this mess.

"So what should we do about it?"

It was a dilemma. A werewolf who issued a challenge to single combat couldn't easily withdraw it. In all the history of the clan, Rainal couldn't remember a single instance of that happening.

"I'm not certain what to do for the best," he admitted.

"In one stroke Markus threatens to ruin all of our work," fumed Verasa. "All we have to do is sit tight in the castle and wait. They cannot take it. Eventually the rebellion would have petered out and by then I'd have had Markus declared Thane. Now he's about to risk his life before Sarapen even arrives."

"Don't you think Markus can defeat Wallace?" asked Rainal.

"No, I don't," replied Verasa. "And I'm not about to let him try."

Verasa paced her chambers, deep in thought. The single combat was due to take place in less than ten hours and she had to find some way of guaranteeing Markus's safety. She poured herself a goblet of wine and drank it down quickly, then lit another cigarette. Finally she told Rainal to send for Markus.

"And remain here when he arrives. If I'm left alone with him I might start breaking the furniture again."

209

Kalix was intrigued by all the events surrounding the gig. She rode in the van while Dominil picked up the other musicians, helping to load their equipment and then carry it into the venue. She watched as the twins set up, then listened to their sound check. It didn't go all that well, and Beauty and Delicious were agitated when they came off-stage. They went downstairs to meet friends in the bar.

Kalix and Dominil had both taken laudanum before coming out. Each knew that the other had, but they didn't mention it. Kalix sipped from a bottle of beer, and studied the inky stamp on the back of her hand. It meant she could come in and out of the gig without paying, because she was helping the band. Again, Kalix felt important. Dominil went downstairs to check that the twins were not getting too drunk, but Kalix didn't have to sit on her own for long. Daniel and Vex arrived early, due to Vex's eagerness to be here. The young fire elemental had never been to a gig before and was feverish with excitement. With her youthful, honey coloured complexion, her wildly spiked and bleached hair, her colourful, mismatched clothes, and a pair of boots large enough to anchor her skinny frame firmly to the ground, she looked strange, but beautiful and exotic. Daniel walked in rather proudly at her side. Kalix asked where Moonglow was.

"She's coming along later," Daniel said. "She's in a funny mood."

Downstairs Dominil was attempting to regulate the twins' alcohol intake. This was difficult because they were at the heart of a great group of friends and acquaintances. The venue was filling up. Despite the bad weather, it seemed there was enough local interest in the notorious Beauty and Delicious to draw a reasonable audience. She was forced to abandon her guardianship of the twins when Thrix arrived. Some sleep, her own werewolf vitality and the expert application of cosmetics had restored the Enchantress to her former golden beauty. Despite the prospect of a confrontation with Sarapen, Thrix had no intention of turning up anywhere looking less than her best. She informed Dominil that her spells were in place.

"You seem uncomfortable," said Dominil. "Is there some problem with the sorcery?"

"None at all," replied Thrix. "I'm uncomfortable because I'm in a bar in Camden with a lot of nineteen year old boys gawking at me."

"I feel this too," admitted Dominil.

At a table in the far corner were four men who Thrix recognised as MacRinnalchs, in the employment of Verasa.

"Our guards for the night?"

Dominil nodded. The Enchantress noticed Dominil's T-shirt under her open coat.

"What's the writing?"

"The band's set list."

Thrix read it with interest.

"*Stupid Werewolf Bitch? Evil White-Haired Slut?*" She laughed. "They wrote two songs about you."

"Three," said Dominil. "They encore with *Vile Werewolf Whore.*"

Kalix arrived in the downstairs room, looking for Gawain. She was disappointed not to find him there, and gravitated towards Dominil. At that moment Beauty and Delicious came over to complain to Dominil that the venue wasn't giving them enough free drinks.

"Then don't drink any more," said Dominil.

Beauty was not impressed.

"That's your solution?"

"Yes."

"You're the worst manager in the world," said Delicious.

The bar was now busy. When the MacRinnalch women came briefly together, the din in the room noticeably diminished. As Kalix, Dominil, Thrix, Butix and Delix talked, all eyes were drawn to them. Young men all around the room lost interest in whoever they were with, and gazed with wonder at the sight. It seemed as if five of the most beautiful and colourful women in the world had suddenly stepped out of a magazine and into the bar. Many people decided there and then that no matter what Yum Yum Sugary Snacks sounded like, they were going to come back and see them again.

210

By the time Markus answered his mother's summons, the Mistress of the Werewolves had her temper under control. It didn't prevent her from lecturing him at length about the stupidity of his behaviour.

"Is this your idea of the modern world? A challenge to single combat? Is this how you plan to run the clan's affairs after I make you Thane?"

"I can't be Thane if no one respects me," protested Markus.

"Do you want to be well respected and dead?" roared Verasa. "Isn't it enough that Sarapen wants to kill you? Do you have to let Wallace MacGregor do his work for him?"

Markus was annoyed.

"I can defeat Wallace MacGregor."

Verasa was about to tell her son that no, he couldn't, but bit back the words. If the fight had to go ahead, there was no point in destroying her son's confidence.

"There's no reason for this," she said, instead. "Once the council votes for you the Baron's rebellion will wither away."

Markus, however, was resolute. He stared at his mother defiantly.

"You can't stop it now."

Verasa lit a cigarette. Unfortunately, Markus was right.

"Very well. If the single combat is to go ahead, it will go ahead in a dignified manner. Rainal, send for Eskandor. We'll issue the challenge to Wallace through Baron MacGregor, as it should have been issued in the first place. The combatants will meet in front of the castle, in full view of the clans. I won't have a combat involving my son carried out like some secret street brawl."

Rainal was taken by surprise. The Mistress of the Werewolves was giving in. She was going to allow the fight to take place. No matter how much disgrace it would have brought on Markus to cancel it, Rainal had not expected her to let it proceed.

Realising that he'd won the point, Markus was pleased. He tried to reassure his mother, telling her that as the son of the Thane, and a MacRinnalch, he could overcome Wallace. Verasa was not reassured, but pretended to have confidence. If the single combat had to go ahead, it would be as well to send Markus out in as good a frame of mind as possible. Afterwards was another matter. If Markus managed to survive this affair, Verasa swore she'd rein him in, and never let such a situation arise again.

211

Moonglow trudged through the snow to the tube station beside the Oval Cricket Ground. Unlike Daniel, she'd never been inside the stadium. The sight of it annoyed her. Anything Daniel liked seemed aggravating just now. Moonglow was feeling hard done by. After all her efforts to help Daniel find some sort of social life, and to make sure he wasn't left out, here she was, going to the gig on her own while Daniel rushed off early with Vex. Moonglow had been tempted to ask Alicia to accompany her. That would certainly teach Daniel, if she turned up with his second girlfriend. How had Daniel managed to secure two girlfriends? It seemed to go against the laws of nature.

It had taken Moonglow a long time to get ready. While making up her eyes she'd had a sudden powerful memory of Markus which had made her cry. While brushing her long black hair she'd felt suddenly annoyed at Daniel, and pulled so hard on the brush she yelped in pain. While putting on her favourite black lace-up spiked-heel boots she'd thought of Kalix, who would no doubt spend the entire evening wrapped around Gawain, completely ignoring Moonglow. The distraction made Moonglow miss an eyelet with a lace, and she had to start all over again. When Alicia phoned, looking for Daniel, and Moonglow was obliged to lie on his behalf, she could barely be civil.

At the end of it all, however, she was looking very fine. Black clad, with dark make-up, her favourite piece of Victorian lace draped over a shiny black corset, a long black skirt, rather tight, and her boots looking dangerously pointed. Moonglow was satisfied when she looked in the mirror.

'I am the spurned woman from hell,' she thought. 'Possibly out for revenge.'

By the time she arrived in Camden the first band had already played, the twins were drunk, and Kalix was sitting on Gawain's lap. Moonglow studied Gawain with interest and thought, as most young women would have, that he was certainly attractive, in a brooding sort of way. If you had to sit on someone's lap, he wasn't a bad choice. Gawain wasn't as beautiful as Markus, but he was handsome, and charismatic.

Daniel and Vex were standing in front of the stage. Dominil was nearby but the white-haired werewolf was too busy to acknowledge her, even though only last week Moonglow had helped her translate some lines of Sumerian. Thrix was surrounded by a gaggle of young men. Moonglow stood on her own, and felt awkward. The second band were coming on. Moonglow watched for a while. She was standing behind a rather nondescript looking man, slightly older than most of the audience, who seemed completely absorbed by their music.

The man was not at all absorbed by the band's music. He was far more interested in the werewolves in the room. It was Madrigal, Sarapen's agent, here to spy. Madrigal was unusually excited, though no one could have guessed. Tonight he was to report to Sarapen. And then, Sarapen promised, he'd make him into a werewolf.

He wasn't the only person in the audience more interested in werewolves than the band onstage. The Guild had two spies here. They were new members of the Guild, and neither of them had ever been close to a werewolf before. There was nothing in their auras or scent to connect them with werewolf hunting. Even the Enchantress, who was constantly checking the venue for signs of trouble, couldn't pick them out as hunters.

Dominil went backstage to check on the twins. They were due onstage soon. With so many distractions in the bar downstairs, it had proved impossible to keep the sisters sober.

"How does this compare with their previous states?" she asked Pete.

"They can still walk. That's better than last time."

While Dominil tried to marshal the band, others nearby were marshalling their troops. Mr Carmichael waited with a group of well armed hunters in a small hotel in Kentish Town, just north of Camden. The hotel was owned by the Guild, and it had been purposely left empty for tonight. Mr Carmichael and his senior officers went round checking that every man's gun was loaded with silver bullets. He made a short speech about how this day would go down in the history of the Avenaris Guild. They were about to kill some of the most highly ranked werewolves in the country.

Sarapen was secreted in a warehouse in King's Cross, just ten minutes south of where the twins were playing. Decembrius was with him, and the Douglas-MacPhees. Sarapen had six personal bodyguards, and fourteen other werewolf warriors, all specially selected for their strength and their ability to transform without the full moon. Twenty-five werewolves in all. More than enough to deal with those who were at the gig.

The temperature in the warehouse rose slightly, and there was a hint of lavender in the air. Princess Kabachetka materialised at Sarapen's side. The Princess wore a dark jacket and trousers, not unlike those of the werewolves who waited to mount their attack, but her hair had already been arrayed for the Sorceress Livia's celebration. It tumbled down in a yellow stream over her shoulders, gleaming under the warehouse lights. Decembrius looked at her with more appreciation than did Sarapen. The Princess kissed Sarapen on the cheek, and smiled as he involuntarily drew back.

"Have you brought everything?" she asked.

Sarapen nodded, and motioned to Andris. The werewolf brought forward a small bundle of herbs, a phial of blood and a silver bowl, which he handled very carefully. The Princess nodded.

"Good. Everything for my sorcery. Will it be soon? I have a very pressing engagement."

"It will be soon," said Sarapen. "Very soon."

212

The Mistress of the Werewolves draped the great green cloak with white fur trimming round her shoulders. It was one of the badges of her rank and though she didn't much care for the garment there were times when it was appropriate. She placed a small golden tiara in her hair, an old piece of clan jewellery that usually resided in the castle museum. It had been given by Thane Durghaid MacRinnalch to his wife on the occasion of their marriage, in the year 1087. Then she took up the broadsword of Avreg MacRinnalch, the great Grey Wolf, Thane in the ninth century.

Rainal had often seen the Mistress of the Werewolves wearing the cloak and tiara, but he was surprised to see her with the broadsword. Avreg MacRinnalch's sword was traditionally only carried by the Thane.

"I am acting Thane," said Verasa, calmly. "I'm entitled to wear it."

They walked together through the long stone corridor that led from Verasa's chambers to the central courtyard.

"Did you ever think of being Thane yourself?" asked Rainal.

"Yes," admitted Verasa. "I considered it."

Of the nineteen werewolves who had been Thane since Avreg, two had been female: Heather Ugraich MacRinnalch, and Eustacia MacBruce MacRinnalch. Both had taken the position after bloody strife against their rivals. In each case there had been no agreed automatic heir to the throne. That was not the case today. For Verasa to seek the position when there were two male children already born would have been a breach of tradition.

"I wouldn't have minded the breach of tradition," said Verasa. "But it's far better for the post to go to someone young and vigorous. Markus will be an excellent Thane."

Now that Verasa had re-issued the challenge in the proper manner, everyone knew of the affair. As night fell and the moon rose, the werewolves in the castle gathered on the walls to look out, and the massed forces of the Barons arrayed themselves in a huge semi circle in front of the castle gates. The atmosphere was one of keen anticipation. Although Verasa had made no agreement to give up the castle if Markus was defeated, just as the Barons had made no agreement to withdraw if Wallace was defeated, it was inevitable that the outcome of the war would be influenced by the result of the single combat.

Buvalis had been incarcerated, along with Kertal, and a new personal assistant, Erenx MacRinnalch, was waiting for Verasa. As the Mistress of the Werewolves reached the castle gates, a platoon of bodyguards fell in around her. When the gates swung open and the portcullis was raised, she strode without hesitation across the drawbridge towards the massed ranks of her foes. Light snow was falling from the pitch black sky and the flakes hissed as they struck the burning torches carried by Verasa's attendants. Baron MacGregor came towards her. Behind him was the young Baron MacAllister with his sister Morag at his side, and beside them was Euan, son of Baron MacPhee. Their attendants followed on.

The Mistress of the Werewolves greeted her enemies with a polite nod. Baron MacGregor, the senior Baron in attendance, hesitated, feeling that perhaps some discussion might be appropriate, but faced with Verasa's calm air, he could think of nothing to say. They were here to oversee a fight, not to negotiate.

"Is Wallace ready?" asked Verasa.

"He is. Is Markus?"

"He is."

From the look on Baron MacGregor's face, Verasa guessed that he was no more keen to see his son Wallace risk his life than she was to see Markus in such peril. But it was done now, and there was no going back. Wallace emerged from the mass of his father's attendants, towering over all of them. At the same time Markus walked swiftly from the castle to take his place at Verasa's side.

Verasa signalled to her assistant Erenx, who stepped forward with a tray on which there were four goblets and a crystal decanter. Erenx poured whisky from the decanter into each of the goblets, and handed them to the Mistress of the Werewolves, Baron MacGregor, Markus MacRinnalch, and Wallace MacGregor. Each of them drank it down in a gulp, and replaced their goblets on the tray. The MacRinnalch whisky was usually a token of friendship; it could also be the sign that formalities were over, and it was time to fight.

Verasa stepped backwards. The Barons withdrew, leaving a clear space for Wallace and Markus. As the combatants neared each other they both took on their werewolf shape. At the same instant, Verasa transformed. So did the Barons, and every werewolf there who could. As a werewolf Wallace was massive. His jaws were huge and his teeth were like two rows of daggers. In front of him Markus suddenly looked very small.

213

Dominil was surprised to realise that she really wanted the twins to do well. It was not particularly rational. After all, it didn't matter to her how they played. Her task had been to recruit musicians and find them a gig. She had succeeded in this, no matter what happened onstage. Her mouth twitched, almost imperceptibly. Dominil was smiling to herself. She wouldn't have thought that she'd ever care about the fortunes of two degenerate werewolves fronting a band called Yum Yum Sugary Snacks, yet here she was, willing them on. Dominil still hoped that Sarapen was going to arrive. But not until after the twins played.

As Beauty and Delicious stumbled on to the stage, the signs were not good. The young werewolves were nervous. The other musicians quickly made themselves ready but both Beauty and Delicious fumbled with their guitars and microphones. They took such a long time over it all that people in the audience became restless. Delicious was-n't happy with her tuning, and wandered to the side of the stage to check it. Two young men in the audience, who probably knew the twins, shouted out some genial abuse. It wasn't meant to be particularly hostile but Dominil noticed that Beauty stiffened up when she heard it. Delicious was taking an age to re-tune her guitar in the wings and Beauty looked like she might want to join her. There were a few more derisive calls from the audience, not so friendly this time.

Dominil frowned. At this rate the girls would never get started. She strode swiftly to the side of the stage to confront Beauty, who had now been joined by her sister. The audience was becoming restless. Something had to be done quickly. The werewolves were behind a speaker stack, hidden from the crowd. Dominil let her face flicker, the first stage of transformation into her werewolf shape, and bared her fangs.

"Get out there and play," she snarled.

Beauty and Delicious stepped back sharply onto the stage. Dominil strode clear of the speaker and made a signal to Pete the guitarist. Understanding her meaning, he started up the first song, *Yum Yum Cute Boys*. The gig was finally underway.

214

Markus was quicker than Wallace, but if he was the more skilful fighter, he hadn't yet been able to display it. After some initial weaving around, Wallace had managed to grab Markus and pull him towards him. He now held him in a bear hug. Markus's feet were off the ground and the breath was being crushed from his body. The werewolves behind the Barons roared Wallace on as he squeezed the life from the pretender to the Thaneship.

Markus gasped, and tried to bring his jaws down to bite at Wallace's face but Wallace buried his snout in Markus's neck and squeezed harder. The Mistress of the Werewolves struggled to keep her composure as she watched her son suffering.

Markus forced himself to think clearly. His youthful struggles with Sarapen had given him experience of fighting a stronger opponent. He swung his right arm and used the inside of his paw to strike Wallace

506

full on the ear and the force of the blow made Wallace loosen his grip. Markus was able to land a raking slash with his talons over Wallace's face. Wallace roared in pain, and dropped Markus to the ground. Markus sprang to his feet, with snow on his coat, and leapt to attack his opponent. He managed to land a few more blows before his massive opponent's strength re-asserted itself. Though Wallace could land only one strike to Markus's three, he finally connected with a great swipe that almost took Markus's head from his shoulders, and Markus crashed to the ground. He scrambled desperately to rise, knowing that if Wallace once got his jaws around his neck, and pinned him to the ground, the fight would be over. Markus was forced to retreat, and Wallace's supporters roared him on as he advanced relentlessly.

Baron MacGregor did not join in with the cheering. He was still concerned over the welfare of his son, though his apprehension was fading. It was clear to every onlooker that it was only a matter of time before Wallace was the victor. Both werewolves had suffered injury but Wallace was obviously the stronger and Markus would eventually fall.

215

Malveria approached the upstairs room where the bands played. She found her entrance blocked by a young woman sitting at a table.

"I have come to the gig," announced Malveria. "Gig is the correct term, I believe?"

The young woman looked at her blankly. Malveria frowned, and wondered who this dull servant was.

"Please tell your master I am here," said the Fire Queen, civily.

"What?"

Malveria's frown deepened. She deplored the practice of putting one's less intelligent servants in positions where they may have to encounter guests. The Enchantress appeared from inside the room.

"Malveria! Are you coming in?"

"This servant is not at all welcoming."

"You have to pay," explained Thrix. Seeing her friend's confusion – Malveria had never paid to enter anything before – Thrix took some money from her purse and handed it over, then escorted Malveria through the door. Once inside she discreetly caused a full glass of wine to appear in her hand.

"There's really nothing worth having at the bar."

Malveria told Thrix that though her carriage was now waiting for her outside her palace, she did not wish to make the journey to Livia's quite yet.

"It would be rather unbecoming for the Queen of the Hiyasta to arrive early, like someone who is eager for a free meal. I shall make them wait a little longer. Incidentally, I had an interesting encounter outside this building."

"Who with?"

"Werewolf hunters, I believe."

"What?"

"Perhaps twenty or so. An unpleasant gathering of men, including several who really should take more care of their physiques. Even if one is dedicated to hunting werewolves, there is no excuse for letting oneself become flabby."

"What happened?" asked Thrix, urgently.

"Nothing, really," replied Malveria. She twitched one finger, creating a little bubble of quiet in which they could hear each other over the noise of the band.

"I sensed your spells of protection and bafflement outside the building. The hunters were confused, but I suspected there may have been one among them who had knowledge of sorcery. Probably rudimentary, but he may have guessed they were close to you. I added a little of my magic to yours and convinced them that the building they sought was some way south of here. They have now gone to hunt werewolves in another place."

Malveria beamed.

"I trust you are not offended by my assistance?"

"Not. I'm grateful. Did you sense Sarapen anywhere close?"

The Fire Queen shook her head. There was an amused gleam in her eye.

"But I do sense the handsome Gawain. You have brought the young wolf here for some later entertainment?"

Thrix scowled.

"If he's entertaining someone later it won't be me."

She directed her gaze to where Gawain and Kalix shared a chair.

508

"Ah," Malveria nodded sympathetically. "He has transferred his attentions to the other sister. I am sorry, Enchantress."

"No need to feel sorry," replied Thrix. "I don't even like him. He was just convenient for a while."

"Indeed," replied Malveria. Showing unusual tact, she said no more, though it was plain to her that Thrix was irritated. Thrix hadn't been in love with Gawain, by any means. Nonetheless, it wasn't exactly pleasant to see the werewolf she'd been sleeping with now having a much better time with her sister. When Gawain arrived he'd greeted Thrix as politely as he could, but it was obvious he was embarrassed to see her.

Malveria's attention was caught by some energetic movement.

"What is my niece doing?"

"Dancing?"

"Dancing? In what way would that qualify as dancing?"

After their shaky start Yum Yum Sugary Snacks had forgotten their nerves, built up momentum, and were now thrashing their way through their set with tremendous enthusiasm. Vex was flinging herself around in front of the stage. She was convinced that watching Yum Yum Sugary Snacks was the finest experience ever had by anyone, anywhere. She was completely engrossed in noise, music and excitement. Vex loved Yum Yum Sugary Snacks, and danced with abandon, completely oblivious to everyone around her.

Kalix didn't feel like dancing – it would have meant letting go of Gawain – but she was enjoying the gig. She didn't like the band as much as the Runaways but she liked them well enough. There was something about the raw noise coming of the stage that stirred her. She held Gawain tightly, and felt happy.

"Our next song's called *Evil White-Haired Slut*," yelled Delicious.

If Dominil minded, she didn't show it. The gig had gone well and the audience had responded enthusiastically. So far, everything was satisfactory. If she could plunge the Begravar knife into Sarapen's heart, the evening would be a total success.

216

Madrigal, a small, nondescript man, but intelligent, and tenacious, drove a motorbike swiftly from Camden to King's Cross. He'd called ahead, and Sarapen was expecting him.

"Well?" said Sarapen.

"They'll finish playing soon. There are nine werewolves in the room."

Sarapen nodded. Nine werewolves. He knew that Butix and Delix could not transform this night. Which left seven. Thrix and Dominil were strong. So was Kalix, in combat. As for the four bodyguards, they were probably experienced fighters. It was not enough to worry Sarapen. He had twenty-four werewolves at his side, plus a powerful elemental princess. With his overwhelming advantage in numbers, he hoped to sweep up his enemies in the space of a few seconds, and end the affair quickly. He planned to attack as late as possible, when the cousins were packing up their equipment and the audience had departed. The only obstacle had been the Enchantress's sorcery. Now that Princess Kabachetka stood at his side, it was no longer a problem.

"Good," said Sarapen. "You've done well. You have always done well for me, Madrigal."

Madrigal stepped forward. He had been waiting for this moment all his life. He was going to be werewolf. The great Sarapen himself was going to share his blood and transform him. Sarapen changed into his werewolf shape. He bent down, took Madrigal in his jaws, and snapped his neck. Madrigal fell down dead. Sarapen looked at the corpse with contempt.

"I would never make a werewolf from a spy such as you," he growled.

"Quite," said Princess Kabachetka. "But could we get on now? I'm planning a late arrival at the Sorceress Livia's but even so, time is pressing."

"We will – " began Sarapen, but halted as the Hainusta Princess held up her hand. She had sensed something.

"Is there any reason for twenty men to be creeping into this warehouse?"

Sarapen reacted instantly.

"Hunters," he hissed. "Everyone get out of sight."

Sarapen's troops melted into the shadows. The hunters from the Guild, confused by the Fire Queen's sorcery, had come further south than they intended. When they reached King's Cross, the one among them with powers of seeing detected the presence of werewolves. The hunters drew their weapons, and advanced.

217

Markus had fought valiantly but Wallace's superior strength was now starting to tell. The Barons' wolves roared encouragement while the MacRinnalchs looked on in mournful silence. Markus was now down on one knee, desperately fending off blows. Blood ran freely down his mane from ten or more cuts. Rainal glanced over at the Mistress of the Werewolves, looking for a signal that he should intervene. If Markus surrendered, his life could still be spared. Verasa remained impassive, and gave no signal. She stood quite still, not even brushing off the snow that settled on her werewolf snout.

Wallace finally succeeded in dragging Markus to the ground, crushing him with his weight, and fixing his jaws around Markus's throat.

"Stop the fight!" hissed Rainal to Verasa. "Tell Markus to yield!"

Up on the battlements, Beatrice MacRinnalch moaned in torment as she watched her lover being savagely mauled, but there was no sound from Verasa. She stood in silence, and watched the fight.

Markus writhed under the jaws of Wallace. His arms flailed but his blows were becoming weaker, unable to hurt his opponent. Or so it seemed, right up till the moment when Wallace dragged Markus's head back to snap his neck. Markus connected with a blow to the side of Wallace's face. It was no stronger than any of the other blows which Wallace had shrugged off, but it seemed to have more effect. Wallace sagged. Markus hit him again, and Wallace sat back, loosening his grip. Markus was able to hurl him off and scramble to his feet. Sensing his opportunity, he threw himself at Wallace, reigning blows on him and tearing at him with his claws. Wallace reeled backwards through the snow, fending him off as best he could.

"His strength has gone," said Verasa, calmly. "I knew it would."

Now Wallace's supporters fell silent as cheering erupted from the

MacRinnalchs on the castle walls. Markus continued to pound Wallace. Though he had been all but spent, the scent of victory renewed his vigour and when Wallace himself sank to one knee, exhausted, Markus leapt on him and fastened his jaws round his neck. Wallace collapsed. His resistance was gone. Abruptly Verasa stepped forward. She hurried across the trampled, blood-stained snow and put her hand on her son's shoulder, then looked up at Baron MacGregor.

"Do you admit defeat?" she called.

Her question was heard by the hundreds of silent werewolves who surrounded the Baron. If the Baron accepted mercy from the Mistress of the Werewolves, the MacGregors could no longer continue to besiege the castle. Everyone knew it. Baron MacGregor walked forward.

"Stop the fight," he said.

Markus allowed Verasa to draw him away. He was satisfied with his victory. He didn't have to kill Wallace. Verasa signalled to her assistant Erenx and she led Markus back into the castle where Verasa's doctor was waiting to attend to his wounds. The Mistress of the Werewolves nodded courteously to Baron MacGregor, turned on her heel, and followed Markus back into the castle.

"That was far too close," muttered Rainal, at her side.

"I had confidence in my son," said Verasa.

"Would you have let him die?"

"Markus would not have wanted me to intervene on his behalf," replied Verasa. "It would have sullied his honour."

Rainal was again impressed at Verasa's coolness in the face of danger. But Rainal was not privy to the Mistress of the Werewolves' every secret. He didn't know, for instance, that Eskandor MacRinnalch was hiding in a tower on the castle walls, with a sniper's rifle loaded with silver bullets, under orders from Verasa to shoot Wallace dead if he seemed to be on the verge of killing Markus. He didn't know that Verasa herself had a small pistol hidden in her cloak, also loaded with silver bullets, which she would have used if necessary. Rather than let Markus die she would have broken all werewolf taboos by killing Wallace, even as the clans looked on. And Rainal didn't know, and would never know, that before the whisky was drunk at the start of the fight, the Mistress of the Werewolves had arranged for the inside of Wallace's goblet to be smeared with poison. The poison had slowly sapped his strength, making it seem as if he was simply worn-out from fighting. Verasa, observing the struggle, had felt a twinge of concern that she might have used too little of the poison. As it turned out, it had done its job perfectly. To those who saw the combat, Wallace had just burned himself out, and the superior stamina and spirit of Markus had carried the day. The poison was debilitating but not lethal. By the time Wallace recovered from his injuries, the substance would have disappeared from his body. No one would ever guess what had happened, least of all Markus.

The Mistress of the Werewolves hadn't told her son of her precautions. Despite this, he'd gone out to fight the fearsome Wallace, and had not hesitated for an instant. Verasa felt proud of him. Few werewolves who watched the single combat now believed he was unworthy of the Thaneship. Many of them might still favour Sarapen, but it couldn't be said that Markus's spirit was weak.

218

Yum Yum Sugary Snacks were finishing their set in fine style. The twins rampaged around the stage, singing, screaming, and knocking things over. The gig had been a great success; much better than anyone previously acquainted with the sisters had anticipated. Dominil was satisfied. In her detached way, she found herself disapproving of the number of mistakes the band made, but she knew it didn't matter. The sisters' raw talent and enthusiasm was enough for tonight.

'Though if I am ever responsible for a studio recording,' she mused. 'I'll make sure it is a good deal more competent.'

Vex was glowing. She hadn't stopped dancing the entire night. Daniel couldn't keep up, and now sat at a table nearby, occasionally bringing her drinks. Further back, Malveria was perplexed. She was used to the stately music played at Hiyasta ceremonies. The sounds emanating from the stage didn't sound like music at all. The Enchantress wasn't enjoying it any more than the Fire Queen. Thrashing guitars had never been to her taste. Besides, she was on the alert for Sarapen or the Guild, and continually scanned the surrounding area, checking that her protection spells were all in place.

Gawain held on tightly to Kalix, and was surprised when he felt someone trying to pull her from his lap. It was Vex.

"Stop being so boring," she was saying to Kalix. "You've been sitting there all night. Come and dance."

"The band's finished," said Kalix.

"They're going to play an encore. Come and dance!"

Vex's eyes shone with enthusiasm. She started tugging at Gawain. Gawain felt awkward.

"I don't dance," he said.

"What do you mean you don't dance?"

"I'm… eh…"

"Brooding and poetic," said Kalix, finishing his sentence for him, and kissing his forehead. Vex looked disappointed.

"You go," said Gawain to Kalix.

Kalix allowed herself to be dragged forward by Vex, just as Yum Yum Sugary Snacks were returning for their encore, *Vile Werewolf Whore,* a particularly virulent denunciation of anything to do with white-haired werewolves from Castle MacRinnalch.

Watching Kalix and Vex dance, the Fire Queen shook her head. She was struck by the huge contrast between Vex's behaviour and her own when she was that age. Then Malveria had been fighting a guerrilla war, dressed in rags and sleeping in a cave with a sword in her hand. Vex slept in a huge bed under a pink quilt and danced without a care in the world. Tomorrow Malveria would scold her thoroughly for her foolish behaviour, and make sure she attended all her lessons. But it was good to see her niece happy.

Thrix glanced at Gawain. He was transfixed by the sight of Kalix in motion. The Enchantress scowled, and snapped her fingers, filling her glass with whisky. She drank it back quickly, then turned her attention back to her protection spells. They were all in order. No enemies were near.

"Yes, I sense nothing out of order," agreed Malveria. "And now it is time for me to go. Soon the appalling Princess Kabachetka will know she has been defeated by the magnificent Malveria Maladisia."

"Maladisia?" said Thrix. She knew many of the Queens names, but had never heard that one.

"One of my most secret names," said the Queen. "I give it to you as a present, because of your tireless work on my behalf. With that name, you can always call me to your side."

As the band's set ended, the audience clapped and cheered. Dominil

514

was gratified. She could report to the Mistress of the Werewolves that her mission had been successful. But as Beauty and Delicious left the stage, she turned towards the entrance and wondered what had happened to Sarapen. She'd been sure he would arrive.

This part of the venue was now closing. Though the band could remain while they packed up their equipment, everyone else had to go downstairs. Dominil didn't want anyone to become separated so she quickly gathered up every werewolf in the room.

"We're with the band," she said, to the bouncer who was asking them to leave. The bouncer shrugged and turned his attention to hurrying the other stragglers downstairs.

Sarapen and his werewolves drove from King's Cross towards Camden. The fight in the warehouse had been brief. The hunters had seemed disorientated as they arrived in the warehouse and they'd been ambushed and slaughtered. The Guild's careful preparations had been fatally disrupted by Malveria's intervention. They had expected to make an attack on a small group of unprepared werewolf musicians. Instead they'd found themselves surrounded by a superior force of trained warriors. Sarapen's wolves had all but annihilated them, and few of the hunters made it out of the warehouse alive.

In the brief melee Sarapen had lost five werewolves. The hunters all had guns with silver bullets, and even the swiftness of the ambush hadn't prevented them from firing a volley, many of them shooting from close range. Inevitably some bullets found their targets. Sarapen's plan was unaffected; he still had plenty of wolves to complete his task.

The rest of their musicians had already gone downstairs and Beauty and Delicious were packing away their guitars. Dominil cast a quizzical look towards Thrix, but Thrix shook her head. There were no enemies nearby. Dominil was disappointed. Vex was still excited.

"Weren't the band great?" she screamed at her aunt.

Before Malveria could compose a suitably withering reply, there was a low growl from the corridor outside. A huge wolf padded into the room. Sarapen was here.

219

Markus's skin was lacerated in many places and he was covered in bruises but he was so elated he hardly noticed the pain. He would have remained in the courtyard, accepting the congratulations of the MacRinnalchs, had Verasa not cut the celebration short, sending her son to his chambers for medical treatment. At the sight of blood flowing from her favourite son, she was moved almost to tears. She waited anxiously outside her son's rooms while the doctor examined him.

"What is taking so long?"

"Doctor Angus is very thorough," replied Rainal. "Don't worry, Markus is fine."

A tear rolled down Verasa's cheek which she wiped away angrily. Rainal pretended not to notice. Finally the doctor emerged. Angus MacRinnalch was grey-haired, old enough to be venerable, older even than Verasa. His manner was slightly brusque, and he dismissed Verasa's fears with a wave.

"Nothing wrong, a few cuts and bruises. Maybe a cracked rib, I'll need an X-ray to be sure."

"A cracked rib?" Verasa was aghast.

"It's a minor injury. If your son insists on fighting Wallace Mac-Gregor, it's fortunate he suffered nothing worse. Once he's rested and had a few wolf changes under the moon he'll be as good as new."

The doctor was spared further anxious questioning from Verasa by the unexpected appearance of Great Mother Dulupina. She moved slowly along the corridor towards them. The old werewolf greeted Doctor Angus before acknowledging Verasa. The doctor had ministered to Dulupina for many years, and she had a high regard for him.

"How is the boy?" she enquired.

"Well enough."

"Well enough for me to see him?"

"For a little while. "

Great Mother Dulupina spoke to the Mistress the Werewolves.

"He did well."

Dulupina, who had never had much regard for Markus, went into his chambers to congratulate him. Markus was lying on his bed. His eyelids were starting to droop, but his head rose sharply as he scented Dulupina. It was something out of the ordinary for her to visit. He struggled to rise.

"Stay where you are. Doctor Angus says you should rest," she said, in her soft, old voice. "I watched from my window. You did well."

Markus acknowledge this with a nod.

"It might now be that your mother can have you elected Thane," continued Dulupina.

She paused, and stared into the distance for a while.

"I prefer your older brother," she said eventually.

Markus wasn't sure what to say, and remained silent.

"I might not object to you as Thane," continued Dulupina. "You've shown you can fight. But I'll never support you if you let Kalix go free."

Dulupina looked at him sharply.

"Will you let her off? If you're Thane will you pardon her?"

Markus shook his head.

"I won't."

"Then I might support you," said Dulupina.

220

In the alley behind the bar in Camden, Princess Kabachetka worked her sorcery while the snow fell around her. It was sorcery not just to break down the Enchantress's spells of protection, and not just to mask Sarapen's approach. It was a spell to remove all sorcery. As the Princess spoke the final words, all magic in the area was nullified. The Enchantress was powerless, and so was the Fire Queen. There was nothing standing between Sarapen and his enemies.

Upstairs, Thrix was shocked at Sarapen's sudden appearance. She didn't understand how he could have arrived without her receiving a warning. It was impossible. But there he stood, in his full wolf form, huge and menacing. Vex was nearest to him. She giggled.

"A big wolf! He's so cute," she said, and started to pat his head.

Malveria spoke sharply to her niece.

"Agrivex. Please do not pat the werewolf. He is a deadly enemy."

"But he's so cute."

"Step away this instant!"

Vex withdrew, grumbling that her aunt never let her do anything.

Sarapen, possibly feeling that his dramatic entrance in wolf shape had been spoiled by Agrivex patting his head, swiftly assumed his human form.

"Greetings Thrix," he said.

"You're late," said the Enchantress. "The band's finished."

"I didn't come here to see the band."

"Just a social call then?"

Thrix stepped forward to confront her brother. She was struggling to remain calm. She tried scanning the area outside but she could detect nothing. Something was interfering with her spells.

"Yes," rumbled Sarapen. "You could say it was a social call."

At that moment Beauty and Delicious emerged from their dressing room. At the sight of Sarapen they froze, petrified. Sarapen looked at them, then swept his gaze over every other werewolf in the room.

"You will all surrender to me."

"Not very likely," responded Thrix, instantly.

Dominil advanced to stand at her side.

"You're surrounded and outnumbered," said Sarapen. "You can surrender or you can die."

"You dare to threaten members of the Great Council?" demanded Thrix.

"As you dared oppose me as Thane," responded Sarapen. "Don't strain yourself trying to eject me. Your sorcery will no longer work."

"Kabachetka!" cried the Fire Queen. "The stink of her cheap perfume is everywhere. She is behind this."

Sarapen nodded, then spoke severely to the Fire Queen. "This is none of your affair. I'll allow you to leave in peace." Sarapen looked towards Moonglow and Daniel. "You also may leave. As for the rest of you, you have a minute to decide your fate. Surrender or die, the choice is yours."

Sarapen changed back into a wolf and padded from the room. The Enchantress whirled towards the Fire Queen.

"Have you any sorcery?"

"Very little."

Malveria waved her hand. A weak beam of green light flickered towards the ceiling.

"And what I have is fading fast. It disturbs me greatly to admit it, but Kabachetka has outmanoeuvred us. She has brought sorcery here which in this realm I cannot defeat. There is nothing to do but leave immediately."

"What do you mean? We can't leave."

"We can," declared Malveria. "I retain just enough power to take me back to the palace. I believe I can carry you with me."

"I'm not leaving!" said Thrix.

"It's foolish to stay," said Malveria. "I sense many werewolves outside. They will kill all who oppose them. I must go quickly to Livia's, but I'll carry you to safety."

"We can't just run away and leave everyone!"

Malveria was unmoved.

"The true warrior knows when to retreat. There's no point in dying needlessly. Come with me now, Enchantress, before my power fades entirely."

The Enchantress refused to go.

"Very well," said the Fire Queen. "I thank you again for the clothes, and I say farewell."

Malveria ascended the thin ray of light, and vanished through the ceiling. There was a brief silence.

"Can we surrender?" suggested Beauty.

"No," said Dominil. "We fight." With that, Dominil transformed into her werewolf shape.

"But we can't transform," said Delicious, and looked scared.

Thrix hurried towards them.

"Get people at both exits," she said to Dominil. "Beauty and Delicious, sit down."

"Why?"

"Do as I say."

The twins sat. They both looked frightened. Kalix told Moonglow and Daniel that they must go.

"We're not leaving you here," said Moonglow.

"You don't know what's about to happen. Get out of here now."

"Kalix is right," said Gawain. "You should go."

"We should," agreed Daniel. He looked appealingly towards Moonglow. Seeing that her expression was set quite stubbornly, he sighed.

"But I guess we're staying."

The Enchantress placed one hand on each of the sisters' heads.

"What are you doing?"

"I'm reminding you how to become werewolf."

"We can't. Not till the wolf nights."

519

"You can. You used to know how."

The Enchantress's powers of sorcery were gone but Minerva had taught her more than sorcery. Before she'd ever shown Thrix a spell she'd taught her ways of controlling her mind.

"Look into my eyes," said Thrix, to Beauty. "And remember when you first ran through the forest."

Dominil was busy organising the defence. There were two doors, the front entrance and the fire exit at the back. She sent the four MacRinnalch guards to the fire exit and took up position with Kalix and Gawain at the front door. Gawain transformed, and snarled defiantly, ready to fight. Kalix remained as human, and seemed almost oblivious to their peril. She put her hand on Gawain's shaggy werewolf shoulder, and kept it there.

Dominil waited impassively. The Begravar knife was concealed in her bag. She transformed into her werewolf shape and discreetly slipped the knife into a harness on her thigh, where it was hidden by her fur. Beauty moaned, and wilted under the Enchantress's gaze. Suddenly she sat bolt upright. Then she laughed, and fell off her chair. As she hit the floor she transformed into a werewolf.

"Wow," she said, and shook her head. She looked up at her sister. "Get werewolfy. It's good."

From somewhere outside howling could be heard. Not the sound of werewolves, but the howling of dogs, terrified as they picked up the werewolves' scent.

"They're coming," said Dominil, softly.

Daniel and Moonglow backed away from the doors. Vex reappeared from the bathroom where she'd been giving her hair some attention. She seemed to have little idea of the danger they faced.

"Where's the big wolf? I want to pat him again."

Moonglow leaned towards Daniel, and whispered.

"So what's it like going out with her?"

"It has its good points," whispered Daniel. "Maybe a few bad points as well. Quite a lot of bad points, actually. You can't talk to Vex about much." His face fell. "It wasn't much of a date, really."

"You should've stuck with Alicia," said Moonglow.

"We don't really get on that well either," admitted Daniel. "I think she thinks it was a mistake when she dreamed about me."

"Thanks for letting me come here on my own tonight," said Moonglow, and managed to sound quite cutting, though they were still whispering.

"You didn't want to come out with us!"

"You didn't ask me. Just waltzed off with Vex before I was ready."

"I'd have waited if you'd said," protested Daniel.

Delicious fell off her chair, changed into a werewolf, and screamed with laughter. The Enchantress changed into her own werewolf shape, tossed some strands of long golden hair from her face, and snarled. It was some time since she'd fought with her talons and jaws but she didn't think she'd forgotten how. If she was about to die she'd take some of her foes with her.

A tiny beam of green light, weak and flickering, trickled down through the ceiling. It was the Fire Queen. She landed heavily on the floor, an expression of utter disgust on her face.

"Really Thrix, I believe you have infected me with this *work ethic* or something equally harmful. It is very bad of you. I should at this moment be riding in my carriage wearing my splendid new clothes and now I've returned to fight at your side. It is the utmost foolishness. We will all certainly die and I am quite powerless to help in any case."

The Fire Queen was carrying a club which a strong man would have struggled to lift. She tossed it casually over her shoulder and looked around her with immense displeasure. The Enchantress put her golden arm around the Fire Queen.

"Thanks for coming back."

Malveria pouted.

"I did not even have time to select a suitable weapon. The ceremonial mace from my carriage was all that was to hand."

Malveria's power was now completely dissipated. The Queen could not work magic and she couldn't leave. Thrix suddenly noticed that Moonglow and Daniel were still hanging around. She put her mouth to Moonglow's ear, and whispered. Moonglow looked surprised. She turned to Daniel.

"We have to go," she said.

"That's what I've been saying all along," replied Daniel, and dragged Moonglow from the room. The Fire Queen slipped off her high heels. She noticed that Vex had re-appeared, and barked at her.

"Agrivex. Find some place to hide and endeavour not to get killed."

"Right," said Vex.

Vex skipped past Malveria and Thrix, heading for the dressing room. As she passed them she halted, and her face broke into a broad grin.

"Wooaahh!" she cried, looking at Thrix. "You've been sleeping with *Gawain?*"

There was a shocked silence in the room.

"Agrivex!" yelled Malveria. "Stop talking nonsense and hide immediately."

"It's not nonsense," protested Vex. "I've been studying auras like you told me. Look, can't you see?"

Princes Kabachetka's sorcery had not only removed the Enchantress's spells of protection, it had also removed the spells she used to cover her association with Gawain. Though Gawain's aura was very faint on her, Vex had recognised it. It was just Thrix's misfortune that Malveria had made Agrivex attend to her studies.

"You most dismal of dismal girls," snarled the Fire Queen. "Can you do nothing right?"

"Hey," said Vex. "You told me to – "

There was a growl from the front of the room. A growl that should only have come from a werewolf's throat, but had come from that of a girl. Kalix's mouth was hanging open and her eyes were wild. She took a step away from Gawain, staring first at him and then at Thrix.

"I'll kill you," she said. "I'll – "

The rest of her sentence was lost as the fire exit burst open and a howling band of werewolves flooded into the room, led by the Douglas-MacPhees. Simultaneously, Sarapen, Andris and a host of others crashed through the front entrance, and leapt towards their prey.

221

The Merchant put down the phone. The telephone, along with everything else in his shop, was very old, a black bakelite receiver such as could hardly be found in the world anymore. The MacDoig preferred it that way.

"It's a strange business," he said to his son. "When a man – or a werewolf – can phone you up from a battlefield and report on affairs so quickly. I remember the days when the womenfolk would wait for weeks for news of the battle, never knowing if their men were alive or dead till a messenger arrived on horseback."

"What was the news?" asked the Young MacDoig.

"Markus MacRinnalch defeated Wallace MacGregor." The Merchant scratched his chin. "All fair and above board, so they say."

MacDoig took up the brass poker and prodded the fire. His ancient shop was draughty in winter, and the fire burned constantly.

"So they say," he repeated.

"You don't think so?"

MacDoig smiled.

"I'd say the chances of the Mistress of the Werewolves allowing Markus to fight Wallace MacGregor fair and square are quite slim, my boy. I've no doubt she worked some sleight of hand to help things along. She's a canny wolf, Verasa MacRinnalch."

MacDoig mused on the news. Verasa had won another round.

"The castle is still hers. That's all right for us. She's a fine customer."

"But Sarapen's a good customer too, father."

"True, very true. He's not a werewolf to scrimp and save when there's work needing done."

The Merchant chuckled.

"He'll be Thane yet, son. Mark my words."

The Merchant sipped his tumbler of whisky.

"Reduce the order for silver bullets. From what I hear, the Guild has a lot fewer hunters who'll be needing supplies."

222

Kalix's battle-madness gripped her as never before. She'd been mad before the battle even started. The revelation that Gawain had been sleeping with Thrix had devastated her. When a werewolf leapt on her, Kalix bit its neck so savagely she almost took its head off. She roared at the taste of blood and threw herself at her next opponent.

The small upstairs room was now a struggling, bloody melee of terrible werewolf violence. The defenders were outnumbered, but the odds were not quite as hopeless as they might have been. Sarapen had lost five werewolves to the Guild. Butix and Delix were unexpectedly in werewolf shape. It was still twenty against nine in Sarapen's favour but his opponents included Kalix, whose rage in combat made her almost unstoppable, Dominil, whose will could not be broken, and Gawain, whose fighting skills matched those of his warrior ancestors. Thrix herself, eldest daughter of the Thane, was immensely strong and savage in combat and even the twins were powerful as werewolves. In addition, the defenders had Malveria. The Fire Queen would have been unrecognisable to anyone who had only ever seen her sobbing over a pair of shoes. Malveria's strength was equal to that of a werewolf, and she had more experience of battle than anyone else in the room. She wielded her club so deftly that she was able to clear a space around Agrivex, pick her up, and throw her to temporary safety at the back of the stage.

"Stay there and – " Malveria's words were cut off as a werewolf leapt on her back, dragging her down onto the floor.

Dominil struggled to come to grips with Sarapen, attempting to batter her way past his bodyguards. Two of the MacRinnalchs who guarded the fire exit had now fallen. The Enchantress tried to bolster their forces at the back of the room but the Douglas-MacPhees pushed her back. More of Sarapen's werewolves forced their way into the room. Kalix slew another opponent then disappeared under two more.

The twins and the surviving MacRinnalch guards were forced back towards the stage while Kalix, Dominil and Gawain were engaged in the most savage fight with seven werewolves at the front of the room. The Enchantress found herself struggling with three enemies at once and she was dragged to the ground. She bit and clawed furiously, seeking to rise, but Andris MacAndris fell on her and fastened his teeth to her shoulder. The Enchantress was buried beneath her opponents and felt their claws and teeth cutting into her hide. The breath was being forced from her body and she couldn't even shout for help.

"Maladisia," she whispered.

Malveria was on the other side of the room, engaged with the enemy. Though the room reverberated with the sound of battle, and the Enchantress had spoken her secret name in a whisper, Malveria heard it. She threw off her attacker and leapt to where Thrix lay. She swung her club in a series of fierce arcs, beating back Andris and his two companions, then grabbed the Enchantress and hauled her to safety. The Enchantress sat gasping on the stage while Malveria stood in front of her, guarding her with her club. They had a second's respite before Dominil was picked up and tossed in their direction, landing heavily with blood seeping from a gash in her arm.

"Retreat," said Malveria. She stepped forward, nimbly avoided Sarapen's jaws, grabbed Kalix and Gawain and dragged them backwards onto the stage. They crashed through the attackers who surrounded the twins and fled across the stage into the tiny dressing room at the back. Once inside they barricaded the door with a stack of heavy crates. Gawain put his shoulder behind the barricade as Sarapen and his werewolves tried to break it down, all the time howling and screaming.

"Thanks for saving me," gasped Thrix to the Fire Queen.

"I gave you my name. I'll always come to your side."

Malveria frowned.

"But I was correct. We should have fled while we had the chance."

The werewolves tried to gather their strength. The door was already beginning to splinter. It wouldn't keep Sarapen out for long.

223

Daniel was relieved to be outside.

"There was nothing we could do. Eh… should we try to get help?"

"What sort of help?"

"I don't know," admitted Daniel. "Maybe call the police?"

"And report some werewolves in trouble? That'll bring a swift response. Anyway, we've got work to do."

"What work?"

"We have to find Princess Kabachetka and disrupt her sorcery."

"What?"

"We have to find the Princess. That's what Thrix whispered to me. You don't think I'd have just left for no reason, do you?"

"We were going to get killed," said Daniel. "That's a reason. What's this *find Princess Kabachetka and disrupt her sorcery?* I don't like the sound of it."

"Come on," said Moonglow, and dragged Daniel along.

"But I don't want to disrupt sorcery," protested Daniel. "It sounds dangerous. And I don't know who Princess Kabachetka is."

"She's another fire elemental. I've met her," said Moonglow.

"What? When?"

"She tried to bribe me into giving away secrets about Malveria's clothes."

Daniel came to a halt.

"What? Why didn't you tell me?"

"You were too busy with Vex and Alicia."

Daniel was still dubious.

"How are we meant to find her? She could be anywhere."

"I'd guess she's in the alley behind the venue," said Moonglow.

They crept quietly along the alleyway. Moonglow stooped to pick up a empty bottle. They tried to move silently but the snow was lying on the ground and crunched beneath their feet. At every step Daniel expected a sorcerous princess to appear, and fire some dreadful spell at them.

"Unless her werewolf bodyguards just rip us to pieces first," he muttered.

Moonglow stopped.

"See, this is why I'd never go out with you," she said. "You're just so negative about everything."

"I'm not negative about everything."

"You are. Nothing ever goes right, according to you. It's just one disaster after another."

"Well, life is hard," said Daniel. "But I don't think I'm that negative. Just realistic."

He paused.

"You mean you'd go out with me if I was more positive?"

"I didn't say that."

"You implied it."

"I don't think I implied it at all," said Moonglow.

"You did so! You said you'd never go out with me because I was so negative. That definitely implies you would go out with me if I was more positive."

"We don't have time to argue about it now," said Moonglow, and walked on. Daniel hurried to catch up. Moonglow was peering round the corner. Half way along the alley, directly behind the venue, a woman with blonde hair and black clothes was staring up at the wall. Moonglow put her mouth to Daniel's ear and whispered.

"It's her. She's concentrating on her magic. Now's our chance to rush her."

"It won't – " began Daniel, but halted as he saw Moonglow's expression. "Well I suppose it might work."

224

"This isn't so great," said Beauty. She was sitting beside her sister in the dressing room. Only an hour or so ago they'd been in here doing their hair prior to walking onstage. They'd drunk beer and joked with their musicians. Now they were bleeding from a dozen cuts apiece and facing death at the hands of Sarapen. She looked towards Dominil.

"Next time we want a better dressing room."

"And more beer," added Delicious.

The Enchantress and Malveria sat next to each other on a crate.

"I'm sorry I got you into this," said the Enchantress. The Fire Queen waved this away.

"I have been in need of activity. And it is a splendid fight, yes?"

Before Thrix could reply, her phone rang. She answered it automatically.

"Hello? No, it's not a very good time. Sorry. Bye."

"Who was that?" asked Malveria, as Sarapen's werewolves pounded on the door.

"Donald Carver. He was wondering if I was free for dinner."

"Ah. Unfortunate timing. Perhaps there will be another occasion?"

"I don't think he'll ask again," said Thrix.

Gawain and the MacRinnalch guard had their shoulders to the door, trying to keep it shut, but any second now it would give way.

"Time to resume the struggle," said Dominil.

The Enchantress rose at her side.

"What's that on your leg?"

Almost concealed beneath Dominil's white fur, there was some sort of strap.

"It holds a knife," said Dominil, but didn't elaborate.

The door burst open. Sarapen threw himself into the room. Dominil leapt at him and they met head on, howling and biting at each other. The remaining werewolves, some fifteen, piled into the tiny dressing room. There was dreadful confusion in the confined space. Kalix found herself assaulted by all three of the Douglas-MacPhees, who still hoped to collect the bounty on her head. She raked her claws across Rhona's face, threw Duncan off and sank her teeth into Fergus's throat. Fergus writhed in agony but could not break free of her grip. Duncan leapt on Kalix's from behind and bit deeply into her back but Kalix wouldn't let go of Fergus. She sunk her teeth deeper and deeper into his neck till his body went limp and she knew he was dead. Then she thrust herself backwards, slamming Duncan into the wall. His grip on her loosened and she whirled to face him, striking him again and again till he sank towards the floor. Kalix opened her jaws and would have killed him had not Rhona smashed a crate of bottles squarely over her head. Kalix sagged at the knees, fighting to stay on her feet as darkness threatened to overwhelm her.

Malveria tumbled through the broken door back onto the stage, pursued by a werewolf. She turned swiftly and clubbed him with such force that he fell to the ground. Malveria raised her weapon again but was distracted as she placed her foot on something soft, which yelled. She looked down.

"Agrivex? What are you doing?"

"Hiding under the drum kit."

"Is that the best place you could find?"

Agrivex's answer was lost as two more werewolves emerged to attack Malveria. She swung her mace mightily, fending them off, but took a raking blow to the chest in the process, which brought blood pouring down the front of her formal coat.

"Argh!" screamed Malveria. "You have destroyed my new coat!"

She swung her weapon, brutally clubbing one of her foes, and set about the second werewolf.

Dominil was grappling with Sarapen. It cost her, as he pummelled her with his superior strength, but she put an arm round his neck, fixed her teeth to his shoulder, and hung on. She reached down to the sheathe at her leg, drawing out the Begravar knife. Sarapen struck her in the face. Dominil spat out blood, and smiled. She held up the knife and spoke the phrase to bring it to life. Seeing the knife, Sarapen took a step backwards. Dominil leapt at him again, and plunged it towards his chest. She didn't quite make it. Sarapen had his guard up, and took the stroke on his arm, but as Dominil sprang away, she was satisfied. She had felt the knife sinking into the flesh and the evil potency of the blade should do the rest. Any deep cut was fatal.

Dominil paused to look at Sarapen. She wanted to see him fall. Sarapen raised his arm, and glanced at the cut. He sneered.

"Not good enough, Dominil," he said, and lashed out with a blow which sent Dominil flying backwards into the Enchantress. This time Dominil struggled to rise. The Enchantress saw the blade in her hand, and recognised it as the Begravar knife.

"No use," she gasped. "No sorcery can work here."

Dominil cursed. Kabachetka's spell had taken away the knife's power. She wearily raised her guard as Sarapen approached. Suddenly the body of a werewolf flew between them. One of Sarapen's followers, dead. A roar, loud even in the room that reverberated with werewolf screams, pierced the air. It was Kalix. She had destroyed another opponent and now hurdled over the body to come to grips with Sarapen. The fury of her assault tumbled him over and they rolled around on the floor, biting and clawing at each other. Kalix's battle-madness was driving her past all barriers of pain or exhaustion. She'd couldn't feel her own injuries. Against any werewolf but Sarapen she'd have been unstoppable. Sarapen, however, was eldest son of the Thane, a werewolf of vast power with enough strength to hold off even Kalix's madness. He tried to use his weight to drag Kalix down him and their jaws met in a dreadful, tearing embrace.

Andris, noticing that Sarapen was locked in combat, ran over and began to strike at Kalix's back. Beside them, Decembrius was struggling with the last of the MacRinnalch guards. The guard had fought valiantly but had suffered many wounds. Decembrius took hold of the guard and prepared to dispatch him. Then Decembrius noticed Kalix's plight, trapped between Sarapen and Andris. Without much thinking what he was doing, Decembrius flung his opponent backwards so he crashed into Andris. Andris fell into Kalix and Sarapen, and as they struggled to their feet they were both swept up in the melee.

Dominil, leaning against the wall for support, found herself confronted by the huge Andris. Sensing her weakness he hurled himself at her. Dominil straightened up rapidly and deflected his assault, sending him crashing into the wall. He whirled to face her and as he did so, Dominil struck him a blow with her claw so fierce it tore through his collarbone and ruptured his neck. He fell down dead in front of her. Dominil bared her teeth, and staggered back into the fray.

225

Daniel gazed at the unconscious figure of Princess Kabachetka.

"I can't believe you did that."

Moonglow had a broken bottle in her hand.

"I had to. She was going to get everyone killed."

They could still hear sounds of fighting coming from above them.

"Do you think her magic has stopped now?"

"Who knows? We should get out of here in before she wakes up," said Daniel.

Moonglow hesitated.

"Maybe we should do something else."

"Like what?"

"I don't know… look for magic stuff, and destroy it."

Daniel made a frustrated gesture.

"See, this is your problem Moonglow. You're never satisfied. You club the Princess over the head and it's still not enough. Now we have to hang around till she wakes up and blasts us."

"I just want to do the job properly," replied Moonglow. "I don't like leaving things half done."

"Sometimes you are so annoying!" yelled Daniel. "You never know when you've done enough. You don't have to get full marks in every exam! Have you any idea how aggravating that is?"

Moonglow felt annoyed at Daniel's criticism.

"You'd get better marks in your exams if you studied occasionally."

"Don't change the subject," said Daniel, heatedly. "You're the one who's being criticised here. Why do you have to do everything so well?"

They made their way back into the street, still bickering.

"You know what it's like living with such an over-achiever?"

"Surprise me," said Moonglow, dryly.

"It's very dispiriting. I can't lie on the couch watching TV without you making me feel guilty by studying all the time. It's unreasonable. And you can't even have a normal boyfriend. Oh no, you have to go out with some fancy werewolf prince."

Feeling that this was stretching personal criticism too far, Moonglow protested hotly.

"Don't you drag Markus into this!"

"Why not? It's all part of the same problem."

"What problem?"

"Ridiculously high standards. You study too much and you only go out with fantastic werewolf princes. No wonder I'm negative. I mean, who can compete?"

Moonglow was now very irritated.

"Will you shut up? Don't talk about Markus."

"Who wants to talk about Markus? Forget he ever existed, I say."

By the time they reached the street Daniel and Moonglow were thoroughly annoyed at each other. They stood angrily on the corner, in the snow, not sure what to do next.

226

When the six fresh werewolves Sarapen had been holding in reserve entered the room, the defenders knew it was over. There was nowhere left to retreat. Thrix, Butix, Delix and Dominil could hardly stay on their feet. The single remaining MacRinnalch guard was alive, but unconscious. Only Kalix, Gawain and Malveria could carry on fighting, and all of them were wounded. They had fought valiantly. They'd killed or incapacitated many of their attackers. Just seven of Sarapen's original force of werewolves were still standing. But Sarapen had hidden six more werewolves in a van outside, not even taking them to the rendezvous in the warehouse. Now they were here.

Dominil hauled herself slowly to her feet.

"You can't finish the job yourself?" she said to Sarapen, mockingly.

"I'll finish it now," replied Sarapen.

Sarapen had fought as werewolf but now he transformed into his full wolf shape. He howled, and led his werewolves in their final assault. Gawain sprang to intercept Sarapen but the wolf-Sarapen was fast, and his teeth were round Gawain's throat in an instant. Kalix felt a hand tugging at her arm. It was Dominil, who was now on one knee, struggling to remain upright. The Begravar knife was glowing. Princess Kabachetka's sorcery was gone, and the knife had now been activated. She handed it to Kalix.

Kalix took the knife and leapt towards Sarapen. Behind her, her fellow defenders were submerged in a murderous tide, but there was some confusion as the knife cast its baleful influence over all the were-wolves. Kalix grabbed Sarapen and threw him from Gawain. As Sara-pen turned to confront her, she thrust the knife deep in his chest. Sarapen howled as the blade burned his insides. Such was the volume of his scream that everyone paused. Malveria attempted to rise grace-fully, but failed.

"Niece," she yelled. "Assist me!"

Agrivex hurried out from beneath the remaining fragments of the drum kit and helped her aunt to her feet. Malveria raised her hand.

"My sorcery has been restored," she gasped, and with a brief wave she threw their assailants across to the far side of the room.

"Of course," thought Thrix. "Sorcery."

Thrix dredged up a spell. It was hard for her to think straight as the confusion cause by the Begravar knife had addled her mind, but she managed to add her powers to those of Malveria, forming a wall of protection around them. All eyes now turned to Sarapen. The great wolf writhed on the floor, transforming first from wolf to werewolf, then from werewolf to human. The knife protruded from his chest and he was unable to draw it out. Sarapen was dying.

The dim room suddenly lit up with a flash of green light. Princes Kabachetka had arrived. She was no longer immaculate. There was snow on her jacket and a trickle of blood on her forehead.

'Although,' reflected Malveria sadly, regarding her own ruined out-fit. 'She still looks better than me.'

Kabachetka hurried to Sarapen's side. She spoke a word and the knife slid from his chest, no longer glowing. She knew, as surely as did the Enchantress, that he was dying. The Princess knelt beside Sara-pen, and cradled his head. She looked up, seeking Malveria.

"You bitch!" said Kabachetka. Then she pointed a finger, though who she was pointing at was unclear.

"I will see you at Livia's celebration," said the Princess.

"I look forward to it," replied Malveria.

Princess Kabachetka unleashed a mighty spell and a great bolt of orange lightning crackled from her finger. It was not directed at Malve-ria, or anyone else in the room. Instead it disappeared through the wall, heading south.

"I fear you may be reduced to wearing last year's fashions," said the Princess, coolly. She dematerialised, taking Sarapen with her.

The Enchantress had by now regained enough strength to stand unaided. She called out to Decembrius.

"Take your wounded and go or I'll kill you where you stand."

Decembrius did as the Enchantress said. They could not continue the fight against the sorcery of the Enchantress and the Fire Queen. With Sarapen gone, there was no point in trying. They departed quickly, though not all quietly. One of the MacAndrises yelled defiantly across the room towards Kalix.

"You killed Sarapen with the Begravar Knife! First your father and now your brother! We won't forget."

Then they were gone. Kalix didn't react. She remained in her werewolf form. Gawain was badly injured, only a few feet away, but she didn't go to him.

"We'd better help the wounded," muttered the Enchantress, looking towards the Fire Queen.

"What was that spell that the Princess used?" asked Malveria.

Thrix shook her head. She hadn't recognised it.

"It had some elements of penetrating a magical defence," muttered the Fire Queen. "But also some elements I have not encountered before. Almost as if it was a spell constructed for – "

She stopped. Colour drained from her honey-toned cheeks.

"My clothes! She has found my beautiful new clothes and treacherously attacked them!"

Malveria forgot her weakness. She snapped her fingers, and vanished. The Enchantress watched her go.

"All right, I'll see to the wounded myself," she muttered.

The Enchantress tried to revive the MacRinnalchs who'd been sent by Verasa but only one of them was still alive, and he was seriously injured. Gawain was also badly hurt. His final confrontation with Sarapen had been very brutal. The Enchantress glanced at his wounds.

"You'll live," she muttered, and turned away. She knelt down beside the MacRinnalch guard.

"I need to take him away for treatment. Is there anyone else about to die?"

There didn't seem to be. Beauty and Delicious were bleeding from cuts all over their bodies, but from the way they'd already hurried to the bar to load up with free alcohol, they didn't seem to be in danger. Dominil had been brutally battered and her coat was more red than white, but she was still in one piece.

"I am fine," said Dominil. She winced in pain.

"Are you sure?"

"I am fine," repeated Dominil, and refused to wince again. "Kalix, do you require attention?"

Kalix didn't reply. She just stood in the middle of the room, staring into space. Her fur was torn and matted with blood and her shoulders were hunched. For a werewolf who'd been fighting so savagely, she suddenly seemed very small.

"I need to get this one back to my apartment," said the Enchantress, kneeling over the guard. She glanced at the bodies which littered the floor. She muttered a spell, and they disappeared.

"The morgue at the castle will be overflowing."

Daniel and Moonglow ventured into the room.

"What happened?"

"We won," said Dominil, and swayed unsteadily. "Take care of Kalix."

Delicious surveyed the wreckage.

"For a first gig, that wasn't bad," she said.

"You're right," agreed Beauty. "Yum Yum Sugary Snacks are really going places."

Dominil ushered the twins out. Gawain was no longer in the room, though no one had noticed him leave. The Enchantress vanished, leaving Daniel and Moonglow alone with Kalix.

"Are you hurt?"

Kalix didn't acknowledge them. Vex appeared from behind the remains of a speaker stack.

"She's okay. She had a bit of a shock. Somebody probably said something tactless. You know how over-sensitive she is."

They led Kalix towards the door.

"Perhaps you should change back to human?" suggested Moonglow. "We're going outside now."

Kalix didn't change. She didn't reply. She seemed to have been shocked beyond worlds.

"So what have you been arguing about?" asked Vex.

Daniel and Moonglow looked at her, both puzzled.

"I've been practising my auras," explained Vex.

Daniel and Moonglow trudged down the stairs, shepherding Kalix along. Vex hopped along behind, talking excitedly about the nights events. Daniel and Moonglow were silent. They hadn't yet made up their argument. As they turned the corner of the narrow stairs they came to an abrupt halt. Standing there was a man whose brawny frame almost filled the staircase. It was Mr Mikulanec. He hadn't died at the warehouse, and he'd not been completely baffled by Thrix and Malveria's spells. He had too much experience of werewolf hunting to be put off forever.

"The werewolf princess," he said, observing Kalix. "I've been looking for you for some time."

Mikulanec took out his knife, and spoke the words to make it glow.

227

Eskandor MacRinnalch rode into Baron MacGregor's camp while the Baron was conferring with Baron MacAllister, Euan MacPhee, and Red Ruraich MacAndris. They were debating what to do in the aftermath of Wallace's defeat by Markus. The MacAllisters, MacPhees and MacAndrises all wanted to press ahead with the assault on the castle but Baron MacGregor insisted that after asking for his son's life to be spared, he could no longer continue with hostilities. They could reach no agreement, but as young Baron MacAllister pointed out, it made little difference. When Sarapen arrived he'd lead them against the castle, with or without the MacGregors.

Eskandor MacRinnalch was a respected member of the MacRinnalch Clan and was greeted courteously by the Barons. He politely accepted the proffered whisky, and sipped from the goblet.

"What brings you riding through the snow to our camp?"

"A message from the Mistress of the Werewolves. Sarapen MacRinnalch is dead. The Mistress invites you to a meeting of the Great Council, to continue with the business of choosing a new Thane."

The Barons gaped.

"Sarapen? Dead?"

"He was killed last night in London, in battle."

"You mean Verasa had him murdered?" roared Douglas MacAllister.

Eskandor MacRinnalch shook his head.

"He was not murdered. He died while carrying out an assault on an event at which members of the Great Council were present."

As Eskandor made his way back to Castle MacRinnalch, the Barons called for their lieutenants, instructing them to contact London immediately, and find out if the report was true.

228

As Mikulanec brandished the Begravar knife, his eyes glinted with cruel pleasure. He knew that Kalix could not stand against it. Kalix abruptly changed from werewolf to human. Blood trickled from her mouth where Sarapen had torn her flesh. Her face was deathly pale and there was no life in her eyes.

"Can you feel the knife, werewolf?" said Mr Mikulanec. He took a step forward. Daniel instinctively tried to block his way but the hunter was far too strong. He grabbed Daniel's shoulder and pushed him down the stairs. Then he raised the knife till it was inches away from Kalix's face.

"Are you ready to die?" he said.

Kalix gazed at the knife.

"Yes," she said, softly. "I'm ready to die. But you're not going to kill me."

Mr Mikulanec frowned. The werewolf should be showing signs of confusion. Kalix did not seem to be confused. When he next spoke, there was the slightest tinge of doubt in his voice.

"Do you feel the knife's power?"

"No."

"How can you not feel it?" demanded Mikulanec.

Kalix shrugged.

"I suppose I'm just too crazy."

With that Kalix transformed back into werewolf shape, and grabbed the hunter's wrist. She dragged Mikulanec's bulky frame up the stairs towards her then fastened her jaws around his neck, moving so swiftly that the hunter had no time to react. Kalix broke his neck with one bite, and let his body slide to the ground. Mr Mikulanec, who had hunted and killed werewolves all over Europe, had finally been defeated.

Daniel picked himself up and hobbled back up the stairs. Moonglow sagged.

"I'm going to be sick," she said. "Let's get out of here."

229

The Enchantress did not have the strength to lavish much attention on the MacRinnalch guard. She was in too much pain herself. She did at least make sure he'd live, boosting his energy and preventing any further loss of blood. He'd wake up battered and bruised, but on the way to recovery.

Thrix was anxious about Malveria's clothes. Could Princess Kabachetka really have located them? Thrix fervently hoped that she hadn't. Despite her weariness, she planned to return to Moonglow's flat to find out. Kalix would be there, and Kalix now knew about Thrix's entanglement with Gawain. The Enchantress anticipated more trouble, but didn't really care. If her young sister felt like making trouble the Enchantress was quite capable of defending herself.

Thrix rarely teleported, not being as gifted at this as Malveria, but now she muttered the appropriate spell to transport herself. The void through which she travelled seemed cold and hostile, and she shivered as she stepped out into the street in Kennington. A cab was drawing up. Daniel, Moonglow, Kalix and Vex emerged. No one spoke. Thrix looked suspiciously at Kalix but the young werewolf hardly seemed to notice her. She was hidden behind her dark glasses, and staring at the ground. Moonglow fumbled with her keys, opened the door and they all trooped up the stairs, in darkness.

"Is that sobbing?" asked Daniel, as they reached the top.

The Fire Queen was huddled on the couch in the living room, and *sobbing* did not do justice to the depths of her grief. Not only her face was wet, but her blouse too, where tears mingled with the blood that still caked her clothes. The couch showed some signs of singeing, as if Malveria had flared up in grief, but the flames were now gone, drowned in her tears. Thrix went to her side and placed her hand on her arm. The Fire Queen looked up.

"They're all gone," she gasped.

"All of them?"

"Burned," moaned Malveria, and was too grief-stricken to say any more. The Enchantress withdrew and hurried upstairs to the loft. Inside there was nothing left. The walls were scorched and the clothes rails were empty. Princess Kabachetka had destroyed all of the Queen's garments. Thrix's work had been for nothing. The Enchantress picked up the charred remnants of an empty hat box, and fought back the tears. She loved the clothes she made. It was more than a commercial enterprise. She could have killed the Princess for doing this.

Thrix remembered how Malveria had recently come to her aid. Feeling that it was her duty to comfort her friend in her hour of grief, she left the attic, though her heart was so heavy, and Malveria's grief so great, that she didn't know what she could possibly say to make things better.

Daniel and Moonglow were sitting in silence. Moonglow was very pale. The sight of Kalix killing Mikulanec had made her sick. It was something she wished she hadn't seen. Kalix had disappeared to her room. Only Vex was animated. The excitement of the gig had not worn off and she was still eager to share it with everyone. Oblivious to the gloom that pervaded the flat, she burbled on about her favourite songs from the evening. Eventually Malveria raised her head.

"Please, Agrivex. For once in your life, be quiet."

Moonglow went off to Kalix's room to see how she was. She feared that she young werewolf might now be cutting her own arm, as if she didn't have enough injuries already. The Enchantress arrived downstairs and put her arm round Malveria.

"I'll design you the most fabulous outfits for the next occasion," she said.

"There will be no next occasion," sobbed Malveria. "I am ruined. I can never leave my palace again."

Moonglow found Kalix asleep, still wrapped in her coat. The room smelled heavily of laudanum. Moonglow removed Kalix's sunglasses and boots, and drew the quilt over her. Then, as she looked round, she saw something which made her smile. She hurried back to the front room where Daniel was helping Malveria lift a small cup of tea to her lips.

"Your clothes are in Kalix's room," said Moonglow. "They're all lying on the floor."

The Queen's eyes widened in surprise.

"Kalix has my clothes? This does not seem likely."

Moonglow and the Enchantress turned their eyes on Vex.

"Well, you know what Kalix is like," said Vex. "Always taking things that don't belong to her."

Malveria rose imperiously to her full height.

"Miserable niece, this is your doing! How many of my clothes are there?"

"How would I know?" protested Vex. "I never went near them. Maybe a few outfits. Kalix made me do it."

By this time Malveria was hurrying through to Kalix's room, closely pursued by the Enchantress. When they got there they found the whole room strewn with dresses, shoes, hats, coats and accessories.

"What has my idiot niece been doing?" cried Malveria, sifting frantically through the crumpled garments.

"Stand back," said Thrix, raising her arm. The Enchantress was a master of all clothes magic, and swiftly cast a spell separating each garment from the others and arranging them into their proper outfits.

"Most of it's here," said the Enchantress. "Vex must have been trying them on and not bothered to put them back."

Malveria levitated several inches off the floor.

"It's a miracle. But they are so creased and wrinkled…"

"Don't worry," said Thrix. "I can fix it."

"Excellent," replied Malveria, who now seemed rejuvenated. "While you do that, I am going to kill Agrivex."

Malveria floated swiftly back into the living room, grabbed Vex by the throat and lifted her off the floor.

"Most miserable of never-to-be-adopted nieces! Even in the murky history of your past crimes, there is nothing to compare with this. You must die. The volcano awaits."

"Stop!" cried Moonglow.

Malveria looked at her politely.

"Yes?"

"You can't kill Vex."

"Whyever not?"

"She saved your clothes."

"It's true," said Thrix, returning to the room. "If she hadn't moved them all, they'd have been destroyed by Kabachetka's spell."

"Exactly," cried Vex, squirming free of the Queen's grasp. "Which is the important point. I cunningly saved your clothes."

"You did not cunningly save my clothes!"

"I did so! I knew they weren't safe in the attic. I was protecting them. I should get a reward. New boots, maybe."

"Pah!" snapped Malveria. "I shall deal with you later. In a harsh manner. Enchantress, what may be saved from the wreckage?"

"Most of it, I think."

The Enchantress was surrounded by a carousel of floating clothes, and was busily checking each outfit.

"Most of your formal attire is here, and everything for the next two days. There are some things missing for day four, but the ball gown is undamaged. I can replace the missing clothes before you need them."

"It is truly the most wonderful outcome!" exclaimed Malveria, still several inches off the ground. "Still I am the mistress of fashion. How Kabachetka will grieve when I appear – late, but not intolerably so – at Livia's celebration, in the full glory of my new attire."

The Enchantress pursed her lips.

"Except for one thing."

"What thing could that be?"

"Your best formal coat. For your entrance. You're wearing it. Or what's left of it."

Malveria looked down at her coat. It was ripped in six places and covered in blood. She descended to ground level, walked over to the couch, and buried her face in a cushion.

"Couldn't you magic it better?" suggested Moonglow. The Enchantress shook her head. Fine tailoring was all-important. Only last week at Malveria's palace, Beau DeMortalis had discarded a very good topcoat which had suffered the slightest of mishaps, no more than a tiny scratch from a thorn bush.

"One cannot go around with magically repaired clothes," he'd said. "Like a common labourer."

Malveria's coat was ruined. Not only that, the Queen had kicked off her shoes before the fight began, and left them in Camden. Thrix frantically tried to come up with an idea.

"Perhaps I could find something at the warehouse?" she suggested.

"Ready made?" gasped Malveria, and began to weep.

"Does it need to be formal?" asked Daniel.

"Very. It is the most formal of formal entrances."

"Oh. That's a pity. Otherwise, what with the blood and everything, you could have made your entrance as Triumphant Warrior Queen."

"Please do not babble," said Malveria. "I have suffered enough from Agrivex."

"But wouldn't just having come back from combat sort of transcend fashion?"

"Nothing transcends fashion."

"Well it might be seen as fashion pretending to transcend fashion," suggested Daniel, who had for some reason been paying attention during his post-modern cultural identity lecture last week. "Act as if you meant to go there wearing a ripped coat."

Thrix was not so dismissive of Daniel's idea.

"It's worth considering. Pretend you've chosen to arrive this way. Get in your coach wearing your blood stained coat and carrying your mace, and arrive as if you're saying, *Here is Malveria, triumphant warrior queen, deliberately dressed in the wreckage of her formal outfit, which is still more glorious than the clothes you're wearing.*"

Malveria wrinkled her brow.

"It is a risky strategy in the face of Beau DeMortalis and his merciless set-downs."

She mused for a few moments.

"It might be possible. No one else could carry it off, certainly. But I am a triumphant warrior queen, am I not?"

"You were fabulous in battle," said Thrix, reassuringly.

Malveria looked down at her torn coat with dissatisfaction.

"But the rips are all wrong. They do not match. And the blood stains are very poorly arranged." She rose, rather nimbly. "Come, dearest Enchantress, you must help me bring some order to this chaos."

Malveria kissed Daniel on the cheek, to thank him for his suggestion. He blushed, as he always did. Malveria laughed, then headed for the attic with Thrix, to re-arrange her clothing. There they set about adding to the damage in some areas to make it more aesthetically pleasing.

"We're going to have to do something about your jewellery," said Thrix. "The emeralds just don't go with the blood."

She thought for a moment.

"Do you still have the necklace Agrivex bought you?"

"The unpleasant trinket featuring axes? Not suitable, surely?"

"Do you have it?"

Malveria brought it out from her bag.

"It appears to be still with me, by coincidence."

Thrix fastened it round Malveria's neck. The Fire Queen nodded. It would do.

"It was cunning of the Princess to construct such a powerful spell," said Malveria. "But have you wondered how she located the clothes? She must have received information."

"From who?"

"I regret to say this, but I can see traces of the vile Kabachetka's aura on Moonglow."

"That's because she encountered Kabachetka outside the gig."

Malveria was dubious. Though the traces were faint and very difficult to interpret, she believed that Moonglow may have met the Princess on more than one occasion.

"Surely you'd have noticed it earlier?" said Thrix.

"If they did meet before, Kabachetka herself may have taken care to remove all traces from the girl."

The Enchantress found it hard to believe that Moonglow would have betrayed the Fire Queen. It would have been out of character.

"Moonglow has been out of character in recent days," pointed out the Fire Queen.

Downstairs, Daniel and Moonglow were sitting next to each other on the couch.

"Do you still feel sick?" asked Daniel.

Moonglow nodded. Daniel put his arm round her, and she rested her head on his shoulder. They sat in front of the TV, and let the trauma of the evening fade away.

230

Two nights had passed since Markus's fight with Wallace MacGregor. With the moon large in the sky, the MacRinnalchs in the castle had revelled as werewolves. News had spread that Sarapen was dead. The besieging forces had not withdrawn but no one now feared an attack; the war was surely over. The Mistress of the Werewolves called a meeting of the Great Council for the night after the full moon and the inhabitants of the castle waited eagerly to see which members of the council would arrive.

There was a wave of excitement when Dominil, Beauty and Delicious walked through the castle gates. Dominil was a familiar figure but the werewolves welcomed her back with increased respect. The story of her part in the battle in London was already well known. Dominil had never been well liked at the castle. Her manner made it difficult to warm to her. However, no werewolf from either side of the dispute could fail to show her respect after her endeavours.

There was widespread amazement that Dominil had somehow persuaded the notoriously anti-social sisters Butix and Delix to return to Scotland for the council meeting. No one had ever expected to see them at the castle again. Some of the younger werewolves, children who'd never seen the twins, hung from their windows around the courtyard, awe-struck at the sight of their great manes of pink and blue hair. Werewolf parents sighed, and told their offspring that no, they could not do the same to their hair, and nor could they leave immediately for London to start bands, live riotously and bring shame on the clan. And they certainly couldn't change their names to anything ridiculous like Beauty and Delicious.

Tupan was waiting to greet his daughter, and they embraced, rather formally, as was normal. The Enchantress arrived a little later in the day. As she entered the castle she was on her phone, talking to Ann about Malveria's outfit for tonight. She regretted taking time out from her schedule to come to the council meeting, but felt she couldn't really miss it. Her mother would complain terribly.

Of the other members of the council, Verasa, Markus, Dulupina, Lucia, Kurian and Kertal were all inside the castle. As Sarapen was dead, Lucia's son Decembrius was due to take his place on the council but the appointment had not yet been ratified. Decembrius remained in London. This left only the three Barons, and Marwanis. Night was falling and the snow was deep on the ground before they arrived. They came together, and entered sullenly through the gates, to be greeted courteously by the Mistress of the Werewolves. The Barons accepted her welcome civilly, even young Douglas MacAllister. Only Marwanis remained aloof. Marwanis would hate the Mistress of the Werewolves forever, and everyone who had contributed to Sarapen's downfall.

Kalix would not be attending. She was still outlawed, and had not been invited.

231

Kalix lay in her favourite clump of bushes in Kennington Park, far away from all company. She stared up at the sky. Overhead there were one hundred and twenty-five billion galaxies. She knew this because Moonglow had been listening to a science programme on the radio. Kalix tried to imagine one hundred and twenty-five billion galaxies. It was such a large number it was confusing to even think about. The young werewolf lay on the ground, looking at the stars, and felt confused. She didn't know what to think about anything. The news of Gawain's affair with Thrix had been too much for her to comprehend. The weight of it crushed her and left her hardly able to move.

She'd had thoughts of attacking Thrix and killing Gawain. These thought were briefly comforting but ultimately more upsetting and they faded away, leaving her desolate. Her anxiety had diminished, pushed out of the way by depression. It didn't feel like an improvement. She sipped some laudanum. Soon she'd need to visit the Merchant, to renew her supply.

Kalix wondered briefly about her family. She'd killed Sarapen. She didn't know what would happen as a result of that. More trouble, probably. Misery over Gawain welled up inside her. She started to cry, even though it was almost unheard of to shed tears while in werewolf form. She became so upset that she did something she'd never done before, which was use her great incisor teeth to cut her own arm. After this, she felt a little better.

As the moon rose high overhead, Kalix changed into her full wolf form, lifted up her head, and howled at the moon. It was a long note filled with pain and misery. Anyone who heard it shivered, and hurried away as fast as they could.

232

Two months ago the Great Council had failed to elect a new Thane. That would not happen again. As Sarapen was no longer here, the vote was hardly more than a formality. Had Sarapen still been alive, the vote would have been closer but in all probability, Verasa would still have had her way. She'd never wavered from her task of gathering support for Markus.

Sarapen's body had not been recovered but he was presumed to be dead. A werewolf could not survive having the Begravar knife thrust deep into his chest. No healing and no sorcery could reverse the effects of such a wound, as the Enchantress attested. Kalix was condemned on all sides for using such a weapon on a fellow werewolf, even a deadly enemy. The condemnation was mitigated a little when Verasa spread it around that the knife had been brought there by Sarapen himself, but there were those who did not believe this, and felt it was more likely that the criminal Kalix had stolen the knife. Dominil did not volunteer the information that she had brought it to the gig, and neither did Thrix.

There were fifteen members of the Great Council in the chamber, Kalix and Decembrius being absent. The atmosphere was less hostile than might have been expected. The Mistress of the Werewolves had treated the defeated Barons generously, welcoming them without any sign of triumph or bitterness. Most supporters of Sarapen now wished for a return to more peaceful times. Of the Barons, only the young MacAllister showed any sign of resentment, and he made efforts to control it. It was his first council meeting and he didn't want to appear unstatesmanlike. Only Marwanis was openly hostile.

When Rainal called for nominations for Thane, no one spoke. Dominil remained silent. Having seen Sarapen defeated, Dominil had lost the urge to nominate anyone. Verasa turned her eyes on Kurian.

"I nominate Markus MacRinnalch," said Kurian.

Kurian was a brother of the old Thane. He was a suitable werewolf to propose Markus. His poor health had rendered him susceptible to persuasion. Besides, he was worried about what the Mistress of the Werewolves might decide to do to his son Kertal, after his arrest. Kertal himself was planning to vote for Markus with a show of enthusiasm, in the hope that his plan to hand the castle over to the Barons might be forgotten.

Clan secretary Rainal counted the raised hands. There were thirteen: Verasa, Lucia, Markus, Dominil, Thrix, Butix, Delix, Kurian, Kertal, Dulupina, Tupan, Baron MacGregor and Baron MacPhee. Baron MacAllister and Marwanis, with no alternative candidate to vote for, abstained.

"I declare that Markus MacRinnalch is the new Thane," said Rainal, thus ending the feud.

"Is there any other business?" asked Rainal.

Great Mother Dulupina raised one hand a few inches from the table. "The continuing status of Kalix MacRinnalch as outlaw," she said.

The Mistress of the Werewolves was taken by surprise. The huge fire in the corner burned brightly but at the mention of Kalix's name the atmosphere in the council chamber grew noticeably cooler.

233

Malveria triumphed at the Sorceress Livia's 500th birthday celebration. There was one awkward moment, when she first arrived in her golden carriage. The great ladies and gentlemen of court were all dressed very formally and as Malveria stepped out of her carriage with her garments ripped and bloodstained there was a surprised hush. Princes Kabachetka turned to Apthalia the Grim to make a crushing comment. Before she could do so, Beau DeMortalis, Duke of the Black Castle and fabulous dandy, was distinctly heard to say to his friend the Molten Lord of Garamlock, "It's a refreshing change of pace." The awkward silence was broken and the assorted guests murmured in admiration at Malveria's courageous feat of appearing at Livia's on the same day as she'd been victorious in battle.

The Fire Queen descended into Livia's underground mansion with her head held high and from then on everything went her way. Once the discerning guests were exposed to Malveria's new, undamaged clothes, her status rose even further. The Enchantress's elegant and beautiful designs were universally acclaimed. They were far superior to anything else on display. Malveria walked through the events of that day and the next with a feeling of blissful superiority. Even when she encountered Princess Kabachetka, she remained tranquil. The matter of the Princess's attack on her clothes was not alluded to. Malveria simply complimented Kabachetka on the beauty of her garments. The Princess, knowing that her wardrobe did not match up to her rival's, accepted the compliments with burning eyes and what little grace she could muster.

At the end of each day Malveria would hurry back to Moonglow's attic to pick up her clothes for the next part of the celebration. She had placed further spells there to protect her clothes, though she did not really fear another attack. The battle was already won.

On the third night of the party, Malveria received a message from First Minister Xakthan, requesting an audience. Malveria was slightly irked. She summoned Xakthan, and explained to him rather testily that she had no time to spare for the mundane business of running a kingdom.

"Day four is still a source of some stress. My hat and shoes for the great chariot race were damaged by the Princess and I am praying that the Enchantress has managed to replace them."

"Forgive me, Queen," said Xakthan. "But we have a report from our intelligence services concerning the attack on your majesty's wardrobe."

Malveria leaned forward on her throne.

"Proceed."

"Our new agent in Kabachetka's household reports that the Princess was indeed given information as to the whereabouts of your clothes. But the informant was not the girl Moonglow. It was a young man of her acquaintance. He is called Jay."

Malveria slapped her palm on the arm of her jewelled throne.

"Jay! I have met this man! He greatly offended me! So it was he who betrayed me? Are you sure of this?"

"I am. Apparently he was upset by Moonglow rejecting him and was thus easily corrupted by Kabachetka's charms."

Xakthan noticed that his words had displeased the Queen.

"Kabachetka's charms being sorcerously enhanced, of course, to hide her true vile nature," he added, tactfully.

"Of course," muttered Malveria. "No doubt she apprehended him in some low tavern where the dim light could hide the repulsiveness of her features. So, it was he and not Moonglow who betrayed me. I am relieved. It would have pained me to take revenge on Moonglow, because she has shown me great hospitality."

"You mean you will no longer break her heart?"

The Fire Queen looked surprised.

"What? Of course I will break her heart. That bargain has already been made. But I will spare her further chastisement. Now I must depart. The shoes must be ready, and they must be brought from Italy. You would be surprised at the trouble this can cause in the human world, with the difficulties involved in the postal services."

"Postal services?" said Xakthan.

"A primitive method for transporting goods. Very often it leads to chaos."

234

The twins were distressed to learn than Dominil was not coming back to London.

"What do you mean you're staying at the castle?" said Delicious. "You can't abandon us now."

"The castle is awful," said Beauty. "All stone walls and battlements. Who needs it? You don't want to stay here."

"I'm very comfortable here."

"But you'll be bored," said Delicious. She looked towards her sister for support.

"Didn't she say she was bored when she was here?"

"She did," agreed Beauty. "Really bored. You need something to do."

"Drink more whisky," suggested Beauty, proffering a bottle to Dominil. "It'll clear your mind."

Dominil regarded the twins, slightly less coldly than normally.

"It was never intended that I would remain with you permanently. It was a task of limited duration."

"Well just extend it a bit," said Beauty. "We need you to organise more gigs and stuff."

"Exactly," agreed Delicious. "There's a lot of stuff to do."

"We need a booking agent. And a website. And internet publicity. And music downloads. You could do that."

Dominil sipped from the bottle.

"I could. But didn't you spend the whole time I was in London complaining about my presence and writing hostile songs about me?"

"I don't think so," replied Delicious. "Beauty, do you remember anything like that?"

Beauty shook her head.

"No, I don't remember that."

"And to be fair," said Delicious. "We never said we liked you. But you have to come back to London."

Dominil declined. She wasn't going back. She planned to return to the tranquillity of the castle and complete her translations of Latin poetry. Beauty and Delicious were annoyed, and went off to complain to the Mistress of the Werewolves. As they tramped around the stone corridors of Castle MacRinnalch they were followed by young werewolves who giggled as they passed, and worked up the courage to ask for autographs. Yum Yum Sugary Snacks were already acquiring legendary status among the younger inhabitants of the castle.

The Mistress of the Werewolves was slightly more sympathetic towards the twins these days. They had, after all, voted for Markus. However, she was not encouraging. She pointed out that Dominil, a werewolf of immense intellect, could hardly be expected to spend all her time looking after Yum Yum Sugary Snacks.

"I'm sure she has weightier things on her mind."

The twins went off, dissatisfied, complaining to each other about how much they hated Castle MacRinnalch and what a waste of time it had been coming here. Markus MacRinnalch had thanked them very graciously for their votes, but what use was that?

"It's okay for pretty boy Markus," said Beauty. "He likes this place. And he's welcome to it. But we've got things to do. And we need Dominil."

The twins put their heads together, and plotted ways of convincing Dominil to return.

The Mistress of the Werewolves had not yet grieved for her eldest son. Perhaps she would tonight, when she attended the memorial service for him. Whether or not she felt grief, it was unseemly that his body had disappeared. She asked Thrix to apply to Malveria for news of Princess Kabachetka, to find out if it could be recovered. Thrix chaffed at the thought, though she felt unable to refuse. The moment the service for Sarapen was over, she was heading back to London and hoped to put all family matters out of her head for a long time to come.

Verasa was satisfied, almost. Markus was Thane. The MacRinnalchs could move forward with the rest of the world, and let the violence of their werewolf heritage pass into history. Her sole dissatisfaction concerned Kalix. The Great Council had refused to lift her condemnation. She was still outlawed, required to be brought back as a captive to the castle for sentencing. Verasa had not been able to persuade a majority of the council otherwise. The biggest shock had been that Markus had not cast his vote in favour of pardoning Kalix. Verasa was very displeased. Perhaps Markus was just making a show of independence, now he was Thane. He wouldn't want it thought that he was too much under the influence of his mother. Verasa was prepared for this. She wouldn't apply too much pressure at first. But in the long run, she had no intention of allowing Markus to run the clan's affairs any differently than she would have done herself.

Verasa's musing was interrupted by the re-appearance of Beauty and Delicious.

"Kalix," said Beauty.

"What about her?"

"She's probably one step away from suicide. You know, with the Gawain thing," said Delicious.

"You know about the Gawain thing, right? With Thrix?"

Verasa did, though it was not something she wanted to talk about. She'd been appalled to learn that her eldest daughter had formed an association with the banished Gawain.

"So you have to send Dominil back to London."

"I'm afraid I don't follow you," said the Mistress of the Werewolves.

"Dominil has a lot of influence with Kalix."

"Does she?"

"She does," said Beauty. "Kalix is always trotting around after her. It's weird, but Kalix is weird. You wouldn't want her to throw herself in front of a train or anything. You'd better send Dominil back to have a word with her."

235

Daniel and Moonglow's lives were returning to normal. Moonglow's anguish over Markus had receded a little. Daniel was no longer seeing Alicia. Malveria was still picking up clothes from the attic but that would be over in a day or two. They were relieved. They'd had enough excitement. They did what they could to comfort Kalix but the young werewolf didn't seem to want comforting, and was rarely at home.

"She should never have fallen in love with a werewolf," said Daniel.

"Well who else did you expect her to fall in love with?" asked Moonglow.

They were sitting on the couch, studying together.

"You think maybe you'd be a good candidate?" suggested Moonglow, teasing him.

"That's not what I meant."

"Well, the way you've been getting through girls recently, what with Alicia and Vex…"

Daniel tried not to look embarrassed.

"Neither of them were right," he said. "They weren't who I wanted."

"They weren't?"

Daniel edged a little closer to Moonglow. Vex suddenly appeared in the room with a crash. Her teleporting had gone slightly wrong and she tumbled over a chair.

"Ow!" she wailed, climbing to her feet. "I bumped my elbow."

The doorbell rang.

"What did you say about our lives returning to normal?" said Daniel, scowling, and trudged downstairs to answer it. He opened the door and took a brisk step backwards. It was Dominil. Her eyes were as black and penetrating as ever, her skin pale and her hair dazzling white.

"I am looking for Kalix."

'It's like opening the door to the grim reaper,' thought Daniel. He welcomed her in, not very graciously. He'd had the feeling in recent days that Moonglow was warming towards him. It had been very significant that she'd agreed to study together on the couch. Had it not been for the unwelcome intervention of Vex and Dominil, who knew what might have happened?

Upstairs Moonglow was rubbing Vex's elbow.

"It's really sore," said Vex, though she didn't look like she was in much pain. "Hi Dominil! Are Yum Yum Sugary Snacks going to play again?"

"Would you like it if they did?" asked Dominil, seriously.

"Of course! It was the best thing ever!"

Dominil nodded.

"I thought they pleased the audience. Rather more than I expected.

551

But I've come here about Kalix."

Moonglow told Dominil that Kalix wasn't around.

"She goes out. We don't know where."

"Is she taking care of herself?"

"Not at all."

It had been the Mistress of the Werewolves' suggestion that Dominil visit Kalix. Dominil had surprised Verasa by accepting the commission. In truth, the white-haired werewolf had swiftly realised that she was bored at Castle MacRinnalch. She wasn't quite ready to return to her private chambers and spend her days translating Latin poetry.

"You should take her shopping," said Vex, brightly.

Dominil stared at her curiously.

"In what way would that help?"

"Everyone likes shopping."

Dominil had no inclination to bandy words with Agrivex.

"I will find Kalix and talk to her," she said, and left without saying goodbye. Daniel shivered.

"She's more likely to push Kalix over the edge than help her."

The doorbell rang. Vex yelped.

"It's Aunt Malvie! I'm meant to be in history class!"

Vex swiftly dematerialised.

"It's your turn to answer the door," said Daniel. Moonglow hurried downstairs. As she opened the door her eyes widened in astonishment. Standing next to the Fire Queen was a woman who was so beautiful, so ethereal, so lovely as to defy all description.

"May we come in?"

Moonglow nodded, too awe-struck by the woman to speak. Her hair shimmered like underwater gold, and her eyes were so large and blue that Moonglow felt she might be swallowed up by them.

"Allow me to introduce Dithean Wallace Cloud-of-Heather NicRinnalch, Fairy Queen of Colburn Wood. She is my guest for Livia's grand chariot race. I am lending her a handbag."

The Fairy Queen smiled at Moonglow. Moonglow stammered to make some reply, but failed.

"Don't worry," said Malveria. "The Fairy Queen always has this effect."

They swept past Moonglow and mounted the stairs. Malveria snapped her fingers as they ascended, illuminating the stairwell.

"You really must buy a light bulb," she said.

By the time Moonglow reached the living room Daniel was on his feet, looking bewildered.

"And this is Daniel," Malveria was saying to her companion. "A most charming young man, though not at this moment displaying himself to his best advantage."

She turned to Moonglow.

"I knew you would be pleased to meet my good friend the Fairy Queen of Colburn Wood. Normally, of course, she prefers to remain at a somewhat smaller size, which is more convenient for most fairy activities. But she has consented to take on her human form, that you may see her."

Dithean Wallace Cloud-of-Heather NicRinnalch smiled at Moonglow and Daniel. They were quite overwhelmed, but managed to smile back. There was a muted flash and the Enchantress appeared in their midst. She wore a very stylish red suit with matching heels and a jaunty red hat atop her hair, which once more tumbled down in a bright golden stream over her shoulders.

"Enchantress!" cried Malveria. "You look splendid. The troubles of the past weeks are quite forgotten and you are again radiant."

Thrix knew the Fairy Queen, and greeted her warmly. They were both Malveria's guests for the chariot races, and were looking forward to the event. Malveria suddenly glanced towards the door, then waved her hand, bringing Vex tumbling into the room.

"Agrivex. When attempting to hide from me, does it never occur to you to travel further than Kalix's bedroom?"

Vex's face wrinkled in pain. She held up her arm towards her aunt, and looked hopeful.

"I bumped my elbow."

Malveria shook her head sadly.

"This, dearest Dithean, is what I have to put up with. Had the fairies stolen my idiotic niece at birth, I would have counted it as a great favour."

Malveria snapped her fingers, sending Vex back to her classroom. Moonglow took advantage of the interruption to approach Thrix.

"We're worried about Kalix," she began.

The Enchantress regarded her coldly.

"What do you expect me to do about it?"

Thrix turned her back, and linked arms with Malveria and Dithean.

"Time for the races?"

"Indeed," replied Malveria. "They are such thrilling events. And DeMortalis is quite trembling at the thought of meeting you again. He is even now working on new ways to flatter you both on your beauty, I assure you."

Malveria, the Enchantress and the Fairy Queen swept upstairs to pick up the handbag for Dithean. Moonglow and Daniel collapsed on the couch.

"Was that really a fairy queen? Here in our house?"

Daniel was still struggling to speak.

"I've never…" he began, but couldn't finish the sentence.

"You've never seen anyone so beautiful?" suggested Moonglow.

"Something like that," admitted Daniel.

"More beautiful than Malveria and all these fabulously beautiful werewolves?" Moonglow sounded cross. "Now I'm feeling frumpy."

"You're not frumpy at all," protested Daniel. "Who said anything about frumpy? I never thought any of the werewolves were that beautiful. And they've all got really bad personalities."

"The first time you met Kalix you described her as a wild beauty," said Moonglow, displaying a memory for detail which Daniel thought quite unreasonable.

"I like you much better than all the werewolves or fairy queens in the world," he blurted out suddenly, then cringed as he realised what he'd said. He waited for Moonglow to withdraw. She didn't. She looked him in the eyes, and edged closer.

It had been kind of the Fire Queen to bring Dithean to meet Moonglow. Malveria knew that Moonglow would be pleased. Of course, Malveria also knew that it was very hard, after being in the presence of a fairy queen, not to feel a great arousal of the senses. Moonglow moved closer to Daniel.

"Perhaps…" she began.

They were interrupted by a gentle cough from the doorway. Malveria was standing there looking curiously satisfied. She directed her gaze towards Moonglow. Her eyes twinkled, but not kindly.

"Take care, my dears," she said. Then she vanished.

"What was that about?" said Daniel, but by this time Moonglow was on her feet.

"I need to study," said Moonglow. "In my room. Right away."

She too departed, leaving Daniel mystified, and not happy.

236

Kalix woke from a curious dream in which the Fairy Queen of Colburn Wood had appeared beside her in the bushes. Malveria had been with her, and they'd looked down at her, and smiled. She woke up feeling slightly heartened. She thought about Gawain, and Sarapen, and all her troubles of the past weeks.

"Stupid MacRinnalchs," she muttered, and stared at her feet.

She sensed someone approaching. It was Dominil, forcing her way into the small clearing. Kalix didn't look up.

"Is it your intention to sit here until you die?"

"Maybe."

"It's a foolish plan."

Kalix raised her head an inch or two.

"I'm fed up with you telling me what's foolish. If you don't like it then go away."

Dominil's eyes narrowed a fraction. The she shrugged, and sat down beside Kalix. She took a small bronze flask from the pocket of her great black coat, unscrewed the cap, and handed it to Kalix. Kalix took a sip.

"The Merchant is surprised we're still alive," said Dominil. "I should kill him for helping Sarapen. But then, where would we find laudanum?"

Dominil told Kalix that the Great Council had not pardoned her. She was still an outlaw.

"In theory, you can still be taken back to the castle for sentencing. In reality, it seems unlikely. The Mistress of the Werewolves will not encourage it."

Kalix professed not to care. A bird sang, somewhere among the cold bushes. They sat in silence for a while.

"I looked for Gawain," said Dominil, eventually. "I promised you I'd talk to him. However, he's gone. He is no longer in his room in Camberwell."

Kalix stared at the ground.

"I did speak to the Enchantress. She regrets what happened. She didn't mean to become involved with him."

Kalix scowled.

"It strikes me that the MacRinnalch feud not only led to many deaths," continued Dominil. "It also had a surprisingly bad effect on the romantic lives of those involved. Markus lost the werewolf he loved, and subsequently broke Moonglow's heart. I doubt he will be happy for long with his current amour. The Enchantress entered into a foolish relationship which did not bring her any happiness. Gawain ended up with nothing, and has fled. Moonglow and Daniel are engaged in some form of attraction which I don't see ending well. And Marwanis and Princess Kabachetka are left pining for Sarapen."

Dominil paused.

"I miss him too."

Kalix looked up.

"What do you mean you miss him?"

"He was a passionate lover, when we were together."

"You tried to kill him."

"Of course. And I was pleased when you did. But I doubt I'll meet anyone else like him."

Dominil screwed the top back on her flask.

"You should take satisfaction from your achievements, Kalix."

"What achievements?"

"You defeated Sarapen. Which means something. No matter how much the Mistress of the Werewolves seeks to modernise the clan, the MacRinnalchs still value prowess in battle. We can't help it."

Kalix nodded. Many things made her feel bad, but killing Sarapen wasn't one of them.

"And you have made progress," said Dominil. "Your mental strength is returning, even if you don't realise it. The moment I appeared you obviously told yourself you weren't going to let me push you around any more. Furthermore, you now have friends. Daniel and Moonglow like you, and you like them. If you didn't like them you'd have left by now. You are no longer quite such a lonely werewolf girl."

Kalix considered this. She supposed it might be true.

"Well so what?" she said.

"So you're stronger and you have friends. I'd say that makes your life better."

"But Gawain…"

"There's nothing to do about that. Just bite it and swallow it. It's not worth killing yourself over. And it's probably better if you live."

Kalix snorted.

"Couldn't you at least pretend you'd be sad if I was dead?"

"Not without straining myself."

Kalix smiled.

"Vex also likes you," continued Dominil. "Though whether that's a good thing, I'm not certain. She suggests I take you shopping."

"She's stupid," said Kalix.

"I won't argue with that. It's also stupid to sit in the middle of this cold clump of bushes. Let's go to the café."

"Okay."

They made their way through the park. The snow had stopped but the ground was still hard and frozen. Only a few dog walkers were about. Their dogs shied away from Kalix and Dominil as they passed.

"How is your reading coming along?"

"A bit better," said Kalix. "Are you going to help the twins more?"

"Probably. They want me to."

Kalix shivered as they left the park.

"This coat is useless."

"I've been telling you that for ages," said Vex, materialising in the street beside them, with no regard for the feelings of passers by. "We have to go shopping. It's an emergency. I can't stay in class while you need a new coat so badly."

"I don't have any money," replied Kalix.

"I thought your clan was rich?" Vex looked at Dominil. "You can get money, right?"

"I have money left over from the sum the Mistress of the Werewolves provided."

"Well that's that problem solved," said Vex, cheerfully. "I already called Daniel and Moonglow. They're meeting us in the café. Then we can all drive somewhere and shop."

They reached the café where Daniel and Moonglow were waiting for them. Vex was excited at the prospect of shopping. Also, she'd never been in a café before.

"I like this. Do they serve roasted oggy monster? No? Okay, what's a sausage?"

She glanced at Daniel and Moonglow. They were sitting very close to each other, though Moonglow seemed deep in thought.

"There's something funny about your auras."

"Never interpret my aura again," said Moonglow, sharply, and moved away from Daniel.

"All right. I'm bored with it anyway. Hasn't this been a great month? Me and Kalix became best friends, you got cable TV, I went shopping in Camden, Yum Yum Sugary Snacks were brilliant. Everything just went really well."

"You seem to be forgetting the violent feud," said Dominil.

"Maybe. But you have to look on the bright side. So, this money you have, does it extend far enough to buy me a few things? Because you know, Aunt Malvie hardly gets me anything. It's cruel the way she treats me, you'd be shocked."

Kalix laughed at Vex. She couldn't help herself. It was warm in the café. She felt better than she had for a long time. And hungry, which was unusual. She felt confident enough to try reading the menu, and managed to make out enough to place her order. She forgot, for a while, her unhappiness over Gawain. She forgot her anxiety, and even found herself looking forward to buying a new coat.

"You see, I knew shopping would cheer you up," said Vex.

"Stop reading my aura you stupid Hiyasta," said Kalix.

"Hey, don't get cranky. Whose clever plan was it to trick Moonglow into getting cable TV?"

"What?" said Moonglow.

"Forget I said that. So this is what a sausage looks like? Interesting. Daniel, that jacket is really bad, you need a new one. Me and Kalix will pick one for you."

"This jacket is not bad," protested Daniel.

"It is," said Moonglow.

"It's awful," said Kalix.

"I agree," said Dominil.

"Everyone stop picking on my jacket."

"We can help you find a better one," said Kalix. "There's no need to get stressed about it."

THE END

558

Martin Millar was born in Scotland and now lives in London. His previous novels include *The Good Fairies of New York*, and *Suzy, Led Zeppelin and Me*. Writing under the pseudonym of Martin Scott, he won the World Fantasy Award for *Thraxas*.

www.martinmillar.com
www.lonelywerewolfgirl.com

Author's agent - Imrie and Dervis
info@imriedervis.com

Cover art by Simon Fraser
www.simonfraser.net